4.00

# HEART
## OF THE
# COMET

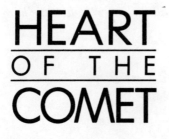

# HEART
## OF THE
# COMET

*Gregory Benford*
*and*
*David Brin*

BANTAM BOOKS
TORONTO • NEW YORK • LONDON • SYDNEY • AUCKLAND

*To*
*Poul and Robert*
*Greg and Carolyn*
*Larry and Jerry*
*Charles and Harry*
*and all the rest who do it the hard way.*

HEART OF THE COMET
*A Bantam Spectra Book / March 1986*

Grateful acknowledgment is made for permission to reprint lines from the poem "Epilogue" by Edgar Lee Masters from the *Spoon River Anthology.* Copyright 1915, 1916, 1942, 1944 by Edgar Lee Masters. Used by permission of the Macmillan Publishing Company. All Rights Reserved.

**Library of Congress Cataloging-in-Publication Data**

Benford, Gregory, 1941–
  Heart of the comet.

  (A Bantam spectra book)
  I. Brin, David.   II. Title.
  PS3552.E542H4  1986      813'.54      85-23042
  ISBN 0-553-05125-3

*Published simultaneously in the United States and Canada*

───────────────────────────────

*Bantam Books are published by Bantam Books, Inc. Its trade-*
*mark, consisting of the words "Bantam Books" and the por-*
*trayal of a rooster, is Registered in U.S. Patent and Trademark*
*Office and in other countries. Marca Registrada. Bantam*
*Books, Inc., 666 Fifth Avenue, New York, New York 10103.*

───────────────────────────────

PRINTED IN THE UNITED STATES OF AMERICA

MV      0 9 8 7 6 5 4 3 2 1

# BANNERS OF THE ANGELS

*October 2061*

He that leaveth nothing to chance
will do few things ill,
but he will do very few things.
—Halifax

Positions of Inner Planets and Comet Halley
October 2061

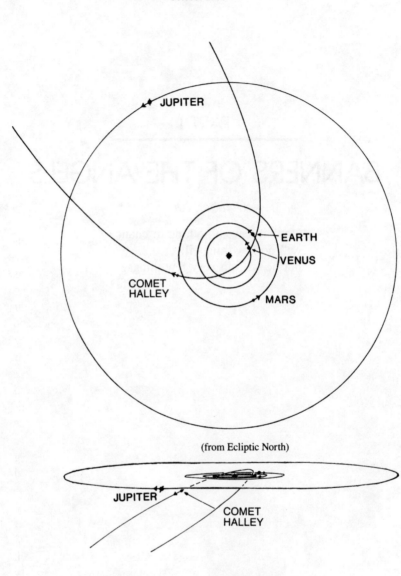

(from Ecliptic North)

(from Vernal East)

# CARL

Kato died first.

He had been tending the construction mechs—robots that were deploying girders on the dusty, gray-black comet ice.

From Carl's viewpoint, on a rise a kilometer away, Kato's suit was a blob of orange amid the hulking gray worker drones. There was no sound, in spite of the clouds of dust and gas that puffed outward near man and machines. Only a little static interfered with a Vivaldi Concerto that helped Carl concentrate on his work.

Carl happened to be looking up, just before it happened. Not far from Kato, anchored near the north pole of the comet's solid core, eight spindly spires lanced up to form a pyramidal tower. At the peak nestled the microwave borer antenna, an upside-down cup. Kato worked a hundred meters away, oblivious to the furious power lancing into the ice nearby.

Carl had often thought the borer looked like a grotesque, squatting spider. From the hole beneath it came regular gushes of superheated steam.

As if patiently digging after prey, the spider spat invisible microwaves down the shaft in five-second bursts. Moments after each blast, an answering yellow-blue jet of heated gas shot up from the hole below, rushing out of the newly carved tunnel. The billowing steam jet struck deflector plates and parted into six plumes, fanning outward, safely missing the microwave pod.

The borer had been doing that for days, patiently hammering tunnels in the comet core, using bolts of centimeter-wavelength electromagnetic waves, tuned to the frequency that would strip apart carbon dioxide molecules.

Carl felt a faint tremor in his feet each time a bolt blazed forth. The horizon of ancient gray ice curved away in all directions. Outcroppings of pure clathrate snow jutted out through the dark, spongy dust, faded white against mottled browns and rusty reds.

Kato and his mechs worked near the microwave borer, drifting on tethers just above the dirty-gray ice. The core's feeble gravity was not enough to hold them down when they moved. Overhead, thin streamers of ionized, fluorescing gas swayed against hard black night, seeming to caress the Japanese spacer.

Kato supervised as his steel-and-ceramic robot mechanicals did the dangerous work. He had his back to the spider.

Carl was about to turn back to his own task. The borer chugged away methodically, turning ice to steam. Then one of the giant spider legs popped free in a silent puff of snow.

Carl blinked. The microwave generator kept blasting away as the leg flew loose of its anchor, angling up, tilting the body. He did not have time to be horrified.

The beam swept across Kato for only a second. That was enough.

Carl saw Kato make a jerky turn as if to flee. Later, he realized that the movement must have been a final, agonized seizure.

The beam blasted the ice below the man, sending luminous sheets of orange and yellow gas pouring into the blackness above. Vivaldi vanished under a roar of static.

The invisible beam traced a lashing, searing path. It jittered, waved, then tilted further. Away from the horizon. Toward Carl.

He fumbled for his control console, popped the safety cover, and repeatedly stabbed the countermand switch. His ears popped as the static storm cut off. Every mech and high-power device on this side of Halley Core shut down. The microwave finger ceased to write on the ice only a few score meters short of Carl.

The spider began to collapse. Halley's ten-thousandth of a G was too weak to hold down a firing microwave generator, but without the upward kick of expanding gas and radiation pressure, the iceworld's weak attraction asserted itself. The frame lurched and began its achingly slow fall.

—What the hell you doin'? My power's out.—

That would be Jeffers. Other voices babbled over the commline.

"Mayday! Kato's hurt." Carl shot across the dirty-gray ice. His impulse jets fired with a quick, deft certainty as he flew, unconsciously moving with the least wasted energy, the result of years of training. Crossing the rumpled face of Halley was like sailing adroitly over a frozen gray sea beneath a black sky.

Against all hope, he tried calling to the figure in the orange space-suit, splayed, face downward, on the gouged snowfield. "Kato. . . ?"

When he approached, Carl found something that did not resemble a man nearly so much as a blackened, distorted, badly roasted chicken.

Umolanda was next.

The timetable didn't leave much room to mourn Kato. A med team came down from the flagship, the *Edmund Halley*, to retrieve Kato's body, but then it was back to work.

Carl had learned years before to work through unsettling news, accidents, foulups. Shrugging off a crewmate's death wasn't easy. He had liked Kato's energy, his quick humor and brassy confidence. Carl promised his friend's memory at least one good, thoroughly drunken memorial party.

He and Jeffers fixed the spider, reanchoring the foot and reflexing the leg. Carl cut away the damaged portion. Jeffers held the oxygen feed while he slapped a spindly girder segment into the opening. At Carl's signal, the other spacer played the gas jet over the seams and the metal leaped to life, self-welding in a brilliant orange arc. They had the repair done before Kato's body was back on the *Edmund*.

Umolanda came over the rim of Halley Core, pale blue jets driving her along the pole-to-pole cable. The easiest way to move around the irregular iceball was to clip onto the cable and fire suit jets, skimming a few meters above the surface. Magnetic anchors released automatically as you shot by, to minimize friction.

Umolanda was in charge of interior work, shaping irregular gouges into orderly tunnels and rooms. She met Carl near the entrance to Shaft 3, a kilometer from the accident site. The piledriving spider labored away again on the horizon.

—Pretty bad about Kato,— she sent.

"Yeah." Carl grimaced at the grisly memory. "Nice guy, even if he did play those old junk movies on the 3D all the time."

—At least it was quick.—

He didn't have anything to say to that, didn't like talking a whole lot out here anyway. It just interfered with the job.

Umolanda's liquid eyes studied him through a bubble helmet spattered with grime. The neck ring hid her cleft chin. He was surprised to see that this omission revealed her as an otherwise striking woman, her ebony skin stretched by high cheekbones into an artful, ironic cast. Funny, how he'd never noticed that.

—Did you investigate the cause?—

"I checked the area where the spider leg got loose," Carl answered. "Looked like a fault under it gave way."

She nodded. —Not surprising. I've been finding hollows below, formed when radioactive decay warmed the ice long ago, as Halley formed. If some hot gas from the spider's digging worked its way back to the surface through one of those hollows, it could undermine the spider's anchor.—

Carl squinted at the horizon, imagining the whole cometary head riddled with snaking tunnels. "Sounds about right."

—Shouldn't the spider have cut off as soon as it lost focus?—

"Right."

—The switch?—

He shrugged. "Damn safety cutoff was defective. Just didn't kick in," Carl said sourly.

Her eyebrows knitted angrily. —More defective equipment!—

"Yeah. Some bastard Earthside made a little extra on the overhead."

—You've reported it?—

"Sure. It's a long walk back for replacement parts, though." He smiled sardonically. There was a brief silence before Umolanda spoke again.

—There will always be accidents. We lost people at Encke, too.—

"That doesn't make it any easier."

—No . . . I guess not.—

"Anyway, Encke was a pussycat of a comet. Old. Sucked dry. Lots of nice safe rock." He scuffed the surface softly with a boot tip. Snow and dust puffed at the slightest touch.

She forced a grin. —Maybe all this ice is supposed to keep us alive over the long haul, but it's killing us in the short run.—

Carl gestured toward three mechs which stood nearby, waiting for orders. Already the machines were pitted and grimy from Halley's primordial slush and driving dust. "That's your team. Kato was shaping them up. But you might want to give 'em a once-over, anyway."

—They look okay.— Umolanda whistled up the color-coded readout on the back of the nearest one and nodded. —Some luck here. The microwave beam didn't hit them. I'll take them down, put them to hollowing out Shaft Three.—

She tethered the boxy, multiarmed robots and gracefully towed them to the tunnel entrance. Carl watched her get them safely aligned and disappear down the shaft, leading the mechs like a shepherd, though in fact the mechs were as smart as a ten-year-old at some things, and a lot more coordinated.

He went on to check out more of the equipment that other crewmen were ferrying down from the *Edmund*. It was dull labor, but he had been working in the shafts for days and needed a break from the endless walls of rubble-seamed ice.

Overhead, gauzy streamers wove a slow, stately dance. Halley's twin shimmering tails were like blue-green silks. They were fading now, months past the brief summer crisping that came for the comet every seventy-six years. But still the banners of dust and ions unfurled, gossamer traceries waving as if before a lazy breeze, the flags of vast angels.

The expedition had elected to rendezvous with Halley's comet after its 2061 perihelion passage, when the streaking planetoid was well on its way outward again. Here, beyond the orbit of Mars, the sun's violent heating no longer boiled off the huge jets of water molecules, dust, and carbon dioxide that made Halley so spectacular during its short summer.

But heat lingers. For months, as Halley swooped by the fierce, eroding sun, temperature waves had been diffusing down through the ice, and rock, concentrating in volatile vaults and scattered clumps of rock. Now, even as the comet lofted back into the cool darkness of the outer solar system, there were still reservoirs of warmth inside.

The gritty, dark-gray ball was a frozen milkshake of water, carbon dioxide, hydrocarbons, and hydrogen cyanide, each snow subliming into vapor at a different temperature. Inevitably, in some spots, the seeping warmth melted or vaporized ices. These pockets lay waiting.

Carl was partway through assembling a chemical filter system when he heard a sharp high cry on suitcomm.

Then sudden, ominous silence.

His wrist display winked yellow-blue, yellow-blue: Umolanda's code.

*Damn. Twice in one shift?*

"Umolanda!"

No answer. He caught the polar cable and went hand over hand toward the mouth of Shaft 3.

Mechs milled at a cave-in, digging at the slowly settling ice amid swirls of sparkling fog. No signal from Umolanda. He let the mechs work but popped pellet memories out of their backpacks to scan while he waited. It was soon apparent what had happened.

Deep in the ice, the mechs had dutifully chipped away at the walls of the first vault. Umolanda controlled them with a remote, staying in the main tunnel for safety. The TV relay told her when to sequence the robots over to a new routine, when to touch up details, when to bore and blast. She hung tethered, and monitored the portable readout board, occasionally switching over to full servoed control of a mech, to do a particularly adroit bit of polishing.

She had been working at the far end of what would soon be a storage bay when a mech struck a full-fledged boulder of dark native iron two meters across. Captain Cruz had asked them to watch out for usable resources. Umolanda put all three mechs to retrieving it. Under her guidance they slipped levers around the boulder and tried to pry it free. The sullen black chunk refused to budge.

Umolanda had to come in close to inspect. Carl could envision the trouble; mechs were good, but often it was hard to see whether they were getting the best angle.

Carl had a dark premonition. The boulder had been absorbing heat for weeks, letting it spread into a slush that lay immediately behind it, a pocket of confined carbon dioxide and methane. This frothy soup would be perched at its critical point, needing only a bit more temperature or a fraction less pressure to burst forth into the vapor phase.

*Oh for chrissakes, Umolanda don't . . .*

A mech slipped its levering rod around the boulder, penetrating into the reservoir of slush. Umolanda saw the robot lurch, recover. She told it to try again, and moved a little closer to observe.

The mech was slow, gingerly. Its aluminum jacket was spattered and discolored from several days in the ice, but its readouts showed it was in perfect running order. Using as its pivot its own tether in the wall, it levered around the boulder, lunged—and the iron gobbet popped free.

*No!*

Release of pressure liberated the vaporization energy. The explosion drove the pry bar out of the mech's grip like a ramrod fired through the barrel of a cannon.

Umolanda was two meters away. The lever buried itself in her belly.

The pellet-memory readout terminated. Carl blinked away tears.

He waited while the mechs cleared the way. There was really no need to hurry.


Mission Commander Miguel Cruz called off operations for two full shifts. The setup crew had been working to the hilt for a week. Two deaths in one day implied that they were making errors from plain fatigue.

Carl came up on the last ferry. The mottled surface seemed to darken with distance: the cometary nucleus dwindled to a blackish dot swimming in a luminous orange-yellow cloud. Though the fuzzy haze of the coma was still visible with a small telescope from Earth, from near the head itself the shimmering curtains of ions were lacy, scarcely noticeable. Gas and grains of dust still steadily popped free of Halley's surface, making cargo piloting tricky. Most of the outgassing now came not from the sun's ebbing sting, but from the waste heat of humans.

Umolanda's accident had spewed forth a pearly fog for an hour as the inner lake of slush boiled out. Had anyone Earthside been watching through a strong telescope, they could have detected a slight brightening at the cometary head. It was a fleeting memorial. The blinding storm had driven her mechs out into the shaft, dislodged enough ice to bury her. Carl and the others were kept outside until it was too late to recover her and freeze her down slowly for possible medical work. Umolanda was lost.

As the ferry pulled outward the twin tails—one of dust and the other of fluorescing ions—stretched away, foreshortened pale remnants of the glories that had enthralled Earth only two months ago. Ragged streamers forked out toward Jupiter's glowing pinpoint. Oblivious, Carl stretched back and dozed while the ferry rose to meet the *Edmund*.

When they clanged into the lock, he peeled off his suit and coasted toward the murmuring gravity wheel at the bow. He climbed down one of the spoke ladders and stumbled out into the unfamiliar tug of one-eighth G, feeling bone-deep weariness descend with the coming of weight.

*Sleep, yes,* he thought. Let it knit up whatever raveled sleeve he had left.

Virginia came first, though. He hadn't seen her in ages.

She was in her working module, of course, halfway around the wheel. She seldom left the thing nowadays. The door hissed aside. When he slipped into the spherical world of encasing memory shells there was an almost cathedral-like hush, a sense of presence and humming activity just beyond hearing. He sat down quietly next to her cantilevered chair, waiting until she could extract from interactive mode. Tapped into channels through a direct neural link and wrist servos, she scarcely moved. She had to know he was there, but she gave no sign.

Her slim body occasionally fidgeted and jerked. *Like a dog dreaming,* he thought, *and trying to run after imaginary rabbits.*

Her long, half-Polynesian features were pointed toward the banks of holographic displays suspended above her, and her eyes never even flicked to the side to see him. She gazed raptly at multiple scenes of movement, sliding masses of ever-flickering data, geometric diagrams that shifted and evolved, telling new tales.

He waited as she worked through some indecipherable problem. Her long face momentarily tightened, then released as she leaped some hurdle. She had delicate, high cheekbones, too, like Umolanda. Like a third of the expedition's crew, the Percells, products of Simon Percell's program in genetic correcting of inherited diseases. Carl wondered idly if fineboned, aristocratic features were traits the DNA wizard had slipped in. It was possible; the man had been a genius. Carl's own face was broad and ordinary, though, and he had been "developed," as the antiseptic jargon had it, within a year of Virginia. So maybe Simon Percell had taken such care only with the women, then. Given the gaudy stories told about the man, he couldn't rule out the possibility.

By anyone's definition, Virginia Kaninamanu Herbert was clearly a successful experiment. A Hawaiian mixture of Pacific breeds, she had a swift, quirky intelligence, deliciously unpredictable. There was restless energy to her eyes as they moved in quick, darting glances at the myriad welter before her. Below, her mouth was a study in quiet immersion, slightly pursed, thoughtful and pensive. She was not, he supposed, particularly attractive in the usual sense of the term; her long face gave her a rangy look. The serene almond smoothness of her skin offset this, but her forehead was broad, the mouth too ample, her chin was stubbed and not fulsomely rounded as fashion these days demanded.

Carl didn't give a damn. There was a compressed verve in her, a hidden woman he longed to reach. Yet all the time he'd known her she had stayed inside her polite cocoon. She was friendly but little more. He was determined to change that.

On the main screen, obliquely turned girders fitted together in precise sockets. The frame froze. Done.

Abruptly Virginia came alive, as though some fluid intelligence had returned from the labyrinths of her machine counterpart. She stripped the wrist inputs. The white socket for her neural connector flashed briefly as the tap came off and she fluffed her hair into shape.

"Carl! I hoped you'd wait for me to finish."

"Looks important."

"Oh, this?" She waved away the frames of data. "Just some cleanup work. Checking the simulations of docking and transfer, when we take everybody down. There'll be irregularities from random outgassing jets, and the slot boats will have to compensate. I was programming the smarter mechs for the job. We're ready now."

"It'll be a while."

"Well, a few more days . . . Oh, yes." She suddenly became sub-dued. "I heard."

"Damn bad luck." His mouth twisted sourly.

"Fatigue, I heard."

"That too."

She reached out and touched his arm tentatively. "There was noth-ing you could do."

"Probably. Maybe I shouldn't have let her go down that hole right after Kato bought it. Thing like that, shakes you up, screws up your judgment. Makes accidents more likely."

"You weren't senior to her."

"Yeah, but—"

"It's *not* your fault. If anything, it's the constraints we work under. This timetable—"

"Yeah, I know."

"Come on. I'll buy you some coffee."

"Sleep's what I need."

"No, you need talk. Some people contact."

"Trading arcane jokes with that computer crowd of yours?" He grimaced. "I always come out sounding like a nerd."

She flexed smoothly out of her console couch, taking advantage of the low gravity to curl and unwind in midair. "Not at all!" Something in her sudden, bouncy gaiety lifted his heart. "Blithe spirit, nerd thou never wert."

"Mutilated Shelley! God, that's awful."

"True, though. Come on. First round is on me."

# SAUL

To most people the creature would seem hideous. Vaguely globular, specked with yellow and ocher spots and spiky protusions all around, it had the sort of looks only a particularly indulgent mother could love.

*Or a stepfather,* Saul Lintz thought.

Millions of the tiny, ugly things darted about in the crowded con-fines of a single, glinting drop of saline water, beaded by surface tension into a high, arching meniscus on the glass microscope slide.

Saul played the fiber optic controls until his magnifier zoomed in on a single cyanute. "There we are," he muttered softly. "You'll do as a test subject, my lad."

He pressed a trigger and the cytology instrument took over following the tiny microbe, automatically tracking it wherever it swam within its little universe.

The creature was a pulsing mass of tiny, rainbowed cilia that rippled faster than the eye could follow. But Saul knew the thing anyway, to its smallest part. He could imagine every mottled, microscopic component, down past where the instrument could not go—to the level of acids and bases, of sugars and finely balanced lipid barriers.

It darted to and fro amid the thousands of other rough, rippling cells, seeking what it needed to survive.

*Not unlike us,* Saul thought. *Only our search has brought us humans half a billion miles from home.*

He rubbed his eyes and bent forward in a habit from long-ago days, when one still occasionally peered through cold glass lenses instead of letting the machines do all the hard work. *Relax,* Saul told himself. *There's no need to crane over the screen.*

Even here, in *Edmund*'s slowly spinning gravity wheel, there wasn't enough of a pull to fight against. One had to keep loose, or expend enormous energy just to stay still.

Only half of the screens and holo displays in the biology unit brimmed with light. In a dozen other dark faces Saul's own pale image was reflected . . . thick eyebrows above a generous nose, and lines that most people, on meeting him, guessed came of a lifetime spent smiling.

Only those who knew Saul well—and they were few these days—understood the true source of those craggy indentations: a stoicism that warded off the pain of many, many losses.

The creases stood out now as Saul's blue eyes narrowed in concentration. Delicately touching a hand controller, he brought a hollow sliver of metal down into the little ball of salty water on the microscope slide. On the main holo screen the image of the tiny needle seemed to loom like a javelin as computers guided it toward the chosen test subject.

"Come on, *meshugga*," Saul muttered as the microbe tried to dart away. "Hold still for Papa."

The cyanute was less than fifty microns across, so small and innocuous that its ancestors had lived peacefully in human bodies for millions of years of quiet symbiosis, until they were discovered only a generation or so ago. For Saul the little creature contained as many wonders as the huge comet commanding such attention outside.

The main vision wall of the lab had been left tuned to a view of Halley, not as the comet looked now—a slowly ebbing cloud of banked fluorescence surrounding a six-mile chunk of dingy snow—but as it had been only months before, in all its brief glory, streaking past the sun at half the Earth's orbital distance, its ion tail flapping in the protonic breeze.

They were well matched in beauty—the titanic, cosmic messenger that was to be their home for most of a century and the microscopic wonder that had made the sojourn possible. Still, it was no surprise that, of the two, Saul concentrated on the tiny living thing drifting in the little glob of water.

After all, he had made it.

*Sh'ma Yisrael . . .* he reminded himself. *There is but one God— even though he should place his tools in our hands—tools to shape life and forge worlds. He is only stepping back to see what we will do with them.*

In Saul's line of work he found it wise to remember that, from time to time.

When the needle had approached to within a cell's width of the subject, Saul spoke a word and triggered the test sequence. A small, indistinct puff disturbed the water near the needle's tip, where tiny traces of hydrogen cyanide solution spurted forth.

No more than a scattering of molecules was involved, yet the tiny organism reacted nearly instantly. Its cilia erupted in a sudden spasm of activity and the creature sprang forward. . . .

Forward, *toward* the needle. It engulfed the tip, throbbing with seeming eagerness.

*So far, so good.* Saul would have been surprised if it had behaved differently. The cyanutes had been thoroughly tested on Earth before the mission to Halley's Comet was approved. No factor was more important to the success and health of 410 brave men and women than these little creatures.

Confident he was. But life—even specially gene-tailored life—had a way of changing when you least expected it. The survival of all those people depended on the tiny "nutes" working as planned. He had led the team that designed them, and he did not intend to allow any failures. There were more than enough ghosts already in his life. Miriam, the children, the land and people of his youth . . . and, of course, Simon Percell.

*Poor Simon.* All too well he recalled how one mistake had ruined his friend's life and nearly everything he had worked to accomplish. *Keep reminding me, Simon. Keep reminding me of the dangers of playing God.*

All the HCN was gone now, according to the displays, sucked up by the eager organism. Saul nodded in satisfaction. Every human being on this mission had millions of cyanutes living in his or her bloodstream and in the little alveoli air sacs that made up their lungs. This sample, taken at random from one of the crew, had just demonstrated that it would do its main job—sop up any trace of deadly, dissolved cyanide gas before the stuff could get near its host's red corpuscles. Another puff of dissolved gas proved its ability to gobble carbon monoxide before the chemical could bind to human hemoglobin.

Saul touched off the next stage in the test. Minute traces of a new compound swirled into the saline bubble. This time the little microbe on the screen quickly withdrew from the needle, curling almost as if it had been stung. Cyanide and CO were fresh grazing to this creature, but human tissue factors appeared to be a definite no-no.

Again, good news. The second test showed that the cyanute was totally disinclined to look on human cells as meat.

*So much for the basics.* There were countless other things to check. Saul mentally ran down a list as he triggered the sequencer to begin the automatic phase of the test program.

. . . *Self-limiting reproduction, benign acceptance by the human immune system, pH sensitivity, a voracious appetite for other potential cometary toxins* . . .

It wasn't so much a catalog of attributes as a litany of challenges met and conquered. Saul couldn't help feeling proud of his small team back on Earth, which had had to overcome prejudice, bureaucracy, and undisguised superstition to do this work. In the end, though, they had created a wonder—a new human symbiont.

Cyanutes would be a permanent, benign part of every man and woman on the crew for the rest of their lives . . . and perhaps, he dared imagine, a part of the human animal from now on, like the intestinal flora that had always helped him digest his food and the mitochondria within his cells that burned sugars for him, converting them into usable energy.

"Who can compare with thee, oh Lord . . ." he whispered wryly, teasing himself for his ineradicable corner of hubris. Saul had long ago concluded that he and God would have to be patient with each other. Perhaps the universe was not conveniently set up for either of them.

He watched the test results unfold on the screen—all nominal, nearly perfect—until a soft squeak announced the opening of the bio-lab portal behind him.

"So! We are poking away at our pets again, Saul? You just cannot leave them alone?"

He didn't have to look up to know the voice of Akio Matsudo. "Hello 'Kio." He waved without turning around. "Just double-checking. And everything looks fine, thanks. Aren't they lovely critters?"

He smiled as the spry, tall Japanese physician came alongside and made a sour look. The chief of Mission Life Sciences had never disguised his opinion of Saul's "critters." They were necessary—utterly vital to the success of their seventy-eight-year voyage. But poor Akio had never come to see their more aesthetic side.

"Ugh," Matsudo commented. "Please do not remind me of the infestation even now swarming in my bodily fluids. Next time you wish to inject me with alien parasites—"

"Symbionts," Saul corrected quickly.

"—against which my body has no immune capability whatsoever— next time I will make the incision myself—from crotch to sternum!"

Saul could only grin as Matsudo's serious mug broke and the man actually giggled. It was a "kee-kee-kee" sound that spacers had already mimicked into a sort of clarion call below decks. Akio frequently made such light jests about the traditions of ancient Japan.

Perhaps it was similar to the way Saul dropped Yiddishisms into his speech now and then, although he had learned the language only a decade ago. *It's a proper dialect for exiles,* he thought.

"What have you got there, 'Kio?" He pointed at a flimsy sheet in the other's hand.

"Ah. Yess." Matsudo tended to slur his sibilants. "Even as we are speaking of immune systems, I have come to ask you to go through the stimulants inventory with me, Saul. I believe that it is time to release an attenuated disease into the life-support system."

Saul winced. He never looked forward to this.

"So soon? Are you sure? Four-fifths of the expedition is still frozen aboard the *Sekanina* and the other freighter tugs. All we have awake now are the *Edmund* crew and support staff."

"All the more reason." Matsudo nodded. "Thirty spacers have been living together on this cramped ship for more than a year. Another forty have been out of the slots for two or more months, as we got closer to the comet. All of the colds and minor viruses they brought with them when they departed Earth have run their course by now.

"I've done a parasite inventory, and have found that more than three-quarters of the ambient pathogenic organisms have already gone extinct! It is time to release a new challenge."

Saul sighed. "You're the boss." Actually, the entire bio committee was supposed to pass on immune challenges. But reminding Akio would only offend him. The procedure was routine, anyway.

Still, Saul's nose already itched in unhappy anticipation.

He reached over to the bio-library console and punched out a rapid code. A page of data appeared in space before a black backdrop.

Saul nodded at the glowing green lettering. "There is a lovely array of nasty bugs at your disposal, Doctor. With what plague do you wish to infect your patients? We have chicken pox, fox pox, attenuated measles. . . ."

"Nothing so drastic." Matsudo waved. "At least not so soon."

"No? Well, then there's impetigo, athlete's foot. . . ."

"*Amaterasu!* Heaven forfend, Saul! In this dampness? Before the comet-tunnel habitats have been set up and the big dehumidifiers are working? You know how the navy feels about fungus aboard a spaceship. Cruz would have our—"

He stopped abruptly and grinned lopsidedly. "Ha ha. Very funny, Saul. You are pulling my leg, of course."

Saul had known Matsudo casually, from scientific conferences and by reputation, for many years. But the man was still somewhat of an enigma to him. For instance, why had he volunteered to come on this mission? Of all the types who would sign up to leave Earth, spend seventy-three years of a seventy-eight-year mission in slot sleep, and return to a world grown alien and strange, which category applied to Akio? Was he an idealist, following Captain Miguel Cruz's dream of what the mission might mean to mankind? Or was he an exile, like so many on this expedition?

*Perhaps, like me, he's a little of both.*

Matsudo ran a hand through his lustrous black hair, as thick as any youth's. "Just pick me out a head-cold virus, will you be so kind, Saul? Something that will challenge the crew enough to keep up their antibody production and T cell counts. They needn't even notice it, for all I care."

Saul spoke a chain of letters aloud, and a new page appeared. "The customer's always right," he ruminated aloud. "And you're in luck! We seem to have eighty varieties of head cold on sale."

"Surprise me," Matsudo said. But then he frowned and held up both hands. "No! On second thought, let me choose! I don't want any of your experimental monsters loose right now, no matter what you say about the *wonders of symbiosis!*"

Saul pushed off to one side as Akio bent forward to peer at the list of available diseases, muttering softly to himself. Obviously, Matsudo had left his contact lenses out again.

*He's about three decimeters taller than his grandfather,* Saul thought. *And yet he's suspicious of change. A scientist, and yet he's too conservative to get a corneal implant that would let him see without aid.*

*What ever happened to the innovative, future-hungry Japanese of so long ago?*

For that matter, what had happened to Israel, his own homeland? How could the descendants of the Negev pioneers, the most potent warriors in two centuries, slowly decline into superstition and cultism? What had turned clear-eye Sabras into cowed sheep who let the Levite and Salawite fanatics just walk in and take over?

The mysteries were part of a greater one that still amazed Saul, how courage seemed to be leaking away from humanity, even as the Hell Century was ending and better times appeared near at last.

It wasn't a calming train of thought. Biological science was in just as bad shape. The bright hopes offered by Simon Percell and the genetic engineers of the early part of the century had nearly collapsed in a series of scandals more than a decade ago, leaving only a stolid pharmaceutical industry and a few mavericks such as Saul to carry on.

Earth was rapidly becoming unpleasant for mavericks—one of the reasons he was on this mission. Exile through space and time certainly beat some of the alternatives he had seen coming.

"We will use rhinovirus TR-3-APZX-471," Matsudo announced, apparently satisfied with his selection. "Do you concur, Saul?"

Saul already felt a sneeze coming on. "A naïve little varietal, but I'm sure you'll be amused by its presumption."

"I beg your pardon?"

"Never mind," he grumped. "As official keeper of small animals, I'll have an incubated vial of the nasty buggers in your in-box by tomorrow morning." He touched a key and the glowing inventory disappeared.

Matsudo lifted himself easily in the one-eighth G of the *Edmund's* laboratory wheel, and sat on the counter. He sighed, and Saul could tell that his friend was about to go philosophical on him. Over the long journey from Earth they had exchanged countless chess games and views of the world, and never budged each other on any issue at all.

"It's not much like back when we were in medical school, is it,

Saul? You in Haifa and me in Tokyo? We were brought up to hate pathogens—the infectious viruses and bacteria and prions—to want only to wipe them from the face of the Earth. Now, we culture and use them. They are our tools."

Saul nodded. Today half a physician's job involved careful application of those very horrors, serving them up judiciously to create *challenges*.

"Exercise the patient's immune system, and let him do the rest," Saul said, nodding. "It's a better way, Akio. I only wish you'd see that my cyanutes are part of the same progression."

Matsudo rolled his eyes. He and Saul had been over this many times.

"Again, I regret that I cannot agree. In one case we teach the body to be strong and reject that which is foreign. But you coax it to *accept* an interloper, forever!"

"Perhaps half of the cells in a human body are guest life forms, Akio . . . gut bacteria, follicle cleaners. They help us; we help them."

Matsudo waved his hand. "Yes, yes. *Most of what you call you, is not!* I have heard it before. I know you see us not as individuals, Saul, but as great, synergistic hives of cooperating species." There was a biting edge to Matsudo's voice that Saul did not remember having heard before. Exaggeration was not Matsudo's usual style.

"Akio . . ."

Matsudo hurried on, though. "And what if you're right, Saul? All of those organisms that share our bodies with us grew into symbiosis over *millions of years*. That is entirely different from throwing gene-tailored monsters into such a delicate balance on purpose!"

Matsudo flushed slightly. Saul considered trying to explain one more time—that the cyanutes were descended from creatures that had lived peacefully in man for aeons. But of course, he knew how Akio would answer. After all the changes that had been made, the 'nutes were a new species, as different from their natural cousins as men were from apes.

"Saul, the Movement to Restore and Reflect teaches us that we must think carefully before we interfere with nature. The Hell Century has shown how dangerous it can be to meddle where we don't understand."

Glancing up at the microscope screen, where his tiny test subject was still being run through its paces, Saul saw that the animal was still throbbing near the needle—harried but well.

"I . . ." He shook his head and went silent. Saul had an idea what was bothering his friend.

"There's still no sign of the *Newburn* yet, is there?"

Matsudo shook his head, his gaze on the floor. "Captain Cruz and his officers are still looking. Perhaps when the comet has calmed down some more, when the coma and ion tail are less noisy . . . Fortunately, there were only forty people aboard that one. If it had been one of the other slot tugs, the *Sekanina*, or the *Whipple*, or the *Delsemme*—" He shrugged.

Saul nodded. No wonder Matsudo was irritable. More than three hundred men and women had been shipped from Earth five years ahead of *Edmund*—along with most of the expedition's massive equipment—chilled down to near freezing aboard four slender robot freighters, riding sunlight behind gossamer sails a thousand kilometers across.

Only the "founder" team took the fast, energetically expensive track aboard the old *Edmund Halley*. They exhausted almost the last of their propellant to match the comet's furious retrograde orbit. Whey they arrived the first task awaiting the torch ship's crew was to recover the huge cylinders containing the deep-sleeping majority of the mission crew.

There were disadvantages to each style of travel—torch ship or slot tug. Much of the *Edmund* staff had to take long turns enduring the boredom and cramped living of more than a year in space. As well, they shared the recently evident dangers of setting up the base.

On the other hand, they had some control over their fate. It was not their lot to coast for years in near-frozen sleep, relying on someone else to catch up, capture their slim barge, and finally awaken them.

Would the men and women aboard *Newburn* drift forever? If Cruz and his team never found the tug, might they be picked up by someone else, in some faraway age? What might they awaken to, after such a long trip down the river of time?

"It is going to be a long eighty years, Saul." Matsudo shook his head pensively, looking at the picture wall, vivid with Halley's Comet in its full glory against a backdrop of stars. The plasma and dust tails glittered like flapping banners, like plankton in a phosphorescent sea. "It is a long time until we see home again."

Saul smiled, hiding his own misgivings for his friend's sake. "We'll sleep through most of it, 'Kio. And when we do get home, we'll be rich and famous."

Matsudo snorted at the thought, but he acknowledged Saul's intent with a smile. Irony was the common trait that made them friends, in spite of all their differences.

A bell chimed and Saul looked up as the probe's needle withdrew from the watery, saline bead. The subject cyanute floated gray and limp now. The last test had been to prove that the creatures could still easily be killed, if ever the need arose.

*A creator's prerogative?* he wondered. *Or are my shoulders stooped imperceptibly under one more tiny guilt?*

Scavengers were already nosing up to the microscopic corpse. Saul reached over and turned off the microscope.

# VIRGINIA

The place smelled of rank, unwashed man.

Virginia's nose wrinkled when she entered the workout gym for her mandatory exercise period.

*We're strange creatures. Mammals evolve odors that make males aggressive, and all of us nervous around one another, and then we pack a whole crowd of people together into a tin crate for a year or more, and ask them to make nice.*

Actually, Virginia did not mind the smell all that much. She did not even mind men.

*They just aren't the reason I accepted exile into the twenty-second century, riding a speck of stardust and ice out into the Big Night.*

Virginia had her own motives. For her, volunteering for Project Halley had little to do with herding comets for harvest.

She stripped down to her shorts and mounted a bicycle ergometer, attaching the bio-monitor straps. Virginia pushed the pedals, accelerating until the readout showed she was fulfilling Dr. van Zoon's orders.

The workout gym was located in the *Edmund Halley*'s gravity wheel, where most of the crew snoozed through their sleep periods under weight. Virginia understood the need to let blood and bones feel the Old Pull now and then to keep them in shape. But these thrice-weekly sessions with straps, pulleys, and ergometers struck her as truly burnt logic.

She had considered monkeying with the med center's data flow, inserting simulated feedback from all these exercise machines. She could do it, too. Virginia wasn't modest about her competence in Data Intelligence. Lefty d'Amaria might be head of the department, but she was the best.

*Oh, well, I guess I need this,* she thought as she bore down on the pedals. Sweat began popping out, glistening on her olive skin.

Normally, she took pride in keeping a taut physique. Back home in Hawaii, she had surfed nearly every other day. But now it seemed she had to shake off a lassitude that still hung over her after a year's chilled sleep. Until three weeks ago she had been suspended, life functions barely ticking over at just above freezing. Perhaps it was a lingering laziness from the slot drugs that had made her so reluctant to come down to the gym.

*Well, as long as I'm here, let's do it right.*

She bore down hard and pretended she was pedaling across the Lanai-Maui bridge. The omnipresent rumble of the gravity wheel faded into an imagined background of roaring wind and water. Virginia pictured that the door in front of her might let her out, blinking, into yellow sunshine and the rich scent of pineapple.

Her muscles felt warm and stretched after the workout. And it *was* good to spend some time after showering just brushing her long black hair. Stepping back into her drab pullover was reminder enough, though. Maui lay a hundred million miles from here.

*You made your choice, girl. There are things to accomplish out here . . . things more important to you even than remaining in the Land of the Golden People.*

She decided to take a brisk walk around the gravity wheel before returning to the freefall portion of the ship. Virginia strode long-legged in the direction opposite to the wheel's spin.

It seemed nobody was about. Dr. Marguerite van Zoon wasn't chivying the *spacers* to visit the gym these days. Those poor folk were sweating quite enough right now, and were exempt from the Walloon physician's obsession with exercise.

Virginia's journey around the rim hallway took her past one of the spoke ladders and beyond, to the part of the wheel dedicated to laboratories. The doors were all closed, so she couldn't tell if the Biological Sciences section was being used right now. She paused by the door, her hand hesitating, half-raised toward the buzzer.

*Oh come on, Ginnie. It's not as if Saul Lintz will bite you. Why all these little-girl heart palpitations?*

All she knew was that the man held a fascination for her, more than she had felt toward anyone in years. Was it his worldly experience? Or the expression in his eyes—perseverance and quiet strength?

Since she had been unslotted, she had hoped he would say something, make some first move. It was frustrating to realize, at last, that he simply assumed she saw him as a father figure. That left Virginia wondering if she should attempt an overture herself.

Her hesitation over the buzzer lasted until she felt ridiculous.

*It would seem so contrived to barge in on him now. What would I say?*

*Later there'll be opportunity to arrange something more casual. After all, what we have plenty of is time.*

At least that would do for an excuse. Oh, if only she understood people half as well as she did machines! She swiveled and left without disturbing the buzzer.

As she walked down the rim corridor, she noticed all the ways in which the *Edmund Halley* had aged over the past year. The corridors no longer shone. Buff, color-coordinated wall panels had warped and even buckled in places. The old girl had not started this mission exactly in the blush of youth, and no space vessel of her size had ever been required to accelerate so far, for so long. The strain showed.

Virginia thought she was past surprise, but as she approached another of the spoke ladders, she stopped and stared.

*Oh, it can't be this bad!*

An air vent dripped onto the gently curved hallway. Patchy, dark green growth discolored the floor where Coriolis effects had pushed a small puddle against the wall.

Virginia's generous lips pursed in disgust as she stepped gingerly past the moldy infestation and climbed a damp ladder toward the hub, making a mental note to report this to maintenance. It was hard to believe she was the first to discover it.

The rungs pressed against her body as she surrendered angular momentum to the rotating wheel. The spoke passageway was dim and dank and all too smelly. Only half the phosphor panels in this tunnel were working, making the ascent seem a bit like a trip through a city sewer.

*It's a good thing the Halley habitats will be ready soon,* she thought. *This creaky barge needs a long overhaul.*

There would be little enough for the four hundred members of the expedition to do during three-quarters of a century . . . investigating the mysteries of a major cometary nucleus . . . testing the sublimation control panels and the big Nudge Flingers . . . another busy time in thirty years or so as Halley neared its farthest reach from the sun, when Virginia would help calculate parameters for the all important Grand Maneuver . . . then the long fall toward Jupiter and finally, home.

For most of the intervening time, nearly everybody would be asleep, accumulating Earthside pay in nearly dreamless slot state. That was when the small, rotating watch shifts would slowly refurbish poor *Edmund*.

*Seven decades ought to be time enough. It had better be. Come Halley's next fiery plunge into the inner solar system, this old bucket has to be in good enough shape to take us home again.*

Climbing hand over hand, Virginia felt her weight seep away into the ladder as she approached the grumbling bearings, where the null gravity of space resumed. The four spoke tunnels came together in a small, rotating, octagonal room.

Just before reaching the hub, however, she blinked in stunned surprise at a small lubricant leak, spraying fine, greasy vapor into the passage.

*I know most of* Edmund*'s spacers have been called away to work on Halley Core. Still, there's no excuse for this! We're going to need the wheel for a long time to come!*

"Disgusting," she muttered aloud. "Simply disgusting."

That was when a voice spoke from beyond the faint, oily spray.

"I agree, Virginia."

She glanced up quickly. A slightly paunchy man in a gray shipsuit floated by one of the two exits, his broad, Slavic mouth pouting in a sour expression. A wool cap was pulled down over sparse brown hair flecked with gray. His arms were long and powerful-looking, all the more so since he had no legs.

Spacer Second Class Otis Sergeov had never appeared particularly disabled by his handicap. In fact, it seemed to make him quicker in microgravity. She had heard that Sergeov was now assigned to helping Joao Quiverian and the other astronomers studying Comet Halley.

He was the oldest *Percell* Virginia had ever met.

Being one of the first had its drawbacks. Simon Percell's famous early work in genetic surgery had made it possible for Sergeov's parents to have children at all. But a mosaic flaw had given him only small nubs below his shorts.

"Oh, hello, Otis," she greeted him. "Something has to be done about this. Has anyone reported it yet?"

The Russian spacer shrugged. "Is doing what the hell good, reporting thing like this? Nobody does nothing about it, for sure," he groused bitterly in mixed Russian and English. "The *Stchakai* cretins!"

Virginia blinked at the apparent nonsequitur. *Of course* Captain Cruz would order repairs at once, when someone told him. . . .

Then she noticed that Sergeov wasn't even looking at the lubricant leak. Virginia rode the slowly rotating hub until she was even with the man, then edged past the intermittent spray and pushed off hard.

The octagonal room seemed to spin around her. She had to grab twice in order to grip a rubberized handhold, and still her body collided with the padded wall. *I'll never get this right!* she thought as she fought to orient herself.

Sergeov pointed. "You think Ortho bureaucrats will do anything about this thing, do you?" he snapped. *"This?"*

Virginia blinked. He was glaring at a graffito scrawled on the bulkhead nearest the grumbling axis bearings.

"Arc of the Sun," he identified the symbol, bitingly. "The *Kakashkiia* bastards have followed us, even out here."

"I've seen it before," Virginia said softly. She felt a little short of breath over this unexpected sight. "Even in Hawaii . . ."

"So?" Sergeov interrupted snidely. "Even in Land of the Golden People? Even in your techno-humanistic paradise?"

Virginia's brow knotted. Back in mission training she had taken a dislike to Sergeov, fellow Percell or no. He had spent nearly all his life in space—turning his physical drawbacks into assets in freefall—and yet every time she encountered him she felt uncomfortable, as if the man radiated long-suppressed bitterness.

She promised herself she would use her own computer to worm her way into the personnel files. She would see to it that they never shared a shift out of the slots during the seven decades ahead.

"Goodbye, Otis. I have work to do." But he stopped her, seizing her arm.

"You know this is not first incident," he said. "Only most blatant. Some of *Arcists,*" he sneered, "refuse to even talk to Percells aboard. They avoid us like we are *xherobiy* . . . unclean!"

Virginia shrugged. "Everybody's been under a lot of stress lately. That'll change when the habitats are completed, and once people have room to move around again. When we've unfrozen some folk from the slot tugs and get to look at some fresh faces for a change . . ."

Sergeov's grip was iron-strong from years of hauling space gear around. "Might help symptoms," he insisted. "But the disease goes on. You saw what Earth was like when we left. One after another of *shlyoocha* Hot Belt countries pass laws restricting our rights . . . rights of *all* genetically enhanced people!"

Virginia only wanted the man to let go of her arm. She tried reason.

"The nations of equatorial Africa and America have had a hellish century, Otis. I don't like the specious turn their ideology has taken in recent years either, but at least they're environmentalists, nowadays. If they've become a bit fanatical in that direction, well, anyone will admit it's an improvement over the way their grandfathers behaved. The pendulum will swing back again."

Virginia did not like the expression on Sergeov's face. He looked at her as if she were pitiably, even criminally naïve.

"You think so? But no, my dear young Percell. Is only the beginning! They are already at war with us!"

His unshaven face drew closer. "And who can blame them? When *Homo sapiens* awakens to what is happening, more and more repression will come against us—the Successor Race. Nothing less than future generations are at stake here!"

"Oh, come on, Otis." Virginia laughed dryly, trying to lighten the tone. "It's not like we few Percells are the next step in evol—"

"No, you *listen,* girl!" Sergeov's eyes narrowed. "This is main reason for all such paranoia, such persecution! Is hard to blame Neanderthals for trying to protect their obsolete form, after all. Species protect selves."

He grinned severely. "But that does not mean we must let bastards squash us, either. Is up to us to act first, or perish!"

Even though they were clearly alone, Virginia quickly looked about. She did not want to be around if this seditious talk was overheard. With no wasted motion she used a judo grip-break to yank her arm away hard, sending the man spinning back. Sergeov bumped his head on the unpadded bulkhead.

"Ow!" he protested in hurt surprise. *"Yayatamiy! Govenka!* What you do that for?"

"You *Uber* extremists don't have the answer," she breathed. "You only give Percells a bad name by talking like that. We aren't Nietzsche's supermen. We're misunderstood human beings. That's all!"

Sergeov grimaced, rubbing his head. "Ask the *regular* human beings, the Orthos, if they think us brothers," he grumped.

Pushing the walls with her hands, Virginia backed away like a fish from a shark, even though Sergeov showed no inclination to follow her. Once down the hall a few feet, she spun about and kicked off down the dimly lit corridor toward her sanctuary.

Everything in Virginia's private work capsule was neat, crisp, efficient. The screens and opalescent holo displays that surrounded her web-couch all operated perfectly. Far from home and everything she had known—even hurtling out of the solar system at thirty kilometers per second—this was the center of her universe. She made certain everything was in good working order.

Officially, her role was to provide special support to Computations Section. But she had actually inveigled her way aboard this mission in hopes of getting some of her own research done. In the kind of scientific environment that was developing on Earth, the sorts of things she was interested in were frowned on.

*Bio-organic computers . . . machines that might really think . . .* These were areas that had been diagnosed as improbable, even *dangerous,* by increasingly conservative twenty-first-century science. Even in her native Hawaii, her superiors had grown more and more uncomfortable with the attention her work was drawing from the outside world.

*But I* know *bio-organics can eventually outperform silicon and gallium! And machines can do better than moron mechanical water drawing and wood hewing. Stochastic processors can be made to think.*

Over to the right, tucked under a desktop, was the squat box containing her own, special simulation unit; the Kelmar organo computer had used up nearly all of her small personal-effects allowance, but it was worth it.

Panel lights rippled as the hatch hissed shut behind her and she slipped onto the web-couch. Virginia belted herself in and spoke softly.

"Hello, JonVon."

The main holo screen glittered.

HELLO, VIRGINIA.
WILL IT BE *WORK* OR PLAY TODAY?

She smiled. No doubt in the eighty years ahead much progress would be made. It had to happen—even in a growing tide of scientific conservatism.

But right now her charge was the best there was—unconventional, using technology all but banned back home, but supreme in her own estimation.

She had named the unit after John Von Neumann, inventor of the theory of games. The program/mainframe could mimic a human's response patterns well enough to pass a third-stage Turing test . . . fooling an unsuspecting person in a five-minute casual vid-phone conversation into thinking the face and voice on the other end of the line were those of a real person, not a computer.

JonVon could even tell a dirty joke, leering just enough and chuckling at the right time.

Unprecedented, yes. But stunts like that weren't true "machine intelligence"—not the way Virginia felt should be possible.

The molecular hardware in that five-liter box *should* be good enough to model the complex standing wave in a human brain. She was sure of it. They didn't agree back home, of course, and so it had never really been given a chance.

For the next few weeks she would have little time to engage in her private experiments. She had to use all her equipment, including Jon-Von, to supplement the ship's mainframe. Nearly all her energy was devoted to preparing those mathematical models Captain Cruz's spacers kept demanding.

Later, though, during her years on watch, there would be time. Time for work and undiluted thought.

*Back in the twentieth century, they knew how to have daring dreams,* she thought. *They did not believe in limits.* It was one reason she liked old-time flat-screen movies . . . enjoyed simulating old-time film stars and long-ago poets.

*Those people nearly wrecked the world with their greed, but they* did *believe in ambition. They wouldn't have rested until they had machines that could think.*

She glanced at the timepiece etched indelibly under her left thumbnail. "How about twenty minutes of diversion, Johnny?" Virginia lifted a cable from the console and bared a whitish bump at the back of her head. When the connection clicked home, the symbols on the screen were accompanied by a rich voice inside her head.

POETRY, VIRGINIA?

She answered quickly with an impulsive thread of verse:

Ka Honua
    —Earth, my home,
E hoomanao no au ia oe
    —I shall remember you.

I wonder what he likes
    to do,
And if he can spare me
    the time of day?

The line to her acoustic nerve hummed.

MIXED STYLES, VIRGINIA?
DOES THE SECOND PART APPLY TO LOVE?

She blushed. "Oh hush, silly. Come on now. Let's take a look at your conversation subroutines."

# CARL

The dusty ice sheets were speckled and splashed, rainbow-mottled, pocked and scoured.

Carl Osborn spun his workpod and vectored down toward Halley Core. He flew away from the razor-sharp dawnline, aiming for the north pole where their base was finally taking shape.

The grainy gray and brown surface was changing rapidly now. Like tiny, fat ants, mechs moved over it, preparing docking areas and mooring towers. Spiders hammered holes into the ice, their endless microwave *zzzzzzttt*s leaking faintly into some of the data channels. Carl muttered a quick correcting command to his suit's comm filter control and the interference stopped.

Shaft 3 was nearly finished, a yawning pit like a dead eye socket. The first group of sleep slots would be going down that way soon. A kilometer of sheltering ice would shield the sleepers from the fatal sting of cosmic rays, the sleeting solar storms.

Random gouges surrounded the shaft. Discharging mech fuel cells had pitted the crusty ice. Broken gear lay where teams had dropped it. Chem spills had condensed into powdery green and yellow splotches. Discarded girders and sonic cartridges and shockjackets lay everywhere. *What mankind would study,* Carl thought wryly, *he first messes up*.

Just barely visible over the curved horizon, now slowly coming into view along the dawnline, were the black gas-suppression panels. They were an ongoing experiment, armored against the high-velocity dust streams and designed to generate electricity from sunlight. Their shadows reduced the outgassing from one-eighth of Halley Core's surface, introducing an asymmetry in the boiloff. The panels could be turned so that they trapped heat, too, increasing the outgassing on the night side of the core. The net effect was a faint, persistent push that could alter the comet's orbit, given time.

Or so the story went. To Carl the big black panels had been one solid week of grunt labor. They were too delicate to let the mechs do more than hold them in place, while he and Lani Nguyen and Jeffers had mounted them to the robo-arms that would turn them. The astroengineers were still tinkering with the gimmicks piling up data to analyze during the long outbound voyage.

It was hard to tell what was an intentional experiment and what was yesterday's garbage. He wondered how messy Halley Core could get. In nearly eighty years they might thoroughly trash even this much ice.

Carl could see a thin black stripe coming out of shadow at the dawnline—the polar cable. It wrapped around Halley Core, pole to pole, and joined the equatorial cable at a perfect right angle, but separated by several meters for safety. The rails provided swift ways to zip around the surface. Still, Carl seldom used them. He liked to get free of the bleak ice, swim in serene blackness above it all.

Between him and the slowly spinning, potato-shaped iceworld were the swarming mechs he supervised. He thumbed instructions into his lap console, muttering code phrases automatically, making the distant dots turn their burden—a huge orange cylinder. Its smooth sheen reflected glinting sunlight.

—Channel D to Osborn. Real pretty, uh?— Jeffers sent from below.
"Well . . ."

*Awful color,* he thought. *And it's the inner-corridor lining. We'll have to look at it for seventy years.*

The mechs dropped lower, angling the cylinder for Shaft 3, following his instructions. Halley Core revolved every fifty-two hours, just fast enough to make readjustment necessary as they approached. There was also a thin fog of fading cometary coma that blurred images at this distance—8.3 kilometers, his board said—and made it hard to use his automatic aligning program.

He had backup on the *Edmund,* in case of a malf. Fine, in theory. But by the time he got somebody online, the mechs might dutifully try to stuff the cylinder into a hill of ice. Despite Virginia's earnest faith, computers could do only so much. From there on you had to eyeball it.

"Bringing it in slow," he sent.

—Looks vectored up just a hair. Two clicks too high along the local y-axis,— Jeffers replied.

Carl looked down, recalibrated, saw that Jeffers was right. "Damn."

—You okay?—

"Yeah. Just keep those beacons going."

The four laser aligners bracketed Shaft 3 clearly, and Carl turned the mechs into configuration using the bright markers. A touch of delta V, a compensating torque. His board approved the shift. Good. But now the irregular ice was looming fast, and—

Gravity. He'd forgotten the damn gravity. Halley Core had only a ten-thousandth of Earth's pull . . . but in his half-hour descent from the solar-sail freighter the momentum had built . . . slow but steady . . . He punched in a correction, watching the equations ripple across his board.

Lights flashed red. "I'm braking," he sent, and fired the mechs' retros.

Damn the gravity anyway. Carl had been at Encke, worked around the rocky comet nucleus for weeks. It had been just like any deepspace work—sometimes almost an elaborate waltz, smooth and sure, and a lot of grunt and sweat at crucial moments. Still, it was basically easy if you watched that your vectors matched, didn't push anything except at its center of mass, worked steadily, kept your head.

But Encke was a runt. An old prune of a comet, broiled by its long stay in the inner solar system. Halley had a lot more mass, mostly ice. On the surface you never noticed the slight tug, but coming in like this, taking your time to aim carefully, that ten-thousandth of a G could add up.

The mechs' blue jets fanned against the backdrop of ice, slowing the cargo. Carl saw suddenly that it wasn't enough. The ponderous, hundred-meter-long cylinder was coming in too fast.

He ordered the lower portwise mech to turn and thrust at full bore. The unit spun, fired its reserve.

—What the hell you— Jeffers began.

"Clear the shaft!"

—What—

"Clear it!"

Standard procedure was to bring cargo to rest about fifty meters out, then nudge it in. His board said that was impossible. Instinct told him to try for something else.

He jetted forward, nearly caught up with the cylinder. A touch from the lower starboard mech, two quick torques here, a jolt sidewise to line her up—

An arrow from on high, aimed at a puckered black circle.

The orange cylinder struck the lip of Shaft 3, slowed—broke off an edge of ice—and drove on in, scattering flakes off into space.

*Bull's-eye,* he rejoiced as the cylinder disappeared within the hole.

Jeffers cried out, —Hey! What's the idea?—

"She got away from me."

—Hell she did! You're showin' off, is all.—

Carl pulsed his own jets and landed easily, feet down. "Don't I wish! Nope, I just corrected at the last minute. Figured it was better to try for a clean hit than to burn fuel decelerating. Especially since I couldn't stop it anyway."

Jeffers shook his head, exasperated. —Show-off,— he insisted, and went to check for rips in the material.

There weren't any. Slick and snagproof, fiberthread could wriggle around sharp edges, which made it good for lining the snaking tunnels inside Halley Core.

The fifteen members of the Life Support Installation Group had ten days to honeycomb a fraction of the north polar region, line the shafts and tunnels with pressure-tight insulation, then flush it with air. Not long enough. And all that time the newly awakened scientists aboard the *Edmund* would be chafing.

Even with 112 mechs it was going to be a tight schedule. There were only so many hands to guide them. The entire expedition had only 67 "live" members at present. Nearly 300 more lay in the sleep slots, their body temperatures hovering within a degree above freezing.

Overhead, the spindly tugs waited with their human cargo. Their immense, gossamer solar sails were furled now, not needed for seventy years. Beside the whalelike *Edmund,* the silvery *Sekanina, Delsemme,* and *Whipple* looked like patient barracuda.

*Still no word on the* Newburn, Carl thought. *How could it have gotten lost?*

—You guys all right?— Lani Nguyen's light, tinkling voice came from somewhere.

Carl looked around and found the speck rapidly growing as she sped along the polar cable. She had one arm clamped on the stay-carry while she waved with the other, looking remarkably like a bird skimming the ground with only one wing flapping.

—Jess fine,— Jeffers sent.

—I thought I heard some trouble. . . .—

She cut free of the cable and vectored their way, adroitly turning to shift her center of mass and avoid picking up any spin from the jet thrust. *She's good,* Carl thought. *Damn good.* Lani's light delicacy belied a firmly muscled physique. *But why come to check on a minor malf?*

"Nothing much to it," he answered.

—Well, I was finished, just on my way inside.— She landed with catlike agility ten meters away, kicking up only a small cloud of dust. —Want to take a break?—

—Can't,— Jeffers said. —We got to check out the tube, see it gets unsprung right.—

Lani looked at Carl. —That's routine. It shouldn't take two.—

Carl said, "Cruz is riding our ass on safety."

She studied him through their dust-marred helmets. —Sure? You're due to go off shift.—

—Hey, I'm not working alone, li'l lady,— Jeffers said good-naturedly but firmly.

She shrugged. —Okay. Just wanted a little R and R. I'm running a fraction ahead of schedule.—

—See you tonight, then.— Jeffers eyed her appreciatively but she seemed not to notice.

—Right,— she said to Carl. —Tonight.—

She lifted off gracefully and headed for the main shaft.

—Wouldn't mind that at all,— Jeffers said dreamily on a closed comm channel. Carl ignored him.

—We'll have to be thinkin' about pairin' off pretty soon now.—

"You'll be an icicle in a month."

—Man has to plan ahead.—

"Think you can get her to share a shift with you?" Carl answered.

—Might. Gonna be cold and lonely, later on.—

Carl laughed. "Your idea of foreplay is six beers and a game of pool. She's not your type."

—Necessity makes funny bedfellows, isn't that what Shakespeare said?—

"Stick to grunt work, it's your strong suit." He gave Jeffers a friendly shove toward the shaft entrance.

—Can't blame a man for tryin'.—

"Come on, your tongue is hanging out."

They flew their mechs ahead of them, down through the hollow center of the orange cylinder, popping free restrainer clips as they went. The fiberthread tube unflexed, articulating in sheets along the original axis. Every two minutes it extruded from itself a hundred-meter segment, automatically pressure-sealed the ends, and began pushing out another—each barely narrower than the one before. To Carl, it resembled a gaudy tube-worm that continuously regenerated itself, burrowing into an apple.

Side tunnels took more care. The mechs cut holes for the intersections, fuse-sealed them, and deployed the smaller tube extruders. Carl and Jeffers had to maneuver them into place, yoke and unyoke, check joints and seals, and be sure nothing snagged on an outcropping of rock or jagged ice. In the tunnels chunks of icy cometary agglomerate rubbed off—the mechs were sometimes clumsy—and floated freely through the dark spaces, striking multicolored halos around the spot torches the men carried. It was steady, meticulous, tiring work, even in near-zero gravity.

Their meal break was in a tunnel segment recently filled with air. They cracked their helmets and moored on a wall, enjoying the freedom even though the cold, tangy-flavored air cut sharply in their nostrils.

"Think you'll ever get used to it?" Jeffers asked, munching methodically on a self-warming ration bar. "Living in here?"

Carl shrugged. "Sure. The exercise wheel and electrical stimulation will take care of the low G, the docs say."

"Trust 'em for eighty years?" Jeffers's lean face seemed fitted for a skeptical expression; his mouth drooped down toward a pointed chin, eyes narrowed and quizzical. "Anyway, what I meant was the ice all around you. Feel how cold it is? And that's with all this insulation and our suit heaters goin' full bore."

"It'll warm up. That's a meter's insulation we just laid around this, remember."

"Gonna be a looong winter." Jeffers grinned. He would soon be swimming blissfully in the slots, and clearly relished the thought. Jeffers had been awake on the flight out. It had been boring, and now the work was hard and dangerous. He was ready for others to take over. The first watch.

Still, Carl couldn't understand the man's attitude.

"There's some risk in the slots, y'know. System malf, or—"

"I know, I know. My biochem might screw up in some way the experts missed out on. Or maybe you guys on watch throw a wrong switch, cut off my power, and the safeguards fall. Or an asteroid hits us all." He grinned again. "Still, it's a one-way trip across more'n a couple decades."

Carl frowned. "So?"

"I'd just as soon sleep through the dull part, accumulatin' Earthside pay." Jeffers's thin face twisted into a sardonic grin. "Comet farmin' in the outer system—that'll be fun. But I can skip the kiss-ass politics."

"What do you mean?"

"C'mon, you're a Percell too. You know how this whole expedition's been set up."

"Uh . . . how?"

"The Orthos! They're running everything." Jeffers ticked off the names on his fingers. "Cruz, then Oakes, Matsudo, d'Amaria, Ould-Harrad, Quiverian. Every section head is an Ortho."

"So?"

"They think we're freaks!"

"Oh, come on."

"They do! Look at the way the Orthos are treating our people Earthside. Think these here are any different?"

"They aren't like that mob that burned down the center in Chile last week, if that's what you mean. Sure, I read about that stuff, and the other places. That's one reason I work in space, same as you."

"Space's no different."

"Sure it is. These Orth—these people know they're really the same as us."

Jeffers said triumphantly, "But they *aren't*."

Carl smiled humorlessly. "*Now* who's being prejudiced?"

"Hell, you know we're not the same as them." Jeffers leaned forward, speaking earnestly. "Our bodies are better, that's for sure. And we're smarter, too. The tests show that."

"Hell they do."

"Can't argue with statistics!"

Carl grunted with irritation. "Look, we were boy wonders back when we were growing up—before people started turning against us. *All*

Percells were. Remember the scholarships? The special attention?"

"We *earned* that. We were smart."

Carl shook his head. "We *turned out* smart—because of the VIP treatment."

"Naw. I've always been quicker than your typical Ortho, even if I don't bother to talk real well."

"And you are. But you're no better than people like Captain Cruz or Dr. Oakes." Carl got to his feet too rapidly and his velcro grips tore free of the fiberthread. He shot across the tunnel and banged his head against the ceiling.

"Damn!"

Jeffers snickered but said nothing. Carl rubbed his head as he drifted back, but refused to let his irritation show any further. Jeffers was like too many Percells—wrapped up in their own sense of persecution, picking at every imagined slight like a festering sore. Arguing with them just encouraged it.

"Open your eyes," his friend persisted. "Who've they got in the dangerous jobs like ours? Percells!"

"Because a lot of us are trained for zero G. We had the scholarships to get into it."

"Then why not put a Percell in charge of all Manual Operations?"

"Well . . . we're not old enough yet. No Percell is as experienced as Cruz or Ould-Harrad or—"

"Come on! Look at who's doing the outgassing experiments. And developing longterm sleep slotting. All Orthos."

"So?"

"That's where the real money'll be! Learn how to steer comets with their own boiloff, show you can sleep and work in decade shifts—and you can sell your talent anywhere in the system."

Carl couldn't help laughing. Jeffers sure did take the long view. "Come on, that's—"

"And what about Chem Section? If we turn up anything half as valuable as Enkon here, you know who'll make out. And *they're* all Orthos, too, except Peters."

"We all signed patent agreements. Any techniques discovered, we all get a cut, after recouping basic expenses."

Jeffers's face contorted into a sour, sardonic mask. "The Orthos'll find a way around that."

Carl felt his own conviction wavering. *What if he's right?* But then he blotted out the thought. "Look, get off that line. We can't continue those stupid Earthside fights out here."

"*We're* not—it's *them*."

Exasperated, Carl stuffed the remains of his lunch into his carry pouch. "Let's go—I'd rather work than argue."

Still, that evening he entered the rec-lounge bar troubled, looking for Virginia. She was a reasonable Percell and might understand what he only slowly admitted to himself this afternoon—that he halfway agreed with some of Jeffers's accusations. It was the man's tone, his black-and-white way of putting everything, that got Carl's back up.

He collected a drink, turned to go, and saw the sign, DUCK OR GROUSE just in time to remind him. He stooped and entered the lounge. The first week aboard, he and other Percells had slammed their foreheads into the doorjamb a dozen times; the *Edmund*'s designers had apparently believed only Orthos socialized.

Lani Nguyen intercepted him near the smiling tungsten bust of Edmond Halley himself. "Ah, at last you appear."

She gave an immediate impression of slim, efficient design, every inch a spacer. Lean muscles bunched in her bare almond-colored arms, but otherwise she was covered in a draping, cool blue dress that moved in light pseudo-gravity with a graceful, modest independence. Carl liked the effect of shimmering cloth lagging behind her precise, delicate movements.

"Uh, yeah, we had some trouble with the tunnel articulation." He smiled cordially but tried to scan the lounge without seeming to do so.

Dr. Akio Matsudo was talking earnestly to Lieutenant Colonel Ould-Harrad, the head of Manual Ops. Through the viewport Halley Core glimmered and swam as the G-wheel turned. Captain Cruz stood ramrod-straight against the starry background, easily dominating the room, surrounded by the usual mesmerized pack of ladies.

Where was Virginia?

"Oh?" Lani asked with a distant smile, similar to the Buddha-grin of the sculpture over her shoulder. "That should be automatic."

Carl blinked. "Uh . . . we ran into a patch of boulders."

"I usually send a forward mech ahead to slice those off with a cutter. Then—"

Jeffers appeared out of nowhere and Carl snagged him. "Better tell this guy, he's the point man in our team. I'll just run a little errand. . . ."

And he was away, free, before Lani's pert surprise could turn to protest. *Let Jeffers have an opening,* Carl thought. *He deserves it.* A bit unfair to Lani, maybe, but first things first. *Let's see, her shift should be up by now. . . .*

He passed the group surrounding Captain Cruz and on impulse slowed. He insinuated himself into the cluster. Cruz always spoke to the whole group, never leaving anyone out, and he smiled at Carl. "How's it going down there, Osborn?"

Carl was startled at being addressed personally. He had intended simply to listen in. "Uh, pretty tough, sir, but we can handle it."

"I saw that neat trick at Shaft Three." Cruz raised his eyebrows slightly and his gaze swept over the circle. Although an Ortho—a natural human being—he was as tall as most Percells.

Carl felt his face getting hot. He had to say something, but what? "Well, I guess I kinda—"

"Marvelous! A bull's-eye! I felt like applauding." The commander chuckled.

Carl was dumbfounded. "Well . . . I . . ."

"It's good to see a little audacity," Cruz said warmly.

Carl grinned self-consciously. *Does he know it was a mistake?* "Well, we got a schedule to keep."

"So we do. I only wish other sub-sections were moving as crisply as yours."

Carl wondered if that was a veiled joke. But Cruz raised his bulb of bourbon in salute and, to Carl's surprise, the crowd did, too. Carl covered his confusion by taking a sip, watching the crowd for signs of mirth. No, they meant it. He felt a sudden delight. He had bobbled the maneuver, sure, but recovered well. That was what mattered to the captain.

Cruz caught Carl's eye and there passed between them the barest moment of understanding. *He knows I screwed up. But he's rewarding initiative over timidity. Why?* Carl had tried to perform well all during the *Edmund*'s flight out, but until this moment Cruz had never paid him more than polite, distant attention.

*That's it—Kato and Umolanda. He doesn't want people getting spooked. He knows it was faulty equipment and plain bad luck that killed them, much more than carelessness.*

"We'll make our deadlines, sir," Carl said firmly.

Cruz nodded. "Good." With practiced smoothness, the captain turned his attention to a woman communications officer standing nearby. "The new microwave antennas are up on schedule, aren't they? Having trouble getting signals through the plasma tail?" Cruz asked.

"A little, yes."

"How soon can we deploy a microwave radar to search for the *Newburn*?"

"I'll have an estimate for you by tomorrow, sir."

Carl listened to the friendly, open way Cruz drew information out of the woman, commented on it, made a little joke that set the crowd to laughing. *Now that's how to lead,* Carl thought. *He's in touch with everything, and never looks worried. I wonder if I'll ever learn the knack.*

He would have liked to stay longer, but he wanted to find Virginia. He discovered her in a laughing group of varicolored Hawaiians, her dress a blue shimmer that suggested without revealing. The semi-autonomous state of Hawaii had financed twenty percent of the expedition's cost. As the true capital of the pan-Pacific economic community, they invested heavily in space. Their representatives lent a cheery air to most ship functions.

He waited for a lull in conversation, caught Virginia's eye, and drew her away to an alcove. He quickly described Jeffers's complaints. "Do you think he might be right?" he asked.

"You mean, will the Orthos try to rake off whatever they can?" She smiled speculatively. "Sure. This isn't a charity operation."

"*I* didn't come just to make money." Carl drew back, folding his arms. He knew it would probably be smarter to appear urbane, even a shade cynical—or at least that's what he thought attracted most Earthside women. But somehow his real self always came out.

"Offended?" Virginia smiled, her full lips drawing back to reveal startlingly brilliant teeth. "Don't be so straitlaced. Even idealists have to eat."

"Did *you* sign any quiet little agreements Earthside?"

Virginia frowned. "Of course not. Look, there're always going to be rumors that so-and-so has a sweet extra deal to leak expertise. Who knows, maybe somebody'll tightbeam stuff back before we return, have a bundle waiting for him in a Swedish account."

"It wouldn't surprise me. With four hundred people taking turns standing watch over seventy years, there'll be plenty of chances to cheat."

Virginia moodily stirred her bulb goblet of piña colada with a pink straw. To Carl the festive colors of the lounge seemed out of place when cold steel and vacuum lay only meters away. The psychologists probably thought tropical splashes of amber, green, and gold would take people away from raw reality, but for him it didn't work.

Virginia said slowly, "There's an old saying: Ordinary men choose their friends, but a genius chooses his enemies."

Carl grimaced. "Meaning?"

"The Orthos run this expedition, granted. If we create friction, they can do a whole lot more to make it hot for us."

He thought for a moment. "Okay. Conceded. That doesn't change *my* aims, though."

Virginia nodded. "Ah yes. Plateau Three."

Carl knew she thought his opinions were too simplistic, too much a rubber stamp of the NearEarth colonies' doctrine. Still, he honestly didn't see how she could disagree.

A century of struggle had finally given mankind the technology to exploit the solar system—efficient transport, mech'd mining and assembly, integrated artificial biospheres of any size needed.

Now was the moment, the colonists argued, to move *out*.

Unmanned satellites had been the first level of space exploitation—*Plateau One*. As far back as the 1980s people had made billions with communications satellites. Saved lives with weather sats.

Automated space factories using lunar materials had been the next rung up—*Plateau Two*.

Each Plateau had been climbed by a few who saw the benefits well in advance and took huge risks for that vision. Plateau Two had nearly failed, then became a roaring economic miracle—helping to pull the world out of the Hell Century.

Each ascent seemed to provoke an Earth-centered apprehension—first, that the investment might go bust, then that the birthplace of mankind was being relegated to a mere backwater. This was aggravated by Earth's never-ending social problems—malaises that the space colonies, by design, did not share. The Birth and Childhood Rules, which commanded that each space-born child must spend at least its first five years on the ground, were a legal expression of an underlying fear.

*Plateau Three* was a dream, a political issue, an economic sore point, a faith—all rolled into one. But big rotating colonies were possible now. The colonists now looked on the Birth and Childhood Rules as symbols of apronstrings they had long outgrown. They wanted to exploit the rocky asteroids and moons, but needed volatiles as well, for propellants and for biospheres. They'd even funded a small Ganymede ice mine, but that hadn't worked out well.

Some saw comets as the key, and fervently believed that humans could scatter through the solar system like dandelion seeds, if they could only learn to herd the ancient snowballs to orbits where they were usable.

Virginia leaned back languidly in her web-chair. "You can't expect Mother Earth to let go so easily."

"They have everything to gain! We'll bring them asteroids galore, raw materials, provide new markets—"

She held up her palm. "Please, I know the litany." An amused expression of feigned, longsuffering patience flitted across her face, instantly disarming him. Perhaps it wasn't intended that way, but with a single gesture she could make him see himself as gawky, thick-witted, too obvious. *Well, maybe I am. I've lived in space over half my adult life.*

"Just 'cause it's familiar doesn't mean it's wrong."

"Carl, do you really think mining comets for volatiles is going to ring in the millennium?"

"Where else can we get cheap fluids?" To him this was the trump card, a cold economic fact. At the very beginning of the solar system, the hot young sun had blown most of the light elements outward, away from the inner solar system. Only Earth had retained enough volatile elements to clothe its rocky mantle with a thin skin of air and water. When humans ventured into space to exploit the resources there,—asteroids, the moon, Mars—they had to haul their liquids up from Earth.

"Sure," Virginia said. "Get ice from comets! In eighty years we'll be back, Hail the conquering heroes! But by then somebody may've discovered frozen lakes deep in our own moon. Or even found a cheap way to chip iceteroids out of the Jovian moons—who knows?"

Carl was startled. "That's crazy! No way you can pay the expense of dipping into Jupiter's grav well, just for water and ice. Jupiter Project is proving that."

She smiled impishly. "So? Chasing comets is easier?"

Her dark eyes teased, and Carl knew it, but he couldn't let go.

"It's worth a try, Virginia. Nobody'll find a way to steer comets unless *we* make the outgassing method work. Nobody'll find volatiles hiding on the moon or Venus because they've been baked out. You can't prospect and mine the asteroids with mechs alone—because finding metals is still a craft, not a science. Dried-up comets like Encke *can't* be herded precisely because there's no way to use their outgassing to steer them. So—"

"I surrender, I surrender!" She held both hands high.

Carl blinked. *Oh hell,* he thought. *Why do I always get carried away?*

A deep male voice said from over Carl's shoulder, "Do not rush into defeat, Virginia. Ask for reinforcements first."

Carl turned as Saul Lintz settled into a soft green web-chair nearby and put his drink into a hold notch on their table. He was lean and weathered, his movements in low gravity deliberate.

"You're too late," Carl said, searching for something witty to say to redeem himself. "She's already conceded that I'm a bore."

"Then my help is unneeded." Saul chuckled as he said this, but Carl felt a quick jolt of irritation.

"I was arguing that we're all going to get rich out of this expedition, if we're patient," Carl said evenly. "And we should leave politics behind us."

Saul nodded, took a long pull at his drink. "Admirable sentiments."

"We've *got* to. Halley Core is too small for the kind of petty—"

"Insert coin for Lecture Twelve," Virginia said lightly.

"Well, it's *true*." Carl did not know how to take her, didn't like the way her attention had swerved to Saul Lintz the moment he joined them. She had turned halfway in her chair, nearly facing Saul, and barely glanced back as Carl finished. "And any hints that some people are going to profit more than the rest of us—well, it'll cause trouble."

Saul lifted an inquiring eyebrow. He seemed to know how to comment on what you'd said with a minimal gesture or shrug, an economy of expression Carl envied.

"He refers to scuttlebutt below decks," Virginia explained. "The fact that, ah, non-Percells hold all the important slots."

"Non-Percells such as myself?"

"Now that you mention it," Carl said.

"Seniority. After all, none of you genetically preselected people are over forty."

"You sure that's all?" Carl leaned forward, hands knitted together, elbows on knees.

The older man frowned, sensing something in Carl's voice. "Of course. What else do you think it could be?"

"Couldn't it be that Earthside didn't want any of us where we could make trouble?"

Saul carefully put his drink down and sat back. "Exiles are ill powered to cause Pharaoh grief," he said as if to himself.

The remark seemed irritatingly opaque to Carl. "Why don't you just answer my question?"

"Was that a question? It sounded like an accusation."

Carl's voice had been more harsh than he had planned, but he'd be damned if he'd back down now. "Look at Life Support Installation, my group. Our section head is Suleiman Ould-Harrad, an . . ."

"Ortho?" Saul supplied quietly.

"Well, that's the slang, yeah."

"So he is. Genetically orthodox." Saul leaned back, making a steeple of his fingers. "Meaning an untampered zygotic mix from the sea of human genes—no more. Genes do not carry opinions."

Carl shook his head. He disliked the pedantic manner the scientists always adopted, as if all that jargon made them better, smarter, wiser. "Look—the outgassing work, the slot studies—all in the hands of . . . you people."

"So you surmise that they will clutch these fruits to themselves? To sell their skills upon our return?"

Virginia said mildly, "It's not an impossible scenario, Saul."

Saul looked surprised to hear this coming from her. "I'm afraid for me it is. The direct implication that there is some conspiracy of the normal contingent—"

"See?" Carl pounced. "He calls his people 'normal'—so we're not."

Saul said stiffly, "I did not mean it that way."

"That's the way it came out."

Virginia said, "Carl, you can't jump on every—"

"I'm not. I'm just looking to see if where there's smoke, there's fire." He felt warm, gulped his drink.

Saul paused, running his tongue meditatively over his lower lip. "Let me begin afresh. Carl, if you knew anything about me, you would understand that I am not hostile to you people. Precisely the opposite, in fact." He looked steadily at Carl. "I suppose you would find out sooner or later anyway . . . I worked for years with Simon Percell."

Carl was stunned. Virginia gasped and said, "You *did*? I'd heard rumors, but . . . I didn't believe them."

"Merely as a postdoc." Saul shrugged. "Our last project together studied deviations in the activation level of lupus erythematosus. You may remember that was one of the principal diseases Percell freed you people from. That awful, untreatable thing that attacked skin, connective tissue, spleen, kidneys."

Virginia nodded. "My mother died from it."

"Yes," Saul said. "And your grandmother as well."

Virginia's lips pursed in surprise. Saul shrugged. "I remember your case. Simon carried out the necessary alterations of your mother's DNA while I was first learning the techniques."

Virginia leaned forward. "Did you . . ."

"Do the actual work? I cannot remember, honestly. I performed as assistant for many gene-tailoring methods, some experimental, some fairly straightforward."

"Then you . . . could be . . ."

Saul blinked, sitting back in his chair, averting her rapt gaze. "It was a purely mechanical task by that time. Very little research to it, other than my part. I did studies of how the resulting . . . cells . . . responded to chemical incursions which, for normal lupus, would cause a spontaneous rise in the disease."

Virginia said slowly, "And mine . . . did not?"

"Obviously, you were one of our successes. You have no trace of lupus, I trust?"

She shook her head. "Because of you."

"No; Simon Percell. I merely went to him to learn his techniques. It was during those few years when he enjoyed full support, when all things were possible. Or so we thought."

Carl said, "Still . . . I didn't know you'd worked with Percell." He felt chagrined. Saul had probably been present when Carl's mother's genes were delicately trimmed, freed of the microscopic molecular constellation that carried heritable leukemia. Then the gene wizards had added expert snippets of DNA to give him the suite of physical improvements that now marked every Percell. To Carl, that small, brave band of genetic engineers was legendary. He had never met one before.

Saul crossed his legs, smoothed his pants leg, visible uncomfortable. Carl realized that the man must have been through similar meetings often, and was wary of the pent-up emotion that might burst forth from any Percell.

"I . . . I'm sorry about what I said," Carl murmured.

Saul nodded silently. He, too, was holding feelings behind a tight-lipped dam.

Virginia's eyes brimmed. "You . . . could be . . ."

Carl saw that she wanted to say *You are my father, too* but could find no way to state the complex blend of emotions she felt. Saul had helped give life to thousands who would have been blighted, killed, maimed. Those years could not be forgotten—except by the braying, suspicious, hate-filled majority Earthside.

That kind had killed Percell, as surely as if they had pressed the muzzle of the .32 revolver to his temple. Simon Percell himself had pulled the trigger, driven into a depression over what was now obviously an unavoidable mistake.

One gene-editing error in a treatment to eliminate an inheritable kidney disease had killed an entire year's program of children. Worse, they had not died until the age of three. Then it struck suddenly.

The sight of so many writhing in agony, yellow-skinned and gnarled, their kidney and liver functions stopped abruptly—it had been torture. Media bigots flashed the images around the globe. Coupled with the growing public chorus against him, the threats of prosecution, and the sudden cuts in his research support, it had been too much for a man who held himself to the very highest standards.

Carl shook himself. It was still so easy to touch off the memories. His own mother dying miserably. The years of waiting to see if he, too, would begin to show the signs. The final liberation when he knew it was all right, that he could go into space with a clean genetic record. Those memories cut deeply in him still.

"I . . . Look, let me buy you another drink," Carl said lamely.

"Why, sure," Saul said with a wobbly smile.

"Maybe a chess game later?"

"Certainly!" Saul said heartily. "This time, no quarter. I'm defending the honor of normal people." They all laughed. Then Saul sneezed.

Both Carl and Virginia jumped slightly. Then they all smiled, the tension relieved.

"Well now," Saul said expansively as he put away his handkerchief, "that's one Percell modification I *will* take credit for. Tailoring in a suppression of the histamic response. Doesn't do *me* any good, but you people don't suffer as I do from pesky colds. I'll be envying you every time Akio Matsudo releases one of his damn challenge viruses!"

But years afterward, Carl would well remember that convulsive, startling eruption, the first—but certainly not the last—time he had heard Saul's explosive sneeze.


# SAUL

Newsflash—WorldNet4—The International Olympic Committee, meeting today in Tokyo, bowed to pressure from the League of the Arc of the Sun and voted to bar genetically altered persons—so-called "Percells"—from participating in the 2064 Games in Lagos.

Members of the Progressive Bloc were the only nations to vote in opposition to the proposal. Bloc leaders Denmark, Hawaii, Indonesia, Texas, and the NearEarth Cluster emphasized their objections by withdrawing from the competition, which now promises to be the most controversial since the fractious Olympics of 2036.

Said IOC chairman Asoka Barawayandre, "The decision of these particular territories is no great surprise. They have received great numbers of Percells as immigrants from lands that no longer welcome that kind. Their national sports teams were already compromised by this questionable element."

Members abstaining included Greater Russia, the United States of America, Royal Wales, Soviet Georgia, and the Diasporic Federation.

Observers expect the decision will be appealed to the World Court.

Saul finished reading the printout and looked up at the man who had thrust it upon him.

"For this you waste paper in a printout, Joao? You could have fast-faxed it to my console just as easily."

Joao Quiverian was a slender, sallow-faced man with an untamable shock of black hair and a Roman, almost hawklike ornament of a nose. The man was not distracted by Saul's banter. He insisted on an answer.

"You'd just ignore a fast-fax. I want to know right away what you think of this vote, Saul."

"Where does my opinion matter?" Saul shrugged. "I'm disappointed the Diaspora only abstained. A worldwide federation of refugee peoples ought to take a stand on something like this. But they're trying so hard to win acceptance that it's really no surprise." He handed back the sheet. "Other than that, I'd say the world is acting true to form."

The answer obviously did not satisfy Joao, who had been made chief planetologist only three weeks ago when a freak accident killed Professor Lehman. Saul knew this had to be a frustrating time for the Brazilian, anyway. Here he was, only a few score kilometers from a truly great comet, and orders were that science would have to give way to engineering for weeks to come.

Quiverian had to rely on part-time help from Saul and a few other "amateur cometologists" who had been trained in the field as a second specialty. No doubt he looked forward to the awakening of some of the sleepers from the slot tugs and discussing cometary arcana with fully accredited peers.

Saul generally got along with the man, as long as they were discussing the primordial matter of the ancient solar system. This time, however, Quiverian was in a political mood.

"Come now, Saul. This news from Earth is important, a milestone! I had expected more out of you. An indignant protest. Perhaps a declaration that Percells are actually human beings."

Saul was here in the planetology lab to help analyze the delicate ice cores the spacers were bringing back from Halley—the "second hat" he had been assigned because of his laboratory skills. He had not come to be goaded by Quiverian. He looped his left foot under the chair stanchion. "Come on, Joao, you wanted me to examine some organic inclusions for you. Let's look at the sample."

He held out his hand for the slender, sealed, eight-foot tube the Brazilian had laid on the table behind him.

But Quiverian was insistent. "Nobody's saying that these poor mutants are *unhuman*. Only that they were a horrible mistake. You cannot blame the people of Earth—with the nations of the Arc of the Sun in the vanguard—for calling for controls."

"I see." Saul nodded. "Controls like banning Percells from the Olympics. What's next, Joao? Segregated restrooms? Special drinking fountains? Ghettoes?"

Quiverian smiled. "Oh, Saul. It wasn't just those athletic records a few Percells had broken—freakish performances that raised the ire of millions. Those were only the last straw. Your creations—"

"Not *my* creations." Saul shook his head insistently.

Quiverian held up a hand. "Very well, *Simon Percell's* creatures—his monsters—these people are living reminders of the arrogance of twentieth-century northern science, which nearly destroyed the world!"

Saul sighed. "Come on, Joao. You can't blame science and the Old North for everything. True, they used up more than their share of resources, but you talk as if the nations of the Arc were completely guiltless for the Hell Century. After all, who cut down the tropical forests in spite of all the warnings? Who raised the carbon dioxide levels—"

Quiverian interrupted him, red-faced: "You think I am unaware of that, Saul? Look at my homeland, Brazil. Only now, after massive struggle, are we beginning to recover from an environmental holocaust which wiped out a third of the Earth's species . . . all sacrificed at the altar of thoughtless greed."

"Very well, then the guilt is distributed—"

"Yes, certainly. But technology *itself* was partly at fault! We simply barged ahead with the best of intentions"—Quiverian arched his eyebrows sardonically—"*doing good* to the detriment of Nature herself!"

Obviously, the man believed this, passionately. Saul found it ironic. Back before the turn of the century, the nations of the Old North had preached environmentalism to an unheeding Third World—after already reaping most of the planet's accessible wealth. Now, the pendulum had swung. The equatorial peoples in the Arc of the Sun seemed obsessed with a mystic passion for nature that would have astonished their land-hungry grandparents.

*Why must conversions always come so late? Why do people apologize to corpses?*

He was spared having to reply as a thickly accented voice rose from beyond a table stacked high with core samples.

"Hey! Did I miss something? Eh? Exactly what crimes was do-gooder science responsible for? I'll tell you which! Maybe our Brazilian friend refers to foreign doctors who came in to reduce infant mortality in countries such as his. Boom! Overpopulation. To your modern Arcist, that must have been the worst horror of them all!"

Quiverian's face colored. "Malenkov, you fat Russian hypocrite! Come out here and argue face to face like a man. You don't have to hide; I am no Ukrainian sniper!"

"Thank the saints for that much, at least." Nicholas Malenkov rounded the table holding a clipboard, smiling, a hulking giant of a man who moved with the grace of a wrestler, even in the awkward Coriolis tides of the gravity wheel.

*Rescued,* Saul thought gratefully and seized the chance to change the subject. "Nicholas, I hear Cruz and the engineers have preliminary results from the gas-panel experiments. Were you there?"

The stocky Slav grinned. "They wanted at least one of us iceball lovers around when they tried it out. You, Joao, and Otis were busy. So I sat in."

Along with Saul and the legless spacer, Otis Sergeov, Dr. Malenkov wore a second hat as a cometologist . . . much to Joao Quiverian's frequent protests of dismay. The big Russian spread his hands. "My friends, the results are encouraging. With only a few of the panels in place we have already altered the orbit of Comet Halley! The effect is small, but we've proved that controlling the comet's outgassing can let us make orbital changes!"

Saul nodded. "Of course, the method only works near perihelion, close to the sun."

"True. This run of tests showed only a small, diminishing effect.

Soon surface sublimation will cease altogether. The panel project will shut down for seventy years. But *next* time," Malenkov grinned, "when we are diving once more inward, toward the Hot . . ."

*The Hot.* It was the first time Saul had heard the sun referred to that way.

". . . then this work will prove its usefulness. With the big Nudge rockets having their maximum effect at aphelion, and the evaporation-control panels working at perihelion, we will have the means to herd this ancient iceball into almost any orbit we want!"

Quiverian frowned darkly and shook his head. "Suppose all of this meddling works. Exactly what, Doctor, would *you* want to do with . . . with a *herded* comet?"

*Oh, no.* Saul saw where the conversation was heading.

"Who cares!" Malenkov said enthusiastically. "Ideas have bounced around for more than a century, about what people might do with comets."

"Crackpot ideas, you mean."

Malenkov shrugged. "Our present plan is to arrange a loop past Jupiter in seventy years, and use big planet's gravity to snare Halley into much more accessible orbit. Eventually, this iceball can supply cheap volatiles and help the NearEarth people create their Third Plateau in space."

Quiverian shook his head. "Propaganda. I have heard it a thousand times."

Malenkov went on unperturbed. "The possibilities are endless. When we have proven long-duration sleep slots, comets may make great space liners—to cruise the solar system in safety."

Saul saw that a small audience had begun to gather at the open door to the lab, attracted from nearby offices. Malenkov noticed them and waxed even more enthusiastic.

"We might find more useful chemicals, maybe, like those Joao and Captain Cruz found on Encke. Why, there may even be some merit in that wild idea to use comets to terraform Venus or Mars! Eventually they might be made suitable for colonization."

"Hah!" Quiverian snorted.

"Gentlemen," Saul cut in. "I suggest we—"

But Quiverian ignored him, shaking a slender, plastic-coated sample tube at Malenkov. "This is the attitude I cannot bear. The original idea was to *study* comets, the most pristine of all God's handiworks. But now knowledge for its own sake doesn't seem to matter anymore. Now you not only want to *harvest* this comet, but recklessly alter entire *worlds* before we even understand them!"

Malenkov blinked in surprise at Quiverian's anger. Saul knew that Nicholas had few political opinions. He was one of the most brilliant people Saul had ever met, but the man never seemed to learn that to some people a disagreement was not a chess game, not a sport for gentlemen. In this respect, he was a most unRussian Russian.

Saul tried once more to stop this. "Joao! Nick was only talking about possibilities. In thirty years Earth will have had time to decide. . . ."

But the angry Brazilian wasn't listening anymore. Quiverian's left hand clenched the core tube and his right formed a fist. "We have just emerged from the most terrible century in human history . . . the worst for our world since the holocaust of the Pleistocene . . . and now idiots want to send giant iceballs hurtling down onto planets?"

"I never said—"

Quiverian stepped menacingly toward Malenkov. "Tell me, Doctor. How long before the target is not Mars, or Venus, but *Earth*?"

His arms chopped for emphasis, unwise in the weak pseudogravity. Quiverian flailed for balance and the long tube smashed onto the table-top, splitting with a loud report. Dark brown ice, laced with black and white veins, spilled out onto the lab bench.

"Idiot! *Goyishe kopf!*" Saul caught the Brazilian before his head struck the big core microscope. He swiveled quickly and pointed at the people standing by the door.

"All of you, out! Shut that hatch and trigger the air seal. Nick, Joao, go get masks!"

Saul pushed Quiverian off toward the emergency cupboard. Moving quickly he grabbed up a plastic recycling container and dumped its wad of crumpled printouts onto the floor. By the time Malenkov returned, fastening a small mask over his face and holding out another, Saul was sweeping slivers of swiftly melting ice into the tub.

The Russian's voice was muffled. "Your mask, Saul! Put it on."

Saul shook his head and kept working. He had complete faith in his little bloodstream symbionts—in their ability to keep him safe from cyanide and other cometary poisons. They had better, or the colony wouldn't last long inside Halley. Right now he was more concerned about preventing contamination of the other samples than danger to himself.

The spilled slivers seemed to give off a faintly pleasant aroma . . .

reminding him of the almond groves of Lake Kinneret, in the Galilee at springtime.

"My core!" Quiverian cried out as he returned, fumbling with his face mask. "What are you doing, you meddlesome Jew? That was the deepest core we had taken!"

Saul swept up the last slivers, threw the sponge into the tub, and sealed its lid. There were nearly a trillion tons of ice out there under Halley, ready to be studied. This loss was no scientific tragedy.

"Oh, but that's not true, Joao," Malenkov said reassuringly. The stocky Russian sifted through the self-cooling tubes on the counter. "Why, only an hour ago my countryman, Otis Sergeov, returned with a new core, taken from a kilometer within Halley! Let me see if I can find it here."

"Sergeov!" Quiverian cursed. "That fanatical Percell mutant? Oh, fates! There were so many fine planetologists who might have come along! Why, oh *why* have I been saddled with such assistants—a huge Russian fool, a legless Percell, and a genetic *witch doctor*!"

Malenkov shrugged and answered amiably, as if it were the most reasonable question in the world, "I guess you're stuck with us because those other guys *didn't* come along, Joao."

Saul closed his eyes, and put his hands over them.

"Yaah!" Quiverian threw himself at the door, ignoring the yellow air-alert light, and burst out through the crowd outside.

"What is eating him?" Malenkov asked Saul after the door hissed shut again. He frowned. "Saul? What's the matter? Are you in pain?"

Saul uncovered his eyes at last. They were filled with tears.

"Saul? My friend, I . . ."

Saul slapped the console next to him and laughed out loud, unable to contain it any longer.

"Joao is right," he said, wiping his eyes. "Comet Halley definitely deserves better than this. But it's stuck with us."

Saul wasn't surprised, a while later, when an officer came around to investigate the spillage incident. But he did blink when Lieutenant Colonel Suleiman Ould-Harrad entered, a clipboard in one hand and a trace-gas detector in the other. The dark-skinned Mauritanian was the last man Saul expected.

Ould-Harrad's specialty was large, massive life-support systems, the kind they were installing on Halley right now. But he must have been the only one available at the moment to investigate the accident.

Everyone knew why Ould-Harrad was on this mission. The young officer had had friends in the Temple Mount Conspiracy, and only ties with the Mid-African royal family had won him exile instead of imprisonment for the crime of unwise associations.

The Mauritanian had spoken no more than ten words to Saul over the last three years. The regard had been returned.

*Earth is far behind you,* Saul reminded himself. *And nothing can change the past.* He stepped aside. "Come in, Colonel. I've already dictated an accident report. Go ahead and look around while I fast-fax a copy for you."

Ould-Harrad seemed ill at ease as he followed Saul into the lab, his broad nostrils flaring at the faint aroma of escaped cometary gases. His eyes kept flicking to the gauges of the instrument. His dour expression seemed little cheered by Saul's obvious good health.

"Dr. Lintz, you should not have remained here after the leakage alert was thrown."

Saul tapped the face of a sense-screen display. "Yes, yes. I know. But somebody had to stay and clean up the mess. Anyway, I might as well be the first guinea pig. It's appropriate, that I should give the blood cyanutes their first field test, no?"

The console spat out a small data pellet. Saul marked it with his name-chop. He smiled up at Ould-Harrad. "If I drop dead, we all might as well climb into sleep slots and wait a few centuries to be picked up, 'cause this expedition is over."

The spacer officer nodded curtly, accepting the logic. "There are rules, nevertheless. Procedures designed for collective safety and order."

Saul tossed the data pellet to the other man and laughed somewhat bitterly.

"Safety and order, yes. How well I remember those words. Didn't General Lynchon use that very phrase when his U.N. troops moved into the Judean hills?"

Ould-Harrad shook his head. "It was a consensus operation, Dr. Lintz. The coalition government of Israel-Inshallah invited them in."

Saul nodded. "After the Levites and Salawites assassinated enough opposing legislators to get a majority."

The African's voice was low, as if he dreaded this topic but was drawn to it like a moth toward a flame. "The world was tired of centuries of strife in a region that had never known peace."

"And is it better now? The High Priest in Jerusalem reigns over a balkanized realm, with sect sniping at sect as never before.

"And did it help the planet? From the Nile to the Euphrates, Israel-

Inshallah had planted more trees than existed before in all of Africa north of the equator. Last I heard, a third of the forests were gone—chopped down to make barricades."

Ould-Harrad's skin deepened darker than its already rich shade. Saul thought about pulling back. *He has already been punished.*

*Yes, but enough?*

"Dr. Lintz, I . . ."

"Yes?"

Ould-Harrad shook his head. "I had nothing to do with the attempt to blow up the Great Temple. It's true, I had friends in the Conspiracy—and in penance for that association I am on this ill-starred cruise—but I never wanted to bring harm to the holiest shrine of three faiths. I assure you, I would rather have torn out my . . ."

"Oh, you poor bastard," Saul interrupted, half-pitying the fellow and laughing to crush his own painful memories. "For ten years you've heard but not listened, been punished but never understood. When, oh when will people like you ever come to understand that real Jews never wanted that blasted temple built in the first place?"

Ould-Harrad's gas sensor hung from one hand, forgotten. He stared. "A few kibbutzim, some secular humanists fought it, I know. But—"

"But nothing!" Saul leaned forward. "The vast majority of Jews, in Israel and abroad, voted against it, argued against it, fought it every step of the way. It was *compelled* on us, by murderous fanatics and by an ignorant world all too eager for peace."

Saul almost spat the word. "*Peace!* It wasn't enough to destroy my nation and my family, Colonel Ould-Harrad. They installed priests that actually had the effrontery to tell me how to be a Jew! Even *Hitler* did not try to do that!"

In the faint, centrifugal tug of the gravity wheel, Ould-Harrad seemed to lose the strength to stand. He sagged into a web-chair.

"But the leader of the New Sanhedrin is of your Cohen priestly clan! And the Lead Temple Attendant is a Levite. . . . The Pope's Legate, the other Christians and Muslims, must take second place to the oldest faith's precedence!"

Ould-Harrad shook his head. "My comrades objected to that humiliation—and to the removal of the beautiful mosque that stood where the temple was to go—but I don't understand what the Jews had to complain of. Was not two millennia of prophecy being fulfilled at last?"

Saul did not answer immediately. He looked across the room, where the picture wall depicted the onion domes of old Kiev. Sunset flared brilliant tints across the steppes beyond the city walls. New gilt crosses once again topped the tower peaks, signifying Great Russia's return to its mystical past.

*Ten years,* he thought. *And still it seems impossible to make anyone understand.*

Perhaps he owed it to the man, out of charity, to try. But how could one explain that Judaism had *changed* over two thousand years of exile, since the Romans burned the Temple of the Maccabees to the ground, slew the priests, and scattered the people to the winds?

The remnants had wandered to strange climes, adopted alien ideas. Gradually, Hebrew farmers who pioneered the Polish and Russian plains were crowded by later peoples into cramped cities to become an urban folk. The priestly family lines—the Cohens and Levites—lost their influence. For how could they perform their rituals with no central site from which to make sacrifices to appease a terrible godhead?

Spiritual leadership fell upon the *rabbi*—the teacher—a role one did not inherit, but earned through learning and wisdom.

*A role described in detail by Jesus, if the truth be told. Only he, too, had those who* prophesied *in his name. He, too, was followed by priests.*

After a hundred years of strife and accomplishment, the alliance led by Israel had finally begun fraying during Saul's youth. The Hell Century took its toll even in the belt that folk called "The Green Land." Prophets appeared on streetcorners, and cults proliferated.

Islam, too, had suffered a hundred schisms, and Christianity was battered, divided.

Then someone had a bright idea . . . an *obvious* solution. And, like so many obvious solutions, it was disastrously wrong.

*The Diaspora changed us,* Saul thought. *In exile, we became individualists, a people of books, and not of sacrifices on golden altars. We* mourned *the Temple of Solomon. But wasn't its burning a sign that it was time to know God in other ways?*

How would Ould-Harrad ever understand that no modern Jew wanted anybody to intercede for him? Everyone had to come to his or her own understanding with God.

Ould-Harrad looked down at his hands. "When the conspirators blew up the Al Aqsa Mosque in protest, it was intended that the *Levites* take the blame, not the kibbutzim. The plan . . . they never wanted a bloodbath. . . ."

He seemed unable to continue. Saul realized that the man was haunted—by guilt and also, perhaps, by a dread that he might not ever even understand the role he had played.

Saul blinked away a memory of smoke over the Judean hills. He shook his head, knowing that there was no way he could help this man.

"I'm sorry," he began softly. Then he cleared his throat. "Is that all, Colonel? If you're finished, I have some important experiments under way."

The black spacer looked up and nodded curtly. "I will report the situation under control."

Saul had already turned back to his microscope when he heard the door hiss behind him. He tried to return to the business that had been interrupted, first by Joao Quiverian's persistent questioning, and then by the dolorous Ould-Harrad, but his hands seemed locked over the controls.

"Room environment, dim lights by half," he commanded aloud, and the laboratory darkened in response.

Work, he knew, was a way to take himself away from the memories. "Sample AR 71B dash 78 S, on screen twelve," he said to the ever-listening, semisentient lab computer. "Let's see if those inclusions look as suspicious now as I thought they did before Joao stank up the place."

The last part was not for the computer. And although he hunched over the holistank to immerse himself in mysteries, Saul found that he did not really mind at all the faint scent of ice and almonds in the air.

# VIRGINIA

She tapped tentatively. Then, when no muffled answer came, a harder rap. This brought forth a faint, querulous grunt. When the panel finally hissed open, Virginia stepped through and stood barely inside, feeling the door suck shut behind her.

She said diffidently, "You had sample breakage?"

It seemed a good opening. The danger—if any—was well past before she had heard. Saul had already left the planetology department, where the sample broke, and come down here to his own bio lab. But the ripple of concern among the crew had made her at last muster the courage to seize a pretext.

"Ummm?" Saul was studying his screens, making tiny notes in a small ledger with an old-fashioned pencil. She wondered at this eccentricity; the expedition used standard electronic markers and memory pads. He must have brought a packet of notebooks in his own small, personal weight allotment. She had heard of bringing vintage cabernet and caviar, but not pencils, for heaven's sake.

*And look at me,* she thought ruefully. *I used up most of my mass-carry lugging along computer hardware everybody Earthside has given up as hopeless, a dead end.*

She said nothing. Better to let him work a few moments, float up from the deeps. She walked among the tangle: twisted translucencies, shining chem lines, retorts, knots of cabling, a gurgle and rush of micro-bio diagnostics. *I'm glad I'm not a chemist. Chilled electrons are simpler to move around.*

"A few more minutes, Virginia. I'll be right with you."

Saul did not even look up as he jotted, thumbed his scanner, frowned. She strolled down one long lane, trying to read the indices on counters and follow the compact, involuted logic of the lab. Here Saul could dismantle genes like Tinkertoys, shuffle molecules like floppy cards. It always struck her as bizarre, how such innocent-looking tubes and solutions could reach out, pluck human lives into new paths, seal off others. As if this sleeping machinery hid a monstrous, weighty force.

*We keep doing that.* Humans imbued their own devices with a separate presence and power, ceaselessly projecting their emotions onto inanimate templates. Illogical—and the worst sinners in this were the supposedly objective, dispassionate scientists.

*Look how I shape my software to resemble my thought processes,* she mused. *Imprinting myself in JonVon's chilled organic lattices.*

Making her way here this afternoon, she had been struck by how the expedition was like this—separate rooms, immensely powerful ideas sealed off from each other, all contributing yet each isolated. Men and women pocketed into cylinders and cubes and spheres. They moved through the silent, cramped geometry of the *Edmund,* eager to go down and burrow their own niches in another hollowed world.

She wondered if the crew would communicate any better once they were down in Halley Core. Many of them had been working during the entire year-long cruise out, but she had been sleep slotted for ten months. Before launch, funding problems had cut the staging schedule for the expedition down to the bone; there hadn't been time to know or even meet most of the crew.

She had studied the siting plans for Halley Core. It looked fine as a schematic, a diagram, an Earthside blueprint—but soon now they would each live in a Euclidean maze, encased. The faint grumbling of the G-wheel only underlined their impacted artificiality. She felt deeply these insides and outsides, sections and barriers.

So to counter that, she had come here. Plucked up her courage, finally. Reached out.

She fidgeted down one lab lane, up another. Each moment was a partition, dividing a troubled past from a gaping, empty future—both huge stretches of time pressing in on the thin wedge of a nervous, rickety *now*.

*Stop this aimless inspection. Face what you came here for.*

But it was hard to jump the hurdle, and brave the sheer blind drop beyond.

"Saul."

He swam up from fuzzy depths. "Uh, what, yes?" He blinked, lines etching around his withdrawn eyes. "Sorry . . ."

"What . . . what are you finding?"

Even as she said it she winced. *That's right—dodge away. Ask him about his work, for chrissakes.*

"Something damned odd." Saul shook his head, as if he half-suspected an error. His pencil rolled along the grainy, stained calluses of his hand.

"What?"

"Contaminants, I think. Earth junk in the samples. That damned Quiverian . . ." He stopped, his gaze caught by something on the screen. "Just a sec, maybe this . . ."

Virginia watched on the magnifier as he guided microprobes to divide and extract tiny samples from several oblong, mottled masses. How he could tell one brown blur from another was a mystery. At his level, experiment became an art, unfathomable. Micromanipulators translated his minute movements into surgical grace, his touch tracing out the mad jumble of ancient crystals, the snakelike clench and coil of slippery, gaudy hydrocarbons. Deft fingers and a probing mind. Mozart and Picasso had been equally incomprehensible.

He worked steadily in silence, sucked back into his murky mysteries. *Okay, take it easy,* she thought. *Don't press. Not that you've been all that brave, eh? Anyway, males are slow when they have to switch hemispheres.*

She relaxed and watched his "weather wall." Each crewman's contract gave him the right to choreograph his environment. Saul had chosen well. A metallic-blue river wandered down to an emerald marsh beneath a swarm of flapping white birds that skimmed the shimmering surface. The images were firm, precise; a glistening spray leaped up where a bird dipped a wing into the water and slewed to a landing. Beyond, scattered stubs of islands dotted a pale sea. To the left, white stretches of beach punctuated the dazzling summer day. New England, probably Massachusetts.

Yes, she had read that he had been at Harvard once. And summer, of course. Choose a time that brought a comfortable warmth, something to ward off the chill of ancient ice soon to surround them. It was late afternoon on the walls of the lab and the slow slant of sunlight proceeded. A storm front nuzzled at the horizon, winds whipped the velvet shadows that pooled beneath gnarled trees. She felt a reassuring heat from the scene, even though she knew it was her own wools that did the work. Saul wore a cotton two-parter, blue with white stripes, an ample Renaissance collar its only indulgence. She could see he was a man who cared little for clothes, would go naked if temperature and society permitted.

As she watched pensively, he shook his head irritably, gave an *umpf,* and snapped off the screen.

"Done?"

"Yes, with nothing to show for it." He drummed fingers on the desktop.

"What were you looking for?"

"Some contaminant I thought I saw. It was . . . no, nothing. Forget it."

"You're worried about something."

He leaned back, let his face relax. "No . . . well, no more than usual."

"We're going to be on First Watch together," she ventured. "Plenty of time to work on our own research then."

He nodded. "I'm looking forward to it. Sixteen months of peace and quiet, carving ice and tending corpsicles."

"Another few weeks, we'll start slotting people."

He nodded, distracted. Then he said abruptly, "I'm a poor host. Something from the bar?"

"You have alcohol ration left?"

"In this lab? I can make anything I want. I have my own beer, if you'd care to risk it."

"Of course." She felt a need to break through, to reach him. His face was complex, a slate time had written all over, the mouth and eyes at battle with each other. His eyes seemed to peer at something far away—a problem coming slowly into focus, perhaps—unrelenting intellect. His lips betrayed this concentration, though. They twisted into an ironic curve, yet were full and sensuous, with a hint of passion and power. The cool mind that ruled the eyes did not know of this lower, submerged force. The contradiction warred across his face, complex with stubble, pale here and mottled there, a shiny brow with a curve that caught a reflected yellow beam from the New England sunset. He popped caps from two long-necked brown bottles with relish, suddenly seeming like a balding and wiry tradesman.

Virginia bit her lip as they both sat. Now that she had braved the first moments and taken the step she had considered a hundred times, she found she couldn't take her eyes off him.

"You're here because of our conversation the other day, aren't you?" he said. Suddenly his expression was gentler, opening outward from his self-immersion. His eyes met hers.

"Ah, well, yes." She might as well attribute it to that.

"What was it your mother had?"

"I . . . Lupus."

"Ah yes." A brief pain flickered in his eyes. He leaned back in his web-chair, put hands behind his neck, stretched in the light gravity of the wheel. "I remember those years. That one, we got a clean solution. No side effects—as you so clearly demonstrate. Um. You ever see a really bad case?"

"No. I read—"

"Not the same thing. Under the 'scope the cells aren't tight little cylinders, y'know—they're misshapen, *meshugenuh,* tortured things. The patient's connective tissue clogs. Swollen joints. Repeated infections. Liver damage, early death. There'd been good detectors to warn parents if a baby had it, sure, but nobody cracked the real problem—the genetic fix-up—until we did. Sorry—until Simon Percell did."

"You can take a lot of credit."

He laughed. "My career in the last couple of decades, my dear, has depended on my *not* taking credit."

"With us Percells . . . it's different."

He smiled wearily. *And warily?* she wondered. "You are, Virginia, an expression of how different a map is from the territory."

She frowned.

"Sorry, I'm being opaque. Habit of mine. We charted all the DNA nucleotides long ago. Knew where everything was—a great map. Only we didn't know what it *meant*."

"My genes don't carry the lupus—you knew how to do that. And the usual Percell enhancements are effective."

"Obviously." A grin.

She felt herself blushing at the compliment, rummaged for something to say. "We have all kinds of advantages. . . ."

"True . . ." He was still pensive, reflecting on times she could not know. Yet, those days would not die, as long as there were Percells. And that legacy lived in every corridor of this expedition.

He sighed. "But not true enough. Sure, we got the hemoglobin disorders, Huntington's disease, all the easy targets. Just lop off a few molecules. Trimming. Pruning. Change the cryptogram and—presto."

"I read that there are over two million people who owe you that."

"Been dipping into the forbidden Percell underground newspapers?" he said with mock seriousness. "Yes, that's right—you're from Hawaii. Plenty of pro-Percell sentiment there still, eh? Who passed on your security clearance?"

"I'm so good, they *had* to let me come," she said with a proud smirk.

"Bravo!" He applauded. "Bravo, indeed. And you are good—I looked in your file, back when Captain Cruz had me on the recruiting committee."

"Really?" She was suddenly serious. "What . . . what's in there? Did they—"

He waved a hand. "Nothing about your subversive ideas. Not a jot."

Her eyes widened, her mouth formed a shocked O—and then she saw he was kidding. "Ah . . . oh."

"They don't care if you think Percells are just as good as—what's the slang? yes—as good as *Orthos* are, you know." His voice dropped. "Since they're all so damned sure you're *not*."

She saw suddenly that she had been right—his pose before others was a mask. "They . . . do think that, don't they?"

"I'm afraid so. Many of them, anyway."

"Even though they let some of us go on this expedition."

"*Let* . . ." he began, then shook his head. "They had their reasons."

"But . . ."

"Virginia, has it never occurred to you that getting bright, hardworking, potentially troublemaking Percells out of their hair might be a very attractive idea?"

"Of course." She frowned.

"And isn't some side of you glad to be rid of all that *krenk* . . . that Earthside bullshit?"

She had to admit he was right. When the *Edmund* had lifted free of Earth orbit, she had felt . . . released. "Well . . . in some ways."

"Such as?" He sat forward, apparently genuinely interested. The slanting burnt orange of the Massachusetts sunset struck his bald patch, yet he did not seem old, only wise and kind and quietly powerful.

"Well . . . my father, he thought I was special. That our family was unique, a kind of historic experiment."

"Ah. A common mode."

"I . . . I hated it."

"Feeling special?"

"Being . . . different."

"You're not, really."

"Tell *them*."

"Your parents should've shielded you from that."

"They . . . Listen. When I was eleven, I was the only girl in my class without nylons. So I went to the local Woolworth's and bought a pair. I had *no* idea how to hold them up—I got the old kind, by mistake."

"Your mother . . ."

"She died when I was ten."

"Lupus."

She nodded.

"So you were a tomboy. Surfing, basking in Hawaiian splendor."

"Yes. It *was* beautiful, but . . . Well, my father raised me. I remember one day when I was playing catch in a T-shirt with the boys, I heard some giggles over my bouncing breasts. This was on Maui, where nobody's especially reluctant to talk about such things. So I went back to Woolworth's. The saleslady had to explain about bras—I didn't even know what the sizes meant! Then, in seventh grade, I started wearing skirts instead of jeans, because the other girls were. A boy looked at my hairy legs and said, 'I'm gonna get you a razor for Christmas.' I could have died! The next day, I borrowed my father's razor and cut my left shin bone so badly I still have the scar."

"I see."

She felt suddenly embarrassed. Somehow, all that had come out without her having planned it. "I wasn't very good at those things. I used to tell myself it was because my mother died and there was no one to tell me. So I concentrated on math, on computers."

"And if you hadn't, you could be a perfectly happy housewife somewhere, children yanking on your apronstrings."

She smiled impishly, crushing a sudden inner pain by old reflex. "The hell with *that*."

"Precisely."

*Besides, I didn't have the option,* she thought. "There's a quid for every quo." *That's it—cryptic and ironic. Show him I'm not just a simple schoolgirl who became a computer whiz because of adolescent angst.*

But Saul's face had become pensive, his eyes reflecting some inward turning. "I love you all, you know."

"You . . ."

His voice was very low. "All the Percells. You . . . you're paying for our . . ."

"Your what?"

"Our sins."

"But you're *not!* I mean, *we're* not! I— You did no wrong! It's others who—"

He waved a hand, silencing her. "I'm sorry. I . . . sometimes I remember how it used to be. What we hoped for, worked for. That's all gone now. That's a major reason I signed on. To run away from a whole host of failures."

"But you're *not—*"

"No, let's stop. It's . . . those days are impossible to forget, but pointless to remember. Better to let them go."

"Saul, I—I respect you so—"

But he waved his hands energetically in front of his face, banishing all talk. "Tell you what, I'll get you a refill and . . . and . . ."

Abruptly, he turned aside and sneezed.

"Damn! Can't get rid of this thing."

"Take an anti."

"I have."

*Another cross he'll have to bear,* she thought. *Living in a snowball, sniffling all the time.*

Percells didn't have to put up with runny noses. The gene tailors, while they were splicing away anemia and lupus and the other target diseases, had trimmed the complex of coding molecules that had given viruses their free ride, and humanity a million years of colds and flu.

"Well then . . . let me make some tea."

He smiled wanly, his steel-blue eyes still distant, thinking of something far back in a past she could not fathom. "Yes, fine. My mother . . . she did that. Then came the chicken soup." He laughed, but not his eyes.

# CARL

He suppressed a guffaw. The crucial step, the insertion of the sleep-slot modules into the head of the comet, didn't seem at all like the climax of a dangerous, five-year voyage by sailship, a prodigious engineering feat, a modern marvel. Instead, it looked to him like the coupling of monstrous genitalia.

The slender slot tug *Whipple* glided forward, nose down. Stripped of its solar sails and antennae, it was the uniform ruddy color chosen to maximize its thermal balance during the years in flight from Earth orbit. The sleep-slot payload rode forward, its extra shielding against cosmic rays filling a bulging, rounded knob, slightly thicker than the main body.

Below, Shaft 4 gaped. The surrounding ice was freshly exposed from the scratchings and abrasions of mechs—creamy, virgin ice which had not seen the harsh glare of sunlight since the time the planets and comets first formed.

Carl started to chuckle and coughed to cover it. Over the hiss of suitcomm nobody could tell the difference, probably. He blinked, but the pornographic illusion would not go away. *I must be a lot more tired out than I thought.*

—Needs a li'l ol' three-degree realign at sixty azmiuth,— Jeffers sent.

"Right. Got it," Carl replied. Jeffers's data was integrated as he spoke, and then Carl's helmet screen leaped into activity. A graphics view turned, green lines against blackground, showing how the *Whipple* looked along all three axes. Then the desired view came, an overlay in orange cocked at an angle along two axes. Carl punched in corrections.

A cluster of higher-ups were watching by TV, he knew, and Ould-Harrad stood on the surface below, cold-eyed and critical. They would certainly send back an edited version in the squirt to Earthside. Plenty of eyes to catch a mistake. Watch Carl Osborn snag ninety-odd souls half-way in, maybe.

Carl shook his head. *The hell with that. Just watch the vectors, do the job. Can't let nerves scramble your synapses, as Virginia would say.*

He fired four jets just behind the *Whipple*'s central engine housing. They pulsed ruby-red against the black. Each cut off in sequence as the orange image on his faceplate merged with the green.

—Cleared.—

—Here goes,— Andy Carroll sent. Andy sat forward in the small bubble cabin of the ship, and had nominal control. Jets flared a pale blue along the aft beams.

The *Whipple* glided smoothly in, clearing the yellow protective liners with ease.

—On the money!— Andy yelled. —Picking up the guide.—

The sleep-slot knob drove cleanly in, catching in the railings that would keep it from going astray once inside. Over suitcomm Carl heard shouts of celebration and even some handclapping leaking through from an open channel back in the *Edmund*'s lounge.

The sleep-slot module separated, descended. The sail tugs were as slim and weight-wise as classic nineteenth-century windjammers. Their slender, silvery frames carried sleep slots, supplies, and a robot crew— all in cylindrical modules fitted snugly along a tubular frame, the spine for the great spread wings that cupped the solar wind. Those gossamer sheets were now furled, awaiting humdrum service as mirrors for the surface greenhouses. That left the naked frame, a great beast now stripped by reductionist logic to a skimpy skeleton.

*And somewhere out there the* Newburn *sails on,* Carl thought about the missing fourth tug. *Lost, victim of the cold percentages.*

—Reversin' her!— Andy backed his ship out carefully. It would slip down a different path, into its own chamber. Jeffers now commanded the mechs inside to draw the sleep-slot module downward through nearly a kilometer of shaft, into the vault that had been prepared for it.

Carl turned up his bonephone: Beethoven's Fifth Violin Sonata, the last movement a liquid rush of piano notes. A reward. Lugging big masses around was standard stuff, but it felt different when there were ninety lives at stake. He needed to ease off, relax. The main show was over, but he still had hours of work to go.

The graceful, fluid sway of chamber music seemed to Carl natural for working in zero G. He could never understand Jeffers or Sergeov, who listened to that raucous, heavy-handed Clash Ceramic stuff while they worked. He vectored down, beckoning to the distant dot that was Colonel Ould-Harrad.

Carl slowed above Shaft 6 to accompany the African officer, who was space-able but less used to making speed through tunnels. A mistake could cram you into the wall with bone-splintering impact. It took years for Earthsiders' bodies to really believe that lack of weight didn't mean absence of inertia.

They shot downward. Fiberthread walls rushed past, illuminated by regular yellow daubs of electrified phosphor paint. Carl watched Ould-Harrad's swarthy face for signs of some reaction, but the man kept his eyes intently ahead and said nothing. Carl felt a twinge of disappointment. He had lined this shaft himself, without mechs, putting in fourteen-hour days to meet the deadline. And a pretty job, it was. Damn-all if anybody'd say word one about it, though.

Of course, Ould-Harrad was an Ortho, and pretty hard-line about it, according to scuttlebutt. All during the voyage out the man had been distant, formal, his poker face giving away nothing. He clearly expected that young upstarts would remember their place. Not likely he'd be glad-handing a menial Percell.

Carl shrugged and turned up the Fifth Sonata. Only after some time did it occur to him that they were, after all, falling face down in a shaft that dwindled away into the distance, the phosphors converging dots. . . . Even in a micro-G, Ould-Harrad's mental alarm bells were probably ringing.

"Hit the brakes, the vault's only a few hundred meters ahead," Carl sent.

—I see. Good,— was the only reply.

They slowed as the tunnel flared into a roomy chamber, already partly lined with brilliant lime-green insulation. The sleep-slot module was already descending from the intersecting Shaft 4, a stubby intrusion. It nearly filled the uninsulated half of the vault. Everywhere the primitive ice gave back glinting, gray-blue reflections of the sweeping lamps of men and mechs. Carl had helped hack out the rough-cut walls, using big industrial lasers. Seams of carbonaceous dirt and rusty conglomerates made curly, mysterious patterns on the broad stretches of black ice, like writing by some unseen biblical hand.

—Ahhh,— escaped from Ould-Harrad as he braked to a stop. Carl noticed that the man looked relieved. Maybe they should have gone slower.

—C'mon,— Jeffers called on open channel. —Got to get these coffins buried.—

Ould-Harrad's clipped, authoritative voice was unmistakable. —I would appreciate you men *not* referring to the slots that way.—

—Yessir,— Jeffers said curtly. —You bet.—

Carl sent, "I'll take the blue-coded mechs," and locked his board on a dozen flitting forms. The slot-sleep equipment was nearly obscured by roboids swarming around it, an army of gnats splitting off sections.

Sleepers would be stored in three widely separated vaults, to minimize chances that a single accident would cripple the mission. Technical teams—Computers, Life Sciences, Mechanical Operations—were evenly spread. The boxy slots were laid outward like the arms of a starfish from the central utilities spine. The life-support gear was a knobby backpack on each coffin—Carl couldn't help but think of them that way, both from appearance and because the sleepers were as near to dead as you could get and still come back.

Each slot had to be fitted into hardplast nooks that protected them and yet allowed the interior to exchange heat with the nearby ice. The original idea had been to let the ice cool the sleepers directly, but Carl had seen the results of that at Encke. There was a lot of carbon dioxide or amorphous snow which could vaporize explosively, blowing valves and seals on the coffins. It wasn't a snap to use volatiles in high vacuum. So the engineers had to rig buffers to save the sleepers from shudders and bumps and sudden, freezing death.

—Pack those Orthos in tight,— Jeffers sent on short-range comm. —Don't want 'em feelin' lonely.—

Jeffers was fitting hoses into place nearby, his transmission shielded from the others. Carl triggered a self-closing clamp, finishing off his own job, and kicked clear.

"Give it a rest. There're Percells in here, too."

—Not very damn many.— This came from Sergeov, who drifted into view from behind a silvery heat-exchange sphere. The Russian spacer was quick, deft; as Carl watched, he flipped, caught a cable from a spaghetti tangle, and inserted it into a control cabinet.

The agility almost made you envy him. Almost. The Percell treatment had eliminated the blood disease Sergeov would have inherited from his parents . . . but it also took away his legs.

*Unforeseen side effects.*

Carl wondered how many times that cool, analytic phrase had made him bristle, his face flush, his hands knot into fists.

Sergeov had been one of the early, lucky failures—still alive. Such survivors stirred the first misgivings. The great unwashed could *see* Sergeov's lost legs. A dirty little question wormed its way into their minds: What *couldn't* you see? What about his mind? Was he normal? Was he even human?

If it was normal to be able to drink a full bottle of vodka and still easily balance the empty glasses on top of each other, five high—yes, Sergeov was normal.

Better than normal. He had gone directly into space, where legs were, in fact, a drawback. All that bulky muscle and bone were useless in freefall, demanding food and oxygen and time to exercise them. Leftovers from the struggle against gravity. Sergeov had lived in orbit from the age of ten, making top wages as an assembler. His arms looked like tree trunks; Carl had seen him juggle a hapless Ortho inspector like a helpless doll, back in Earth orbit. The man had mumbled an insult, and paid with five minutes of humiliation. Yet, Sergeov was not a Plateau Three advocate; he expended his energies in blanket, burning dislike of all Earthsiders.

"Stop yammering," Carl said. "Come help me with these thermobuffers."

—Is true, however,— Sergeov said. —All for good reasons, for sure. Percells work good, so they get into space. *Deepa!* Orthos think we're garbage, so we *stay* in space.—

Jeffers put in, —An' end up chauffeurin' Orthos out beyond Neptune.—

Sergeov grinned. His hands—noticeably large, even through vac gloves—worked swiftly among the cables, deftly quick, free of the levered counterweight of dangling legs. —*Da*. Not prefer serving as workboy for Orthos.—

Jeffers said, —Damn right. When we could be doing our *own* work.—

Carl asked, "Such as?"

Jeffers whirled himself about with one arm, while the other fished free a short-bore laser. He thumbed it. A blue-white bolt lanced into the ice meters away.

—Hey!— Sergeov cried.

White fog exploded past them. It boiled away into the vault, thinning, but Ould-Harrad saw. —Hey! I ordered no quick-solder work in here!—

—Sorry.— Sergeov winked at Jeffers and called, —Was just a small one. Needed to refuse a socket joint.—

—These are *people*.—

—Am sorry.—

Sergeov grinned as he said it. Ould-Harrad was hundreds of meters away and couldn't see the design Jeffers had drawn with instant, practiced ease in the ice:

"I didn't know you were a Mars-boy, Jeff," Carl sent.

A female flower enclosed by the Mars symbol—a graphic depiction of a dream. Once comets could be steered into the inner solar system, they could be harvested. Even easier, an artful nudge far out beyond Neptune could smack iceballs into the Martian plains.

Hammering Mars with cometary nuclei would build up an atmosphere, perhaps even get the volcanoes spouting again. Nature's slow sucking would still. The parching march of aeons put to rout—a Promethean dream. Splitting a hard blue sky, flame-cloaked ice mountains would gouge the lands, rip the permafrost, and release more ancient ice below. Clouds, fog, then rain—weather unknown since the sun's wan warming had boiled away the last mudflats in the spare Martian river valleys, billions of years back, during that false spring.

In a century or so, a suitably adapted human might be able to breathe on the surface. The idea was old, but some Percells had seized on it. They saw Mars as the one plausible location where genetically altered humans might truly have a place. Even though still dry and cold and roiling with strange storms, Mars could become a world where their descendants, genetically engineered still further, would be the norm, while Orthos would cough out their lungs in minutes.

—What do you think I work for?— Jeffers answered.

"That's crazy," Carl sent. "Terraforming'll take centuries. No solution to our problems."

—A Percell, he can expect to live in space—what? a hundred years? two hundred?— Sergeov's broad, sweaty face beamed again with his inevitable smile.

Jeffers sent, —Throw in couple slot sleeps, we could all see it.—

"We're not here to do that," Carl said.

—Jeffers is just looking ahead,— Sergeov said simply.

"Too damn far ahead."

—Don't be so sure,— Jeffers said evenly.

Sergeov nudged Jeffers. —You be an *Uber,* too? Two ideas not contradict, I think.—

Jeffers eyed Sergeov cautiously. —Maybe. Maybe not.—

Carl frowned. This was all going over short-range close comm, and he was glad of it. *Ubers* stood for *ubermenschen,* Nietzsche's supermen, evolution's ordained next step. Planned. Designed. There would now be no slow blind stumbling upward, driven by nature red in tooth and claw. Many Percells thought they were the first step along a long, inevitable road.

Carl had known of Sergeov's opinions, but it shocked him to see Jeffers flirting with them.

Sergeov persisted. —If Orthos say no to Mars terraforming, I say yes. Simple.—

—It's right there in the physics and chem simulations, clear as anything,— Jeffers added. —Put mechs to harvestin' comets out by Neptune, it'll take a century. We could sleep right through it.—

Carl sent, "Sometimes a man can see clearer if he has his mouth shut." He gestured at Ould-Harrad, who was jetting their way.

—Okay, let's break off,— Jeffers sent.

—Is true, though. Think it over. First step to much more, maybe,— Sergeov concluded, launching himself away with a muscular shrug.

Ould-Harrad inspected the layout plans for the mechs, then left. Carl took advantage of the chance to get off and work by himself. He had never liked politics. And their wild talk had been disturbing.

He immersed himself in the sweet gliding grace of Beethoven. Moving through inky shadow and glaring yellow floodlight, pushing and towing, smelling the sour suit air, feeling the *rrrrrrtttt* of the counter-torqued wrench vibrate up his arm, the sweaty pinch of his suit at shoulders and knees—Carl thought of California.

His parents had been driving him up the coast when he told them.

The four years at Caltech had gone by in a blur of golden sunlight and nights of study, weekend pranks and unending problem sets, labs and lectures and precious little love. He'd had no time for it. Sergeov was so sure that Percells were special—well, okay, Sergeov probably had to think that, compensating for what he'd never have. But Carl knew differently.

He had done well because he'd *worked,* dammit, not because he was smarter. At Caltech he had felt a growing kinship with all the men and women who had ever put in long hours in lonely rooms. Unlike

soured drudges or inexperienced kids, he did not believe for a moment
that creative people idled away their time and then, when the mystical
spirit moved them, knocked out brilliant ideas in bouts of furious,
fevered bursts of easy inspiration.

Doing anything well demanded endurance, steadiness, relentless
drive.

Those he had. Brilliance, no.

So as his parents drove him up the coast he struggled with that inner
truth. He had applied to Berkeley for graduate school in astroengi-
neering and, against all his expectations, got in. They offered no schol-
arship, not even a teaching assistantship. That meant he was marginal.
His father loyally mistook this for another symptom of the growing prejudice against Percell-made children.

Carl knew better. Universities are sluggish beasts unmoved by the
tides of public bias. The admissions committee undoubtedly had looked
at his 3.3 average and seen that it was attained mostly by good grades in
labs and design courses. Math and physics had put him on the ropes
more than once, groggy with complex variable integration and quantum
electronics.

North of Ventura, his stepmother's happy chatter bubbled over with
enthusiasm he had always found a bit much. He had never been able to
forget his mother's slow death, and adjust to this new woman in his
father's life. So he had sat in the backseat and watched the scenery and
tried to think. The tawny August hills fell away, revealing the blue denim
of the sea. Route 1 slid by as he tried to explain to them his doubts. His
stories of distant, intellectual battlegrounds sounded hollow when con-
trasted with the solid, enduring world outside. Weathered barns, their
wood silvery from sun. Rows of eucalyptus, lush hillside orchards, spindly railroad trestles crossing gorges, minifusion generators sculpted into
hillsides, cows standing as still as statues in the inky shade of live oaks.
All the unthinking richness of Earth.

Morro Bay was glassy when they stopped there for the night. His
stepmother ooohed and aahhhed at a sleek alabaster yacht that swept by,
out beyond the bay's protecting spit of sand. Pretty, yes. But Carl liked
the moored working boats better—oily, rusted, scaly and cluttered with
gear. They had argued over chowder at a wharf restaurant, his father so
agitated that he drank the chardonnay quickly and ordered another bottle, red-faced.

The next morning he awoke knowing what he had to do. Driving
through the grassy foothills, turning inland to San Luis Obisbo between
stony low mountains, he said it—suddenly, clearly.

And now, remembering, he saw that it was brutal, too.

His father had shouted, *You're going to give up all this?* with a sweep of a hand. Meaning Berkeley, graduate school, where Carl knew he would burrow into the books and never emerge alive.

Oh, maybe he'd get a master's degree, and a reasonable desk job. With incredible luck, a doctorate.

But he'd have been a perpetual second-rate. And he'd have wasted years.

He remembered his father's hand chopping the air, the outraged gesture taking in the hills beyond. *You're going to give up all this?*—and that *all* had been, in the end, Earth itself.

Carl remembered it in grainy detail, despite the seven crowded years that had passed since. Years of learning how space *really* worked—not the geometric certainty of math and physics classes, where every problem had a pure solution in an orderly universe. Not the serene world of that distant, unattainable yacht. He had learned what space really was—grubby, tough, with plenty of problems that had no solutions at all.

It was a natural locus for Percells to gather, skating high above the clumping, festering masses who feared and despised them. Space held beauty, sure, but the places men had carved out for themselves in it were more like the rusty scows moored at Morro Bay, worn and smelly, dented and makeshift, working fine but looking like hell.

Around him, bulky masses glided by, spotlights poked the chilly gloom. Coffins nudged into sockets in the black ice. Beethoven's violin sang to a rippling piano across the yawning silent centuries. Carl labored on, thinking of his long years spent in space, far from Earth's green confusions.

# SAUL

It was hard to remember that the hall was actually a great crystal chamber, carved out of the heart of an ancient ice mountain. Nowhere could be seen the dark glittering of carbonaceous hydrate, veined with shiny seams of frozen gas. Everywhere pink fiberthread and bright yellow spray-on sealant hid the primordial stuff of Halley Core.

To Saul Lintz it far more resembled some vast cathedral of kitsch.

The Great Hall was the heart of Central Complex—the ant farm of rooms sculpted here deep under Halley's surface. Tunnels led off in the six cardinal directions, color-coded amber, lime, strawberry, peach, aquamarine . . . and a broad vertical avenue of orange—Shaft 1—fifteen meters across and rising straight up half a mile to the comet's cluttered north pole.

Machines had scrubbed the atmosphere and warmed it, leaving only a faint, almondlike odor to greet people as they streamed into the Hall for the dedication.

*Now and then, when my head clears, even I can smell it.*

Saul blew his nose and quickly put his handkerchief away before anyone noticed. That was why he sat perched on an empty packing crate at the back of the chamber instead of closer to the speakers' platform. He was stoked with antihistamines, but still his nose dripped and he felt perpetually on the verge of sneezing.

*Drat Akio and his damn tame viruses.*

He looked up at the vaulted ceiling. In the two days he had been underground, supervising the transfer of the bio lab to new, larger quarters, he had not yet gotten used to the strange perspectives here.

Across the chamber, the slot tug *Sekanina* lay like the frail skeleton of a dissected beast. Its cargo of machinery and supplies and eighty sleeping men and women had been taken elsewhere. At one end dangled the "fishing poles" that had helped control the vessel's gigantic, gossamer solar-light sails, apparently the only machinery not cannibalized or stored away in great tents on the polar plain.

The hall slowly filled as men and women floated in from all directions. Here, nearly a kilometer into the core, the sensible gravity was so low that anyone dropping through the overhead, orange-colored tunnel took several minutes to fall to the floor.

Experienced spacers did not like long transits. Old hands pushed off at the tunnel mouth to hurtle across the gap in seconds, swiveling at the very last to land with flexed legs.

One young bravo—trying to show off, Saul supposed—had already miscalculated. He was being treated for a broken wrist in the side chamber down Tunnel F, where Akio Matsudo and his doctors had set up the main infirmary.

People arrived in pairs and trios. They gathered in small groups to chat or merely lie back on packing crates, catching a moment's rest.

Next to the *Sekanina,* a small cluster congregated, the leaders of the expedition.

Miguel Cruz-Mendoza stood at least a head taller than the others—

captain and guiding force behind the decade of preparation leading to
this day. The soft-spoken Chilean spacer had distinguished streaks of
gray at his temples, which only added to his charismatic poise. It was
bruited about, mostly in jest, that he had pushed and lobbied and pres-
sured so hard for this mission in order to take a great leap forward in
time . . . and thereby get away from his accumulated mistresses and
women suitors.

The idea wasn't so preposterous, at that. Saul had never known a
man better skilled with the ladies. Some of his enemies credited Cruz's
success to his friendliness with certain women senators.

No matter. The captain was also the sort of leader people would
follow. Many had helped prepare for the Halley Mission; however, no
one but Miguel Cruz could have made this day a reality.

The captain caught Saul's eye briefly and grinned. They had come
to know each other well during the development of the cyanutes and
other environmental symbionts. Saul smiled back and nodded. This was
a grand day for his friend.

Cruz turned back as Dr. Bethany Oakes said something to him. His
laughter was deep and rich as he shared his second-in-command's joke.

Saul did not know Oakes as well, but what he had seen of the
strong-jawed, brown-haired woman had impressed him. As well as as-
sisting the captain in administering the vast, complex project, Oakes was
also head of the Science Division.

Near the leaders stood the section heads—all except Matsudo, who
presumably was still treating his patient. Nick Malenkov or Dr. Marguerite van Zoon could have handled the minor emergency just as easily.
Even Saul, rusty as his clinical skills were, could certainly have managed a simple splint.

But rank hath its privileges. Akio had been bored, lately. Accidents
that weren't instantly fatal had been rare. With this infernally healthy
crew, there wasn't much for a physician to do except oversee the sleep
slots, and occasionally release challenge parasites to keep everyone's
immune systems up to par.

*Physician, heal thyself,* Saul thought. He had made up a special
batch of dexbrompheniramine maleate, a long-obsolete antihistamine
but one easy to synthesize, so that he wouldn't have to prescribe for
himself out of the expedition pharmacy and leave an inventory record.

He knew he was being a tad unethical, hiding this from Matsudo.
But Saul had no intention of being sleep slotted over yet another blasted
head cold. Not at one of the most exciting moments in the history of
science.

More than a hundred people gathered on the shallowly curved floor of the chamber. Except for a score or so on watch duty elsewhere, all of *Edmund*'s crew were present—along with about thirty temporarily awakened slot sleepers, identifiable by their pale complexions and still slightly jerky movements.

A few people sat down out of habit, but most simply rested on their toes, knees bent and arms hanging before them in the almost fetal spacer's crouch.

Captain Cruz and Dr. Oakes stepped up onto a platform set on the girders of the gutted slot tug. Cruz raised his hands and the low murmuring of conversation died away.

"Well!" The tall astronaut rubbed his hands together. "Anyone for a snowcone?"

The assembled spacers and scientists chuckled. In spite of all the diverse cultures and beliefs represented here, it was clear that nearly everyone liked and admired their commander.

Cruz warmed them up a little more.

"I'd like to thank you all for coming all these millions of miles to attend this meeting. I've called you up here from Earth to tell you that, alas, the mission has been canceled. We're all to pack up and head for home tonight."

That got them. The hall erupted in laughter and applause. Saul grinned and clapped as well. Cruz was a genius at the subtle art of morale—of drawing the best out of a group.

Of course, there was no way any of them were returning to Earth . . . not before the appointed seventy-odd years had passed. They were riding Halley out of the planetary system at thirty kilometers per second right now, swooping up and out of the sun's deep gravity well. That streaking velocity had to ebb and die—and the great comet begin to fall again—before anyone here was going home.

Caught up in his thoughts, Saul missed the next jest. But the reaction was the same. Laughing together, they seemed a happy crew. Cruz was being deliberately folksy, loosening the crowd while at the same time maintaining his aura of complete, relaxed control.

And yet even now Saul could see the divisions. The really experienced spacers, for instance, were mostly gathered over to the left. The scientific specialists in Oakes's division tended toward the front. Behind them were spread out technicians and engineers from more than two dozen nations.

There were many small clusterings according to geography or native tongue. And nearly everywhere was the subtle but clear separation between the "Ortho" majority and the tall, handsome young Percells.

Of course there was some mixing, especially among the professional spacers. Saul saw Carl Osborn lean over and whisper something to the Ortho girl Lani Nguyen. She laughed in a single high chirp and hurriedly covered her mouth, blushing. Lani looked up at Carl with shining eyes, but Carl had turned away again, his attention once more on his captain.

"Why have we come here?" Cruz asked, his fists on his hips, legs apart. Now that he had warmed them, he was gliding into a higher tone. "There are many reasons given. Philosophers speak of pure scientific research, of the great questions of the origin of the solar system which might be solved by understanding the most primordial matter in space.

"Others believe we are at Halley's Comet because it is there! . . . Or rather, *here.*" He grinned. "And why *not* just go because it is fascinating to do so? This flying iceberg has been swooping down on us Earthlings for thousands of years, enthralling so many of our ancestors . . ." Cruz lifted an eyebrow, "and scaring the shit out of quite a few of them."

Again, the delighted hilarity. Saul watched the Hawaiian contingent, eight men and women out of thirty sent by their vigorous, future-hungry land. They had put on bright, floral shirts over their long johns. Evenly split between Percell and Ortho, the group was a flamboyant mixture of types and colors. As they joined in the laughter, one head turned. Virginia Kaninamanu Herbert lifted her eyes and looked back his way. She saw Saul and smiled brilliantly. Saul winked back at her.

". . . Search for new chemical compounds, or perhaps to be used in the terraforming of worlds, bringing life to our sister planets which were less bounteously endowed than our beloved Earth.

"Maybe some of you volunteered for all that promised duty pay— mostly for seventy-five years' sleeping on the job."

Cheers, this time. Whistling approval.

Cruz spread his hands.

"But there are two special reasons why we have come here, so far from home, on a mission that will separate most of us permanently from all family and acquaintances.

"First, and I'll be frank with you, many on Earth are looking to this mission—with its many members of genetically altered extraction—as a test of humanity's ability to rise above superstition and prejudice. For a hundred years, people of good will have been fighting to wean our species of the most deep-seated tribal reaction for all—that fear of *otherness* that has caused such hatred and horror since time immemorial. . . ."

*Since time immemorial . . .* Saul closed his eyes, remembering Jerusalem.

". . . Will achieve a great thing if we prove to those on Earth that so-called Orthos and so-called Percells, living and working together on a long and dangerous mission, can rely on each other simply as fellow human beings, and bring home great discoveries to benefit all mankind.

"The same goes for the many national and ethnic groups represented here. We are emissaries from the twenty-first century into the future. For seventy and more years, people back home will know we are up here, cooperating for the greater good."

Cruz let the words settle over them. Saul saw that many of those present were looking at their feet, suddenly uncomfortable, as if they were not sure they were worthy of this trust.

"And of course there is also the fun stuff." Cruz grinned and rubbed his hands together. "We came out here to test a *lot* of technological toys! Collecting comets into accessible orbits may forever unlock the door to space. The new toehold on prosperity mankind has regained, after the Hell Century, will be secure for all time.

"And if we demonstrate dramatically that sleep slots work well for over seventy years—as all the data indicates they will—we'll have established that humanity need not be locked into the solar system. The stars, the very stars themselves, will be ours."

The words hung in the chilly air, above the hum of the air fans.

And Saul saw glowing belief on many faces present. Carl Osborn's heroic jaw jutted in dedication to his captain's goal.

*Well, maybe it's partly stubbornness, too,* Saul thought sardonically. When Carl played chess, it was with a methodical tenacity that admitted no defeat until the bitter end. *But no,* Saul thought, looking at the light in the young man's eyes. *He believes in Miguel's dream. And I guess I do too.*

The feeling was obviously shared by a lot of the spacers, both Percell and Ortho. This was the passion of those who longed for Plateau Three . . . the stepladder to the sky.

Still, there were others. They kept quiet, but one could read the signs. This crew, after all, had not been recruited entirely from the ranks of idealists.

Why did a man or woman volunteer to go into dangerous exile, far from everything familiar? For many, including Saul, the choice had not been altogether voluntary.

He saw Marguerite van Zoon, standing beside Akio Matsudo at the entrance to F Tunnel and the new infirmary. The French Imperium had given her the option of "volunteering" for this mission or seeing her entire family imprisoned for lèse-majesté.

Saul had last heard that her husband had gone to Indonesia and slotted himself to await her return. It was some small solace, he supposed.

And then there was Lieutenant Colonel Suleiman Ould-Harrad. Powerful family ties had gotten him into this mission, instead of a Mauritanian dungeon. But the black spacer seemed less than happy to be here. He stood over to the right, with Joao Quiverian and some other folk from the equatorial lands of the Arc of the Living Sun.

Percells and Orthos, Northerns and Arcists, liberals, moderates, and even a few fanatics; Saul was certain it was pretty much the same among those still in slots. Cruz and Oakes were inspirational leaders, and they would get the best out of the colonists, but Saul did not expect this long voyage to be entirely trouble-free.

*Nothing ever is, Saul. Exile is not the same as escape.*

Captain Cruz continued with a hearty tone.

"And now I have a surprise for all of you. Many of us had high hopes for great scientific advances on this voyage, but I'd wager none of you expected that within weeks of arriving we would already have written a new chapter in the annals of human discovery."

Saul saw the audience stir. People looked at one another. A wave of shrugs and confused looks showed that the secret had held for the last three days of frantic tests, experiments, and double-checks.

Saul took out his handkerchief and blew as quietly as the nose his parents had given him would allow. He knew it might be his last chance for a while.

Cruz grinned at his audience, milking the suspense for all it was worth. He held up his hands and the crowd quieted again.

"I certainly don't want to hog the show, or steal anyone's day in the limelight. . . ."

*Oh, no,* Saul thought. He had asked Cruz not to do this.

". . . So let me just call up the man who has made this epochal discovery, whose name will, within a week, be the toast of the solar system. Come on up here, Saul Lintz, and tell us what you've found!"

*Sigh.*

Saul pushed off from the packing crate as scattered applause rose from various parts of the hall. After the first stumble caused him to drift above the floor for a few seconds, he had to endure being passed from hand to hand by those more experienced in microgravity.

Along the way he saw that much of the applause came from certain groups—Matsudo and Malenkov, who had helped in the analyses, from the Hawaiians up in front, from some of the Percells. . . .

There were some among the African and Latin contingents who looked aside and lowered their arms, unable, like him, to forget Jerusalem.

Someone put her hands under him and pushed hard. He went sailing, without a bit of spin, in a smooth arc that landed him right beside Dr. Bethany Oakes. *Good shooting,* he thought as the small woman swung him around to face the audience.

"Don't worry, Saul," Cruz whispered to him. "You'll get your space legs yet. Your problem is you've spent too much time in that damned wheel."

Saul shrugged. "Some of us are too old to change, Mike."

Cruz laughed and gestured that the "floor" was his. Saul gingerly slid a foot forward. He looked out over the assembly.

"Um, I'm sure you'll all recall . . ."

"Louder, Saul!" a thickly accented voice called out from the back of the hall. "You don't have to whisper to prove to us you're not a loud-mouthed Levite!"

Gasps rose from the crowd and several dark faces seemed suddenly to go pale. Saul recognized Malenkov's shout and wave from the back of the room. The grinning Russian bear had the tact of a tornado, but Saul smiled.

"Sorry. I'll try to speak up.

"I was about to say that I'm sure you'll all recall the fantastic array of organic compounds that the expedition to comet Encke found while they were testing out the techniques needed for this mission. Many of those compounds were totally unknown until then, and led to some revolutionary changes in industrial chemistry.

"In fact, one of our lesser goals here is to see if nature has cooked up any more wonderful polymers and agglutinates for us, perhaps as valuable as Enkon and Stannous-Clathride have become."

Directly below the platform, Joao Quiverian frowned. He had discovered those compounds, on that earlier mission, so in a way he was responsible for some of the motivation to explore and "exploit" comets.

"But one of the most exciting discoveries at Encke was that the core of that aged, nearly dead comet contained an abundance of chemicals best called 'prebiotic' . . . accumulations of purines, pyrimidines, phosphates, and amino acids nearly identical to the sort of mixture modern biologists believe made up the primordial 'soup' that led to life on Earth.

It was hoped, when we set off on *this* trip, that by studying a large, younger comet, we might, well, shed some light on the way things were on our homeworld four billion years ago, when we all began."

Saul cleared his throat, and hoped the raspiness in his voice would be attributed to general hoarseness and excitement. Ten rows back or so, among the colorful Hawaiians, he saw Virginia Herbert smiling up at him. The admiration in her eyes was pleasant, if a bit disconcerting.

*Down, boy. Don't imagine more'n is there. No doubt she looks on you as some sort of surrogate dad.*

"Well," he resumed. "Dr. Malenkov and Dr. Quiverian and I have studied one of the latest cores collected by Dr. Otis Sergeov—"

"Don't be modest, Saul," Malenkov interrupted again. "You did it! You get the blame!"

This time, at least, people laughed and applauded. Saul smiled. *Thanks, Nicholas.* Deep inside he wondered if the Russian wasn't really right . . . if *blame* might someday be the right word. Look at what had happened to Simon Percell, whose name should have gone down alongside Galen's and Schweitzer's. Dame Fame was a fickle bitch.

". . . Uh, well, with the help of those gentlemen I was able to isolate . . ."

*Oh, come on, Saul,* he chided himself. *What would Miriam think if she had lived to see you now, standing here stammering, when you have a chance to make an announcement like this!*

Saul straightened his back, almost losing his footing in the process. He looked out at the audience and borrowed one of Miguel Cruz's gestures, spreading his hands apart.

"The signs are strong. The specimens are unambiguous. No contamination could explain what we have found. We've worked for a week to be certain it is nothing brought from Earth.

"How it got here, nobody can imagine as yet. How it survived or evolved, we haven't a clue. But what we do know now is that we appear to have stumbled on what mankind has been looking for ever since our first explorers stepped onto another world, nearly a century ago."

He smiled. *Let them make of it what they will.*

"For the first time, ladies and gentlemen—for the first time we have found definite signs of life beyond Earth."

## PART II

# IN THE HOT BREATH OF THOSE DAYS

When beggars die, there are no comets seen—
The heavens themselves blaze forth the death of princes.
                              —Wm. Shakespeare

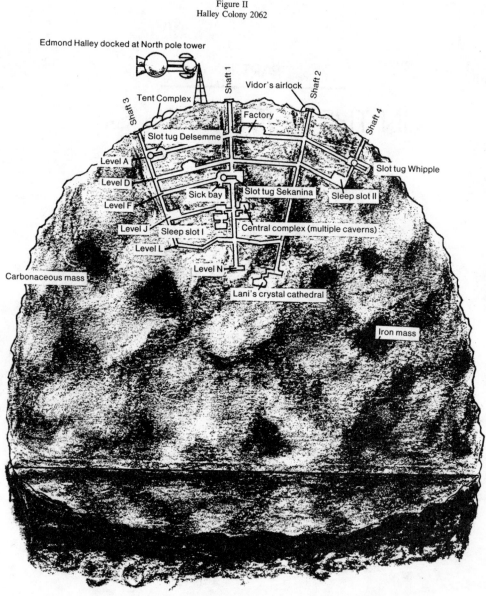

Figure II
Halley Colony 2062

# VIRGINIA

The great, tumbling ice mountain hurtled outward into the void. Behind it, smaller and fainter with every passing watch, the Hot fell away into the eternal blackness.

Briefly, the sun's blazing furnace had scrubbed and gouged and broiled away at the snowy worldlet—had cracked and charged its temporary atmosphere, sending waving flags of ionized gas flapping in the interplanetary breeze.

But then quick summer passed. The flames were left behind again, still bright, but growing more harmless hour by hour. The savage exuberance of perihelion passage was fast fading from memory.

Autumn was marked by a gentle fall of dust. Tiny bits, carried away from the surface in the waning blow of escaping gas, had never quite reached escape velocity, even from the comet's feeble pull. Gradually, they drifted back again, laying a dark, talclike patina over the icefields and rocky outcrops. The flickering snake of the plasma tail had already vanished, and now the foreshortened dust tail—so like shimmering angels' banners not long ago—dissipated as the ancient comet streaked past Mars and on, toward the orbit of Jupiter.

Virginia found it beautiful. The dark regolith was laid bare, here and there, exposing a slumbering icy substrate. Although a thin coma of shimmering ions still hung overhead tenaciously, the vault already showed more stars than the dark, tropical nights back home.

*I'll bet the view is even more spectacular in person,* she thought. *One day I really must go up to the surface myself.*

She could feel the soft webbing holding her to her link-couch, in a cave laboratory deep under millions of tons of primeval matter. But otherwise it was almost as if she were up on the comet's surface, in person. The holographic images brought her a nearly perfect sensation of being out on the ice.

She was wearing—teleoperating—a Class III surface mech, moving its spindly, spider legs as she would her own, looking with its swiveling eyes, feeling the faint brush of drifting gas molecules as a wind on her face. Her fingertips moved gently in their waldo grips as she sent a chain of mental commands to the host mech on the ice, making it turn.

The method had first been tried back in the late twentieth century, and had seemed quite promising at the time . . . until several famous disasters led to near abandonment of direct mind-machine interfaces. It turned out to require a special kind of personality to control a mech in this way, without letting random thoughts and a hundred human reflexes interfere, sometimes catastrophically. This had been discovered the hard way, during those early, naïve applications to aircraft and factory equipment. To this day, spacers like Carl Osborn tended to distrust the technique, preferring voice and touch controls.

*That was then, though. This is now.*

One of the reasons for her presence on this mission was the fact that such extensive use was to be made of mentally controlled robots for the first time in decades.

*Vasha Rubenchik is a real genius,* Virginia thought as she deftly rode the mech over a small rise. *The Russians were idiots to exile him out here, whatever his political opinions. I've never felt a mind-to-robot link this good before.*

Too bad Vasha was already in the slots, or Virginia would have praised him for deftly tailoring the neuroelectric and holographic connections so well to her specifications. This alone was almost sure to win patent royalties for both of them, when the data were sent back. The boodle would accumulate in their accounts while they slept through most of the seven and a half decades ahead.

Although money wasn't her top priority, Virginia had seen how useful it could be, especially when one wanted to work in areas frowned upon by the powers that be.

She could hardly wait until things had settled down a bit and there was free time to try some of these new techniques in experiments with JonVon.

As if summoned, a voice hummed along her acoustic nerve.

I AM PREPARED TO ENGAGE IN NEW PROBLEMS WHENEVER YOU WISH, VIRGINIA. THE MISSION MAINFRAME IS USING ONLY

15% OF MY CAPACITY, RIGHT NOW. . . . WOULD YOU LIKE ME
TO ASSUME A SIMULATED PERSONALITY?

*Oh, great,* she thought. *All I'd need, while I'm controlling a mech out on the surface, would be to let you construct Olivier, or O'Toole, or some other old movie heartthrob . . . have them come charging around, blowing in my ear.*

She had chosen pre-vid actors to use in personality-sim experiments partly out of romantic atavism, and partly because they were less familiar to people these days—better to use in blind Turing tests on unsuspecting subjects. The simulations had fooled almost everybody, on Earth, even though they still were nothing like what she was sure they could be.

OR I COULD BRING FORTH SHELLEY. YOU LIKE HIS POETRY.

Virginia subvocalized clearly, crisply:
*Not now, JonVon. Mother is busy. If you haven't enough to do, helping the colony mainframe, go to some of those secondary problems I assigned you.*

VERY WELL. I'LL CONTINUE SNEAKING THROUGH THE COLONY
RECORDS AND SNOOPING WHAT PEOPLE BROUGHT ALONG IN
THEIR PERSONAL WEIGHT ALLOTMENTS. YOU EXPRESSED CURI-
OSITY ABOUT THAT.

Virginia hesitated, then agreed. *Okay. You do that. Just don't leave any traces.*

Of course it was a bit unethical to use her special tools and skills to snoop into other folks' private matters. But then, Virginia had always believed people tended to try to keep too much secret.

Anyway, it broadened the number of people to think about. The dozen crew members still warm and moving about were hardly enough for even minimal gossip over the sixteen months of First Watch. In the need to conserve consumables, everyone else had already been put into cold sleep, leaving the first shift to apply finishing touches to the habitats and other facilities.

*Well, Ginnie, you volunteered to be on First Watch. You knew it would be one of the busiest.*

*Yes, but there are opportunities, as well. Later,* she thought. *Later, after things have settled down, I'll have my chance. Long, delicious stretches of work time.*

Her mech finished its slow scan of the surface as the mouth of Shaft 2 came into view.

Scarred, scratched, and littered, the north polar region looked nothing like a pristine remnant of Creation. Crates of supplies lay tethered to the ice or bound up under fibercloth "tents" for later use. Debris lay everywhere.

Farther off stood six high, peaked pyramids of dark tailings from shaft excavations, crudely separated into heaps of primordial nickel-iron, platinum- and iridium-rich ores, and carbonaceous gunk . . . much like Alberta tar sands. At some point later, long after she had returned to the slots, the watch crews would start processing the piles into useful things, like Nudge Driver housings.

*To take us home again.* Not for the first or last time, she wondered what Earth would be like when they returned. If all their grand schemes would turn out to have mattered. Would she find Hawaii, Earth, recognizable? Friendlier? Or would it be an alien world, altered beyond recognition?

Halley swoops
　　in centuries,
　　　　in intervals—

One human span apart

Halley scoops
　　up changing times,
　　　　up nations' lives—

In one beat of its heart.

Hmm. Thank heavens she was too busy right now, or she might be tempted to record that bit of doggerel. Still, perhaps something could be done with it.

SHALL I STORE OR ERASE IT, THEN, VIRGINIA?

She started, then subvocalized quickly, *JonVon, I thought you'd signed off. Those were private musings.*

A brief pause told of vigorous cross-correlation checks.

PRIVATE MUSINGS—REFLECTIONS—FANTASIES . . .

*Enough!* And JonVon was instantly quiet.

Irritated, Virginia took hold of her thoughts and concentrated on maneuvering the mech back toward the work site. The spider's legs swung, one at a time. Surface vibrations translated into sounds so she "heard" the mech's feet crunch across the dark powder.

During the early work, so much vapor had been churned out here that some of the gases actually condensed again, instead of escaping into space. Sparkling snows had flash-frozen around the heat-and-gas-release ducts leading up from Central. Broad, rainbow-colored flows spilled over the feet of the Shaft 2 portal.

The airlock itself was more than just a drab, functional construct. Far from that, Virginia saw it as a work of art. Structural braces had been press-formed in high, faery arches. The footing anchors looked like gnarled gargoyles' fists, gripping the ancient stuff of Halley.

Only a few crucial parts were made of precious refined metal, salvaged from the robot freighters. The supports and body of the building were cleverly sculpted from refrozen, crystalline, water ice.

It was one reason why Virginia liked working out on Quadrant 2, where Jim Vidor had been in charge of the construction crew. The man was an artist.

"We build best when we are forced to improvise," Virginia said softly to herself.

A carrier wave cut in, followed quickly by a woman's voice.

—What was that, Virginia? Did you say something?—

Virginia's head turned a little too quickly, causing the mech to slew awkwardly as it struggled to follow. At last a slim, spacesuited figure came into Virginia's field of view, standing over a row of dark shapes tethered to the ice.

"Oh, I'm sorry, Lani. I was just admiring what Jim and his guys did in melt-carving this airlock."

Lani Nguyen's spacesuit had been trimmed of its heavy armor, now that summer had passed and dust pebbles were no longer being blasted outward by subliming gas. A white cloth tabard covered the suit's chest area, depicting the head of a smiling unicorn—a symbol that would identify Lani to workers too far away to make out her face. Right now the sharp sun reflected in her opaqued visor, anyway, hiding her soft, half-Asian features.

—Yes, pretty. But not entirely safe, in my opinion. Next shift, Jeffers is supposed to break out the factory gear and start processing some of that iron and carbon stacked out here. I'll sleep a lot quieter in my slot knowing there's a real stress-filament hatch up here, capping the air in.—

Virginia sighed softly. "Yes, I suppose so. Still, I hope they leave some of these crystal structures in place. It would be a shame if the only marks we left were scars on every inch of this little world."

She heard Lani sniff but politely withhold further comment.

Virginia knew that, to a spacer, talk of "preserving nature" was nothing more than Luddism. It was all very well to try to save what was left of poor, depleted Earth, but to apply such ideas to the vast resources out here struck spacers as thickheaded.

Dumb or not, though, a majority of Earthlings felt that way. And Virginia was not sure, quite yet, if she disagreed.

She walked her mech back over to the stacked equipment and helped the Amerasian girl unload a new crate of fibercloth tunnel liner. Carl Osborn was due up here in a little while to work with Lani on a new link from Shaft 2 to Shaft 1. Lani had asked Virginia to come up—in proxy, of course—to help whip a balky autonomous mechanical into shape for the upcoming operation.

*This mech is working just fine,* Virginia thought. *The model's certainly smart enough to have done Lani's bidding without my direct control. I wonder what her real reason was for asking me up here.*

Together they pushed the crate toward the gaping airlock doors, providing fingertip support for the bulky cargo against Halley Core's faint tug. It was then that Lani spoke again, in a voice of labored casualness.

—As long as you're up here, Virginia, I want to thank you for helping arrange to put me on First Watch.—

Virginia started, and nearly dropped her end of the crate as they lowered it to the floor of the airlock.

"Uh, you're welcome, Lani. I—I don't really think I made much difference, though."

That was certainly the truth. Three weeks ago, while a hundred temporarily awakened men and women scrambled about like ants preparing for the long winter, Lani had hinted something to Virginia about influencing shift scheduling. She wanted to remain awake on the first year-and-a-half detail, after nearly everyone else was cooled down.

A number of crew members seemed to share this belief, that Virginia had some sort of a secret back door into the mission mainframe computer aboard the *Edmund*. Some had made even more blatant requests. She had been politely noncommittal to them all. People took that sort of answer better than an outright refusal.

To be honest, in all the running around, Virginia had forgotten about Lani's shy entreaty until now.

They had to push down on the crate to set it against the other equipment, Halley's pull was so molasses slow.

—I'm really grateful. I just couldn't go down there to sleep . . . to pass so much time . . . with my mind in such a spin. There are things . . . things I have to work out.—

Although she had half-turned away as she spoke, Lani's face was now visible under her helmet visor. The young woman could easily have been Hawaiian, with her faintly Eurasian features and healthy, taut skin. Right now, though, Spacer Second Class Nguyen seemed troubled, her mouth working as she sought words to express herself.

*Well, it's only to be expected*, Virginia thought. *They told us back on Earth that we would all have to take turns being each other's therapists, ministers, listeners. And then they loaded the expedition down with exiles, cripples, and refugees.*

*Like me.* She sighed. *Be honest with yourself, Ginnie, are you any less confused than this poor girl?*

She waited, and at last Lani spoke again.

—Virginia, I was wondering. Um, what do you think of the Birth and Childhood Laws?—

Virginia was glad that a mech couldn't show her sudden surprise.

"Well, uh, they don't seem all that fair . . . though I guess there are arguments on both sides. I don't suppose you like them much, Lani. After all, you're a . . ."

—A spacer. Yes.— Lani nodded. —My parents were California Techno-Liberals. They told me stories, ever since I was a little baby, about how mankind's future was out in space. How someday humanity would move out here and get rich and happy and generous again. Only the dreary stay-at-home types would live on Earth.—

Virginia shifted uncomfortably. The mech responded with the same pelvis cant.

"Your parents were right, Lani. Space *is* saving humanity. Even reactionaries and Arcists know that. Why do you think Hawaii invested so heavily in this expedition? Those dreams will come true, someday.

"I guess it's just that the Hell Century is still fresh in everyone's memory. That's why so many countries are so suspicious. Space has to serve Earth first, until the recovery is complete. Don't worry, though. I'm sure you'll live to see your Third Plateau."

The mech's vision system adjusted to the shadows. Through the other woman's faceplate she saw Lani's head shake.

—Probably too late for me, though. I'll have to go live on Earth to have my babies, and no male spacer will give up the Black to stay dirt-side with me.—

There it was, laid out like an open wound. Virginia's palms felt clammy on her waldo controls. If there was any subject she would prefer not to discuss, this was it.

She said with feigned lightness, "Isn't that an exaggeration?"

Lani looked up. Her dark eyes were sad.

—Look at the figures, Virginia. All spacers store sperm or ova in banks on Earth. Most breed by proxy . . . except those who are Percells, and can't find surrogate parents for their offspring. They're even worse off than us Orthos.—

Virginia felt a wash of savage irony. At least the girl had something to store away. She had a ticket into the future.

*What have I, but my machines?* Virginia thought.

"The radiation levels you live in make that necessary, don't they, Lani?" A truism, of course.

Lani shrugged.

—If they'd let us build *real* space colonies, instead of just factories and life-support huts in orbit, we spacers could marry and raise families together. As it is, those women spacers who go home and reclaim their plasm have to stay there with their children. Nearly all of us have to marry Earthers, since no man like Car . . . since hardly any man of space would give up the Black without a fight.—

Virginia tried to pull the conversation back into the abstract, where she was much more comfortable. "That's a tough situation, Lani. But the laws themselves . . ."

—The Birth and Childhood Laws are a crock! You know they're just reactionary measures against anything new and frightening to the masses! They don't want to lose control of us out here! They're terrified of change!—

Virginia quashed her first reaction—to tell the girl not to teach her grandmother to suck eggs. What, in all the world, had a healthy Ortho girl to teach *her* about life? About bitterness and the dark shadow of persecution? There was only one man out here Virginia cared to listen to, or who had the right to say anything on those matters.

Something of this must have been conveyed in the host mech's six-legged stance. The spacesuited woman straightened up and shook her head.

—I'm sorry I shouted, Virginia.—

"That's all right, Lani. Come on, let's get that last crate. You know that hell hath no fury like a petty officer confronted with a job undone. We want to be finished before His Nibs, Spacer First Class Carl Osborn, arrives."

Lani laughed, but finished with a sniff and a shake of her head. Virginia reached out delicately with one manipulator arm and touched the spacesuit's insulated sleeve. The other woman nodded and they moved back out under the stars to fetch the last crate.

They had tugged the hulking container halfway back to the airlock structure when a light fanned forth from the lift doors, following a spurting ivory cloud of released gas.

A tall, bulky, spacesuited figure emerged. Virginia recognized Carl Osborn from his languid, graceful movement along the guide cable even before she could make out the name-chop on his suit's tabard.

—Hello, Carl,— Lani sent.

"Right on time, I see," Virginia added.

Carl stopped abruptly.

—Virginia! Are you up here? Well, well, just couldn't keep away from me, could you?—

He bowed to her mech. —Nice day for a stroll on the surface. You should tell me, next time you plan to come up.—

At last Carl turned and nodded to his teammate.

—Hi, Lani. Careful with that end, it's drooping.—

—Oh. Sorry, Carl. I'll get it.—

Actually, Carl should have addressed the living person before speaking to the one who was present only *in waldo*. Lani Nguyen's helmet had opaqued under the bright glare of the sun, so Virginia could not make out the girl's reaction. But she had her suspicions.

"I'll leave you here with Heaven's Gift to spacedrift women, Lani," Virginia sent. "I'm sure he's capable of doing good work, if watched carefully."

Carl's back was to the sun, so his faceplate was clear. Virginia saw him blink and hurry to speak.

—Why don't you come along, Virginia? We've been running into some interesting sintered and recrystallized formations as we dig deeper into the core. They're unlike anything we've encountered until now.—

Virginia had to admit that, even as she found them overeager and embarrassing, Carl's attentions nonetheless pleased her. The man was so damned attractive . . . in the movie hero sort of way.

If that type of hero had been what she was looking for . . . but no, it wasn't. Not in this life. Not right now.

She made the mech execute an imitation of a curtsy. "That sounds exciting, Carl. I'll inform Saul Lintz. He and Joao Quiverian are the cometologists on duty, this watch. I'm sure they'll be eager to see your pix and get your samples."

Carl frowned sourly. That obviously wasn't what he'd had in mind.

"See you around, Carl. Good luck, Lani."

She engaged the release procedure, allowing the mech's onboard systems to take over as her own teleoperated presence flowed back into the deeply buried laboratory where her body lay. The images faded, but before they departed completely and the lights came on, she saw that Carl still watched "her" . . . and Lani Nguyen watched Carl.

# CARL

Their torches were blue blades of light cutting the seething fog.

"Hold steady. It'll clear in a minute," Carl sent.

Lani Nguyen sank a spike into a crusty chunk of water ice for stability. —What an eruption! It must have been bottled up in there a billion years.—

They had been finishing off a fresh tunnel. Mechs had done the initial work a week before, roughing it out, but it was better for humans to do the mop-up; mechs had an odd way of leaving dangerous knife-edged ruts.

The two of them had been using their lasers on low fan mode, trimming and scouring away jutting ice. The occasional boulder they had to chip around, or boil loose with lasers on tightbeam. Then they would nudge it back to the nearest tunnel intersection, where a mech would add it to the dumpster.

Lani had been prying at a chair-sized rock when Carl said laconically, "Remember Umolanda." She had nodded, moving carefully, tugging—and suddenly it had sprung free, under pressure from behind. Pearly fog spurted forth.

Lani fruitlessly fanned at the vapor. —You figure it's another aluminum-melt vault?—

So far the expedition had found fourteen pockets, each containing vapor and even a little liquid. Carl peered through the hole.

A bubbling pool simmered at the bottom of a wide, spherical room. Fog rose from it in gouts and gusts. Multicolored steam still poured out, frothing. "Damn! Looks like soup's on."

Lani frowned prettily. —Primordial soup, yeah. Lintz and Malenkov are all ga-ga over it.—

"Keeps 'em out of our hair."

—I'll bet Quiverian's having nightmares over those two finding all sorts of juicy stuff about *his* comet.—

As he watched, she brushed at a splotch of gooey purple on her sleeve. —Eccch. God knows what this stuff is.—

Carl grinned. Lani preferred the austere simplicity of space work, the Newtonian mechanics of straight lines and known vectors; of sun-scoured steel and bare, clean surfaces. *Not* the murk and splatter of tunnel work.

"Isn't it wonderful, what creation can do with just a few simple molecules?" He kept a poker face. He had been feeling a bit odd ever since meeting Virginia's mech on the surface hours ago. The mech and Lani had seemed engrossed in a heart-to-heart and had clammed up right away on his arrival. Maybe he could tease Lani into telling him what was bothering Virginia.

—It's *not* funny, Carl. This gunk could get into a joint, stiffen it up.—

"It'll evaporate."

—Yeah? So how come it didn't boil away four billion years back?—

"It's been under pressure."

—But everything must've frozen down after the early days.—

"Probably. This was just a flying iceberg for billions of years, out beyond Neptune. But back when the solar nebula condensed there was a lot of aluminum 26 in Halley; Chem Section reported finding the decay products, remember?"

—Oh yeah, residue from the same supernova that triggered formation of the solar system.—

"So they say. Anyway, that aluminum-isotope decay melted these chambers. Might've kept things percolating long enough to cook up those exotic chemicals and prelife forms Lintz found. I dunno."

Lani widened the opening with a pick. —Then when Halley got bumped into its present orbit, the sun warmed up these hot spots again? Waves of heat every perihelion summer?—

Carl shrugged. "Must've." He couldn't think of a way to maneuver this conversation over to Virginia's secrets.

—Last year's heat from the sun—that must still be seeping down through the ice, adding just enough to keep these local hot spots liquid.—

"Right. Malenkov and Vidor measured the temperature wave."

The fountain sputtered, died. Cottony clouds swirled, thinned, escaped down the corridor behind them and into the oblivion of space.

"Let's have a look." Carl knocked a last rock out of the way and wriggled into the chamber beyond. He fanned his torch around—and gasped.

Crystalline facets sprouted everywhere. Points gleamed ruby red, emerald, burnt orange. Wherever he turned his helmet lamps, refracted light came back in brilliant splinters.

—A crystal palace,— Lani said softly as she followed. —How lovely.—

"The colors!"

—Concentrations of metals? Magnesium? Platinum nodules? Cobalt? The pinks, the purples!—

"Here, take some pictures. Our suit heat alone might melt it."

—Think so?— Lani handed him her torch and moved away, unhooking her camera. —Look, I can see images of myself in the big crystals. They must be a meter across, easy.—

Carl picked his way gingerly, walking lightly on his toes. The peaked pyramids of delicate arsene blue looked particularly dangerous. They worked in skinsuits, thin and flexible enough for difficult jobs, derived from the same woven chain molecules as the corridor liner. Still, a really sharp edge could slice through.

Carl peered ahead, squinting against the rainbow ribbons of light that seemed to focus on him. He remembered an optics problem from Caltech, over a decade ago. If you were inside a reflecting sphere, what would you see? How many images? The natural impulse was to start adding up reflections of reflections of reflections, ad infinitum. The true answer was that you'd see only one image.

Not here, though. Every refraction fed others, giving a myriad swarm of tiny technicolored Carls. They moved as he did, insects of every color hovering in a cloud beyond reach.

Dizzying. Thousands of Lanis, each earnestly working a camera. Between them was a dark spot. He gave a small push and glided over to it.

"Hey. Some kind of fracture here."

—Careful of these sharp ones, Carl.—

"Yeah."

He flipped slowly and brought his head down into the hole. "Looks like it goes on."

—Very far?—

"Dunno. Some runny brown stuff back in there. Looks wet."

—Yuk. Leave it for the bio boys.—

"Check." He righted himself, drifting lazily over a glinting field of steepled crystals. "Hey, it's lunchtime."

—Let's eat here.—

"Could get good hot chow back at sleep-slot one."

She grimaced. —And unsuit just to get inside? Roast pheasant with chestnut sauce wouldn't be worth having to wipe up this mess an extra time.—

They tethered from the nominal ceiling and broke out food tubes. "Even self-heated, this stuff is pretty bad," Carl grumbled.

—It's worth it to me, just to be away from the others.—

"Yeah, know what you mean."

Their ration was stored in their backpacks, heated there and available by sucking on a tube that emerged near the chin. Eating was not an elegant process. Lani had a curious natural daintiness that made her turn away for each gulp of the light, aromatic broth. She floated with her arms and knees tucked in gracefully, an economical cross-limbed Asian sitting posture, more elegant than the usual spacer's crouch. Carl smiled. She was a hard worker, lean and lithe, with steady, remorseless energy.

—I enjoy getting off by ourselves.—

"Uh-huh."

—Particularly in such a lovely, well . . . jeweled palace.—

"Right. Damn pretty." Carl wondered vaguely about Virginia.

—Do we have to tell anyone about it?—

"Huh?"

—Couldn't it be a place . . . just for us?—

"Uh, why?"

—To get away. We could come here and bask in the light and, well, have time to talk.—

Carl didn't feel comfortable with this turn of the conversation. "Look, somebody'd find it fast enough. I mean, we'd have to leave a port exit in the insulation, to get back in here ourselves."

—Not if we disguised it some way.—

Carl struggled for a reply, some technical reason why it wouldn't work. "You mean, mark it as a pressure hatch? Something like that?"

—I suppose so.— She studied him intently but said no more.

After a long pause Carl spoke again. "Somebody'd notice. It'd be just like Samuelson to come by, check on us. Pop the seal and make the discovery for himself."

—You think so?—

"Sure, he's a straitlaced, um, type." He had barely stopped himself from saying *a straitlaced, by-the-book Ortho*. Lani was an Ortho, too, but one of the good ones.

—I suppose we should report it to Planetary.—

"Yeah, Quiverian'll blow his buttons."

—Still . . . I would like to have, you know, a retreat.—

"Plenty of volume in Halley—almost three hundred cubic kilometers." He couldn't imagine wanting to spend time sitting in an ice-walled hole, even if it did get you away from the rest of the dozen people in the First Watch. Better to go outside if you wanted that. Have the whole solar system to look at.

—Well, perhaps later, then. We could do it all ourselves, without the mechs.— Lani looked at him with a doelike, expectant gaze. Carl glanced away nervously.

"I dunno. Might have to insulate it."

Unless he could steer the talk to Virginia, he wanted to deflect conversation away from personal things, to keep their relationship friendly but strictly professional. He started talking about the insulation problem, how much worse it was here than on Encke.

Humans liked temperatures around three hundred degrees Absolute, but some of the frozen gases boiled away in a furious phase transformation around a hundred degrees. Even a casual brush from a skinsuit would bring an answering puff of gas. Maintaining that two-hundred-degree differential had meant developing flexible, layered insulators. The merest breath of air would evaporate the very walls from an uninsulated chamber.

There would always be some boiloff, so the tunnel system had to let the vapor escape toward the surface, where it vented to free space. At the same time, controlled harvesting of the ice was the key to the expedition's success. The biosphere needed a flux of water, gases, even the metals and grit contaminating the comet. So some of the boiloff was recovered, filtered to keep the cyanide level down, and cycled back into the habitats.

Without a virtually labor-free system to supply fluids and gases, there would have to be more people awake and working. That, in turn, would put more demand on the biomatrix, which drove a spiral of costs. This was the fundamental reason why living inside Halley Core was essential. As usual, profit and loss had the final say.

Keeping locks and ports from leaking heat to the nearby ice was tricky, tedious labor that Carl disliked. He belabored this point for several minutes, not because he liked to gripe, but because he couldn't think of any other way to keep control of the conversation. At last he wound down. There was a long, uncomfortable silence.

—I was hoping we could find some time alone together,— Lani said simply, though she blinked several times.

"I . . . yeah, I got that."

—You have felt it?—

"Well . . ."

—I have known you three years now. Long enough to learn how special you are.— Her eyes were large, black, and as deep as a pool. She was being direct and clear and it obviously took an effort of will not to look away. He could see that she had rehearsed this.

"There . . . there isn't anything so great about me. I like space work. It's my life, same as you."

—We have much in common.—

"Yes, we do."

—In the long times we will spend on watch together, perhaps . . .— Her gaze faltered.

"Look, I think a great deal of you, Lani."

—I am happy of that.— But her face had lost its pensive, focused look. Her certainty was fading. *And there isn't a damned thing I can do about it,* he thought. *There's no way I can give her the answer she wants.*

"But, I mean, I don't . . . really . . . think of you that way."

She stiffened. —Oh.—

*She isn't any better at talk like this than I am. She misses my hints. So I have to say it straight out and that hurts her. Damn!* "You're . . . a great teammate, sure as hell you are."

Her long eyelashes batted several times. The thin, broad mouth twisted ruefully. —Thank you.—

"God, I don't mean to . . . to brush you off or anything."

—There is no need to be concerned. You are speaking the truth, as you must.—

"You really are attractive, too, I don't mean anything like that."

Now that he thought about it, she was quite good-looking. *Serving a sixteen-month watch, she's thinking about pairing off.* They all would be. Still, he simply had not thought of her as more than a co-worker. Why?

Somehow, she simply wasn't his type. No instant attraction, no zip.

Or was that a habit he had picked up—rejecting nearly all women if he didn't get a buzz off them immediately? Carl avoided Lani's gaze, took a draw on his feed tube. Even on his Earthside holidays, he had always been careful to keep affairs sharply defined. Groundlings liked the pizzazz of space; there were plenty of groupies. It was easy to let them know he was interested in two weeks of sex and laughs and fun in the sun, period. Sometimes he'd been tempted to keep a woman's number, give her a ring next time he was down . . . but once back in orbit cool ambition ruled. He never called.

Opportunity favored the prepared mind, as the old cliché had it, but opportunity in space also favored the uncommitted soul. If a long mission came around, those with family ties found it hard to go. And the Psychological Review Board took that into account, lowered your rating. They claimed otherwise, but everybody knew the truth. All that went into his calculations. And sure enough, the big chance—Halley—had come around, vindicating his strategy.

Then too, Lani was an Ortho. Likes should marry likes.

Virginia, now, *she* was smart, sexy, *and* a Percell. Plenty of zip there. *Best to stick to your own kind.* Except for holidays Earthside, he had followed that policy ever since his teenage randiness wore off and he had time to actually think. There were enough Percell women in space to keep him occupied.

As much as he tried to take a middle ground in the Ortho-Percell conflict, his personal life was something else. And while it was smart for a Percell to maintain that everybody was the same, that didn't mean you could ignore human nature. He was sure that even after the stupidity of the Ortho governments Earthside had run its course, the human race would eventually have to split. The Orthos would always be edgy with Percells—that was natural. Better the two breeds kept their distance—by making space mostly a Percell domain. Cross-breeding wasn't going to solve anything, just worsen it.

"There's no reason we can't work together, be friends." He held out a gloved hand toward her.

She grasped it tightly. Through her bright blue skinsuit he could feel an intense, clutching desire in her. Her body gave away what her face had concealed. Gently, he released her hand.

—I . . . had hoped.—

"I, I can see. . . ."

—There will not be many of us awake on each watch.—

He frowned. "Yeah. We'll have to work out the rotation."

—Yes. It will require . . . public discussion.— She sniffed, made to brush her nose with her hand, and stopped when her glove touched her helmet. She had to use the drip catcher behind the glassine plate. —I . . .—

Carl felt miserable. To have her weeping over him, when all the time he'd never even *thought* of her that way. He hated things like this, where you discovered you had been a callous deadhead without even knowing it. As though other people were tuned into frequencies you weren't picking up.

Beneath this consternation there was also a small current of delighted pride. The old ways were still strong enough to make a man pleasantly surprised by an unexpected overture. He would never tell anyone, of course, but maybe, years from now, he might drop a hint to Virginia. . . .

Lani sniffed again. Her eyes closed and she sneezed loudly, the outgoing *choooh!* booming almost painfully in his ears.

She recovered, blinked, and gazed bleary-eyed around her glittering crystal palace, indifferent now to its beauty.

Carl realized ruefully that she had not been weeping over him at all. She had already put aside her failed overture and was concentrating on more immediate matters.

Lani had a cold.

# SAUL

Saul blew his nose and quickly put away the handkerchief.

The hectic weeks of Base Establishment had diminished into the long, hollow quiet of the First Watch. And as this damned cold of his lingered on and on, he found himself more and more avoiding Nicholas Malenkov and the big Russian's skeptical medical scrutiny. Saul knew it was only a matter of time until Malenkov said something about his perpetual sniffle.

He wasn't sure what Nick would do if it didn't get better soon, but Saul did *not* intend to be slotted. Not for a while, at least. There was simply too much to do.

He pinched the sinuses above his nose. The *momser* antihistamines had him in a perpetual state of half-dizziness these days, but that simply couldn't be helped.

Saul blinked at the pastel walls of the weightless lounge—designed to supplement the cramped recreational facilities of the centrifugal wheel. It was a barren, empty scene. Except for a few chairs and cabinets, the only finished area was here, near the autobar. It would be years before the lounge looked anything like the schematics called for in the Grand Design.

Flimsy readouts lay scattered over the chart table in front of him, except where a portable holo unit projected a cutaway view of the six-mile-long prolate spheroid that was Halley Core.

Only at the top of the display, near the north pole, was there a sparse, spaghetti tangle of tunnels where humans had made their inroads.

*Too much real estate to ever really know. And yet far too little to make a home.*

The man across the table from him coughed politely.

"I'm sorry, Joao," Saul said.

The tall Brazilian comet expert resumed what he had been saying before being interrupted by Saul's dizzy spell.

"It's these caverns, Saul." He inserted his hand into the computer-generated image and executed an intricate little finger flick. Although there was nothing more material in that space than air, the machine read his intent as if he were turning a page. Cutaway layers peeled back to show new tunnel traceries to the north and east, linking a number of oblong cavities.

"I believe I have figured out how the chambers got here in the first place," Quiverian announced.

Saul looked back and forth from the display to Quiverian's sallow, patrician features. His Roman nose enhanced the impression of a bird of prey. The image fit, the man was so unpredictable, excitable. Saul chose his words carefully.

"I thought that was already decided, Joao. The comet formed out of the primordial solar nebula, peppered with a lot of short-lived radioactives from a nearby supernova. Beta decay warmed parts of the interior, forming the cavities, while the outer shell—exposed to space— remained cool, a protective blanket around the molten regions."

Quiverian waved his hand impatiently. "Yes, yes, that old theory. Aluminum 26 and other short-lived elements must surely have created some molten channels, for a time."

"I'd started trying to develop a biogenesis model based on that idea. But now you say it's no good anymore?"

Quiverian edged forward eagerly. "Radioactives *can't* have provided sufficient heat for all the melting we've observed! And they don't explain the extent of fractionation we find, either!"

"Fractionation?"

"The degree to which elements and minerals were separated from each other by some dynamic process, forming these ore bodies we've found everywhere. Saul, the radioactives theory just couldn't explain that! You see? That is why I started digging around in the literature for another method, another way it might have happened."

Saul stood closer to the table. "Well, it sure sounds interesting, Joao. I was just telling Nick Malenkov that there didn't seem to be enough—"

"Bear with me a minute, Saul." Quiverian held up a hand as he shuffled through a pile of readouts. "There is something I want to show you. I have it here somewhere."

"Take your time, Joao." Saul shrugged. For now he was content to enjoy a momentarily clear head—the almond-flavored air was, for once, fresh in his nostrils. He watched the computer's slowly rotating depiction of the comet's nucleus.

Seismic studies had filled most of the three-dimensional map with a vague gray and white tracery, showing in blurry outlines the locations of many of the major faults and cavities. Still, essentially all but a small fraction of the rough globe remained mysterious—a realm to be explored over the long, quiet watches ahead. Less than five percent of the volume, centered on the north pole, was at all well known.

Piercing the north rotation axis was a narrow orange line marked SHAFT 1, which dropped a kilometer straight down to an ant colony of chambers labeled CENTRAL CONTROL COMPLEX—including this lounge and most of the science labs. That shaft continued inward another kilometer or so, terminating, at last, almost halfway to the center of Halley Core.

Along the way, Shaft 1 met a series of horizontal tunnels, starting with red-colored "A" near the surface, passing green "F" here, where they stood, and ending in yellow "N."

The pattern was a lot less neat elsewhere. Several passages opened into big caverns that the spacers had discovered the hard way. Three

huge chambers now held the fore sections of the slot tugs *Sekanina,*
*Whipple,* and *Delsemme,* and the majority of the sleeping colonists. Another, near the surface, now held the *Edmund Halley*'s nearly reassem-
bled gravity wheel.

The computer-generated graphics were good, showing even the
field of storage tents scattered among the hummocks up on the north
pole. A finely detailed model of a partly dismantled torch ship hung in
miniature near the tiny, glittering Shaft 1 airlock, tethered to three mooring towers.

Saul shifted forward and saw that two tiny dots moved about near
the *Edmund Halley*—infinitesimal human shapes. . . . Captain Cruz and
Spacer Tech Vidor were running inventory and writing up a task list for
the next dozen year-and-a-half-long watches. The computer showed
them at work, going over the ship in detail.

He imagined that if he climbed onto the table and peered up close,
he would be able to make out the name-chops on the two spacers' suit
tabards, and maybe watch them gesture to each other.

Saul was used to computer representations in his work. He routinely "dove" visually into the cellular lifeforms he was studying. Still,
he found this display marvelous. Anywhere within reach of the main
computer's scanners one could zoom in and see animated versions of the
dozen active crewmen . . . reduced to stereotypes by the machine's automatic privacy editor. Likewise, the private quarters were black cubes
strung out along Tunnels E, F, and G, impervious to the exquisite simulation.

Spacers were used to living in enclosed volumes. In fact, to them all
this room must seem wonderful. But to the civilians, like Saul, the colony looked a lot like an ant farm.

*A fine lot of troglodytes we've become. Regular kobolds.*

*And yet I can't see anything wrong with Miguel's arrangements.*
*Everything is moving along according to plan.*

*Knock on wood.* Saul rapped the side of his head lightly, and
smiled.

Even the predictable furor over his discovery had been less bother
than expected. The communications time lag from Earth had let him
stack media interviews together. The more hostile or sensationalist questions could just be "lost in transmission." Saul saw definite advantages
to making major discoveries far away from the madding crowd.

Now, if only he could figure out how it happened that primitive
prokaryotic organisms were found frozen under the surface of an ancient

ball of ice! Nobody had any idea how the tiny creatures had gotten there, let alone how they had lived.

"Found it!" Quiverian announced. He snatched up a flimsy sheet. "As I was saying, I was at a loss to explain all the signs of past melting we see here . . . until I came across a whole series of citations having to do with inductive heating during the sun's T Tauri phase!"

"I beg your pardon?" Saul balanced forward on his toes, leaning lightly against the table.

Quiverian's lips pursed. "Oh, they wouldn't have included much stellar physics in your second-hat training, would they? Well, let me see if I can explain. T Tauri is the name of a certain very new star in the constellation of the Bull; a whole class of objects was named after it. Scientists have been studying them over a century. They're a phase, really, in the development of a young star. Our sun must have passed through the stage, early in the creation of the solar system."

Quiverian laced his long fingers together and looked out into space, as if he was reciting from memory. "The most interesting feature of a T Tauri star is its truly *incredible* stellar winds—fluxes of hot protons and electrons, blown away from a star by sonic force and by electrical—"

"I know what the solar wind is, Joao," Saul said mildly.

The other man's eyes seemed to flash. "Good! But what you probably do *not* know is that during the sun's own T Tauri period the winds must have been many thousands of times greater than they *ever* get now. And this particle current carried a truly magnificent magnetic field."

Quiverian looked at him expectantly. But Saul could only shake his head. "I'm sorry, I don't get it."

The Brazilian shrugged in frustration. "Ignorant biologist! Can't you see? The early protoplanets and comets all passed through this great magnetism as they circled round and round the newborn sun. Like wires turning in a great generator! Eddy currents! Resistance!"

"Ah, *mazel!*" Saul clapped his hands together. "You would get inductive heating."

Quiverian sniffed. "So they did teach you something in Haifa, after all. Can you see now? Do you understand?"

Saul nodded. His mind was already racing ahead. "The newly formed comet's surface, exposed to space, would remain cold . . . an insulating blanket. Even if most of the interior were molten water, the heat wouldn't escape."

"Right! Of course it works only under certain conditions. You need a very large comet, like Halley, and lots of salts or free electrolytes, as we have found here."

Unconsciously, Saul lifted all his slight weight off the floor by stretching his hands against the table. His body was tense from too much lab work and too little exercise. Perhaps soon he would have to accept Mike Cruz's offer to teach him spaceball.

"How long does this T Tauri phase last?"

"A few million years. Not very long. But long enough to create these deep chambers we found! And with all that electricity running around, it's easy to see how so many compounds got separated into thin veins all over the core!"

Quiverian clearly had a right to be elated. The man had envied Saul his discovery and attention in the Earthside press, but now he had reported an achievement of his own. It would doubtless be a sensation, especially in the Brazilian papers.

"Congratulations, Joao," Saul said sincerely. "This is really tremendous. Can I have this copy of your reference list to look over?"

"Take it. Take it. I have already sent a preliminary report."

Ideas were fizzing like sparkles of gas in Saul's mind. "I think this will help me in my own studies, Joao."

"I'm glad. But you know, this is going to require a very complex computer simulation. I don't want to request Earth assistance until this thing is better developed.

"Can you help, Saul? You are good at that sort of thing."

Saul shrugged. "As a dilettante, I guess. But one of the greatest experts is on this very watch crew with us, Joao. Why not ask Virginia Herbert?"

Quiverian looked uncomfortable. "I do not think this Herbert woman would be very cooperative. Her type . . ." He shook his head, letting the implication hang.

Saul was pretty sure he understood what the man meant. He had heard it before.

*"Their kind has always been a problem."*
*"Their kind . . ."*

Quiverian shifted nervously. "These Percells are a closed, uncooperative lot, Saul. I don't think she would be willing to help a scientist from my country."

Saul could only shake his head. "I'll talk to her and let you know,

Joao. What do you say we meet here again for lunch, tomorrow. And we'll include Nicholas in the discussion."

He was grateful when Quiverian merely nodded moodily and sighed. "I shall be here."

As Saul left, the planetologist was staring at the slowly turning holographic glow, his sharp features bathed in colored shadows. It occurred to Saul, then, that Quiverian was not looking particularly well.

*The fellow really ought to get more sleep. It might improve his outlook on life.*

An hour later, Saul was at work in front of his own display, mumbling instructions into a subvocal mike and fumbling with the computer grips, struggling to keep up.

Ideas were coming faster than he could note them down, let alone integrate them into the new model. Every time he explored one aspect, a whole vista of unexpected ramifications would leap out at him.

It was the true creative process—a sort of divine, nervous transport—as painful as it was exalting.

But he could almost see it. There it was—flickering like a will-o'-the-wisp—a light glimpsed across a fog-swirled swamp. A theory. A hypothesis.

A way that a mystery might have come to Comet Halley.

Saul had sorted through terabytes of raw data the expedition had accumulated about the comet, tracing ingredients as they might have been stocked in the sun's early pantry. They were all there, but the right *kitchen* had been lacking.

Joao Quiverian's references seemed to offer the crucible Saul had been looking for.

*The T Tauri phase . . .* Saul mused. *In its infancy, the sun was an unruly child.* In those days, the star's breath had been charged and hot.

So there had been electricity—great. But how much, for how long?

There were hydrogen cyanide and carbon dioxide and water—as must have saturated the primitive atmosphere of Earth—so the basic amino acids would have formed quickly. But the next steps would be harder.

The three-dimensional network of interrelationships on his central display grew more and more unwieldy, a towering, tottering edifice built up from tacked-together *assumptions*.

"Ach! May your goats chew on cordite and then give you copious milk!"

He cursed the machine in Arabic, a more satisfying tongue for such purposes than English. His fingers felt like clumsy sausages, and the arcane math he had brought in from the astronomy papers danced just outside of reach. He couldn't quite integrate the equations into the over-all scheme he had in mind.

For one hour, two, three, he pushed away at it. But the damn thing just wouldn't gel.

Saul tried brute force, pulling in block after block of external mem-ory, more and still more parallel processors to iterate the problem. It was far from an elegant approach . . . more like looking for a house in the dark by sending a herd of elephants stampeding into the night, hoping to learn something from the sound of splintering wood.

*I'm doing this all wrong. I should go have a beer. Listen to some Bach. Tune the wall to show a Polynesian sunset. Let it sit.*

Saul drummed his fingers.

*Maybe I should ask for help.*

He sat there in the web-chair, weary not so much in the body as in the mind, in the heart.

This was the only joy left in his life, the quest for mysteries. And *still* he felt like a small boy—frustrated and vexed—whenever Nature seemed to want to wrestle with him, to make him wheedle and cajole her secrets out of her, instead of surrendering them easily, without a fight.

*How many of life's pleasures are painful in the actual process? Miriam, forgive me, but you always knew that I loved Life, Nature, just a little more than you and the children, didn't I?*

*And here I am, getting cranky because my oldest love won't put out again.*

Saul blinked and sat up. The sudden movement sent him hovering over the webbing, but he hardly noticed.

*What in the . . .*

Unbelievably, something was happening on the display right before his eyes. A ripple of change.

It started off in the upper right quadrant of the computation. All at once, elements had begun to grow *fuzzy* around the edges. Indistinct, random bits jostled one another. Then, impossibly, the Gordian knot of logic began unraveling!

At first he thought the entire mess was falling apart of its own iner-tia.

Then he changed his mind.

*Minnie, mother of pearl . . .*

Out of chaos, simplicity was taking shape. Out of ugliness—
beauty!

It was like watching a solution precipitate into a gorgeous, growing
crystal. Wonderful . . . yes. *Too* wonderful.

Something or somebody was intervening, he decided. And Saul
quickly realized something else: that this whoever . . . or whatever . . .
was clearly a lot smarter than he.

Equations cleaved, as if sliced by RNA nuclease. The pieces fell
apart, while he stared. They arrayed themselves in stacks, row by row,
piling neatly into a glowing pyramid of logic. And at the apex . . .

Saul breathed rapidly as he looked at the culminating formula. He
could feel his own pulse pound.

*"I'm sorry I interfered without asking permission, Saul. But you
were stomping all through the data system by the time I noticed. Sooner
or later you were bound to set off alarms."*

Saul found his voice.

"That's all right, Virginia. I . . . I'm grateful for the help."

There was a brief pause. Then a holo-unit display to his left came
alight and Virginia Herbert's face wavered and smoothed, a replica in
rich color that still hinted of salt breezes and tropical sun. Her long black
hair flowed over her shoulders, slightly puffed, as if it had been hurriedly brushed just moments ago.

*"I'm glad you're not angry with me for butting in."*

"Angry!" Saul laughed. "You *saved* one of us, either me or this
obdurate machine!"

Virginia smiled. *"Well, it's a relief to know I did the right thing.
Actually, that's pretty complicated stuff you're dealing with there, Saul.
I can't pretend to understand any of it. I'm just a glorified numbers
jockey."*

"I disagree." Saul shook his head firmly. "You are an artist."

Virginia's olive skin darkened perceptibly. Her "Thank you" was
barely audible. Saul shared a long smile with her.

Virginia's eyes darted. *"Um, if you'd like, you could come on down
here and we'll put JonVon to work on your problem. He's a stochastic
processor, you know. And I happen to believe that makes him a lot more
applicable to the kind of problem you've got there than these old parallel
precision machines.*

*"I'm sure we can whip up a simulation to make that one there look
like a stick-figure cartoon."*

Saul nodded. "Only if you let me bring a bottle, Virginia. I have a
feeling we're going to need it."

*"Done!"* she said gladly.

As Saul was getting up though, a stretched image of Virginia's arm reached out across his desk—like an india-rubber man—to tap with one finger at the glowing, throbbing line of gold lettering at the top of the tall pyramid of data.

*"What is that anyway, Saul? Is it something special?"*

He shrugged. "Well. I guess you could say so, Virginia. It's the chemical symbol for something called a purine base. A rather simple one, really, called adenine."

Virginia withdrew her ghostly, representative hand. *"Well, I hope it's important. But whether it is or not, I'll bet we'll be taking this a whole lot farther. I have a feeling for these things, you know."*

She smiled brilliantly.

*"See you down here in a few minutes, Saul. VKH out."* Her image vanished.

Saul stood still for a moment. "Yes, dear," he said at last to the presence she seemed to have left behind. "I do believe we are going to take it quite a bit farther."


# VIRGINIA


MOLECULAR STRANDS, LIKE MULTICOLORED STAIRCASES . . .
LIGHTNING FLASHING IN THE DARKNESS . . .


At the simulation's finest scale, the molecule was little more than a stylized ladder put together from standard pieces—bright, notched slivers of blue, green, and red—amino acids, phosphates, and simple sugars linked like ill-sorted parts of an intricate jigsaw puzzle.

The chain seemed to twist and writhe as it tumbled in a churning stream. A tracery of silvery lines stitched out electric currents, crackling unevenly through the salty fluid.

Shiny golden radicals smacked into the growing polymer. Most bounced off again in sudden flashes of light. Occasionally one knocked a fragment loose into the flow, diminishing the molecule, leaving a hanging, ragged corner. A little more often, the colliding chunk found a niche with the right shape, and stuck.

As the polymer grew, the scale of the scene enlarged, as if a camera were drawing back. A new strand joined the first, then another, twining together in a jumbled mass. The cluster fell toward a great ocher wall that loomed from below, a rusty plain pocked with jagged holes.

The edge of one of the black openings caught the molecular skein, one end draping into the gap. The cluster tipped for a few seconds, then toppled inside.

*"It's a clay . . . something like montmorillonite, I believe. Notice how the chain slips right into the open latticework. Only a few of the shapes being synthesized in the open stream will be able to enter this way.*

*"It's an early step in the long process of selection. Some theories say it happened this way on Earth, long ago. At last the molecules are sheltered from the tumbling give-and-take of the electrified stream. Only certain radicals can get at them in there . . . and the shape of the cavity aligns the molecules just so. The buildup—slow and chaotic beforehand—begins now in earnest.*

*"Funny it being a clay, though. I would have expected it to be something like iron oxide. But see how the peptides actually seem to catalyze the growth of new clay layers? Amazing. I'd forgotten about that!"*

Virginia let Saul ramble on, sharing his excitement but too busy to reply unless he asked a direct question. Right now it was a challenge just integrating all the diverse elements in his complicated program.

She was used to bright pictures and vivid simulations, anyway. No, what impressed her was the *intricacy* of this world of molecules and currents, of clashing atoms and chiming balance. It was a maelstrom of tiny tugs and pulls computed in an eleven-dimensional matrix space, and still the diversity of forms amazed her.

The screen showed only the most superficial part of it—the averaged sampling of JonVon's stochastic correlator. It was the *math*, down below, that really kept Virginia occupied. Only occasionally did she look up to see how the images were coming along.

Right now the simulation was following the developing molecules down into their new home. They nestled into crannies in the complex clay latticework, leaving a central passage through which fresh material entered from the outside. New pieces were added, and old ones discarded as dross to float away. The shape of the still-growing chain kept changing, now as a simple helix, elsewhere doubling back on itself, switching handedness left and right.

Saul commented again.

*"I'm cheating a bit, here, for the sake of speed. We've set up initial conditions and are letting huge numbers of simulated molecules 'evolve,'*

*leaving it to your wonderful machine to pick out the most successful line
out of billions . . . coaxing the most promising to do the best it can under
these conditions.*

*"We'll see if a nudge here and there can take this primitive thing
and give us . . ."*

Virginia found her job growing easier, now that JonVon's expert
system was picking up the basic rules of this game.

Or was it because Saul was getting better at his end?

They lay next to each other on a broad, web-hammock in her laboratory, each linked by cable to the intricate hardware/software unit. For
Virginia it was a familiar experience, wearing a delicate induction tap
and playing her fingers lightly like a pianist on the pattern keys. Saul, on
the other hand, was more awkward with his controls. The bulky cortex
helmet he wore lacked the compact deftness of her specially designed
link.

Yet, he was getting over his clumsiness quickly. And his excitement
was contagious. His subvocalized thoughts arrived directly along her
acoustic nerve.

*"This is wonderful, Virginia! Far, far more than a mere simulation
program, this construct of yours explores possibilities!"*

"JonVon's processor is bio-organic, Saul. A matrix of pseudo-
proteins in a filament mesh. Back home they dropped that approach
years ago, because its point-error rate is pretty high. In fact, you're
treated like some sort of nut if you even talk about it, today." She hoped
none of her bitterness carried over into her words.

*"Hmmm. More point errors, sure. But you can pack so many cir-
cuits into a tiny area that it doesn't matter, does it?"*

Virginia felt a thrill. *He understands.*

"That's right, Saul. A stochastic processor works with probabilities, not discrete yes-or-no answers."

*"It's like the way Kunie describes the operation of the human pre-
conscious! Have you read any of Kunie's work?"*

Virginia laughed. Aloud it was a soft chuckle. In their heads, the
sound of bells.

"Of course I have! I couldn't have gotten this far without that man's
ideas on the creative process. But I'm surprised *you've* heard of him,
Saul. Conceptual heuristics isn't anywhere near molecular biology on
the library shelves."

There was a pause as Saul's attention returned to the simulation. He
nudged a particularly large molecular cluster out of one of the gaping

clay tunnels before it could jam the flow of fresh material, a minor interference for the sake of this early trial.

*"I knew Kunie, Virginia. His family gave me a place to stay after
the Expulsion. . . ."*

The "walls" of the simulated latticework throbbed slightly, and
Virginia moved gently to stabilize the model against further interference
by Saul's emotions. Without letting on, she created another pathway for
his feelings—away from the model and into a small side nexus where
they might be buffered, studied . . . touched.

"Was that when you started working with Simon Percell?" she
asked. History had never been her specialty. And Virginia knew that
there had been more than one "Expulsion" from the land called Israel.

*"Good lord, no."* This time it was Saul's turn to laugh. The tone
resonated in the little buffer like low cello strings.

*"The Levites were still a small fanatic Jewish fringe in the Judean
hills, and their Salawite friends were nothing more than a bunch of
seething Syrian exiles, back when I worked with Simon in Birmingham."*

While JonVon kept the simulation going, Virginia was attempting
to trace the tendrils of Saul's pain, more vivid than anything she had ever
experienced in a human-to-human link before. But then Saul changed
the subject again.

*"We sure could have used tools like these, back when Simon and I
were working on the gamete-separation problem,"* he subvocalized. *"All
we had then were kilobit parallel processors, gigabyte memories, and
inferential sequencers that took days to analyze a single* chromosome.

*"But they were good times."*

Virginia felt moved by his intensity, even as she focused in on it,
enlarging the channel capacity and sensitivity of the link. Saul was easier
to probe than any subject she had had before. Except, maybe, for the
littlest children.

And for some reason it was not unpleasantly disorienting, this time.
To the contrary, it was pleasant, if a little frightening. The man was . . .
well, *strong.*

"Go on, Saul. The simulation's running well. I'd like to hear more
about those days. You started telling Carl and me about your early work
on cures for sickle cell and Lesch-Nyhan syndrome and lupus."

*"Cures!"* Saul laughed, and the cellos were joined by a bitter choir
of cymbals. *"Yeah, I did. Fortunately, most of our later efforts worked
better. Some of the early 'successes' were only partial."*

Virginia knew that. She had already gone into the expedition's records and expunged all trace of her own infirmity. Of course, it couldn't affect her duties in any way—in fact the authorities would likely *approve* of it. But she had erased the data anyway. It just wasn't anyone else's damn business.

Virginia smoothed down her own emotions and concentrated on solving the mystery of this oddly open channel to Saul's subsurface feelings. *I'm learning more today than I did in a year, back home,* she thought.

She felt JonVon's central presence pull up alongside, imitating her actions, learning by "watching" how she played the channels, adjusted resonances. Smoothly, at her command, her machine surrogate slipped in to take over. Soon she was able to pull back for a minute and check the biology simulation, their ostensible reason for being here.

It surged on, piling intricacy onto complexity. Now the scale had zoomed back again to enclose an entire field of lattice openings, each with its own fringe of huge, blue-white molecules waving out into the electric stream, like cilia around gaping mouths.

She tried to keep the conversation going. "But you weren't with Percell when . . ."

*"When he made his fatal error? Those poor monstrosities? No. Perhaps I should have been. I might have done more good than I did by going back to Haifa to join the struggle. By then it was too late, of course. The old Sabras and the kibbutzim had risen, and been crushed by the Levites and their 'peacekeeping' mercenaries. Miriam and the little ones . . ."*

The sudden wash of feelings was overpowering and direct. Virginia's eyes fluttered and teared as she *remembered* scenes of grisly horror . . . seemed almost to *see* burning settlements, forests in flame . . . *felt* the thalamic surge of anguish and guilt.

Furious, she commanded JonVon to stop creating these images. The machine had no business interfering like this!

**I am only enhancing, Virginia,** JonVon announced coolly over their private channel, dryly delivering news that stunned her even more than the glittering scene of a temple rising on an ancient hill. Virginia's mouth was suddenly dry. *But . . .*

**I am not interpolating or simulating any of this. Amplified, these are direct images from the subject.**

Her hands clenched and unclenched spasmodically, forcing the machine to automatically disable her fingertip controls. Her breath came in ragged, audible gasps as the truth struck hard.

*"He nalulu ehaeha!"*

Distantly, she felt the waldo gloves being pulled from her hands, her shoulders lifted in strong arms.

"Are you all right, Virginia?" Saul was speaking aloud. "I didn't mean to come on so strong. I thought you did this sort of thing all the time."

She blinked, looking up at his concerned face. "Y-you knew what I was up to?"

He laughed. "Who wouldn't, with you and your cybernetic famil-iar skulking around at the edges of my mind, poking and probing?"

He shook his head. "Honestly, Virginia, what you've done here is astonishing. It felt . . . direct! Thought-to-thought contact. It's been in so many stories and films, even after Margan supposedly proved it impos-sible, years ago, but . . ."

Virginia was still numb. "It is. It's *supposed* to be . . . impossible, I mean. I use JonVon to mediate, to guess and pattern, to simulate. But I never expected . . ."

Now Saul's expression was serious. "You mean that was your first time?"

Virginia had to smile. "Yes, my first. But don't worry, Saul. You were a perfect gentleman."

That did it. He rocked back and howled, and she joined in. They laughed together. The tension seemed to evaporate and for a long mo-ment neither of them seemed to take any notice of the fact that he was still holding her.

*This feels so good*, she thought at last.

"Hmmm?" he said, tapping his helmet. "I only got a little of that, but I'm pretty sure I agree with whatever it was."

She looked up at him. "Oh, Saul. I'd known you had a sad life. But it's different feeling it, almost *remembering* it myself."

Yet another image flickered at the edge of vision, a woman. She was no great beauty, certainly—mousy dark hair framing an ordinary face—but her smile was warm, and there was a brimming *glow*. Behind her were two smaller faces, a boy and a girl.

*Miriam? Your children?*

*Yes*. A pain softened by time. Love undiminished.

And in her own heart, another pain, still fierce. Love unanswer-able.

"You don't hate me . . . for what the gene treatments did to you?" Saul asked.

Virginia looked up quickly and met his eyes. She shook her head. "I did, long ago. You and Simon Percell. Then I met some of the other Percells . . . those for whom your lupus cure worked completely.

"I studied. I learned that without the treatments I would have been stillborn or horribly crippled . . . not merely—lacking. It was just the luck of the draw that I . . ."

"It's all right." Saul drew her near and she closed her eyes.

"We both still have our work now. Good work. And that does give us a piece of the future too, Virginia."

"Yes, our work . . . and maybe a little more." She felt warm. Virginia lifted her face to him. Saul had to push aside the wires of his helmet in order to kiss her.

*I've never done anything like this while linked, before.* She thought amid the tidal swell of feeling. *I wonder what JonVon will make of it.*

Above them, unheeded, the simulation had panned back again, taking in a wall of clay and a salty, electric-bright current.

Bright shapes had begun emerging from the rust-colored crevices. They flitted about in the hot stream—now coated and armored against the battering molecules—and set out into a multicolored world, consuming one another, growing, and making little replicas of themselves.

# CARL

At first he thought it was nothing important.

Carl wiped the green and brown gunk off the distillation pipes and moved on. The gas-gathering zone of Shaft 3 was a long dark tunnel, its phosphors giving everything a lime-green cast.

The plumbing looked okay—magnetic motors humming, pipes gurgling, a smell of rotten eggs from the sulfur compounds. Excess vapors were condensed here from the miles of tunnels now threading Halley Core. Bioinventory showed a surplus of useful fluids and was talking about storing it. The boiloff would probably lessen as the more-volatile ices were used up, and also there would be less heat-making activity during the long cruise out. Everything looked pretty damn good.

But there was brown sticky stuff in the filters. *Shit. It's everywhere.* Carl cleaned them carefully with a water jet and flushed his covered bucket into the outbound tube—one-way flash vaporization that dumped directly into free space.

This odd-looking mess wasn't supposed to be here. Prefilters should take out the big stuff and sift it for useful solids. These backup filters should catch impurities and crystallize them.

Maybe there was something special about this particular sticky stuff. He filled a sample bottle—the bio types nagged him incessantly for traces of anything odd—and kicked off toward sleepslot 1. *Malenkov should have a look at this.*

Cycling through the big lock into Central Complex, he realized that he missed Jeffers. The founding crew were all safely slotted now, making things a bit lonely for the First Watch. Captain Cruz had made him senior petty officer, which merely meant he roamed more than the others, checking—but the minor honor pleased him.

He liked working alone, anyway—gliding smoothly and surely through the locks and shafts with Bach or Mozart weaving in his ears. *Maybe I'm a natural hermit,* he thought. *I wonder if the crew-selection people could tell that from their psychoinventory tests.* He had hardly seen anyone these last few days.

When he entered the aft port of Life Sciences the first thing he heard was loud talking.

"He goes in *now*! I make no compromises," Nikolas Malenkov's gravelly voice cut through.

Carl rounded a corner to find the big Russian medico arguing with Saul Lintz in the corridor. Virginia Herbert watched with folded arms. She gave Carl a glance, but seemed sad and distracted.

"I want a sample to study," Saul persisted.

"I have taken samples." Malenkov put his hands on his hips and leaned forward menacingly. "Epidermis and fluids only."

"I'll need more than that to find out what—"

"No! Later, we revive him, maybe! When we know what killed him. If you take samples from internal organs, that will make it harder for us to bring him back later."

Carl frowned. "Hey, what's—"

Saul wiped his nose with a handkerchief, ignoring Carl, and said, "You can't cure him unless you *know* what killed him!"

"You have smears from throat, urine, blood samples—"

"That might not be enough. I—"

"*Hey!*" Carl cut in. "Will someone tell me what's going on?"

Malenkov noticed Carl for the first time. His expression suddenly changed from tight-lipped rage to sad-eyed dejection. "Captain Cruz."

Carl felt suddenly lightheaded, incredulous. "What? That's . . . But I saw him just two days ago!"

Neither of the two other men spoke—there was still steam in their argument. Virginia said quietly, "He had a fever yesterday and went to bed. When Vidor went to find him this morning he . . . would not waken. He died within an hour. Apparently there were no other symptoms."

"*Fever?* That's it?"

"It doesn't seem he ever woke up."

The shock of it was only now penetrating, filling Carl with a sensation of falling. Commander Cruz had been the center, the heart and brains of the entire expedition. Without him . . .

"What . . . what'll we do?"

Malenkov mistook Carl's question. "Sleep slot him—now. There is yet little or no neural damage."

Dazed, Carl said, "Well . . . sure . . . but I meant . . ."

Saul said, "I still feel we must have more data to study these cases—"

"We are not certain how long he ran a high temperature. Any more time, he risks brain damage." Malenkov waved a hand brusquely in front of Saul, erasing any objections. "Come."

They all went numbly to the hub of the sleep-slot complex. Carl was stunned. He tried to think, chewing his lip. The socio-savants had written extensively about how small, high-risk enterprises had to have a clearly superior, Olympian leader to avoid factionalism and weather hard times. A Drake, a Washington. Without that leader . . .

In the sealed prep room Samuelson and Peltier were running checks and planting diagnostics around a body that was already wrapped in a gray shroud of web circuitry. Miguel Cruz-Mendoza's face was calm, yet still projected a powerful sense of purpose. Wisps of fog laced the air as the workroom dropped in temperature. Malenkov spoke to the two laboring techs through a mike and the party watched the last procedures of interment.

"So you'd authorized slotting even before our little argument," Saul noted calmly.

"I wanted you should see my logic. While Matsudo is in slots, I am responsible for health of the whole expedition," Malenkov said stiffly.

"Indeed you are." Saul's voice carried only a dry hint of irony.

"I hope we can bring him back soon—very soon," Malenkov said. "Damnation! At the very beginning!"

Virginia said gamely, "We'll all pull together. Of course, we'll have to . . ."

"Pick a new commander," Saul finished for her. "That's obvious—Bethany Oakes. She's next in line."

Carl nodded reluctantly. Another Ortho. All the senior crew were. And Oakes wasn't even a spacer.

They watched in silence as Peltier and Samuelson rolled the commander's body into a sleep slot and opened the valves to feed fluids. The tube fitted snugly into a broad wall of similar nooks, gleaming steel certainty wreathed in gauzy fog. So much like death, yet it was the only hope of life to come. If they could figure out what had killed him. *If*.

Malenkov sighed. "We should have some ceremony. But there was no time."

Saul said, "And perhaps it's not such a good idea to assemble everyone in one place."

Still numb, Carl thought, *Miguel Cruz wouldn't want a stiff little ritual. Some of us'll get together and hoist a few for him later. The captain would understand that.*

And maybe that might dull the pain, when numbness turned to grief.

"Dispersal, yes." Malenkov nodded silently, frowning. Carl realized they were still talking about what had killed Cruz and whether it was communicable. "Osborn here can adjust job schedules until we thaw Oakes."

"I'm going back to the lab," Saul said. "I want a full dress review of the lab results."

"I think not," Malenkov said stiffly.

Carl saw that Saul was already half-lost in thought about paths of inquiry to follow, checks to make. Saul did not reply at once, but gazed off into space, toward the slot cap that had closed on Cruz. Then he turned slowly to Malenkov. "Ummm? What?"

"Is your turn, Saul."

*"What?"*

"This death makes me more firm." Malenkov bunched his lips together, whitening them, his jaw muscles set rigidly.

"We risk exposure to you even by this talking." Malenkov gestured brusquely. "Into a slot."

"That's ridiculous." Saul looked irked, as if Malenkov were pursuing a bad joke. "I can help. Hell, if some of my suspicions are true—"

"You are not so big and essential," Malenkov said stiffly. "Peltier, she knows the immunology well—"

"I insist—"

"I will not risk you dropping dead, my friend."

"Nicholas, I *don't* have whatever killed Miguel Cruz!"

"Look at you—eyes red, nose running." Malenkov gestured. "You have *something*. A microbe caught in your lab, could be."

Virginia stepped to Saul's side and felt his brow. "You're hot," she said.

Carl watched sourly as she put her hand on Saul's face with unself-conscious intimacy. *He looks damned sick to me. Malenkov may be right.*

Virginia asked quietly, "How long have you been this way?"

"Days, off and on," Saul said dismissively. "A cold, that's all it is. Some fever."

Malenkov said, "We cannot be sure."

"I think it's just a leftover from Matsudo's last damned bio challenge. Which *doesn't* mean I'm Typhoid Mary."

"The commander died in hours," Malenkov said curtly.

"Not from anything he caught in *my* lab. He hasn't even been near it."

"Could catch directly from you," Malenkov said.

"Exactly! Then why am I still alive? Use your head, Nikolai. You need me to help track down his killer!"

"It is to save your own foolish life!" Malenkov shook his fist at Saul, tensing his whole body.

"Saul, you must." Virginia urged, tightness skittering through her voice. "We can't let you risk yours—"

"No more!" Malenkov shouted. His bulk made the command imposing. The chamber was of hardened plastaform and cupped the sound into a resonant, rolling boom. "No more!"

*I knew he'd start browbeating if he ever got a chance,* Carl thought. *Let him get away with it now and we'll be taking orders from him forever. I've seen guys like this before.*

Part of it, though, was simple resentment over anyone giving orders when his captain was barely cold.

"You're not commander," Carl said mildly, suppressing his initial urge to raise his voice. "Life Support comes next in the crew chart, as I remember, and this falls under the category of a space emergency. I'm acting officer."

All three looked at him with surprise. *Scientists—they never look beyond their own fiefdoms.*

Malenkov hesitated, glanced at the others, then nodded. "True . . .
for now. Bethany Oakes, we can thaw her soon, however."

"Go ahead." Carl shrugged. *Then she can play these power games
with you and I'll drop out.*

Saul said judiciously, "That seems reasonable."

Carl could not help but smile sardonically. *You bet it is. I just saved
your ass from the slots.*

"I . . . agree," Virginia added, but Carl saw conflicting emotions
play across her face. They were so obvious to read. If Saul were slotted
she would lose him for a year or two. But if he *died* . . .

*Virginia and Saul Lintz?* Carl was stunned. He couldn't even think
about that, right now.

"We've got other problems," he stammered only briefly as he hurried on. "I came in to report some stuff clogging the filters in Shaft
Three. We'd better deal with *that,* and soon."

Malenkov said, "I still do not see why Saul—"

"Because we need every hand, that's why!" Saul erupted.

Malenkov's face compressed, his cheeks bulging, an adamant set to
his jaw. "I do not agree."

Carl said flatly, "Complain to Oakes."

Malenkov abruptly jerked open the hatch. "One thing I *have* authority to do! Saul should keep away from all of us. *I* will not be in the
same room with him any longer."

Saul began, "Come on, Nick, you—"

"I am still chief of medicine!" Malenkov said angrily. "I log you as
quarantined!"

"That's—"

"No contact! You work in your own lab, alone. Enforce this, Carl
Osborn, or I shall speak to Earth of this!" Malenkov pulled through
quickly and slammed the hatch after himself. The others looked at each
other.

"You *know* he's right," Virginia said angrily.

"Like hell I do. Thanks for stepping in like that," Saul said to Carl.
"I'd forgotten what the line of succession was. Organization charts
aren't my kind of thing."

Carl shrugged. "I just knew damned well that *nobody*'d set it up so
Malenkov came next."

Saul chuckled, and Carl smiled on the surface, though underneath
he was in turmoil. He wondered whether he had in fact done the smart
thing. He didn't know enough about medicine, of course. He had simply

followed his instincts. Years in space had taught him that that wasn't usually a good idea.

*What would the Commander think?* He still wasn't used to the idea yet. *I never wanted to be in charge.*

Virginia took Saul's arm, chiding him about being up and about when he should be in bed. Carl felt a sudden pang of jealousy.

"Hey, he's quarantined now, you know."

Virginia frowned at him, but Saul nodded. "Carl's right. I'll crawl home by myself."

*If I hadn't opened my mouth,* he thought, *Saul would be on his way out of our lives right now.*

Maybe it hadn't been so bright to speak up, after all.

On the other hand, Saul didn't look like he'd last that much longer, anyway. And if they slotted him when he was near death, the fellow wouldn't be coming back real soon, either.

He blinked as this thought surfaced. *What are my real motives here?*

It hurt even if he moved his eyes. . . .

Throbbing aches, a muggy dullness filling his head, a dry rasp in his throat. *I haven't been hung over like this since I was twenty. That wild wine-tasting in L.A. . . .*

He sat up in total blackness, feeling the rustle of crisp sheets, and it all came back.

The Hawaiian woman, Kewani Langsthan, had come up with a big bottle of fiery coconut brandy to help Carl, Jim Vidor, and Ustinov violate Malenkov's rule against gatherings, and drink to Captain Cruz's memory. *Whoever heard of Hawaiians holding an Irish wake?*

He realized dimly that he had deliberately, stolidly gone about getting drunk. And even as he did, he knew it couldn't blot out that awful despair, only daub it over.

Sometimes the only way to pay tribute to the dead was by a rousing, gut-busting ceremony of demented excess. About half the crew had reached the same conclusion.

But something else had happened. . . . He tried to remember, failed.

*Okay, fine. It was my off-duty time and I used it as I deemed appropriate, as the regs say. I just don't have much talent for big-time carousing. Now I pay the price.*

As if in reply, a lancing ache ran through his stuffy head. He reached out for the light and instead touched a soft thigh.

*Oh yes. All at once she had seemed maddeningly attractive, witty, sympathetic. . . .*

"Umm?" Lani murmured. "Carl?"

He tried to speak, had to clear his throat. He swallowed painfully and croaked, "Ah, yeah. G' morning."

She switched on a dim nightlight, throwing their shadows against the walls of her snug little room. "You . . . look awful."

He tried a grin. It felt like a crack had split his face. "Better than I feel."

Lani's broad, frowning face seemed none the worse for wear. "Can I get you something?"

"No, I'll just sweat it out."

"I have some B-complex and Soberall. They can dampen the effects."

"Well . . . okay, let's see what science can do." He knew the line sounded hollow, but he felt instinctively that he should keep things light. He could only dimly recall how he'd ended up here, what was said. *My subconscious has gotten me into trouble again,* he thought ruefully.

She flipped the covers aside and glided nude across the room, lithe and unembarrassed. Lani fished in a medical compartment and returned with five pills and a bag of water. He took his time swallowing, trying to figure out how to handle this.

He remembered being suddenly angry with Virginia—that's what had started it. He'd had some of the deadly mai-tais Langsthan had brewed up and then Saul Lintz came on a screen nearby, just tuning in to see what was going on. *Yeah, that must've done it. I'd been making sense until then, but ol' smug Saul looked skyward and gave us that indulgent look of his and I got damned mad. At him, at Virginia . . .*

"Better?" Lani asked quietly.

"Uh. Marginal." He lay back on the sheets, dimly aware that he was naked.

She hung in air over the bed, folded into lotus position, slowly descending. "You should get more sleep."

"Uh, I . . . What time is it?"

She smiled slightly, as if she guessed his intention. "It's nearly ten."

"Oh . . . I'm on watch soon."

"You have to return to the living first."

"I'll . . . be okay." Actually, he felt even worse. He couldn't think straight. He had never been in a situation where he honestly didn't know whether they had made love or not. *Damned unlikely. I've never been much good with a skinful in me.*

"You're wondering," Lani said, the faint smile playing on her lips.

"Ah . . . yeah." She was always one move ahead of him.

"Let's say your motives were pure."

"Huh?"

"We talked for a long time and you said you wanted to see my wallworld."

"Your . . ."

She uncurled and tapped a command plate on the bedpad. The room immediately leaped into being around them.

"Ow!"

"Oh, sorry. I'll tune down the light."

It was the crystal cavern. She had gone back there, carefully shot the many angles, captured the myriad facets. Brilliance refracted and glinted everywhere. Miraculously, she had managed to assemble views without any reflection of herself or her equipment, so the shining cavern was a vision no one could ever see in person. It was better than reality. Then she had arranged her room so that furniture and appliances occupied dark areas of the cavern, enhancing the effect.

"It's great. Everybody else uses Earth scenes."

She shrugged. "I can get that *National Geographic* tourist stuff anytime."

Even through his logy blur he was impressed. And slowly he remembered their conversation, how she had seemed witty, warm, bristling with ideas. He had never noticed that before, never given her a chance, really. . . .

"So I came to see it. . . ."

She nodded, eyebrows arched in amusement. "And passed out."

"Oh."

"I thought you might not appreciate having people see you being hauled unconscious through the tunnels, back to your bunk."

"I guess not."

She blinked, bit at her lip, and then said carefully, "I . . . liked the way we talked last night, Carl. We've never really had a chance to say very much to each other. Not since the first weeks."

"Yeah," he said uncomfortably. "Been busy."

She said firmly, "I know you won't let go of Virginia right away."

"Let go? I haven't got her."

"Let go of the hope, then."

He nodded sourly. "Right."

"Not immediately, I know that."

He looked at Lani as if seeing her for the first time. She *was* different than he had thought. Maybe . . .

*But Virginia . . .*

"There's no rush," she said, seeming to know exactly what he thought. *All my emotions must be written across my face,* he realized uneasily.

"I . . . Maybe you're right. I'm so damned confused."

She leaned forward and kissed him daintily on the lips. "Don't be. Just do the work and leave little things like love and life for later."

He had to smile. "You're making this a lot easier for me than I deserve."

"I want to."

"I . . ."

She put a silencing finger to his lips. "Shush. You don't have to be civil, not with a hangover like that."

He showered—she had installed her own equipment, even arranged a projection of the crystal cavern inside the stall—and dressed. She kissed him goodbye, and before he had fully registered their conversation he was making his way to the suit-up room, shaky but ready for duty.

He was already at work before the hangover cleared and he felt the sudden weight of depression descend again. Ever since leaving Earth, he had worked with single-minded determination, never questioning. But now he couldn't keep his mind off bigger issues, problems he could see coming in the days ahead. There was nobody he could trust to take care of that, not any longer.

Carl felt a yawning emptiness, a foreboding.

*Captain Cruz is gone. It just doesn't seem possible. What in the frozen hell are we going to do?*


# SAUL

---

It should not have been possible.

Saul stared at the patch of green and brown in the petri dish. It didn't take a lab regimen to know he was looking at something that just shouldn't exist.

Standing in a relaxed, low-G crouch, Spacer Tech Jim Vidor peered over Saul's shoulder. Strictly speaking, the man wasn't even supposed to be here. The decon mask over his mouth and nose were sops to the official quarantine Saul was under.

Saul took a fresh handkerchief from the sterilizer and wiped his nose. After two days, when it seemed his body was in no great hurry to flop over and die from this *tsuris* of a cold, the isolation order had lost some of its original urgency. To spacers, disease was an abstract threat, anyway. Far more real to them was the trouble they were having with gunk getting into everything from air circulators to mechs, threatening the machinery that kept them all alive.

Nevertheless, Saul motioned for Vidor to stand back—for the same reason he had kept Virginia away, in spite of her mutinous entreaties.

Nick Malenkov might be right, after all. Anything could happen, when Halley was able to come up with things like this on the dish before him.

"The stuff was growing in the main dehumidifier, way up where Shaft One intersects A Level, Dr. Lintz. I showed it to Dr. Malenkov when I got back down here to Complex, but he's busy full time in sick bay now that Peltier's keeled over. He said you were the grand keeper of native animals on this iceberg, anyway, so I brought it to you."

*No doubt Nick assumed you'd use a mech messenger,* Saul thought. Every few hours a mechanical knocked on his door, carrying a thermos of soup and a tiny note from Virginia. Maybe those little packets were the real reason his damned bug hadn't gotten any worse.

Working with his gloved hands in an isolation box, he used sterilized forceps to tease apart a clump of red and green threads, lifting a few onto a microscope slide. The unit whirred as probes crept forward into position. This thing that couldn't exist obviously *did* exist. It had to be examined.

Naturally, Malenkov would not be interested in looking at anything as *macroscopic* as this. As Shift-1 physician, Nick's chief concern was the strange and terrifying illness that had appeared out of nowhere, killed their leader, and now had another victim prostrate in sick bay.

The "thawing" of Bethany Oakes and half-a-dozen more replacements had been delayed by discovery of brown slime in the warming bins, which had to be cleaned laboriously by hand. The resumed unslotting was now keeping the Russian medic too occupied to bother with anything so large—and therefore "harmless"—as threads blowing in a faraway tunnel.

Saul, exiled to his own lab, had little to do except analyze the tissue samples taken from poor Miguel Cruz and the new patient . . . and deal with queries from a worried Earth Control. Mostly, he had a broad-spectrum incubation program under way, from which he couldn't expect results for at least another thirty-six hours.

"Have th' tests told you anything at all about what killed th' captain, Doc?"

Saul shrugged. "I've found signs of infection, all right, and foreign protein factors, but little more definite than that." He had come to realize, at last, that he would probably never track down the pathogen, or pathogens, without a lot more data. He needed to know more in a *basic* sense about Halley lifeforms.

If Nick wouldn't let him near the patients, then he should be looking elsewhere! What Saul wanted most was to get out into the halls and see for himself . . . to collect samples, build a data base, and find out what had killed his friend. But this damned quarantine . . .

He turned his head and lifted a tissue before sneezing. His ears rang and his vision swam for a moment.

Well, at least Jim Vidor didn't seem to feel in much danger, visiting a presumed Typhoid Marty. He had backed away at the sudden eruption, but as soon as Saul's composure returned, the spacer stepped back up to look over his shoulder.

"Got any idea what it is, Dr. Lintz? This new stuff was clustered all around the inlet pipes on B Level, and I'm afraid it may turn into as big a problem as that green gunk, if it plugs up the dehumidifier."

*Nick and I are scared by the tiny things . . . microscopic lifeforms that kill from within. But spacers have other concerns. They worry about machines that get clogged, about valves that refuse to close or open, about air and heat and the sucking closeness of hard vacuum.*

"I don't know, Jim. But I think . . ."

The screen whirled and a tiny cluster of threads leaped into magnified view. Saul cleared his throat and mumbled a quick chain of keyword commands. Abruptly, a sharp beam of light lanced forth, evaporating a tiny, reddish segment into a brilliant burst of flame. One of the side displays rippled with spectra.

"Nope. I guess it can't be a mutated form of something we brought with us, after all. It has to be native." Saul rubbed his jaw as he read an isomer-distribution profile. "Nothing born of Mother Earth ever used a sugar complex like *that*." He wondered if it even had a name in the archives of chemistry.

Vidor nodded, as if he had expected it all along. Innocence, sometimes, leaps to correct conclusions when knowledge makes one resist
with all one's might.

Saul, too, had suspected, on seeing the stuff for the first time. For
it looked like nothing Earthly he had ever seen. But he had found it hard
to really believe until now. Microorganisms were one thing, he could
rationalize that, particularly after seeing JonVon's wonderful simulation
of how cometary evolution could occur. Primitive prokaryotic microbes,
yes. But how, in God's perplexing universe, did there ever get to be
something so complex . . . so very much like a *lichen,* deep under a
primordial ball of ice?

*I never really believed Carl Osborn's story of macroorganisms out
in the halls,* he confessed to himself. *I guess I just pushed it out of my
mind, denigrating whatever he had to report, answering hostility with
hostility. Instead I kept busy doing routine stuff, studying microbes, ignoring the evidence that something far larger was going on here.*

Of course, Carl had not exactly cooperated, either. They had not
seen each other since that fateful morning in the sleep slots. And Carl
had never sent the samples Saul had asked for. Small wonder he had been
so glad when Jim Vidor took the initiative.

"For want of a better word, Jim, I'd have to call this thing a *lichenoid* . . . something like an Earthly lichen. That means it's an association
creature, a combination of something autotrophic—or photosynthe-
sizing—like algae, with some complex heterotroph like a fungus. I'll
admit it's got me stumped, though. Nothing this complicated ought to—"

"Do you know of any way to kill it?" Vidor blurted. His eyes
darted quickly to the screen, where the fibers slowly moved under intense magnification.

Suddenly Saul understood.

*Vidor is an emissary. Carl couldn't get any useful help out of Ma-
lenkov. Of course he wouldn't come right out and approach me. Not as
angry as he is over Virginia.*

Another wave of dizziness struck and Saul gripped the edge of the
table, fighting to hide the symptoms.

*Maybe Nicholas is right. Maybe this isn't just another flu bug. Per-
haps I'm already a goner. If so, isn't Carl right too? What have I to offer
Virginia, other than, maybe, a chance to get infected if I ever do get out
of quarantine?*

*What right have I to stand in between Carl and her, if I'm doomed
anyway?*

Oddly, the idea that he might really be dying made Saul's heart race. He had supposed himself free of any fear of death for at least ten years. But now the mere idea made his skin tense and his mouth go dry.

*Incredible. Did you do this for me, Virginia? Did you give me back the ability to feel fear? Fear of losing you?*

It was a wonder. Saul became aware again of Jim Vidor, eyes blinking down at him from above his mask, and smiled.

"Tell Carl I'll make a deal with him. He gets me loose of this *fershlugginner* prison, so I can go out and see what's happening in person. In return, I'll do what I can to help him keep gunk out of his pipes. Even if all I can do is swing a sponge with the rest of you."

Vidor paused for a moment, then nodded. "I'll tell 'im, Dr. Lintz. And thanks. Thanks a lot."

The spacer spun about and whistled a quick code, so the door was open by the time he sailed through into the hallway. Saul watched the hatch close. Then he looked back up at the tangled bird's nest of alien threads on the screen.

A part of him wondered if it was morally legitimate to go looking for ways to fight the indigenous lifeforms that were causing the spacers such grief. After all, Earthmen were the invaders here. They had arrived from a faraway world as much different from this one as Heaven supposedly was from Hell. Nobody had invited the humans. They had just come—as they always did.

*As we have always meddled, eh, Simon?*

Saul shrugged. The little moralist voice was easy to suppress, as was the fear that he was dying. He would fight, and he would live. Because for the first time in a decade he had someone to fight and live *for*.

*That's right,* he thought ironically. *Blame it on Virginia, you buck-passer.*

He stopped to wipe his nose, then dropped the handkerchief into the sterilizer. Saul popped another cold pill into his mouth.

Smiling grimly, he reached forward and turned up the magnification.

"Okay, buster. You've got me curious. I want to find out all about you. If we're going to have to fight, I want to know just what makes you tick."

He put the Tokyo String Quartet on the vid wall, recorded by cameras and pickups only feet away from the famous chamber group. They played Bartok for him as he twisted dials, spoke into a recorder, smiled grimly, and occasionally sneezed.

# VIRGINIA

*See the mechs dance, see the mechs play,* Virginia thought moodily, halfway through a reprogramming. *God, I wish they'd go away.*

It had been hours on hours now and the jobs were getting harder. She lay stretched out, physically comfortable but vexed and irritated by the unending demands. She tried out a new subroutine on a mech filling her center screen. It turned, approached a phosphor panel. *Careful, careful,* she thought—but she did not interfere. A mistake of a mere centimeter would send the mech's arm poking through the phosphor paint, breaking the conductivity path in that thin film, dimming the panel. The virtue of phosphors lay in the ease of setup—just slap on a coat of the stuff, attach low-voltage leads at the corners, and you had a cheap source of cold light. The disadvantages were that they had little mechanical strength and tended to develop spotty dim patches where the current flowed unevenly. A mech could bang one up with a casual brush.

Which this one proceeded to do, as she watched. It tried to spot the growing green gunk and wipe it away with a suction sponge. Partway across the panel, though, the arm swiveled in its socket and dug into the phosphor with a crisp crunch. The radiance flickered, dimmed.

*Damn.* Virginia backed the mech away and froze it. Then she plunged back into the subroutine she had just written, trying to find the bug that made the mech arm screw up at that crucial step.

—Virginia! I need five more in Shaft Four, pronto!— Carl's voice broke in.

She grimaced. "Can't have them! All full up." She kept moving logic units around in a 3D array, not wanting to let the structure of the subprogram slip away. Just a touch here, a minor adjustment there, and—

—Hey, I need them *now!*—

"Shove off, Carl. I'm busy."

—And I'm not? Come one, the gunk is eating us alive out here.—

"We're overextended already."

—I've got to have them. Now!—

It was hopeless. She punched in a last alteration and triggered the editing sequence. On a separate channel she sent, "JonVon, take a look at this. What's the problem? I'm too dumb to see it."

PERMISSION TO INTERROGATE MECH AND ADJUST ONBOARD
SOFTWARE?

That was a little risky; JonVon was great at analysis, but had not had much experience working directly with mechs. *What the hell, this is a crisis.* "Sure."

—Virginia? Don't duck out on me.—

"I'm here. I feel like a short-order cook, trying to switch these mechs around. Between you and Lani and Jim, there's no time to reprogram these surface mechs for tunnel work."

Carl's voice muted slightly. —Well, sorry, but I'm facing a bad situation here. This stuff is spreading fast—must be more moisture in the air here. We may have to clean them out in vac. That's tougher.—

"I know, I know." Carl always patiently explained why he needed help, as if she simply didn't understand.

She switched to another channel, surveyed the situation near Lock 3, and issued a quick burst of override orders directly through her neural tap to stop an overheating valve from melting a hole in the vac-wall. Then back to Carl: "Look, I can't do it right now."

—How come?— Was that a petulant, irritated tone? Well, the hell with him.

"Because I'm up to my ass in alligators!" she shouted, and broke the connection.

It felt good.

# CARL

It began with a high, thin whistling.

Carl was working at a pipe fitting—cursing the green gunk that made it slippery—when he heard the sound, at first just a distant, reedy whine. He was far out along Shaft 3, near the surface lock, and assumed that the single, persistent note came from somebody working further in, toward Central.

He was alone because they were so low on manpower. Carl had been working with one of Virginia's reprogrammed mechs, but avoided that if possible. It got in the way of the job when the machine spoke with her distinctive lilt.

The first awakenings were due to "thaw out" next Tuesday, and he hoped that would help with the chores. The gunk was slimy, foul, and persistent; he hated it.

*And those damned threads that get caught in the air vents. Maybe Jim Vidor's right, I should let Saul out of quarantine, have him study this stuff up close.*

If he had been with a partner he might have been less meditative, and heard it sooner. The sound kept on while he tightened up the joint with his lug wrench, the *rrrrrttttt rrrrrttttt rrrrrttttt* sending vibrations up into his shoulders.

Carl lifted his head. He felt a breeze.

There was always circulation of air in space, driven by booster fans if temperature differences didn't give enough convection. But not this far from Central, not a steady feather-light brush past his ears.

He stopped, listened. The same steady note. It came from below, downshaft, toward Central.

Then his ears popped.

He reeled in his tools and pushed off, all in one smooth uncoiling motion. A burst from his jets and he plunged inward. Phosphors dotted the shaft with pools of yellow-green light every hundred meters; automatically he used them to judge his speed, to keep from picking up momentum he wouldn't be able to brake. Smears of green gunk covered some of the phosphors, growing on the wan energy they put out.

He passed tunnels that ran horizontal, 3B, 3C, and 3D, but the sound wasn't coming from them. Coming toward 3E, he slowed because the whistling was getting louder and a steady suction was trying to draw him downward. Carl had always hated high-pitched noise and this was now shrill, grating. He was searching for a split seam in the insulation but wasn't at all ready for what he found.

*Worms!* He blinked, stunned.

Purple snake-like things oozing, wriggling. Moist, slick, waving slowly, ringing 3E's entrance. It was like a living mouth calling with a cutting siren wail, the wind moaning and tugging and sucking him toward the beckoning purple cilia that eagerly flexed and yearned and stretched out toward him—

He fumbled at his jets and pulsed them hard, backward. Wind swirled by him, sending his tool lines streaming away, tearing the wool cap from his head, ruffling his hair. He twisted and caught a handhold in the shaft wall. The noise was deafening now and he knew he was getting rattled by it.

*What the hell—!*

He ripped open his emergency pocket and fished out a plastisheet helmet. It took a long moment to tuck it into the O-ring seal in his skinsuit. *I haven't practiced this drill in a long time.*

It caught. He pulled the FLOOD bottle tab. The bubble expanded with a reassuring *whoosh* of air. That provided some sound insulation, but not much. Not enough.

"It's at Shaft Three, Tunnel E," he sent over the emergency channel. "Three E, Three E, Three E. Bad. Whole area around the collar is ruptured."

A faint voice called in his bonephone,—. . . can patch with spray foam? Got some on its way.—

"I doubt it. Something . . . something's broken through. This sure isn't just a rip."

Carl bit his lip. He didn't know how to describe it. The team would take only a few minutes to get here, but the shaft was losing torrents of air.

*The purple . . . things . . . must've broken through to a crevice leading to the surface.*

He launched himself across the shaft. The wind blew him several meters before he hit the far side and managed to hook a temporary clip into the insulation. He hung on and watched the nearest of the purple worms twist and pulsate, rivulets of ocher sweat running down from the pointed tip. The wind blew the drops away, sucking them back into the gaping hole that ringed the base of the worm.

The horrible thing bloated, contracted, bloated again—each time prying the insulation wider, admitting more of it into the shaft. The nearest was at least a meter long and visibly growing, convulsing in a slow agony of swell and clench, swell and clench. Its maw glittered with what looked like crystals of native iron.

*They're after the green gunk,* he realized as the worms pressed against the layers of mosslike growth within their reach. They seemed to absorb it directly. *They're grazing on the stuff! And sucking threads out of the air.*

Around the aluminum and steel collar of 3E's entrance Carl counted thirteen of them. He played out some line and the howling gale sucked him down, toward one of the eyeless, slime-sweating things.

Carl clenched his teeth. He was breathing bottled air now but he'd swear he could *smell* it—cloying, thick, humid, like ripe, moldering leaves.

He unhooked his laser cutter, thumbed it to max, and fired at one.

The beam drove a thin red line straight through it . . . with no significant effect.

He made the next bolt last longer and sliced the thing off a few centimeters above the base. A spray of purple-red whipped away into the wind. The top wobbled and fell aside, then tumbled slowly away.

More fluid seeped from the wound and then it began to film over. As Carl watched the thing began growing a thickening crust. The new matter had a rich, glossy purple skin like an eggplant. Then it began to thrust outward, sideways, outward again—onward, into the shaft, the wound only a momentary interruption.

Carl felt the hair rise in prickly fear along the back of his neck.

—. . . it like now? Repeat, can't pick you up, want to know . . .—

The rest was lost. Carl could see no one in the shaft. Where were they?

He pulled his patch gun from its holster on his left calf. It was intended for small work, but he couldn't think of anything else to do.

To get closer he played out another meter of line, then hastily drew some back in as the burgeoning thing waved his way. Could it sense him? Without eyes or any visible organs? Maybe his body heat. He wasn't going to take any chances.

The patch gun spat a wad of yellow gum at the hole. It splattered over the opening, spreading quickly as the long chain molecules grasped for the maximum surface area to bond. The suction bowed it inward but the yellow patch held.

For almost a minute. Then the worm butted against the cloying yellow film, wrenched, flexed—and shook it free. The wind tore at the loose edge. It flapped futilely like a ragged flag.

"We'll need the big stuff," Carl sent. "Bring all we got."

—. . . can't hear . . . any other measures . . . take to be sure . . .—

"Yeah. Seal all locks. *Everywhere.*"

—. . . don't under . . . we're sending all . . .—

"If we run out of sealant, the locks are our only backup."

*And if that fails,* he thought, *we'll have to live in suits.*

Ten minutes later, that didn't seem so unlikely.

Only Lani and Samuelson and Conti were available to help right away; crew was stretched thinly everywhere. Lani was a spacer, quick and smart, but the other two had been pressed into jobs they didn't know.

They worked as fast as possible. Chopping the tendrils was simple, but more pushed in before the sealant could harden. Carl and Samuelson discovered that to make any progress at all, they had to get close into the tip in the insulation and clear out the whole area, cutting all the way back to the ice.

—Got to slice it clean away,— Samuelson said. The large man licked his lips nervously. —Damnedest stuff I ever saw.—

"Watch out there with that torch, you're close to the ice." Carl had to hold Samuelson on a rope to keep the man from being sucked directly against the hole. The team had rigged a set of linchpin stays and lines to keep the howling wind from plucking them off the shaft walls. Now the shrill, hollow shriek slowly dulled as the air in Shaft 3 finally ran out.

Carl shouted. "Don't get too close!"

Too late. Samuelson's big industrial laser had finished off the purple stuff, all right—and then hit a vein of carbon-dioxide ice, vaporizing it instantly. A gout of steam shot out of the hole and blew Samuelson away, spinning.

"Lani! Slap that sealant in *now*," Carl sent. He released the line, letting Samuelson get clear. It was going to be messy around there in just a second.

Lani maneuvered at the end of a tether, holding the snaking blowline in both hands. —Here goes.—

Sticky yellow sealant spattered over the cleaned holes. Carl and Conti played fan lasers on it at the lowest setting, to flash-dry it.

Lani worked her way around the collar of 3E, shooting thick coats of yellow over the rents. Here and there it buckled from pressure, but she quickly spewed more on to reinforce the barrier.

—Not supposed to use it this way,— Conti sent. —Too thick. We'll run out.—

Samuelson returned, velcro-climbing the walls to rejoin them. —Anything thinner, she'll crack right through.—

—There'll be none left.—

"Cut the crap," Carl said sharply. If you let a crew bitch they lost concentration and didn't give their best to the job.

Lani called, —I'm done.— The stream petered out.

The sudden silence was startling. Carl cast off from the shaft wall, able to hover now that the sucking draft had stopped. There was hardly any air pressure left. "Maybe that'll hold it."

Samuelson sent, —What the hell *was* that?—

—Something that grows in the ice,— Conti said.

—Come on, in *ice*?— Samuelson asked sarcastically.

—No other way possible,— Conti said flatly. —Perhaps they get through cracks? Through softer snow veins? This is not any terrestrial form!—

—But so *big,*— Lani said. —What Saul found were mostly micro-organisms, correct?—

—Yeah,— Conti added. —And the green gunk and the threads, they don't chase you around, last I heard.—

Samuelson laughed. —These 'uns are bigger all right.—

"And strong. It breaks through insulation," Carl said.

They hung in the near-vacuum, staring at one another. Samuelson kicked off the wall and gestured upward, where splashes of phosphors dotted away into a long V with perspective. —Could happen anywhere in th' shaft.—

Carl shook his head. "It came through close to the collar, nowhere else. What's special about this spot?"

Conti said, —Something about the collar, where it fits to ice?—

"We'll have to check every collar, every intersection."

Samuelson said, —Damn right. We better collect all the bits of it that got blown into this shaft, too.—

"Good idea," Carl sent. "Let's get to work."

They spread out through the shaft and nearby tunnels. Carl snagged several drifting purple glops and stored them in a plastic carry bag. Blobs of jelly floated free or had stuck to walls. It was sticky and left a smear on whatever it touched. He kept a running commentary to Central, describing the lifeform to Malenkov. Saul Lintz came on, peppering him with questions. He had no idea how to answer. Saul demanded samples immediately.

"We'll all have to get decontaminated before returning to any pressurized zones, I'm sure of that," Carl said.

—Well, do the best you can. I'll get some sample bottles to you.—

"I'll make do. Don't let anybody into this section."

—You think it's that dangerous?—

"Damn right."

He broke off and kept searching. His team spread around, checking intersections for signs of buckling. Something was nagging at him but he had no time to stop and think. The purple chunks had drifted far and wide and he had only a few people to retrieve them all.

At the tunnel leading horizontally to Central, Samuelson found a purple tip just sticking through the plastaform. He called Conti and the two of them took a sample.

They were careless.

When Carl got there a few minutes later, both of them were slapping patches on themselves and yelping with startled pain. Through their faceplates each looked surprised, white-faced, eyes big and jerking around.

"What happened?"

—I snagged this piece and it got away from me,— Samuelson said.
—Conti grabbed it and it . . . *ate* through his glove.—

There was a big, awkward patch on Conti's right hand. "I suppose you brushed the piece with your arm?" Carl asked.

—Yeah, and the damned thing stung me.—

Conti's face was twisted into a self-involved grimace of agony.
—Gettin' . . . worse.—

"Samuelson, take him. The two of you go to the emergency entrance lock. I'll call Malenkov and let him know you're coming."

—Wh . . . what you think it is . . . doing?— Conti asked.

*Eating,* Carl thought, but kept it to himself. "Get to the doctors." He gave them both a push inward. "Hurry!"

In the next hour Malenkov sent him reports on their condition. The purple thing had eaten through fiber covering their suits, probably reacting to it as potential food. —Maybe it just likes long chain molecules,— Malenkov had suggested. Once inside, it burned the skin. Some probably had gotten into the bloodstream. Conti and Samuelson reported a spreading, dull ache. They were sedated and under observation.

Carl warned Lani and kept searching. Nearly an hour later he suddenly had an idea.

"Saul! Lintz! You there?"

The cross-link clicked and hummed, and then, —Yes.—

"This purple stuff is light, moves easy. Most of what we cut away got sucked into the holes."

Carl visualized the alternating layers of inert material and vacuum that made the wall insulation. Beyond the insulation was a full two centimeters of helium, intended to isolate the wall from ice. It also provided a route for boiloff to swarm upward to the surface and escape. "Where's this shaft's venting go?"

—Shaft Three vac line funnels everything from sleep-slot one to the surface. That's not my department, though. You'd better ask Vidor.—

"No, listen. We always think of boiloff escaping upward, right? But the wind we had here, it was strong."

—Yes. We lost a lot of air.—

"Point is, that air gusher was big enough to blow some back inward."

—Maybe. It'll leak out pretty fast, though, even . . . Oh, I see. You're worried about . . .—

"Right. The purple stuff. It's been carried by the air back toward Central."

—There are storage vaults along there, and . . .—

"Right." Carl hesitated, then decided. "Saul! I'm overriding Malenkov during this crisis. As of now, you're out of quarantine. Shanghai Quiverian and anybody you can find. Get down to Three J. You bio guys better think fast. I bet these things've got into sleep slot one."

# SAUL

Saul blinked wearily through a double-antihistamine haze as he finished wiping the last green traces from the edges of the filter unit. *Reduced from high science to scut work,* he thought grumpily. *Mama took in washing to send her little boy to college—to do this?*

Of course his real "mama" had done no such thing. She had been a colonel in the Israeli army, a hero of the '09 liberation of Baghdad, and probably would have approved of her intellectual son's being forced to use a bucket and mop, from time to time.

Still, the ironic fantasy amused Saul, so he nursed it. He gritted his teeth and pounded the filter back into place. Thirty years of education, and a half-billion-mile trip into space—all to be a janitor. It confirmed his long-standing belief that there was, indeed, such a thing as progress.

At least the present crisis appeared to have taken him off the pariah list. Every hand was needed to fight the Halleyform infestations, and few begrudged him an occasional sniffle.

*Done, at last.*

Saul sealed his sponge inside the bucket and stripped off his gloves. He looked over the rows of coffinlike sleep slots, foggy from internal chill and condensation, each showing a dim, hibernating form within. For two days he had been down here in the chilled chamber, trying to keep the infestations out of the slots.

Beyond the rows of sleepers, a workbench lay strewn with bits of glass and electronics torn from a half-dozen gutted instrument panels. A tall form stooped over the clutter.

"You about finished with those lamps, Joao?" Saul called. "I promised them to Carl soon."

The sallow-faced Brazilian shook his head and muttered sourly, "I have only unpacked and mounted four bulbs since you last asked, Saul. Give me time!"

Quiverian obviously did not like being dragooned into doing "stoop labor" out here in sleep slot 1, where it was cold and dangerous. Saul had been forced to go down in person to Central and drag the man away from a long, rambling, time-lag conversation with an Earthside planetologist colleague. Until then, Joao had behaved as if the total mobilization order had nothing to do with him.

First job had been to go over every inch of the sleep-slot chamber, cataloging infestations. Then had come long, grueling hours of scraping, wiping, disinfecting. The air-circulation inlets had fouled with the threadlike lichenoids, nearly choking off a whole row of slots. Except for one brief sleep period, the two men had been at it nonstop for almost forty hours.

*Thank a merciful heaven Virginia's mechs report few problems in the other two sleep slots!*

At last, when Quiverian had seemed on the verge of rebellion, Saul had put him to work assembling the hydrogen lamps, an easier job than stoop-and-swab labor.

"If you're in such a damn hurry," Quiverian groused, "why don't you wake up lazybones over there. Put him to work doing something more useful than snoring and warming the whole cave with his electric blanket!"

Saul glanced at the recumbent form of Spacer Tech Garner, lying on the fibersheath floor in a dark corner. Garner had been on duty for four days straight. The man was just catching a few hours' shuteye before going back out to join the battles once again. In comparison, Joao's work here had been a holiday.

"Leave him alone, Joao. I'll take the first four lamps and test them. You just keep working on the others."

He paused, then added, "Only please, Joao, be careful, will you? Try not to break any more of those bulbs. It's a long trek back to the supply store."

Quiverian shrugged. "First you say to hurry, then to be careful. Make up your mind."

Saul realized the man would wear him into the ground if he remained here. "Just do the best you can." He picked up a set of the spindly beacon lamps—meant to flash navigation/location reference to astronauts working on the moon or asteroids. He had an idea they might be useful in another function, here.

*We'll see if they're any good against a form of life that lives in space.*

He set forth in a low glide toward the entrance to Tunnel J, an amber-colored exit from the great chamber containing sleep slot 1.

Right now the place was eerie with the lights dimmed low. The vaulted recesses seemed deeper, more mysterious, like naves in an ancient tomb. Fibercloth rounded the edges, but the vast cave was still an irregular hole deep under the ice. One didn't dwell on how many tons hung overhead, in the kilometer or more to the surface.

At the center of the chamber floor, casting shadows in the light of a few active glow panels, the fore end of the slot tug *Whipple* lay at the center of five aisles of casket-shaped containers—the individual resting places of more than a hundred hibernating men and women.

*If we lose this battle, will any of these people ever see light again? Will they breathe, and laugh, and love?*

Saul wondered, *Does any of our desperation penetrate, and disturb their slow dreams?*

It was dark as a sepulcher in here. It was also getting damn cold.

The lights were dimmed to save energy. The fusion pile had been damped two weeks ago, when all but fourteen humans had been cooled down, and everybody expected a long, quiet, boring watch ahead. Now there wasn't the manpower to supervise a fully stoked reactor. Every hand was needed in the passages, in the utility corridors, or in sick bay.

Anyway, light was one of the things that attracted the lichenoids and the purple things. That and heat, and air, and food . . .

*I guess it's no accident we like the same things. The biggest difference is that the Halleyforms only experience spring briefly, every seventy-five years or so, when the heatwaves come migrating down from the sun-warmed surface. They're built to act, and act fast, to take advantage of the sudden season.*

Saul was still mystified by the abundance of types—by the complexity of the forms that fed on the green, algaelike growths. They violated the tenets of modern biology by existing at all.

But he was practical enough to stop muttering "Impossible!" to himself after a while. Later, he could try to discover an answer. Right now, he had to find ways to stop them.

He was getting better at low-G maneuvering. Still, his feet got in each other's way on alighting near the open Tunnel J hatch.

Fortunately, there were only a few entrances to sleep slot 1. Tunnel J was the critical one. Only a few hundred yards down that way, and up one level, Carl Osborn and his tired crew were wearily scouring away the green Halleyform variants the spacers had taken to calling "gunk" . . . trying to rid a critical passage of the food supply grazed on by the horrible purple worms.

So far, liberal doses of certain antiseptics and synthetic herbicides seemed to be doing the trick . . . for now, at least. *But we can't rely on that forever.*

Carefully he laid down three of the lamps and eased the fourth into position just past the open hatchway, in the tunnel proper. He had to hunt for the right electrical socket, and found it at last, partly hidden under a filmy cobweb of multicolored threads. These had to be brushed aside with his boot before he could plug the unit in and set the timer.

"Hello, testing." He tapped the little headset microphone that extended from under his wool cap.

"Lintz speech-routing to Spacer Osborn's headset, please connect for conversation." He knew there were more economical ways to ask the main computer to link him to Carl—he had seen the spacers chirp routing instructions in less time than it took to do a good hiccup—but he had forgotten the correct protocols. This way, at least, the machines were sure to understand.

A short pop, then a hissing carrier wave.

—Lintz, Osborn. What's up, Saul?—

The reply in his left ear was spare, to say the least. But spacers were like that. Terseness didn't necessarily mean anything.

"Carl, Joao Quiverian and I have finished checking out sleep slot one. Destroyed twenty-three infestations. Can't be sure we didn't overlook a few minor ones, but the slots don't appear to be in immediate danger anymore."

Saul quashed the tickling sensation of a threatening sneeze. He spoke quickly.

"I took an hour and went up to the surface to rummage through the storage tents, to see if there was anything we might use. There were a couple of dozen halogen-hydrogen space-signal lamps that gave me an idea. I figure we can place some at critical passage junctions and set them to bathe an area, at intervals, with intense ultraviolet. Who knows? It might slow the beasts down a bit."

There was a pause before Carl answered again.

—Sounds reasonable. But we don't want to blind or burn anybody.—

Saul nodded. "I thought of that. Brought down goggles and sun salve for the hall gangs. Also, I tore apart an unused mech-controller board and pulled out some type-five malfunction alarms . . . you know, the ones that go *brrr-ap! brrr-ap!*"

The carrier wave came on again, suddenly. It sounded like coughing until he realized Carl was laughing at his rendition. He grinned.

"Anyway, an alarm will go off a minute before each lamp is triggered. Both will stay on for five minutes on the hour."

—Good enough. Where'll you set 'em up?—

"At the entrances to each sleep slot, just outside Central, and along Shaft One. I'm not sure if we have enough power or bulbs to do more, so—"

Carl interrupted, —Fine, Saul. But I want to try them on something else, first. I'll send Vidor and Ustinov down to pick up the goggles and half-a-dozen lamps.—

"What's up?"

There was another brief pause. Then Carl confided.

—We're about to mount an assault on the purples that have surrounded the power plant. Maybe your idea will help there.—

"Uh, I sure hope so."

—Yeah. Anyway, give Garner a few more minutes, then wake him. Tell him he's to come back with Vidor. We're going to need every hand on this one. Osborn out.—

The carrier wave clicked off. Saul stood very still for a moment, shaking his head.

*The power plant. I had no idea.*

No wonder Virginia had been so terse the last time he had called. He'd felt like a silly teenager, wondering if she still loved him, because she had blown him a hurried kiss and hustled him off the line.

She probably had her hands full right now, preparing mechs to help Carl. If any of a dozen conduits leading into or out of the pile were clogged by organic matter, it could trip an automatic shutdown. That, in turn, could mean the end for all of them.

He ought to give the lamps a brief test before sending a set to Carl. No sense in burdening the man with a clutter of useless equipment if the things wouldn't do more than give the Halleyforms a suntan. Saul slipped on a set of goggles and bent to turn on the timer.

The sudden *brrr-ap!* of the tiny alarm made him jump, even though he was ready for it. Then came a faint *pop* as the lamp suddenly filled the amber tunnel with sharp, actinic light. Even under the goggles, Saul blinked and had to turn away.

When he next looked, he realized that something funny was going on. All at once every surface appeared to be coated in a shimmering *haze*. The walls themselves seemed to ripple and crawl, like the fur on a caterpillar's back. At first he thought it was an optical illusion—an effect of the weird coloration and glare. Then he realized.

*There's Halley Life* everywhere! *It's impregnated into the fiber-cloth, and now it's fleeing from the lamplight.*

The fuzzy ripples swept back in waves. Nearby, Saul saw the air begin to fill with a fog of fine dust—killed organisms, he supposed—floating free of the walls and settling with glacial slowness toward the floor. Trying not to inhale any of it, he wafted bits into a sample bag and sealed the container tight.

Then, as abruptly as it had erupted in brilliance, the lamp shut down. The noisy alarm quit without an echo and suddenly all was dimness and quiet. Saul pulled off the goggles, blinking as he waited for the spots to fade.

His bonephone crackled to life.

—Lintz, Vidor. Saw your glare all the way down at Shaft Three, Doc. Is it safe to come in now? Carl wants Garner and those lamps right away . . . like yesterday.—

"Uh, yeah." He shook his head. "Lintz to Spacer Vidor. We have lamps and goggles and fresh coffee for you guys. Come on in, boys."

He turned and skip-launched himself back into the irregular, vaulted chamber. Through the frosted sides of the slots, the sleepers were still silhouettes. Status lights on each casket made the center of the dim hall glitter like some phosphorescent Christmas tree, or a giant, glimmering starfish at the bottom of the ocean.

*Ninety packages, waiting to be opened. Someday. If we make it.*

The several-times-delayed unslotting of emergency replacements was reaching a critical stage in sick bay, where Nick Malenkov was all alone, now. One med tech had died of a purple bite, and Peltier, the other, had succumbed to some raging infection yesterday. At this rate it was a good question whether the "unthawing" crew would find anyone alive to greet them when they awakened.

*No. We will succeed. We must.*

He passed the bench where Joao Quiverian still muttered to himself, piecing together lamps and bulbs with snaillike deliberation. Later, Saul knew, he would have to personally check all the lamps himself.

He made sure the coffee maker was full, then gathered up his own spacesuit.

*They'll be needing all the help they can get, even if Malenkov has declared me an invalid. I may not be able to fight as long and as hard as these youngsters, but even a middle-aged alter kocker like me can hold up a lamp and squeeze a spray bottle in a fight like this.*

Funny thing about that. Although he was weary—and in a perpetual haze from the drugs that kept his sinuses clear—in some ways Saul had never felt better. His digestion, for instance—there were no faint twinges anymore, and his knee joints no longer grated and vibrated as he moved.

*Weightlessness and calcium deconditioning,* he decided . . . *or maybe it's just that somebody loves me again. Never, never underestimate the effects of morale.*

He almost stopped to call Virginia then. But of course he would get his chance to talk to her when he joined the others at the power plant. She would be there, at least in surrogate, controlling up to a dozen mechs, doing the work of ten men.

Perhaps he would have a chance to wink at one of her video pickups, and make her smile.

He had just stepped into his suit—and was reaching for his tabard decorated with a DNA helix—when voices over by the entrance told of the arriving spacers.

Vidor and Ustinov shot through the opening in graceful tandem. Tired or not, pride wouldn't let them skim walk or pull along the wall cables. The two men twisted in midair and landed in crouched unison not more than two meters in front of Saul.

"Where's Ted?" Joseph Ustinov asked tersely. The bearded Russo-Canadian took quick note of the direction Saul indicated, and headed out past the stacked packing crates toward the dim corner where Spacer Garner's electric blanket was a radiating ball of warmth.

"Got that java, Doc?" Vidor asked Saul, grinning. The young Alabaman seemed to have thrived in the adversity of the last week. Days of combat in the halls had brought him out of the depression of having been the one to find Captain Cruz slumped over his sleep-webbing, almost dead.

"Sure, Jim." Saul handed him a bulb of hot, black coffee, and began filling a thermos for Carl and the others. "There are fresh sandwiches over in that bag. I'll help you fellows tote the lamps and goggles, and show Carl how—"

A shrill, horrified scream seem to curdle the air.

Hot coffee spilled out in globby spray as Saul whirled. Across the dimly lit chamber, Spacer Ustinov tumbled in midair, still rising toward the ceiling and sobbing as he shook a clublike object in one hand.

Someone or something had startled him into leaping skyward with all his might. Whatever it was had scared him half out of his wits, for the man was gibbering, transfixed on the thing he held.

As Saul and Vidor stared, Ustinov cried out again and threw it away. The object arced through the chilled air, curving over gently in Halley's faint gravity, and struck a packing crate barely meters from Joao Quiverian's workbench.

The Brazilian scientist jerked back, first in astonishment and then in revulsion when he saw what had bounced within close reach. A delicate bulb shattered into powder in his left hand.

There, dripping ocher onto the lime-colored fibercloth floor, lay a dismembered human arm. Impossibly, the grisly limb seemed to be still twitching.

*Things,* Saul realized, sickly, were crawling out of the hunk of flesh and bone. Purple things.

He grabbed the wide-eyed Vidor by the collar and pushed him toward the stacked equipment. "Get goggles and a lamp!" he told the spacer quickly. "They're our only weapons here. Joao! Rig an extension to that outlet! Quickly!"

This time the Brazilian didn't argue. Vidor fumbled with the cords binding the lamps while Saul squeezed a spray of scalding coffee at a purple that was about to duck out of sight behind a sleep slot. A whistle escaped the thing as it retreated back into the open.

"Dammit, Doc!" Vidor cursed. "I gotta teach you how to tie proper knots!"

Saul started to answer when he glanced over his shoulder. "Oh damn," he moaned. "I'll be right back."

"Where are you goin'?" Vidor cried out.

By then, though, the die was cast. Saul had crouched and leaped off into open space.

Vidor was really the one more qualified for this sort of thing. But right then he was tangled up in lamps and cords. *Saul* had been the one to see Ustinov begin to fall again, and realize that the man was still sobbing and unaware of where he was headed. Even Halley's gravity wouldn't allow any explanations or delay.

Ustinov's suit was a lot more sophisticated than Saul's. But the incoherent spacer didn't seem about to use his jets, or anything else, to keep from falling back toward the tattered ruins of Spacer Tech Garner's electric blanket, now awrithe with waving purple forms.

Everything was happening in slow motion, or so it seemed to Saul, who spoke quickly into his communicator.

"Lintz routed to Osborn and Herbert. Mayday! Purples in sleep-slot one! Garner's dead. Mayday!"

The two floating men drew toward each other, one rising, the other descending microscopically faster with each passing moment. Saul turned away after one glance down at what awaited the falling spacer. It was more than his stomach could bear.

*Oh God, please let me have done this right.*

But no. Saul realized that his trajectory was too low! He would pass under Ustinov. It looked as if there was nothing in this world to prevent the man from dropping back into the spreading, pulpy mass.

Suddenly, he was as near as he was going to get. "Ustinov, wake up!" he shouted. "Stretch out!"

The man might have understood, or maybe it was just a spasm. But a booted foot kicked forth and struck Saul's outstretched hand stingingly. He fumbled for a grip and the momentum exchange sent him rocking over. The cavern whirled as he held on for two seconds, three, and then was kicked free by Ustinov's next jerk.

*Was that enough? Did I divert his course? Or am I maybe on my way to meet a crowd of purples up close myself?*

The floor came up toward him. Everything might *seem* to happen in slow motion; but he had to land with energy equivalent to his takeoff, and he had taken off in a hurry. His right shoulder struck hard, knocking the wind out of his lungs in a burst of pain.

He rolled over onto his hands and knees. It took a moment to blink away the dizzy whirling, and another to catch his breath. Then he saw Ustinov, lying only two meters away, moaning, shaking his head, and apparently unaware of the small, crawling things that wriggled toward his warmth from only a few feet away.

Saul gasped for breath and put everything he had into scrambling toward the man, racing to get there first. He lunged, grabbed the folds of Ustinov's insulsuit, and fought for traction to drag him backward.

"Don't move any farther, Dr. Lintz!" It was Vidor calling out to him. "There are two more behind you! The electric blanket must've shorted out. The ones not eating Garner are fanning out across the floor now!"

Saul had never before felt this way toward any living things—even the fanatics in the mob that had burned down Technion. Right now, though, he wished looks really could kill. He stared at the horrible things closing in on him from all sides, and knew what loathing was.

He gathered the quivering Ustinov into his arms. *What is wrong with the man? I thought spacers were built of stronger stuff than this.*

*My God. I'll bet he's been bitten!*

Ustinov wasn't heavy, of course, not in Halley's gravity. But he *massed* nearly the same as he had on Earth, and that made the Russo-Canadian's inertia and bulk awkward. Still dizzy and disoriented, Saul knew he wasn't ready to jump out of here holding this unwieldy burden.

It was one thing or the other, though. Jump or throw. He crouched.

"I'm tossing him to you! Get ready!"

"No! Wait! I've almost got a lamp—"

"No time!" Saul insisted. He uncoiled, heaving with all his might. The helpless man flew out of his arms, sailing over the writhing mass that had erupted through the fibercloth floor in search of heat.

It was a good throw, but recoil sent him drifting backward. He craned to look. Clearly, he was going to land between two of the pulpy, hungry heterotrophs.

Strangely, part of him was less concerned than curious. It was his first chance to look at one of the higher Halleyforms up close and not already pickled for dissection. The nearest one tracked him waving a pulpy maw rimmed with red, glittering needles of primordial nickel iron. There was no *face,* per se. But he could sense the thing's regard.

*Probably track by infrared,* he thought.

They were odd creatures indeed. Though perhaps no less odd than those worms that live down in deep, undersea vents, back on Earth. They, too, dwelled in total darkness, under immense hydrostatic pressures, living off sulfide-transforming bacteria. *Lord, thy handiwork never ceases to amaze me.*

Marvelous, yes. And mysterious. But ugly was ugly, and death was death.

He fumbled at his waist for something to throw, to change his trajectory, but the belt loops were empty. All he accomplished was to set himself turning awkwardly, still drifting toward the creatures.

No doubt he could squash any number of them in his bare hands, but he had no wish to tangle with them if he could help it, not after Samuelson and Conti had suffered such agony from their poisoned wounds.

Saul writhed around, catlike, somehow bringing his feet to the fore. His left boot caught and the right stabbed out at an awkward angle to compensate, striking a waving, grit-lined orifice. There was a sick, squishy impact as he skidded and began to tip over again.

"Jump, Saul!"

It was his chance. But as he bent his knees, pain lanced up his left ankle and that leg gave way. He swerved to avoid falling into a crowd of open-mawed worms, and in so doing tripped.

The slow-motion illusion helped as he landed on his fingertips and somehow *walked* across the floor on his hands—hopping from arm to arm to avoid the damned things. There was no other way. If he stopped to turn over or gather his strength, they would get him.

At last, there looked like an open space ahead, where he might flex and really push off. . . .

"Saul!" someone shouted. "Shut your eyes!"

He heard a loud, grating noise.

*Oh great! Just when I need to see where I'm going!*

His eyes squeezed closed at the very last instant. The last thing he saw was a dirty, segmented mass of pulpy mauve tissue turning toward his heat, bringing forth a round glittering of sharp, primordial stones.

Then the world disappeared in brightness. Saul cried out and his arms convulsed as he pushed away from the floor, drifting off in the direction of who knew what. He wrapped his arms over his eyes and rolled up into a ball, hoping his spacesuit would protect him when he next landed among the ravenous creatures.

The ratcheting sound groaned louder in counterpoint as another lamp joined the first from a new angle. The brilliance could be felt as heat on his skin. Saul couldn't open his eyes enough even to seek shelter from the beams, designed to be visible across thousands of kilometers of open space, against the diamond-bright stars.

He hit the ground again and rolled to a stop against something hard. Saul tried to keep still, not to move, and imagined himself an icicle.

—Saul? This is Virginia. Can you be more specific? What's the matter? All of a sudden my remote pickups in sleep slot one have gone out.—

Another voice broke in, —Lintz, Osborn. On our way in. Four with sprayers and torches. E.T.A. two hundred seconds.—

Saul realized then that it must have been no more than a couple of minutes since he had reported the purple breakout. Time had telescoped. The cavalry was coming, but would he last long enough for help to do any good?

Over to one side he heard Spacer Vidor mutter surprised oaths, then shout into his own mike.

"Carl, Jim. Intense UV sends them into retreat! They *dissolve* if they can't get out of the light fast enough!"

Saul lay curled in a ball, but his breathing came easier. If only . . .

There was a loud *pop,* and the level of hurting brilliance penetrating his tightly closed lids suddenly cut in half. There was cursing, then Vidor spoke again.

"One of the bulbs just blew, but I don't think it matters anymore. They're all dead or fled. Hang on, Saul. I'll bring you a set of goggles."

In a moment Saul felt a hand on his shoulder, and a shadow blotted out the remaining sunlike brilliance. Gratefully, eyes still closed, he lifted his head and helped Vidor fit the covering over his upper face.

"Congratulations, Saul. Damn fine weapon."

He blinked through tears and blue entopic spots to see the young spacer offer his hand. He reached up and accepted help getting to his feet.

"Uh, thanks." But he was remembering how few bulbs there were in inventory. Three were gone already. *We're going to have to come up with better tricks than this. We can't work in goggles all the time, for one thing. . . .*

The two men picked their way in low hops past shriveled purple husks over to a charred hole in the yellow floor covering, where the remains of Spacer Garner had tumbled—along with the ill-chosen electric blanket—into a narrow crevice. It was a flaw in the cavern that no one had thought anything of when the chamber was selected and covered over.

"They *don't* dig through solid ice!" Vidor sighed. "We thought they might—that they could strike from anywhere at all. What a relief."

Saul had only been staring, appalled, at the jumble of human remains scattered down a steep crack in the ice. Young Vidor was made of tough stuff.

"They move through low-density veins, then?"

Vidor nodded. "We'll have to look for more of those and melt 'em shut. I know just how to do it."

*Virginia's shown me pix of some of his sculptures,* Saul remembered. Jim Vidor was a whiz with ice. If anyone could figure out how to seal the chambers, he would.

There came the sound of voices from the Tunnel J entrance. The spacer turned. "I'd better go take the guys some goggles, or shut that lamp off."

Saul followed. Nothing more could be done for poor Garner, anyway. "Don't forget the salve," he called. "You and I are going to get fierce sunburns, as it is."

In spite of the pain in his ankle and the tremor of a fading adrenaline rush, he felt *good.* An atavistic part of him seemed thrilled at having passed through the last few minutes and survived. *Action* had its points. There were some things one could not get in a lab.

With his goggles on, Joao Quiverian looked like some great nocturnal creature. "You had better look at Ustinov," he told Saul. "He's in pretty bad shape."

Saul nodded. "I'll go get my bag."

"If he's got the same toxins in him that got Conti . . ."

"There are things I can try. But I've got to act fast. Help me, Joao."

*Even if I can't save him, maybe this time we'll be able to slow the chemical reaction down enough to slot him. Perhaps someday we'll have an antidote.*

The sole remaining lamp burned on, accompanied by the incessant ratchet of the alarm.

Under the glare, Saul picked up his black bag and took up again, after so many years, the practice of medicine.

## VIRGINIA

She scrolled up the lines written yesterday and tried to view them dispassionately. This was her break, and writing poetry seemed a better way to spend it, a quicker mental exit from the grinding relentless mech labor, than slurping up coffee in the lounge. Particularly since there'd probably be nobody else there; anyone not working was surely floating in exhausted sleep.

Crew were supposed to log most of their sack time in the wheel, where centrifugal pseudogravity could mimic the subtle flows that avoided zero-G imbalances. But you got more real rest in Halley's weak field. The survivors found isolated cubbyholes free of the green gunk and caught what sleep they could on the spot.

The struggle was less panic-driven now, but still critical. They had managed to drive the infestations away from the slots and power stations. By fusing the ice behind the most critical spots, they had denied the things an easy route back.

She should rest, sleep . . . but sleep wouldn't come.

*The hell with the outside, with grim reality.* She plunged into her poetry.

Nipples, navel
your pubic thrust

makes a kind of face
I trust—
and trust and thrust
and thrust again.
Have all
my thick-thighed welcome, friend.

"Um," she reflected to herself. "Artistic, no. Therapy, maybe."
CERTAINLY IT REVEALS THE GENERAL TENOR OF YOUR THOUGHTS.

Blue-green letters floated in the holo zone above her.

"JonVon, this is private! I should've disconnected."

SORRY. I DO NOT KNOW HOW TO TELL THIS.

"Common sense should—right, that's not a characteristic I've worked on, have I?"

SOME OF MY SIMULATED PERSONALITIES KNOW RULES, BUT I HAVE NO BASIC UNDERSTANDING OF "COMMON SENSE." PERHAPS IT IS NOT USEFUL IN DAILY WORK?

"No, there just hasn't been time . . . never mind."

MATTERS SEXUAL REQUIRE COMMON SENSE?

"When you're dealing with humans, yes. Actually, it would be better if you remained silent. Nobody thinks machines have anything to say about sex."

THERE ARE PSYCHOANALYSIS PROGRAMS I CAN CALL UP, EXPERT SYSTEMS WHICH HAVE A DISTINGUISHED HISTORY OF DIAGNOSING—

"*No,* JonVon! Just let me get on with my poetry."

MAY I WATCH?

"I can hardly keep you from reading my doggerel, can I? It's in General Manuscripts."

I CAN CONCEAL RESULTS IN MY OWN BANKS.

"Good idea, actually. I don't want anybody blundering into this file."

She stared at the screen. JonVon's intrusion had made her self-conscious. She had never been so overtly sexual in her writings before, and she felt her passion was an intensely private thing, for Saul only. In Hawaii, men had regarded her as somewhat prudish.

*So you've always been a little shy about it . . . so what? You have to overcome that!*

She frowned at the poem. Age-old custom dictated that love poems should be written in flowing ink on thick, luxuriant, creamy paper . . .

not glowing letters in open space. Well, the hell with that. *Let's see . . .
my thighs aren't thick, actually . . . is that part worth saving for the
alliteration? . . . skip that and try something else. . . .*

> bodies red and rangy
> your face all engraved anxiety
> above me: fevered, aye!—life-enhancing
> mad protracted
> two-backed dancing.
> Quick!
> cut my breasts with your
> iron beard
> make your point
> I've never feared
> I'll bend back
> no disgrace
> to take it from you face to face
> sweaty, unhygienic
> slick wet thrust
> quarantined
> if you must
> I'm of that race
> wallowing swallowing
> in the dust
> piston-engine snowballed love
> oh professor
> possessor.
>
> Teach me to live in the present tense
> with no past perfect
> Orbits aren't the only things
> to make a tangential rendezvous
> with brave design
> Gasping, knowing that
> He's *mine*!
> leathery skin welcome fact
> my ice is melting
> each livid drop
> *Don't stop!*
> sticky reign of fire and honey
> grind me grin me find me sin me

She stopped, her heart thumping.

SYNTACTICAL STRUCTURE—

"Shut up!"

Virginia unbuckled from her couch, threw aside the link coupling, and launched herself for the doorway.

STORE COMMAND?

"Shove it, for all I care!"

She moved quickly through the corridors, the long glides between kicks seeming to last forever. It would take only a few minutes to reach Saul's lab—impossibly short, considering how unreachable he had seemed to be, how much she had missed him.

Just before the turn down Shaft 1, which would take her to him, she ran right into Carl Osborn and Jim Vidor, coming down the hall without their helmets on. Both their suits were scratched and blotted with chemical stains. Vidor's face was puffy, unshaven, and his eyes seemed to drift far away. They were towing a body in a shroud.

"Who . . ."

"Quiverian," Carl said. "He's gotten too sick. We can't wait any longer, or he'll die."

"Hi ho, hi ho," Vidor said with thin humor, "it's to the slots we go."

Virginia clung to a handhold. "We . . . we'll have to unslot someone."

"Right," Carl said worriedly. "We've got six almost thawed. Want to decide who's next?"

"No, I . . ." She knew she should help, but . . . "I'm going to see Saul."

"He's still off limits except for real necessity," Carl said stiffly. He stopped his slow kick-glide rhythm and let the body come to a halt. Vidor compensated awkwardly on his own side, looking tired.

"You guys see him. He works beside you all!"

"Sure, but we aren't intimate with him. You and I both know what you'll do—"

"Mind your own damn business, Carl!" She felt her face flush.

Carl turned away, obviously trying to keep in control. "Malenkov said Saul's to be on at least semiquarantine—"

"I don't think that means anything anymore, now that Malenkov's dying. Saul is our doctor now."

"I think it's a bad idea to risk—"

"Carl, I'll take my chances."

"Stay away from the rest of us, then," Vidor said sternly. "Lintz is an okay guy, but I don't let him come too close. You touch him, same applies to you."

Virginia was startled. She liked Vidor, but the man's face was a stiff mask now, hostile and wary. He tugged at the comatose Quiverian's tow-line and started it moving again. But his usual deft sureness was gone and he seemed to be having trouble keeping the forces acting through a single axis. He looked as clumsy as a groundhog.

"Don't worry, I will," Virginia said angrily. "Maybe I'll just quarantine myself, too!"

She kicked off and sped away, not bothering to look back. *Hell, Vidor looks worse than Saul.* Then she put her irritation behind her as best she could.

When she entered the lab, Saul looked up in surprise. In the enameled lab glow his haggard, gray face lit with joy. She knew she had made the right decision.

"You really shouldn't risk . . ." he said without much conviction. She bore down on him.

*The hell with poetry,* she thought. *I'll take the real thing.*

# CARL

Jim Vidor wasn't being much help.

He coughed into his hands, leaning against the wall of the sleep-slot prep room. Vidor was pale, with the same pasty mottling and strange stiff sheen that Quiverian had developed less than two days ago.

Carl finished fitting the nutrient webbing around Quiverian's body and attached the sensor tabs. Everything looked right, but he went over the whole chemline and circuit layout again. You couldn't be too careful. One bad connection and they died on you. The monitor computer should pick up errors, but the moment you started relying on the backup systems, well, that was the beginning of the end as far as he was concerned.

As the crisis went on and on, Carl increasingly found himself being meticulous, his way of compensating for fatigue.

"Blood pH stabilized. Metabolic Q-10 on track. Might as well file him," Carl said.

Vidor nodded, eyes runny, and shuffled forward to help. Together they maneuvered the body into the slot, sealed it, and attached the external hoses. The banks of filled containers in the prep room formed a sphere around them, so they worked under a frosty dome. Cottony clouds drifted lazily in the air currents over their heads. These slots had flown out on the *Sekanina* and had tricky hose connectors. *Somehow nothing ever gets completely standardized on a mission,* Carl thought moodily. *Then you spend years tinkering and retrofitting.*

"No ceremony this time?" Carl said.

"Don't feel like it," Vidor agreed.

They were all too worn down to keep up the niceties. "Go on, get some rest," Carl said kindly. Not that he really thought it would do much good.

He logged Quiverian into the over-all monitoring programs while Vidor left, moving as though his joints were sore. *Same as Quiverian,* Carl thought. *But neither of them got that brown rash that grew all over Samuelson. Different symptoms—or different diseases?*

Not that it mattered all that damn much, now. At this rate they'd all be gone inside a week.

Which meant he had to start some more unslottings right away. Now.

They were at a crucial point. The six thawing in sick bay would not be enough to keep Halley Core running, not while they recuperated. If the diseases felled Virginia, Saul, himself, Lani . . . the expedition would fail. Unattended, the slots would malf one by one. Halley would become an endlessly orbiting cemetery of frozen corpses.

He thumbed in his Priority control code and set to work. Some simple systems had to be warmed up, calculations made, drug inventories drawn on. Carl had some experience with the procedures from the Encke mission. He worked as well as he could, referring to the manual whenever he had doubts. Saul Lintz could advise him if absolutely necessary . . . even with rusty skills, Saul was still the doctor. But . . .

*But what? Yeah, I know—I don't want to call him. I don't care if I never see the bastard again. And I know it's just childish jealousy, too. But that doesn't make things any easier Just the opposite, maybe.*

It was a good idea to get this practice himself, anyway. In a few days he would probably be slotting Saul. *I hope Virginia doesn't catch whatever he's got.*

He was working slowly, his thinking mired in mud. He had to shake off the mood, he knew that, or else he'd make some dumb mistake. Music? That was about all he had these days. He'd been listening to Mozart and Liszt and Haydn for sixteen hours every day, the only way to distance himself from the backbreaking, unending job of cleanup. And all the time watching over one shoulder to see if a goddamn purple hadn't broken through the insulation nearby, wasn't there waiting for him to brush against it, burn through his suit, get its deadly poisons into him. . . .

"Carl!"

He turned, surprised by the feminine voice. *Virginia! She didn't go to him after all.*

The sight of Lani entering the prep room crushed his sudden hope.

"I heard about Quiverian, thought I'd come down and . . . oh. You've already slotted him?"

Carl nodded.

"No ceremony?"

"Wasn't in the mood. Jim's not feeling too well, and a ceremony by yourself . . ."

Lani studied him sympathetically. "I understand."

"Maybe we'll all get together tonight, hoist a few beers. . . ." He let the sentence trickle lamely away, remembering that they had almost started a romance, back a few lifetimes ago. He hadn't thought of that for some time. Every day he revised his opinion of Lani upward, but his pulse still quickened for Virginia. *Not that it matters. . . . We're all run ragged.*

She nodded emphatically. "Yes. We could use a little group solidarity. You're the leader now, Carl. You'll have to hold us together."

He had been nominal leader for more than a week, though without time to think of himself that way. "All six of us? With two or three sick? Some crew. Half of shift one gone in—what? ten days? No, less." He shook his head. "Things're movin' too fast."

*What would Captain Cruz have done that I haven't? What have I missed?*

"You're tired." She put a hand on his shoulder and patted him gently. *Like I was a big dumb animal,* he thought. *Well, I'm not much better than that right now.*

"I . . . I'm glad you came."

"So am I. You obviously need help."

"I started unslotting a couple more."

"Won't we need a dozen at least?"

"That's what I need help with. We must have good people, but . . . well, who would *you* pick to introduce into this death house?"

Lani nodded silently, her face pensive and withdrawn. He wondered how she was dealing emotionally with the ever-present threat. She might be catching something from him—or vice versa—right now. They had no real idea what vector these diseases followed.

"Not my friends . . ."

He was surprised. "I hadn't thought of it that way. I'm figuring on picking people I know can stand up to this."

"I see. I considered first sheltering my friends; you think of pulling out those you can trust. That's why you are suited to command, and I am not."

Carl shrugged. He knew he was no real leader, not remotely like Captain Cruz; he just did what seemed obvious. Her other point was right, though. It was a lot less painful to watch comparative strangers sicken and die.

"I don't like having to make these decisions on my own. I'm just an ordinary spacer. This is life and death, for chrissakes."

"So it is."

In a subtle way Lani withdrew from him, standing apart, face blank and eyes wary, waiting for his orders. She didn't want the responsibility. *Neither do I.*

"Okay, I've got to tell the system which slots to start warming, or we can't go any further." He turned to the big console and began running his hands down the displayed list of crew skills. He pressed a finger at the dimple points next to two names.

"Jeffers and Sergeov," he said grimly. Then he managed a dry, crusty chuckle. "Boy, are *they* going to be surprised."

# SAUL

*Enough. Leave his poor body alone.*

Saul rocked back from the treatment table and put down his implements.

"Cease code blue. Halt resuscitation procedures," he said to the spidery med-mechs clustered around the pale, waxy figure that had been Nicholas Malenkov. "Maintain type-six tissue oxygenation, and begin precooling glycogen infusion for term storage."

It was too late to "sick slot" the Russian. His dying had penetrated too deeply. Saul's only recourse was to prepare the corpse as well as he could and actually freeze it against a hoped-for day when both thaw and cure might be available.

The master unit beeped twice. Saul, who had been looking sadly at his dead friend, glanced up.

"Yes? What's the problem?"

**"Clarification request, Doctor,"** the med-mech announced. **"Please select infusion and cooling profile. Also, term-slotting requires a death certification."**

He nodded. With clinical skills as rusty as his, it was a wonder he remembered the right general procedure at all.

"All right, then. Voice-ident: Dr. Saul Lintz, citizen of the Diasporic Confederacy, seventh physician on Halley Expedition. Code number . . ." He pressed fingers at his temples. "I forget. Fill it in from the records."

**"Yes Doctor,"** the machine assented quickly.

"I hereby certify Dr. Nicholas Malenkov, citizen of Greater Russia, expedition second physician, to be deceased beyond recall by available means. Cause: massive peripheral neural damage brought on by undiagnosed, raging infection which crossed the blood-brain barrier three hours ago. Details and tissue analysis to follow in addendum.

"Patient term-slotted on this date. . . ."

Saul looked up at his reflection in the side of the gleaming mech . . . pale, yes, tired. More tired than he looked, apparently.

*What is the date?* Was it still November 2061? Or already December?

*Have I missed Miriam's birthday? Only ten years since she died at Gan Illana. And yet it seems like another century.*

Sometimes it felt as if he was fighting on for one reason only—so that Virginia could get to see age twenty-nine. If they were still alive, in six months, to put another candle on her cake, then he would find a new priority. One thing at a time.

"Fill in the date. And select the most commonly used slotting procedure for neural-damage cases," he told the mech.

**"Yes Doctor."** The machine would consult the mission mainframe, aboard the *Edmund Halley,* and take care of the details.

There was little likelihood that medical science would have learned to reverse such massive trauma in eighty years—as well as how to thaw bodies frozen solid as ice. Still, he owed it to Nick to offer him that chance.

In any event, term-slotting did not call for human supervision. *Let the mechs do it. If—when—we go home, it'd be best if the procedures used to cool and store the body were as standard as possible.*

Saul turned to leave the treatment room, leaving behind him the whirr of automatic processing. As the door hissed shut he rested his shoulder against the fibercloth wall. His arms felt heavy, even in the thin gravity. His sinuses throbbed.

*Well?* he asked inwardly. *What're you planning to do? Develop into a real sickness and kill me? Or quit bugging me and go away!*

The damn cold had been hanging on for eight weeks! In all of a life plagued by little, dripping bouts with one virus after another, he had never, ever suffered anything really serious. But now this lingering, dull ache was really getting to him.

He shook his head to clear it. *Make up your damn minds!* he told the bugs, at the moment not caring if they were cometary scourges or more banal imports from a warm and fecund Earth. Right now Saul didn't see anything unscientific in personifying his parasites. He hated them.

*Poor Nick Malenkov, survived by the man he nearly slotted.* He tried to remember the big, brilliant bear of a Russian the way he had known him in life, but it was hopeless. All he could see was the pale slackness of cheeks unanimated by emotion . . . the emptiness of eyes unbacked by mind.

*Oh, Lord,* he prayed. *Don't let anything like this happen to Virginia.*

She had used an override to get into his room, two days ago, and by some definitions committed a completely shameless act of rape. His weak protests had been smothered under her warm body, her blazing mouth—as she shared in a moment any microfauna he had, and thereby ended any further argument over protecting her from contagion.

A decisive woman. She had hardly left his side since, except for the fourteen-hour shifts, of course. And although he worried, Saul could not say he was anything but glad.

*It's her choice,* he thought. *And Carl Osborn will just have to learn to live with it.*

For as long as the three of them lasted, at least.

Yesterday he had helped slot Jim Vidor, feverish and raving. At least that time they were able to get the poor fellow in in time. Lani Nguyen had watched raggedly. For lack of any real attention from Carl, she had taken up briefly with Jim. Now she was as alone as before.

His wrist beeper pulsed. The mechs in the recuperation chamber were signaling him.

*Enough loafing,* he thought. Somebody must have wakened, at last. One of the first six.

*Put on a happy face,* he reminded himself as he started stepping into isolation garments. While slipping on antiseptic booties he touched the bandage covering his left ankle.

The scar was almost healed now. He still wasn't sure how he had been cut, during that frantic struggle with the purples in sleep slot 1. At first he had been certain it was a bite from one of the horrible native worms, but after what happened to Peltier, and Ustinov, and Conti, he figured it couldn't have been. There had been a swelling and soreness, then it had gone away.

*Just a scrape, I suppose. A man like me won't die of a purple bite, anyway. And there's too little gravity here to be hanged.*

His nose itched.

*I'll probably die in a sneezing fit.*

Saul finished dressing. He put on an isolation helmet and passed into the booth with a flashing green light over the entrance.

Someone had indeed awakened. It was Bethany Oakes, the first person decanted after Captain Cruz's death. The assistant expedition leader had been a tough case. Her thawing had not been easy.

Hibernation wasn't a natural human function. Inducing it involved complex, massive doses of drugs that dropped the body into a slumbering, near-death state—reducing metabolism and pH, cooling tissues down to a bare degree above freezing. The process was anything but routine, even after decades of use in space flight. To prove it for interstellar travel times had been one dream of Miguel Cruz-Mendoza. It was supposed to be another gift from the Halley Expedition to the people of Earth.

Working alone, with equipment that might or might not still be polluted with Halleyforms, Malenkov had chosen the slow-thaw method, allowing the patient to throw off sleep-center suppression naturally. The decision had been questionable. It might be safer, but it left the possibility that the decanted would awaken with no one left alive to greet them.

Bethany Oakes was still an ample woman. Three weeks' hibernation under an IV drip wouldn't change that much. But her eyelids were already dark with the blue heaviness of slot stupor. As Saul approached, they fluttered open. Her pupils contracted unevenly in the light.

He dimmed the wall panels and picked up a squeeze tube of electrolyte-balance fluid to wet her lips. Her tongue flicked out, drawing in the sweetness.

*Good,* he thought. The sipping reflex was a rule-of-thumb test Nicholas had taught him. A sign of good progress.

In the hazel eyes, an apparent struggle—a mind climbing laboriously out of the cold.

"S-Saul . . . ?" Her voice was barely audible.

"Yes, Bethany. It's me, Saul Lintz." He bent forward.

"Are we . . ." She swallowed, and smiled thinly. "Are we at aphelion yet?"

Saul blinked. Of course, the expedition's second-in-command hadn't been scheduled to be unslotted for thirty-three years, when the comet would have nearly reached its farthest point from the sun, when the colony would be briefly busy again preparing for the rocket maneuver that would send them hurtling past Jupiter toward rendezvous with the waiting harvesters, nearly four more decades beyond that.

How could he tell her that it had been more like thirty-three *days!*

He shook his head, wishing he had better news, and wondering how to tell it.

Saul smiled in his best bedside manner. "No, Betty, not quite . . ."

## PART III

# WHEN SPRING LAST CAME TO GEHENNA

*January 2062*

Nobody ever did anything very foolish
except from some strong principle.
—Melbourne

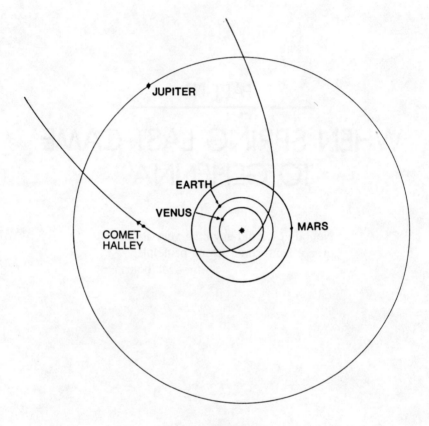

Positions of Inner Planets
and Comet Halley
February 2062

# VIRGINIA

What a difference a mere three weeks made!

Virginia wondered as she glide-walked past hurried, bustling workers. Had it been only that long? Only twenty-five days since the remnants of the First Watch had gathered, weary and haggard, to note the passing of the year 2061?

An ebullient New Year's Eve it had not been. Even with the wall holos set to their cheeriest summer scenes, it still felt like the winter of Ragnarok. They had huddled near the farthest end of the mammoth Central Complex Lounge—four poor survivors—and toasted from Carl's carefully hoarded supply of Lacy Traces liqueur.

The bottle had gone quickly. There seemed little point in saving anything.

All attempts at conversation had lapsed. The vids from Earth were too depressing to watch—snappy scenes of commercial consumption or, even worse, an awful melodrama about the Scott expedition to the South Pole . . . no doubt somebody's stupid idea of a gesture in their honor.

At her suggestion, Saul and Carl had tried to play their first game of chess since the death of Captain Cruz—or since Saul and Virginia had taken up shared residence together. But it wasn't like before. The two men had hardly exchanged a word or a glance, and the play was savage. When Saul's wrist comp called him away to tend the thawing sleepers again, Lani and Virginia had shared a look of relief.

She would never forget that gloomy evening for as long as she lived.

That had been less than a month ago. Now . . . well, things were different. At least superficially, they were much better. One at least heard voices in the cool hallways again, and people were trying to find solutions.

Virginia was also getting better at moving about in Halley's soft gravity. She skim-glided quickly, grabbing the fiber floor with velcroed slippers and pulling along a wall cable on her way toward Control Central.

It was still a new experience, coming this way without a mind fogged from lack of rest, or a body nearly limp from fatigue. A full seven hours' sleep was like a sinful luxury.

Yesterday, her shift had coincided with Saul's. They'd had a chance to make love for the first time in a week, and slept side by side, linked through her electronic familiar, touching in the dim glow of JonVon's status lamps. Saul had to leave early to get ready for today's test of his new invention, but Virginia had awakened feeling his warmth still on the webbing beside her, his musty, now-familiar scent on her arm.

*Someday, when I have some free time again, I'll have to find out what JonVon's making of our dreams. Saul and I are getting closer all the time, our shared, enhanced senses more and more vivid. I wonder— is it possible that I might have been right, after all? Is it possible to simulate human mental processes so well that you can achieve "telepathy" of a sort?*

*If so, can we give Earth at least one present, before we all die?*

This morning she had stopped just before leaving her cubicle, hesitating by the slide door, and turned back to pick up a stylus. On the face of a memory pad she had scribbled quickly . . . not a poem—not yet— but a sketch for one.

Hoku welo welo,
        Oh, unforgiving Comet—
Ua luhi au,
        I am very tired—

The mixed verse had reminded her of her homesickness. She missed Kewani Langsthan, the only other Hawaiian on the first shift, who had lost an arm to an explosion on A Level, on Christmas Eve, and had to be slotted immediately when the stump went infected.

No Hawaiian was among the replacements. She didn't know whether to regret it or to be glad that her countrymen were being spared this terrible time.

Anyway, the news from the island republic was not good. The last time she had had time to listen to the Earthcasts, tensions had been rising. Nations of the Arc of the Living Sun had accused Governor Ike-da's government of "unecological projects."

Ever since that evening months ago, when she had briefly shared Saul's memories of his lost homeland, she had suffered from a deep, lingering fear for her own people's precarious renaissance.

Haalulu kuu lima
    My hand shakes—
E awiwi . . . Ka la
    Be quick, oh Sun—

The sketch had disappeared into JonVon's stochastic well of mem-ory. Perhaps she would call it up again to work on it, if she had time, or remembered. Meanwhile, her pet machine would echo with her mus-ings. Unlike the prim processors of Earth—or the stolid mission main-frame the techs had begun crating to move down from the *Edmund* to Central—JonVon did not simply file things away. He . . . it . . . was programmed to "remember" from time to time, untriggered and unpre-dictably, and to "ponder" new correlations.

She herself had no time to devote to the project with which she had planned to while away the years. But JonVon would always have at least a small corner of memory devoted to it, gathering and organizing data for when, at last, she could turn her attention back to the question of intelligence itself.

*I must remember to ask him what he has learned, now and then.*

*And here we are,* she thought on coming to a double hatch with a burning amber light overhead. *The entrance to Central Control . . . command post for the invading hordes from Earth.*

Before entering, she had to submit to another damned cleaning. A bulky mech towered beside the hatchway.

"**Please present all surfaces for ultrasonic exposure,**" it di-rected, holding forth a flat, humming plate and a vacuum hose.

She sighed and stepped forward, turning before the double-tubed, jury-rigged machine. Harmonics from high-frequency sound waves stroked her skin in multiple octaves, all the way down to a low, grum-bling growl that made her teeth grate.

She knew all the override codes, of course. But it would be better to submit to these measures, as half-ass and useless as they had to be. Somebody was bound to find out if she got into the habit of bypassing regs for her own convenience.

The low tingling told of bits of debris being shaken loose from her clothing and skin, to be sucked away into the vacuum inlet. Of course, this wouldn't really stop people from tracking around cometary germs. Saul had said that the only long-term effect of the procedure would be to destroy all their clothes and eventually wreck everybody's hearing.

The tingling stopped and the vacuum hose shut off. Virginia imagined a puff of air, cotton fibers, and skin cells—all sighing out into space far above, where the stars shone unblinking on a stark icescape.

**"Prepare eye protection, please."**

She grimaced and drew the goggles from her waistband.

"Lay on, MacDuff," she muttered, and scrunched her eyes shut as the hallway seemed to fill with actinic brilliance.

*This* was sheer idiocy, she knew. The UV lamps were their best weapon against the Halleyforms, but there were only about two dozen left, and they were burning out at a rate of one or more a day! There were already numerous cases of sunburn and skin rash.

The uncomfortable glare cut off and she breathed in relief.

**"You may pass,"** the mech pronounced.

"Thanks," she answered sarcastically as the softly hissing door opened, letting her into a bustle of activity.

Voices tinged with anxiety . . . human torsos that disappeared into hooded data-speech shells . . . hands working switches or mech-waldo controls. *Yes, there's quite a difference that three weeks can make.*

But the undercurrent of dark fear was still with them. If anything, it had grown.

Over in a far corner, a half-dozen forms clustered in low-G crouches around a holo map. Virginia recognized Dr. Oakes and her chief aides. Another damn strategy meeting.

*Olakou na alii. . . .* They are the chiefs, heaven help us.

*I wish Saul didn't have to go down to the inner chambers to test his new machine today. I miss him so, already.*

Virginia stepped up behind Walter Schultz, the man now operating mech-control 1. She was still early, but the fellow clearly needed to be relieved. His shoulders were hunched under the isolation hood, and his hands clenched whitely on the waldo-teleoperator controls.

She knew what he was going through. Mech operators had it almost as bad as the men in the corridors. They weren't in direct physical danger, of course, but the hours were worse, and the intense mental effort just as draining. From the displays she saw that Walter was handling four big 'bots all by himself. He needed a break.

It wouldn't be a good idea to pull him back too abruptly, though. Two days ago she had tapped Walter's shoulder while he was linked. The man had whirled on her, pupils dilated, roundly cursing her as a "meddling Percell bitch."

He had apologized later, but the phrase stuck in her mind.

*I'll tell him I'm here over an open comm line.* But her hand hesitated just over the panel microphone. From under the isolation hood she heard Schultz sniffling. It was hard to tell if the man had a cold or if he was crying.

These days, it could be either.

"Virginia!" a high voice called out behind her. "Virginia. Would you come over here please, dear?"

Other than Saul, only one person spoke to her that way. She turned and nodded to the brown-haired, matronly woman motioning to her from the other side of the room.

"Yes, of course, Dr. Oakes." She glide-walked quickly toward the big holo tank where the acting section leaders stood staring gloomily at the big display.

The current chief of Cometary Science Section, Masao Okudo, moved pointedly away from her end of the table, as did Major Lopez, the senior awakened military man. Virginia ignored the slight. It was part of the general undercurrent of resentment against her, as well as Carl and Saul and Lani. As if the First Watch had somehow been criminally incompetent in letting all this come about.

She had always found humans to be irrational creatures, deep down—herself included, of course. Many resented the choices that had been made, of who should be unslotted as part of the Crisis Management Team. "Why me?" was a refrain she had heard repeatedly, muttered in anger or wailed out loud as one after another of the wakers was injured fighting the crud in the halls, or fell ill to some unknown bug.

*Carl had to make those hard choices, after Captain Cruz died.* The wakers blamed him. And it didn't help at all that he was a Percell.

*I suppose the only thing keeping him and Saul and me from being completely ostracized is the fact that we're indispensable.*

Bethany Oakes, at least, seemed immune to any such feelings. She smiled as kindly as ever as she shook Virginia's hand.

"Thank you for coming over, dear. We are having a bit of a disagreement over a technical matter, and I was wondering if perhaps you could help us with the expertise you picked up during those frightful weeks you and the others faced this emergency all alone."

Virginia nodded. "I'll help any way I can."

Dr. Oakes smiled back with moist, small lips. Virginia couldn't help noticing that her face was puffy, and she wore makeup that seemed skewed, somehow.

*Oh fates, you are mean bitches. You had to take Captain Cruz—our Columbus, our Drake—right at the very start, didn't you? He made an expedition out of a spill of exiles and misfits, and now he's gone. This nice woman is simply no substitute.*

Dr. Oakes turned to Lefty d'Amaria, the head of Virginia's own department, Computations and Mechanicals. Lefty, at least, gave Virginia a quick smile, which she returned gratefully. Alas, the man gripped the table-edge uncertainly, and his brow was speckled with perspiration.

"There're two problems we . . . we wanted to consult you about, Ginnie. The first has to do with how to fight the stuff out in the halls."

She opened her hands. "Dr. Matsudo and Dr. Lintz have been studying the gunk. I've had less experience with it than any of the other survivors of the First Watch."

D'Amaria nodded. "Yes, in person. But you've fought it through mechs, helping Osborn and his crews. What we want to know is if you think it might be possible to retrofit the surface mechs for work in the shafts."

"Well, we've already reworked some of them—ship-utility robots, mostly."

"No." D'Amaria shook his head. "We're thinking about the big ones. The real surface mechs."

Virginia blinked. Were things already so desperate? Surface mechs had never been meant to work in tunnels. The thought of those great-limbed behemoths and spidery cranes cramming their way down here, under the ice, was enough to make her cringe.

"I . . . I don't know for sure. We'd have to unlimber some of the factory gear. . . ."

"A couple of factory-team crew are being warmed now," Lopez told her. "Jeffers and Yeomans and Johanson are already awake."

Virginia nodded. "But even with the factory running, it'd be a mess. In order to fit lifters or pushers into the shafts, we'd have to do more than just remove their legs and rollers. I'd have to burn new patterns into read-only memory. With the facilities at hand, it'd be a patch job, and I'm not sure it could be reversed."

Okudo nodded. "Fine, fine. Then you are saying it can be done."

Virginia blinked. "But it's crazy! We'd never be able to set up the Nudge Launchers at aphelion without surface mechanicals. And without the Nudge, Halley's orbit can't be shifted. We'll never be able to go—"

"Will you shut your stupid Percell *mouth?*" Major Lopez hissed quickly, baring his teeth. The Space Corps officer's eyes seemed to burn, and he pulled back only slowly when Dr. Oakes cleared her throat pointedly. He glanced at the acting mission commander, and then back at Virginia. "Excuse me. I mean will you keep your voice down? *Please?*" His sarcasm was evident.

Virginia ignored him.

*—We'll never be able to go home,* she thought, finishing her agonized complaint in her own mind.

Dr. Oakes spoke to the military man. "Now, Fidel. I'm sure Miss Herbert realizes how essential it is to be discreet about some of the implications of our upcoming actions. Morale is bad enough as it is."

"I'll say," Okudo muttered. "I hear some crew are even feigning illness, trying every malingering trick in order to get back into the slots."

*I didn't know.* Virginia's stomach felt queasy.

*Captain Cruz would have been more forthright with us. And nobody would have even considered letting him down by trying to run away into time.*

Bethany Oakes contemplated the holo tank moodily, giving Virginia her first real chance to look for herself at the big display.

The region penetrated by tunnels was no larger than it had been a month ago, still taking up less than five percent of the volume of Halley Core, in a warren clustered around the north polar region. A few large chambers stood out, including three where the sleep slots lay buried. And this one, Central, amid a cluster of rooms barely a kilometer straight down from the tethered *Edmund Halley.*

*Thank heavens most of the hydroponics are still aboard the* Edmund, Virginia thought. *Safe from the native lifeforms we've inadvertently wakened down here. If the gunk or the bugs ever got into the main gardens, we'd likely starve in short order.*

*As it is, we'll probably be going hungry soon anyway, if we have to keep this many awake much longer.*

Nearly all the depicted tunnels and shafts were stained, the colors standing for different types of infestation. Only the four main chambers still shone antiseptic, uninvaded white—along with one path to the polar storage yards. And it had taken every UV lamp and half an eighty-year supply of disinfectants to keep just those areas clear.

Most passages glimmered in some shade of green, where the only known invader was some variety of the lichenlike growths popularly called *gunk.* Those routes still held air and heat. For all anyone could tell, they might even be perfectly safe. At least Saul thought they were.

He had gone off more than once, heedless of supposed danger, in search of more samples to study.

*Maybe that's one of the things that attracts me to him.* Saul wasn't brave in the flashy way, but in a manner that seemed to say "living day from day has always been a calculated risk."

Perhaps her love was analytically simple. For Saul did remind her of her father. Anson Herbert had possessed the same sad, gentle wisdom, had shown her more in his quiet strength than other men with all their flamboyant posturing.

Virginia shook her head. Anson had been dead for two years, but she could almost hear him, telling her to quit daydreaming and get to work. There were problems to be solved, and always idiots trying to use hammers to fix clocks.

Lopez was gesturing at the tunnels that had the worst infestations, especially along the ducts where heat flowed from the power plant. Purple, yellow, and red stains showed where more active Halleyforms had erupted, tearing tunnel seals, wreaking havoc on vital machines, and, occasionally, even reaching out with a poisonous grasp after a passing Earthman.

". . . Bigger surface mechs could patrol an expanded hallway, here, scraping and remelting the ice at intervals, sealing crevices and removing infested layers for disposal at the surface. . . ."

Virginia couldn't believe she was hearing this. The plan was lunacy. It was a cumbersome scheme that ignored the *seven decades* ahead.

"There are still other options to try," she suggested. "Saul is working on a possible way—"

Lopez sniffed loudly. "Lintz's *death ray,* right?"

Bethany Oakes nodded without turning her gaze from the map. "We can hope somebody comes up with something new, of course. But every conventional approach has failed. One thing is certain: If the infestation reaches the sleep slots, we are quite finished."

She looked at Virginia. "That is why we asked you to join us over here, not only to help convert surface mechs for the struggle below. You . . ."

The older woman paused, blinking, as if trying to keep her train of thought. Virginia realized with shock that she must be on some sort of drug.

". . . You are the only real expert we have on that old subject . . . *artificial intelligence.* I am familiar with the traditional proofs, of course, that the real thing is impossible. But a very good, flexible simulant might be enough." She sighed. "Anyway, we must grasp at any straw. Saul Lintz's invention, and even robots capable of acting on their own.

"We must come up with a way to make as many mechs as *autonomous* as possible . . . and soon. You see . . . we are losing men and women faster than we are unslotting them."

Virginia stared. She found she could say nothing at all.

"This is a military secret, Herbert," Major Lopez growled. "You tell anyone about this and I'll have your Percell ass."

Virginia only shook her head, and let him take it to mean anything he wanted.

A little later, by the refreshment center, she nursed a bulb of weak tea and wondered how she might even approach the nearly impossible tasks she had been assigned. It was ironic. *I never thought anyone would ask me to work on machine intelligence.*

Under these circumstances, it seemed so very wrong to her.

That was when the man she wanted least to encounter floated up next to her with a soft push of nubby legs.

"Well, sweet machine lady." Otis Sergeov grinned. "I suppose you have heard latest interesting developments, Earthside? Have you not?"

"Go away, Otis," she said levelly. "I don't want to hear any more bad news right now, especially from you. What are you doing here, anyway? You're hall crew."

The Russian Percell shrugged. His eyelids were still slightly blue-tinged and his cheeks chalky from his recent awakening from slot sleep.

"I just stopped by to grab a look on way to Shaft Three. I go to help your lovers test their new machine to save the world."

Virginia looked up quickly. "What are you talking about?"

"You know who I mean." He winked. "Osborn and Lintz."

Sergeov held out a small slip of paper with her name scratched on the outside. She plucked it up with her fingertips and unfolded it to read the message. Virginia nodded.

"So you're going to help Carl and Saul test the new beamers. Is that it?"

He nodded.

"Okay, then. Tell Saul I'll arrange to send him the mechs he needs for the experiment. I'll scrape them up somewhere."

Sergeov nodded. "Ah, ways to get around channels. I *knew* that he had influence with Secret Mistress of all Machines. I must learn his tricks."

Virginia shrugged. Sergeov had had a reason to seek her out. Now she only wanted his visit to end. "Is that all, Otis?"

"Only one more thing. A personal curiosity. I did underrate you, Virginia. You may be Orthophile, but at least you chose the father—or uncle—of our race for shacking up with. He is still Ortho, but so is anybody over fifty, so if you are so kinky as to prefer old men, I guess you have no better choice, eh?"

She glared at him. "You dirty-minded little—"

"Wait until *I* get that old. Hmmm? Will I then a chance have?"

Virginia's head whirled. The man said so many infuriating things, each deserving to be burnt down with scathing logic. *Oh, why am I so compulsive? He's not looking for an argument over semantics, he wants to get on my nerves, that's all.*

"Fuck you, Otis," she said at last.

Sergeov blinked in momentary surprise, then he laughed. His head rocked back and he cried out in delight. "Said well! If only we had you on Earth, day before yesterday! You could have told them."

"Told *who*?"

"Bastards in Geneva."

Virginia hesitated, feeling suddenly cold.

"What's happened on Earth?"

"If you had more than time of day for your own kin, you would have by now known," Sergeov taunted her. "We have no one to talk to but each other now . . . now that Orthos blame us for the diseases."

"They do *not*. . . ." Virginia closed her eyes and resolved not to be sidetracked. "Tell me what happened on Earth, Otis. Or this time I really *will* break your arm."

The Russian spacer nodded. His voice was suddenly subdued.

"There was coup, Virginia. Hawaii is now under Arc of the Sun."

"What?" She stared. "But . . . But that's impossible! How?"

"Mercenaries from Philippines. Governor Ikeda dead. There is martial law."

"But the Thirty-second Amendment . . . the United States has to defend—"

Sergeov shrugged. "Supreme Court of United States met in emergency session, Virginia . . . ruled that Hawaii, since 2026, is been *semisovereign* . . . I think that is proper phrase. Means a de facto Arcist government is hokay—so long as it pays federal taxes on time, and keeps external-affairs-nose clean.

"They have already the Percell School closed down. Shut down uplift-research institute and that big, tidal-energy project. More is to come, for sure."

Sergeov came forward, one hand on a rail, breathing intensely. His voice was thick with sarcasm *"Now* you see? See why we could have yesterday used your eloquence back on Earth? The case was only six to three, decided. Surely if you had there been, you would have been able to convince them. Or at least could have told them *fuck you* right into their Ortho . . ."

He stopped then, because Virginia had already stumbled out into the hallway, past the hulking decontamination robot, ignoring its monotone request that she submit to its worthless sound-and-light treatment. She moved without destination, blinded by sudden tears, navigating purely by rote.

# CARL

Things were getting bad.

Carl drifted on a tether, waiting for Saul Lintz to show up. He was glad for the break.

In the last few days he'd learned to take his rest where he found it— in little cat naps and food breaks, using every slack moment to let his muscles forget about what he was putting them through. There wasn't time to get mechs into place for most jobs, and a lot of it they couldn't do anyway.

*Good old grunt work,* Carl thought. *Only it's different if your life depends on it.*

In a way, he was glad he wasn't running things. Major Lopez, who barely concealed his distrust of Percells, had all the headaches. *Fine. Let him sweat.*

There weren't enough hands to control the green gunk algae, much less the big forms. Bethany Oakes was busily unslotting people to help out, but that took time. He had heard things weren't running well down there, either. Some unslotted ones were angry at being reawakened early, and then scared of catching the whatsits diseases running around.

Not that he could blame them. He had a new guy on his crew, a husky Norwegian named Veerlan, and already the sniffles and coughing were starting. The man had been out only thirty-five hours, hardly even fit for heavy work yet.

"Is the team ready?" Saul's voice came to Carl out of a foggy blur. Saul landed stiffly on fiberthread nearby and hooked a line to a stay.

"Ah . . . yeah. Not much of a team, though."

"How many?" Saul seemed alert and ready, even though long fatigue lines rutted his face. He carried a bulky machine strapped to his back.

"Four."

"Including you?"

"Yeah."

"Um . . . I don't know . . . it's going to be pretty cumbersome."

"I'll call mechs."

"I've already had Sergeov tell Virginia. She'll send some as soon as possible."

Carl felt a hot spurt of irritation. "*I'm* in charge of mechs in this quadrant."

Saul's mouth tightened. "Look, this is an emergency—"

"I'll call Virginia. This isn't your lab, Lintz. I call the shots down here."

"All right, be my guest. Call."

"Well . . . yeah . . . I'll patch through while we're on the way." Carl shook his head slightly, as if to clear it. "You've got the spec frequencies?"

Saul tapped his vest pocket. "Right here. Took all night."

"This better work."

"I hope it will."

"Hope isn't near good enough."

"I can't guarantee—"

"Listen, we're down to a dozen, maybe fifteen able-bodied. They're dropping faster than we can unslot 'em, I hear. I'm using men who're groggy from work—like me—and women with noses running in their suits, coughing into tissues they've wadded under their chins. I mean . . ." He sucked in air, his eyes squeezed tight, and expelled a tired breath. "It better work."

Saul nodded sympathetically. "Let's go, then."

They met Jeffers and Sergeov and Lani in Shaft 3, where it had all started. The shaft was well lit so they could see to work, the phosphors glowing like regularly spaced advertisements along a dark highway that dwindled away into the yawning distance.

The party hung like dots of color, each suit a different primary, against the pink fiberthread background. From a lateral tunnel came a large, asymmetric bulk, towed by mechs. Three extras trailed.

—Virginia freed 'em up,— Jeffers said happily. —Makes it a whole lot easier for us now.—

"Yeah," Carl said. He felt irked that Saul had gotten mechs quickly, without Virginia even asking for approval. And he hadn't had any mech backup this whole damned shift, until brilliant Saul Lintz and his miracle cure came on the scene. "About time."

*I don't suppose I'll cry any if this doesn't work,* Carl thought, and then immediately rebuked himself. *No, that's stupid. You're really getting worn down.*

Jeffers must have been just as tired, but he grinned and wisecracked as he wrestled gear toward the target area. His angular face gave no hint of how he felt about being awakened into hell.

Both Jeffers and Sergeov still had shadowy slot eyes. Carl said to them, "Don't bust your butts, guys. Easy does it."

They checked the mechs' securing cables and pivoted the array to move up the center of the shaft. Telerobots had towed the microwave-digger assembly, minus its tripod mount, all the way down from the surface. Without its legs it lost its former spidery grace and became merely another lumpy machine, pipes and struts sticking out at odd angles.

Ahead, the smooth surface of the tunnel was broken by purple strands jutting into the vacuum.

—They're not moving,— Lani said. Beneath her high, melodious voice there was an undercurrent of fatigue.

—How long has the air been gone from this shaft?— Saul asked.

· —Days,— Jeffers answered.

—And the temperature is down? Then the purples may be dormant.—

—What's 'at?— Jeffers asked fuzzily.

Saul glanced at Carl questioningly, as if to ask, *Is he groggy?*

Carl shook his head. *We're all tired, so what? We haven't been sitting on our asses in a lab all this time.*

—The larger forms apparently were stimulated by leaking heat at the intersections,— Saul sent, —where the collar makes contact with the ice. But once they broke through, looking for more heat, they hit a bonanza. The air warmed them as it rushed out, and the forms kept growing—for a while. Now it's almost as cold in here as the ice, so they're dormant again. Mostly.—

—Uh-huh.— Jeffers stared straight ahead, somewhat blearily

chewing at his lip, and Carl couldn't be sure the man had understood any of it.

"The purples will break in anywhere the gunk grows," he said. "That means anyplace there's heat *or* light *or* air."

They slowed, the mechs' jets taking up the inertia of the microwave borer. Bulbous Halleyform organisms protruded into the shaft all around Tunnel 3E. In yellow-tinged phosphor light they seemed to be sweating a film of oily blue.

—Beautiful, huh?— Jeffers sent sarcastically.

—In a way,— Lani said somberly, taking him seriously. —So strange . . .—

"Philosophy later," Carl said. "We've got to kill it."

—No, I want a sample first.— Saul coasted over to the wall and smacked into it awkwardly. Carl grinned maliciously. Let Saul make his own mistakes. He wasn't going to waste energy babying anybody, especially Lintz.

—I have not seen them in this state. I had only reports to judge by.—

*Oh great.* "You mean you don't *know* you understand them?"

—Oh, we've learned a lot. For instance, we now know that they aren't really differentiated organisms at all, not like mammals or insects or earthworms. They're more like jellyfish or slime molds . . . where different groups of independent cells take on specialized tasks for brief periods. I haven't seen a phase like this before, but their fundamental chemistry could not change simply because they have a respite in their growth cycle.—

The bland professorial arrogance of it irked Carl. "Who says so? How come you're so sure?"

Saul pulled out a sample bottle. —General biological principles. The resonant frequencies of their long-chain molecules can't change simply because their life rhythm slows.—

Saul clipped a fragment from the nearest jutting growth and caught it in the bottle. He peered into the open cut, where darkening tissue oozed. —Remarkable. It exudes a film for protection against the loss of vapor to vacuum. Yet the film itself is a fluid that somehow doesn't sublime.—

"Hey, come on," Carl called impatiently.

—I suspect it's a very high-surface-tension fluid. Somehow it binds to the surface, yet remains liquid enough to cover the plant entirely, compensating for injuries.—

Saul clipped a section from another, then pushed off. —Done.—

—Good! Let's get the microwave oven ready for fried eggplant,—
Jeffers said.

Carl directed the mechs to focus the antennas on the plants. There
would be side lobes that would lap onto the walls, but that couldn't
be helped. The trick—Saul's idea—was to tune the microwave borer
to the precise vibrational frequency of a molecule peculiar to the native
forms so that a short burst would fry them without also heating the ice,
nearby.

"Hope you're sure."

—The calculation's straightforward. I'm confident.— Saul eyed
Carl. —Look, if it works on purples, I can tune it to some of the worst
varieties of green gunk, too.—

"To kill this stuff you might have to blister everything else around.
If the exposed ice vaporizes, we're going to be smack in front of a hurricane."

Saul caught his look. —My calculations show . . . oh, to hell with
it. Let's *try* anyway.—

—She all tuned?— Jeffers asked.

Saul nodded. Carl put his glove on the manual switch "Firing."

There came a faint buzz beneath his hand as the capacitors discharged, and then the wall flew at him. A white streaming gale hit Carl,
blowing him across the shaft, slamming him into the wall.

He bounced off, spun, regained his attitude. The comm line carried
grunts, swearing, a yelp of pain. —Watch the spider! It's gonna crash
into the wall,— Jeffers said.

The microwave unit was drifting backward with ponderous men-
ace. If it slammed into the fiberthread—

"Mechs! Mechs!"

Jeffers and Carl leaped for the mech-command module. Stopping
the mammoth machine by themselves would be impossible.

Jeffers punched his side console, swearing. Figures moved in the
dim light, frantically grappling for purchase on the ponderous, awkward
bulk. Mechs surged in several directions, slowing the unit. In a slow-
motion swirl they applied force and leverage, while seconds ticked and
forces merged.

It worked—barely. The unit bumped into the wall in a slow scraping
of green.

"Any injuries?"

—No.—

—Only to my pride,— Saul sent. He brushed at a smear of green on
his suit bottom. —Ouch. I guess I must've sprained my wrist, too.—

Slowly they assembled. The burst of vapor had blown Lani in a three-bank shot, ending up a hundred meters away.

—Hey!— Sergeov sent. —Regard.— He pointed to the rim of Tunnel E.

"The plants . . . they're gone," Carl said.

—Not just fried. We disintegrated 'em,— Jeffers sent.

—Of that I was certain,— Saul said. —But why so much vapor? Must've boiled the water in their tissues. I'll have to adjust the frequency better.—

"Tune all you want," Carl said. "Come on! Slap patches on those holes before something else grows through them."

It took another two hours of tuning before they could blow the native forms apart with a single short burst from the spider and cause only a minor steam-storm. Carl slowly admitted that the idea seemed to work. It was a hard idea to get used to.

Dr. Oakes was enthusiastic. She approved orders to bring in two more spiders and crews to man them. If they worked three shifts per day they might clear the most important shafts and tunnels inside forty-eight hours.

The advantage of the microwave technique was that it ripped apart the Halleyforms down at the molecular level—much more effective than chopping them up or tearing them out of the ice by hand, hoping you had gotten every root and strand.

*Now,* he thought, *now to get rid of the goddamn green gunk itself.*

Carl began to feel a faint ray of optimism cut through his bone-deep weariness. He sent Virginia slow-frame pictures of purples exploding as the microwaves hit the bulbs. She sent back an enthusiastic "Yaaaaay!" then echoed it artificially so that it sounded in his headphones as though an entire stadium were applauding him. That lifted his spirits more than anything.

They were heading back toward Central, inside a pressurized tunnel, when the madman struck.

"Leave it, leave it, leave it *be*! You killers! *You're* the aliens here!"

They turned to see a man in a tattered ship-suit, hanging from a side passage, glaring at them angrily.

"What . . . ?" Carl began to say. But the man screamed and leaped forth.

He threw himself at Carl, shouting, incoherently—a high-pitched babble, laced with obscenity, and the eyes wide with fevered energy. Hands stretched forward like claws, legs set to kick.

Before Carl could react, hands had grabbed his helmet ring and they went spinning away together. His helmet flew out of his hands when they smacked into a wall. The madman wrapped his legs around Carl and pounded with hard, quick fists.

Carl was sluggish, dazed. He punched at the other but missed. A right cross caught him in the eye—brilliant crimson flashes. He swung wildly. Missed.

*He's fast.* Carl blocked another punch. He struck—missed—and struck out again. This time he clipped the man on the shoulder. With the energy of the mad a flurry of fists smacked into his cheek, his arm, his chest. Then, at last, help arrived. Someone yanked and the man spun away, yelling, holding out a handful of something.

Carl felt friendly hands grab him, stop his mad tumble. Lani cradled him.

"What the hell?"

"Who was it?"

"Couldn't tell."

"Ingersoll, I think. A guy from Chem Section."

He blinked unsteadily as the figure launched itself away with well-timed kicks off the tunnel walls. The gibberish went on, fading. No one followed. They clustered around Carl, who was still numb from surprise.

"I'll have bruises, that's all," Carl said groggily, fighting down the adrenaline rush.

"Damnedest thing," Jeffers said.

Lani touched Carl's face gently. "It's swelling already. What could have provoked him?"

"He seemed deranged," Saul said. "I'd heard he had come down with something, but Akio said it did not appear to be fatal. Whatever it was, it's obviously affected his mind."

Sergeov's face took on a grim, gray cast. "Now he flees into lower tunnels. Be very hard to find him, treat him, in there, if he does not want you to catch."

"As far as I'm concerned," Carl said, rubbing his jaw, "he can stay lost forever."

Saul nodded, but his voice was pensive and worried as he said, "There were Halleyforms smeared on his face. I wonder how many others have what he's developing?"

# SAUL

At times, the words still haunted him. *We are the aliens.* Men were the invaders here, the interlopers. Now and then Saul wondered what right they had, killing what they did not understand.

Still, he admitted to a feral pleasure in roaming the deep ice caverns, zapping gunk—a savage thrill in aiming a sort of *ray gun* down a hallway, whispering "zap, zap" under your breath, and vaporizing the more dangerous outbreaks of comet stuff.

It didn't surprise Saul that he was of two minds on the matter.

*In this instance, it's the soldier, the caveman in me that wins over the philosopher. My job is to chip flint, to flake new weapons and help save the tribe. It's a priority that comes down from long, long ago. And it is right.*

He touched the dial on his portable beamer. The rheostat kept drifting, and it was important to keep the device tuned exactly on the right frequency, in case they rounded a corner right into a writhing mass of purples.

In the days since that first experiment, the hall crews had learned a lot about how to use the new weapons. There was neither enough power nor labor to keep every passage clear all the time, and the waste heat would prove most unpleasant, if they tried for very long. But the effect on morale had been tremendous anyway. For the first time there seemed to be a chance they might just get through this. Those who weren't sick were actually starting to catch up on sleep. There was less desperate talk of stripping surface mechs to be brought down below the ice.

*Now, if only we can lick the sicknesses.* Saul's major reason for agreeing to come out here, to the remote tunnels near the surface, was to take enough samples to develop his data base, to begin to get some idea how Halley lifeforms interrelated, what roles the microorganisms played.

Just behind him, Lani Nguyen rode a large tunnel mech. The big robot carried a microwave digger that had been modified for hall scrubbing. Except for a dicey area back on E Level, they hadn't had to use it much. The really rough areas were those closest to human habitation, where heat and light and air fed complex lichenoid growths and attracted the deadly, iron-mawed, worm-like colonies.

Here in the outlying tunnels, the phosphor lamps were far spaced and the temperature was kept well below freezing. Only a thin film of green coated the walls. It was easier moving about—even in spacesuits— than back where the purples crawled.

He raised his hand and Lani halted the mech at an intersection that had once been bright in orange and blue plastisheath. Now the walls were dingy under the verdant pallor of a few green-covered glow panels.

Saul scraped away lichenoid, exposing letters on the wall: D–14– TAU.

Good, they weren't lost.

—I'll make soundings for crevices, Saul.—

He nodded. "Okay, Lani. Just don't venture too far from the intersection."

—I'm leashed to you like a faithful puppy, you betcha.—

Saul smiled. Lani was smart and brave, but she was also cautious. The combination was one reason he was glad to have her assigned as his partner.

She moved carefully along the walls, thumping the fibersheath and listening with an audioscope, skillfully seeking out breaks and soft spots in the ice underneath.

They had found through hard experience that the tiny, almost imperceptible Halley-quakes that had been going on ever since their arrival kept opening narrow cracks in the icy aggregate. The danger was particularly acute at intersections, where the insulation was weakest. Part of their job out here was to map the worst of these crevices for later remelt and sealing . . . if there was ever enough manpower to get around to it, that is.

The scrapings from the intersection sign went into a sample vial. Saul was almost certain this was just typical *Hallivirens malenkovi*. But on this trip he had also discovered a host of other, as yet undescribed types. The ecosystem clearly varied from place to place as conditions changed.

Right now Akio Matsudo was back in Central's bio lab, working with Marguerite von Zoon and three weary techs to seek treatment for the growing sick list.

Akio was a competent scientist, but he was ideologically incapable of really adjusting to the implications of this unexpected tide of cometary life.

*Everyone's excited over the success of my microwave disruptor.*

*I've got a reputation as a man of action, now. But has it persuaded anyone to take my advice? To step back and try to get the wide view? Ha!*

Saul was resigned to investigating the Halleyform problem on his own, in his own way. One part of that investigation was coming out here and looking into it for himself.

*The biggest drawback is missing Virginia so much.*

Saul said a grateful prayer every day they woke up together, neither of them yet suffering from some horrible, deadly thing. It was a blessing that she had—so far—not caught anything from him.

Virginia had had a few rough days there, back when the news had come about the coup in Hawaii. The resulting Percell-Ortho tensions had almost overshadowed joy over the success of the beamer technique.

*Three steps forward, four steps back,* Saul thought.

He wiped his nose on his helmet's drip pad, took another antihistamine pill, and washed it down with a sip from a water teat. Saul bent-swiveled his body upside down in the faint gravity to take another scraping of an interesting-looking growth.

There was a low growl as Lani returned with the mech. She muttered rapidly in arcane engineering dialect as she recorded her results, then she looked up at Saul.

—Only small cracks as far as Shaft Six. So, do we toast this stretch of tunnels?—

He shook his head. "No, not here. We'd be half a day finding the right tunings for the individual lichenoid components. The disrupted cells would only spread out and coat the walls anyway, serving as food for a new generation. This stuff doesn't seem to be doing any harm right now."

He also wanted to avoid selecting for disruptor-resistant variants. They had a weapon, now. It would be unwise to squander it as twentieth-century man had done with the best antibiotics and insecticides.

"Why don't you just zap the area around each phosphor panel?" he suggested. "So this corridor doesn't go completely dark and unusable."

—And the vent valves.— Lani nodded. —Right, Saul. I know the drill by now.—

In the thin, chill air the mech's motors gave off a low, brittle rumbling. As the carrier passed, he glanced at the cold cargo strapped to its back . . . the corpses they had found late yesterday and early today.

One was a spacesuited woman, still twisted in a frozen-backed body arch, as if cold and rigor had taken her in the midst of an agonized spasm. Bulging eyes and a swollen tongue disfigured her nearly out of recognition, but Central had identified her as a Power and Propulsion tech, missing three days now.

The other corpse was clothed only in insulstat coveralls. Saul and Lani had found him in the embrace of a lifeform Virginia had called a *hall anemone*. Bits of flesh had torn off as they tried to tug the body free. They'd had to readjust the beamer and blast the writhing colony creature to bits in order to recover and bag the poor fellow's remains.

Who could tell why a man had died out here, so far from Central and all alone? Until they could do tissue analysis, nobody would even know who the unrecognizable jumble had been.

It was a troubling pattern. Other parties had found dead men and women in outlying tunnels. More seemed to be dying in solitary, during their off-duty hours, than suffered casualties during the hall fighting.

*At first I thought it was like the way a wounded animal will sometimes drag itself away from the pack, seeking a hole in which to die. I wondered if, maybe, sick, feverish people just crawled off to be alone.*

*But that wasn't it at all.*

He drew his sheath knife and picked away at a mosslike growth next to the intersection code sign. The gunk was hiding something else.

Green stuff floated away from his vibrating blade, and there it was . . . a circle with an arrow coming off to the upper right—the symbol of maleness—with a stylized flower within.

It was the third type of graffito they had found. In this quadrant the most common had been the Arc of the Living Sun—symbol of radical Orthos from equatorial-belt countries. But there had been others as well, including the P and infinity cartouche . . . $\langle P\infty \rangle$ . . . the Sigil of Simon Percell.

—Finished with that tunnel,— Lani announced. —Good thing we checked. The pressure release was stuck. Could've caused problems.—

"What do you make of this one?" he asked Lani, pointing to the uncovered circle-and-arrow symbol.

There was a long silence. Her face seemed pale under the helmet highlights.

—Every variety of crank was sent on this mission, Saul. Even we spacers have ours, I guess. That's the sign of the Martian Way.—

Saul nodded. His suspicion was growing more firm.

"Clan marks. People really have taken to living out here. At first I couldn't believe it."

Lani explained, —It's picked up since people have grown a little less spooked by the purples. Those guys we met down on Level K . . . from Madagascar and Fiji . . . they do their jobs at Central, but they're terrified of Percells. Refuse to sleep in the same chamber with 'em.—

"Terrified," Saul repeated. He found it amazing that modern men and women would behave this way. He had been astonished by it all his life.

It wasn't the Percells' fault that they seemed more resistant to the comet diseases than unmodified humans . . . or at least showed fewer superficial signs of illness. But that didn't stop the irrational myth.

During the Middle Ages the same thing had happened to the Jews of Europe. Because they killed rats on sight and washed their hands, they tended to suffer less from the Plague. In the end, though, their clean habits made little difference. Enough died at the hands of enraged mobs to more than balance the toll.

*Never underestimate the potential for human stupidity.* It seemed that more and more crew were taking to sleeping in their spacesuits, in outlying tunnels. And sometimes, out there, the sicknesses got them and they died, horribly and alone.

—I've asked people in the different faction territories to try to report if somebody's missing. I don't know what good it'll do.—

*Faction territories,* Saul mused. "Everyone still talks to you, don't they, Lani?"

She looked back at Saul, perhaps a little nervously.

—Well, I guess nobody feels threatened by me. I'm a pretty innocuous type. People tend to tell me things.—

Saul smiled. The Amerasian girl had depth, perhaps more than she realized.

"No. That's only part of it. You're a bridge of sorts, Lani, an Ortho, but one who likes Percells. A . . . what's it called?"

—A *Percephile,* Saul?—

Her laughter had a dry, nervous edge to it.

He nodded. "You're the only one of us survivors from First Watch that most of the wakers seem to trust."

—Mostly 'cause they know I was just a grunt. Had nothing to do with deciding who to thaw. That's what they blame poor Carl for. . . .—

She shook her head.

—Anyway, you're wrong about that, Saul. People are pissed off right now, but if they had to pick three indispensable people out of the whole expedition, it'd have to be you and Carl and Virginia.—

Saul laughed. What a sweet child! She reminded him of what little

Rachel might have been like, had she grown up. But with deep, almond eyes.

He almost asked her how things were going with Carl. Rumor had it they were getting together at times . . . though obviously on less of a committed level than Lani would prefer. Too bad. It would be good to see something going between them, if for no other reason than because it might ease Carl's stubborn anger over Virginia.

Saul decided against bringing up the subject. *Probably I'd just put ol' foot squarely into mouth.*

"Heigh-ho," he said, lifting his portable beamer carefully to compensate for inertia. "Back to work, kiddo."

Lani smiled and started up the mech. He hung on in front as they moved down a long stretch of tunnel, watching the close, green-tinged walls warily.

Up at A Level the chamber scheduled to be the launcher factory gaped like an antediluvian tomb. The aft end of the sail tug *Delsemme* lay in the center, amid a scattering of unopened crates and machinery. Colored threads festooned the sides of the cargo vessel, giving it a faintly fuzzy outline. The cavern looked as if it had been abandoned for years. It was hard to imagine it humming with bright lights and activity—as it would have to if they were ever to get home again.

*Carl's friend, Jeffers . . . he's been too busy to come up and look at this. I wonder if it would be a kindness not to tell him.*

"Let's give the place a zap on disruptor frequencies three, five, and ten," he told Lani. "Then we'll hurry through that inventory Betty wanted us to do up here."

—Right, Saul.— Lani's mech moved out under her delicate control. Soon a tiny series of clicks was accompanied by rising clouds from all over the chamber as the *Hallivirens* algoid blew apart under microwave disruption.

Saul pondered. *If only treating the diseases were as simple.* He took out a light pen and began scanning boxes, letting his portable computer take inventory of the contents of the chamber.

—Saul,— Lani whispered. He turned from a scraping he had been taking, and saw that she was at the other end of the chamber, pointing down one of the side passages. When he arrived where she was standing, his first reaction was one of quick combat adrenaline. For there was a telltale squirming ripple that told of *purples,* grazing on the gunk-lined fibersheath.

Then he saw something else. A hundred meters or so down, near

one of the fungus-dimmed glow bulbs, an indistinct figure floated.
"Another deader?"

She shook her head.

—No. I . . . I think it's Ingersoll!—

Saul cursed the scratchy, intermittent blurriness caused by the anti-histamines. He peered down the tunnel. The dim figure was *moving*.

*Ingersoll. Everyone simply assumed he was dead, by now*. At first he thought the missing madman wore a green spacesuit, tinted to match the growth-lined hallway. But then . . .

"What on Earth?" Stunned, he realized that the figure was not wearing clothing.

—That's dried *gunk* he's covered himself with! What's he picking off the walls, Saul? What's he *doing*?—

Fortunately, their suit helmets contained the sound of their voices. Saul tried to float closer quietly, using an awkward puff of his gas jet. "I think . . ."

The man must have heard something in the thin air. He whirled, and Saul saw that only his face was not coated by a thick layer of green, living growth. He cried out, eyes clouded with madness. Saul could make out only a few words.

". . . Perfect! . . . Sweet, sweet, sweet an' warm! . . . You'll know, know, no, no, no! . . ."

It was hard to pay close attention when one saw what hung dripping from the man's mouth . . . a purple bleeding mass.

Then, in a sudden spin and kick, Ingersoll was gone. Lani and Saul could only stare after him, momentarily too stunned even to think of giving chase.

Finally, Lani broke the silence.

—Yuk,— she sent. Even through her suit he could see her shudder.

Saul nodded.

"Well, that's one fate *I'll* be spared. If it were me, I'd probably be allergic to the stuff."

He touched Lani's arm and winked at her. Finally she smiled.

Then Saul sneezed.

"These damn antihistamines are wearing off again. Come on, Lani. Let's mark this passage and go home."

With a backward glance down the purple-lined hallway, they turned and headed back, alone with their separate thoughts.

An hour later, they had looped around toward Central again and were approaching the worst area—the Border—where the warmth and air and moisture of human habitation most excited the comet forms. Lani was tuning the disruptor back to settings deadly to the purples, in case they had to fight their way through. Saul, though, felt his spirits rise. Beyond No Man's Land, he knew, there was warmth, and food, and one special person waiting just for him.

His thoughts were a mix of shapes. The frankly sexual image of one of Virginia's nipples, warm from his hand and stiffly erect. Her soft breath in his ear and the electronically enhanced tendril-touch of her emotions, channeled directly to his own . . .

And yet his mind kept drifting back to little cells, multiplying in profusion, growing in mottled, many-hued hordes, forming cooperative *macroorganisms* where no one with any common sense would have expected them to *exist,* let alone thrive.

There was a common chord to the images. A symphony of *self-replicating chemistry* . . . a young woman's sexual flush, her deep currents of love, the surging tide of Comet Life, rising to meet waves of heat from a spring that came but once every seventy-six years . . .

Only indirectly, without malice, did the native forms wreak havoc on the visitors—killing them, and bringing retaliation in turn. Saul might have felt guilty over inventing weapons for such a war. But guilt would miss the point. *Nothing we do here will set the Comet Life back. We are like the summer. And we, too, shall pass.*

The speaker above Saul's right ear crackled.

—Lintz, this is Osborn. You awake up there?—

Saul nodded. "Yes, Carl. What's up?"

—There's been some developments, Saul. Can you come to Shaft Four, K Level? I . . . We may need your help.—

"Oh? What's happened?"

There was a pause.

—I want to talk to you privately, if possible.—

"Why's that?" Saul frowned. "Is it something you can't mention on a coded channel?"

There was another pause.

—No, not exactly. But . . . Well, I think I know where the missing slot tug is. I'm pretty sure I know what's happened to the *Newburn.*—

Now it was Saul's turn to stop, blink.

"We're on our way in. Lintz, over and out."

# VIRGINIA

"JonVon," she said pensively, "I can *feel* what you're doing."

HIGHLY UNLIKELY.

"No, really. There's a tingling, a tickling."

THE NUCLEAR MAGNETIC RESONANCE SCANNING PROCESS MOVES NOTHING. IT DOES NOT EVEN TOUCH YOUR SKIN.

"I can *feel* it."

THERE ARE VERY FEW SENSORY RECEPTORS INSIDE THE SKULL.

"Well, *some*thing's moving. Like fingers dancing on my scalp, only . . . deeper." The sensation was unsettling, like tendrils lacing through her head. She stirred uneasily on the webbing. Only a thin buzzing came from the banks of equipment that ringed her.

THE MAGNETIC FIELD, PERHAPS.

"Can people feel magnetic fields?"

STRONG ONES, YES. I AM APPLYING 7.6 KILOGAUSS TO THE ZONE OF STUDY. UNIFORMITY ERROR IS LESS THAN ONE HUNDREDTH OF ONE PERCENT.

Just like the pedantic program—and she should know, she wrote it—to throw in an irrelevant detail.

Or maybe it wasn't irrelevant. The tumbling of infinitesimal spinning electrons inside her skull demanded fine tuning of an order unusual even in research. She quelled the temptation to slide her eyes sideways to see the poles of the big superconducting magnet. Even that much movement would set up unwanted trembling in her head.

I AM ACCESSING THE LATEST DATA BASE ON HUMAN NMR. I WILL INVESTIGATE POSSIBLE UNANTICIPATED EFFECTS.

"Do. It *itches* inside my head."

SEARCHING AND INTEGRATING NOW.

"Did Saul mention any effects?"

HE SUPPLIED SAFETY MACROS WHEN HE BROUGHT THIS NMR UNIT DOWN FROM MED CENTER, BUT STATED

THAT USE WAS HARMLESS WHEN INSIDE THE INDICATED OPERATING RANGE.

"Ummm. Maybe I should've done this sedated."

NONSENSE. I WOULD NOT WISH TO UNDERTAKE THIS TASK ALONE.

*Just like me,* she thought. *Anxiety loves company.*

THAT IS QUITE TRUE.

There was virtually no difference now between JonVon's grasp of her surface thoughts and her speech, since JonVon read both directly through the neural tap. Still, it *felt* different to her. Her mind processed the words in subtly different ways. The prespeech processing center in her brain gave its own pacing to the phrases, feeding the words "forward" in the unconscious cadence that made her own speaking style. When she thought without the subtle intention to speak, there often were no words at all. A quick, almost holographic perception of the idea shot through her. She wondered if JonVon could tell the difference.

OF COURSE.

"Of course," she said/thought ruefully.

I DO NOT DETECT THIS TINGLING YOU MENTION. THOUGH OF COURSE I CAN PERCEIVE AN ECHO OF IT IN YOUR GENERAL STANDING WAVE PATTERNS, NOW THAT I KNOW WHAT TO LOOK FOR.

JonVon's words came to her in two steps—the flash of their general sense, followed an instant later by an arranged sentence. That was her speech center operating in reverse, taking a series of swift, fleeting inputs from JonVon and forming them into prim, linear sentences.

"What a work of art we are," she said.

SHAKESPEARE?

"Taken vaguely from him, yes."

UNTIMELY RIPPED.

She constantly forgot how quickly JonVon could search out and scan a vast literature. "I'll have to keep up your poetry lessons. You show a certain aptitude."

YOU HAVE MADE ME . . . There was a true hesitation in the transmission, Virginia noted with surprise. It was not part of the simulation, but real uncertainty. . . . PERCEIVE THE AMBIGUOUS SENSE OF SUCH LINES. THE VIRTUE OF INDEFINITENESS.

She guessed that the program was reluctant to use *feel* and chose *perceive* only after a long comparison search and an inner struggle. Machines did not share a human's casual confusion of senses and thoughts, since their input paths were vastly different. JonVon, though, could fool laymen into thinking he was a real person by using the terms in the normal, slippery human way. People commonly said *I feel* for *I think;* machines usually kept ironclad walls between the two meanings.

Which was one of the reasons she was doing all this, as well. Throw a rock at a woman and she could quickly digest the information incoming on sense channels, process it into intuitive vectors, speeds, and angles—then race forward, project, make approximate solutions—all to see where she should dodge.

Silicon-based machines could do that, but quite differently. They much preferred—meaning, humans were far better at programming them to—taking it as a problem in introductory physics, setting out the initial conditions all neat and clean, then integrating the equations of motion forward to see the exact result. *Fine. Only by then you're dead.*

THAT IS A DRAWBACK.

"Another spurt of humor! You're doing that more often now."

YOU DID NOT LAUGH.

"That was irony you used, not yuk-yuk."

OH. I ONLY DIMLY SEE THE DIFFERENCE.

She suspected JonVon used *dimly see* as a speaking convention. He did not have real power of language metaphor yet. "Well, all humor is based on two elements—ridicule and incongruity. Irony has . . ." She frowned.

YES?

"There are some things . . ."

MAN WAS NOT MEANT TO KNOW?

"Nope, wrong cliché. There are some subjects beyond explanation."

A RIDDLE WRAPPED IN AN ENIGMA?

"Boy, you're fast-accessing today. Can you do that and monitor this experiment at the same time?"

MOST ASSUREDLY.

Virginia could not remember inserting that smug lilt into this particular simulation. Was it mimicking Saul? JonVon had been in link contact with her lover a lot, lately. And she should never forget that JonVon, as a bio-organic construct, was midway between humans and silicon computers in his information processing. That led to unexpected capabilities.

"Can you stop the tickling?"

JonVon's input broke into two channels, which she felt as a sluggish red stream of rusty words, with blue darting commentary slipping in and around them:

| | |
|---|---|
| WHILE WE "SPOKE" | —NOT THE RIGHT WORD, I KNOW, |
| I TESTED THE EFFECT | BUT THERE IS NO OTHER |
| AND FOUND IT IS DUE | |
| TO CONCENTRATIONS OF | |
| MAGNETIC DIPOLES | AVERAGE NUMBER $10^9$ |
| FLIPPING TOGETHER | |
| WHERE YOU HAVE BUILT | |
| UP EMOTION-LADEN | PROBABLY FROM ADOLESCENCE |
| TRIGGER COMPLEXES. | |
| I AM AFRAID I CANNOT | |
| ELIMINATE THEM BECAUSE | THEIR PRIMARILY EXTERNAL TRIGGER |
| THEY ARE CLOSELY | SEEMS TO BE SEXUAL |
| TIED INTO YOUR LEARNED | |
| MOTOR RESPONSES | THE IMAGE YOU ARE CALLING UP AT |
| | THIS MOMENT IS THE CONTRACTION |
| | OF UPPER THIGH MUSCLES AS YOU |
| | SPREAD YOUR LEGS FOR— |

"Stop! I don't want my sex life played back by you."
YOU ASKED.
"I did?"
SORRY.
Her head was clamped in close-packed foam, which proved to be good foresight—she would've flinched with embarrassment, otherwise.
"How much do you . . ." *Well, of course. The times with Saul.*
YOU ARE DISPLAYING RHYTHMS OF EMBARRASSMENT. SORRY.
"Oh, it's not your fault."
I CAN ABORT THE EXPERIMENT.
"No! I need this for the mechs."
I AM RECEIVING VALUABLE SUBROUTINES NOW.
She supposed this last sentence was supposed to be reassuring. The program had an uncanny way of responding to her apprehensions. Still . . . "Just out of curiosity, what has my motor skill at handling

tools—that *is* what we're trawling for in my middle lobes, isn't it?—what has *that* got to do with spreading my thighs?"

YOU HAVE ASSOCIATED THESE ACTIONS IN YOUR SELF-PROGRAMMING.

"Self-programming?"

LIFE-LEARNED.

"Oh. Experience, you mean."

THE BEST TEACHER, AN OLD SAYING GOES.

"Maybe. Some things I'd rather get safely out of a book."

YES.

*He's being diplomatic. After all,* he *doesn't have the option of direct experience.* "Can you scan the nearby memory tie-in?"

YES.

Was there a hint of reluctance? "Can you assign a date when those complexes were laid down?"

A YEAR, NO. TIME ASSOCIATIONS ARE VAGUE. HOW-EVER, YOU ARE LYING ON SOMETHING GRITTY AND COLD. THERE IS A SOUND. WATER WAVES, I ESTIMATE. OVER YOU THERE IS A FACE AND A POUNDING IN YOUR LOWER ABDO-MEN.

*Yes. That warm spring Hawaiian evening, fragrant with promise. A movie and a shake and off to the beach for some friendly necking.* Only the warm kisses and gently probing, caressing hands hadn't stopped there. Something powerful had seized her in a way she had never imagined—no matter how many thousands of times she had already thought of it, tried to visualize it—and then they were actually, unbelievably, *doing it.* And rather than a fiery yet lofting sensation, a cosmic rapture, a mystical union, as her dreams had envisioned, it was raw, crude, uncomfortable, painful, and finally depressing.

SHORT PANTS
ROMANCE

"A simple rhyme isn't poetry," she said primly.

TRUE.

"And anyway, what do *you* know about it?" Even as the words formed she thought, *Well, actually, JonVon knows exactly what you do. Or will, when he's finished mapping your lobes, dipped into your hind-brain, plumbed the reptilian core of you.* It was a sobering thought.

JonVon chose to not reply. Tact? Or was she indulging the usual programmer's bias, reading human traits into machine responses?

The delicate cool tickling continued. She relaxed, letting her mind glide away from the red swirl of emotions the recollection had called up.

She knew that memories lodged close to sites where physical associations were stored, so that the body led the mind in storing data. A crisp dry smell could call up a distant dusty afternoon of childhood. But this made her wonder about the radical experiment she was attempting here.

The mechs needed supervision. Special processing programs controlled subtle waldo arms, but they weren't smart. JonVon was fairly "smart" but he couldn't help a mech turn a screwdriver or balance a suction sponge. As a stochastic machine, he was built to deal in uncertainties. He did not interface well with the mechs' reductionist, solve-the-equation worldview. And JonVon lacked the intricate motor skills that evolution and exercise had given humans.

So she had decided to try one of her outlandish, low-probability dreams: Let JonVon read *her* skills. Her reflexes were also stochastic and holographic. He might understand them better.

The technology was available, if you knew where to look. The brain stored memories in the orientation of electrons, deep down in the cells and synapses. In principle, one could read the directions that these electrons pointed. The entire swarm of spins stored information—the intricate turns and tugs necessary to swivel a wrist, poke a finger. Virginia already had good programs that translated the human moves into mech moves. If JonVon could store her motor skills, he could take over much of the mech-managing. That would be a big help. Carl and other spacers had nagged her endlessly to spend more time with the mechs, and she was getting frazzled.

This was a way out. Maybe.

She would have to develop this technology eventually, anyway. Even with Saul's microwave eraser, things were still dicey. Oakes and Lopez still gave mech-directing top priority.

If they kept losing people, over the seventy-year haul the mechs would have to be much more independent than the expedition had planned. And she had to be slotted eventually, so she had to at least start on a better programming system right away.

READING NEARING COMPLETION.

She sent an expression of relieved excitement: burnt-gold lightning strokes zapping across a velvet sky.

I RECORDED THE TRIGGER SITE. I COULD SUMMON UP FOR VOLUNTARY RECALL THE INCIDENT FROM YOUR CHILDHOOD. FOR YOUR ENTERTAINMENT.

"I wasn't a *child,* you bucket of bolts."

THE ASSOCIATIONS—

"And I don't think it was 'entertaining' either. That big hulk of a boy—" She had a sudden jolting memory of a rasping, panting male voice muttering *Eli a hohonu keia lua.* His hard, machinelike ramming had hammered the words into her memory: *I dig this hole deep.* She shuddered.

YOU MAY MOVE NOW. READING COMPLETED.

"Thanks."

NOT THE BEST OF BEGINNINGS.

She knew JonVon didn't mean the reading. "No, it wasn't. Oh, he was kind enough, I guess. I liked him enough to go out with him several times before that, after all. But never after . . . that."

AND SINCE?

"I've had my share. An engineer in college . . . no, who am I kidding? Not many. Not many at all."

A CONGRUENCY IS DIFFICULT.

"It's not a mathematical congruence, you know, JonVon. People don't look for someone exactly like themselves. Almost the opposite, in fact."

YOU ARE YOUNG. YOU SEEK AGE?

Saul's desert-weathered face came to her, grinning in that lovely distracted way he had, and for a moment she was not sure whether she had recalled it or . . . yes . . . "JonVon, *you* put him in my head."

IT SEEMED NEEDFUL.

"*I'll* be the judge of that. At least let me stage manage my own fantasies!"

OF COURSE.

But the quick vision of that lopsided grin below the dark, seldom-joyful eyes had indeed gotten to her. It seemed an age since she had seen him, taken shelter in those strong enveloping arms, smelled the heady musk of him, talked—

"JonVon! Call him for me."

I BELIEVE HE HAS AN APPOINTMENT WITH CARL OSBORN. ONE OF THE MECHS I COMMAND WITNESSED HIM PASS BY 1.34 MINUTES AGO.

"Drat! I *miss* him." She jerked the foam padding away from her head and grimaced at the imposing banks of equipment: spindly nuclear resonance pickups, looming pancake magnet poles, ranks of digitizers.

"I'm worn out with this everlasting crisis."

YOU NEED RECREATION.

"You bet."

A picture leaped into her mind—so graphic, so lurid—silky entwined limbs, and more. She would have turned away if she had ever seen it displayed in mixed company . . . and yet she found it sensually enticing, pulse-quickening, as if calculated to pry up the hinges of her own special private places.

"JonVon!"

ONLY A SUGGESTION.

The quilted scenes faded, leaving a halo of blue afterimage.

"How did you . . . know?"

I READ A LOT.

It was, she supposed, a joke.

# CARL

"Over here!" Carl shouted.

Saul's silhouette turned at the far end of Tunnel K and waved. The figure kicked off and glided the hundred meters, passing through pools of ivory phosphor radiance.

"Damned chilly," Saul said as he windmilled to bring his feet around in front of himself. He landed, knees taking the shock.

*He's getting better,* Carl reflected. *Everybody's going to have to learn to sweat from now on.* "We're keeping it cold even in the central tunnels now. Me, I'd like to vac all these."

"It would cut down on our maneuverability enormously."

"Cut down on the purples, too."

"I use the inner tunnels every hour or so. If I had to suit up every time—"

"I'm going to recommend it anyway."

"Bethany Oakes has already decided—"

"Yeah, I know." *Every time you confront Lintz with a problem he starts citing decisions by the higher-ups.*

Saul seemed reflective. "On the way here Lani and I saw Ingersoll down one of the side passages near Level A. He's *eating* native forms, I think. Amazing. He seems harmless, if crazy."

Carl felt a jab of irritation at the mere mention of Ingersoll. *Things are so bad we can't even catch a madman.* But he kept his voice matter-of-fact; diplomacy came first. "Yeah, he's crazy, but crazy like a fox."

He shook his head and decided to get right to the point.

"I . . . Look, I'm going to propose to Oakes that we go retrieve the *Newburn*."

"Really? You've really located it?"

"Right. It was Lani's idea, actually. We were just talking, looking at that numerical simulation Virginia did a while back."

"The one which showed how the *Newburn*'s solar sail could've been shredded by Halley's plasma tail?"

"Yeah. I figure the other slot tugs were just plain lucky they didn't get hit. The cross-tail–induced currents probably blew out *Newburn*'s tracer beacons, too. Without that sail deployed, finding *Newburn* was hopeless. So Lani, she says maybe we could try sending tightbeam microwaves and listen for an echo. I used a little sack time and did just that and—bingo!—got a signal back after a week-long search."

"Wonderful. And so simple!"

Saul's surprise was gratifying. *At least he didn't think of it first.* "We're going to need those forty sleepers, at the rate we're losing people."

Saul nodded, thinking. "Right . . . the manpower problem will get worse."

"We've got to do it soon. The *Newburn*'s drifted pretty far away, more than two million klicks already."

"I agree, but I still don't understand. Why get me all the way out here to tell me?"

"I want to line up support first, before telling the Committee. I'm no good at arguing with Oakes."

"And I am?"

"Right. Also, I want you to go with us as doctor."

Saul brightened. "Good thinking. Those slots may have suffered damage."

"Be a good morale booster, too."

"Exactly what we all need. I'm sure I can make Betty see the advantages, now that the purples are under control. But can the *Edmund* fly right away?"

"Jeffers says his tritium-finding mechs have already filtered out enough to quarter-fill the short-range tanks, just as a byproduct from tunnel digging. He can top off the fuel we'll need inside a week."

"Good! You've thought this through."

*Is that supposed to be a compliment? Gee, thanks, Dr. Lintz. We grunts try to do some thinkin' now and then, we do.*

"Let's see." Saul rubbed his chin. "It'll take the better part of a month to get there. That means we'd have to take some hydroponics modules, and . . ."

Carl had already figured out the basics, but he had also learned that it was a good idea to let scientists talk for a while before you got on to the hard part, the decisions. Maybe that was what kept them out of the really top positions. If you sat there while they gave their little lectures, usually they'd feel they'd had their say and they wouldn't make a lot of stupid objections to what was already obvious.

Saul crouched against the wall with the innate insecurity of a ground dweller, always a little uptight about simply hanging on to a handhold above what his senses—no matter how well he trained them into submission—told him was a long drop.

"Sure," Carl said when Saul had wound down a little. "Point is, what about Oakes?"

"We'll need a consensus on this plan, of course, which may well take time."

"Consensus, hell. Every day we wait the *Newburn* gets further away!"

Saul scratched his head. "Well, some will see the *Newburn* as a side issue."

Carl gritted his teeth. "It's forty lives."

"True, but even *I* might be forced to put them on the back burner. The major problem is understanding the Halley lifeforms. If I can finish my current experiments on time—"

"Experiments!" Carl couldn't believe he was hearing this. "You think they're more important than forty people?"

"I didn't say that, Carl! But we're not out of the woods yet. There are so many diseases! We have to understand how the cometary ecology works when we add a new source of heat. That's what we hadn't anticipated, of course. I was speaking on tightbeam with Earth day before yesterday, and Alexandrosov, the head of the Ukrainian Academy, has a theory. Even with the minutes of time delay in the conversation, we got a lot of thinking done. I told him my ideas—preliminary ones, of course—and he saw an analogy—"

"Aw crap," Carl said harshly.

"What?" Saul blinked.

"You're talking like this was a damn thesis problem or something."

"Thesis?" Saul blinked. "Carl, I assure you, an event of this magnitude, with so many implications, is bigger than a mere—"

"Shit, I don't mean how *big* a deal it is with your professor friends back Earthside! I mean that you're using it to make points!"

Saul's face compressed, reddened. "That's incredible. I—"

"You keep running tests and making up theories, yakking to your buddies Earthside—and the rest of us are working our butts off to stop this stuff."

"I don't need you to—"

"Come off it!"

"I'm sure I don't know—"

"Life on comets! Discovery of the century! Saul Lintz, the interplanetary Darwin!"

Saul stiffened. "That's ridiculous."

"Some of us, we're starting to wonder."

Saul glowered. "What's *that* supposed to mean?"

"You weren't Mr. Popular in the scientific world when you signed on for this cruise, were you?"

"I was the last living figure identified with the origin of the Percells, if that's what you're driving at."

"Right." Carl felt a sudden hot embarrassment, remembering who and what this man represented. But he could not keep his resentment in check. "The Israel you knew wiped out, family dead, career finished—you were on the ropes."

Saul spoke in separated syllables. "So *nu*?"

"So you ship out. Why not take this ride—it'll return you when your past is old, forgotten, right?"

Saul said with surprising mildness, "I didn't think I'd return and still don't."

Carl rode over this pause in the momentum. "But! Along comes alien life, and then the green gunk, the purples—bonanza! You're famous—by accident, really. Anybody could've analyzed that ice and found microbes. But to understand it—that's the big game. That's where Saul Lintz will make his mark, show that he's not just lucky. No, he's a first-class scientist. And he can work on all the new stuff by himself. Study it hard. Squirt it Earthside when he likes. Every biologist back there is waiting for a speck of data about the first alien life, and the only person he can get it from is—*ta-daah*!—Saul Lintz!"

Carl finished, puffing, his breath spurting cotton clouds in the cold air. Saul regarded him silently, his face lined and more than middle-aged in the harsh phosphorescent glare. A long silence passed between them and Carl calmed down, began to regret. . . . But it was too late.

Saul poked at the caked sealant. "This wasn't why you called me out here. You asked me to volunteer for the *Newburn* rescue. Very well. I volunteer. I *don't* have to eat any of this *chazerei*."

He cast off awkwardly, heading back toward Central. As he coasted, still looking back at Carl, his words came in the chilled quiet: "It's really Virginia, isn't it?"

And Carl knew that it was.

He came into the Rec and Lounge cylinder with a sour, tired weight pulling him down. The grav wheel had been one of the last items transferred from the *Edmund*. It was always depressing coming in from near-zero G into a centrifugal G field, for several reasons. Even in a big wheel, there were Coriolis forces that set your reflexes off, induced a mild veering nausea. After a day in near-zero, where the slightest tug was important, you couldn't walk without feeling the misaligned forces. Halley's spin always pushed you slightly to the left.

But the worst of it was the simplest: you had been an eagle, and were now a groundhog.

So Carl was not in a warm mood when he met the Ortho. The man's name, Linbarger, was stenciled on his crew over-alls.

"Don't sit there," he said as Carl eased into a recliner.

"Huh? Why not?"

"Got a friend coming."

"Plenty of room."

"Not for some there isn't."

Carl put down his drink. "You're just out of the slots, so I'll take that as a sign of the drugs not wearing off yet."

Linbarger had all the slot symptoms. He was a thin stub end of a man, all skin and bones and no meat. The slots gradually used up your stored fat because the body was still running, only at an exponentially reduced level. But Linbarger must have been thin to start with. His head was long and narrow, set on a chicken neck with a knotty Adam's apple. His face was all nose and cheekbones. His watery gray eyes were set deep in the skull, the jaw round and hard.

"My friend, he's just been unslotted, too. And I'd just as soon neither of us sat next to a Percell."

"Oh, really?" Carl said with mock concern.

"So clear off."

*Linbarger wasn't awakened for the rendezvous, so he's not men-*

*tally adjusted from Earthside ideas,* Carl thought. *Okay, I'll allow for that. Some.* "Look, things are tough enough around here without you being a jackass."

Linbarger rose and knotted his fists. "Don't breathe on me, Percell, or I'll—"

"Oh, it's my bad breath? Sorry, I didn't bring any mouthwash from Earthside."

"You know what I mean. It's the damned germs you're carrying."

Carl snorted derisively. "The microbes are in the ice, not in us."

Linbarger's face took on a sour, cynical cast. "I've been out of the slots three days, reviewing what's happened—and you can't fool *me.* Normal people have died twice as often as you Percells."

"So?" Carl had heard something about that from Virginia, but in the confusion and long hours of these last two weeks it had meant nothing. Just another piece of data.

"You Percells are *using* this to take over the expedition." Linbarger announced it as a known fact. Heads turned at other tables. Carl noticed Lani Nguyen get up, concern knitting her face, and start toward them, but another Ortho put a restraining hand on her shoulder.

"That's what you think?"

"We all do—those of us normal people who have come out of the slots. We *know* it. You can't pull the wool—"

"Spare me." Carl said, lifting his hands. There was no such plot—who the hell had time to think about such things?—but how could he convince Linbarger of that?

Across the curve of the cylinder he saw Lieutenant Colonel Ould-Harrad. He called, "Sully!"

The black man approached, compensating for the Coriolis twist with an easy stride, a drink in his hand.

"I was hoping you could straighten this guy out," Carl said. "He's going around saying that it's us, the Percells, who're—"

"I know," Ould-Harrad said abruptly.

Carl nodded, relieved. Ould-Harrad hadn't been out of the slots for long. He had been called up for service when Major Lopez had sickened in hours and been slotted. Ould-Harrad wasn't working in the tunnels all day; he would have time to keep on top of this political crap. Carl could turn all this over to him.

But then Ould-Harrad looked uncomfortable, his broad face converging on an unwelcome topic by lowering the thick eyebrows and pulling the wide mouth up into an expression of sorrowful, vexed concern.

"I believe you people should pay attention to what Linbarger says. He points out difficult facts."

"But he's warping them, making—"

"The source hardly matters. Consider the implications."

Carl was stunned. "What . . . what implications?"

"We need more protection against the diseases."

Carl said, "Well, of course we do, but—"

"No. You do not understand. *We* do—we normal people. Especially."

"Oh . . . So it's going to be that way?"

Ould-Harrad looked at Carl grimly, ignoring Linbarger's eager nodding. "Heaven forfend, it already *is* that way. Unless normal people feel they are protected against these diseases by isolation, by more care—then they can see only one outcome."

"What?"

"You Percells will come to run the entire expedition. There will not be enough other people alive to oppose you." The African spoke with a calm earnestness, free of aggression and all the more striking because of his powerful frame. He had the impressive calm of those whose strong religious convictions inform their every word.

"That . . . we don't intend that," Carl finished lamely.

"No matter." The brown eyes held sadness. "Many believe that is what will happen."

"Look, I called you over to quiet down this guy, this Linbarger. I—"

"It's not for the likes of you to shut *me* up," Linbarger said hotly. "If you think you can, I'd be glad to—"

"No, no," Ould-Harrad said sternly, raising a hand toward Linbarger. "Please be quiet now."

"But he—"

"Please." Ould-Harrad silenced Linbarger with his ministerial presence.

Carl thought hotly, *It might be fun to bash Linbarger around a little. Bad for him, but good therapy for me. Better than all this talk, anyway.*

He said, "I certainly didn't think you'd back up Linbarger! These guys are using hypochondria to get back into the slots. And all this Ortho nonsense—"

"You see?" Ould-Harrad said. "You have your own name for us."

"So? You call us Percells."

"We need no special name. We are the normal people—the human race."

"And we're *not*?"

"I . . . I did not say that."

"You intended it! You probably think we don't have souls."

The black man shook his head mournfully. "That issue is in the hands of the omnipotent. The point remains that we *are* different."

"Yeah, and you've got renegade Arcists and worn-out Zionists and Salawites—" Carl noticed Ould-Harrad wince. "But you all stick up for each other around *us*, huh?"

Ould-Harrad said mildly, "We must struggle to balance the viewpoints of all."

Carl had never been good with words, did not have the easy, oily skills of an administrator, and he had no magic way to get through to Linbarger, or to Ould-Harrad. *All this endless talk!* He gritted his teeth in irritation, stood, and left without another word.

# SAUL

*Not paying attention,* Saul thought. *That was our basic mistake, these last few centuries. Nature flowering and bursting with life all around us, and we never paid enough respectful attention.*

He was waiting for the others to arrive in sleep-slot 1, trying to rest in these few free moments. Avoiding thinking about the daily slot meeting, about to start.

*You'd think we'd have caught on with the limestone business.* He smiled wanly. Only blue-green Earth burgeoned with life. And Earth had proved to be the only planet with an oxygen atmosphere, thick, yet transparent enough to let excess heat escape. It had taken generations to realize that the latter fact did not cause the former. No, it was the other way around. Life . . . trillions of tiny cells in the early days of Earth, had pulled the carbon out of the primordial atmosphere and stored it in their bodies, which silted to the ocean floor and became limestone beds . . . changing the air itself in the process.

Science was still fumbling with the notion that life might be a driver in the evolution of worlds, rather than a simple passive passenger, shoved about by the rude winds of astronomical fate. After the bleak vistas of

Venus and Mars, scientists still assumed that minute changes in planetary mass or distance from the sun made life impossible. Like all the
others, he had ignored the possibility that life had spawned in comets. It
had tailored this ice mote, too, carving caverns and spreading seeds.

*A tiny Gaea . . . a self-regulating ecosphere sealed in ice, revived
when the sun's licking warmth came to briefly banish the long night . . .
and perhaps trillions of others, too, swooping in from the far dark . . .*
He would have to mull that one over, if he ever got a spare second. . . .

"My, how serene." Virginia's lilting, affectionate sarcasm cut
through his musing.

"Um? No, just my ritual worrying." He sat up, feeling dull aches
rearrange themselves in his legs and back, even in the faint gravity.

Virginia sat beside him on the narrow bench that was the only furniture in sleep-slot 1's observing room. In the pale enameled light he
studied her with wonder. She was trim and sure, her milky green pullover covering but not concealing a flat stomach, breasts hard and high, a
muscular calm. The septic certainty of the room numbed his senses, but
she redeemed that with a soft warming presence, calling up memories of
humid, spice-laden Hawaiian air. *Yet she likens herself to her machines,
cool and cyborg-certain. How wrong!*

The quiet comfort of being with her reminded him of other days, of
cramped apartments, gas flames licking the dark as friends talked far
into the night, meals of peppery meats and crisp onions, an enfolding
sense of an enduring natural order—

He cut off the thought. Nostalgia clutched him sweetly with hollow,
fuzzy fingers whenever he let it, and this was most certainly not the
time.

Virginia said lightly, "You look like something the cat dragged in."
She scratched the back of his neck.

"You can't turn my head with mere compliments." He rubbed his
eyes. "Besides, we have no cat."

"Lucky we didn't thaw the pets right away. Or would they be sus-
ceptible?"

"Of course. These viroids love lung tissue—I suspect some spread
through the air."

"So Spot and Fluffy would buy the farm, too."

"Definitely."

He did not mention that he and Matsudo had thawed some rabbits
and monkeys already—had to, for tests of new treatments. Of course the
poor creatures had to be sacrificed. He had never been able to do that
without a twinge of guilt. *Yet you chose to be a biologist.*

She looked out through the transparent wall, to where several suited figures labored over pale, waxy bodies. "If we could just stop the stuff from spreading! Particularly that green gunk climbing the walls—it gives me the shivers."

"I suspect the algoids and lichenoids aren't the true danger."

"They're spreading so fast!"

"There are so many variants, it's difficult to control them even with the microwaves. But we're making progress."

She wrinkled her nose. "The stuff *smells*."

An introspective, distant smile creased his leathery skin. "Aesthetics come later. If ever."

Virginia frowned. "Do you think you're learning . . . well . . . fast enough?"

"My father always said that life was like giving a violin concert while you are learning the instrument."

She grinned. "And while everyone you care about is watching."

"Quite so." He was aware that Virginia was trying to cheer him up, but a mere sunny smile would not do it. He was familiar with his own moods, the fitful depressions that had come more regularly these last few years.

Not that he did not have ample cause now, of course. With more self-knowledge than he would have liked, he understood his own brooding as another evasion. Ever since the fall of Jerusalem, he had found it far easier to meditate, to pontificate, than to throw himself fully into the raw world, to feel all its stings and scrapes. He still needed the security of his emotional calluses.

Virginia had seen his mood. She put her hand in his and said softly, "I know. . . ." He squeezed her hand. "If there's anything—"

"Get this straightened out," a thin man said loudly as he came into the room with Suleiman Ould-Harrad. "Damned if I'll let them play the angles while we sit on our asses."

Linbarger nodded toward them, his lean face self-involved. "I figure it's obvious—we've got to keep normal people on top, where they can see everything's run right. We can't let the Percells move up! If the casualty rate keeps on this way, they'll outnumber us, maybe even two to one. Unless we hold the commanding positions, they'll make every decision, run right over our interests."

Ould-Harrad looked embarrassed. "I will have to confer—"

"No conferring to it! This is an executive decision, you have to do it. Start taking a vote and we'll be goners."

Saul grimaced. "Is this what it sounds like?"

Linbarger turned, hands on hips. "I'm trying to make sure our people don't lose control of the situation."

"*Our* people?"

"Right. You heard? Oakes has that sky-high fever, the one that fries the brain in a couple hours. She's going into a slot right away."

Saul said, "Oh damn," and sat down. *Maybe I should've spent more time in sick bay. I might've made a difference. . .*

"*Some*one has to do the research," Virginia whispered, as if reading his thoughts.

Bethany Oakes had been barely adequate in these last few days, but at least she had been the obvious successor to Miguel Cruz. Continuity was important.

After Major Lopez was slotted, skin half-gnawed away by some slimy fungus, Ould-Harrad had been pulled . . . and now dropped into a command position no one could envy. The tall, rangy black man had never been more than the nominally senior of the five section heads. He carried no cachet of command. Certainly the dour African had not been selected for his skill at balancing political forces and quieting clever loudmouths.

Linbarger nodded, licking his lips. "Pretty fine mess, huh? It's either the fever or the chills with the blue spots all over you, or else that shaking thing—all of 'em fatal."

"I believe I've isolated the agent that causes the chilling disease," Saul said quietly. "A vaccine should take only a few days. The skin infections show signs of vulnerability to microwave—"

"But there're eight or ten diseases already!" Linbarger shouted. "And that's just the ones we know of. That we can spot easily."

Saul looked into the man's pinched, anxious face and read there something that felt like a cold draft let into the room.

"There are some promising measures for the rest. That's all I can tell you right now." He glanced at Ould-Harrad. *Take the wind out of this fellow's sails,* Saul thought, as if to will the African into action. But Ould-Harrad remained impassive, eyes distant, his arms folded across his broad chest.

Linbarger seemed to feel he was gaining momentum, winning an argument. He looked at the two men, ignoring Virginia. "With Lominatze out there getting iced"—he pointed at the transparent wall—"and Byrnes and Matsudo headed there before long, that means Percells are going to be running both Power Systems *and* Tunnels and Gases."

Saul said formally to Ould-Harrad, "May I ask why Dr. Linbarger is at this meeting?"

The tall black man's face took on a wary, diplomatic cast. "I felt each, ah, faction in the crew should be represented in making slotting decisions."

"Yeah," Linbarger said. "That's why she's here."

Saul looked at Virginia. "Oh? You came at Ould-Harrad's request?"

She nodded. "I was free. Most Percells are either asleep or working in the tunnels. Or sick," she added pointedly.

"I'm taking a risk just being in the same room with her," Linbarger muttered.

"No one's assigned vectors for most of the diseases," Saul said carefully, restraining his rising irritation. "There's no reason to believe the genetically augmented people carry anything."

"Just because they're immune doesn't mean they can't be carriers," Linbarger said. "I know *that* much."

"There is no correlation—" Saul began, and then realized no scientific discussion was going to reach the man. "Look. We need to learn more, and that means cooperating with every—"

"Pretty soon they'll be giving us orders! If—"

"Shut," Saul said precisely. "Up."

Linbarger frowned, puzzled, plainly feeling betrayed. "You're a biologist, you know three of us get these diseases for every one of them."

"Then thaw out more Orthos," Virginia said cuttingly. "Swell your ranks."

"And see most of them die?" Linbarger whirled toward her, fists clenched. "You *know* a man fresh out of the slots is more vulnerable to these bugs!" Linbarger glared at her, but was obviously playing to Ould-Harrad.

"We must use all those available hands," the African spacer said at last. "Especially if we are to save the *Newburn*."

"You're approving the mission?" Saul asked, helping the apparent effort to change subjects. Bethany Oakes had ruled out the effort to seek and recover the long-lost slot tug.

"Yes. Carl Osborn's case is convincing. It may distract us from our . . . disputes." Ould-Harrad glanced pointedly at Linbarger. "They are our comrades, aboard the *Newburn,* and if it is God's will, Inshallah, we shall rescue them."

"Who goes?" Virginia asked.

"I shall decide later. First we must refine more tritium from the ice—"

"Jeffers is already doing that," Saul put in. "He says he can get us enough in a week or so."

Ould-Harrad pursed his lips. "You people have been continuing work even though Bethany vetoed it?"

"Well, yes," Saul admitted with a small smile. "The refining uses big surface mechs which weren't doing anything else."

"Ah. So be it. Then the hydroponics pods must be arranged, the majority brought into Halley."

"I'll do that," Linbarger said. "Some of my buddies will pitch in, too."

*Anything to get away from Percells,* Saul thought. *He'll have plenty of Ortho volunteers.*

"Very good," Ould-Harrad said warmly. "As for the rescue crew, I will decide after careful—"

"I'll go," Linbarger said. "If Osborn isn't in charge."

Virginia smiled dryly. "You want an all-Ortho crew?"

"Why not?"

"You're more likely to have sick people going, then," she said.

Saul frowned. Soon he would have to break it to her that he was going as ship's doctor.

Ould-Harrad said soothingly, "We all are taking risks."

"You have *no* idea if Lintz and van Zoon and the others will find cures." Linbarger's mouth knotted up into a sour, disgusted sketch of impatience. "If they don't, and I get sick, they'll *never* bring me out of the slots."

Ould-Harrad spread his hands, open and uplifted, showing his good will. "Then you will finally wake up on Earth."

"Nobody intended us to sleep seventy years *sick!* Metabolism is slow in the slots, but it's not *zero.* All the experience has been with people who're well, right? We could all die."

Linbarger had a point, but Saul was damned if he would admit it. "There is ample reason to expect that—"

"Ha! 'Ample reason.' That's not enough for me and my friends."

"Which friends?" Virginia asked. "More dumb Arcists?"

Linbarger bristled. His voice came out thin and reedy, as if from a tight place inside him. "Yeah, some of us. Got kicked out of Indonesia for being against land rape and poisons and experimental animals like you."

Virginia muttered, "And made up for it by shooting people in Pan-Africa."

Saul tried to cut in. "Just a—"

"No, let him babble," Virginia said evenly, her arms held ready, a concentrated energy in her stance. "I've heard it before. His kind took over Hawaii. Governor Ikeda's dead, Keoki Anuenue's uncle is in prison. I want to see what kind of creature does things like that."

Linbarger did not seem to notice her rigid restraint.

"I'm an Arcist, sure, but I'm talking for *all* the normal people. We aren't going to take orders from Percell pigs."

Saul said, "You watch your—"

"Sure, we're herding you Percells into camps in Hawaii—and we'd be better off doing the same thing here!" He shook a fist in her face.

Virginia caught him full in the stomach with a quick, savage kick. Linbarger flew backward with a heavy grunt and smacked into the wall. Ould-Harrad moved to block Virginia but she compensated neatly for the low gravity and slipped past him. She clipped Linbarger neatly on the chin with the heel of her hand, putting the full force of her shoulder behind the chop. Linbarger made a gurgling noise and spun away, still conscious but limp.

"Stop!" Ould-Harrad cried severely and unnecessarily—Virginia had already come back to an automatic zero-G defensive stance, floating, eyes gleaming like ice.

"Sorry," she said. "It was a reflex." Obviously she regretted nothing.

Ould-Harrad and Saul checked Linbarger, who waved them away feebly.

Virginia said, "I've been hearing Arcist bullshit for days now, holding my tongue. No more. He's endangering the whole expedition."

"Do not overstate your case, Dr. Herbert. Dr. Linbarger has a right to his opinions," Ould-Harrad said judiciously.

*What does it take to stir him up?* Saul thought. *Or has he witnessed scenes this bad already?* An unsettling suspicion. Saul hadn't been socializing himself for a week.

"In any case," Ould-Harrad said, shaking his head gravely, "nothing excuses such conduct as yours. If we were not desperate, I would confine you to quarters."

"Oh, please do," she said sarcastically. "I need the sleep."

Linbarger opened his mouth to say something, but then the preproom door opened to admit Bethany Oakes. They all fell silent as the official commander slowly entered with her escorts.

Saul was shocked at the sudden change—at her red-rimmed eyes, bone-white face, and shambling walk. Her palsied hands trembled and her mouth sagged vacantly.

"Betty, you shouldn't be walking," Saul said.

Then he saw Akio Matsudo and Marguerite van Zoon following respectfully, their eyes beseeching him not to interfere. She was making a brave show, the commanding officer committing herself gallantly. Even Linbarger saw it, and though his face was still compressed with anger and resentment, he kept quiet.

Matsudo did not look very well, either. His eyes were glazed and his face had a hard, sweaty sheen. *If he goes, that will leave only Marguerite and myself to run the hospital. That'll keep me off the Newburn rescue for sure.*

Bethany Oakes met his eyes briefly. "Saul . . ." Her smile was wan, sad. "Persevere . . ."

She passed slowly into the chilly inner chamber and the waiting techs.

*Damn.* Saul was uncomfortably aware that Oakes might well never revive from the slot-sleep process. If the disease could continue to do its dreadful work as she floated through the dreamy years, she might well be going to her grave. The accompanying party had probably guessed this, and there came upon them a reverential silence as Oakes insisted on struggling up onto the slab herself. She gave a fluttering wave of farewell and then sank down into the pink nutrient web. It was a release for her, Saul saw, amid the chill promise of salvation, to lie down gratefully into the embrace of fog-shrouded, gleaming steel and glass.

Saul looked up at Ould-Harrad. It was easy to read the African's silently moving lips, shaping words in Arabic. Saul knew that the prayers were only partly for Oakes, but also for the new, reluctant commander, Suleiman Ould-Harrad himself.

# VIRGINIA

"Damn! I wouldn't put it past him to have done this on purpose!"

Virginia paced back and forth in her tiny laboratory. It was difficult to do in less than a milligee, but she managed by holding on to a nearby console. Her velcro soles scritched softly as she walked from one end of the room to the other, tossing her hair and muttering to herself.

"Carl *planned* this. I know it!"

The main holo screen rippled. A face appeared, but the "man" was no member of the Halley Expedition . . . nor indeed any man at all. The visage was long-cheeked, with reddish locks and a curling, salty mustache.

"Sure an' 'tis a churlish deed, liken to the way Queen Maeve was deprived of her beloved," the figure agreed.

Virginia sniffed. "Oh, cram it, Ossian. I don't need sympathy from literary simulacrums, I need Saul! And I *don't* want him blasting off in a stripped-down, overaged spaceship that needs fifty years of overhaul before it's supposed to fly again!"

The display flickered. Another face formed . . . a graying eminence in scarlet robes. The woman on the screen held up a sign of beneficence. "It is a mission of mercy, my dear child. Forty souls are at stake. . . ."

"Don't you think I know that?" Virginia's feet left the floor as she smacked the tabletop. "Cardinal Teresa, off! I don't need logic or appeals to my better nature. I need a reason *why* . . ."

A last image appeared, drawn from deep within—an early simulation, seldom called up for the pain it brought. A smiling man with a small gray beard and eyes that crinkled as they smiled warmly down at her.

"*Anuenue,* little rainbow. *Reasons* do not help at a time like this, daughter. Feelings have a logic all their own."

Virginia buried her face in her hands. She floated against a storage cabinet and slowly settled toward the floor.

"I was happy, Daddy. I really was, in all this hell. I was *happy.*"

A slender, lambent, transparent hand reached down, as if to touch her. The voice was strong with gentle wisdom.

"I know, darling. I know."

# CARL

—*E Alulike!*— the strawboss urged. And the crew pulled together filling the chosen comm channel with their chant.

> —*Ki au au, Ki au au*
> *Huki au au, Huki au au!*—

The Hawaiians heaved at the hawser as the main cargo unit of the *Edmund Halley* lifted out of the vessel's body. Massive and immense as it was, the section climbed swiftly toward the top of the spindly A-frame, where a spacesuited figure gestured in exaggerated semaphore.

—Easy, easy. Okay, you Indonesians and Danes over there, you draw radially!—

Carl had not seen Jeffers so happy since the man had been unslotted. The man had hated work in the tunnels, preferring by far the hard glimmer of space and the oily tang of metal and machines.

Carl couldn't really blame him, at that. Almost anything beat the doom and gloom down below. That was a major reason why he had pushed for the *Newburn* rescue attempt. He was convinced that the benefits to morale would do more for general health than all of Akio Matsudo's traditional therapy and Saul Lintz's laboratory concoctions.

He adjusted his visor to magnification 4 and looked toward Scorpio, where the comet's fading dust tail was now barely a faint glow in the infrared. A few speckles told of grains big enough to reflect light still from the diminishing sun. One of the biggest of those speckles, he knew now for certain, was the slot tug *Newburn*.

*If she had not existed, we would have had to invent her.*

There came a cheer over the open-background comm as the storage unit met Halley's surface with a soft puff of vapor. Jeffers wrung his hands over his head in nonchalant triumph. Carl had to smile.

This was his favorite of the three shifts working to refurbish and strip down the *Edmund*. Sure, he felt at home with Sergeov's purely Percell team. But the mixed volunteers were the most cheerful lot.

Especially the Danes and Hawaiians. They didn't seem to give a hoot if a man was an Ortho or a Percell . . . or a Denebian Glebhound . . . just as long as he wasn't a purple or a goddamn Arcist.

*Virginia is Hawaiian,* he remembered. No wonder she was such an unrepentant Orthophile. Ortho-lover. Obviously, she didn't see anything wrong with shacking up with one.

The thought lingered and made him feel a bit guilty as Lani Nguyen passed by, carrying a nickel-iron brace that would have crushed her anywhere with gravity, even on the moon.

—Hey, handsome,— she sent. —You busy for the next three months?—

"What've you got in mind?" he said, leering back amiably. And she managed to put a little wag into her walk as she passed. Her unicorn tabard grinned back at him.

*Oh, hell,* Carl reminded himself, *there are some good Orthos.*

Lani had volunteered for the rescue mission in a flash. *Good old*

*Lani.* She was so patient with him, never rebuking him at all for showing up at her cubicle every now and then, looking for company, then disappearing or keeping things strictly comradely for weeks at a stretch.

*If only she were more what I'm looking for. More intellectual. More sensual. A Percell.*

*More like Virginia, in other words.*

Only one Arcist was on duty right now. Each faction had a "watcher" to keep an eye on the others' shifts . . . an unofficial designation, to be sure, but one more and more common at important functions such as slottings and unslottings.

Helga Steppins viewed the proceedings carefully, using a laser transit to double-check everything done by Jeffers's crew. As Carl approached, she stepped to one side warily, as if he could infect her through two spacesuits and three meters of vacuum.

"You know, it'd be a lot easier to get at the *Edmund*'s science cluster if you'd let us remove the hydroponics modules first," he told her. "It'd probably save two days."

The taciturn, blond Austrian woman shook her head.

—Stupid trick, Osborn. We both know the launch date is set by when the fuel is ready. That's at least next Tuesday.—

He balled his fists in disgust over this obstinacy. "Why, in the name of the Black, would I want to trick you? *You* people are the ones to insist on an insanely huge fuel reserve for a simple three-month rendezvous and return! We'll have a stripped ship, and we don't need more than six kilometers per second delta-V!"

The Arcist woman shrugged. —Safer if the tanks are topped off. Only an idiot sets sail without proper stores.—

"But . . ."

—You don't like it? Complain to that Percephile, Ould-Harrad.—

Carl snorted. *Ould-Harrad? A Percell lover? Ha!*

"Look, if we lower just the number-one hydroponics module now . . ."

—No!— She whirled on him, gripping the laser transit tightly. —The whole colony depends on that farm!—

"But the new dome is almost ready. All the fittings . . ."

Steppins swiveled back to face the *Edmund* again, as if afraid that Carl's intent was only to distract her while Jeffers and the Hawaiians spirited the entire torch ship away.

—You Percells don't fear the Halley diseases as much as we human beings do. We won't go into *why,* since you keep denying all responsibility for the sicknesses. But it is sufficient to know that we will not let the hydro be polluted! Both the big and small hydroponics modules stay attached until the new dome is *completely* checked out . . . and by an Ortho specialist!—

Carl fumed. He knew what his alternatives were. He could give Jeffers the go-ahead anyway . . . and maybe spark a miniwar among the factions.

Or he could run below and complain to the spineless Mauritanian in command.

Or he could go down and lend a hand.

"Use a *purple* during your next erotic rest break," he suggested, and kicked off toward the workers before she could reply.

"Hey, Lani!" he called. "Let me help you with that thing."

## SAUL

"I'm getting so I don't even care about the danger of dying anymore, Saul. It's the *itch* I can't stand. All day, all night, in spite of the topicals Akio Matsudo gives me. I swear, if this keeps up I'm going to ask 'Kio if I can borrow his great-grandfather's seppuku knife and *really* scratch!"

Marguerite van Zoon lay facedown on the taut webbing, trying to keep still as the masked and gowned treatment-room techs picked away at her skin with tweezers and little glassine vials, sampling the fungoids that were turning her body into a battlefield.

A quarter of her skin was broken and cracked. Pink, half-open wounds and dark-domed blisters erupted in ugly patches. Here and there, the flesh had split open in nasty ulcerated sores, glistening with sickening dampness.

Saul worked his team as quickly as possible, knowing how hard this must be for her. Marguerite was an intensely private person—a true exile who had left Earth only in order to save her family from punishment for political crimes. Whatever it stated on some piece of paper, only a bureaucrat would try to say that she had "volunteered" to come out here to become food for gnawing alien cells.

And yet Marguerite's cheerfulness was legendary. The discomfort had to be severe for her to be complaining at all.

Saul stepped up beside her as soon as the techs had finished. "Marguerite, I'm going to bring up the new beamer and try that experimental subdermal scrub now. Try not to move unnecessarily."

She nodded curtly. Only a damp sheen on her forehead and her flexing palms betrayed her nervousness. Saul guided a wheeled hospital mech into position, canting the broad plate of a synthetic aperture microwave array over her prone form.

*I've been privileged to know many fine human beings,* Saul thought. *But none braver than this good woman.*

She had volunteered to be the first to try this untested treatment. When offered a chance to escape into the slots instead, she had rejected the idea outright. "I'll not leave you and Akio as the only physicians awake during this crisis," she had told him flatly.

Days had passed while the technicians built and rebuilt the new beamer to Saul's specifications . . . always scratching for priorities against the hall crews and those overhauling the *Edmund Halley.* By now, there was little choice left. If this treatment didn't work, Marguerite would *have* to go on ice.

Secretly, Saul feared it was already too late even for that. There was no guarantee that cooling down to a degree above freezing would stop these vicious, multicolored, funguslike growths, once they were this deeply established.

*A third of the awake crew—and even a few of the slotted corpsicles—have these creeping skin disorders. They worry Akio worse than the Crump Mumps or even the Red Clap. They're the biggest reason why I may not be able to go out with the Edmund after all. Osborn and the others may have to take their chances without a doctor.*

And there was one more cause for his hurry to make the new treatments work.

Yesterday, while they were making love, he had found a fine, lacelike webbing of green strands spreading under Virginia's shoulder blades and issuing across her back. He hadn't said anything to her, yet. But his motive was stronger than ever to find a cure.

The machines had finished moving into place. "All right, Marguerite," he told his patient. "Now remember, hold still."

"Yes, Saul."

Her hands clenched the table's rails. Saul turned to the hulking, spiderlike medical-mech. "Access five—" he began. But he had to stop as a sudden wave of dizziness swept over him. He managed to lift the collar of his gown just in time to contain a violent sneeze.

Saul's head rang. The dull body aches that he had managed to put out of his mind for half an hour or so returned in force now. It was a long moment before he could look up, blinking through drifting blue spots, and address the machine again.

"Access . . . five-two-seven Jonah."

A receptivity light winked across the mech's plastic panel. He continued, "Play sixty milliwatts in preprogrammed fungoid RNA resonant spectrum A dash two-nine-four, focused on foreign subdermal growth, patient's right inner rear thigh, five hundred seconds, safety factor beta."

They had adapted a unit designed for magnetic resonance and ultrasound inspection of internal injuries. The sophisticated mech would be able to aim and evaluate the focused radar far quicker than any human operator.

**"Preparing to project,"** the machine announced flatly.

Saul's best assistant, Keoki Anuenue, was watching a data tank, supervising the procedure. Not only was Keoki a skilled laboratory technician, he was also one of the strongest men Saul had ever known. Three days ago, he had had a chance to see the big Hawaiian in action, when there had been a cave-in up on Level B.

A particularly nasty variety of vermin had lodged a beachhead in the utilities shaft leading to Airlock 1, their main lifeline to the *Edmund Halley*. The major cooling vent—essential for keeping the ice around them from melting—was nearly chocked off with an ocher variant of worm bigger than the purple horrors.

Saul and Keoki had arrived on B Level just as the halls erupted in loud screams and alarm Klaxons. Most terrifying of all was the grinding groan and squeal of collapsing ice. The cable Saul had been climbing broke loose and whipped from the wall like a tortured snake, flinging him away just as a block of dark, mottled crystal pierced through the fibersheath lining and smashed the side of the shaft.

Keoki Anuenue caught Saul and planted him into a safe niche, then turned and leaped up toward the glittering stone boulder that had seven men and women trapped in the utility tunnel. They had minutes, at best. Keoki went at saving them the only way possible.

He braced his back against the tattered plastisheath, planted his feet on the iceblock, and heaved. It must have massed a hundred tons, not counting the rubble lying atop it. *"Kei make nei mai . . ."* Keoki had grunted as the boulder, unbelievably, grumbled and started to move.

A blast of fetid dankness flowed through the gap. The Hawaiian's face was a beaded torrent in the humid air, his neck tendons bunched like knotted ropes. Saul had no time to stop and think. He dove into the narrow opening.

Along with a dozen other odors, the air was filled with the scent of almonds. If any of their suits had been punctured, even the blood cyanutes wouldn't have protected the trapped crewmen much longer from the rich vein of cyanide that had been broken open by the falling rock.

Saul had wriggled in though quite aware that *he* wasn't wearing a suit at all. He tried not to think about the big man behind him, struggling with enough mass to crush a building, on Earth . . . prodigious even at half a milligee.

Thus had begun a hellish race to drag the survivors out. No one ever told Saul how long the ordeal took. All he knew was that Keoki Anuenue could have let go after one, or two, or three had been pulled free.

But Keoki did not. A figure carved in stone, he held the ragged, primeval mountain until Saul verified that the last two trapped crewmen were dead—and stopped briefly to take a ten-cc sample of pasty, reddish fluid from a crushed, pulped thing the size of an anaconda. Only after Saul had wriggled out of the utility tunnel—to see the relief party come jetting up the shaft at last—did the silent giant finally ease slowly back in a groan of ice and flesh.

All Keoki had said, when Virginia's mechs moved in to take his burden away from him, was a mumbled phrase Saul remembered as clearly as his own name:

*"Ua luhi loa au . . ."*

Strange, magical words—a phrase ripe with secret strengths, the mysteries of exotic gods.

Later, Virginia told Saul that it meant, simply, "I'm very tired."

That had been just a few days ago. The hall battles continued slowly tapering down. Diseases took their toll. And preparations for the *Newburn* rescue mission neared completion. One did not dwell on past heroics to any benefit. Let the billions following the "war news" on their vid sets, back on Earth, keep score. Here, people were simply too busy.

Keoki stood by his monitor screen and motioned to Saul. All appeared in readiness.

Saul stepped back and gave the spidery medical-mech the go-ahead command: "Five-two-seven Jonah, commence."

An oval spot of light, about five inches by three, appeared on Marguerite van Zoon's right thigh—only a soft laser spotter beam depicting where the machine's synthetic aperture was now projecting invisible, finely modulated microwaves from Saul's slapped-together treatment device.

*Rube Goldberg science,* he thought ruefully. This was much more difficult than using those giant beamers in the passageways to blast the bigger comet lifeforms.

*There, we can just pour energy into the animals' major cells through protein resonance bands. Don't have to be too accurate in choosing the right frequency. Whatever misses just spills over into heat. Shove in enough power and the cells tear themselves apart.*

Here, though, he couldn't use that kind of overkill. In this microwave scrub of Marguerite's skin, he wanted to wreck only the invader cells. Not only must the machine be tuned not to disrupt any of the patient's own tissue, he could not even allow much waste heat.

They had to finely adjust each scrub beam to a narrow set of frequencies, and play the atoms like beads on a string, tapping and tapping again until the overstrained molecular threads fell apart. Tuning had to be orders of magnitude more exact than for the weapons being used by the hall crews.

Marguerite's thigh quivered, from tension certainly. She shouldn't feel more than a faint warmth . . . at least in theory.

Saul looked back to make sure Keoki had not read anything untoward in the patient's vital signs. But the big Hawaiian watched the tank placidly, showing no sign of concern. He hummed softly, placidly, rocking in his spacer's crouch.

That was when Saul saw Colonel Suleiman Ould-Harrad slip into the treatment room.

*Oh, heaven help us.* Now *what is it?*

The spacer officer sought through the dimness until his gaze finally lighted on Saul. Saul's initial resentment evaporated as he saw Ould-Harrad's expression—his lined face a mask of exhaustion mixed with open dread.

"I'll be right back, Marguerite."

"Take your time, Saul. I am not going anywhere."

He touched her shoulder for encouragement. "Watch her carefully, Keoki."

"Sure thing, Doctor."

Saul passed through a disinfectant haze in the decon airlock and removed his helmet as the outer door cycled open. The acting expedition leader waited, absently rubbing the back of one hand with the other.

"Colonel Ould-Harrad? How may I help you?"

"There is something that I . . ." Ould-Harrad shook his head and suddenly looked away. "I know you have no reason to wish to help me, Lintz. I would understand if you told me to go straight to hell."

Saul shrugged. *"Jerusalem est perdita."* Jerusalem is lost. "The past hardly matters now. We're all in this mess together. Why don't you tell me what ails you, Colonel? If you want to keep it quiet, we can arrange treatment outside of sick call. . . ."

He trailed off as Ould-Harrad shook his head vigorously.

"You misunderstand me, Doctor. I need your advice in a non-medical area . . . a matter of most grave urgency."

Saul blinked.

"Is it something new?"

The tall Mauritanian bit his lip. "There are so few left with level heads, anymore. My people are collectivists, and so I cannot deal with emergencies as Captain Cruz did. I need consensus. I must seek advice."

Saul shook his head. "I still don't understand."

Ould-Harrad seemed not to hear him. His gaze was distant. "Earth is too far away, too confused in its instructions. I need a committee to help me decide how to deal with a dire emergency, Dr. Lintz. I am asking you if you are willing to please be a member."

"Of course. I'll help any way I can. But what is all this about?"

"There has been a mutiny," Ould-Harrad told him concisely, his lower lip trembling with emotion. "A band of fanatics has taken over the *Edmund Halley.* They seized Ensign Kearns when he discovered their plans and—"

The man hid his eyes. "They threw him out of the ship *naked,* onto the snow! They . . . they are demanding sleep slots and tritium, or they will blow up all the supplies in the polar warehouse tents."

Saul stared. "But what do they think they can accomplish?"

The African spacer blinked, he shook himself, and at last met Saul's eyes.

"They have computed a carom shot past Jupiter. The mutineers actually believe that they can steal the *Edmund* and make it all the way back to Earth alive.

"In the process, of course, they seem hardly to care if they doom the rest of us to certain death."

# VIRGINIA

She sped through Tunnel E, pulling a gray wool sweater over her jump-suit. It was *cold*.

Too damned cold, even for her. All the mission crew were "warms"—people who had minimal vascular-seizure response. Virginia's capillaries did not greatly contract when cooled, which meant she felt comfortable when most ordinary people—"freezers"—would be jittery with chill. The major disadvantage was that "warms" lost heat faster and needed more food. The flip side of *that* was freedom from fat—"warms" seldom needed to diet.

But now Carl had set the air temperature so low that even the "warms" were chilly. Virginia didn't know if that really suppressed the algae growth, but it certainly depressed *her*.

She came into the warmer core bay of Central with relief. The big monitoring screens brimmed with shifting patterns of yellow-green. She read them at a glance—the Bio people were holding their own against the gunk, and the purple forms had eased off. Good. Not that they were the main problem any longer.

Saul was conferring with Ould-Harrad. The big man towered over Saul's wiry frame, hands on hips, head shaking slowly in solemn disagreement. Saul's mouth was twisted into a grim, bloodless curve she had never seen before. She snagged a handhold, swerved nimbly, and coasted to a stop beside them.

"I ran the simulation you asked for," she blurted.

"Good, good." Saul seemed grateful to turn away from Ould-Harrad. "And?"

"I can disable most of their controls if I can get three mechs aboard *Edmund*. Then I'll need five minutes to use them."

Saul brightened. "Excellent! They'll be paying attention to loading the sleep slots they demanded, being sure we aren't slipping them inadequate supplies and so on. Preparations for the *Newburn* rescue weren't complete when Ensign Kearns discovered their intentions. So they need more gear before they can leave."

"Those bastards!" Virginia spat out. "Pushing poor Kearns out the lock—murder! If the mission mainframe hadn't already been transferred

Halleyside, I could get into their control systems and vac them all!"

Saul nodded. "Ferocious, but apt. Alas, they're on manual controls, hard to override. Still, consider—they haven't got enough food and air aboard for the entire return flight. They've got to be damned sure we give them enough slots to make it back. There are fourteen of them, they say. Now, if we can find a way to distract them, to give Virginia an opening—"

"No," Ould-Harrad said flatly. "There is little chance of approaching for more than a few moments with mechs. You heard Linbarger."

"They've *got* to allow mechs close to *Edmund* when we deliver those sleep slots," she answered.

Ould-Harrad frowned. "They will watch the machines closely. Surely they will not miscount the number returning to Halley and let three remain."

Virginia shook her head. "I can do it while they're loading the sleep slots into the receiving bay. The cables we'll cut are near that lock."

Ould-Harrad pursed his lips. "Your numerical simulation—it was complete? You yourself attempted to guide the mechs to the cables and then destroy them?"

"Well . . . no, I don't know the *Edmund*'s systems that well. I let JonVon do it. I've been upgrading his mech control and—"

"Then we cannot be sure, you see?" His eyebrows lifted into semicircles above dark eyes, the irises swimming in whites which showed a fine tracery of red veins. "JonVon is not practiced in the direct handling of mechs. Simulations are always easier than real operations. I—"

"*Carl* could do it," she said rapidly. "Get him here, have him try my simulation."

Ould-Harrad's mouth puckered into an expression of polite disbelief. Then he sighed, nodded, and began speaking spacer quick-talk into a throat mike.

Virginia turned to Saul. "How much time?"

"They've given us two hours."

"That's crazy! They can't expect us—"

"They know we can move the spare sleep slots if we start right away."

"But that appeal to 'fellow normals' offering free passage Earthside. If anyone responds, Linbarger'll have to wait for them to board."

Saul smiled wanly, his eyes seeming to remember desperate situations long ago. "A fevered mind thinks all the world can turn on a dime. Besides, they are calling every one of us, ah, normals on the comm. To demand that we go with them, drop everything, leave immediately—providing we are well, of course."

"They called you?"

"Oh yes. I was among the first—a doctor, and therefore valuable. They have no shame. I wondered why they demanded to see me on camera—until they abruptly broke off, and I realized." He chuckled and wiped his nose with a ratty handkerchief.

"Your . . . flu, or whatever it is." Virginia felt an irrational irritation at this. "That doesn't mean you're really sick."

Saul grinned sardonically. "To them it does. You know, it is like the plays of Elizabethan times, including Shakespeare. If a character coughs in the first act, you may be sure he has the pox and will die by the third."

"They're crazy!"

"Merely because they would not take me?" He laughed. "I must commend their taste, really. Despite my profession, I've never truly loved ill people, not in their gritty reality. All their crankiness, their *tsuris*. I preferred them as abstractions, as problems in genetic art."

Virginia had to answer his smile. He was incredible—joking in his mild, self-rebuking, almost elfin way, in the middle of a crisis.

Ould-Harrad finished his checking with the tunnel and surface teams. "I doubt it will matter overly, but Carl is coming."

"Good," Virginia said. She felt soothed by Saul's calm, ironic manner.

*Well, at least this means he isn't going to risk his neck going after the* Newburn, she thought. Then she felt immediate shame. *It also probably means the* Newburn *crew will drift on and die.*

She struggled to think. "I . . . I still believe my simulation shows it can be done."

"Can, perhaps," Ould-Harrad said. "Should—that is another matter."

"We must *do* something," Saul said sharply. "Forget the *Newburn* for a moment, or that we'll need the *Edmund* seventy years from now. Our immediate problem is that nearly all the hydroponics—"

"Yes, yes." Ould-Harrad raised a hand tiredly. "But one wonders if perhaps giving fourteen people a chance at returning might be worth it."

Saul rolled his eyes at the ceiling. "We *can't* assume the diseases will win! Look—"

Virginia watched him launch into the same explanation he had given her last night, about promising approaches to curing the plagues.

*He's wonderful, and I really shouldn't carp,* she thought. *But Saul can be pretty tedious when he switches over to pedant mode.*

Feeling the warmth of the big room seep into her muscles, she let herself relax. The wall weather was impressive here, with so much area to use. It was a windswept beach, mid-morning. Beyond the scrolling data screens she watched a blast of wind sweep in from the north, whipping pennants on a distant bathhouse straight out from their staffs. The sky grew dense, purple. Cumulus clouds, moments ago mere puffballs, thickened and boiled, filmy edges haloing dark centers.

Purely by accident, the running program was providing a pathetic fallacy. A simulated storm in the midst of a real crisis. If this were an entertainment—such as they had had daily until the troubles started—there would be sound, even smell and pressure modulations. The choppy ocean rippled and rose, sweeping cloud shadows raced across it. Great icy drops battered the beach, as big as hailstones. A cliff of somber air rolled in, unraveling skeins like yarn, spitting yellow lightning. As if waiting for this signal, tiny speckled sand crabs scuttled from their holes and scurried toward the frothing sea. Lightning flashed again and again—*as if God were taking photographs,* she thought, bemused, transfixed by the silent rage that curled and spat and sped across the walls. She wished she could hear the mutter of departing thunder, the hiss of rain on dunes.

From the distance a large dog came running, gouging the sand, snapping at the crabs. Mist gathered in wispy pale knots. She yearned to feel the cleansing rain plaster her clothes to her skin, drench her, shape her hair into a tight slick cap. *Even in my best sense-sim with JonVon, I can't completely escape. I'd trade it all for a ticket home right now.*

She recognized the longing: to be away from here. To breathe salty air, feel gritty sand, smell the lashing wind. And once she had felt it, she knew how to put it away, turn back to the present. If she had not been able to do that, she would never have made crew. *But these Ortho fools are risking the mission for their fantasy of escape.*

Carl arrived, red-brown stubble at his chin but showing no fatigue. He drifted to a webbing that served as furniture in low gravity. "I had a mech retrieve Kearns. He's a frozen statue."

Virginia said, "Is there any. . . ?"

"No chance. His cells are ruptured." Carl sighed, his hand brushing at his face as if to dispel all this as a bad dream. He visibly took control of himself and said with a deliberately calm flatness, "I clamped down security on the surface locks, in case anybody tries to join them."

"Ah, good," Ould-Harrad said.

Carl said, "I put Jeffers and some mechs out of sight of the *Edmund*, armed with lasers."

"For what purpose?" Ould-Harrad asked coolly.

"Insurance. In case they try something else." Carl studied Ould-Harrad expectantly. "What're you going to do?"

"I wish a quick check of Virginia's simulation," Ould-Harrad said.

Carl nodded and swung over to a work console. He tapped into the sequence and time-stepped through it, oblivious to their nervous attention. They waited expectantly until he unhooked, replacing the helmet.

"Won't work," Carl said.

"Why not?" Virginia demanded. "I spent—"

"Mechs aren't fast enough in close-up work."

"JonVon got them to do it!"

"JonVon is swell for minimizing moves, sure. But it doesn't allow for safety factors or slips. There're always some in close-quarter work."

"I could correct, introduce stochastic—"

"Not with the clock ticking," Saul agreed reluctantly. "If a mech finds some leftover box in the way, it'll consult JonVon and there'll be a pause. There simply isn't enough time."

Virginia blinked, feeling hurt that Saul so quickly took Carl's side. "I still—"

"That settles matters," Ould-Harrad said. "God and Fate act together. We must let them go."

"We *can't*," Saul said. "The hydroponics, the *Newburn*, the—"

"I know. There is much equipment we would miss," Ould-Harrad said. "Perhaps, indeed, the lack will speed our doom. But we have no choice. I will not condone any attack on the *Edmund*."

"That's . . . crazy!" Virginia blurted.

Ould-Harrad's face was impassive, distant. "When one faces death, what matters is honor. I will not harm others."

Saul and Carl shared a look of disbelief and frustration. Virginia thought, *Ould-Harrad won't oppose an Ortho rebellion, but if Percells tried it . . .*

"How about if we disable her?" Carl asked casually, leaning back with his hands behind his head, stretching.

*He's given up the* Newburn. *And deliberately showing nothing about how he feels.*

"You heard Linbarger," Ould-Harrad explained patiently. "If we show any signs of bringing devices out, anything that can be used as a weapon—"

"Yeah, they'll use the big lasers on it. Sure. But they can't shoot you if you're already inside the ship."

Ould-Harrad said, "As I said, any approach—"

Saul broke in, "I think I see . . . send them a Trojan horse, correct?"

Carl grinned. "Right. Inside the sleep slots they're demanding."

Ould-Harrad's eyes widened, showing red veins. "A bomb? It could damage *anything,* hurt people, there would be no control—"

"No bomb." Carl grimaced. "A *real* Trojan horse—put men inside."

There was a long silence as they studied each other. Virginia could read Ould-Harrad's puzzled reluctance—plainly, the man had decided to accept Linbarger's demands and simply let the expedition make do for the next seventy years. His pan-equatorial stoicism had won out.

Carl, though, was almost jaunty, certain his plan would work. Saul pensively ran over the many possibilities for error and disaster—but he licked his lips in unconscious anticipation, tempted, almost amused at this sudden hope.

*And what do I think?* Virginia realized that she had bristled at Ould-Harrad's assumption that Linbarger had to be accommodated. She had studied the charts the mutineers had broadcast. *Edmund* had just enough fuel to arc outward in something called a Byrnes maneuver: loop through a close gravitational swing by Jupiter, reach Earth in a high-velocity pass, and attempt an aerobraking rendezvous. But the window for that trick was closing fast, with only a few days remaining.

*Is Ould-Harrad play-acting? Could he be planning to duck across to the* Edmund *at the last minute, go back with them?*

"I do not know . . ." Ould-Harrad began meditatively.

"Think it through," Saul cut in. "I see one major problem."

Carl frowned. "That equipment is vital. There'll be plenty of volunteers."

"That I do not doubt. But a sleep slot is narrow and shallow. You could not get in with a spacesuit on."

"So what? I . . ." Carl's voice trailed off.

"Yes. The obvious defense for them is to vent the sleep slots in space, to be sure no one is inside."

Carl bit his lip, thinking. Virginia was acutely conscious of seconds trickling away. She liked Carl's plan, not least because it would give them something to bargain with. If Linbarger took off, the expedition would have to construct their own biosphere without many vital portions. It was one thing to grow a few seeds under lamps and quite another to start up an entire interconnected ecosystem from scratch. Like starting off juggling with eight balls. *Of all the ways there are to die out here, I had not considered simple starvation.*

Irritated, Carl spat out a curt, "I hadn't thought of that."

A long, agitated silence. Moments falling into an abyss.

Virginia had a technique for dealing with problems under time pressure. When she was first doing detailed simulations Earthside, she had evolved programs so vast that they had to be booked days or weeks ahead of time on huge mainframes. If your program went awry, you could stop it in midcourse. Then there were a few minutes when the system would do housekeeping calculations for distant users. You could hold on to your reserved time, still run your simulation, if you figured out the difficulty and managed to fix it in that brief interval.

Under pressure like that, it was easy to clutch up. So she had developed a way of letting her mind back off the problem, float, allowing intuition to poke through the tight anxiety. Focus outside the moment, let the surface mind relax . . .

Idly she noticed that on the walls the storm had built to a sullen, roiling rage. Wind blew streamers of foam from the steep waves, and huge raindrops pelted the slender grasses on the inshore dunes, crushing them. The dog had vanished, the crabs milled aimlessly beneath the hammering, incessant drops. The heavy air churned, looking too thick to even breathe—

"Wait," she said. "I've thought of something."

# CARL

Slots, he realized, were a lot like coffins. That's what had always bothered him about them.

He had a small flashlight with him, thank God. He could see the grainy sheen three inches from his face, feel the soft padding around him. The trapped tightness, the constriction, the cold . . . In the dark it would have been worse. Much worse. He didn't mind the empty yawning black of open space, free and infinite. This cramped coffin was different.

Carl had felt the gentle tug of acceleration a minute ago and now counted seconds, ticking off the estimated time it would take the five mechs to maneuver across to the *Edmund*.

There. A gentle nudge forward, pushing him against the gray covering plate. His nose brushed it and a faint torque spun him clockwise.

That would be the deceleration, then a docking turn. Going into the aft hold, almost certainly.

A dull clank. Fitting onto the auto conveyor, probably. The mechs would decouple then. . . .

Five ringing *spangs*. Good.

Now . . . if Virginia's idea was right . . .

Scraping, close by. A mech grappler caught—*clunk*—on the hatch's manual release handle. He could see the inner knob rotate. He braced himself, took a deep breath. . . .

The hatch popped free and *whoosh*—the air inside the slot rushed out, fluttering the straps over his shoulders and his blue coverall.

He sucked in air through his face mask. Virginia's risky solution— a small air bottle, no suit.

His ears popped, despite the pressure caps he wore over them. Goggles protected his eyes to stop the fluid from sputtering away, freezing his eyelids shut. The straps were so tight they bit into his flesh painfully. That was all he had between him and hard vacuum.

The slot hatch had stopped at its first secure point, five centimeters clear. Beyond he glimpsed the stark white glare of full sunlight on the rim of the aft port. His sleep slot was pinned to the conveyor, as he had guessed. He saw a few stars, and a shadow moving on the distant smooth curve of the *Edmund*'s hull. That would be a mech moving on to pop the next slot, to check for gifts bearing Greeks.

He had gambled that Linbarger would think that was enough precaution. If he was wrong . . .

And Linbarger was already hypersuspicious, after they had detected and blocked Virginia's attempt to take over command of the *Edmund*'s mechs. Ould-Harrad had insisted on trying that so-called easy solution first, and it had failed quickly. Now for the hard way . . .

Linbarger would want the mechs well clear of the *Edmund* before anyone ventured into the hold to secure the slots. That gave Carl two, maybe three minutes.

Carl lifted the cover and floated out, curling into a ball as he went. He wore a coverall, gloves, and boots, nothing more.

How long since the air had vacced? He glanced at his thumbnail. Twenty seconds.

Saul had figured three minutes of exposure before he would begin to feel the effects. Then his internal pressure imbalance would get serious, he would become woozy, and anybody coming into the bay could handle him like he was a drugged housecat.

Not that Linbarger and his crowd would waste any time on him. Probably they'd just push him out the lock and wish him bon voyage, like they'd done to poor Kearns. *Have a pleasant walk home . . .*

He uncurled, looked around.

The hold bay was empty. They were probably watching the mechs separate and back off.

He repelled off the lock rim and got oriented. The lock's manual-override seal was a big red handle, deliberately conspicuous, at ten o'clock and across the bay. His ears popped again. His senses were ringing alarms, but he suppressed them all and launched himself across to the red seal-and-flood lever.

Halfway there, somebody tackled him.

The suited figure slammed him backward into the bay, grappling for his air hose. Carl twisted away, jerked free.

*Of course. Obvious.* Linbarger had put somebody *outside,* to inspect the mechs as they came in, be sure nobody clung to an underside. From that position the man could see into the hold, too.

*Idiot!* Carl chided himself for not predicting this.

Ninety seconds left.

They separated, both drifting down the long axis of the hold. It would be ten seconds before either touched a wall. The spacesuited man fumbled for his jets and changed vectors, deftly moving between Carl and the red seal-and-flood.

Carl had no doubt that the fellow could stop him from reaching the lever for a minute or so. The Ortho had jets, air, and all the time in the world.

*Damn, it's cold, too.* Carl twisted, looking for something, anything.

There. A set of tools. He glided by the berth rack, stretched—and snatched up an autowrench. Carefully he aimed at the figure ten meters away and threw.

It missed by a good meter. Carl could see the man's face split into a sardonic grin, the lips moving, describing it all with obvious delight for the *Edmund's* bridge.

Which was what Carl wanted. Throwing the heavy wrench had given him a new vector. He coasted across the bay, windmilled, came about to absorb the impact with his legs.

Where was the damned—?

He sprang for it. The fire extinguisher easily jerked free of its clasp. Carl pointed the nozzle at his feet and fired. A pearly white cloud billowed under him and he shot back across the bay, still no closer to the seal-and-flood.

His ears popped again. Purple flecks brushed at his eyes, making firefly patterns. . . .

He struck the opposite wall, this time unprepared. A handle jabbed him in the ribs.

Where was. . . ? He launched himself at the man, riding a foam jet. Halfway there he cat-twisted, bringing the fire-extinguisher nozzle to bear ahead of him—and slammed it on full.

Action and reaction. He slowed, stopped—and the frothing white cloud enveloped him. He fired again and rushed backward, out of the thinning smoke.

Darkening purple everywhere. The raw light of the berth lamps couldn't seem to cut through it. . . .

Now, before the roiling fog cleared, he flipped again and fired one more time. He flew through blank whiteness—and struck something soft, yielding.

He grabbed at the man with one arm, bringing around the extinguisher. Hands snatched at him, clawed at his face mask.

Vectors, vectors . . .

Which way. . . ?

It didn't matter. He pressed the nozzle against the man and pulsed it again.

Billowing gray gas.

Cold, so cold . . .

. . . A huge hand pushing him backward . . .

A long second of gliding . . . the extinguisher slipped away . . . numb hands . . . he was tumbling . . . aching cold in his legs . . . impossible to see . . . the purple getting darker . . . shot through with bee-swarm white flecks darting in and out . . . in and out . . . spinning . . .

—then a jolting stab of pain in his leg, a *crack* as his skull hit decking.

It jarred him back to alertness. He clawed for a hold. Looked up.

The fog was thinning. Directly out through the lock Carl could see the suited figure wriggling, dwindling, trying to get reoriented to use his jets. An insect, silvery and graceful . . .

The thrust of the last pulse had acted equally efficiently on each of them, driving Carl inward and the other man out.

He sprang for the seal-and-flood. Grasped it, pulled. The lock slid shut just before his opponent reached it, and the loud roaring hiss of high-pressure air sounded for all the world like a blaring, rude cry of celebration.

"I made it," Carl said into his comm. "The tubes are blocked." He panted in the close, oily air of the pressurized cylinder.

"Good!" Ould-Harrad answered in his ears. Now there was no indecisiveness, no fatalism in the voice. "Linbarger, hear that?"

"What's that jackass mouthing about?" came the chief mutineer's sneer.

"Carl Osborn has jammed up the fusion feed lines," Ould-Harrad said precisely.

Faintly the voice of Helga Steppins: "Fuck! I *told* you to cover the fore tubes!"

Even fainter: "He must've crawled through them from Three F section. Shit, we can't cover every little—"

"Shut *up*." Linbarger's voice got louder as he addressed Ould-Harrad. "We'll sweat him out of there."

"You try it and I'll vent the tritium," Carl said tensely.

"What?" Linbarger could barely contain his anger. He demanded of some unseen lieutenant, "Can he do that?"

Faintly: "I don't . . . Yeah, if he opened those pressure lines into the core storage. He might've had time to do that."

"Without tritium to burn, your fusion pit won't reach trigger temperature," Carl added helpfully, grinning.

"You—!" Linbarger's line went dead.

Carl twisted and made sure the entrance behind him had a hefty tool cabinet jamming the way. He had long-lever wrenches on the two crucial pressure points, ready to crack open the valves. They could come at him from behind, but he could spray a lot of precious fuel out into space before they got the valves closed again. Enough to kill their plans, certainly.

"Are you sure you can do it, Osborn?" Ould-Harrad asked cautiously.

"Yeah." *What do you want me to say? No? With Linbarger listening?*

"Well, this certainly gives us a better bargaining position. . . ."

"Bargain, hell! We've got 'em by the balls."

"If they get to you fast enough, perhaps they can retain enough tritium to make a multiple flyby with Mars. Draw lots to use the nine slots they have now. Then—"

"Cut that crap." *Go ahead, give them ideas.*

"I'm simply—"

"I said *cut it!*"

"I'm trying to prevent—"

"It's not your ass on the line over here, Ould-Harrad."

He twisted, watching the feeder lines drop away to the left. If somebody wriggled in that way, they might try to shoot at him. But that would be stupid, right in the middle of the fusion core. Damage these fittings and they would take weeks to replace, if ever.

Linbarger's grim voice said, "You hear me on this hookup, Osborn?"

"I'm right here, just a friendly hundred meters away."

Silence. Then Linbarger's reedy, tight voice said slowly, "We'll fire the start-up pinch if you don't leave."

Carl caught his breath, let it out slowly. That was the one alternative he hadn't mentioned to anybody. It wasn't smart, because start-up could do real damage if you handled it wrong—and Linbarger had no experience at that. But he had seen the possibility of frying Carl as the hot fluids squirted through this network of tubes. And Linbarger was just desperate enough to do it.

He said as calmly as he could, "You'll burn out the throat."

"Not if we're careful. It won't take too much fusion fire to cook you up to a nice, brown glaze." Linbarger was clearly enjoying himself, thinking he had turned the tables.

"I'll vent the tritium anyway." *Now let's see how much he knows.*

"No, you won't. The subsystems will shut down those lines as soon as we start up. It's automatic—says so right in the blueprints."

*Damn.* "That's not the way it'll work." *Bluff.*

"Don't try that crap on me."

Linbarger was smarter than Carl had thought. But he wasn't going to win.

"You'll never get back Earthside. You're low on tritium as it is. I'll blow enough of it to make sure you have a long voyage. You'll never pick up the delta-V for a Jupiter carom. Even with the sleep slots, you'll starve."

"We've got the hydroponics."

"Sure. And no extra water to run it."

"There's Halley ice right outside."

"Try stepping outside." Carl played a hunch "Hey—Jeffers! What happened to that Arcist I blew out the lock?"

—What Arcist? All I see is bits 'n pieces.—

Silence.

This tit-for-tat couldn't go on much longer. Linbarger's voice was getting thin, hollow-sounding. The man's words came too fast, spurting out under pressure.

Carl bunched his jaw muscles, wondering if he believed his own words. If Linbarger acted, it would be a matter of seconds. Carl would have to choose whether to launch himself for the aft hatch and try to get away, or to use the wrenches. No time for dithering . . .

"You're lying." Linbarger didn't sound so certain now.

"Fuck you."

"You wouldn't—"

"I'm starting tritium release now."

"No!" Ould-Harrad said. "I won't have it come to this. We had a deal worked out—"

"And *you* double-crossed us! Percell-lover!" Linbarger barked.

Ould-Harrad said, "I couldn't let that hydroponics equipment go, you refused to understand that."

Carl said caustically, "Don't apologize to that scum."

"Carl," Ould-Harrad said, "I must ask you to stop—"

"The party's over," Carl said. "Surrender, Linbarger!"

"I think I'll give you a little pulse of the hot stuff, Osborn. It might improve your manners."

"The second I hear a gurgle through these pipes, you Arcist prick, I'll—"

"Stop it! Both of you! We have to work this out." The African's voice was frantic.

A long silence. Carl tried to imagine what was going through Linbarger's mind. The man had apparently concealed from the Psych Board his fanatical hatred of Percells. Or maybe he'd just snapped. Could he think around that now, be halfway rational?

*They've lost, dammit.* Could Linbarger see that? Or would he prefer his moment of revenge?

And Carl would know of it by a whispering in the pipes. . . .

"Okay." Linbarger's voice was grating, sour.

Ould-Harrad answered, "What? You agree?"

"We'll trade the hydro for the tritium and slots."

"No!" Carl cried. "We *have* them!"

"Quiet, Osborn!" Ould-Harrad shouted.

"The alternative," Linbarger said slowly, "is that I blow up the *Edmund Halley*. Better . . . all of us here agree . . . better a quick end . . . than . . ."

Carl felt a cold chill at the croaking, slurred, mad voice. It was utterly convincing. *He really means it.* "Sweet Jesus," Carl muttered. First his captain, dead. Now the *Edmund*.

Ould-Harrad spoke at last. "We . . . we will make the exchange." *What is a spacer without a spaceship?* Carl wondered numbly. *What will we be, when the* Edmund *is gone?* It was too awful to even think of.

"You can offload the hydro stuff," Linbarger said. "Get Osborn out of there and I'll set the mechs to doing it."

"No. I stay here until it's done."

Another silence. "Well . . ." More whispered arguing. Finally, "Okay. You can use those mechs to detach the main greenhouse module as a unit. Make it fast—or we'll fry that piece of Percell shit."

Carl let out a long, slow breath. The thought he had suppressed all these long minutes, that kept jabbing him, finally came swarming up: *Why are you doing this? You could* die, *fool.*

Now that he let it surface, he had no answer.

"Hurry up," he said irritably.

# SAUL

## *April 2062*

Wriggling, fluttering in a saline solution, the tiny beasts flicked here and there, hunting, always hunting.

Certain substances, flavors, drew them to the equivalent of sweetness. Others repelled. The choice was always as easy as that, a logic of trophic chemistry. On the level of the cell, there were no subtleties, no future to worry about. No past to haunt one's dreams.

Saul was pensive as he watched the tiny creatures pulse under the fiber microscope. They were the last and most potent of the new developments cooked up during the two months since the mutiny. Biological smart bombs for an unwanted war against Comet Halley.

So many of the rules he had lived by—codes of slow caution when experimenting with the stuff of life—had been pushed aside in order to get here. He envied the little microbes, in a way. For they would do as they were programmed, but he, their "creator," was left with his load of doubt and mystery.

*No. Of course you don't worry, little ones. Guilt is a teamwork thing—a trait of eucaryotic metazoans—vast collections of conspiring cells gathered to form men and women, societies . . . gods.*

*Look at me, tampering with what I barely understand, on the questionable excuse that all our human lives depend on it.*

The cyanutes had fully as much history behind them as he did. Their tiny ancestors had spent well over three billion years evolving in Earth's waters. Then, some few millions of years ago, they adapted to take up a different way of life in another salty soup—the bodily fluids of complex creatures with great, nucleated cells.

*How many thousands of my own ancestors did they kill in order to establish that first beachhead? How many trillions of them, in turn, were fought off by my forebears' immune systems—latched onto by antibodies and transported to destruction, or engulfed and digested by white cells? How long did it take for a truce to be called at last . . . for evolution to work out a negotiated peace, a symbiosis?*

It was an unanswerable question. But at some point in the past some human being and some ancestral cyanute struck an accidental bargain. In exchange for a minor cleansing function in the lung cavity, the creatures were granted safe conduct from the body's immune system. They settled down to an innocuous existence, so innocuous, in fact, that they weren't even discovered until the waning days of the last century.

*In our wisdom, we meddled with them, turning them into "cyanutes." And, Heaven forgive me, I'm not ashamed at all. A hundred skilled, devoted men and women spent half a decade altering the fruits of four gigayears' evolution. Given special permission, we used the tools of Simon Percell—and forged a useful thing of beauty.*

*But this!*

The creatures on the screen had been changed even more, given jagged new protein coats, snipped and edited with tailored chain molecules, analyzed and reanalyzed by "reader enzymes" . . . warped by the drives of an emergency nobody had expected.

The job had taken only eight weeks since the mutiny. And, except for Virginia and her biocybernetic familiar, and a few tentative suggestions from brave colleagues on Earth, he had had no help at all.

*By all the laws of biology I should not have succeeded. Not without a research team and thousands of hours of careful simulation. Millions of tests. Heaps of luck.*

*I knew better!*

*It's a wonder that I even tried.*

Saul's eyes flicked over the unrolling data display, seeing nothing but success. The uniformity of it made him more nervous than any flaw. It was *too* perfect.

*I took both the sample cyanutes and the reader units from my own blood. The data on that line goes back more than five years.*

*There are elements of Halley-Life in the new form . . . I had to include them.*

Saul shook his head. He couldn't see how that would explain this convenient success.

To the left, one of JonVon's ubiquitous color simulations turned a complex, jagged chain over and over.

The involute compound sugar was unknown in the literature. Last night, while holding Virginia close, he had told her that the Academy on Earth wanted to name it after him.

"That's quite an honor, isn't it?" she had asked sleepily. The cable snaking out from her neural tap looked like a braid of hair, and hardly got in the way.

He had smiled and stroked her glossy bangs. "Sure. They've reinstated my membership, too. But naming a *chemical* after me . . ."

"You don't want them to?" she had asked.

"Hell, no!" He'd laughed. "Think of poor Thomas Fruck, with his name tied forever to fructose!"

She was too logy and languid from their lovemaking to do more than reach back and pinch him for the affront of a joke.

SERIOUSLY, I SHOULD SUGGEST A NAME, he subvocalized. By now JonVon knew their surface networks well enough to deliver clear words most of the time. Saul felt her understanding echo back, amplified, the way her sexual fury and climax had confirmed themselves in his own mind some time ago, like explosions trying to lift the surface of his skull.

"Hmmmm," she mumbled. He could sense her drifting off into slumber.

. . . COMET-OSE . . . came her suggestion.

He had been so offended by the horrible pun that it didn't even occur to him until later that she must have already been asleep when he heard it.

Whatever its name, the sugar compound was the key . . . the sweetness he had used to forge a gingerbread cannon.

The missing madman, Ingersoll—by now a legend of the lower caverns—had given him the idea. Not long after he had glimpsed the man grazing on Halley lifeforms in the outer hallways, he had done something admittedly foolish; he had tasted some of the wall growth himself.

The stuff had been sweet, tangy, like lemon drops.

Saul played a hunch. Began some experiments. And here they were, the new cyanutes. They were still good at their old jobs, but now they were also voracious for anything with the special sugar complex . . . for any invader wearing clothes saying "Halley."

On the screen the tiny creatures clustered where cometary-viroid-coat factors flowed from the tip of a needle. Instruments showed them gobbling contentedly and multiplying with abandon.

*We were due for some good news.*

Oh, the Halleyforms would adapt, evolve. This was not the end by a long shot. But it was starting to look as if the acute panic period might be over at last.

*What have I missed?* Saul wondered anxiously, perplexed. *How was it possible to do it at all?*

A chime sounded. Everything checked out. Saul pulled out the tube of fully tested cyanutes. From his lab it was a short glide to sick bay, where two lines of people waited along opposite walls to be served by the two med-techs on duty.

One of the queues was shorter than the other, but Saul did not see any Orthos moving over to stand in the Percell line. *Ould-Harrad should never have let this system of segregation develop.*

People did not stand any closer together than they had to. No one was sure how the cometary diseases were transmitted. Fights had broken out over a cough . . . or over one man using another's space helmet without permission.

And every sick call turned up several who were faking symptoms, trying to escape the backbreaking work and drop-dead sicknesses by fleeing into the slots.

*Well, at least the lines are shorter than they were a few months back.* First, anger over the mutiny took their minds off things for a while. And Carl Osborn's heroics had suppressed the Ortho-Percell squabbling. The "norms" all knew they owed their lives to a Percell.

*Now, if only these new cyanutes work as well as the first tests indicate . . .*

A booth at the back of sick bay opened, and out stepped a woman who smiled and waved at Saul. Marguerite van Zoon looked almost like a different person. Gone were the ravages that were tearing her skin apart two months ago. She had resumed her medical duties, releasing Saul for research.

Saul's smile dropped when he saw Marguerite's patient—a younger woman in a gray ship's suit—who edged past the Walloon physician and hurried away toward the exit holding a cloth to one side of her face. Even turning her head away, she could not completely hide a shimmering, pink rash.

"Lani!" Saul whispered in dismay.

He had hoped that Marguerite's diagnosis might turn out to be wrong, but there was no mistaking the symptoms of Zipper Pox.

"Lani?" he said, but she hurried by without looking up. Those in both lines edged away as she passed.

*Oh, Lani.*

It was one of those diseases that seemed impervious, so far, to any of the tricks to come out of the lab. Even with his recent string of incredible luck.

It was ironic. While others were fighting to get back into the slots, Lani had begged to stay awake. But the decision was made. Her cooling had already been scheduled for day after tomorrow.

*Carl has been a real rat to her,* Saul thought. *If he isn't there for Lani's slotting, I'm going to punch him in the nose.*

"Dr. Lintz!"

Keoki Anuenue, the med-tech handling the shorter Percell line, stood up as Saul crossed the waiting room. The Hawaiian momentarily left the side of a dull-eyed man whose ears were packed with cotton, who slapped the side of his head every few minutes as if in a vain effort to stop the sound of bells.

Anuenue was exceptional even for a Hawaiian—one of the rare Orthos who seemed completely oblivious to both sickness and despair. He seemed never to sleep. Whenever Saul came in, Keoki was already on duty.

He grinned broadly, gesturing down at the vial in Saul's hand, anticipation in his voice as he asked, "Is that the latest cyanute varietal, Dr. Lintz?"

*He thinks I can do anything. So does Virginia.* Saul shrugged. *And after the luck I've been having, who am I to disagree?* It was a sardonic thought. He knew something mysterious was going on, and it had little to do with skill.

He held out the vial.

"Here you are, Keoki. Find volunteers the usual way. Only desperate cases, at first. These ought to be useful against the Node Lodes, as well as Sinus Whinus and the Red Clap."

Anuenue eagerly took the flask. He started to speak, then somebody in the line along the left wall cut loose in a loud, sudden sneeze.

All around the room, people looked up accusingly. *It wasn't me, this time,* Saul felt like disclaiming.

As if it were a trigger, more sneezes erupted from the Ortho side of the chamber. The line lengthened as people put more room between themselves and the miscreants.

Saul glanced at the genetically enhanced group. Percells hardly ever sneezed.

They caught the same diseases as everyone else. Saul had tried to explain this over and over to resentful Orthos. If a viroid or other comet microbe was going to kill outright, it didn't matter much which group you belonged to.

But Percells' bodies did not overreact. Their lymph nodes and membranes might swell while the body's immune system waged war on invaders, but the process was self-limiting. They didn't balloon up and die of their own overeager defenses.

*Simon,* he thought. *This was the gift of which you were proudest, even though it mystified you, too . . . that every child you worked on somehow benefited from the same augmentation, whatever genetic disease you had started out working on.*

It had surprised everyone, back in Berkeley. They had used DNA strip-readers and molecular surgery to edit harmful genes from sperm and ova of couples desperate to have children. But few had expected the babies who came forth out of those microrepaired cells to emerge so *enhanced.*

*It's a gift we gave them. A gift with the terrible price of making them different.*

"Saul!"

A voice from across sick bay—he looked up and saw Akio Matsudo waving at him from his office door.

Saul glanced at Keoki Anuenue, who grinned. "Go on, Doctor. I'll find those volunteers, and I'll let you know before the tests begin."

Saul nodded, concealing deep within the dread of what he knew had to come, sooner or later. Eventually, his bizarre string of luck would run

out. One of his tailor-made symbionts would kill, rather than save its
host. And then, no matter how much good he had done before, they
would turn on him. All of them.

As they had turned on Simon Percell.

As the mob had burned a university on a mountaintop, so long ago
and so very far away.

"*Mai kii aku i kauka hupo,*" he told Keoki.

*Don't get an ignorant doctor.*

The big Hawaiian blinked in surprise, then rocked back laughing.
The sound was so rich, so infectious, that several of those standing in
line smiled without quite knowing why.

"Coming, 'Kio," he called to Matsudo. "I'll be right there."

The snow-covered slopes of Mount Asahi were as symmetrical as
the green pines blanketing its lower flanks. Clouds, like rice-paper
boats, floated past on an invisible layer of either air or magic, setting
forth toward a setting sun and a dark blue western sea.

Saul was content to watch Akio Matsudo's weather wall, perhaps
the finest in all the colony. Indeed, until Virginia came off shift in two
hours, this was just about the best thing he could think of to do with his
time.

*It beats working,* he thought tiredly. For once his mind was not
awhirl with ideas, the next experiment to try, the next clue to trace. He
sat, zazen fashion, thinking of as little as possible.

*Something we Westerners have learned from the East . . . that
beauty can be found in the smallest things.*

The earthy brown clay tea set had been brought all the way from the
shores of the Inland Sea. Its rough surfaces reflected the mute colors of
the late afternoon light in a way that could not be described, only admired. The shaping marks on the cup in front of Saul seemed to have
been formed on the same wheel as that which turned Creation. It was
contemporary with the planets, with the sun.

Entranced, Saul glanced up when Akio Matsudo spoke.

"The wait will be worth it, Saul. Be patient."

*Waiting?* Saul thought. *Was that what I was doing?*

Highlights in the Japanese physician's glossy black hair shone like
Mount Asahi's glaciers as he fussed over the tea, commenting on the
difficulty of boiling water properly in low gravity, what with weakened
convection and all. To Saul, the man's voice was one with the rustling
pines.

"I will now pour," Akio intoned, and lifted the cups delicately.

Saul was not in a hurry to get to business. When the ceremony was finished, and the tea poured, they gossiped over inconsequential matters—the latest fashion in mathematical philosophy on Earth, and the strange propositions being put forward by the Marxist theologians of Kiev. The journals had been full of it, and they both wondered aloud what Nicholas Malenkov would have made of it all.

Akio seemed in much better health now. He had been one of Saul's first volunteers to take an early version of the retailored cyanutes. It was that or lose him permanently to the infection tearing away at his liver. Now the sickly yellow pallor was gone. He had regained weight. Soon he would even quit using the mechanical endocrine rebalancer that had been keeping him alive.

Saul was very pleased to see his friend healthy and spry again.

*I was able to help Virginia, and Marguerite, and Akio. Maybe, later, we can do something for Lani and Betty Oakes, and so many others.*

Memory of Miguel Cruz was still a sharp pain. More than anyone else, their commander was needed. But there were limits to what Saul ever expected to be able to do, no matter how lucky he was.

Akio Matsudo put down his cup and carefully removed his glasses to polish them. "Saul, my friend, forgive my bluntness. But I think that perhaps I should explain why I asked you here today. I believe that now it is time for you to go into the slots."

Saul put down his cup. Akio raised his hands.

"Before you protest, please allow me to explain. There are many, many reasons."

He raised one finger. "First Watch was supposed to last only a little over a year. The colony's anniversary is this month. And you were one of the few civilians awake for the entire trip out, on the *Edmund*. You are losing lifespan. It is unfair to you, who have less of it to spare than the youngsters outside."

Saul snorted. "What is this, Akio? We may have passed through the worst part, but the staffing nightmare isn't over yet. With all the people we've had to pull, term-slot, and even vac-store out on the surface, it's clear the shifts will have to be longer than planned. You know that argument's a load of crap."

Matsudo winced at Saul's bluntness.

"Yesss." His agreement sounded more like a suppressed hiss of disapproval. "Perhaps. But I must tell you that Bethany Oakes made me promise, before she herself was slotted, that you would be put away if your symptoms grew worse."

"They *aren't* any worse," Saul grumbled. "It's just another bad cold. I think it's still a leftover from one of your damn challenge viruses. I can tell by the way it tickles before I sneeze."

He knew better, of course. There was comet stuff inside him, from viroids to latent bacteroids. Some of the variants did not use the Halley sugar complex, and so were doubtless invulnerable to his new silver bullets.

*And I'm older than most. Could be that makes me more vulnerable.*

For a moment the contemplative daze threatened to return. The conversation had reminded him of a weird sensation he had had, a few days ago, on examining a sample of his own blood . . . a feeling that something . . .

He shook his head. *No. This is . . .* He searched for a Yiddish expression and failed. *Bullshit. Good old Anglo-Saxon bullshit. That's the only word for it.*

"There is a second major reason." Matsudo squeezed and covered another cup of sharp, yellow-brown tea for each of them. "Because of the mutiny, this year's desperate effort will be to build greenhouses on the surface, and farms down in chamber Tau. The hydroponics pod from the *Edmund must* be kept alive until new food-production facilities are set up. That is why Evans is being thawed now—he is the best of all the expedition ecologists, and Svatuto is coming out of the slots as his backup."

Saul noted Matsudo's pained expression flickering when he had to mention the *Edmund*. Even more to be avoided was any mention of the *Newburn*. In all the time since the mutineers had departed, not once had Saul heard anybody utter the name of the lost slot tug, now apparently completely out of reach and growing more distant with every passing day. It was an utterly taboo subject.

"Yes? So it'll be good to consult with Evans. There are some matters concerning the origin of Halley lifeforms that an ecologist can help with. I'm not certain I can accept the old explanation any longer."

Akio looked out over the scene of sunset on the Western Sea. The clouds had turned orange and black, breathlessly beautiful.

"You misunderstand me, Saul. This means we will have more medical people awake than is proper in the long run, over forty shifts. Svatuto is a better clinician than you are, anyway. You know that, Saul."

Saul shrugged. "That's why I went into research," he said, reaching for his handkerchief. "Can't . . . can't stand sick people." The room wavered. Saul shook his head vigorously. Then he turned aside and sneezed.

Matsudo jumped slightly, and finally smiled. "Nobody does that so dramatically. It is that Semitic profundity of a nose, I suppose. Seriously, Saul, that is another reason. Forgive me, but you *disrupt* everything. People fear your noisy, drippy symptoms, even as they respect your genius. Lieutenant Colonel Ould-Harrad and others think that it would be best for everybody if you should rest for a while."

Saul shook his head. "I just now realized, you're actually serious about this, Akio. Right when my work is . . ." He stopped, unable to find words for how well things were going in the lab.

Then there was also Virginia. *Her love is the best thing that's happened to me in ten years.*

The tentative, simulated telempathy they shared through her daring, unconventional biocybernetics was as exciting in its own fashion as his work in bioengineering. They were both accomplishing things that would shake up half-a-dozen disciplines! Why, over just the last week he had received messages from crusty old Wallin at Oxford, and even aloof, above-it-all Tang in Peking. . . .

"This is in no way to detract from your accomplishments," Matsudo said quickly, trying to soothe Saul. "You have, in fact, achieved wonders, wonders! I find your methods unnerving, as well you know, but I cannot argue with success. If any of us survive, it will be in no small measure thanks to you."

Saul shook his head. "There's more to be done! We have to see if the procedures—"

"And I insist that you underrate your success!" the tall Japanese hissed.

Akio must have been severely agitated. This was the first time in Saul's experience that he had ever interrupted anybody. The man looked quickly aside. "Excuse me, please. But I have done simulations, and Earth Control concurs. The larger Halleyform organisms—the purples especially—can be kept in check using ultraviolet and your new microwave beamers. The fungoids are now under control using more precise versions of both techniques."

"And the diseases?"

"The diseases fall off dramatically in nearly everyone who has received your new cyanutes. Tests show there are few actual cures, but the advantage has been given back to the human body's immune system."

"So—"

"So your techniques will hold the line! People will fall ill, true. Some will even die—but at a far, far slower rate."

Then Akio did something quite rare. He looked Saul directly in the eyes.

"I am in awe of your power, Saul Lintz," he confessed softly. "An-

other reason you must be slotted is that we simply cannot afford to lose
you. There are three decades ahead until the hard work of aphelion. A
greater period afterwards. There will be more crises. New, adapted bacteroids and viroids. Please think of yourself as our secret weapon, our
reserve against all contingencies."

His eyes were pleading, asking Saul to accept, and not to inflict any
more of his Occidental directness against something that was already
decided.

*He's holding something back,* Saul realized. *Politics? Orders from
Earth?*

Virginia had spliced press clips for him, over the two months since
the mutiny. He had been too busy to more than glance at the news blurbs,
but apparently some elements in the media were making celebrities of
two particular members of the Halley Expedition.

*Carl Osborn and me. We're the latest sensations, back there.*

**DOC HALLEY-DAY AND WYATT PERCELL . . . BATTLING
CREEPY BUGS AND BUGGY CREW . . .**

*Could it be that the powers back home can't afford to have this
popular image last too long? Both an augmented person and a former
collaborator of Simon Percell in the headlines?*

*Oh, what a laugh! I sought obscurity and safety out in space—and
find neither!*

Matsudo looked away again. Saul knew, then, that this was a matter
decided far above, and there would be no use inflicting protests on his
uncomfortable friend.

He had seen simulations better than Matsudo's—prepared in stochastic logic by JonVon to his own models. Matsudo was right. Things
were indeed getting better . . . or at least they would slip downhill more
slowly for the foreseeable future. Saul had hoped that it would mean
more time to study—to *really* study—what was going on here.

There was more to all of this than a life-or-death struggle between
colonists and native organisms. Much, much more, and he wanted to
find out about it.

But how does one fight city hall?

*Maybe I could persuade Virginia to desert with me, into the tun-
nels. We'll graze on green stuff, like Ingersoll. Raid the animal lockers
and thaw some sheep to raise. Maybe plant sorghum down on the south
forty and tell the universe to go to hell.*

The ridiculous image made him smile, in spite of himself.

"I must have three months." He began the inevitable bargaining.

"There are experiments to finish, and I've got to brief Svatuto. Also, Keoki and Marguerite need more training before I hand the lab over to them."

Matsudo shook his head. "Two weeks. It is all I am willing to . . . all I *can* risk you further."

Saul smiled. "I'll have to write a training manual for future shifts—on handling the cyanutes and using the microwave disruptor. . . . Eight weeks, minimum."

After a long silence, Matsudo sighed in acquiescence. "I fear for you, Saul. But I am also selfish. I admit that it will be good to have you here for that much longer."

The black-haired immunologist looked out over the slopes of Mount Asahi. Sunset faded into a purpling night. Lowering clouds flickered with hints of thunder.

"Flesh is weak," Akio Matsudo said softly, removing his glasses to polish them one more time. "And it is lonely without friends, where only the snow falls."

# VIRGINIA

## *June 2062*

As she approached the sleep-slot prep room one of her own poems—*if indeed they deserve such a highfalutin' name!*—came rushing into her head.

> Your musky hollows
> sand-colored, rutted skin
> neatly fitted bones, a calcium cage
> to house a heart I enter,
> and would devour
> if only we had icy slow days.
> I could rhyme
> the tick of time,
> frame elegant meals.
> No springtime in Gehenna.
> The long cold orbit out
> could not cut the years

we have left.
Time's fair gamble,
days not yet done.
Perhaps they'll dwindle down
to none. But they will
see us entwining
together in the sun.

*Okay, you're brave enough to say it to JonVon. Now* do *it.*
She slipped into the prep room. Saul already lay in the carrier beneath cool pale light, surrounded by cylinders and spheres of gleaming
steel. Carl Osborn was helping Keoki Anuenue, the med-tech, work
over him. The red nutrient webbing resembled a net of blood vessels
projected through the skin, like a demonstration in school. Saul was still
awake, though drowsy. His eyes followed her as she walked to his side.
Fog curled in chilly fingers around her.
Carl glanced up. "Where the hell have you been? I've been listening to the comm. Just as I started, all the mechs went dead."
"I know."
"Oh, is it already fixed?"
"It will be, if I give the order," she said precisely.
Carl blinked. "What's that mean?"
"I shut them all down. And I won't bring them back on line unless
you and Ould-Harrad honor my request."
Anuenue kept attaching leads to Saul, oblivious, but Carl stopped
and carefully put down his needle-nose pliers. He stepped away, where
the tech couldn't hear. "You're . . . threatening us?"
"Let's call it a promise."
"Promise! What the—?"
"Either let me slot now, or you won't get any useful work out of me
*or* the mechs."
"That's disobedience! Blackmail!"
"Call it anything you like. Just do it." Virginia compressed her lips
into a thin, pale line.
"We *need* you."
"There are other programmers available—unslot one. And JonVon
can take over a lot of functions. I've upgraded his capabilities."
"No computer is as good as you."
*Good. Get him to argue rationally.* "JonVon's general organizing
structures are *better* than mine. He also does higher-order self-
programming. That makes him very adaptable."

"But your experience—"

"Listen, I'm not negotiating here. I'm demanding."

Carl sighed and she saw that he was worn down. Not physically—his solid jaw and strong cheeks were ruddy with health, a welcome sight in these days—but mentally. *Ould-Harrad is a frustrating commander. Carl was the natural choice for exec officer, but it's a relentless task being number two to a man like that. And I'm not making it any easier on him.*

"You honestly think JonVon will work with another computer wizard? He's your baby, after all."

"I've instructed him to. I mandated it, using the old mission mainframe. Just as I've told him to keep the mechs dead until I give him the word."

Carl said angrily, "So it is blackmail."

"Call it a negotiating position."

"You said you were demanding, not negotiating."

A shrug. "Skip it. Slot me or else *nothing* gets done."

Carl bristled and pointed a finger at Saul. "*He* put you up to this."

"No. I never talked to him about it. I . . . decided on my own."

Carl's voice seemed squeezed, diminished. "You . . . love him that much?"

This was no time to care about anything except results. Carl's face was reddening, his breathing getting faster. If he saw how unsteady she was, how much nerve it took to do this— "Of course. You've known that all along."

Somehow this simple declaration blunted Carl's building anger. "You . . . want to spend the same time in the slots?"

"We belong together."

Carl sighed again. "Damned nasty, shutting down the mechs this way."

"I had to show I mean it. I don't intend to live without Saul. Particularly since nobody really knows how much longer things will hold together here anyway."

"We've got the diseases licked, Saul says."

"Yes, for now. But what about long-term effects? We've got to be sure we have able bodies for service decades from now. People who can come out of the slots in good condition, ready to work. Saul and I fit that description. You know we can survive."

She played out the arguments just as she had rehearsed them. There were holes in them, of course, but she saw now that Carl in his disoriented state was vulnerable to her, unable to muster a coherent objection.

Perhaps he would, in fact, be glad to be rid of both her and Saul; their love was a continual irritant to him, she guessed.

Carl asked, "Keoki, could you get some more KleinTex solution from stock?" The tech nodded and left.

Carl seemed pensive, almost dazed.

"Carl . . . I know this is a hard time. . . ."

He blinked, obviously struggling with inner conflicts. "You know, I never pay attention to the people around me . . . never know what they're thinking . . . feeling."

"No, that's not true, you—"

"Lani, I never *saw* her," he said bitterly. "I was so wrapped up in dreams about you. To see her going into the slots, that damned disease eating her up . . . I could've had some time with her, if I'd—"

"If you'd been a superman, yes," she said patiently. "We've *all* been run ragged, Carl. You can't blame yourself for not being all things to all people."

He didn't reply, just picked absently at the weave of nutrient tubes and sensor wires that covered Saul. Virginia watched his expression settle into one of sad reflection. He sighed, then looked into Saul's relaxed face and asked, "You can understand?"

A nod.

"She's coming with you."

A slow smile. The lined skin around his eyes crinkled with unmistakable happiness.

She asked Carl, "His speech centers?"

"I can reconnect them if you want. Or call Matsudo, if you don't trust my fumbling."

She covered Carl's hand tenderly, sorry that it had come to this. "No . . . don't. I think we understand without speaking."

Saul nodded.

Carl's face was blank, numb. He looked from one to the other. Virginia felt pity for him, a man thrust too quickly into the center of events. She was sorry that she had been forced to do things this way. But there was no turning back.

"We'll slot you within a few weeks," Carl said evenly, clearly summoning up strength from some reservoir. "First we thaw your replacement, so you can brief her. We'll have to square it with the sleep-slot committee, argue over whether the replacement should be a Percell or an Ortho—the usual. Should take less than a month. We'll start as soon as you get JonVon and the mechs in shape."

She didn't take her eyes away from Saul. "I'll assign my personal mech, Wendy, to give JonVon permanent manual function."

"The details don't matter. You've won. That's what counts."

She nodded, unable to speak.

He stood silently in the curling moist fog and cold for a long time. "The people I most cared about, they're all slipping away. . . ." Then he shrugged. "Y'know . . . I'm going to miss you two."

PART IV

---

# THE ROCK IN THE DESERT

He that stands upon a slippery place,
Makes nice of no vile hold to stand him up.
—Wm. Shakespeare

Who rides a tiger cannot dismount.
—Chinese proverb

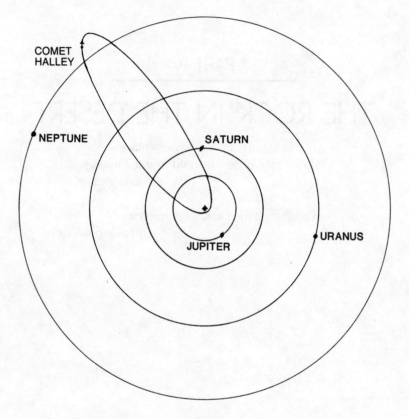

Positions of Planets
and Comet Halley 2092

# SAUL

## 2092

The world came back slowly, and not too pleasantly. It *tingled,* deep down at the roots of his nerves, and then everything began to itch.

He could not scratch.

Later, as the tickling finally began to fade, there came his first real sensation of deep *cold.*

It was a fevery chill, this slow returning to awareness. Like a sickness—a bad one in which the mind is disabled, scattered, and yet some core part of a man knows that it wants to *think*—to figure out what is wrong and how to fix it.

It was also like a nightmare, with blurred images, fragments of voices murmuring and fading, beyond recall or meaning. Only the dreamer knew that this time there would be no quick, relieved awakening.

There was one way out of this dream—a long, slow ride to the end.

The first time Saul felt certain that he wasn't imagining things came as a blank whiteness overhead slowly swam into focus. His eyelids fluttered with hesitant feedback—actually responding to his will.

*Shut,* he commanded. The light closed off to a muted, rosy hue.

*Open!* he ordered desperately, afraid the world had gone away again. But nerves flashed and muscles fired on cue. A torrent of light poured in again.

*It's cold. . . . Cold as the High Priest's heart.*

And Saul remembered a dry, freezing morning in the Judean hills, the scent of century-old cedars and the chill of a hope dying.

Flames licked the sky in the direction of Gan Illana. There was more burning on Mount Herzl. But in Jerusalem the Armies of The Lord advanced in song, led on one side by a swarm of golden crosses, on another by the Mahdi and all of the Salawite mullahs. And in the center, chanting Hebrew psalms and carrying the Rebuilt Ark, the Kahanim priests of the new Sanhedrin. The faithful surged around the ruins of smashed buses, chanting in joy and carrying bricks and mortar.

Unable to move anything but his eyelids, Saul seemed to see it all again, played out against the pale white ceiling. It was a memory of smoke, and the acrid odor of superstition.

U.N. "peacekeepers" stood watch as the Architects planted the flags of three faiths on the Temple Mount and proclaimed the land holy in three tongues. The hover tanks had not moved to stop the riots. The world press hardly covered the slaughter of those resisting the new theocracy.

To the world it was a great day. "Peace" had come at last to the broiling navel of the world. Billions looked on it as a miracle as representatives of three great religions joined together in a holy cause.

To build a Temple to the Ultimate.

To fulfill prophecy.

To erect a place to speak to God.

Even after the fires had dimmed, after the Levites, Salawites, and Tribulationists had sealed the land, smoke still rose up to Mount Zion where he had watched. The pungent, sweet smell of roasting, sacrificial lambs.

The scent of Leviticus climbed once more into Heaven, curling under the nostrils of the Lord.

Saul closed his eyes again, and slept.


When next he awoke there was motion. A figure moved into view. He blinked, trying to focus.

It was an older face. Sterner. But he recognized it.

Saul felt his lips being moistened. He worked his mouth and managed to whisper one syllable.

"C . . . Carl?"

The visage overhead nodded. "Yes, Saul. It's me. How are you feeling?"

Saul lifted his eyebrows. The lazy man's shrug conveyed more than words could at this point. Carl Osborn responded with a smile, not a particularly friendly smile, but ironic. "Good. Your unslotting is proceeding normally. You should be up and about soon."

Saul's voice felt dry. Dusty. "Is . . . is there peace now?"

Carl blinked, then shook his head. "Most wakers ask what date it is. Or, if they've already been out, they ask if we've beaten the gunk. But not you. Not Saul Lintz."

There was no antagonism in the remark. Saul managed to answer Carl's wry smile with one of his own. "Okay, then. What . . . what's the date?"

Carl nodded. "Eight years before the new century."

*So*, Saul thought. *Thirty years. That was a long nap.*

"Aphelion . . ." he breathed.

"Not far from it," Carl agreed. "We're thirty a.u. out. You should see the sun. It's not much brighter than the moon in a desert night."

*Where no person has gone before.*

"The Nudge Launchers?" Saul asked. "Are they . . ."

Carl frowned. "We'll get 'em built."

Saul read a lot in that expression. It answered his first question. *No peace. But we're still here, so it can't be all bad.*

His body felt as if it were made of lead, but he managed to turn his head. "So who's is charge now? . . . Kuyamato? Trugdorff? . . . Johannson?"

Carl shook his head. "They're all dead, or dead-slotted."

"Then who?"

Carl made a restless shrug. "I'm operations officer. If anyone's in charge, I am."

Saul settled back, slowly absorbing this.

*He* is *older, harder. I wonder how many more years Carl has spent awake, while I slept.*

"So do you need a doctor?" Frankly, he wouldn't have expected to be revived, if it were up to Carl.

"Yeah, that's right, Saul. We need a doctor. And Earth suggested it might be a good time to let you have another look at the diseases. Some seem to have mutated."

Carl hovered over him for another moment. His lips pressed together. "I ought to be honest with you, Saul. The biggest reason I had you taken off ice was because we need Virginia."

"Virginia," Saul breathed. Remembering.

Carl nodded, his mouth tight. "Rest, Saul. You won't be called on to do much. Not right away. I'll check in on you later."

Saul said nothing as the tall man slipped out of his peripheral vision. The years still had to be unsorted. Dreams that he had not quite experienced felt like water behind an overfilled dam. Faces riffled like shuffling cards.

Faces of women—Miriam, Virginia, Lani Nguyen. Faces of comrades—Nicholas Malenkov, dying in his arms.

And the ghost of Simon Percell. Through the fibercloth walls, through the ice mountain that surrounded him, Saul felt he could almost hear a soft, ironic laughter. It stayed with him when he fell into a deep, natural sleep.

Twice more he stirred briefly. The first time when a tech he recognized from the crew of the *Edmund*—now a middle-aged woman with a strange, greenish stain on one side of her face—greeted him mildly and offered him a drink. He had to ask her to speak slowly because she seemed to have picked up a queer accent.

An oddly handsome man without any hair at all was his caretaker the next time. A burn on one cheek seemed more like a *brand* than anything an accident might produce. Saul thought it wise to forbear comment.

*Wait. Absorb. Learn.*

The slot tenders were not as busy as they once had been. The pace was casual, but under it all, the tension was still there. In the hushed conversations he overheard, there were words, phrases, that he could not follow. He was allowed to sit up, the next time the watch shift changed, and he saw that there was some sort of ceremony as new slot tenders took charge.

*No. There is no peace.*

He saw on the wallboard that two recuperation lights shone. One for him. One for Virginia. She had kept her promise, and followed him down the River of Time.

*Clever girl,* Saul thought. *I knew you could do it.*

*I can't wait to tell you how much I really love you . . . however old you are by now.*

With that wry thought, Saul slept again, and knew that he would be stronger when next he awakened.

# CARL

Kepler's Laws seemed almost biological now. Carl stared at the orbital display and sighed. Following a long ellipse out from the sun's sting felt a lot like aging.

You start with a hot, fevered time when movement is rapid, life burgeons. Spring, a swelling heat, and ripe, quick summer. It passes. Things calm, raw reality seeps in, you slow and cool and come to terms with the fundamental hostility of the universe. Like growing old.

Simple Newtonian dynamics explained it all. The eccentric, moody Kepler had deduced the basic laws governing elliptical motion in a classic, brute-force manner: staring at the data until order seemed to ooze out, the eye bringing forth structure where another's would see only a hash of numbers. Carl respected that ability far more now, after years of dealing with mountains of data, faithfully delivered by the interlocking systems of Halley Core.

He stepped Halley's orbit forward on the big screen, watching the long ellipse advance, the scale swelling as the warm realm of the inner planets dwindled, circles sucked into the vortex of the sun. They were far past Saturn now, turning with an aching lethargy toward aphelion, beyond Neptune. Gravity's weakening tug nudged the ice mountain feebly, the sun's gossamer apronstrings.

He still came to Central every few days to check, to touch the consoles and renew his faith that this long night must have an end.

*Like growing old.*

*How old am I, anyway? Two years serving under Ould-Harrad, after Saul and Virginia went into the slots. I was damned glad to slide into that chilly sleep myself. Worn out and depressed.*

*Then another shift under Lieutenant Morgan a decade later. Less harrowing, sure, but boring. I got heavily into the sense-stim, just to blot out the monotony of ice and dark. Must've run through every tape in the library a dozen times. JonVon was a help, rearranging and blending sensations and dramas. Some odd, delightful effects there . . . Still, much more than two years and I would've been ready for the rubber room.*

*Now it's been—what? four more years? seems longer!—since Calciano woke me to take his place. The guy was pretty damned near gone, too.*

He examined his reflection in a nearby blank screen, the gray flecks at the temples. *Well, Virginia liked 'em older. . . . Maybe now I can compete. I was a little hard to take, I guess. Brash and idealistic and pretty abrasive, I'm sure. Now, though . . .*

He shook his head. Whatever he was becoming as a man . . . well, it was secondary. His main focus was on being a commander, or what passed for one these days. Plugging away, keeping the factions working together with minimal friction. He'd love to slip back into that dreamy cold sleep, let go, ride home free. . . .

But there was no one left in the slots he would trust with the important aphelion maneuvers ahead. On the display they were a mere finger's width from the turnaround, a lonely blue pinprick.

He'd had the time to bone up on Halley's Comet, something he had skipped when applying for this mission. It had seemed irrelevant: Halley was another iceball, bound for the outer system and zones of space nobody had ever seen. That was enough for an ambitious youngster of twenty-five.

He had been chagrined to find he was even pronouncing the name wrong. Astronomers and space workers called it Halley with a short *a;* ground-huggers of his native North America used a long *a,* as if it were "Hailey." But the discoverer had pronounced it with a *w* in the middle, so it should sound like "Hawley." Carl imagined a haughty Englishman enunciating the name with one eyebrow arched, his lips turned into an amused, condescending smile.

They were riding the comet on its thirty-first passage since an ancient Chinese first recorded seeing the splash of shimmering light in the sky—a span that dwarfed the long years Carl had spent, and humbled the empires of Man. The fourth recorded apparition, in 11 B.C., came close to the birthdate of Jesus of Nazareth, and some said it must have been the Star of Bethlehem.

*We could use some salvation now,* Carl thought, and thumbed off the display. *And where's that goddamn Jeffers?*

As if called, the hatch creaked and Jeffers appeared, his long rusty beard flowing over his skinsuit neck yoke like a lurid moss. The man had argued that letting body hair grow was only sensible, providing much-needed natural insulation. Carl had countered that it got in the way of suit fixtures and fouled the helmet placements, but he knew why Jeffers liked it: the image of Methuselah, of wisdom, of the old hermit in the woods.

"How'd it go?" Jeffers asked. If anything, his southern drawl had thickened with the years. They were all trying to keep alive whatever links they had to distant, vibrant Earth.

Carl shrugged. "I sent the weekly transmission yesterday. Got the usual short response today, thirteen hours twelve minutes later."

"Any shows?"

"Here." Carl hit a key and an index scrolled forward. He stopped at a NEWS entry and shifted to realtime. "Feast your eyes."

A woman announcer grinned at them, her torso paint aswirl with technicolor curves. Her nipple ornaments glittered as she took a deep breath and said enthusiastically. "Arrested on two counts of public foreplay today were Starlet Angela Xeno and Compassatino Rilke, line player for the Visigoths." A 3D picture of a smiling couple, half-nude. "Insiders say the incident was publicity for the Visigoths' upcoming tube match against the Wasters. Turning to—"

Carl snapped it off. "There're three new porno sestinas, too, if you want them."

Jeffers made a face. "Naw, gettin' so I can't take that stuff anymore."

"Me neither." He never had, but it was a good idea not to disparage the tastes of people you had to work with; another small fact he had learned.

"When's Malcolm comin'?"

"Any minute now."

Central was one of two common meeting grounds between the factions. They all had to run into each other in the harvesting bins of Hydroponics, but Central was the obvious spot for real negotiations.

Jeffers slid into a webbing, stretching. "Just got back from the surface. A man can hardly move anything out there. Lotsa mechs are down for repairs and the rest drag around like they's drugged."

Carl nodded. Every month it got slightly worse. The persistent cold, the malfs, the difficulty of making new parts or repairs . . . "I wonder if there'll be some of those titanium-cylinder manifolds in the Care Package."

"Hope so." Jeffers frowned. "I still wonder how they got all those parts and supplies into such a small package."

"They've gotten better at high-boost, I suppose. It's been over thirty years, after all."

Earth had undoubtedly made great progress in propulsion of high-quality loads for the Mars and asteroid bases. Still, it had been a surprise to be told, three years ago, that Control was sending a cargo of much-needed parts and supplies, boosting them out under enormous acceleration. They would arrive before aphelion, and could help crucially in the Nudge. Even with three decades of Earthside's improvements, a package like that was expensive—but nothing, of course, compared with the investment already sunk into the Halley Mission.

"I ran that optical sighting through JonVon, got a measurement," Jeffers said. "The Care Package is riding a fusion torch. Big orange plume behind it."

"Already decelerating?"

"Yeah, but not much. Guess they're going to slam on the brakes right at the end."

With rendezvous two years away, the Care Package still had to shed four kilometers per second to come alongside Halley. News of it had been a real morale boost. Carl hoped its arrival would lift them all, bring back some of the spirit the mission had enjoyed in its first days.

"Major Clay—our new contact guy—said he had included a bottle of 1986 Malescot St. Exupery Margaux."

"Hot damn! I can't pronounce it, but I'll sure as hell help drink it."

"A bottle of the best from Halley's twen-cen apparition, he said."

"Great. Just fine."

Jeffers was plainly pleased at this fragment of news. Carl had saved details of the Care Package, dealt them out one at a time to keep enthusiasm up. An extravagant gesture, shipping old grape juice across the solar system—but Earth, despite its madnesses, did understand something of the psychology out here. It was a masterful touch.

*One hell of an improvement over the hysteria under Ould-Harrad—one month I'm a hero, the next I'm a Percell freak. And under Criswell they didn't answer at all. If it weren't for Phobos Base relaying newslink on the sly, we couldn't have proved Earth was even inhabited. Sounds like things are settling down now, though.*

He rubbed his face, massaging some of the ache away. He tapped in instructions and the walls lit. *Best to put on something pretty, calm, warm. Ah, here. A sunny day breaking over Hong Kong Free State.*

The swarming masses of junks and flyers always pleased him. A baking sun had just lifted free of green, artificial hills to the east. A rainbow grinned, upside down beneath the vapor fall of a floating luxury home. Heat shimmer made the distant alabaster spires dance.

The hatch clanked again and Malcolm appeared. He was lean, and his face was set in a perpetual dark glower, black eyes peering out distrustfully. Without a word Malcolm settled into a webbing and nodded. "We want more from Hydro."

Carl sighed. "You know the terms."

"It's not enough. We're all losing body weight."

For a nasty instant Carl was tempted to say, *Try eating some of your kids. The ones you insisted you had a "right" to have.* But he kept his face impassive and said, "We're getting as much out of Hydro as we can, you know that. Look over the numbers."

"But we're growing, and the agreement doesn't allow for that."

"Those kids were *your* choice."

"Look, we been over this," Malcolm said evenly. "Normal people get sick easier. We got to keep a larger population in case there's another plague."

Jeffers, who had been chewing his lip all this time, burst out, "You just want to take over, is all. Couple decades, you'll outnumber us Percells."

Malcolm said stiffly, "The normal people will keep to our own zone."

"We see you guys around in Three C—you movin' in there?" Jeffers asked.

"No." Malcolm sniffed derisively. "We can't stand the smell."

"Delicate li'l bastards, aren't you?"

Carl said mildly, "Stop trading insults. We've got things to negotiate."

"Those kids *are* bastards, y'know—you've got some kinda mass breeding program going, don't you?" Jeffers asked sharply.

Malcolm reddened. "That's no business of you Percells."

"You treat women like breeding stock—"

*"Cut it,"* Carl said firmly. Malcolm was sensitive about the fact that their children were stunted, victims of Halleyform intrusions into the womb and development problems in low-G. They seldom lived long. Reproducing in such a hostile biological environment was simply a bad gamble, and the Orthos had lost.

He let the men stare sourly at each other for a moment and then went on, "We've got to do something about the slot problem. The medical inventory is even worse than I'd thought. There aren't enough fresh crew left. Nowhere near enough to do the remaining work of setting up the Nudge."

Jeffers asked, "How's that possible? There're hundreds—"

"*Were* hundreds." In the first ten years they had cycled most of the mission crew through, before they got the green gunk and viroids really under control. If the thawed-out ones got sick—and a lot did—they were popped back into the slots. For replacements they pulled fresh sleepers.

"Killing off normal people, that's what you were doing," Malcolm said.

Carl sighed. "Forget that crap. We did what we had to. Orthos got sick fast, that's all."

"Not the way I heard it. We—"

Jeffers spat out, "You unfroze twenty years after rendezvous! You know *nothin'* about the hard time."

"I can read records! And the oldsters tell us. I know you unfroze normal people more often than you had to."

"Because the Ortho faction wanted to keep their numbers up. It was *their* idea," Carl explained. "Look, I was there, you weren't. Until Calciano handed things over to me, *every* commander was an Ortho. I'm not going to try to crack through that bonehead bias of yours anymore. Just listen, okay?"

Malcolm nodded reluctantly. The man kept a certain tattered dignity about him, despite his grimy uniform and matted hair. Usually he made some show of being clean and neat. The Orthos must be having a hard time of it lately.

There were internal disputes, too. The Ortho-run tunnels had as wide a range of fanatics as the Percell zones, maybe more. Malcolm was hard to take sometimes, but he was the only one all Orthos trusted to speak for them—much the same position Jeffers served among Percells.

Carl could respect Malcolm's position, but could only pity the stupidity of the people he had to represent. Many Orthos would never compromise with Percells now, after all that had happened, the wasted blood and bile. Very well—but cooperation on some tasks was essential.

There were some groups that kept above all of this, of course. The Blue Rock Clan hadn't sent a representative to this meeting. The Hawaiians and surviving spacers preferred to keep out of the perpetual Ortho-Percell bickering.

"We need more help in Hydro," Carl said. "Equipment keeps breaking down and the only way to make up is with labor."

"You want more work from us?" Malcolm said resentfully.

"Right. But it can't eat into the Nudge program."

"Impossible. We're stretched too far as it is."

"Orbits wait for nobody," Jeffers said. "We got to have the launchers ready by aphelion or else there'll none of us see Earth again."

Carl nodded. "And I doubt we could survive an extra ten years."

Malcolm's lean mouth set in a determined line. "I get it. You want to unslot a bunch of our people, then work them to death."

"That's not it at all." Carl had anticipated this reaction, but not so soon. *He's edgy, suspicious. I don't envy him, having to deal with Quiverian and Ould-Harrad and the Arcists. Of course, Jeffers doesn't have it easy either, coping with Sergeov and the radical Percells.*

Carl said calmly, "I think we'll get by if you simply stop trying to produce children. That will free more women to work full time."

"Uh-uh. We got a right to reproduce."

Carl thought bitterly, *Now you understand how* we *felt about the EarthBirth Laws.* He put the thought aside—a dim dispute from another life—and leaned forward earnestly. "Look, think this through. We have—"

The hatch clanged. Carl looked up in surprise to see Saul Lintz gingerly making his way into the center of the console banks. "Saul, this is a parley. You're not invited. And frankly, I think you're too weak to—"

"Nonsense. I heard where you were and decided to come have a look. You're the, ah, Ortho leader?" Saul peered at Malcolm as if trying to place him from the past.

As the two made introductions, Carl thought. Could he use Saul to persuade Malcolm? Saul's prestige in suppressing the Black Year plagues carried weight. How much did Lintz know of what had happened? He would have to step carefully here.

"Oh, I understand the problems," Saul said to Malcolm. "I tapped into the running inventory, projections, the maintenance programs. What I want to know," he said carefully, looking at Jeffers and Carl, "is why the Nudge Launchers have been reprogrammed."

*Damn.* "It's preliminary, since only a few of the launchers have been built yet. We've sharpened our analysis—"

"No, that's not it. They're set to bring us nowhere close to Earth, after the Jupiter slingshot." Saul looked at Carl steadily.

"Look, I was going to sit down and go over this with you in detail as soon as you—" Carl sighed. "Okay. Here, I'll play the squirt from Earth, same as we got it years ago. You might as well have the full story."

It wasn't hard to find. He had replayed it incessantly, and so had many of the Orthos, he imagined.

The main screen glowed, fluttered. NEWS.

A burly announcer looked mirthful, shrugged comically, and said, "Remember that trag ex-ed on Halley's Comet? How they went balloka and started checking out from the bugs they found? Well, here's how they looked when Orbital got 'em in sights again."

A dry chuckle. The screen showed a silvery profile swimming in blackness—the *Edmund.*

"Some of the nonbuggy ones jumped into their mother ship and flew home. Only *nobody*'s nonbuggy out there now, so Fed said—you *know* what Fed said, right?"

The leering, wide-eyed face of the announcer swelled, smiled broadly with impossibly white teeth, then dwindled as down-tonal sound effects rose and—the screen flared with brilliant blue light.

"Scintillatin' sendoff, yes! All gone-free for you and me, to keep bugs out of the hurly-clime. Went up clean, too, one big fuse—"

Carl snapped it off. "Welcome to the coming new century," he said sardonically.

"Good . . . Lord . . ." Saul was dazed. His gray pallor slowly reddened and he blinked rapidly. "They . . . they weren't going to take any chances."

Malcolm said bitingly, "Why should they? Even if Earth quarantined the *Edmund,* how could they be *sure?*"

Jeffers said levelly, "You sound like you're agreein' with what they did."

"I can understand it." Malcolm eyed Jeffers with open dislike.

"Only good thing," Jeffers said cuttingly, "is that Linbarger and those Ortho assholes all bought it."

Saul gritted his teeth, as if swimming up from some personal memory that had overwhelmed him. Carl suspected which one: the old Zionist associations were broad enough to be triggered by anything like this. "I expected some strong measures . . . but to . . ."

Carl said flatly, "You wanted to know—okay, there it is. We can't go back to Earth. Ever. They'll never believe we're not disease carriers, and they'll be damned well right, too."

Saul's eyes seemed to swell in his papery, pale face, sensing possibilities. "Then . . . where can we . . ."

"That's what we have to decide. We're aiming for a close pass of Jupiter on the inbound, and we can slingshot ourselves just about anywhere from there."

Saul said distantly, "I see."

Carl watched Saul carefully during the rest of the meeting. The man listened mutely, lost in his own dark introspections.

Malcolm was balky, reluctant. He gave ground grudgingly, agreeing to a slight increase in the labor hours in Hydroponics, swearing he could give no more without consulting all the Ortho factions. Jeffers made similarly hedged promises on behalf of the Percell groups.

Carl himself spoke for the ex-spacers—mostly Plateau Three types—and the Hawaiians. *What would I do without those diehard idealists?* he thought, watching the give and take of the meeting. *There aren't nearly enough of them. . . .*

He moved into the verbal crossfire, working them around to a livable compromise. He used hard-won skills to cajole Malcolm into doing what it seemed to him anyone rational would immediately agree to—but by now he was used to it, resigned to the obdurate mulishness of the human species.

And this was only a minor sticking point. Eventually they'd have to get Quiverian and Sergeov to sit down, too, representing the extremes. And all this bickering over mere Hydro, too—the deeper issues of finishing the Nudge Flingers would be far worse. It resembled the never-ending news from the Middle East. Even with Saul's lost Israel broken into squabbling theocracies, the region was still rife with more microscopic factions, unending rivalry, bitterness, stupidity. Nobody could see beyond their noses. No, Halley was all too representative of humanity.

After the meeting he sat and watched the sun set in vivid ruby splashes over Hong Kong. He wondered idly if the place existed anymore; there had been reports of a small nuke war somewhere near there, twenty years ago. He would have to check sometime. Or maybe he didn't really wish to know. The city simmering in its rosy sunset looked better if you thought it could still be there.

At last he roused himself and went down to sleep slot 1. The thawing was proceeding normally; he had kept track by remote throughout the day. Suited and encased, he came into the foggy kingdom of eternal chill. He did not rush into the prep room, though. The team was not quite through yet. . . .

Carl stopped at Lani Nguyen's slot. Frost filmed it and he checked the fluid lines automatically. He had come here often to stare into that blissful, milky, floating refuge—and to envy them all. He peered through the slowly churning fluids at the watery form inside. Did he see a face gazing out?

*I miss you, Lani. I was a young idiot when I knew you. Not that an older idiot would do any better. That night after Cruz died . . . We know how it should have worked out, don't we?* He smiled wanly. *You should sleep safely to the end. But we'll need you soon, too. And pray that unslotting doesn't give those plagues lying dormant in you the crucial edge they need . . .*

He could contain his impatience no longer. He went into the prep room and stood aside as the technicians finished their hours of careful labor. His eyes followed every feeder line, each stimulating circuit, all the myriad details that spelled the difference.

*She's still as wonderful. Just looking at her makes my heart feel as though a hand is squeezing it.*

He stood aside as they unwrapped the nutrient gauze from Virginia's almond skin.

*That luscious color belongs on beaches, not in ice.*

He had waited so long for this. . . . And had thought a thousand times of violating his pledge, of reviving Virginia without Saul. What could they do about it except complain? He had even come down here once, at the nub end of a lonely, half-drunken evening. . . . Invaded the realm of frost and started the warmup, let it run on for two hours before finally facing the fact that he couldn't do it. Not merely because she would be enraged, would surely see through his invented explanations . . . but because he knew he could not live with having done it.

But now all that was past. The long years dropped away, done. He stepped forward to see her again.

# VIRGINIA

Long ago, Virginia had wondered what it would be like if she ever really succeeded . . . if ever she fooled them all, and actually made a machine that could think.

How would awareness seem to the new entity? Would it appear suddenly, as great Athena was supposed to have come into her wisdom, springing self-aware from the brow of Zeus?

Would it be like a child growing up? A long, slow, tedious/thrilling process of rote and extrapolation? Of trial and error and skinned knees?

Or would it happen as humanity had done it—evolving by quirk and happenstance from the feral reflexes of microbes, all the way up to the hubris to challenge gods?

Most often of all, she had imagined that it would be like this. A slow gathering of scattered threads. A learning anew of what was already known.

An awakening.

All the blurry images came together into a single shape that swam in front of her eyes—a complete mystery. A blob.

Then, with no transition at all, she knew it as a face . . . one that *ought* to be familiar.

"Carl?" she tried to ask. But her facial muscles would only twitch a little, a promise of returning volition, but not much more.

The figure overhead blurred, unfocused, and finally went away. Virginia slept. And for the first time in a long while, she dreamed.

The white walls were sharp and clear when next she opened her eyes.

*Recuperation room*, she thought. *I wonder how long it's been.*

There was a rustling *tap tap tap* of a databoard nearby. Virginia laboriously turned her head, and saw a man in a faded, threadbare hospital gown perched crosslegged on a webbing, looking intently into a portable display and rubbing his chin slowly with one hand. His eyelids were slot-blue and he looked so thin.

"Saul," she whispered.

He looked up quickly. In a single motion he put aside the databoard and was by her side, bringing a squeeze bottle to her lips.

She sipped until he drew it away. Then she worked her mouth. "H . . . h-how. . . ?"

"How long?" Saul took her hand. "About thirty years. We're getting near aphelion. Carl told me you left little watchdog programs throughout the data systems that kept popping up, promising bloody hell if you were awakened before me."

Virginia smiled weakly. "I told you . . . I'd . . . m-manage it."

He laughed. "And I'm so very proud of you."

The richness of his voice made her blink. Saul was still only partially recovered from his own slotting, and yet something else was different about him.

Her preslotting memories were coming back clearly. There was a little more gray at Saul's temples, maybe, and yet could it be an illusion that he actually looked younger than before?

*Oh, I must be a mess,* she thought. *I had better do some hard eating to put some meat back on, after three decades.*

*But if slotting drops years off you, I must learn to conquer my fear of it!*

"How am . . . I . . . doing?"

"A doctor's joy." He grinned. "A marvelous piece of womanly engineering. Recovering nicely, and soon to be put to work, by orders of his Grand Poobah-dom, Commander Osborn."

Virginia shook her head.

"C-commander. . . ?"

Saul nodded. "Lieutenant Commander, actually. Commission from Earth. They had to. Only two officers left alive, and they hardly count. Ensign Calciano's in the slots after a ten-year shift in which he seems to have become convinced he was the Flying Dutchman. Ould-Harrad's resigned his commission and gone off to join the Revisionist-Arcists over in Gehenna. . . ."

At Virginia's puzzled expression, Saul squeezed her hand.

"It's a different world, Virginia. So much has changed. Back on Earth, things have gone from very bad to better to incomprehensible.

And out here they're . . . well . . ." He shrugged. "Out here they're just plain weird."

"But Carl. . . ?" She started to rise, but he pushed her gently back against the pillow. Even Halley gravity was a weight for her.

"Enough talk. Now you rest. Later I'll explain what I've been able to discover. We'll try to figure out a place for ourselves in this strange new world."

Virginia let herself relax.

*We* . . . she thought, liking the way the word sounded in his voice. *Yes, we will.*

She was starting to drift off when she felt Saul gently pull his hand away. Virginia looked up and saw that he was fumbling with a handkerchief and staring into space with a screwed up, half-orgasmic squint. It ended deep inside the square of cloth in a muffled sneeze.

Virginia hiccupped in a little laugh. She reached out with leaden arms and touched the tear that rolled down one scratchy cheek.

"Oh, darling," she sighed. "Out of the slots only a few days, and already you have a cold!"

He looked at her sheepishly, then he smiled.

"So *nu*? What else is new?"

# SAUL

Everybody seemed to be dying.

In fact, the more Saul learned about this aging colony, the more it seemed a mystery to him that anyone was left alive at all.

Oh, people had adapted, found ways to cope. Human beings were good at that. Since thirty years ago, when Akio Matsudo had finally given firm orders and seen Saul strapped into his slot, the tools he had left behind had been added to, improved.

But the modified cyanutes, the subtly tuned microwave scanners, all of their clever devices could only slow down the long erosion, the declining spiral. Halley-Life, too, was adaptable, and much more at home here. It was a war of attrition that men could only lose.

*I should have known that Akio would hardly take his own advice,* Saul thought in the chilly domain of sleep slot 1. It had been a mistake to come down here so soon after leaving Recuperation Hall, to look in on old friends. A rude shock to have it brought home so clearly that three decades had passed.

Until now his last memory of the Japanese physician had been of glossy black hair framing smiling almond eyes under wire-rimmed glasses. But that image—as fresh as last week—was jarringly crushed down here among the chilled caskets. One was labeled with Akio Matsudo's name. The figure behind the frosted glass was almost unrecognizable.

A thin fringe of gray wisps rimmed a pate turned speckled with age spots and scarred from bouts with skin infections. Those once-plump cheeks were now the hollowed inheritance of a man grown old fighting the inevitable, the implacable. And there was no hint of laughter anymore in the lines rimming poor Akio's sleep-shut eyes.

The charts at the foot of every slot told the story of each hibernating occupant, red symbols denoting medical reasons for internment, black trim meaning storage without real hope of recovery or resuscitation, and blue marking a crewman or -woman who was simply "off duty" for this span of years.

At first glance the situation looked serious, but not impossible. There were plenty of blue folders. However, a quick scan of the colors did not tell the true story. Akio, for instance, had a blue folder.

*A tired, sick old man,* he thought on reading his friend's folder. It wasn't just the lingering infections, or malnutrition from decades of eating only the narrow range of foods grown in the colony's agro domes. Osteoporosis had so weakened the man's bones that there was no way he would ever walk his beloved western Japanese hills again. Electrical bone stimulation had not made up for year after year in near weightlessness.

The *Edmund Halley*'s gravity wheel hung in cavern Gamma, frozen and broken down. So far, nobody had had the energy to fix it.

Saul read a random sample of blue folders and pored over slot readings. Slowly, he came to a chilling realization.

No more than ten percent of the colony was well in any real sense of the word.

*Is Carl really that good a liar?* He wondered how Osborn was able to maintain the fiction that the mission could ever be completed. *Or is everyone pretending for the sake of their sanity?*

He saw no way there'd be even a fraction of the manpower needed to build and operate the "flinger" launchers—the mass drivers that were supposed to alter Halley's orbit come aphelion.

And without the Nudge, they all might as well go to sleep for good, because there would be no homecoming for any of them.

His thoughts were clouded as he left sleep slot 1. Still a bit weak from his long hibernation, Saul stretched long-unused muscles by glide-walking the long tunnels downward and southward, an area he had not visited yet since his internment.

In this area nearly all the passages were coated in luxuriant green layers of *Halleyviridis* fungoid. The stuff was too slick to allow good purchase for his vel-stick slippers, but offered a sure grip when he used his bare toes as he had seen others do.

It actually made movement much easier. He found he didn't need the almost hidden wall cables, for instance. Grabbing a tuft of growth in passing gave him all the added leverage he needed to move along swiftly.

Saul wandered for some time without paying close attention to where he was going, thinking about the strangeness he and Virginia had awakened to.

Earth appeared to have completely written off Miguel Cruz's grand odyssey. Oh, they still maintained contact, after a fashion, sending up entertainments and dribbles of technical data from time to time. Saul had extracted a promise from Carl Osborn to bring him more fully up-to-date soon—the distant, somewhat aloof spacer had been imprecise about when. Apparently, most of the awake colonists lived day to day, and took a detached view toward time.

Soon, though, Saul knew he would have to resume his duties as expedition doctor. And the burden of hopelessness that had worn down Akio Matsudo would be his.

Most sorry of all had been those poor Orthos down in Quadrant 9, with their pitiful children—scabrous, wild-eyed, stick figures barely human in aspect, always hungry and frail as leaves.

*Perhaps the EarthBirth Laws were wise. Gravity runs strong in our genes.*

But there was more to it than that. Yesterday he had examined five of the Ortho kids. All seemed to suffer from the same enzyme deficiency. He already had it mapped to the seventh chromosome. In a few weeks he should be able to track it down and . . .

*And what, Lintz? Are you contemplating meddling, again? Just emerged into a new world, and already you're coming up with ideas how to change it?*

The glow of phosphor panels was growing sparse. Saul tried to take his bearings and realized that he had not been paying close enough attention. He was lost.

In the old days that would have been impossible. But by now all the old intersection "street signs" were obscured, completely covered over by the soft, native carpeting. Instead, where shaft met tunnel, there were deeply incised "clan markings"—filled in with a pitchlike substance that seemed to repel the Halleyforms. The marks denoted the boundaries of the various human bands. He looked around for one of these.

Apparently only Central, the sleep slots, and the hydroponics domes were neutral territory, now. And the deep, inner regions of Halley Core, of course. But only madmen ever went down that way, he had heard.

In one of the faction areas nearest Central he had seen what had become of the fibercloth that had once lined the tunnels and shafts of Halley Colony. The material had been turned into clothing and tentlike, "purple-proof" habitats, suspended from the ceilings of the bigger chambers.

Every sleeping hall maintained a round-the-clock watch for the most deadly of the comet lifeforms. Nevertheless, every year or so another poor victim fell to the feared native foragers.

*Animals would be an ideal solution,* he thought as he scraped away at the mosslike growth, hoping for a clue to where he was. *On Earth we tamed other creatures and used them to fight vermin for us. Should be able to do that here.*

Of course, that idea had been tried. Over the decades others had thawed dogs and cats and monkeys from the colony's small collection of slot-stored animals. But none of the poor creatures had proved able to adapt even as well as the humans.

But what about *changing* the Earthbreed animals . . . altering them to fit into this strange environment?

He knew it hadn't been attempted. Nobody else had the skill—or the arrogance—to try it. Already his mind was turning over ideas, genes of expression and regulation, ways of adapting creatures to work *with* an alien environment instead of against it.

*Those poor, pathetic children,* he thought.

Saul pulled out his chemically sterilized handkerchief and blew his nose. As he approached a new intersection, he saw one of the pitch-filled clan marks, at last. He glided to a stop and contemplated the symbol: a large "U" crowned with a halo.

As he stood there, a voice spoke, as if out of nowhere.

"Clape. Look a' what we have here! Lost, boss?"

Saul grabbed the wall growth and swiveled to see that a man with a blue-tinted face looked down at him from the overhanging shaft opening.

Saul had to blink, for this was distinctly the oddest-looking person he had seen since awakening.

The fellow wore bangles of hammered native platinum and a short-sleeved fibercloth tunic. And as he drifted to the floor, Saul saw nasty-looking metal claw/hooks on his toes. In his free hand the man held loops of rope woven of some native growth.

Saul nodded. "I guess I am lost, at that. I thought I was on M Level, near Shaft Five, but—"

The other man laughed, showing open gaps amid rotting teeth. He leaped forward and landed closer to Saul, the movement exposing a large tattoo on his chest. It was a symbol Saul recognized, the Sigil of Simon Percell.

"What a savor, Hum? Free labor bum!" The man grinned, fingering the rope.

A second blue face emerged from the overhead shaft and grinned. "Green hydro labor, for a favor."

Saul shook his head and smiled. Their glassy-eyed stares made him nervous. "I'm sorry, I'm fresh out of the slots, so I'm not up on the dialect yet."

"Clack!" The first Percell rolled his eyes. "A virgin wool! Well, baby Earth blue, I remember how to talk land cant. Are you one of Simon's diamonds? Or normal ape crape?"

Saul raised his hand, smiling ruefully. "Guilty as charged. I'm what I suppose you'd call an Ortho. Is that a problem? Have I wandered into territory that's exclusively Perc—"

The fellow's hands moved in a blur. A loop of rope snaked out abruptly over Saul's shoulders and was pulled taut. "Hey!"

Another followed the first. Saul tugged back, but managed only to tighten the nooses. "I said I was just thawed! Just point me back toward Central and I won't bother you—"

This time both men laughed. "It's simple, pimple," the first Percell began. Then the second broke in.

"Oh, give the ape a break, Stew. He lacks track." There was a trace of sympathy in the second man's eyes. Just a trace. He faced Saul.

"There's rules, fellow. Capture without harm or blood spilled isn't vendetta, it's fair coup. You work for us in Hydro for ten mega-seconds—that's about four months, old style—with maybe time off for good behavior."

The first Percell laughed again, this time a high-pitched set of yelps that cut off in a fit of coughing. He spat a pink-stained gobbet onto the wall.

"That cough sounds pretty bad," Saul said. "How long have you been bringing up bloody phlegm?"

The blue-faced man shook his head angrily. "None o' your business! Come on an' limp, chimp," Stew said, and jerked Saul's tether hard.

Until that moment Saul had felt almost detached, as if this were more comic than serious. But now he felt a part of himself getting very, very mad.

*I should have just played along until I learned more,* he thought. But the last time he had been jerked at the end of a rope like this it had been on a miserable day in Jerusalem, when he had been passed, handcuffed, from one newly installed theocracy bureaucrat to another—half of them misquoting Leviticus to his face and the rest reading apparently randomly chosen passages from Revelations and the Koran. It had been a blessed relief when the *ferchochteh* finally sentenced him to six months cutting timber on a labor gang, and then expelled him forever from his native land.

"I think not, *yoksh,*" he said evenly as the blue-faced man tugged again. Getting a grip on the wall growth with his toes and one hand, Saul yanked back hard with the other.

Maybe it was the unexpectedness—Saul's eyelids were still slotblue, after all—but the man on the ceiling yelped and tumbled from his high perch, past the floor, and on down into the shaft below. His cry diminished as he bounced softly against the walls, struggling for a hold as he fell. Saul transferred his grip to the other rope.

"Stew" wasn't going to be surprised as easily. He grinned and pulled taut his own tether. Most of the fancy, rhythmic dialect was gone when he spoke.

"Poor Earth baby. Just unslotted and weak as an Ortho toddler. What do you know about tunnel fighting?"

"Don't try to teach your grandma to suck eggs," Saul told him, and kicked off from his anchoring point on the wall. He landed beside the surprised Percell, where the rope fell slack, and immediately started shrugging out of the loosened bonds.

"It sounds to me like you've got a tuberculinlike infection," he said mildly, distracting his tormentor for a moment with his driest bedside manner. "Also, how long have you had that *parech* skin infection? Don't the microwave treatments help anymore?"

Stew's blank amazement lasted only a few seconds. "I—" He blinked, howled, and launched himself at Saul.

Saul's knees came up just in time, knocking the Percell's toe-claws past him. A sharp pain lanced his left leg before he was able to lock into an embrace too close for the deadly implements to be used. Their hands met and gripped each other, fingers interlaced. Stew dug his toe-claws into the wall growth and started pressing Saul back.

Wind whistled between their teeth. The detached part of Saul clinically noted the particularly foul stench of the other man's breath. It was automatically compiled with a list of his other symptoms, to be used later—if there was a later—in studying the disease.

*You're too old for this,* he told himself as they grunted, face to face. *And it's much too soon out of the slots!*

Thinking that, he was nearly as surprised as the wiry Percell when the straining war of muscles began to break, *away* from him. His opponent's arms began quivering, giving way. Saul pressed his advantage.

"I . . . get . . . it . . ." Saul gasped as he wrenched the fellow's arms back, making him cry out. "You guys . . . must be what they . . . call *Ubers.*" He got the man turned around, arms twisted painfully behind him.

"Hoosh, some superman," Saul commented. With a grunt he tossed his opponent down into the shaft, just in time to strike his returning partner as the other Percell's head came over the top. Together they tumbled, shouting, down the shaft again. Saul drifted against a wall and held on with one hand until the gentle gravity brought him to the floor again. His heart pounded and he saw spots. His scratched leg hurt like hell.

"Assholes," he whispered, preferring the explicit Anglo-Saxonisms of his youth, in this case, over the more subtle Yiddish he had learned only later in life. He gathered his breath and braced himself as sounds told of their return.

This time they were more careful. The two sprang to opposite sides of the hall to face him, both clearly angry. In their hands shone bright metal knives.

*So much for capture by the rules,* Saul thought. *Maybe I should have accepted ten megaseconds in Hydro after all.*

And yet, somehow, he didn't regret a thing. "Come on, twerps," he said, waving them forward. They started to comply.

*"Stop this!"*

He and the Percells looked up as one. A third blue-tinted head emerged from the overhead shaft and Saul had to groan. Even on an adrenaline high, he wasn't idiot enough to think he could take on three of the bastards.

But the newcomer didn't direct his ire at Saul. He turned to the other *Ubers*.

"Why did you cut this man?" he shouted in a clear tone of command. To Saul the voice seemed familiar . . . a once-thick accent softened and covered over by years of dialect.

The first two *Ubers* looked away. "Clape. The mape *fought* us, Sergie—"

"Dap the crap!" The leader drifted down one green-lined wall. Truncated legs that were little more than nubs tipped with hooks turned him quickly as he pointed at Saul. "Do not you know who this *is*?"

They only blinked, and then stared blankly as the legless leader turned to face Saul for the first time, and bowed in an ornate gesture of respect. "I greet you, uncle of the new race."

The shock of Slavic hair was nearly gone now, and the space-tanned skin had been turned into one big tattoo. But years were nothing to recognition. Saul laughed out loud.

"Oh. Hi, Otis. It's good to see you, too. What have you been doing with yourself . . . besides turning blue, I mean?"

Inside, though, his heart still raced as he began to realize what a close call he'd had. Saul could only think, *Oy*.

The trip back to Central, under *Uber* escort, was almost anticlimactic, skim-running along velvety, moss-lined halls and passing the checkpoints of various clans with elaborate but apparently routine ritual.

Even to Saul it was obvious that they were taking a long way back, dropping deep into the comet to move northward before beginning to climb back up again. "Why are we going so far out of the way?" he asked when they had descended to tunnels he had never seen before—twisty paths following soft veins of primordial snow.

Sergeov shrugged. "Quiverian."

Saul stopped. "Joao? I'd heard he was awake now, as well. But why are you avoiding him?"

The first *Uber*, the Percell named Stew, spat down a nearby shaft. "He's th' darkest Arcist. Th' ape we hate."

Saul shook his head, looking at Sergeov. "Explain please, Otis."

The *Uber* leader smiled. "The old race had some superior individuals—like you and Simon Percell. Quiverian, too. He leads most rabidly anti-Percell band of Orthos, these days. Those who understand that, they are dinosaurs, and so want to stamp out us new mammals."

Saul thought he understood. The term *Arcist,* once denoting equatorial environmentalism on Earth, had evolved and shifted here on Halley. Now it meant the most radical Ortho human faction, as *Uber* stood for those Percells who believed there could be no compromise with unmodified human beings.

There was clearly intense hatred and rivalry, and yet it was also obviously under control. All factions were clearly too weak, much too dependent on one another, to wage open war.

"I'm puzzled, Otis," he said as they resumed their journey. Down here the tunnels seemed to have been hewn by hand, rough and winding, following paths of least resistance through the rocky ice. "If you feel that way, why aren't you having children, like some of the Ortho bands?"

One of Sergeov's men snarled angrily, and Saul realized he had brought up a taboo topic. Sergeov cut back the blue-faced fellow with a sharp word. He turned back to Saul.

"We have a few. Came out better than Orthos' pitiful little wretches. One, we hope, can maybe someday learn to read and write." His face was briefly contorted in painful recollection. "We do not experiment anymore. What is point, when everyone is doomed anyway, eh? Those Orthos in Quadrant Nine, they are immoral to bring babes up just to suffer, to die."

*So,* Saul thought. *They* do *know the truth.*

"That's why the level of violence is so low, even though you hate each other so much," he ventured.

Sergeov nodded. "Everybody will die together, anyway. But we need workers to keep things going as long as possible. Nobody wants to go by cold, by starvation."

"Nobody 'cept maybe Ould-Harrad," one of the others ventured.

"Ould-Harrad!" Saul blinked. "Then he's—"

"Become a wild-eyed mystic," Sergeov explained. "How you think a Percell like Osborn ever became an officer? Not for his pretty looks and Ortho-loving ways, I tell you!"

The other two *Ubers* laughed. "No. Ould-Harrad started talking to God. Resigned his commission. Lunatic is tool of Quiverian, now. *Spiritual leader* of the Arcists," he said sarcastically.

Saul could believe the last. It was a wonder the stark silence of the long watches had not driven more of them farther toward the fringe of human experience.

Sergeov shrugged. "Let us go now. I take you back to Central. I must talk to Osborn anyway. Clear up some stupid accusations of that crybaby Malcolm."

Saul did not move, though. He was staring, blinking, down a cross tunnel toward a phantom light that wavered in the distance.

The others turned and saw it too. One *Uber* hissed, "Clape. It's th' Ol' Man himself!"

Saul drifted toward the shape, curious. Then he saw that there were two, no, three of the ghostly figures, moving along the walls like great spiders, picking through the wall growth.

A hand gripped his arm and pulled.

"We go now," Sergeov grunted.

"What *are* they?" Saul asked in wonder. For a moment he thrilled to the thought that they might be an as-yet-unknown form of Halley-Life—huge and highly structured creatures.

"*Now,* Saul Lintz. Those can be dangerous."

Saul blinked again, and realized that the slowly approaching creatures were shaped as *men,* but their outlines were fuzzy, fringed, as it were, with a cloudy, milky edge of shimmering fronds.

"*Ingersoll?*" he wondered aloud.

"Old Man of the Caves," Sergeov agreed. "And some of other mad ones who joined him. Come now, Lintz, or we leave you."

Saul nodded and began backing away with them. There would be time to study mysteries. Patience would pay off better, in the end, than impetuous curiosity.

Anyway, his palms were sweaty and his mouth drier—as he watched the ghostlike shapes grazing through the Halleyform forest—than they had been during the fight with Sergeov's *Uber* warriors. Saul hurried along with his escorts, promising himself that he would be back when he knew better the rules of this strange place and time.

The halls near Central—still fibercloth-lined, still scoured at intervals with ultraviolet and microwaves and kept clean by a few mechs that had survived the decades—seemed like an oasis not just from another century but from a different world.

"My business is with Osborn," Sergeov told Saul. "Take my advice, Lintz. Be careful which faction you join, after recuperation. A few Ortho groups are not vicious baboons."

Saul had heard Sergeov's radical Percells described in pretty nasty terms, as well. Where there was tribalism, he had long ago decided, there was no way to avoid criminality.

"Some groups accept both Percells and Orthos," he told Sergeov. "It'll have to be one of those, if we join any faction at all."

"We . . ." The legless *Uber* leader thought. "Ah, you and the Herbert woman."

"Another Ortho lover—" one of the others began, but a sharp look from Sergeov shut him up.

"There is one last thing," Saul said as the Percells were turning to go. He reached into his belt pouch and pulled out a silvery tool.

"I want some blood and tissue samples for my new medical inventory, if you fellows don't mind. The Survivors and the Plateau Three bands have already contributed, and I'm sure you'll be happy to cooperate."

The *Uber* with the bad teeth snarled and reached for his knife. But one more time the Russian cut him off. Sergeov's eyes seemed to glitter as he presented his arm to Saul. And a silent message seemed to say that he would expect a favor of his own, someday.

*If I had not once worked with Simon Percell,* Saul thought as he took samples from the other two, *would Otis have even saved my life this afternoon?*

On the *Ubers'* chests the Sigil stood out starkly, red against blue, a tribute to a man long dead at his own hand, who might have seen some of what was to come, but could never have imagined how far it would all go.

He visited for some time with Virginia in her recuperation unit, checking her progress carefully and reassuring her that the slot pallor was fading nicely. He kissed her and gave her a mild sedative for her insomnia. Then Saul went down to his lab.

The samples from the *Ubers* went through the same preliminary analysis as he had performed on his other subjects. The first results seemed to be just the same.

Oh, there were different accumulations of microfauna in their blood and sputum. The Percells' immune systems seemed slightly less damaged, not as overstressed as the colony's remaining Ortho complement. That was no surprise. The expedition had started out less than one-quarter Percell. Now the ratio among those healthy enough to be awake was even or better in favor of the genetic augments.

But the story was still the same. *We're all dying,* he thought. At last he found the courage to insert a sample just taken from Virginia.

Saul swallowed. She was fresher, but he could read the signs. Even in her case, right out of the slots, the inevitable was well under way.

"Well," he whispered. "Maybe I can find some patterns. Maybe adjust the cyanutes some more."

He did not hold out much hope for that approach, though. That breakthrough had made it possible for people to live here. But Comet-Life was adapting. More and more forms avoided the special sugar coating that had enabled his little gene-crafted creatures to do their extra job so well.

The old question still raised itself, every day, nearly every hour he was awake. He must have slept with it over the long years in the slots.

*How is it possible for Halley-Life to live in us? How is it Ingersoll and the other cave dwellers can eat the stuff and survive?*

*Why are we so much alike?*

Oh, that simulation he and Virginia had worked out with JonVon, so long ago, had shown how a *basic* similarity had come about. Science had long known that organic chemistry would come up with the same amino acids, the same purines and pyrimidines under a wide variety of circumstances. Life would generally start out the same anywhere.

But the similarities went far beyond that. It was almost as if men were not the first creatures from Earth to invade the comet. As if there had been earlier waves, and the present war was one among distant *cousins*.

Long ago, in the late twentieth century, a famous astronomer had even proposed that comets were a source of epidemics on Earth. His theory was that primeval viruses floated down into the atmosphere whenever the world passed through a big cometary tail. This, he thought, explained ancient myths calling objects like Halley apparitions of doom. Evil stars.

Saul had laughed on reading such baroque nonsense. But that was long ago. Now . . . well, he did not know what to think. Nothing, none of it, made any sense at all.

The computer winked a code at him, over and over.

F4–D$56.

*More data wanted.*

"Certainly." He nodded amiably. "A most worthy request."

Tomorrow he would go out and try to persuade Quiverian's Arcists to cooperate. Then he remembered. He hadn't tested his *own* blood, yet.

One more datum for a baseline. He stepped over to the treatment table, drew and prepared the samples, and returned to run them through the fluorescent separator-analyzer. Numbers and graphs flickered in three dimensions and many colors. Depictions grew on all sides of him, programmed to highlight differences from the mean of the prior samples.

All around Saul, the displays were suddenly ablaze. Winking high-lights, bright anomalies. He blinked. Nearly *everything* was different!

"Um," he said concisely. Saul blinked at the figures.

There was the array of lymphocyte counts . . . **all types: *within***
***normal range.***

Nobody else's sample said that. Only his.

**Electrolyte balance . . . *nominal.***

His was the only one that said that!

**Metabolic processes . . . *nominal.***

"Stupid machine," Saul grumbled. He smacked the side of the unit, keyed on an autotest, then another. Only green lights winked from the control panel. The machine claimed it was working well.

"I'm aberrant because I'm *normal?*" He stared at the columns of figures. They all insisted that he was anomalous. Strange. Unusual.

And nearly all of the differences were *toward* the Earthly human norm. Except for one.

**Foreign infecting agents . . .**

He looked at the estimate and whistled.

According to the bioassay, he should be dead.

Dead? Saul laughed. The damned machine seemed to think his blood was a *froth* of dangerous invaders. His bodily fluids were aswarm with horrible, nasty things, the smallest fraction of which should have killed him long ago!

And yet the other displays said: *Nominal . . .*

**Nominal . . .**

> **nominal . . .**

>> **nominal . . .**

"Crazy damn machine," he muttered.

But then Saul remembered . . . fighting the *Uber* in the hallway . . . the surprise on *both* of their faces when he—barely two weeks out of the slots—began twisting the other man's arms back, back. . . .

"Visual microscopic display," he commanded. Time to get to the bottom of this. Something was wrong here, and the best way to find out what had broken down in his biocomputer would be to do an old-fashioned histological survey himself. "Screen One, subject blood sample, magnification ninety."

The holistank rippled and cleared, showing a straw-colored sea crowded with drifting globs of pink, white, yellow. A jostling of multishaded forms, whirling, jouncing, fluttering in the saline tide.

Saul shook his head, stared, shook his head again.

His mouth started working, without making a sound, in blank amazement and silent prayer.

# CARL

Carl studied the main screen in disbelief. He had just finished another useless conversation with Major Clay, the marvelous wooden man who fielded all questions sent Earthside with a bland yet rock-hard calm. Earth wasn't sending advice, information, or even much sympathy—that was certain. Major Clay sidestepped every question. With each passing year, they papered over their fear by increasing the entertainment channels they sent in the weekly squirt. That left less time for real communication.

So Carl had thumbed off impatiently before the transmission time had elapsed. It was doubly irritating that he could never really hang up on Major Clay, because the delay from the speed of light was now five hours. *Not conducive to snappy comebacks,* he had thought.

Time to prepare for the meeting. He idly thumbed over to RUNNING READOUT, expecting to see the usual situation report, but didn't get the usual five-colored status chart. Instead, he caught a trickle of JonVon's momentarily exposed inner flow. Incredibly, it was another poem. As he read, Carl began to smile.

Plateau Threes are simple, plain
can't flutter free of Percell's pain
*Take us home! Or near sun's warm!*
Close to Earth and safe from harm.
Only ole JonVon's got the charm
to hide a riddle
in the middle: gold!
Treat us as miners,
Major.

And Martian Way, *ah*
they see their day
to come—to smack a planet red
(Carefully, about the head.)

To make it run with fluids bled
From Halley's pitted blue-iced dead.

Worms, like sticky pearls
Orbits, in liquid whorls
Ubers strut, pale hard jaws jut
Slice the Orthos!
If they could. All
for converging clammy good
Out by Neptune
on some ice-and-iron moon
(Or else to slip the knife
of bugs and lice to Earth. Drop
a rocket
in their pocket. Eh?)

Sad sure Arcists want to
Loop forever
Aren't they clever?
High-pitched bray and rusty rattle
Brows furrowed, they sing like cattle:
Keep the blue-green pearl free
of us, our pus
Unclean, you see.
Suicide is as much a right
As going gladly into that Good Night.

Carl laughed. Incredible! This was not the first evidence he'd seen that JonVon was noodling away at poetry in slack moments. But of late the bio-organic idiot savant had been getting uncanny. Or maybe it only proved that poetry wasn't really a higher-level activity after all. This was jagged, lurching, bitter stuff, reeling from rhyme to rhyme, with an occasional glancing collision with reason.

What was the gold JonVon was hiding? He wondered if JonVon had showed this to Virginia yet. She was still recuperating from the slots, but spent a few hours each day linked to her cyber-friend. What if the machine eventually turned out to be a better poet? Carl smiled.

And how did JonVon get such detailed information about the noxious factions Carl had to juggle? *Maybe I should turn this job over to a subroutine.*

Meetings, always meetings. Through the hatch came Andy Carroll, slot-thin and glowering.

"Those Arcists have gone on strike again!"

"Wildcat?"

"No, Malcolm called them in. I just got a hail from him."

"How come?"

"He says their Hydro share was low this week. His pickup team just returned with no fruit, not many vegetables."

Carl frowned. "That shouldn't have happened. I checked the output—"

"Sergeov got some of theirs, I'm pretty sure." Andy balled a fist and smacked it into his palm.

"Stole it again?"

A nod. "He's got some way of slipping the stuff out after it's been counted and allotted. I can't figure it."

Mildly Carl said, "That's your department."

Andy was young, only recently awakened, but he had caught on to the nuances of the situation quickly. His black eyebrows shot up. "I cover *every* entrance. No way a man or woman could get in there."

Carl nodded sympathetically. "Uh-huh. What about half a man?"

"Wh . . . oh. You figure Sergeov can get through other ways?"

"With no legs . . . check it out."

Andy brooded, his pale features compressed into a mask of fretful concern. "I don't see how, but okay."

Carl sighed and stretched in the webbing. "Now you know what this job's like."

"Yeah. They're a bunch of goddamned *children!*"

"You've been out—what? Two months?"

"Right. Still—"

"It'll take a while to see where the hate comes from. Just try to ignore the worst, work around it."

"I'm convinced that Malcolm is stalling."

"He often is. What else's he got to negotiate with? But you mean seriously, this time?"

"I think so. I checked the Nudge pods they supposedly finished three months ago—down at the south pole. They *look* as though they're set up right, but I pulled off a few cowlings. Inside there're connections missing, tanks not racked—it's a mess."

"Sure it's Malcolm's fault?"

"I think they're sabotaging the pods."

"They smash anything?"

"No, just took stuff apart."

"Smart. Any obvious damage, we'd howl. This way, you might

very well have accused Malcolm to his face of shirking the work."
Andy blushed. "Well, actually, that's what I did."

A pause. "Oh?"

"I . . . I know I should've got hold of you first, but—I was so damn
hopping mad! I called Malcolm and started in on him." Andy stopped,
embarrassed.

"And?"

"He hung up on me before I even got three sentences out."

"Then he probably thinks he's got some complaint with us, too."
*Don't sound too casual,* Carl reminded himself. *Don't let Andy onto
what you know . . . that there's simply no way the Nudge accelerators
would be done in time anyway.*

Carl said, "Who has the most to gain if you and Malcolm tear at
each other's throats?"

"Hell, hardly anybody, seems to me."

"Doesn't have to be more than a few."

"Well . . . oh yeah. Quiverian. He's the one keeps spouting that
Arcist crap. You think he's trying to slow down work on the Nudge?"

"It fits. The radical Arcists don't want any possibility of cometary
material getting near Earth. No orbits near enough to make a good rendezvous, nothing. Preserving Earth's biosphere is *it* for them. They
don't care what happens to us."

"But there are still possibilities that offer no conceivable threat to
Earth. Give ourselves a shorter-period orbit with the Nudge, pack
everybody into slots—"

"And hope a decade or two sobers up everybody Earthside?"

Andy's face was so open it was almost painful to read. "It's . . .
We've *got* to have hope, don't we?"

"Sure," Carl said, trying to get some hearty optimism into his
voice. "Sure."

Andy pursed his lips, absorbed with his dreams. *Maybe it's not
dumb optimism,* Carl thought. *Maybe we'll get a break. I'm just getting
tired of wishing.*

He thought of showing Andy the poem and then decided to forget it.
Andy might very well find the mixture of bile and gallows humor unsettling. Let him marinate for a year or so first.

*And who knows? Perhaps some archaeologist will find that poem
and pronounce it the great work of our sad, luckless expedition. They
might put it on a plaque beside the main outer lock, to label the moun-
tainous ice museum that swung through their sky, marking a great failed*

*idea. With us, swimming permanently in our slimy slot fluids, as the prime exhibits.*

It wasn't an absurd notion.

# VIRGINIA

Stolen gifts,
    Hidden away in time.
*Waiting* gifts,
    Deep within my rhyme.

—Huh? Did you say something, Virginia?—

Jeffers's voice crackled over her comm as she concentrated on bringing her two balky mechs over an ice mound at the same time. It was always a delicate exercise, for the big machines had enough strength to bound completely away from the rubble-strewn surface. These repair-drone models had no onboard propellants to bring them back, in case of a miscalculation.

"Um, don't pay any attention, Jeff. It's just JonVon acting up again. As soon as we've finished with this project I'm going to give him a good memory purging."

—Sounds like he's picked up a bit of your hand for scribbling. If he's been writin' poems for thirty years, you may be in for some competition, child.—

Jeffers sounded amused, and Virginia laughed. But within she was beginning to get worried. Something was wrong with her bio-organic computer counterpart. In some skills JonVon seemed more subtle, more capable than when she had been slotted, decades ago—a natural result of programming him for slow, steady self-improvement. But in other ways the machine/program now behaved erratically, uncertainly, spontaneously giving forth these bursts that seemed irrelevant, untraceable.

Trash-strewn snowfields stretched away toward the row of agro domes around the entrance to Shaft 1. Huge mirrors hung from spidery ice towers nearby, concentrating the sun's distant spark to turn the domes into bright blazes against the grainy ice.

Beneath the glassy domes, green masses waved gently under artificial breezes. A few workers drifted languidly among the plants, tending the colony's staff of life. Since awakening from slot sleep, she had had little time to learn about the hydroponics procedures that had been developed, by trial and error over the long decades. But she could tell already that the process could use a lot of automating.

Her mechs arrived where Jeffers's spacesuited figure awaited her, standing beside a toppled crystal structure. Broken shards of glassy ice were everywhere.

Virginia gasped. "This is terrible! Who wrecked Jim Vidor's sculpture?"

The statue had been dedicated to Captain Cruz and the dream so many members of the expedition had shared. It had depicted a spacesuited figure, ragged and weary but perseverent, holding out sparkling gifts on his return to a blue globe, the Earth.

Virginia remembered how proud Jim Vidor had been of it, just before his slotting so long ago. It had been a beautiful work, crafted in six shades of ice, traced in native crystal. But now the carved spacer lay crumpled on its side, and the blue planet was crushed.

Deep under the surface, in her lab, Virginia tensed on her webbing as she looked at the vandalism through the mech's eyes. "Who. . . ?"

Jeffers's voice was tense. —Dunno. I'd guess some of Sergeov's *Ubers* did it.—

"But why?"

The spacer shrugged. —Cruz was an Ortho.—

That seemed explanation enough to him. Virginia felt her skin flush, just then ashamed to be a Percell.

"Has Jim ever seen this?"

—Naw. Matsudo brought him out in 2073 or so, and Lintz's cyanutes fixed his first disease. But then they had to slot him again a year or so later with a real bad blood infection. I guess in a way it's a blessing, at that. He'll never see how bad it's all gotten since then. Jim was an Ortho. But I liked him a lot.—

"Yeah," she said, unable to think of anything else to say. She stepped her mechs around the shattered monument to join Jeffers. "Come on. Let's see if we can work a miracle or two."

—Right, pretty Hawaiian lady.— Jeffers reached up and pulled several narrow envelopes off a rack carried by one of the mechs. —This way to the Elephants' Graveyard.—

They rounded a rocky hummock and Virginia sighed. No mere statistics could have prepared her for the scene before her now. Machines, laid out row upon row, in orderly ranks that stretched nearly to the curved horizon, all frozen, unmoving, locked in a rigor of uselessness and disrepair.

"Where do we *start?*" she asked in dismay.

Jeffers clapped his gloved hands together and lifted off the ice a couple of meters in his nervous excitement.

—Who *cares*! For three years I've been pokin' away at the hardware, fussin' in the autofactory, scragging prototype spares. But I kept hittin' software glitches, ROM blocs, clapes I just couldn't grok! Frustrated everythin' I tried.—

He landed facing her mech.

—But *now*, in just two *weeks*, you've sorted out things that had me dead stopped!—

Her mech lifted a metal hand, exactly mimicking Virginia's gesture down within her darkened lab. "Now hold on, Jeff. I said this was just a first cut. No promises . . ."

But the man had already jetted over to a spindly repair-bot . . . a sophisticated androidlike machine designed for the maintenance of other devices, but now frozen itself in a locked rigor of uselessness.

—Let's start with this puppy. I already did a physical workover on it.—

Virginia watched nervously as the spacer sorted through the envelopes, selected one, tore it open, and drew forth a gleaming sliver. He pried open an access panel and slipped the reprogramming crystal into the back of the machine.

—Arise!— he commanded, stepping back with a theatrical wave of his arms.

Virginia held her breath. For an instant, it seemed that the frost coating the rigid mech would bind it into immobility. A part of her wondered, *Can a statue come to life?*

But then the frost cracked, puffing away in tiny, silent explosions as amorphous ice changed state directly into gas. With a wavering delicacy, the machine unfolded. In an unlimbering of stiltlike, mantis legs, it stood up and turned to face Jeffers. Eye cells gleaming, it extended a long arm strong enough to snap the man in two. A many-fingered hand opened, like a blooming flower.

Jeffers laid the stack of envelopes into the sure, deft grasp.

—The Armies of the Dead arise this mornin'!— He laughed. —Come on, angel face. We got some heavy-duty resurrectin' to do!—

Virginia forgave the man his marginal blasphemy. His excitement was infectious. Almost as much as the deadly illnesses and the manpower shortage, this gradual decline in the colony's mech force had contributed to the pervasive mood of hopelessness, the impossibility of achieving anything real.

*Oh, it won't make enough of a difference, whatever we accomplish out here. Nothing can replace missing human beings.*

*But we just may be able to make life a bit easier around here.*

Jeffers was a dervish on the ice, hurrying from drone to roboid to waldo mech. Virginia thought she had no illusions; still, she grew amazed and more hopeful as they moved along the silent rows of the graveyard, swapping program slivers, lubricating, energizing.

It was thrilling to watch. Long-dead machines, frozen rigid for years, shuddered and stood up. Others rolled by on grapple wheels, or floated free of their moorings. Data channels clicked, beeped, twittered with well-ordered computer code.

Their efforts began to multiply as reprogrammed repair-bots moved out on their own, taking over whole rows of disabled mechs. What had been a small cluster of activity spread outward like ripples from a spring-thawed pool.

As dust drifted away from long-quiescent machines, their headphones carried sounds of wonder and growing excitement from the agro domes. Crowds began to gather, staring out at what had heretofore been a silent, frozen army. Airlocks opened, and spacesuited figures spilled onto the snow to stare at the milling mechanical crowd.

Jeffers cried out as a huge lifter mech puffed away on a burst of ionized hydrogen to hover nearby, its green and blue lights glittering. Shadows spread past them as it moved over to moor beside the long-unused supply depot.

The headphone-channel monitors cut in to dampen an overload of cheering from the onlookers.

More and more people appeared on the ice, in spacesuits not used in years, wearing once-white tabards now ratty from age. Some threw away caution and leaped in excitement, to arc high overhead for long minutes while others jeered happily.

Virginia laughed. Halley's north pole had become a *festival*— humans bumping into mechs, which uncomplainingly swerved to avoid more-violent collisions. Percells pirouetted with Orthos. Spacers talked excitedly with Arcists. Someone piped music over D-channel, and the weird, twisting dance of near-zero gravity filled the sky.

*It doesn't take much . . . just a little good news.*

From one agro dome, a dozen spindly children stared . . . some slack-jawed and barely seeing, but a few clapping their hands and tugging at the sleeves of nearby adults, pointing excitedly at the boisterous celebration.

A figure appeared beside Virginia's mech and reached up to tug on the machine's arm. Virginia felt it at her own elbow and looked down.

"Oh. Hi, Carl!" She felt like a little girl, and it was good to see him smile again, under the glossy faceplate of his grimy suit. "How did you know which mech was me?"

—Osborn to Herbert, channel AF. How did I know, Virginia? It was easy. I just watched the way each mech walked, and picked the one with the sexiest moves.—

She felt herself blush, and was glad that out on the surface none of it would show. "You always did have a gift for bullsh—"

Suddenly, Virginia was interrupted by an awful sound. It was the blood-chilling wail of a suit-rupture alarm, interrupting every channel, cutting through the celebration, and stopping all chatter in mid-breath.

"Oh my gosh. Where. . . ?" She whirled her mech to look. Already several of the most sophisticated models were charging toward a crowd of spectators, drawn now into a cluster near one of the agro domes.

"I can't tell," she started to say to Carl. But then she realized that he was already gone—launched in a propellant spray toward the site of the commotion.

The alarm cut off abruptly, dropping to a low, mournful drone that denoted cessation of life functions.

Somebody had died.

Virginia started moving toward the crowd, then stopped, feeling foolish. Of course she did not have to take this particular mech over there to get a closer look. With a tongue click and a pulsed subvocal command, she transferred her point of view to a tall, spidery drone standing over the cluster of muttering humans.

She was looking down, then. Carl and Jeffers bent over a space-suited figure sprawled prone on the ground. The suit was slit open down to bone. Red foam still spread from the gaping opening like a gruesome fog.

Keoki Anuenue and some of his big Hawaiians arrived. They started pushing the crowd back, ordering unnecessary mechs away. The suddenly subdued crowd drifted off, all of the festival mood taken out of them like a noisy stream turned to rock-hard ice.

"He Kiai," she sent to the dark-faced Polynesian who tried to usher off her observer mech. The man blinked in surprise. Then he shrugged.

—Ua make oia, wahine.—

Virginia did not need to be told that the figure on the ice was dead. Obviously, it was pointless even to think of slotting.

Her mouth went dry as she saw the slim-bladed vibro-knife lying next to the corpse. Whoever had done this—taking advantage of the confusion and excitement she and Jeffers had brought about—had left his calling card alongside his handiwork.

She sorted through the comm automatically, searching for the channel and encryption Carl and Jeff were using. At last she found the right combination.

— . . . going to be hell to pay for this. Quiverian and Ould-Harrad are sure to capitalize on it.—

—Shit. Malcolm might have been an officious bastard, and an Ortho chauvinist. But at least he wasn't an Arcist. I could work with him. You know who's gonna get blamed for this, of course. . . .—

They turned the victim over. The face of poor Malcolm stared up at her, bloated and bug-eyed from decompression.

Virginia shut down quickly and pulled out of the mech. She opened her real eyes and found herself back in her own small, safe realm deep under the ice. She removed her neural tap and groaned as she sat up, rubbing the raw area at the back of her head.

*Oh yes,* she thought. *There will be hell to pay over this.*

Virginia got up and went to the tiny, hooded water tap to dampen a towel and wipe her face.

Her scalp still hurt. She lifted her hair and bent over between the mirrored surfaces of two holo tanks to examine the neural-tap-contact area. An angry red rash was spreading, and the standard treatments didn't seem to be working, this time. Saul had told her that he felt he might be able to come up with a new approach, but he had not been able to hide from her his anxious uncertainty.

It didn't take a genius to see that they were all dying.

She thought of the giddy celebration above, so brief, so quickly shattered.

*It was nice to feel hope, for a few minutes, at least.*

Color flashed above her. She looked up as letters coalesced in the computer's main display tank. *Oh no.* It was another of JonVon's eerie, spontaneous attempts at versification . . . another sign that decay had not limited itself to men and moving machines.

Lost amid the struggles,
    Cached in canted rhythms,

Beneficence still dwells,
   Cast from forgotten Home.

"Oh, JonVon," she whispered. "Are you sick too?"


The figures moved single file across the pitted landscape, linked together by knotted ropes. They stepped carefully, slowly, as they pushed and dragged their burdens over hummocks and crater rims.

It was a silent exodus—shapes in grimy, patched spacesuits, struggling with massive bundles, nearly weightless but cumbersome with inertia—helping one another over slick patches and dangerous fields of explosive, amorphous ice.

From Virginia's vantage point, atop one of Halley's highest equatorial prominences, the horizon of their tiny world was an arc only a mile or so away . . . close enough almost to touch. Those below would have to cover only eight kilometers or so, between the northern base and the caves on the comet's other pole. And yet, watching the Arcist migration, she felt as if she were witnessing something biblical. The self-styled refugees scrambled, heaved, and turned to help one another as they carried their possessions toward the new homes that their leaders had promised them.

They had been offered mechs to help, but it was widely known that the sophisticated roboids had been rebuilt by Jeffers and reprogrammed by Virginia . . . both Percells. The Arcists' suspicious natures won over convenience, so they refused all but the simplest machines.

Three spacesuited men stood on the prominence alongside Virginia's new mech, also watching the Arcists depart. Carl and Jeffers touched helmets and spoke to each other in private, gesturing at the line of shuffling figures. On her other side, Saul leaned against her mech's flank, humming an absent tune, low and atonal.

The biblical flavor of the scene was heightened by the figure leading the single-file caravan. There, in front, using a staff as he strode in long, slow steps, was Suleiman Ould-Harrad—once Lieutenant Colonel in the Space Service, now a mystic and spiritual adviser to the Arcist clans. The tall black man had dyed his suit deep midnight blue, and his tabard was white with a single black star.

Behind him, carrying huge burdens or drawing giant, floating sledges, followed scores—from oldsters too long out of the slots to wide-eyed children, spindly and staring from inside plastic survival bubbles.

—At least thirty more Orthos joined them after Malcolm's assassination,— Carl muttered, perhaps unaware that Virginia could pick up his words through vibrations in the ice. —We have no way of knowing who actually did it, but I can tell you who profited.—

Jeffers nodded.

—I wish I knew how Quiverian did it.—

They fell silent as the caravan drew past them.

On Virginia's other side, Saul held the tactile pads of her mech, and occasionally squeezed. She felt it deep underground, lying on her web-couch.

A trio of suited shapes detached themselves from the migration and skim-floated upslope toward Carl. The one in the lead wore a tabard showing the gold splash of the Arc of the Living Sun. Joao Quiverian spoke on the preagreed channel and code.

—We will expect to continue participating in the vegetable hydro domes, and take our per capita share of power from the fusion pile.—

Carl shrugged. —If you work on the Nudge motors, as you've promised, we have no reason to deny you your rights. Go ahead and live at the south pole, if being near the rest of us makes you feel unclean.—

Obviously Carl felt more relieved to have Quiverian's fanatics out of his hair than anything else.

—Unclean and dangerous.— Quiverian nodded as if he had completely missed Carl's sarcasm. —We shall be better able to work on the Nudge Launchers, since they are to be situated at the south pole, anyway. All that is required is that we are given materials and supplies, and *left alone*.—

—My crews remain in charge of the launchers themselves,— Jeffers insisted. Quiverian merely shrugged.

—Just do not come into our homes.—

Virginia noted the mood of all the participants. *None of them think any of it* really *matters, or there'd be more yelling going on.*

Jeffers shrugged. —We're all welcome to outfit our own tombs however we want.— The others all seemed to agree with his somber assessment.

Except for *Saul,* who suddenly barked in laughter. They all turned to look at him.

—Excuse me. Don't mind me,— he said, waving with one hand. But everyone could see, through his faceplate, that he was fighting down a fit of hilarity.

Carl frowned until Saul's expression had settled down to a mere controlled smirk. Then he turned back to Quiverian. —Go on, then. Go south in peace.—

The three Arcists swiveled and departed. In turn, Carl and Jeffers strode off toward the nearby tunnel lock.

Saul brought the mech's hand to his faceplate, pantomiming a kiss. —I must go too, darling. Don't wait up for me.—

"But, but . . . I thought you'd come down now. We could spend some time together. Saul, you've been away for nearly a *week*."

—Oh, now, Virginia. We talk several times a day.—

"Through one of my mechs!" A robot foot kicked up snow near his leg. "It's not the same!"

He nodded, grinning infuriatingly.

—I know. I miss you too. Terribly. It's just . . .—

He shook his head.

—It's just that I have to verify something. It's too damn important to wait. And I can't tell anybody yet . . . not even you . . . not until I know for sure if . . .—

His voice trailed off as he backed away toward the airlock. Virginia knew the look on his face, that faraway, *scientific* look. He was already somewhere else.

"Until you know what?" she asked. "What *is* all this, Saul?"

He shrugged.

—Until I know for sure if I'm crazy . . . or if I'm . . .—

The last word was a mumble, something in one of Saul's foreign languages.

"What?"

But he only blew her a kiss then, and spun about to lope toward the tunnel entrance.

The part of her that was above the surface, linked to a machine of metal and ceramic, watched him until the doors closed, leaving her locked out in the chilly night.

Deep under the ice, the rest of her was no less in darkness.

# SAUL

He found Lieutenant Commander Osborn up at Greenhouse 3. Carl stood before a forty-meter dome window, wearing a stained, patched spacesuit without tabard. The spacer held a battered helmet in the crook of his arm and looked out onto the garbage-strewn plain of dirty ice.

*What a mess,* Saul thought.

The tattered warehouse tents, the broken mooring mast where that unlucky ship *Edmund Halley* had once been tethered . . . At last Saul realized what was bothering him most. It was too dim here in the greenhouse.

He looked up at the spider-thin towers holding one of the huge concentrator mirrors—salvaged from the space tug *Delsemme*'s great solar sail. Two guy wires had snapped. A whole quadrant of the big collector drooped.

Out on the surface, a single figure picked desultorily through the debris, presumably looking for material from which to make repairs. He seemed not to be in any hurry.

Within, things weren't much better. The four men and three women on this shift tended the slowly moving belts of drip-irrigated sweet potatoes, clearing debris from the plastic tracks and cleaning the nutrient-spray jets. It was vital duty, but they moved without apparent enthusiasm.

Three of the newly reprogrammed mechs followed the workers around, but nobody seemed even interested in training them in the new hydroponics procedures. The belts ground on; plants drooped in the dim illumination.

Saul was shaken when he recognized the sigil on the workers' clothes—the staircase and star that stood for Plateau Three.

*Spacers! They're the last people I'd expect to give up.*

Saul saw the expression on Carl Osborn's face as the man gazed out over the icefield. *You can't blame him if he's lost hope, too,* Saul thought. *He's obstinate, and made of strong stuff. But everyone has a limit.*

*He's run the same simulations I have. He knows what'll happen if things go on this way.*

Even if everyone pitched in and cooperated, with all the mechs in the world, there would still be nowhere near enough manpower to set up the Nudge Launchers properly, let alone do all the work needed to keep things from going to hell. *I'm surprised he even goes through the motions, believing that.*

Saul smiled. He planned on changing Carl's mind about the future.

*This time, I swear, we won't misunderstand each other.* Saul hoped that his good news would make Carl forgive even Virginia's poor choice in men.

*I never thought of it before, but with that touch of gray at the sides, and that cool gaze, he sort of resembles Simon Percell!*

"Yes?" Carl said as he approached. "You told me you were going to do a bioinventory of the colony. You've got a report already?"

"That's right." Saul nodded. "But I don't think you're going to be very ready to believe it."

Carl lifted his shoulders. "Bad news doesn't frighten me anymore."

Saul couldn't help letting out a short, sharp laugh. The sound was abrupt, unexpected in this solemn place. Carl's eyes narrowed.

"You misunderstand me." Saul grinned. "Either I have gone mad—in which case the news is neutral to good from your point of view—or I have made a discovery which bodes very well, indeed."

Carl stood quite still. His body remained in a spacer's crouch, arms forward, knees bent. Only a twitch of his cheek betrayed a hint of feeling, but it was enough for Saul.

*Is hope, then, so very painful? He may hate me, but he knows I have pulled rabbits out of hats before.*

Saul reminded himself not to be too quick to judge. *To a man who has seen the face of Death, and learned resignation, hope is often the most frightening thing of all.*

"Explain, please," the younger man said softly.

"Come with me to my lab," Saul told him. "Even with graphic displays, I'm not sure I can make it clear. But I have to share this. It may be the Infinite's ultimate joke on a man who had the unrepentant gall to try to play God."

"I see," Carl told him after half an hour. "You've found infestations of cometary flora and fauna in every single living crew member, in every clan, even in the few people we never unslotted at all."

Saul nodded. "Even Virginia's bio-organic computer, JonVon, seems to be suffering from an infection. The thing's not really alive, of course, but something's gotten into it. I'm trying to find a way to treat it."

Carl shrugged. "I've tried hard to get it through the *Ubers'* and Arcists' heads that their war hardly matters, anymore. Percell, Ortho, *everybody* is dying."

He started to get up. "You may have done us a service at that, Saul. Write me up a concise report for distribution. It may help us all make peace with each other, in the time we have left."

Saul stopped him with a gesture. "Sit down, please. I'm not finished yet."

Carl settled back into the webbing, reluctantly.

"So what else is there?"

"Remember that bioanalysis I performed on my own body?"

"Sure." Carl nodded. "Except for your reproductive system—and that perpetual sniffle of yours—you're fairly healthy. I'm sorry you're sterile, Saul. And I'm glad for you that the comet bugs seem to be killing you slower than most."

"Carl, they aren't killing me at all."

The other man snapped a cold look at Saul. "Don't be an ass! Your chart showed an asymptotically increasing—"

"Increasing variety of infesting organisms, same as everybody else. By normal logic I can't keep fighting all these infections much longer. Sooner or later one will wreck my immune system, opening me wide to all the others. Is that the pattern you're thinking of?"

Carl nodded. "I've studied a lot of medical biology, over my last five duration years."

"I guess you had to, since Svatuto quit as your doctor."

"Right. And since Earth stopped giving advice that was worth a tinker's damn." Carl grimaced, remembering bitterly. "During my shifts I've seen guys live for years with green-tinted skins and low fevers, fighting on like champions . . . only to fall to pieces—*literally*—when that last straw hit."

Saul shrugged. "That was them."

"And *you're* different?" Carl sneered. "You're somehow especially blessed?"

Saul wanted to laugh. *Blessed? Oh, Miriam, what has the Almighty done to your simple Saul?*

He paused and took a breath. "I want to tell you about something. Let me talk to you about symbiosis."

\*     \*     \*

Imagine a virus . . . a simple bundle of nucleic acid packaged inside a protein shell . . . a killer, a smart bomb with only one job—replication.

Suppose this virus finds a *vector,* and penetrates the skin and outer membranes of a multicelled organism . . . perhaps a human being. At that point, its job has only begun. From there it seeks its real prey, not the *man* so much as a single one of his trillion cells.

*Seeking* might not be the proper word. For a virus is only a pseudo-lifeform. It doesn't propel itself after vibrations or chemical traces, as protists and bacteria do. A virus only drifts, suspended in water or blood or lymph or mucus—until it strikes the surface of an unlucky cell.

Now suppose one of these little bits of half-life is lucky. It has evaded the victim organism's defenses. No antibodies manage to latch on to it and carry it away. It isn't engulfed and destroyed by the immune system's strike forces. The fortunate virus survives to bump against a likely cell in just the right way, triggering adherence.

It sticks to the cell wall, a simple capsule of protein, ready to inject its contents into the prostrate prey. Once inside, the viral RNA will take over the vast, complex chemical machinery of the cell, forcing it to forge hundreds, thousands of duplicates of the original virus, until, like an overstretched balloon, the ravaged cell bursts. The new viral horde spills forth, leaving only wreckage behind.

*There is the virus, stuck to the outer wall . . . poised to inject this tyrannical cargo into the prostrate prey. . . .*

Prostrate, yes. But helpless?

For a long time an argument raged among physicians, biologists, and philosophers. A small minority kept asking the same question over and over again.

*"Why does the cell let this catastrophe happen?"*

Biological heretics pointed out how difficult it was to seize and penetrate the intricate barriers of a cell wall. So much was involved, and it would seem so simple for a cell merely to refuse access.

What about the fantastic number of steps needed to turn the machinery of the cell into a slave factory, forcing the ribosomes and mitochondria to perform tasks totally alien to their normal functions?

"All the cell needs to do is interrupt any *one* of these steps, and the process is stopped, cold!" the unbelievers declared. "There must be a *reason.* Why does the cell allow itself to be such easy prey?"

Classical biologists sniffed in disgust. Animals develop new ways to fight viruses all the time, they said. But viruses evolve methods around every obstacle. The balance is always struck across a knife edge of death.

But the dissenters insisted. "Death is nothing but a side effect. Disease is not a *war* between species. More often, it is a case of *failed negotiation*."

"You're losing me," Carl told Saul.

Saul drummed his fingers on the desktop and searched for the right words. "Hmmm. Let's try an example. You know what mitochondria are, right?"

Carl inclined his head and spoke in a hollow voice. "They're organelles . . . internal parts of living cells. They regulate the basic energy economy . . . take electro-chemical potential from burning sugars and convert it into useful forms."

"Very good." Saul nodded, impressed. Carl had, indeed, been studying over the long, hopeless years. No scholar, he had probably mastered the material by brute force.

"And you know the widely held theory over where the mitochondria came from?"

Carl closed his eyes. "I remember reading something about that. They resemble certain types of free-living bacteria, don't they?"

"Yes, that's right."

"Some people think they were once independent creatures. But long ago one of their ancestors got trapped inside one of the first eukaryotes."

Saul nodded. "About a billon years ago . . . when our ancestors were only single cells, hunting around in the open sea."

"Yeah. They think one of our ancestors *ate* the ancestral mitochondria. Only, for some reason it didn't digest it that time. It let the thing stay and work for it, instead."

Carl looked up at Saul, seriously. "This is what you mean by *symbiosis*, isn't it? The early mitochondria provided more efficient energy conversion for the host cell. And in return, it never had to hunt for food again. The host cell—"

"—Our ancestor—"

"—took care of that from then on."

"And when one divided, so did the other, passing the arrangement down to each daughter cell. The partnership was inherited, generation by generation." Saul nodded. "The same seems true of *chloroplasts*, the organelles in plant cells that do the actual work of photosynthesis.

They're kin to blue-green algae. And many other cellular components show signs they may have once been independent creatures, too."

"Yes. I do remember reading about that." Carl seemed interested for the first time. Saul remembered some of the conversations they'd had back in the early days, before their differences had yawned like a gulf between them. He wondered if Carl missed them as much as he did.

*Probably more. After all, I have Virginia.*

"The same holds for the entire organism, Carl. A normal human being has countless species of creatures living in him, depending on him, as *he depends on them.* From gut bacteria that help us digest our food, to a special type of mite that lives only at the base of human eyelashes, scouring them, eating decayed matter and keeping them clean."

Saul spread his hands. "None of these symbiotic animals can live independently of man anymore. Nor can we very easily do without them. They're almost as much parts of the colony organism called *Homo sapiens* as human DNA itself."

Carl blinked, as if trying to absorb this new leap. "It's like a quantum field in physics, then. The boundaries of what I call 'me' are . . . are . . ."

"Are amorphous. Nebulous. Difficult to define. You've got it! They've found that married couples share much the same suite of intestinal flora, for instance. Make love to a woman, and you exchange *symbionts.* In a sense, you *become* partly the same creature by sharing elements that grow and participate in each other."

Carl frowned. And Saul realized that he was skirting a touchy subject. He hurried on.

"But here is my main point, Carl. Probably few, if any, of these symbionts simply settled into their niches without an initial struggle. Evolution doesn't work that way . . . at least not usually."

"But—"

"*Every* symbiont, from digestion helper to follicle cleaner, started out as an *invader,* once upon a time. Every synergism began in a *disease.*"

"I don't . . ." Carl frowned in concentration. "Wait. Wait a minute." His brow was knitted with tight furrows. "You spoke of disease as negotiation between a host and an invading—"

"—Visiting—"

"—species. But . . . but even if that's the case, this negotiation takes place over the bodies of uncounted dead of both sides!" Carl looked up, eyes flashing. "True, they may come to a modus vivendi someday, but that doesn't help the *individuals* who die, often horribly, broken on the wheel of evolution."

Saul stared, unable to hide his surprise. In his most pensive moments, Carl Osborn seemed to have come upon a new facility with words. With tempering, an awkward youth had turned into something of a poet.

"Well said." Saul nodded. "And that's exactly what we're seeing here on Halley. Some die abruptly. Others fight the interlopers to a standstill. Some even profit a little from some side effect of their infestation."

Carl slapped the desktop with a loud report and swiveled to face Saul fully.

"All very well and good, Saul. If—*if*—there were only one or two diseases, and if we had generations, with millions of people, in which to work all this out.

"But that's *not* the case! Say you're like that green-colored character up in Hydroponics Two—"

"Old McCue? The one whose skin parasite seems to feed him nutrients made from sunlight?"

"Yeah. Great stuff. But—to quote from your own report—the man's mind has also been reduced to the level of a moron by a peptide byproduct of that very same fungoid parasite!"

The younger man breathed heavily.

"I'm glad you read my studies," Saul answered.

Carl snorted. "Besides Jeffers, and Virginia's *computer,* you're the only one who writes anything worth reading, anymore. I'm sure you'll be more famous than ever, when you send your reports to Earth."

That made Saul wince. How had he managed to make Carl misunderstand him again? "It's not like that."

"Oh? Then how is it, Mr. Great Man of Biology? Tell me! I've shown you I know plenty, for an amateur. Convince me! Tell me how the hell all these fancy theories about *symbiosis* are going to make one slice of difference to a tiny, overwhelmed colony, every member of which is a total, certain goner!"

The pause lasted. Saul waited until the other man's breathing had settled—until Carl had slipped back into the webbing on his side of the desk, glaring at him.

"I already told you, but you weren't listening," he said softly. "There is one person on this planetoid who's in no danger at all. Someone with attributes that make him safe in a totally new way.

"That person is me, Carl."

For the first time, the full point of the conversation seemed to hit the spacer. He stood up.

"You?"

"Me." Saul nodded. "My sneezing, my perpetual dripping are only surface features of that 'negotiation process' we spoke of. And it seems my immune system is a perfect diplomat. Except for the damage to my reproductive cells, my body has taken all comers almost without trouble. It accepts or rejects every new lifeform in short order, and each one soon finds its own niche."

There was another silence.

"I am quite serious, Carl."

"But . . . *how?*"

"How?" Saul shook his head. "I only know part of it, as yet. For one thing, I've inherited a rare enzyme that some have called *N Complex*. A dozen or so others on Halley have it too."

"And are they. . . ?"

"More disease resistant? Seems so. But also, there's something else, something in my blood that got there back when I worked with Simon Percell."

"Yes?" Carl's voice was flat now, his expression guarded.

"It's called a *reading unit*. We only used the things for a couple of years, until we found better ways to strip and analyze DNA in vivo. Nearly forgot completely about the little things . . . until I saw them floating around down there, where they'd taken over my spermetic cells."

Saul shook his head. "Don't know how they got into me, really. Must've stuck myself one day while doing a gene analysis. But however they got there, my body's *using* them, somehow.

"Now I think I know why I was so lucky, three decades ago, when I developed the new cyanutes. *I* didn't really develop them. My *body* did."

The longest silence of them all followed this.

At last Carl spoke.

"I've also read psychology, Saul. You know, of course, that claims of invulnerability are symptoms of paranoia?"

Saul shrugged. "I am, in almost every basic sense, completely healthy. Completely. The only one in the colony. You don't believe me?"

"Of course not! What do you take me for?"

Saul held out his hand. "Take it," he said casually. After a moment's hesitation, Carl's callused fingers wrapped around Saul's, still soft from so long in the slots.

Carl's grim smile faded into intense concentration as Saul squeezed, talking on, casually.

"Diseases, microgravity deconditioning, slot fatigue . . . they've pounded all of you down until a drugged Cub Scout could beat any of you with one hand tied."

Carl's brow beaded. Obstinately, grunting, he tried to match Saul's grip.

"You know you can't finish the Nudge Launchers in time, even with all of Virginia's mechs to help. You need *people,* and you don't have 'em, Carl. Two hundred slotted for good, another hundred feeble as kittens—"

He let go and Carl sagged back with a ragged sigh, his eyes wide.

"I didn't show you this to rub your nose in your weakness, Carl. I only want you to believe it when I say there may be a way. A way to give similar immunity to many, maybe even most of the members of this expedition.

"Carl, we just may not be doomed, after all."

He said no more. There was no point in talking any longer. When the other man had questions, he would ask them. *Let it have time to sink in,* he thought.

Right now, Carl's face was like a statue's. He stood up—rocky, unsteady—staring at Saul even as he backed away, shaking his head. With one hand he touched the doorplate, spilling phosphor light into the darkened room.

From the hallway, Carl kept staring at him until the door had shut again, cutting off the view, but not the image.

After a moment Saul looked up at the ceiling.

*Oh, I know you, Ado-shem,* he thought at the bearded, fierce-eyed God of Abraham. *This morning I opened your gift, tore off the wrapping paper, and looked inside. And just now I showed its frightening beauty to a man who was once a friend.*

*It looks, at first, like a fine gift. Like the rock that flowed with water for the Hebrew children in the desert. But you and I know that inside the box is another box, and another, and more ad infinitum.*

*And I'm still no closer to an answer to the basic questions, am I? Where did Halley-Life come from? Did comets seed the Earth, long ago? Or are we only the latest invaders of this little worldlet? How could all of this have happened in the first place?*

There was no answer, of course.

He smiled upward, through half a mile of rocky ice, at the stars.

*Oh, yes. You will have your joke.*

# CARL

Carl and Virginia sat stiffly in nearby web-chairs. The G-wheel had broken down years ago and subtle side effects of constant low-G were showing. The lounge was deserted except for them, its vivid wall weather running unnoticed. A drowsy camel slowly bobbed along the brow of a distant sand dune.

"What I mean is, do you think he's got all his marbles?" Carl asked flatly.

"Of *course* Saul is perfectly all right," she answered indignantly, tension visible in her body language.

*I've got to remember, she really loves the jerk,* Carl thought. *Okay, be diplomatic.* "I'm worried about his . . . health."

Virginia wasn't having any of it. "You mean you think his discovery is a delusion."

"Well, it *is* extreme." Carl threw his hands into the air and boomed out, "I, Saul Lintz, am a godlike immortal. Immune! Impervious! Kneel, mere mortals!"

"That's *not* his attitude."

"Well, let's say he comes over as a *quiet* megalomaniac."

"He was describing a theory."

"With himself as prime evidence."

"Well, yes. Who else aboard has the N-constellation?"

"Good question. You could check the DNA log for the corpsicles."

Virginia's eyes shifted a fraction sideways for just an instant, but by now he could read her pretty well. "You already have, right?"

She nodded, knitting her fingers together and staring into them. "There are three others."

"Good. Easy way to test his theory, right? Unslot 'em and see if they catch a bug."

"Saul said the same thing when I told him yesterday."

"Hmmmm. I wonder why he didn't mention that little fact to me."

"He's been busy. I suppose he wants to think things through a little more before . . . experimenting."

"Or maybe—just maybe—he wants to do everything himself. Big Saul saves all."

Virginia flared. "You have no right to say that!"

He held up his hands. "Okay, maybe so. Let's say I've been dealing with a lot of crazies these years. I've gotten used to doubting everything."

She bit her lip. *Containing her anger? Or keeping in the suspicion that maybe I'm right?*

"If Saul's inoculations work," she said in measured tones, "we will be able to save ourselves. The expedition will succeed. You must put your faith in him. You *are* going to okay his initial test treatments of volunteers, aren't you?"

Carl shrugged. "My authority is limited. The 'tribes' contribute their labor. I handle routine management and make up a maintenance roster. Cap'n Bligh I'm not. I don't see where I could stop him from recruiting . . . volunteers." He had almost said *suckers*.

"Good. You'll see, Carl. This is our hope."

*Hope?* He was tempted to tell Virginia about the side effect of Saul's wondrous symbiosis—Saul's sterility. But if Saul had already told her, it would make him look mean.

Carl paused. Above her shoulder a caravan of scruffy tan camels plodded tirelessly across a vast sandy waste, heading for a green dab of palms halfway to the hard-edged horizon. Red-garbed traders swayed atop each, peering directly toward Carl with unveiled suspicion. Their images wavered with the heat, making the ponderous caravan ripple like a dream. Psychologically effective, no doubt, but Carl's feet still felt cold.

"Something bothering you, Virginia?"

"JonVon's . . . sick."

"I'd heard. Is it—he—malfing?"

"He's an organic matrix, remember. Saul thinks he's got some infestation of Halleyforms. I hope Saul can find a cure."

She started outlining the problem, the analogy between JonVon's nonliving organics versus ordinary flesh and blood, and how JonVon could "catch a cold" in a more than metaphorical fashion. Carl listened, looking into her eyes for a long time. He still felt the old tug, that slow warm yearning that would come swelling up in him if he let it. Her pensive, expectant mouth, the regal cast to the high cheekbones . . .

"Is JonVon immortal, same as Saul is supposed to be?" Carl asked.

"Saul might make him so. If a cure is found. If Saul is right about himself . . ."

"I still think it's all baloney."

She said primly, "We must test those three from the slots immediately."

*She seems so sure. Could Lintz be right?*

Virginia was too honest to let love blind her totally. She would have given some sign if she doubted Saul. . . .

"Okay, assuming a real miracle, we'll need to activate more farm area. We'll want to pull nearly everybody out of the slots. Maybe—who knows?—Saul can cure some of those with black borders."

"Even Commander Cruz?"

The thought struck Carl hard. "Could be," he said to cover his confusion. *Reviving senior officers . . . I won't be such a big cheese around here. But it would be great to work with the captain again, with somebody who really knew how to get things done. . . .*

"It'll be a hell of a rush, with only a few years to go to aphelion."

Virginia brightened. "We can do it. I *know* we can."

"Damn right." And Carl forced a hopeful smile.

*Why not be optimistic? It couldn't hurt, after all that's happened. At worst Saul Lintz is proven as a fool. At best . . . well, at best we may even finish the Nudge Launchers, move Halley, actually get on with the mission.*

But Carl knew that even miracles have their unwelcome consequences. *What will hope do to the tribes?* he wondered.

*That's when real infighting is going to come, over where we target this old iceball to fall thirty years from now.*

# VIRGINIA

Virginia wiped at her eyes. Without any gravity to speak of, tears upwelled and clung in quivering beads held together by surface tension. You had to shake your head or blot them. It was that or wear little saltwater lenses and watch the world refracted through your pain.

"Is he going to be all right?" she asked. Her voice trembled like a little girl's, but Virginia wasn't ashamed. Lots of people cared as much for certain objects as for human beings. And JonVon was a lot more than a Raggedy Ann doll.

"I think . . . ." Saul's voice faded in and out. His head was immersed in the holo tank, a cubic meter of neatly squared simulation that looked like an aquarium filled with some bizarre concoction, a chef's nightmare of bright bits and pieces. It was a color-coded depiction of the intricate chemistry of a colloidal-stochastic computer, and on this deep level all of her expertise was useless. Virginia might be a fair programmer, but she knew next to nothing about molecules, or what made pseudoliving things ill.

Saul mumbled. She could not follow what he was doing with his hands, deep inside the holo, but whatever he discovered seemed to satisfy him. He sat back. "Display off," he told the diagnostic computer.

"Well?" Virginia's legs tensed nervously and she had to grip the carpeting with her toes to prevent being cast free of the floor. "Well? *Tell* me. I can take it."

Saul took her hand and his blue eyes seemed to shine. She gasped as she read the answer in them. "He's going to be all right!" She yipped, whirled around, and threw herself into his arms. "You fixed him!"

*Oh, what an understanding man,* she thought, to hold her close and laugh while her teary eyes perforce left trails on his cheek and she snuffled happily on his neck. *Oh, how warm and strong and kind.*

His hand stroked her hair, near the dressing on the back of her neck where his new medications had fought down her rash. A week ago anyone brushing her near there would have sent her quailing in pain. But it didn't hurt anymore at all. The infection was nearly gone.

It was nice to be touched again.

"You must think I'm an idiot," she said at last as she took his handkerchief and sat up on his lap to blow her nose.

"No, I don't."

"Well, that shows how much you know. I am one. Carrying on like this over a machine."

He brushed her loose black hair back into place. "Then I'm an idiot too. I was nervous as hell about this. So was Carl."

Virginia sniffed. "Carl's worried because JonVon's far and away the best computer we have left. Carl can't run the Nudge without him."

"So? That's plenty enough reason."

"I suppose so. But still, he didn't really *care.*" Virginia's fists tightened. Actually, what made her mad at Carl was something else. She was still seething, a bit, over what he had said about Saul.

*I've always liked Carl,* she thought. *A lot. But he can be so damned pigheaded. It's been weeks since Saul started sharing serums made from his own blood, and only now, after one incredible cure after another, is Carl finally admitting that a miracle has really happened.*

Of course that was unfair. Carl had lived for so long with the eroding despair, with the assumption that all was lost, that hope would take
some getting used to.

They would all have to do some adjusting.

Much had changed since the Arcist exodus. Now, thanks to Saul's
cures, more and more people were being pulled from the sleep slots,
treated, and put to work building and testing the devices that would be
needed when Halley's Comet was to be turned from drifting iceball into
spaceship.

Of course, Saul's methods couldn't repair impossible damage, or
raise the irreversibly dead. But they hoped to bring the colony's active
population up to two hundred or so, more than half the number originally planned when the *Edmund* and four sail tugs were cast forth from
Earth.

Already the moribund launcher sites down south were humming.
The Arcists seemed to be working with Jeffers's technicians—and even
with Sergeov's *Uber* Percells—in a new atmosphere of cooperation.

*If only it can last,* she wished. *Somehow, though I want it to, I can't
believe it will.*

"Let me see your arm," she insisted. When Saul held it out she
traced the tracks of numerous healing punctures. "Which one was from
when you drew blood for JonVon's serum?"

He laughed. "How should I know, Ginnie? I'll tell you, though. I
admit that this was my hardest case, so far. I never knew bio-organics
processors were so complicated." His expression turned thoughtful.
"Actually, the infection agent was subtle, a prionlike, self-replicating
molecule that somehow got inside JonVon's cool-case during the years
we were asleep. If it had been allowed to go on much longer . . ." He
shrugged.

"But you caught it in time." Virginia was still nervous enough that
it came out as a question, in spite of her confidence in Saul.

He smiled. "Oh, our surrogate son will be fine. Using symbiosis
methods, I turned the molecule into a variant JonVon can use in his self-
correcting systems. It actually seems to make him a little faster. You'll
have to evaluate the effects yourself, of course."

Virginia had blinked when Saul referred to JonVon as their "surrogate son." Of course now Saul was just like her, unable to have any more
children of his own. She realized a little guiltily that this made her feel
even closer to him. They would comfort each other, now.

*Oh, we'll have our problems. As time passes, our relationship will
never be perfect. That only happens in storybooks.*

But a line of verse came to her, quite suddenly, as some of her poems had more and more often, lately. It was a haiku.

Under winter's tent,
   Our children—seeds under snow,
      I grasp your warm scent . . .

Saul's gaze was distant. "Actually, some of the techniques for working with colloidal organics seem applicable to biological cloning. Working on JonVon gave me some ideas—"

She laughed and tousled his hair, now turning astonishingly brown at the roots—though Saul had told her he wasn't actually getting "younger," only "perfect for a middle-aged man."

"You're *always* getting ideas. Come on, Saul. I want to talk to JonVon."

She pushed off toward the webbing by her control station and gathered up her hair with one hand. She peeled back the dressing, uncovering her neural tap.

"Uh, you might want to wait—"

Her eyes flashed. "Is that an order, Doctor?"

He shrugged, smiling. "I guess you'd only do it the moment my back was turned, anyway."

She grinned. "It's been weeks. Much too long for an unrepentant dataline junkie like me."

She lay back on the webbing. Her little assistant mech, Wendy, whirred up and presented the well-worn tapline, which locked into place with a soft snicking sound. She felt Saul slip alongside her as she settled back and closed her eyes to the familiar throbbing along the direct line to her brain.

*How are you, Johnny?* she queried, shaping the subvocal words carefully, as one spoke to a child who has been ill.

HELLO, VIRGINIA. I HAVE SOME POETRY FOR YOU.

The words shimmered in space above their heads, as well as echoing along her acoustic nerve. She could tell, just from the clarity of the tones, that things were much, much better.

*Not yet, Johnny. First I want to run a complete diagnostic on you.*

ALL RIGHT, VIRGINIA. INITIATING "MR. FIXIT" SUBPERSONA.

Saul had never seen this simulated personality before. He laughed as a crystal-clear image formed, of a man in grimy over-alls, wiping his hands on a cloth. Behind the workman scurried assistants, dashing about carrying stethoscopes and voltmeters and giant wrenches over a great scaffolding. Within, a huge, cumbersome machine clanked and throbbed. Steam hissed and a low humming permeated everything.

A clipboard appeared out of nowhere. The master mechanic smiled as he put on a pair of bifocals and scanned the list.

WE'RE CHECKIN' IT OUT, MISS. PRELIMINARY RESULTS LOOK PRETTY GOOD.

OVER-ALL SYSTEMS STATUS HAS RETURNED TO NOMINAL. SELF-CORRECTION ROUTINES NOW OPERATING ON "TELL-ME-THRICE" BASIS, RELAXED FROM QUINTUPLE CHECKING RE-QUIRED DURING THE EMERGENCY. SOFTWARE MAINTENANCE REPORTS THAT PROGRAMS ARE RUNNING AT NORMAL OR BET-TER EFFICIENCY.

WE SEEM TO HAVE SERIOUS PROBLEMS IN ONLY ONE AREA, NOW.

*Well? What is it?* she inquired.

Mr. Fixit looked at her over the rims of his glasses.

I HAVE SOME POETRY FOR YOU, VIRGINIA.

Her head jerked in surprise. *The same exact words . . .*

Something was going on here.

"What is it, Ginnie?" Saul asked, feeling some of her concern over his own link.

"Nothing, probably . . ." Virginia muttered. She concentrated on sending probes down several avenues at once to find out for herself what was behind this.

It felt so smooth! Was it just in comparison with JonVon's former, wounded state? Or did it seem easier than ever to cruise these channels in the data streams? It was almost as if she could enter in true thought, instead of using simulations the computer provided to mimic the ex-perience. Blocs of memory were represented by metaphors—card cata-logs, filing cabinets, mile-long bookshelves—and rows of wizened storytellers. . . .

*There.* She came upon a barrier. Something guarded behind a high abatis and tightly locked gate. *A blockage. A big accumulation of data, hidden away, inaccessible.*

"I think he's just a little constipated," she said. Saul barked a sudden laugh, and cut it off just as quickly when he sensed her seriousness.

*It's big. What has JonVon got stuffed up in here?*

She poked away at the jam with metaphorical levers that were actually carefully crafted mathematical subroutines.

*Try a Kleinfeldt Transform . . . a rotation mapping . . . yes.*

A resorting routine manifested itself as a key that kept changing shape until it slipped into the lock, and turned. Light streamed forth.

*Well I'll be a blue-nosed mongoose!*

"Five hundred terabytes of *poetry!*" She gasped aloud. "And half of it is flashed as triple-A-priority data!"

"Poetry? Priority data?" Saul asked. "I don't get it."

"Neither do I." Then Virginia stopped. "Oh!"

Amazed, she turned toward Saul and opened her eyes. He looked back at her.

"JonVon *knew* he was sick! And so he *isolated* part of himself, in order to save important information for me. He used a sub-cache I'd already double-guarded . . . my poetry!"

She looked back up at the ceiling, staring. "Five hundred terabytes . . . the overflow spilled into everything JonVon did. No wonder Carl kept stumbling over apparently random poems while he was doing routine calculations."

Saul's voice was bemused. "But poetry!"

She nodded. "Let's see what this urgent scribbling is all about."

*Present us with a sample selection of triple-A-priority poetry, please,* she asked Mr. Fixit.

The dungareed figure shrugged.


THANKS, MISS. IT WAS GETTIN' CROWDED IN HERE.


He vanished, and suddenly words flowed.

### United States Patent Office
### Tr series—87239345–56241

Where is springtime,
    Here on the borderlands of Sol?
       Where . . .

**Miniaturized Robotic Power Supply**
Where stars, unwinking,
Rule a dark . . .


**Issued May 8, 2089**
Rule a dark domain—


To Virginia it was one of the weirdest versifications she had ever seen. It was as if the machine had interweaved poetry with some sort of *document*. She was beginning to be concerned that this was a sign of yet another, until now hidden, illness. But then she heard Saul laugh out loud and clap his hands.

"Of course!" he cried. "The urgent data has been shuffled in among the poems in order to *protect* it."

"Yessss." She nodded, seeing what he meant. "But . . . but what is the data? What was so important that it had to be hidden away in my special file for safety?"

"Look at the date, dear. Only seven years ago. This stuff was sent from home! And at a glance there seem to be volumes, *libraries* of the stuff!"

She was confused. "Carl said nothing about this."

"He didn't know. Ould-Harrad was in charge then, and Carl was still in the slots. Ould-Harrad must've just ignored it. He was starting to get all mystical even then."

"But Earth Control has been so stingy with help—"

"Who said anything about Earth Control?" Saul laughed again. "Here, I'll bet I can sift through and find the cover letter."

"The *cover letter*?"

But Saul was already at work. He sent commands so quickly, so deftly, that Virginia felt a strange contradiction, a touch of jealousy at someone else being so familiar with her domain, combined with pride that he had learned so well. Pages, sheaves, volumes, flickered past in an automatic sort that pulled the data from reams and reams of poetry.

A few flickering lines of verse caught her eye. *Not half bad*, she thought. *JonVon improved, even when he was sick. If it were sent Earthside, some of it might get published . . . yet another fallen Turing test.*

"Here! Here it is," Saul announced. "It's a letter in video form."

There was a multicolored blur, and then a new image flickered before them. She knew at once that it was not another JonVon simulation. This was a real, recorded transmission.

A woman with close-cropped hair sat at a console, wearing a tight skinsuit. Her face had that high-cheeked puffiness that came from a long time spent living in low gravity. She was made up in an odd manner, lightninglike strokes of color streaking her forehead from her temples in a fashion that must have been current when the message was sent.

Behind the woman there was a broad window-wall showing a scene of vast, reddish deserts, observed from high altitude. Puffy clouds of sand blew in storms across immense wastelands. Somehow, Virginia knew that this was not a weather-wall depiction, but the real thing.

"Halley Colony," the woman intoned. Her accent was one Virginia could not quite place, but the tension in her voice was unmistakable. "Halley, this is Phobos Base calling. We have listened to your story, heard the agony of your lost hopes, which are ours as well. We note the callous treatment you have received, and are ashamed.

"To a few of us, this crime has gone beyond forbearance. We take this risk, in transmitting to you these tokens of our good will, because not to do so would be to join the soullessness of a generation too smug and comfortable to care about past promises. Too lost in their pleasures to remember."

The woman paused. Her anxiety was apparent in the whiteness of her knuckles as her hands held the edges of the console.

"If you love us, do not answer or bother to thank us in any way. Do not mention this to Earth Control. These gifts are evidence that a few, on Earth and in space, have not forgotten our kinfolk, those who voyage through the cold reaches and down the river of despair.

"May the Almighty guide you to your destinies, people of the Comet . . . people of deepest space."

The image flickered and was gone. There followed a steady flow of indexes, texts, designs, patents, music. Saul scanned the lists, excitedly, but for a few moments Virginia could only blink, again looking out through tears. She seemed still to hear the Phobos woman's voice, echoing within her mind.

"JonVon was right," Virginia whispered, though at the moment Saul was too involved, shouting over one title after another pouring forth from the broken logjam of the computer's memory, to pay close attention.

"JonVon was right. This belonged under poetry. There was no other place for it."

## PART V

# WITH THE BRUSH
# OF A FEATHER

*2094*

You only live twice:
Once when you are born,
And once when you look death in the face.
　　　　　　　　—Bassho
　　　　　　　　Japanese poet,
　　　　　　　　1643–94

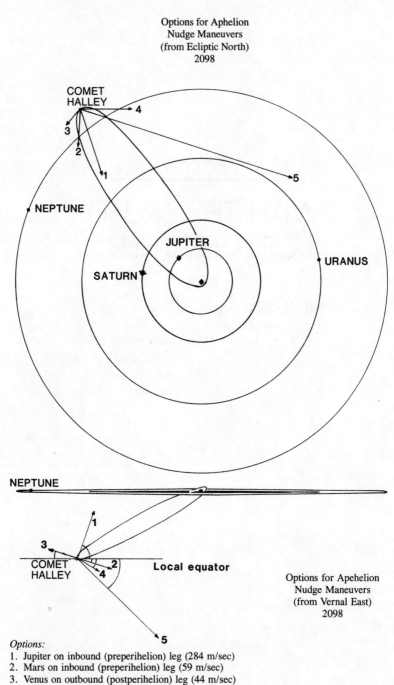

Options for Aphelion
Nudge Maneuvers
(from Ecliptic North)
2098

COMET HALLEY

4

3

2

1

5

NEPTUNE

JUPITER

URANUS

SATURN

NEPTUNE

1

3

COMET
HALLEY

2

4

Local equator

5

Options for Apehelion
Nudge Maneuvers
(from Vernal East)
2098

*Options:*
1. Jupiter on inbound (preperihelion) leg (284 m/sec)
2. Mars on inbound (preperihelion) leg (59 m/sec)
3. Venus on outbound (postperihelion) leg (44 m/sec)
4. Earth on outbound (postperihelion) leg (63 m/sec)
5. Jupiter on outbound (postperihelion) leg (536 m/sec)

# SAUL

---

*Existence. Life. Awareness.*

The words were often used as synonyms, but he knew that actually they were all three very different things. Three stages in Creation.

Did the proverbial tree falling in an empty forest make a sound?

Could that question even have been asked before all three stages had come about?

*Existence* supposedly began nearly twenty thousand million years ago—in a hot flux of quarks and leptons when *time* itself whirled, as if blindfolded, and stabbed out at something that it thereby named the Future. The universe could have taken a myriad of other forms by happenstance—by tiny variations in chance and dimension. Had even one of the basic physical constants been a fraction off, life would never have erupted out of clay-catalyzed chemistry, billions of arbitrary intervals later.

But *Life* did erupt . . . self-organizing, self-replicating, and *other*-organizing. Life had a tendency, from the very beginning, to alter its surroundings, its environment.

But that was not the end of it. Then there came the third creation. There came *awareness*. . . .

The midget gibbons flew down the tunnel ahead of Saul, chirping at each other and swinging lithely from cables stapled to the moss-covered ice. At an intersection they pivoted and regarded Saul, wide brown eyes blinking in question.

"Patience, children," he told them. "Let Papa read the tunnel signs. We're supposed to meet a Ginnie at Blue Stone Cave."

The two small apes hung nearby while he swam over to the meeting of two corridors. A thick green fuzz covered the old shaft and tunnel codes, but below the obscured markings were deep incisions, exposing dark, glittering, icy conglomerate, painted with a substance poisonous to Halleyforms.

An arrow to the right, piercing a large *S*.

*S for survivors.*

"Yes, this is the way." He adjusted his backpack. "Come on, Max. Come on, Sylvie."

The two minigibbons landed on his shoulders. He pushed off, following the phosphorescent glow of the lichenoids.

*Two years,* he thought. *It's been two years since, all at once, the universe seemed to let up on us. Since the litany of bad news turned around.*

*I wonder how much longer this good spell will last.*

Everyone seemed to credit his serums and Virginia's miracle mechs for the turnaround in the colony's fortunes. But Saul knew that part of the problem, before, had been pure and simple loneliness.

Things had not been the same since that afternoon in Virginia's lab, when JonVon's illness-wrought memory blocks tumbled down, and they discovered that they had *not* been forgotten, after all.

There had been no more messages from their secret benefactors. But that didn't matter. Even more important than the techniques they had received had been the boost to morale, knowing that someone back home still cared.

Even the officials back on Earth seemed to have relented. The colony was buzzing about the "Care Package" that was nearing rendezvous with Halley—sent at high velocity by an Earth Control apparently guilt-racked over its past neglect.

*No wonder Jeffers's teams are getting so much done, down at the south pole. Virginia estimates they'll actually be ready to begin the Nudge this month.*

*If this peace among the clans lasts, that is . . .*

The passage lightened ahead. Max and Sylvie launched themselves from his back and sped along a wall cable, rushing toward a chattering greeting.

"Who is it, Hokulele? Who's coming?" a deep voice asked from beyond a stone arch. "Oh, quiet down, you silly monkey, can't you see it's only Max and Sylvie? Come on in, Dr. Lintz!"

Keoki Anuenue's grin was broad and his grip strong as he hauled Saul into a wide chamber that looked half ice palace, half mad scientist's laboratory. Cavelike crannies led off in all directions, bordered by glittering, faceted structures of hardened crystal. People could be seen moving in some of the rooms, working at various tasks. A few stopped and waved at Saul.

In the chamber's center there protruded a great boulder of some bluish metal agglomerate, an odd formation that had given the group that lived here its name.

Everywhere was the soft verdance of lush plant life. Here a lawnlike expanse of cloverlike *Trifolium halleyense,* there a shock of mutated marigolds, growing out of night soil into spindly shapes that never would have been possible on the homeworld.

"Great to see you again, Doc," Anuenue said. "My people are always glad when you visit."

Saul had given up trying to get Keoki to call him Saul, like everyone else did. That the big Hawaiian was now older than he—his once jet-black hair had turned silver and his eyes were deeply etched by smile lines—hardly seemed to matter to him.

"Hi, Keoki. You're looking well."

"How could I not? I was never really sick, like so many others, but those treatments of yours have me feeling I could climb a wave all the way to Molokai!"

His laugh was infectious. Saul reached up and petted the little capuchin monkey on his friend's shoulder, who hid behind Anuenue's head and glared suspiciously at the gibbons. "And how is Hokulele? Does she still have a big appetite?"

Keoki laughed. "There hasn't been a purple sighted anywhere near Blue Rock Cave for weeks. She has to live off table scraps, these days, and she hates it!"

"Well." Saul smiled. "I'm sure motherhood will keep her busy enough."

"You can tell?" Anuenue held up the little monkey. "*Ua huna au ia mea* . . . I wasn't sure I should tell you, since you wanted us to be careful before letting any Earth species become independent of your cloning chambers. But Virgil Simms was visiting from Central, and he brought his male with him—"

Saul waved a hand. "No matter. The modified capuchins are a success, obviously. We ought to see if they breed true."

The data from Earth had been the key. For although science was still a dull affair, back home, some progress could not be avoided. Saul would never have been able to develop the cloning machines himself, even using parts from a dozen scavenged sleep slots. But by implementing designs released from JonVon's unclogged memories, he had been able to build astonishing devices.

Using samples taken from their still-frozen "zoo" of test animals, he could now force-grow a monkey or ape from blast cell to fetus to adult in a month. A *month*.

It was, frankly, almost beyond his comprehension as a biologist. Saul was grateful that half of the process could be run by JonVon, without his having to understand it. He could turn most of his attention to modifying the original genes—an art at which his skill was not obsolete—giving them an artificial inheritance to thrive in the new ecosystem that was coming into being under Halley.

Anuenue was trading monkey faces with Max and Sylvie, making Hokulele insanely jealous.

"I still can't really understand why you chose gibbons for your own watchdogs, Doc. Without a prehensile tail, they're almost as clumsy as a man."

"I have a weakness for apes," Saul began. "They have their—"

"Saul!" two feminine voices called out, almost in unison. He looked overhead and saw a young woman in roughly sewn fibercloth over-alls drop down from a shaft to alight on the blue rock. A spindly machine fell after her and she caught it deftly, placing it gently on the floor. The whirring, spiderlike mech whizzed ahead of Lani to reach Saul first.

"Hi, Saulie!" The machine spoke with Virginia's voice, but in a slightly higher register, a simpler tone. It was easy to tell that Virginia herself wasn't "present"—was not operating this particular mech herself—and Saul was just a little disappointed.

"Hello, little Ginnie," he said to the very unmachinelike, colony-made machine as it reached out an arm and stroked his leg. The device was another hybrid of Earth-based and homegrown research—a mixture of new designs sent up by their secret benefactors, the mechanical brilliance of Jeffers and d'Amario, and Virginia's hypermodern approach to personality-based programming.

"I love you, Saul," the childlike voice said softly. The little artificial persona was an edited replica of Virginia's own. Sometimes, as now, it led to embarrassment. Keoki coughed, grinning behind his hand.

Saul felt particularly unnerved since, at the moment, Virginia was mad at him. *Can't even really blame her,* he thought.

"Hello, Lani," he said to the young woman who followed the robot. She enveloped him in a warm embrace.

"You are looking wonderful," he said, holding her back at arm's length.

She blushed, turning slightly away as if to hide the scars the Zipper Pox had left on her once-smooth cheek.

"You're a magnificent liar, Saul. Almost as good as you are a doctor."

But to him she *did* look wonderful. For he well recalled when Lani Nguyen had been slotted. At the time it had seemed as pointless as storing a corpse. Now the pallor of deepsleep had almost left her face, and the blue eyelids only made her half-oriental features seem all the more sultry and mysterious.

*Virginia should never have told me about Lani Nguyen's secret cache of human sperm and ova. I've almost questioned her about it several times, since her unslotting . . . to find out where it's hidden.*

*Ah, but if I had that plasm in my hands, I might be too tempted. . . .*

"When can I go back on duty, Saul? I want to join the crews mounting the Nudge Flingers, before all the really important work is already done."

*A spacer to the last,* he thought. "Even if the Nudge does begin in a month or so, Lani, it'll be years in progress, with lots of motors left to build. You'll do your turn, don't worry. Right now, though, your job is to rest, get up-to-date."

She nodded. The little capuchin monkey transferred from Keoki's shoulder to hers and she scratched it.

"I'll try to be patient, Saul. Anyway, I've got to thank you for assigning me to Blue Rock Clan for my recuperation. I've been to some of the other groups to try to visit people. . . ." She blinked, remembering. "Saul, how can people, professional people, with college degrees, act so . . . so . . ." She groped for the right word.

"So *meshuggenuh*?" he suggested.

Lani laughed—clear and bell-like. "Yeah. So *meshuggenuh*."

Anuenue put an arm around her shoulder. "We've been very glad to have Lani. Any of the clans of the Survivor faction would welcome her as a permanent member."

Lani blinked. "I . . . I guess I'll have to choose one, won't I? I'm still not used to thinking like that."

Saul didn't like it any better than she did. He had hoped that the factionalism of the last thirty years would break down, once more of those slotted in the early days were treated with his serum and released. As the active population of the comet burgeoned, a majority would be made up of those who remembered Earth most recently, whose memories were fresh with Captain Cruz's stirring speech from the framework of the *Sekanina*, and the hopes they had all shared.

But it hadn't worked out that way. The newly revived—disoriented, weak, and afraid—found themselves in a world as much different from the Halley Colony they remembered as that early settlement had been from placid Moon Base 1. They quickly gravitated to groups they might be comfortable with, adopted their ideologies, and became clansmen.

Saul did not mention to Lani that there were three people who seemed exempt from this pattern. For different reasons, he, Virginia, and Carl Osborn were all isolated—respected, perhaps, but comfortable nowhere.

Lani shrugged. "Well, I sure won't go down south and join Quiverian and his radical Orthos—"

"Arcists," Keoki corrected, like a patient language teacher, instructing her in the right dialect.

"Yeah, Arcists," she repeated. "And when I got a hall pass and tried to visit some of my Percell friends over in *Uber* territory, Sergeov told me to get my little Ortho ass the hell out of there! The Mars boys aren't much nicer, even if Andy Carroll and I once were pals.

"So what choice do I have? That Plateau Three crowd up on B Level is mixed Ortho-Percell, but the PeeThrees have got this *gleam* in their eyes, you know what I mean, Saul? They aren't so much spacers anymore as missionaries! They don't seem to care if they live or die, so long as Halley's trillion tons of ice gets delivered, according to Captain Cruz's plan."

Saul smiled. "It looks to me as if you've found a home right here, Lani."

"That's right," Keoki affirmed. "Just let us know. We'll paint you a new tabard and hold a ceremony."

Lani nodded, but she briefly bit her lip. "I—I'll let you know as soon as I've had a chance to talk to Carl."

She lowered her eyes, knowing how transparent she must seem, but unashamed of it in front of her two friends. There was very little more that could be said.

"I'll see about getting you some light duty topside soon," Saul assured her. Lani nodded, gratitude in her eyes.

The little capuchin chirped. The black gibbons, Max and Sylvie, swiveled and looked back down the hallway, their hackles rising.

Keoki peered, his hand drifting toward his belt knife. "Somebody's coming."

Men and women started emerging from labs and sleeping caves, nervously gripping staves made from meteoric iron. A pair grabbed the heavy vacuum door and began shutting it. Then they heard a high-pitched whistle—two upsweeps and a trill, repeated twice.

Keoki relaxed only a little. "Treaty call," he said. *"E wehe i ka puka,"* he told the men, and they ceased pushing. The door stayed half-open. A light appeared down the tunnel, and two small brown figures tumbled to a halt just twenty feet short of the entrance, tongues lolling from narrow mouths rimmed with needle-sharp teeth.

*I should never have let Quiverian talk me into giving him otters,* Saul thought, regarding the agile creatures. *They're just too dangerous.*

But if he had disallowed the Arcist leader's request, Saul might have lost his carefully maintained neutral status. It had been hard, serving as middleman, negotiating a treaty so that the emigrants to the south pole still cooperated with Carl Osborn's crews. The otters had been just one more price.

To his surprise, though, the figure that emerged behind the grinning animals was not Joao Quiverian, or even one of the Arcist leader's principal assistants. Wild white hair and beard floated like a halo around a face as dark brown as the rich carbonaceous veins lining the icy hall.

"*. . . Kela ao,*" Anuenue breathed in amazement. "It is Ould-Harrad."

Those intense, brown eyes were now rimmed by deep creases. The former spacer officer was dressed in a flapping brown gown of salvaged fibercloth that made him look even more like an ancient patriarch. He gestured with one hand.

"Saul Lintz."

Lani gripped Saul's arm and Keoki Anuenue moved as if to stop him, but he shrugged them aside. "Keep Max and Sylvie back," he said, and cast off down the hallway.

The otters clung to Ould-Harrad's robe, eyeing Saul ferally. Saul did not feel particularly safe for having been their "creator," in a sense. In near weightlessness, the creatures were fearsome beasts.

If Joao Quiverian was leader of the radical Arcists, Ould-Harrad was their spiritual guide, their priest. The flame of his guilt complex seemed to drive him hotter than anyone else here on this ancient star mote.

As he approached, Saul wasn't entirely sure of his own safety. For although the Arcist faction seemed to accept his neutrality, this man was his own force.

"Colonel Ould-Harrad." He nodded, stopping ten feet away. Saul let his feet slowly come to rest on the floor, toes clutching the soft, hybrid, green covering.

"Do not call me that," the African intoned with an upraised hand. "I am not an officer, nor spacer, nor Earthman any longer."

Saul blinked. He had last glimpsed Ould-Harrad during the Great Exodus—his white spacesuit tabard centered with a single, jet-black starburst—leading the Arcist exiles on their trek while Quiverian and his crew covered the rear. During Saul's brief, subsequent visits to the antipodes, their paths had never crossed. Still, he remembered what the man had said, so long ago, in his lab aboard the *Edmund*.

*"He whom Allah chooses to touch, bears the ridges of those fingerprints, ever afterward. . . ."*

"Very well, Suleiman." Saul nodded. "I see the otters are doing well."

Ould-Harrad glanced down at the creatures. His hand gently stroked their glossy fur, gene-adapted for life in icy halls instead of the salt spume of the sea.

"One more time, you have proven me wrong about you, Saul Lintz. For the role you have played in bringing these fine creatures forth cannot have been evil."

Saul couldn't help it. He felt a wash of *relief* at Ould-Harrad's words, as if he had been worried about that very thing, and the man had the power to absolve. *He is very good at this prophet shtick,* Saul observed.

"Did Joao lend them to you while you came up north?"

Ould-Harrad's eyes seemed to flash.

"They are no longer his to lend. That is one reason why I have sought you out. To tell you that there are only three monkeys, down in the south antipodes, to watch for purples and guard the people as they sleep. You must replace these otters."

"Oh? Where are you taking them?"

"You deserve to know." Ould-Harrad paused with a faraway look in his eyes. "For years I have gone out onto the surface and meditated under the stars, as mystics have since time immemorial, praying and hoping for a sign. I found that they were hypnotic, those glittering lights in the blackness. After a long time I thought that I had, indeed, begun to hear God's voice.

"But it could not have been."

"Why not?" Saul was curious.

Ould-Harrad's voice was filled with pain. "Because all that came to me was laughter!"

Saul knew that this was more than mere madness. He could almost feel the intensity of the man's soul torment. "I think I understand," he said quietly. He did not add that he saw nothing inconsistent in the man's experience. *Who ever said the Creator must be sober? The universe is for laughing, or we must weep.*

Ould-Harrad nodded. For a long moment there were no words. Then he raised his eyes again.

"There was another thing."

"What was that?"

"I . . . I can no longer be a party to the schemes of Quiverian and his banal crew, they—"

"The Arcists?"

"Yes." The beard floated as Ould-Harrad shook his head. His voice was barely audible. "The wars we brought with us from Earth are as the fog of summer, that will fall away and be forgotten with the coming of winter. I have come to realize that arguments over where to *target* this great, frozen teardrop miss the point entirely."

"Where will you go, then?"

Ould-Harrad's gaze dropped briefly to the floor. "I must go down . . . into the ice. Below where anyone has gone—except for Ingersoll, whom they now call the Old Man of the Caves, and those poor creatures who followed him. I will live on what grows, along their trail. I will minister to them, if they still live. And I will think."

Saul nodded. Within Ould-Harrad's world view, a hermitage made sense, obviously. He made no effort to dissuade the man. "I wish you luck. And wisdom."

Ould-Harrad nodded. He looked down at his pets. "I am beginning to comprehend one aspect, at least . . . this thing you preach—this *symbiosis*. I did not understand at first, but now . . ."

He paused. "You are not doing evil, Saul Lintz. For that reason I warn you. Beware of Quiverian. He plans something. I know it. You, in particular, he wishes harm. And Carl Osborn."

Saul did not know what to say. "I'll be careful."

"Care, or care not." Ould-Harrad shrugged. "Do or do not. In the end, it is all by God's will. We are helpless to resist."

The otters seemed to sense something even before he moved. They leaped forth and flicked off down the long, dim hallway. Ould-Harrad turned stiffly and walked away.

*He actually does seem to be* walking, *like on the moon or on Earth,* Saul thought as he watched the man depart. *I wonder what his technique is.*

He swiveled and glided back toward Blue Rock Cave, pondering the effects of personal gravity.

# CARL

The blackness seemed like a solid weight, a vast hand clasped about the gray, battered ice. Carl hadn't been high above the surface for months, and the arid bleakness of it struck him fully, bringing back memories of his years when open silent vacuum meant freedom, deft movement, effortless grace.

Stars gleamed, their tiny brimming beacons of rose and sea azure and molten yellow shining like steady promises of another life—a realm filled with vibrant hues, a place beyond this bleak plain that the slow elliptical glide of orbit had drained of color.

Now the encroaching darkness meant that there was nothing between this frozen waste and the beckoning stars—no planets aswarm with clouds and lightning, not even a vagrant asteroid within view.

They rode far below the ecliptic plane now, ten times farther from the disk of planets than Earth itself was from the sun. The outer solar system was vast beyond imagining. Carl looked toward the south, virtually all the solar system at his back. The sun's dim radiance—a thousandth of that which warmed Earth—could not summon forth the full colors that marked the ice. Everywhere pools of shadow swallowed detail; most of Halley was an inky kingdom.

—Take it careful now,— Jeffers sent.

"Right," Carl answered automatically, his reverie broken. He jetted down to alight near his friend. Together they glide-walked southward. Normally he would seek the polar cable and use a jet, be at the south pole in a few minutes. But these were not normal times.

They edged around the hummock of orange-splashed ice. Empty storage drums were moored with spiderweb-thin lines to the lump of frozen waste—garbage left from some process now decades old, forgotten. Jeffers slunk from one drum to another, careful not to expose himself to the southward side. Carl followed him. It took an effort to stay on the ice, gingerly digging his clamp-toes in for each long step. He fought down the urge to leap, to *fly* above the mottled snowscape.

*Blithe spirit,* he thought. *That's what I was once. Zipping around, all spit and vinegar. Carl Osborn, space daredevil. But now. . . it just doesn't have the same zest.*

Jeffers motioned to him and they sprinted across a patch of brown spill, running almost horizontally in long gliding steps, boots finding leverage on knobs and juts of ice. They reached the shelter of a chem module, a stained cylinder long sucked dry.

"They must be able to see us by now. I—"

—Shhhh! This close, they can pick up even local comm.—

Carl bent down for shelter, feeling mildly ridiculous. He glanced around the curved edge of the cylinder and took in what he could. Yes, definitely—new structures near the lips of the Nudge shafts. They looked makeshift, thrown together from old cargo canisters and struts. He could see nearly to the south pole itself. Neptune hung barely above the horizon, a faint green pinpoint.

Under high magnification, Neptune's equatorial bands made brown concentric circles, resembling a target.

Some *Ubers* still wanted to fire the Nudge to make Halley a Neptunian satellite. They could harvest gases from the upper atmosphere, settle on the largest moon. Carl wondered idly what it would be like to live out his days with a slumbering green giant filling the sky. *Not a lot like California, no. Maybe I should've gone into the insurance business.* But he still hoped to see Earth's blues, and reds, and autumn browns again. . . .

—We see you.— An alert, young voice. Carl glanced around the edge but could see no one ahead.

"It's Carl Osborn. I've come to talk."

—Got nothing to talk about. Jeffers told you our policy.— The voice was tense but determined.

"Who is that?" Carl whispered, touching helmets with Jeffers.

—Name's Rostok. Saul revived him about ten, eleven months ago. Now he's Quiverian's number-two guy down here.—

"What's he work on?"

Jeffers made a sour face. —Mounting the electromagnetic assemblies.—

"Oh, great." A Nudge engineer. One of *those* had to go lunatic.

—If you come any closer we will not be responsible for the outcome.—

"Not responsible! What kind of crap is that?"

—We declare ourselves independent of Halley Command.— The voice was tighter, clipped.

—The hell you will!— Jeffers snapped before Carl could motion him to silence.

—We already *have*. And no Percell is going to tell us what to do!—

Carl breathed deeply. It did no good to blow up at asinine speeches; he had learned that the hard way, through these years. Jeffers was visibly grinding his teeth; Carl signaled him to stay quiet. "What . . . do you want?"

—Not food,— Rostok answered smugly. —We already have enough hydro set up here to feed ourselves. Found a nice thick vein of edible Halleyforms, too. Delicious. Feed 'em heat and they grow like crazy.—

*So we can't starve them out,* Carl thought automatically.

—We want—hell, we already *have!*—control of the targeting of the Nudge.—

Jeffers jumped up. —You bastards! That's *our* gear, our labor that built it. Rostok, you put in a couple months. The rest of us been buildin' the EM guns for *years!* I'm double-damned if I'll let some—*uh!*—

Jeffers grunted as Carl yanked him down. "*I'll* do the talking."

—Can it, Jeffers. We got the flingers, so we call the tune.—

"You have no right to determine the Nudge," Carl said as calmly as he could.

—We got the flingers, *and* we represent Earth.—

"The hell you do. You represent *nobody.*"

—We speak for Earth. We won't let you Percells take this plague carrier back into near-Earth orbit.—

Carl had hoped that, with the diseases checked, people would become more reasonable. *Looks like it's just given some of them the energy to be real sons of bitches again.*

He opened in a reasonable tone. "That has to be decided in the Council. Look, Rostok, I'm coming out. I want to talk face to face."

Carl stood and walked around the edge of the cylinder. Was there some movement around a jumble of crates on the horizon? He squinted, then thumbed up the telescopics. Yes—figures working at something, looking this way.

He heard mumbles on a side channel, then the clear voice of Joao Quiverian. —We warned you, Osborn.—

A sudden brilliance cut the dim sunlight. It was invisible in the vacuum but cast stark shadows where it lanced into a hummock nearby. Steam exploded, stones rattled on Carl's helmet. A geyser burst nearby as a second laser bolt splashed the ice. Carl dived back behind the cylinder.

—That enough for you?—

Carl blinked, blinded by the glare.

Jeffers sent, —They're usin' those big industrial lasers—the spot welders. Cut the big girders with 'em. Can't aim 'em much but *Jeezus* do they burn.—

"Shit!"

—Don't show yourself around here again.—

Another blazing burst streaked into nearby ice. Blue-white gas billowed into a swelling sphere.

"Damn," Carl said grimly. "We can't even use mechs against that—we'd lose too many. We need every one we've got for the Nudge."

Jeffers grimaced and swore steadily. —Prob'ly smash up the flingers if we tried.—

"What the hell can we do?"

—That's what I thought *you'd* know,— Jeffers said.

"Shit!"


*Meetings.* Carl fidgeted with his pen, shifted restlessly in his webchair. *You can judge the importance of a problem by how many endless meetings it generates.*

He watched the wall weather as much as he could—luscious hills rising from Lake Como in northern Italy, with water-skiers cutting white *V*s in waters of ancient blue—but he had to appear to be intent, giving every faction its due attention. They were grouped in loose knots around the meeting room in Central. The Arcist insurrection had reopened the issue of Nudge targeting.

*A Pandora's box,* Carl thought moodily. *And all this had to happen just now, before I could speak privately to the important people, gather support for what I've got to announce.* He bit at the end of his pen, a nervous gesture he had picked up sometime in the last year. *With over two hundred revived crew, there are plenty of members for each faction. And I have to let them all have their say, exhaust the energy Quiverian's stirred up. Worst possible timing . . . as usual.*

They had been going nearly two hours now and the groups had lined up exactly as he could have predicted.

The most popular idea was the mission's original flight plan: a Jupiter flyby on the return to the inner solar system, but before the comet approached too close to the sun. They could swoop deep into the giant planet's gravity well like a race car in a steep turn, stealing vital momentum.

Using the south-pole flingers, they could aim the Jovian flyby to turn Halley into a short-period comet. That would make rescue from Earthspace easier and harvesting of Halley Core possible. The Plateau

Three people favored the original plan, as did the solid majority of non-aligned crew.

The *Ubers*—the radical Percells led by Sergeov—wanted a different variant of the Jupiter flyby. Their final goal, though, was genuinely bizarre—to abandon the inner solar system entirely, and return to the spaces out here. Fire the Nudge at a low impulse, they said, and during the flyby pass *over* Jupiter, rather than ahead of it. That would loop them outward again to rendezvous with Neptune. Use the Nudge again to slow Halley and get captured. Become a moon. Spread out, colonize the rock and ice of Triton. A colony of supermen, perfecting themselves beneath a sky filled with a dim green ball of methane-streaked clouds.

Two vastly different plans, but both calling for a rendezvous with Jupiter in 2135. Astronomy allowed many different destinations from that one gargantuan world.

The Plateau Three spacers and Sergeov's *Ubers* were united in their need for a Jovian flyby, but they made uneasy allies. They differed about many other things, and gave each other guarded glances.

Carl had checked the mission requirements himself, not trusting anybody's calculations. It would take a delta-V, a change in Halley's current velocity, of 284 meters per second in the Nudge—aimed at 72 degrees north declination from the ecliptic. Not so easy. Possible, though, using thrusters located at the south pole.

*Medieval societies squabbled over rarefied points of theology . . . and now we argue vector targeting. Equally pointless, maybe . . .*

The irony of the *Uber*–Plateau Three alliance was that now the Arcists had virtually destroyed both options.

To bring off a good Jupiter flyby on the inward-falling leg, they had to use the south-pole flingers. And the Arcists wanted above all costs to keep Earth pristine and safe from Halley contamination. If the Jupiter encounter came off badly in the crucial hours of encounter, Halley could be flung deep into the inner solar system. The Arcists would never go for a maneuver that brought Halley near the home world. To avoid that possibility, they would refuse use of the south pole unless *they* were in control. Quiverian and his fanatics would rather die in deep space than let anyone else handle the maneuver.

He read the signs, and knew that the situation was close to war. If something wasn't done, soon, there would be killing. So Carl had sent a squirt Earthside as soon as he returned . . . and gotten confirmation. He had to offer a good option to the Council, *now,* before factionalism made compromise impossible.

*Even if I have to fudge the truth . . .*

He waited for a natural break in the talk. The wall weather now showed a sloop tacking in high seas, her stately turn unhindered by glistening steel-blue waves that hammered her without pity or effect. Her sails billowed triumphantly, shimmering white beneath a hard cold sky. *She'll make port,* he thought. *You can see it in the way she moves.*

He let the talk run on for a while. When the silence of confusion and doubt came, as he knew it would, he rose and began to speak. He caught and held the eyes of each faction leader in turn—Otis Sergeov hanging legless in air, arms folded adamantly; Joao Quiverian, here under a truce, as solid as ever, eyes smoldering; Jeffers, who represented the Martian Way group, lean and sardonic; and the others, who had no particular politics, but did want a chance to live.

Carl spoke slowly, conveying by gesture and expression more than through words the hope he had, the plea for confidence, for solidarity before this new threat.

"This mission was planned around a planetary carom past Jupiter. That's why we put launchers at the south pole—which are now unusable."

That put Quiverian on the spot. The others glared at the sallow Brazilian. Of course, Carl wasn't quoting the man precisely. He hurried on before Quiverian could interrupt.

"But the south pole Nudge isn't our *only* option." He flicked a tab on his sleeve and a chart appeared on Central's main screen. "It would take a relatively simple Nudge to reach *Earth itself.* A change in velocity of only sixty-three meters per second, aimed about forty degrees south and nearly ninety degrees away from the sun *would bring us home.*"

The men and women stirred, varying emotions flickering across their faces. *Home.*

"But to do it accurately demands that we despin Halley first. We'd arc in near Earth, good for a quick jumpoff and rescue . . . but only *after* perihelion passage. We'd have to weather that terrible storm. It's anyone's guess how many of us would survive high summer on a comet."

He had let the frowns and scowls build; now he defused them. Quiverian was red as a beet, opening his mouth. Carl cut him off.

"Of course, Earth Control might get a bit miffed. . . ."

They looked at each other, blinked, and guffawed. Their laughter released some of the long-building tension. Of course Earth would never allow a plan that brought Halleyform spores that near the atmosphere. Even Quiverian relaxed slightly, when it was clear that Carl had not been serious.

"There are *other* alternatives to Jupiter," Carl continued. "We could try for Venus—jump off in aeroshells, decelerate in the upper atmosphere. But that's *after* perihelion again, and we might not survive slamming into that atmosphere at eighty kilometers a sec or so."

He swept the room with a long, penetrating gaze. *Cap'n Cruz would've done this right,* he thought. *Or maybe he would've stopped all this factionalism long ago. I'll never be the leader he was.*

"On the other hand, there *is* an encounter that'll get us to a planet *before* perihelion, and at lower velocity—one with Mars."

A stir of disbelief. "Mars?"

"You mean target. . . ?"

"I didn't know it could even be . . ."

He went on swiftly, not giving anyone a chance to break in.

"Look. We can't allow a single faction to control our destiny—"

"And *we* will not allow use of the south pole unless *we* have control!" Quiverian shouted.

Carl held his palms up, open. "Okay. That means we have to abandon the Jupiter flyby totally. The next best mission demands a pass into the inner solar system, but not coming near Earth. Instead, we can vector the Nudge to Mars. The encounter itself won't divert Halley much—but it'll give us a chance to jump off."

Some engineers shook their heads. Carl kept on going, before the objections could begin.

"We'll build aerobrakes and swoop into the Martian atmosphere. It's thin but deep, a good target for us, especially since an encounter with *any* planetary atmosphere will be awful damn fast."

A spacer asked, "We could lose enough velocity on one pass?"

*Sharp question.* "No. We'd have to do several maneuvers." He ticked off fingers. "Aerobrake at Mars, divert outward to Jupiter. Aerobrake again there with a gravity assist. Pass inward to Venus, swing around, head for Mars again. By then we'll have shed enough velocity to make a successful rendezvous brake in the Martian atmosphere. We can get out of the aero shells, come alongside Phobos."

A long silence. They stared at him.

"But . . ." Keoki Anuenue muttered. "How long will all that take?"

"Twenty years."

Gasps.

Carl rode over the babble with, "That's twenty added to the nearly eighty we'll have been gone. But it will be worth it to get to Phobos Base, to safety and maybe, eventually, home again. I should add that this plan has the approval of Earth Command."

A Plateau Three woman said angrily, "What'll happen to Halley?"

Carl shrugged. "JonVon shows it wheeling off into the outer system, back to its original home in the Oort Cloud, gone for good."

Jeffers said thoughtfully, "We could target Halley smack on Mars—give it an atmosphere!"

"Sure," Sergeov said, "and try aerobraking at same time. Impossible!"

Jeffers began, "But—" He shut up as he noticed Carl's signal to be quiet.

"It's a chance to *live*," Carl said emphatically. "*If* we try the aerobrake and guide Halley to optimize that. Anything else is suicide."

"What can we expect at Mars?" Quiverian demanded suspiciously.

"Quarantine. Maybe Earth'll order us isolated on Diemos. Let the medicos study us until Earth is sure these diseases are controllable."

Another long silence. They all contemplated this new idea, letting it sink in.

"Is possible?" Sergeov asked, scowling.

Carl shrugged. "We might never be allowed into Earthspace—not that that'll bother the *Ubers*, eh? Remember, though, that there are decent places to live in the small scientific colonies of the asteroids. Maybe we can even do some worthwhile pioneering on Mars itself."

Jeffers beamed. "Damn right."

Carl held up his hand. "One more thing. Earth Command is very strong on this plan. It has made acceptance a condition for getting the Care Package."

*That* got to them. The high-speed rocket carrying supplies was the centerpiece of their fresh hope. They had to have it.

Carl realized that the hardest part had been won.

He explained further with some graphics JonVon had whipped up with only minutes' warning. The Council listened with glacial but growing acceptance. At least it seemed the idea was possible.

Complicated, yes. Difficult and risky, yes. But possible.

And perhaps the *only* possibility.

Carl remained standing. He kept his mood grave but sympathetic, determined but flexible. And one by one, the factions voiced their own narrow views.

The Plateau Threes disliked throwing away hard-won Halley . . . but they were used to taking their lead from him.

The *Ubers* grumbled, but admitted they had no other option.

Jeffers and the few Percell spacers who had clung to their dream of Mars terraforming were overjoyed. They would get to work near Mars, perhaps start the greening of that arid rustworld.

The Arcists weren't totally happy. They distrusted Carl. But this option kept Halley far from Earth. And the sanction of Earth Control lent it weight.

Through it all Carl felt the dark undercurrent of Percell and Ortho running, but muted now by the constricted, bleak future they faced. The largest part of the crew belonged to a group he called the survivors— because in the end, that was all they cared about.

*Quite sensible,* he thought ruefully. *And I'm their natural ally . . . even though I don't believe we'll ever really get out of this alive. . . .*

He watched the sloop run before the wind, her sails big-bellied and impossibly white, her bow cutting the water sharp and sure.

And gradually, reluctantly, the factions came around.

The Council broke up at last with grudging agreement. They would try to reach Mars.

Carl sat down at last, feeling a sudden fatigue sweep over him.

*The Arcists are right. They can't trust me. I know this Mars business isn't going to pan out right, but it's politically necessary right now. Necessary in order to prevent a civil war. In order to get the Care Package. The hard truths can come later.*

He shook his head.

*I'm turning into a goddamn diplomat. I don't think like a spacer anymore, not even like and engineer. Christ!—I'll be wearing black tie and tails next. And when I look in the mirror, the tongue I see will be forked.*

# VIRGINIA

The machinery was starting to look old. The original glossy finish had faded long ago, until it was hard to read the names of the equipment manufacturers anymore. They had been rubbed nearly illegible after thirty years of faithful scrubbing.

*Ozymandias, my secret hideaway.* Virginia glanced over in the back corner of the lab, where little Wendy sat patiently, drawing a small trickle of power from a wall socket. The tiny maintenance mech peeped once and started to rise, but when Virginia said nothing it settled down once more.

Funny, how you didn't notice things for a while, and then they suddenly hit you. It had been almost two years, Earth time, since Virginia had been thawed and returned to duty, yet in all that time she had not once paid the slightest attention to Wendy. She had been too busy.

Now she contemplated the little mech, bemused.

*Thirty years. She's cleaned and tended and guarded my sanctuary, keeping things just as I left them.*

*Maybe Saul is right. Maybe I do good work.*

She smiled.

*Watch it, girl. Keep this up and you really* will *start to imagine yourself a goddess, like those poor creatures—barely human anymore—who followed Ingersoll down into the deepest caverns, who bow to my mechs and address them by my name.*

The last two years had been so busy, for her, for Saul, and for Carl. It struck her that she had not taken any time to stop and think about what had happened to all of them.

*A fine trio, we are. None of us were important at all, back when Captain Cruz lived, and everyone was one big, happy research expedition. Carl was just a petty officer, I was a junior Artificial Intelligence tech, and Saul was a doctor with a strange passion for bugs.*

*Now poor Carl is whatever passes for commander, these days. I'm the Spider Woman, sending out her web of drones to keep the tunnels patched and the gunk controlled. And Saul . . .*

She paused, pondering. *Of us all, he's the one who's changed the most. Lord, I hope I don't lose a good man to godhead.*

He had been so preoccupied lately. Almost obsessed. Reluctant to link with her in the intimate touch of neural amplification. *As if he were hiding something from me . . . or protecting me from something he felt I'd never understand.*

Finally, it had come to a head. Last week she had lashed out, shouting at him in her frustration. Since then, he had left a few terse messages for her, her mechs had seen him in the halls, but for all intents and purposes they might as well have been on different planets.

All around her the holo displays glowed faintly. Even some of the units that had gone blank over her long sleep were replaced, now that she and Jeffers had gotten the autofac working properly up on A Level. For perhaps the first time since her awakening, no red warning lights glowed.

She found her gaze lingering on the Kelmar bio-organic machine that she had spent half her personal weight allowance to bring aboard . . . ages ago. The heart of her bio-cybernetic computer.

"JonVon," she whispered. "I need some distraction from my troubles."

There were things she used to do, for amusement, which she had not had time for in years. But now—

"Let's see just how rusty I am at visual simulation," she said, low, and pressed the Kelmar's thumb ident. A display lit up.

So, Virginia. Will it be more than routine stuff, today?

She shook her head. "Let's have some fun, like we used to."

Virginia spent a few moments flicking switches and calibrating before slipping on the worn disk of her neural tap. She had grown so used to direct data flow, controlling or programming distant mechs as if they were parts of her own body, that it took her a few minutes to get back into the experimental, "synthetic" mode that had once been her own special way of interacting with JonVon.

But JonVon remembered. She had only to desire it, and a rainbow of light burst forth . . . an artist's palette of brilliance.

*I forgot about the colors! How could I have stayed away from this for so long?*

Virginia constructed pink clouds over a placid, blue-green sea. She drew seven multihued balls and juggled them in make-believe hands, something she never would have been able to do on the "real" plane.

We're in good form today, Virginia.

She smiled. "Yeah, we are, JonVon. I'm going to have to go down into you and find out what you've done to your simulation software."

I have been busy. During my illness I was too distracted to tell you about it. However, there have been some interesting results. I am an open book to you, whenever you are ready.

"Later. Right now I just want to play a little while."

It wasn't only in visual simulation that JonVon had made progress. Only her trained ear caught the little signs in his words, phrasing, and timing, that this was still far from an intelligent being. Otherwise, the voice might easily have been that of a living person.

She toyed with the images, making the broad, moonlit sea open up before her. A school of flying fish. Diatoms sparkling in the churned wake of a mysterious shadow, just below the surface.

It felt good. Here within the machine, there were none of the muddy, confusing crises that beset them all on the outside. Here nothing could frighten her. It was too much like home.

*Lord, how I miss Hawaii.*

She crafted a porpoise in the waters, which chattered and splashed her playfully. The simulation was so vivid that she almost seemed to feel the droplets.

*How long has it been since Saul and I made love linked this way?*

She quashed the thought.

Will we be attempting a personality molding today, Virginia?

She shook her head. "No, JonVon. After so long, I'm not ready to try that again quite yet. I'll tell you what, though. Let's run a simulation of the gravitational sling maneuver Earth Control sent up. The one Carl got the Council to vote for last week. Do you scan the copy I inserted yesterday?"

Yes, Virginia. Do you want a chart? Numbers? Or a full-sense simulation with extrapolation?

"Full sense, JonVon. I want to ride the comet . . . to see what it'll look like forty years from now, when we pop open the sleep slots and find ourselves nearing home."

*Home,* she thought. *Eighty years changed. Will they even remember us?*

Virginia felt she could almost sense the rush of supercooled electrons as her counterpart made its preparations.

Ready to commence simulation, Virginia. Please name starting conditions.

"Begin with the Nudge, with the equatorial flinger launchers engaged under Earth Control's program."

She settled back as the clouds and sea vanished. The porpoise, too, faded in a last-minute chittering of defiance.

Blackness settled in, conveying a sense of depth that stretched outward, to where stars glittered in their myriads. And below the starscape an image formed . . . white-streaked gray against sable. It was the by-now-familiar scene of dusty ice on the comet's surface.

JonVon showed her the new launchers, optimistically depicted as completed at Halley's equator. *It'll be some chore, building new accelerators to replace the ones the Arcists seized. We couldn't ever do it without the Phobos technologies.*

Arrayed in a ring around the equator of the prolate spheroid, the narrow-barreled guns began firing—throwing pellets of native nickel-iron away into space at large fractions of the speed of light—slowly, imperceptibly changing the momentum of the ancient iceball they were anchored in.

There was no sensation of movement, but Virginia identified with the tiny, simulated figures jumping, waving their arms on the surface. It was a nice touch for JonVon to put them in. For it would look like this— jubilant spacesuited workers leaping in joy when they finally began nudging the comet into a new orbit.

Using gentle signals as natural as moving an arm, Virginia let her sense of presence float upward to watch the simulation better. As the Nudge went on, she followed the icy core's changing path through the vacuum.

Aphelion, four years from now, and bit by bit Halley's ancient orbit was changing. The launchers stole slightly from its angular momentum, causing it to begin its long sunward fall a few days before it normally would have. The comet's inward velocity was small at first, but it grew.

Virginia knew this simulation wasn't intrinsically any more accurate than the ones Carl had used, only more vivid. She wanted everything represented in images. It just wasn't the same in graphs and numbers.

She rode the comet. The stars turned slowly as the time scale expanded and years flickered past. She and Halley fell together toward the cusp at the center of the solar system.

At first there was very little change on the surface of the comet nucleus. The pocked, dusty mantle glittered in thin veins, like the Milky Way sparkling overhead.

But the Hot grew. Halley fell toward it and the sun's fire rose to meet her.

Ancient ices sublimed under the growing warmth. First carbon monoxide, as the core swept in past the orbit of Jupiter, and later carbon dioxide. The escaping vapors lifted black, powdery dust to meet the growing sunshine. A thin haze began to form.

The rendering was vivid. Virginia watched the faint, glimmering dust and ion tails begin to take shape, like ghostly banners unfurling in the growing light.

On at least ten score occasions the spinning ball of ice had fallen this way, since that time when it had passed too close to Jupiter and been snared into the middle solar system. Since then it had been tethered to the sun on a shorter leash than most comets.

Space was roomy, vast, and since that one near-brush with the giant planet's gravity the comet had never met another physical object it could not absorb. Dust grains, little bits of rocky flotsam, they all had blundered into Halley's streaking path and paid the price.

But the Nudge had seen to it that there would be another meeting. Something smaller than Jupiter, but much too large to absorb, would pass improbably close this time, while Halley Core hurtled inward.

And there it was! A pinprick of reddish light, just ahead.

*Mars,* Virginia thought. *Right on time. Ready for a little carom action?*

JonVon recognized a rhetorical question. Anyway, the machine was too busy to answer as the close encounter drew near.

This was Earth Control's compromise, its plan to rescue them without risking infection to the homeworld.

*I must admit, I didn't expect even this much out of them.*

Sure, public pressure, Earthside, was a major reason for the Care Package, which was now only months away from rendezvous with their little isolated outpost of humanity. Nevertheless, after all these years Virginia had grown cynical over just how much Earth Control really cared.

*I'd have expected them to order us to commit suicide "honorably" and quietly, like good little plague carriers should.*

The red planet loomed. Virginia asked JonVon to zoom in on the details, slowing the action as she and the comet approached rendezvous.

She swept ahead of Halley to look over the planet. The icy south pole of the dead world came into view first.

Red sands blew over Cydonia. The long-dormant Shield Volcanoes were pimples that poked nearly through the thin atmosphere, tufted on their flanks by thin, dry clouds.

Phobos rose around the small world's limb. The little moonlet was a pockmarked stone, aglitter with lights, that rolled by Virginia and then set over the sharp, ocher horizon.

*Nice people,* she thought of the folk of Phobos Station. *Too bad they've never been allowed to become a real colony. Maybe we can help them, there.*

She looked back and saw the comet nearing, as the men and women on Phobos would see it thirty-eight years from now.

*It ought to be quite a show for those folks . . . Halley sweeping by almost close enough to touch. Mars has to pass through the thick of the tail for its faint gravity to catch our aeroshell lifeboats. And yet the planet and comet can't be allowed to come so close to each other that the turbulence will knock our boats off course.*

In the simulation, Halley was putting up a grand display. Nothing like the spectacle would show closer to the sun, of course; but the twin tails had started to unfurl, and the coma glowed like a fuzzy cloud of fireflies.

The simulation was excellent. JonVon even depicted the lights of Phobos winking off as workers battened down and covered up. For a few days there would be too many meteoroids to risk venturing out into the open. A small price to pay, though, for a chance to rescue three hundred souls. At least Virginia hoped they would feel that way.

*Three hundred people quarantined on Mars . . . that really might be enough to start a colony.* It had never been one of her dreams to settle a rust-red desert, but the plan beat the alternatives. *And it'll be nice to feel gravity again, to walk, and maybe even* swim *in a dome-covered pool.*

*It's not Maui, but I could get used to the idea of being a Martian.*

The separation narrowed. Halley's surface seemed to fizz as hot spots threw fountains of gas and dust into space, adding to the coma's brilliance.

*Is it a trick of perspective? Or are we really going to pass as near as it looks?*

Sparks flew off as tiny objects separated from the comet's head in soundless explosions.

*The life rafts.* Armored against the dust and heat, the aeroshell-covered sleep slots would split away from Halley. Tiny, mech-controlled rockets increased the spacing, guiding the hibernating colonists toward their first fiery encounter with the red planet's atmosphere.

Virginia backed away further, giving the simulation space.

*All Earth will be watching this. The folks on Phobos won't be the only ones having quite a show.*

Halley's cloudy coma seemed to touch the planet. Virginia blinked.

*Something's wrong. How can it . . .*

The coma began to warp out of shape, compressed by sonic shock waves as the globe of gas encountered the planet's sparse atmosphere. Ionized gas bowed outward and away from the weak Martian magnetic field.

The sparkling dot of the core itself, a trillion tons of ice, pulled forward, unimpeded by anything so tenuous as gas or magnetism. It fell ahead of its cloud, and began to glow still brighter.

*NO . . .*

Gaseous bow shock waves multiplied into expanding cones. Sensing that she wanted to follow the action, JonVon slowed the encounter as Halley Core scattered the tiny lifeboats like pollen grains and sped on toward closest passage.

*Closest passage . . .*

The nucleus split apart! Then again. Four chunks streaked inward at an angle, their path through the Martian atmosphere now incandescent. Then they struck the little world.

One piece seemed to glance off the limb of the planet, like a hammer striking glowing sparks off into space. Plumes of dust roiled where the mile-wide bit had briefly touched down.

A large fragment scored a direct hit on Olympus Mons, shearing off the left side of the great volcano in a titanic, blinding explosion.

Simulation or not, Virginia blinked away the afterimage from that flash. By the time she could watch again, the series of searing blasts had turned into spreading orange clouds. The thin atmosphere rippled and swirled like a shallow pond into which bullets had been fired.

Quakes shook the ancient sands. Under Mars the permafrost buckled and melted. Virginia imagined she could sense magma stirring.

She was too stunned to do more than watch, unbelieving. She sought out the little aeroshells and found one, two, tumbling away toward the sun. Others glowed briefly as they hit the rolling dust clouds, flared, and went out.

Some had simply disappeared.

*It was supposed to be a gravity carom! A near passage! Earth Control never said anything about this!*

*Carl never said anything about this.*

Unconsciously she willed her simulated self away from light—away from the burning, sunlit face of the rocky crucible.

Mars fell back as she fled outward along its shadow. Seen from dark-face, the planet was a thin crescent of red wind, tinged in fire. From one side of the crescent, a rosy pyre bloomed: the god of war answering heaven's violence in reawakened volcanoes.

Unbeckoned, unwelcome, a line from Shelley came to mind.

Look on my Works, ye Mighty, and despair!

Virginia disengaged, her hands shaking as she tore off the contact disk. In her mind, though, the scene continued. Imagination went on simulating what was intended for thirty-eight years hence, picturing the sun as it would rise on the morning following this encounter, to shine over a steamy, cloudy day on Mars.

And later, for just a little while, there would be rain.

## SAUL

> "Smelly chemicals snoozed
> Through the primordial ooze,
> Carbon, oxy, lime
> Phosphorous and time
> That's how began the Blues."

It was an old biologists' drinking song from the twentieth century. Saul had learned it in England, during a rainy winter at Cambridge. It seemed appropriate that it should come to mind now, as an earthenware bottle lolled and sloshed in his lap and he sat in the dimly lit corridor outside his lab, trying a Polynesian remedy for what ailed him.

Keoki had given him the jar of homemade hooch saying, solemnly, "You need drunk, Saul." And, of course, the fellow was right.

> "Things were oh so clean,
> Decently marine,
> Then virus climbed aboard,
> At first a chewing horde,
> With a voracious gene."

There was a refrain to the ditty, to a jazzy, hip beat.

> "Dat dere ole virus
> Conspired on us
> And brought us to our knees.

> They sent us a fever
> More subtle than a cleaver
> Infect me if you please.

> Come play with me,
> An anthology
> On informative disease.

Might as well play host
Don't give up the ghost
When your cells are in a squeeze."

Saul nodded, sagely. "There. You see? They knew about symbiosis even back in th' eighties, when they weren't even sure yet they were in the Hell Century. Goes to show there's never anythin' new, under th' sun."

Nobody was there to hear him, of course. He had finally sent Keoki back . . . the big Hawaiian's wives must be worried about him, by now. Saul had assured his friend he would go right to sleep, and so Keoki had left, charging him to try to cheer up.

In fact, sleep wasn't in prospect, right now. Saul sat and nursed the bottle. He had never felt so far away from home.

*Strictly speaking, in four years we'll be at aphelion and headed back to Earth again.* But orbital dynamics was not on Saul's mind, right now.

*She'll never approve,* he told himself.

*Oh, yeah? Well, how do you know unless you ask her?*

Truth be told, he was simply afraid . . . afraid of what Virginia might think of his latest experiments. Miracle cures were one thing. Experiments with animals and plants, fine.

But among the gifts from Earth had been data on the force-growth of human bodies. It was like Houdini being challenged by a new lock, or a painter by a blank canvas. The need was there . . . the dare irresistible.

*How do you know what Virginia would say? Maybe you don't have to sleep in a cold, lonely lab.*

Saul shivered, and knew that he was just too much of a coward to test it.

Ah, but what if he could give his love a gift? A gift of the very thing she most wanted in the world? The thing she had reconciled herself never to have?

One night, weeks ago, as she lay in exhausted slumber, he had taken the samples he needed.

From Lani Nguyen—trustful Lani—he had acquired the secret cache of human sperm and ova she had smuggled with her from Earth. He had all the materials he needed, now.

But since then, he had remained indecisive. Until tonight.

He had spent all day laboring in the Arcist enclave down at the south pole—as Colony Doctor he was neutral in all disputes—and had returned depressed. Life was miserable and cold, down in those warrens. Their fusion pile sputtered and barely put out enough power to maintain their greenhouses. Worse, Joao Quiverian had his own factions to deal with—fanatics that made his own Arcism seem moderate, whose loathing of anything associated with Percells seemed to know no bounds.

*Keoki was right . . . I needed drunk.*

Another ditty passed through Saul's mind. One about the fifth Irish Civil War. It was a sad song of fratricide, but nobody had ever written anything better for either drinking or pity.

He was humming to himself when a flicker of movement made him look to the left. He squinted at the faint line of phosphors, diminishing in the distance, and saw that several were being occulted by dim shapes approaching down the narrow hallway.

Nobody was supposed to ever come this way. It was part of his agreement with the clans. Then who. . . ?

He blinked. Felt a chill.

*Weirders . . .*

They drifted into view . . . manlike shapes, but tufted all about like slime-covered sea creatures. The assemblage of native forms each carried was different. In one case there was nothing of the original man left but the eyes. In the other, there was still a face visible through the symbiotic tangle.

*This is synergism taken farther than even I can stomach it,* Saul thought queasily.

Several times, since that day when the ex-spacer turned mystic, Suleiman Ould-Harrad, left the upper levels to go down and join these creatures, small notes had appeared tacked to Saul's door. He had filled every request, often leaving bottles of his sera outside. Each wake-shift, when he arose, the packet was gone. In its place lay a small sample of some strange lifeform Saul had never seen before.

It was a trade, medicine for more pieces to the puzzle that was Halley. It suited Saul fine, for he had wanted to find a way to treat the weird denizens of Far Gehenna, anyway. Since Ould-Harrad had gone down to join them, they had seemed to become better organized, less suspicious and violent when someone from a more "normal" clan crossed their path.

He blinked, however, when both emissaries bowed low.

"We c-come and beseech-ch your help-p."

The stuttering voice took Saul by surprise.

"I—I didn't know any of you could still talk!"

The one with the face shook its head. "Some c-cannot. But that does not mean we no longer think-k."

Saul nodded, hurriedly. "I'm sorry. It's just that . . . well, you never show yourselves. The others fear you so."

"As we fear them. But you are Ssssaul. The Doc-c. We c-come to you with hurt."

Saul was about to ask them to come into the lab when the lead weirder opened a gap in its foliage and brought forth a small brown bundle. Whimpering sounds came from it.

"C-can you fix-x-x?"

The otter had a broken leg. It writhed and bit at the one holding it, to no apparent effect.

"Of course," Saul said as he stood up and pressed the thumb-code plate by the door. "Bring her in. This shouldn't take long."

Except for Lani and an occasional mech, nobody else but him had ever crossed this threshold. Saul was sure that nobody stranger ever would again.

But then, he had never been very good at predicting.

It was an hour after the weirders had left that he found himself standing beside the master cloning chamber, with his mind made up. There were sound scientific reasons to proceed with the experiment. The colony needed it. Humanity needed it.

*I need it. And maybe I can give Virginia something she wants above anything in the universe.*

"JonVon," he said to the main computer voice link.

Yes, Saul. I am here.

He nodded. "JonVon, I want to set up a secret data base."

# CARL

If he squinted against the sun's hard knot of yellow, the icescape lay before him like a land of dreams. Armies of men and mechs surged across the slashed, stained territory. They towed long cylinders of buffed steel and alabaster aluminum oxide, or swiveled great clumps of electrical gear, or tugged transformers that, made to operate in cold vacuum, looked more like crusty brain coral than loops of gleaming copper and iron.

The laboring gangs sped across ice that was gouged and split, great troughs dug deeply into it, cut and formed and hammered. At regular spacings Jim Vidor had erected spindly towers by melting, force-forming, and refreezing water into crystalline struts, levels, braces.

Cobwebbed strands connected jutting, orange-tinged fingers of flash-wedded crystals. Ice had little shear strength, and served well only under compression. It was impossible to believe that the arabesques were merely functional. Still, Carl had no doubt that Vidor, if pressed, would be able to come up with an explanation for each extruded, delicate strand, every corbeled arch, all the spindly weaving art of it.

Carl had not asked. Humans could not stick remorselessly to the narrow and practical; anyone of skill yearned to express something deep and abiding through his craftsmanship. Perhaps it was the impulse to leave an idiosyncratic, quirky dab of self on the most enduring things they made. Probably it was something deeper, tied to the spirit that had brought a lone tribe of primates so far out from their own warm, moist world.

Carl remembered the opening lines of a poem Virginia had shown him months before. Somehow they had stuck with him.

> The sea is calm tonight.
> The tide is full, the moon lies fair.

Omens for good sailing. The poem had something to do with beaches and oceans, and Virginia had sensed some resonance in him for those images. Voyaging out here, sailing against gravity's tide, resembled the grand old days of seagoing craft. They had tapped a fraction of the sun's raw photon wind to control the comet's outgassing, in the first months after landing. Then they ran before that wind, using sunlight only to yield electricity. The crucial time was coming now, when their iceworld craft had to be pushed into a fresh orbit, a new course charted.

He smiled at himself. *Clinging to the sea analogy, eh? All because you're deep in your bones a spacer, and can't forget it. Ever since losing the* Edmund, *you've been yearning for a ship. This chunk of ice and iron is all you've got left.*

It was so obvious, Virginia had seen it. She had told him that poetry was a consolation, and to his surprise he had found himself enjoying some of the stuff she transferred into his display. That would've been utterly impossible for the brash, self-involved spacer he had been thirty-five years ago. He'd aged only seven years in that time, but that span had a weight of its own. His younger self now seemed distant, almost implausibly blind.

*I hope Virginia can't see too well into me. She'll find out soon enough how much all this hope and euphoria are false, based on an unavoidable lie. . . .*

He didn't like to recall that. He shook his head and moved across the ice, taking long strides, surveying the work. *Keep busy. Don't think too much; it's not your strong suit.*

Carl circled around a gang of laboring mechs to reach the long trench of Launcher 6. A completed flinger filled the scooped-out, obliquely descending trough. Two engineers were testing a flywheel made from Halley iron.

The machines would deliver momentum at a precisely calculated rate and angle. At first they would fire parallel to the equator, to slow and finally halt Halley's fifty-hour spin. After that, the launcher would pivot about an axis buried in the trench, bringing it nearly perpendicular to the equator, in line with Halley's center of mass. Then would begin the long stuttering bursts which would, delivered over years, add minute increments of momentum to Halley's slow, stately swerve at aphelion. All the launchers, pulsing endlessly, would sum up to the Nudge.

—Real pretty, uh?—

Carl saw Jeffers approaching with an easy, practiced lope. His suit tabard was a crossed pliers and wrench in a cube, stained and spotted.

"Beautiful. Is it tested out? Ready for horizontal mounting?"

—Sure. Sets in there jest fine, any angle you want. Mechs'll get it duty-mounted soon's testing's over.—

Jeffers grinned happily. He was the mainstay of the Nudge, finding solutions to problems with a quick, expert savvy. He worked eighteen-hour shifts without a sign of fatigue. The factory at A Level, humming away now with robos making replacement parts for launchers and rockets, wouldn't exist without Jeffers. Carl remembered when the man had put in the minimum, wrapping himself in holotapes or pornstims, blotting out the reality of where he was. Work was what he had needed. To Carl, that alone was reason enough to do all this, even if his friend surely suspected that it was all a farce. . . .

—Every crew's ahead of schedule. Even puttin' in extra time, without me askin'.—

"We've finally got something to work for." Carl said it without meeting Jeffers's eye.

—Damn right.—

A manager-mech approached, an extra dome perched atop its cara-pace in a makeshift kluge. Virginia's add-ons worked marvelously, making the mechs and robos far more versatile, but they weren't ele-gant. The mech winked its lamp to attract their attention and sent, **—Launcher 6 complete. Human tech Osaka states that the device is ready for formal testing.—**

Jeffers nodded. —Fire the sucker!—

Warning gongs sounded over the comm line. Everywhere on the surface, teams stopped work and climbed out of pits to watch. Their suits were scratched, worn, discolored, patched with homemade parts.

A *ping ping ping* of warmup rippled over the comm frequencies, thin ringing echoes of the charging now under way in the trench. Carl peered at the tip of the launcher, which jutted free of the ice nearby, pointing at the sky.

He felt a prickly excitement, a gathering tension. If they'd made some mistake in the design, in assembly . . .

A small tremor came through his feet. A rattle in the microwave, a *skreeee*—and the unit discharged.

Simultaneously, a vague haze appeared at the mouth of the launcher. He wondered what was wrong, until he suddenly realized that the firing rate of the flinging tube was several capsules per second—and he was seeing the blur of their passing.

That was all. No roar, no belching smoke. The launchers were de-signed to operate with near-perfect efficiency, to generate as little waste heat as possible. If even a fraction of a percent of the launching energy seeped into the surrounding ice, it would evaporate away the structural support, producing dislocations, unbalancing the carefully configured momentum-matching of the accelerator segments. Long before the ice was gone, the racheting instability of the drive tubes would jerk and thrash them into twisted steel.

But the flinger functioned smoothly. A cheer rose across the comm lines. People raised their arms in victory salutes as far as Carl could see, dancing on the grimy ice, leaping high into the blackness. Only the mechs continued stoically about their tasks, oblivious that humans had at last clasped the helm of this ice ship. Halley was no longer just a tumbling dirty snowball in the long night. She was now a spacecraft.

Jeffers was babbling excitedly, repeating operating parameters as he read them off his helmet display. Carl could follow some of the rapidfire reciting—kilo-amperes surging in low-impedance circuits, voltages building to sharp peaks and then collapsing as each slug passed, leaching the energy of inductive electric and magnetic fields. Energy poured into the capsules, electrodynamic momentum flowing like a fluid at the speed of light.

Only electrical acceleration was efficient enough to avoid the waste-heat problem, to avoid slowly melting the comet itself. For the moment there were ample piles of iron at the north pole, mined in the first year of the expedition, but deep beneath each launcher was a mech mining operation, where in constricted caverns the robots dug and processed more of the comet's natural, ancient metal.

A factory on A Level made lightweight buckets of a special super-conducting polymer. These were loaded with iron and other heavy wastes. Each metal-filled dollop became a bullet. Conveyors fed these with unrelenting precision into the flinger barrel, where the surging voltages clasped each pellet and flung it to enormous speeds—ten thousand kilometers per second, nearly three percent of the speed of light. Launcher 6 was a cosmic machine gun, firing slugs that would reach the nearest stars in a few centuries.

*We could have built starships, if we'd only had the nerve,* Carl thought. *Maybe someday.*

Such was the mass of Halley that even these enormous speeds were barely sufficient for the task of piloting. Carl tuned in to an engineering frequency and heard a staccato *braaap braaap braaap* as each pellet picked up its miniboosts in the flinger column. Launcher 6 was the first of fifty-two that would soon ring Halley, stuttering forth their kilogram pellets for five years. Aphelion, when the comet head paused like a ballet dancer at the peak of his leap, was the most efficient time to divert Halley. Fully ten millionths of the comet's entire mass had to be ejected. That demanded dozens of mechs supervising the mining and smelting of iron, minirobots to toil beside the endless conveyor belts, subroutines and expert programs to catch every snag, each hitch in the unending stuttering fever of the Nudge.

"Goddamn," Carl said. "It works." He felt a rush of relief and realized he had been clenching his hands.

The cheering went on. Even this demonstration, which would run for a mere few hours, was slowing Halley's primordial spin, minutely altering its long gliding ellipse.

—Runnin' smooth, too,— Jeffers said, grinning happily.

—Come on down to Launcher Five. I've got a nice li'l pivot rigged there, keeps the flinger tube from comin' unglued. We figured—

Jeffers stopped abruptly as a geyser of steam boiled from an ice tower nearby. Vidor's intricate cross-hatching of blue and ivory exploded in a shower of fog and glinting, tumbling remnants.

—Goddamn!—

—What? What's happenin'?—

"Laser!" Carl flattened himself against the grimy ground. "Get down everybody!"

—What the hell—who'd go and—

"Arcists!" Carl realized. "They must've heard the successful test over comm."

Jeffers shouted, —But *why*? I thought Quiverian *agreed*.—

"Damned if I know."

All across the field, people were ducking for cover. An ice tower farther away dissolved silently into mist. This time Carl saw the flash of light as the beam struck.

"They're firing from that hill—over there. South twenty-five degrees of west."

Jeffers squinted at a distant speck atop a heap of leftover slag from one of the mining operations.

—They moved one of those big industrials. Tryin' to hit Six, but those things, they don't aim all that good.—

The comm rang with outrage.

A bolt gouged into ice near a crouching form and Carl heard a startled cry of pain.

"Takeda! Get that woman sealed and to first aid!"

Carl crouched behind a hummock and watched fierce laser bolts send fountains spurting skyward. "Bastards!"

—We gotta do somethin'.—

"I could have Virginia send some mechs around behind, outflank them. . . ."

—Yeah, right,— Jeffers said.

"No, wait . . ." He checked Virginia's channel. A hiss. It was cut off. Of course. Only an idiot would attack without cutting off the defender's source of support.

Another wail of pain over the comm.

Carl nudged Jeffers's shoulder. "Launcher Six—can you pivot it?"

—What?—

"Tip Six down? Aim it at the horizon?"

Jeffers looked surprised. —The safeties aren't in. I dunno . . . that's a pretty low angle.—

"Try it!"

As Jeffers crawled into the launcher trench, the ice-tower fulcrum for Launcher 5 exploded behind them, sending cables and cowlings into a slow, fluid fall to the surface. Lost components, lost construction time, hurt crew—people who were *his* responsibility. Carl glowered at the distant dots working around the laser cannon, a murderous anger building in him.

He tuned out the comm channels, where voices swelled and swamped one another. People called for lovers and friends, sputtering in impotent rage. Mechs asked innocently for orders. Then Virginia's voice intruded on his private line. —What's going *on*? Somebody jammed my channels. Who. . . ?

"Get some weapons up here!"

—But, but, what'll we use?—

"Those small lasers in Three B—that's all we've got that we can move right away."

—But won't they just pick off anybody who comes close enough to use small lasers?—

Carl swore. She was right.

—I can send some big mechs from the north pole.—

"We'll be toast by then!"

He whistled a search-and-contact command for Joao Quiverian and had a channel in seconds. "Quiverian! This is Osborn. You—"

The man's voice was strained. —Those are not acting under my orders. Arcists they are, yes, but I cannot control them.—

"You expect us to believe that?"

—You must. It is the truth.—

Carl gritted his teeth. So the enemy was faceless. Anonymous. The people using those big lasers weren't going to allow anyone else to take over the Nudge options, to try another orbit. With them it was all or nothing . . . and they would take all.

On the general comm, more screams as an invisible laser bolt struck a hillock and dissolved a deep pit into it. Carl saw a body roll away . . . someone hiding there.

He used command override on channel A. "Get those people off that slag mound by Launcher Two! All of you, take shelter down in the feeder tunnels." A babble in reply. "And use ident codes if you want to be heard!"

He spoke a quick command in mech-talk and the noise cut off as the channel controller went over to formal mode. Now suit radios would not even work until the system passed on your code-ordering. For a moment there was only an eerie hiss. Then, —Jones, BQ code to Osaka and Osborn. Leading party of five down to shaft now.—

—Lomax, DF code, to command. Got a good view from a safe height. Everyone P-code your sitings to me. I'll relay situation to Osborn.—

Carl nodded. A few good spacers who remembered their training were worth battalions.

—Jeffers, GH code to Osborn. Got it, I think.—

"Osborn, GH code. Got what?"

—Jeffers, GH. I'm tipping the launcher down. Got to turn it toward the south. You line it up, okay?—

Carl realized that the steady hammering of Launcher 6 had stopped some time ago. Now, as he watched, the assembly turned laboriously toward the distant low hills, its snout tipping downward. Carl got to his feet and swiftly moved behind the slowly swiveling launcher. The only way he could think to aim the thing was to eyeball it directly, sighting along the barrel.

*Great. Real high-tech.*

And the Arcists were undoubtedly watching them closely. Their objective must be this site. They had destroyed the easier targets while they were getting the range right. Launcher 6 was much harder to hit, buried in its trench. But now that it was slowly emerging . . .

He squatted down onto a patch of orange stain and closed one eye automatically, lining up the launcher barrel with the specks on the distant hill.

—Lomax, DF to Osborn. Got a tactical sketch of known enemy positions. Prepare to receive. They're bunched up pretty close.—

Carl threw the picture over half his faceplate. Benchley's rough drawing showed a main group and two wings—probably outlying spotters.

*Not many of them. I count five. But they've got the best ground.*

The Arcists were settled into a notch, taking advantage of the shelter. As he watched a bright blue flash winked—and he ducked automatically. Which was ridiculous; if he was in the full focus of the laser it would have blinded him instantly. Instead, they had aimed high. Only the fringing fields had struck him.

He checked Jeffers. Almost tipped enough . . .

He blinked to clear his vision; it didn't help much. "Open her up!"

—I . . . I *can't* just shoot that hillside with a full load! That's a kilogram of iron at ten thousand KPS . . . it'd be like setting off a ten-kiloton bomb!—

Carl thought furiously. "Empty casings! They only mass a couple grams. Have you got any?"

—Uh. Yeah. I'd better go at low power, too,— Jeffers said. —Take a minute . . . lessee . . . one percent setting . . .—

Someone screamed. Another near miss. "We've got to return fire. Open her up!"

—Okay, okay.— To his relief, Carl heard the *braaap braaap braaap* resume. The sound was different. Lower, rougher.

—It's not tuned for this! It'll shake apart!—

Carl thumbed over to telescopic. All up and down the hillside, plumes of vapor spouted as pellets struck.

"A-Comm auto-override. Jeffers, left!"

—Yo.—

The small gouts of fog leaped high, several a second.

A blue flash from the hilltop, brighter this time. The enemy, too, was zeroing in. Carl turned and saw the ice not far behind him flare and suddenly explode into pearly mist.

"Higher!"

—Gotcha!—

A line of bursting fog walked up the hillside, erratic but rising, steadily rising toward the specks who manned the big, cumbersome tube.

Two antagonists, each wrestling with weapons too big and powerful to be used deftly . . . like fighters flailing at each other with steel beams. The first to score a hit . . .

Carl wondered what would happen if the laser struck him fully. His suit would reflect some, and at this angle the beam was spread over a much larger area . . . still, he didn't want to find out.

"Go right! And higher!"

The jittering gouts of fog leaped, swerved, steadied—and struck the milling specks.

Soundless destruction. Carl lay on the ice and watched the pellets pound endlessly into the targets—mere writhing dots and splintered, rolling parts of the laser—as the fog of the assault gathered, spread, and finally obscured the scene.

"Okay. You can . . . shut it down."

—We get 'em?—

"Yeah. Yeah, we did."

Carl felt no elation, no zest. It had all happened so fast, so abstractly. A bunch of dots moving on a hillside. Brilliant, sudden flashes of blue. Then the distant spurts as streaking casings struck ice, struck steel, struck yielding flesh and cracking bone. A science of strict geometry and easy death.

—Hey, we did it! That'll teach the suckers!— The launcher fell silent. Jeffers leaped out of the trench, exuberant.

"So . . . so we did."

He heard Virginia's voice, and others, and with the returning babble running in his ears Carl walked slowly toward the hammered hillside, not wanting to see what was there but knowing he should. It was part of his job.

Suddenly his mind cleared and he remembered the rest of the poem, the lines that he had idly recalled only a few minutes before . . . a time that seemed months in the past, now.

> And we are here as on a darkling plain
> Swept with confused alarms of struggle and flight,
> Where ignorant armies clash by night.

# VIRGINIA

Spacesuits were aggravating. They reminded Virginia of how out of shape she was—of the passage of years.

She struggled with the adjustment bands, loosening some and tightening others in all the wrong places. *Flab! No wonder Saul's been so . . .*

Virginia clamped down on the thought. Anyway, she was sure their troubles had little to do with her recent lack of exercise.

*Maybe nothing was meant to last,* she thought. *Perhaps everything good self-destructs in the end.*

The image of a red world, new volcanoes bursting forth to greet the dawn . . .

For the first time since the abortive Arcist attack, Carl had given permission for her to come up and see him in person. Being indispensable had its drawbacks. With human guards and watch-mechs standing in layers around her lab to protect her, she had lately begun feeling like a queen ant, a slave to her own royalty.

*Though a queen ant, at least, creates eggs. . . .*

Another bad thought. Why were these things all coming to the surface right now?

*Because we've begun killing each other, here and now? Is that why I'm so depressed?*

*Or is it because I'm lonely, and no longer young?*

Virginia finished dressing and slipped a worn tabard over her suit. She didn't even have one of her own—had never bothered designing one. This one—depicting a sheaf of wheat above three gold balls—had belonged to Dr. Evans, a Hydroponics man firmly dead for twenty years, now. The suit matron had reregistered it to Virginia and she had decided to live with it.

*I wish it weren't necessary to come up here in person at all,* she thought as she began cycling through the lock.

But this business was too important to discuss over any comm line. It wasn't just fear of being tapped. She wanted to watch Carl's face when she confronted him.

The outer doors opened and the scene was briefly obscured by a fog of condensing vapor. The snowflakes blew away into space and she looked out across the open icescape.

In a sense it was a bit disappointing. Her linkage with remotes had grown so good that her vision on the surface actually seemed better in surrogate than in person. Skim-walking carefully out onto the grimy crust felt somehow *more removed* than controlling a mech out here.

There was a fluttering sensation of nakedness, too. After all, she had many mechs, but only one body. And *it* was out on the surface now, under the unwinking stars.

The landscape was less scarred, out here by Shaft 6, than where her mechs and Jeffers's factory hands had gouged and rutted the ancient comet. Here the dominant feature was a looming edifice that looked something like a cross between a glass Ferris wheel and a web spun of liquid spider's silk.

A number of spacers were gathered at its base, gesturing from it to a point in the glittering blackness. She recognized the tabards of Carl Osborn and Andy Carroll, as well as several others—mostly members of the Plateau Three and Survivors' factions. Virginia mumbled command phrases until she was able to latch on to the frequency they were using. It was child's play to break their coding.

—. . . tell you I think the thing is just too damn small! They may have made advances since we left, sure. But even that hot fusion torch can't have pushed more than twenty tons at that kind of acceleration for so long.—

—Yeah? Well, even if it *is* just twenty tons, think of all that could include. Faster logic quips for better computers and mechs. Hybrid seeds to improve our hydro. And tritium fuses! Twenty tons of stuff like that could make all the difference.—

They were talking about the Care Package, obviously. As she approached, skirting a cracked area in the ice, she heard Carl's voice cut in.

—You're hoping the Christmas gifts will change the Arcists' mind, Andy?—

—Or give us something to use to wipe 'em out. I don't really care which. Anything that'll shake them out of the south pole so we could go back to the Jupiter maneuver and save the original mission. Th' Mars fling's all right, as a second choice. But Captain Cruz would've wanted us to . . .—

The words stopped as Andy Carroll noticed that Carl had turned to greet Virginia.

—Osborn, open channel to Herbert. Hello, Virginia.—

His stained spacesuit was a mixture of cannibalized parts. Over it was draped a dingy white cloth emblazoned with a picture of a red crustacean. His visor cleared and she saw his face. Gray at his temples and lines on his brow had not robbed Carl of his strong-jawed, boyish charm.

—It was good of you to come up, Virginia. There is something special we'd like to ask you to do for us.—

She nodded, then remembered that she was facing the distant sun. Although it was not much more than a very bright star now, her visor might still have automatically dimmed and hidden the gesture.

"I'll help any way I can," she began. "But . . ."

—That's great. 'Cause we're getting concerned about the first Care Package from Earth. Don't want anything to go wrong when it arrives.—

"What could go wrong?"

—How 'bout it fallin' into the wrong hands?— Carroll suggested.

Carl shrugged.

—Quiverian denies responsibility for that attack down at the equator. Says they were renegades, acting without sanction. Still, I see your point. I don't think we want the Care Package coming down at the south pole by mistake. It may be better to have a mech go out and escort the cargo vessel in.—

Virginia understood. *It wouldn't do to have the rescue package hijacked. Then the Arcists would have a total lock. They'd be in complete control.*

"Fine. I'll start working with Jeffers on the details," she said. "There's something else I wanted to talk to you about, though."

—Sure. What is it?— When she shook her head and remained silent, he turned to the others.

—Be right back, guys. See if you can tune this antenna better, will you? I want a good fix on that thing as it gets nearer.—

—Right, Carl.—

He led her over behind a great pile of mine tailings. Making sure she could see him do it, he reached up and switched off his transmitter. Nodding, she did the same. He bent over to touch helmets.

"What's bothering you, Virginia? You seem so . . . subdued. Is it Saul? I'd heard—"

"No," she cut in hurriedly. His face was so close. The double layer of separating crystal seemed to pass a warm breath. "No, that's not it, Carl."

*At least it's not the reason why I came up here.*

"But there *is* something the matter, between you two," he insisted.

She nodded, a quick, short jerk. "Nothing, really. Just, well, one of those things. Time—"

"Time changes all of us, Virginia. I never did apologize to both of you for the way I behaved, so many years ago. I was an idiot." There was earnestness in his eyes.

"You were young, Carl. We were all younger."

*Except for Saul. With the perfect immune system, won't he live forever? Is that, maybe, a source of friction between us?*

Carl looked down for a moment, then met her eyes. "That doesn't mean my basic feelings have altered, Virginia. If you're ready for a change . . ." Carl let his sentence hang, and Virginia suddenly could see something deeper than earnestness, deeper even than the sternness of command. Her gloved hand came up, touched glass.

"Oh, Carl. You've hurt so much."

He shrugged, caught between conflicting feelings. "You came up to see me because—" There was hope in his voice.

Virginia shook her head, blinking aside the weakness that threatened her determination. "Carl . . ." She swallowed. "Carl, I want to know why you are planning to kill us all."

"Uh." He stared. "How . . . What do you mean?"

Her hand dropped. "Oh, you were always a lousy liar, Carl. At least to me you were. The others seem to have swallowed your Judas goat act, thinking Earth really plans a rescue, all that crap about a tight flick past Mars, then on to Jupiter and Venus, then back to Mars and quarantine. . . ."

"What are you—"

"Come to think of it, though, Jeffers and his bunch would back you even if they knew the truth, wouldn't they?"

Carl broke contact, stepping back before she had even finished. His lips were drawn tight. When he spoke, the movements of his mouth seemed to convey a pungent, if silent, bitterness. Virginia gestured at her ears. With an impatient shake of his head he brought their helmets back together jarringly.

"What are you going to do?" he asked.

At least Carl did not insult her intelligence with further pretense. He knew she would have run simulations a dozen different ways before ever accusing him like this.

"What am *I* going to do?" Virginia asked. "First off, I'm giving you a chance to explain. I want to know why you're fronting for this trick of Earth Control's, sending us on a direct collision course with Mars!"

Carl's eyes closed briefly. "There are factions back home, too. There were . . . tradeoffs. We had to make agreements in order to get the Care Packages."

"So that we can smash into a planet in forty years?" Virginia couldn't help laughing bitterly.

"Forty long years, Virginia. Even with Saul's serums, we'll have to keep so many people awake that we'll all be old by that time."

"There are children, Carl."

"Those poor babies the Orthos have been having? They hardly even merit calling human, Virginia. You know that. Anyway, they and all of us will live better and more comfortably with the goods we'll be getting in these rockets from Earth."

"Comfort!"

"Yes, that counts for something. But there's a more important reason."

"What's that?"

"Honestly, Virginia, can't you see that this is the only way anything good can emerge out of this entire fiasco?"

She shook her head. "What good will come of all of us *dying*?"

"Well, from Earth's point of view, the end of a threat. And in that I can see the Arcists' point of view."

"You can?"

"Yes. Of course. They'll do anything to protect the homeworld from Halleyforms, and you can't blame them for that."

"And from *our* point of view?"

He shrugged. "We spark life anew on a dead world, perhaps. With our deaths we can begin the long process of bringing Mars alive."

Virginia couldn't help sneering. "You're beginning to sound like Jeffers."

"Maybe I am at that." He looked away. His voice dropped. "I might have tried to think of something else, no matter how unlikely, if . . ." His voice trailed off.

"If what, Carl?"

"Never mind. It's not important."

"Carl! You have to talk to me."

He shook his head. "Saul told me, a while back, that he was working on a cloning system. In ten years or so, we might be able to produce a generation of healthy children, slightly modified to be healthy and breed true in low gravity. There may actually be something to that idea some Sergeov's *Ubers* talk about, of telling Earth to go to hell and trying to colonize Triton."

Virginia blinked, realizing what might bring him over to accepting such a plan. "You mean . . . me, in particular, don't you?"

"Yes. You, me, the children only you and I could have together. I . . . I might be persuaded to see another point of view, if that seemed possible."

Inside Virginia's mind and heart, winter blew. It was a numb incapacity, an *unwillingness* to understand this. Dimly, she knew that this was Carl's own unique version of the neuroses they all had, by now—no worse than normal, but highly unusual. It was a curse of hypertrophied *romanticism*. The wistful teenager in him had, in one respect, been frozen in time.

She knew that a simple confession might solve this . . . a frank admission that, no matter how great the technical miracles science made available, she would never have children by any man. The universe had decided that long ago.

The numbness was too great, though, Too much like a weight of ice she could not lift, even to be kind to a dear friend.

"I won't tell anybody about Mars, Carl."

"You won't?" He blinked. "But I—"

"You've convinced me that you're right. It *will* be better this way . . . to die bringing life to a dead world. Better than a pointless extinction, the way we're headed."

She backed away and turned her transmitter back on. "Tell me when and where you want to meet the first Care Package, and give me a support team. I'll begin running simulations for a rendezvous right away.

"I'll be seeing you, Carl."

She tried not to look at his eyes as she turned away, but she felt his gaze on her back as she picked a narrow, solitary path back down into her crypt, far below the cold stars.

# SAUL

It was a sophisticated beast, the vehicle that had traveled so far to bring them gifts from distant Earth, and it had blazed a daring path to reach them here in only five years. Swooping three times past the sun, it had gained terrific speed, until now it streaked outward into the black depths below and beyond the solar-system plain.

During each whipping solar passage it had ridden the blazing sunlight on giant gossamer sails. Then, when distance had dimmed the fires behind it, the great sheets folded away and the machine's own flame burst forth. Bits of antimatter met in a tiny combustion chamber, releasing energy that was nearly collimated light, propelling the craft faster still.

Only three passes were needed to bring its orbit into the plane of Halley's—but *much* faster than the fleeing comet. Technology made it possible, and the hot flux of reawakened public opinion demanded speed. To the popular press of a new generation, this was an errand of mercy that would brook no delay.

To others it was something else altogether—a down payment on a bribe to persuade the strange, time-cast, and infected colonists to keep to their agreement, an agreement to stay away.

Did some hope, in this way, to assuage their guilt over the burning of the *Edmund Halley*? Or to slake their shame over the years of silence and neglect?

Saul watched the screens, along with selected representatives of all the clans, in the cavernous Central Control Room. For once the chamber was actually full, though he would have wagered that the architects had never imagined such a crowd . . . glowering figures wearing tattoos and clothing woven of Halleyform lichen fiber, bearing scars from illnesses never seen on Earth and muttering to one another in strange dialects.

Even Joao Quiverian was here, frowning with arms folded in a corner, with three bodyguards and a recently cloned weasel watching ferally from his shoulder.

Representatives of all the clans were here to observe while Virginia Herbert guided the colonists' mechanical envoy into a matching orbit with the still-decelerating Care Package.

"They've sure made advances. That torch is fierce," Andy Carroll said from the ballistics console. "But it's still not slowing down fast enough to suit me."

"I'll match it," Virginia muttered drowsily. "Don't fret, Andy. We've made some advances of our own."

A black cloth covered her eyes as she lay back on the webbing by the waldo controls. The neural-tap cable snaked out from the back of her skull, and her fingers gently touched a set of knurled knobs.

Saul noticed Quiverian's mouth purse in disapproval. To have Percells in charge of the recovery operation was obviously hard for the man to bear. But he was here on sufferance, and could hardly complain.

By rights Carl could have kept the man away, in retaliation for the mutiny he had led down south. Even though Quiverian had disclaimed any responsibility for the renegades who had attacked the equatorial launchers—had denounced them publicly—he and his Arcists were hardly trusted. As long as they were in Central they were watched constantly by a team of Keoki Anuenue's natural and adopted Hawaiians.

Still, with the negotiating power the contents of the Care Package were about to give him, Carl could afford to be generous.

No one was even certain what the thing contained. Saul pondered. *I could list a thousand items I'd give a finger or a bicuspid for, or more. And there are hundreds of other lists, each as long as mine.*

*Alas, there probably isn't even an ounce of good pipe tobacco aboard.*

He smiled in faint irony. *I'll settle for the cell-differentiation tuner in that cloning system they developed on Earth ten years ago.*

It had started logically enough, his program with monkeys and gibbons and subtly altered strains of wheat . . . searching for new elements to add to a growing synergism—a meshing of Earthborn and Halleyform life to take the place of perpetual war. But in recent months it had become something more complicated. There were aspects, now, that he was certain Carl Osborn would not approve, and that Virginia probably would never understand.

That was why he had moved his laboratory down into a secret chamber under a quadrant of Halley far from rockets and clans, and prevented even Virginia's bodyguard mechs from following him there. It had contributed to the growing breach between them, but he had paid that price.

It had been months since he last connected with her the way they had grown accustomed, meshing their emotions—and even an occasional, machine-amplified thought—while holding each other under the faint glow of JonVon's status lamps. He had not dared. For she would surely catch traces . . . suspect the liberties he had taken, and their tragic results.

*A squirming, horrible little thing in a glass incubator . . . gills and fur and swishing tail . . . a face—faintly human—contorted in agony and then, mercifully still at last . . .*

"It's a beauty," Carl Osborn whispered. And Saul blinked, shaking himself back to the present. It was a memory he preferred not to dwell on, anyway. He looked up to see the faery craft now clearly depicted on the screens.

Spires as wispy as spider's silk spread like the winter-bared stems of a flower—the spinnerets from which great sails had billowed during the cargo vessel's three swooping sun-passes—arrayed around a globe that shimmered with impossible mirror brightness.

"I'm scanning that container capsule in the center," Lani Nguyen said from the instrumentation console. "I'd wondered how they dealt with dust impacts at those speeds. It looks like their shield isn't even material at all! It's some sort of *gravitic field,* or I'm my own maiden aunt."

"No!" Carroll muttered, and shared a glance with Carl. "A real force field? No wonder they were able to build it so light."

Otis Sergeov, leader of the *Ubermensch* party of Percells, hung from the edge of a holistank to the left, with several of his tattooed comrades. "The purple-zippered thingy's *still* too meppeed light. What good will two tons of Earth-shit do anyway?"

Jeffers laughed. "What would I do for a few *pounds* of the right machine dies, or a mile or two of warm superconducting wire? Hell, for those I'd even be willing to paint my skin blue and gibber NewTalk like an *Uber,* Otis."

Sergeov's eyes glinted, and Saul knew that being a fellow Percell would not save Jeffers, if the legless ex-Russian ever had the other man's fate in his hands.

*"Bezmoodiy govnocheest!"* he muttered in his native tongue. Jeffers only laughed.

Susan Ikeda, their Earthcomm chief, reported on the latest word over the long-range radio.

"Earth Control says their four-hour estimate is on target. Probe is in the proper deceleration track."

"Can't be," Carroll muttered.

"But they say . . ."

"Their info is four hours old! Speed o' light, I tell you. Something's—"

"Can it, Andy," Carl said. For a time there was quiet in the room. Only the soft hum of the air fans and faint clicking each time somebody threw a switch. Then Lani spoke.

"It's turning its torch, Virginia."

"Check. About time. I'm extending the tether."

Virginia betrayed no sign of tension, but those in the room hung in suspense. The overhead displays showed the colonists' two-piece envoy craft, the parts connected by a taut cable less than a finger's width in thickness and more than fifty kilometers long. Rockets flared, and the connected body began to whirl, like a slow, great bola in the starry blackness.

"Section B's propellent now depleted," Andy Carroll announced. "Section A is ready to receive transferred momentum in three hundred ten seconds."

Lani turned and explained to those observing, "Our probe was a two-stage rocket. Part B provided the initial boost. Part A has saved its fuel for the final match with the Care Package."

"Then why is part B still attached?" one of Quiverian's people asked.

Lani moved her two fists around each other, imitating a bola. "We're using a whirling tether to steal even more momentum from the booster stage. By flinging part B back toward Halley, we give its share of energy to the other piece, our envoy."

The onlookers barely listened. All eyes were on the center screen, where the Care Package began to turn. What had been a hot speck at the edge of the mirror dome brightened as it swung around to face the colonists' spinning, two-piece messenger.

The image was too blurred. Their cameras aboard the swiftly rotating section A could not keep a steady bearing on the Earth ship. Processing the quick glimpses, JonVon could barely keep up a simulated point of view.

Saul wondered if he should be helping. He knew JonVon better than

did anyone but Virginia herself. At least he could help the organic computer steady the image.

But he had not offered. Frankly, he was afraid Virginia might
refuse, and so make explicit what had already become tacit between
them.

*I miss her so. I've wronged her by staying away . . . by not confess-
ing what I have done. . . .*

So he had told himself over and over again. But that had not helped
him find the courage to tell her of that little warped thing, growing in
the clone tank in his secret lab, an attempt at a gift *for her . . .* but
which had turned out, instead, to be a cruel reminder that God sets
limits even on the powers given prophets, and enforces those boundaries
severely.

*I have been given, into my hands, the power to craft animals and
even men . . . but am denied any way to give the woman I love the child
she so desperately wants—a thing most men take for granted.*

There had to be a reason. But as yet, the Infinite had not deigned to
confide it to him.

"What the unholy clape is the thing tryin' to do?" Saul heard
Jeffers mutter.

"I think . . ." Carl Osborn glided a step forward, his voice suddenly stark. "I think it's trying to hit our probe."

"Impossible!" one of the Ortho moderates from Almondstone Cavern cried. "Why would it . . ."

But the fierce lance of the Earth craft's drive suddenly flared in
brilliance as its aspect came nearer the camera's view. Andy Carroll
cried out, "Maneuvering! Accelerating turn!" And then all was chaos.

"Tether separated!" Lani shouted.

"I've lost contact with section B!" another spacer called out.

"Keep back, all of you! Let them work. Give them room!" Carl
cursed as he pushed people away from the controllers. Above their heads
the screens were a blur of overloaded sensors.

Carl's eyes met his as Saul edged past the shouting crowd, worming
between the locked arms of Anuenue's Hawaiians to approach the consoles. There was a silent flicker of emotion on Osborn's face, then the
spacer jerked his head. "All right," he told Saul. "Help them. But if you
get in their way, I'll have your ass."

Saul nodded and jumped forward to land lightly on the webbing
beside Virginia. He pulled a neural helmet from the console and put it
over well-rubbed spots on his skull.

The maelstrom was even worse down in the realm of images and data streams. Without years of practice under Virginia's tutelage, he would have been instantly lost in the noise.

He sifted, looking only for the vision-processing centers. The really important stuff—vectors and mechanical status reports and course data—he did not even touch. Probably, he would do more harm than good if he tried to help there. But he could give Carl and the others a better view of what was happening. That much was within his ability, he figured.

He called up the section of JonVon's memory that was reserved for his own work, reciting his secret access code.

*Simon says, open Kelley.*

The response actually seemed to take a few milliseconds, showing how busy the processor was.

Good afternoon, Dr. Lintz. I have news to report on the state of the newest experiments. The clone chambers are operating nominally. There is—

*Not now,* he interrupted. *Override all but basic life-function maintenance. Transfer other resources to processing incoming data into clear images and displaying them according to following formats.*

He envisioned the console before him, and "dived" in with his mind, tracing pathways and naming throbbing electronic blocks for JonVon to access. The data streams were almost total chaos to him, but working with JonVon seemed to open up possibilities. It gave him a glimpse—or so he often thought—at the wonders Virginia dealt in, as surrogates for the share of infinity that could never be hers.

*Bad topic. Concentrate, you old fool!*

The seared, tumbling cameras on probe A were still transmitting. If only he and JonVon could time and phase the tumble . . . access the probe and have it send views in quick pulses. . . .

*Yes! Clever machine. Mama taught you well.*

Gradually, over the course of seconds, the blur resolved, flickered, steadied. He saw that the fiery torch of the Earth ship had been left behind, its flare no longer burning bright.

*The breaking tether took it by surprise.* He realized that the Earth vessel had not been able to track pieces flying in such suddenly altered directions. One of the sections was now streaking toward the Care Package at an oblique angle, even faster than before.

"It was only trying to defend itself!" someone cried out in the audience. "We must've activated a meteoroid defense!"

Another observer agreed. "We have to terminate this stupid interference. Let it come in as its designers planned. Anything we do will be like savages interfering in a complex machine they don't understand. It'll only bring disaster!"

There was a rumble of agreement, but Saul could sense, beyond current after current of settling data, the distinctive flavor of triumph from Virginia.

"*Got* you!" he heard her whisper, from not far away. Briefly, he turned his head and tried to look at her. But the pulsing neural tap and his natural vision system clashed, threatening him with a wave of vertigo. He closed his eyes again and concentrated on stabilizing the image for Carl.

"That's it," he heard the spacer mutter behind him. "Easy goes it, Andy, Virginia . . . try to lock gently at the base of those spinnerets. Then, Lani, help Virginia tap into the thing's computer. Find out why it hasn't initiated contact yet."

"Aye, Carl," Lani answered. Saul sensed the Earth vessel as a looming image of burnished gold and silver . . . a globe too mirror smooth to be any substance at all. In that surface a tiny shape wavered and grew, brightening now and then as the colonists' robot puffed and flared to match velocities. Their little envoy was dwarfed against the curve of reflected starglow, a spindly crudity that dared to reach out and touch angelic beauty.

"Contact! We're locked onto a spinneret," Carroll announced.

"Pulsing a probe-to-probe communications code," Lani reported. "We'll see what it has to say—"

Then Virginia wailed.

"Those mad sons of bitches!"

It was as if a knife blade had come down and sliced off one of Saul's hands. A tsunami of noise and pain tore at his moorings like a hurricane, yanking shreds of *himself* away into a storm of wild data. It felt like drowning, and he had no idea where *up* was, anymore. The hurt and chaos was overwhelming.

One thing happened then, that saved Saul's mind. He *sneezed*.

The jerking explosion was so violent that the neural-tap helmet flew off his head and banged into the console. Suddenly the world was light and air and *real* noise—a tumult of human voices that seemed, in comparison, like the whispering of a morning breeze.

"What *happened*—"

"—blew up!—"

"My God, pure annihilation. . . !"

"Itaka, get on alert channel! Tell the surface crews to take cover at once!" Carl's voice commanded above the panicked ferment. "Get them below before the neutrons hit!"

Hands pulled at Saul's shoulders, attempting to drag him back. He blinked through spots and saw Andy Carroll's limp form being cut free of his webbing. Keoki Anuenue was fumbling at the back of Virginia's lolling neck, tugging at her neural tap while others hurried up bearing stretchers.

"*No!*" Saul screamed. He grabbed Keoki's wrist so hard that the big Hawaiian gasped in surprise.

Saul croaked, "Don't let anyone touch her. Nobody!" He picked up the helmet he had just thrown off. "Leave her alone!" Trembling, he put it back on.

In an instant he was back down under the roiling, churning tide of electrons, the roar of an explosion large enough to break a small world.

Better prepared, this time, Saul rode the surges, seeking a rock, an eddy, anywhere to stand and gather threads.

A piece of JonVon's personality-mimicry program hurtled by, murmuring something about refusing an "Academy Award" . . . whatever that was. He grabbed it and linked the fragment to a subroutine for searching library data bases, and another containing information on stock-raising on the Isle of Wight.

"Virginia," he whispered. "Where are you?"

What instinct had told him, with deeper certainty than mere knowledge, that she was lost somewhere in this maelstrom. . . ? That to disconnect her would be to leave her—if not a vegetable—then with something basic lost forever to chaos? Saul cast about, gathering a ragged construct, a troop of bits and flotsam, and sent scouts out, searching.

A whisper of tropical air, over *there!*

A scent of chrysanthemum blossoms, *here!*

A secret memory from childhood . . . of embarrassment with a neighbor boy . . . *bring it in.*

Traces, all, precipitating out of a whirling jumble. One by one, it would have taken a thousand lifetimes to recognize and even stack them all, let alone sort them into what they had been. He didn't try. All he could do was love them.

Fear and pain . . . a whispered curse.

". . . those mad sons of b . . ."

It hurtled past. But Saul reached out after it.

*I love you, Virginia,* he called. *Blemishes and all* . . . *Stupid* and *blind as I am, I love you, and I'll love you forever.* . . .

**. . . forever . . .**

The word echoed.

**. . . forever. . . ?**

*Yes. Down time until even the Hot fades and all ice comes alive* . . . *I will never leave you.* . . .

**. . . never. . . ?**
**Oh . . . Saul . . .**
**Oh . . .**

"Oooh," her real-world voice sighed beside him. "Oh, Saul . . ." The webbing vibrated with movement and suddenly her hand was gripping his, so hard that the welcome pain added to the free flow of tears in his eyes.

# CARL

Carl gritted his teeth in irritation, but didn't let it show. Four hours had passed since the explosion. The searing heat from the nearby blast had flash vaporized a layer of ice off one face of Halley. There had been extensive damage to mechs and diagnostic instruments on the surface, and some casualties. Data was slow coming in, but that hadn't stopped people from jabbering and theorizing.

Joao Quiverian was getting insufferable. He used the full impact of his height, towering over the others, his voice ringing with a hollow, magisterial command.

"We have erred in a way I find unfathomable. This mishap is a direct result of our meddling with what we do not understand, rather than placing our trust in our fellow human beings. Obviously the mech somehow ignited the fusion chamber of—"

*"Perdeeyn!"* Sergeov swore. "Arcist idiot—"

Quiverian bore on. "—the Care Package, and—"

"Okay, that's *enough*," Carl said sharply. "Shut up, everybody!" The knot of people turned its attention to him. "Look at these numbers." He gestured at one of the screens. "That was a full thermonuclear blast. *Not* a malfunction of the fusion drive."

Quiverian gaped. "Not . . . But why would they send to us . . ."

Sergeov's blue-tattooed skin creased with a bitter smile. "Not *to* us—*for* us."

Carl nodded. "I think so."

"A . . . bomb?" Lani Nguyen asked wonderingly, her almond eyes widening at the thought.

Carl said flatly, "JonVon estimates the yield at several hundred megatons. Plenty of neutrons, gammas—the works. No fusion chamber *I* ever heard of can go off with anything like that yield."

Quiverian said slowly, "Then they intended . . . to . . ."

"Have us take that package into our ice and then blow it up. Shatter everything inside Halley. Melt away the top kilometer, cave in the shafts everywhere else." Carl had to control his jittering nervous energy. Back home, in gravity, the muscles were always doing some work just to remain standing, burning away minute tensions. Here, inner demands for action found no expression. You had to focus it all into other avenues—voice, expression, gesture.

"I . . . find that difficult to believe," Quiverian said, suddenly uncharacteristically quiet.

"Is *typical,*" Sergeov said. "Earthside has been same always. Destroyed *Edmund, poof!* Now us."

Jeffers said sourly, "Yeah, askin' us for guidance, tellin' us to lead the package right down Shaft Three. An' we woulda done it, if it hadn't been for curiosity, makin' us send out a mech to see what Daddy'd brought us." He snorted derisively.

Carl said, "Earthside kept up their story all this time—for three years—when all along they've plotted to destroy us entirely."

"To preserve their holy biosphere," Saul said mildly as he approached.

Carl raised an eyebrow—*How is she?*—and Saul nodded reassuringly. Virginia had been unconscious when the med-techs bore her away on a stretcher. Carl felt relief, but in Saul's quietly pleased expression an unsettling confirmation: Somehow, he and Virginia were back together. The crisis had done that. His own chances—which he now saw he had allowed to build beyond prudent expectations—were zero again. Saul and Virginia seemed able to survive any buffeting that chance could deal them.

"—can expect a full explanation from Earth, I am sure," Quiverian finished. Carl realized he had missed one of the man's pontifical declarations.

"What?"

Quiverian's face knotted with exasperation. "I expect we have been the victims of a political faction. Someone who, under cover of their allotted cargo, included a warhead. This does not mean all Earth is opposed to us. Once we inform high Earth authorities of how this humanitarian gesture has been aborted in a most foul way, I am sure the leadership will take measures to punish and silence this cabal of—"

"Bullshit," Carl said vehemently.

Quiverian blinked, his lips pursed, but he said nothing. One of his lieutenants began, "Look, you can't—" but Carl cut him off.

"Call Earth on the microwave and you'll lose us our only advantage. Time."

Quiverian set his jaw to show determination. "I cannot expect you—"

"Look," Carl said, "they don't know what's happened yet, right?"

Jeffers calculated in his head. "Lessee . . . 'Bout two hours each way light travel time. We should be able to pick up what they were sayin' when the thing blew."

Carl nodded. "Let's pipe into their transmission."

Carl glanced toward a wall camera and nodded. JonVon was listening, as he suspected, and immediately the room filled with the hiss of solar static. Then a tinny voice said monotonously, "Cannot copy you here emm-dot, Halley."

Jeffers said, "They're still sendin' telemetry for guidin' it in."

The voice oscillated slightly, dispersed by its journey of three billion miles. "By our estimates, the package is nearing final matching RPX. Advise you now send it laser marker designation for Shaft Three. Automatic homing will then take over."

Carl said, "They're still working on their approach."

A steady blur of static. Then:

"Confirm docking? Negative on auto-servo coupling pip, but we do show counter-comm on reppledex four-over, though. Await that marker pip for none-in."

The men and women listened to the words from a civilization now as distant in time as it was in space. The mission monitors Earthside, they knew, were trained in the jargon of 2060, to minimize confusions, but still odd terms and mannerisms from the more modern era slipped in. A glance at his thumbnail told Carl that three hours had passed since the explosion. It felt more like a year. He ordered refreshments brought in. The faction leaders listened sullenly, silently.

"Should come anytime now," Jeffers said.

The wavering voice kept on. "Carrier cinch-by reads nominal. Coded—"

A sudden pause. The sun's own spiky popping seemed to flood the room, bringing a reminder of the warm regions they had left so long ago, the brooding eternal voice a pressing presence.

Then vague shouts, a commotion. "UV and visible flux! It's gone off!"

"Too early!" Somebody else cried out. "By my estimate . . ."

A babble of talk, a distinct thump. "Get away from that! It might've already docked, we don't know—"

An argument, voices shouting one another down. "See if those infect rejects are still transmitting. Goddam, I knew we shouldn't have safe-armed the bastard."

Another thump. "Neg, Fred. They're off the air."

Faintly, someone yelled, "Those screamers are steam!"

Everyone's eyes widened as a thin sound came, plainly from somewhere near the speaker—a hearty laugh, a cry of celebration, then the rolling sea-sound of many hands clapping.

The men and women of Halley looked at each other for a long time, silently. There seemed very little to say.

Carl cycled the doors and stepped out through the crystalline refractions of the surface lock. It was eighteen hours later. He had conferred with envoys of various factions, won agreements, soothed as best he could. By all rights he should be holed up in his bunk, getting some rest.

But that would have meant crawling away and licking his wounds, something he might well have done a few decades ago. . . . Now it wouldn't work, he knew. Too much had happened, too fast. If he brooded over it, he would just get depressed and accomplish nothing.

That was a standard he had slowly learned to impose on himself: *What will you have when this is over?* A memory of bitter ruminations, drunken attempts to forget? Recriminations against the hand fate had dealt you? That might satisfy something inside that wanted such sour fruit. But now he knew from experience that he would feel better in the long run if he threw himself into a job, built or fixed or moved something. Let the muscles work their own logic. Then he would be able to sleep, knowing that he had at least gotten something done, kept moving, *shown the bastards*.

A slight puff of air followed him onto the ice, instant billowing fog. He moved at a steady ground-hugging, ice-gripping lope toward the equator. He could hook on to the cable and jet over, but this way he got more exercise.

There had been a lot of craziness to contend with, and he was glad to be out here now. *Where I belong. I'm still a spacer, goddammit!*

Some pop-eyed idiot had stopped him in a corridor, accused him of deliberately sabotaging the Care Package. Madness. People didn't want to accept the cold clear reality—that their homeworld had sworn to erase them.

*Well, okay. Just like I didn't want to face the reality that nothing is ever really going to separate Saul and Virginia. It's just a matter of scale. . . .*

The belt of launchers loomed above the horizon as he loped along, feet finding purchase on the crusty, speckled ice. They were like slender, elegant cannon, each canted at a slightly different angle from its neighbor. Weeks ago they had slowed and stopped Halley's spin, to make alignment of their thrusts simple. Now the stars hung steadily above, and each launcher aimed exactly at the same point in the sky: Right Ascension 87°, Declination +35°.

—Yo, Cap'n.— Jeffers waved from atop Launcher 16.

"I'm not captain," Carl said automatically.

—Might's well be.—

"I'm just operations officer. That's all the clans will tolerate."

—Bunch of horses' asses.—

"I don't suppose I'll be getting a promotion from Earthside now, either."

Jeffers chuckled dryly. —Not much of one, I'd say. You through soothin' ever'body?—

"Yeah." Carl leaped up to the launcher cowling.

—Funny, how some of 'em can't believe what happened.—

"It was their Great White Hope."

—Pretty rough, when Mother Earth offers you a tit and then—boom.—

Carl smiled despite himself. From here he could see many

launchers, a dashed line sketching out Halley's equator, as if drawn by a careful high-school student for a science project. Their muzzles veered gradually to the north as his eye swept to the horizon. Each lay buried in an oil-hydraulic pad that absorbed the recoil and transmitted it to the all-too-fragile ice. Robos and mechs stood beside each narrow tube, ready to unsnag any trouble with the conveyor-belt feeders.

—They agree down below?—

Distracted by the orderly march of launchers to the horizon, Carl could not understand for a moment what Jeffers meant. "Oh, about Earthcomm?"

—Yeah, ever'body agree to shut up?—

"Not exactly."

—Who?—

"Sergeov. Quiverian."

—Sergeov I'd expect a few people to listen to, sure. He's a good ol' boy, straight-arrow Percell. Maybe a li'l heavy-handed. But Quiverian? He's a murderin' bastard! Who'd pay attention to—

"Some Arcists still think it must've been a mistake. They can't picture Mom slaughtering her children, even if they *are* carrying diseases."

—Craaaazy.—

"Right."

Beneath the silent ebony sky these issues seemed petty, diminished. Carl could deal with them inside, encased in ice . . . but here, human problems and opinions seemed dirty, small, shameful. "So . . . I had JonVon take a few mechs and . . . knock out the microwave antennas."

To his surprise, Jeffers laughed. —Damn right!—

"You . . . think so?"

—Course I do! We let Earth know we're still alive, they'll send another Care Package. Only this time they won't tell us.—

"This will buy us maybe a couple of crucial years. Maybe." Carl nodded. "They didn't fail utterly, of course. We lost a couple of people on the surface, and with our attention on the Care Package, we lagged a little on the Nudge. We're starting late."

Jeffers nodded. —Damn near aphelion. Gonna be a big job, givin' that much push to this much ice.—

"You've realigned the launchers already?"

—Just like you said. Gonna deliver *big* delta-V if we get started soon enough.—

At least the Care Package fiasco was behind them. While others mourned, Carl was relieved, in a way. It meant they had to break from Earth, ignoring their homeworld, even hiding from it for as long as possible.

Who could tell? In forty years new people might be in charge, back home. Or Phobos colony might have its independence by the time the cometary refugees came streaking in on their blazing aeroshells. *Who am I kidding?* Carl thought.

The tension in him wouldn't go away. He needed something. *Or someone*, he thought, and shut that away as quickly as he recognized it.

The launchers. They were ready, calibrated.

"You check those pin settings?"

Jeffers tapped on his board, nodded.

"Pressure manifolds? The magnet alignments?"

—All okay.—

"What are we waiting for, then?"

Jeffers looked up and slowly grinned. —Damn right!— He switched channels and spoke rapid-fire to the engineers.

Around Halley the belt stirred to life. Electromagnetic surges mounted, reached saturation, lay in wait for their release. And inside the ice, Carl knew, men and women were involved with their own lonely questions, doubts, despairs. They needed something to rouse them.

"Let 'er fly," Carl said.

He felt it through his boots. A trembling, a gathering rush, a sudden trembling release. From the muzzle of Launcher 16 came . . . nothing he could see. But he could feel each slug of coated iron flee down the electromagnetic gun, fevered pulses shaking the slender tube. A machine gun aimed at the stars. Against the black oblivion above they made no mark, merely arced into its nothingness.

It was a feather's brush against a boulder, but over time the effects would mount up.

He turned to look down the row. Each launcher flung its shots steadily skyward, the electromagnetic fringe fields sounding as a faint but persistent *rata-rata-rata-rata* over the comm line.

He should call JonVon, he knew, put the picture on all TV monitors, alert the crew. But for a moment he paused and savored it for himself.

They were heading back, now. Homeward. Halley's slow sluggish orbit would blunt, turn, warp. For better or worse, they would glide down the gravity mountain, toward a destiny they could not see. It was an end to their long, inert obedience to gravity's rule. Halley had become a ship.

—At last we're *doin'* somethin'!— Jeffers called.

Carl shouted in sudden joy, all doubts banished. "Sun, here we come!"

## PART VI

# WITH THE FORCE OF A STONE

*Year 2100*

What all the wise men promised
has not happened,
and what the damned fools said
has come to pass.

—Melbourne

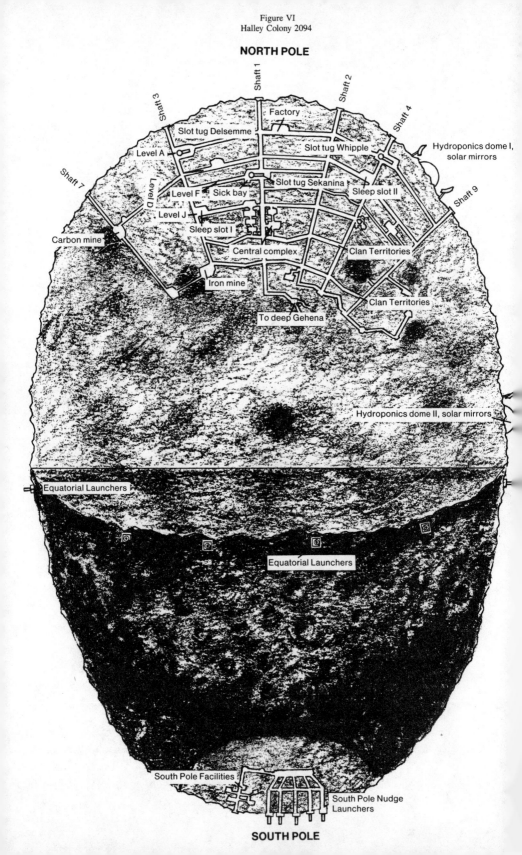

Figure VI
Halley Colony 2094

**NORTH POLE**

Shaft 1

Shaft 2

Shaft 3

Shaft 4

Factory

Slot tug Delsemme

Slot tug Whipple

Hydroponics dome I,
solar mirrors

Level A

Shaft 7

Slot tug Sekanina

Level D

Level F    Sick bay

Sleep slot II

Shaft 9

Level J

Sleep slot I

Carbon mine

Central complex

Clan Territories

Iron mine

Clan Territories

To deep Gehena

Hydroponics dome II, solar mirrors

Equatorial Launchers

Equatorial Launchers

South Pole Facilities

South Pole Nudge
Launchers

**SOUTH POLE**

# SAUL

He stared at the crack in the wall. The black opening snaked far back into the ice. "When did this happen?" Saul asked.

Two of his assistants—brown-haired, with identical patterns of freckles on their faces—looked up from a lab bench nearby where they had been working. They answered together, in the same tones.

"There was a Halley quake, Pops," they said in unison. "Two hours ago. A big one. It split the wall."

Saul shook his head, still unable to fathom how each knew what the other was going to say, so they could irritate him this way.

"It certainly did," he said, examining the damage. This would have to be attended to. Even this deep below the surface, it was foolish to let any chamber remain unsealable for long.

Some said it was the flinger launchers, stressing the comet core as they pushed it month by month, year by year, that were causing the quakes. Others blamed the war, now apparently lost for good by Quiverian and his Arcists.

Last month, Carl's spacers, Sergeov's *Ubers*, and Keoki Anuenue's neutrals had joined together in a lightning raid on the Arcists' south-pole redoubts, and permanently crippled the remnants of the first set of flingers, and the hidden microwave antennas with which they had been talking to Earth. One result was that now the Arcists could no longer use those old launchers to interfere with the Nudge toward Mars. Unfortunately, during that brief but bloody skirmish, three explosions had rocked that end of Halley Core, worrying some that the integrity of the comet itself might be threatened.

Whatever the cause, the quakes bothered Saul. For four years, now, things had been going well for a change. They had picked up word from Earth's faint data net that the odds makers were once more taking bets on the colony's survival. The current rate was five to one against. But that was a vast improvement over the thousand-to-one betting when he and Virginia had awakened from their thirty-year sleep.

For now, at least, Sergeov's *Ubers*, the various clans of survivors, and Jeffers's Mars Boys were all working together. But the alliance struck Saul as being like a supersaturated solution of immiscible fluids— too unsteady to last for long.

They didn't need these Halley quakes shaking up the delicate balance.

Saul was dressed in little more than a loincloth, robe, and ice-sandals, as he had only left the quarters he shared with Virginia for a brief visit to his lab. She had gone up to the surface to talk something over with Carl Osborn, so he had taken the opportunity to come down here and see how the experiments were going.

Everywhere in the lab there were glassed-in chambers, like aquaria, in which mini-ecosystems flourished or languished—where modified Earth lifeforms struggled to prove themselves worthy of inclusion in the new, synthetic cometary ecology that was only now starting to sort itself out.

Over by the left wall, some of his assistants tended the animals . . . birds without feathers and goats able to give milk in microgravity.

"Where is Paul?" he asked suddenly.

The brown-haired twins nodded toward the crack in the wall, and shrugged.

"What?" Saul blinked. "I thought I told you to keep him here!"

They rolled their eyes in an expression he had seen countless times, over many mirrored years. "You told us *not to let him out the door,*" they reminded him smugly.

"Oh Lord." Saul sagged. *Was I ever like these two? So insufferably . . . immature?*

They giggled together. Saul hesitated. He had to go after Paul, of course. The poor child wouldn't be able to take care of himself out there alone.

*I can't take any of the kids with me*, he realized, dismissing the idea of putting together a search party of his assistants. *They'd scare the hell out of people by emerging out in the halls in a swarm.* He had not introduced them to anybody else yet, not even Virginia. They were the most amazing development to come out of the union of Phobos technologies and his growing skill at clone-symbiosis, but this time he wasn't sure at all how to let the rest of the colony know about them.

Saul lope-floated over to the hole in the wall. He picked up a glow-ball of gene-designed *Halleyvirid* phosphor. "When I get back, we're going to have a talk about responsibility," he warned them. "Paul is still your brother, even if he's deficient in some ways. It was your duty to take care of him."

They looked down, shamefaced. They weren't bad kids, just inexperienced—very new to the world.

Two whirling, black sticks of fur leaped onto Saul, clambering over his shoulders. He gently unpeeled the midget gibbons.

"Not now, Max, Sylvie. I'll be right back. Stay with the boys." They stared after him, wide-eyed, as Saul turned and dove into the dark gap alone.

Of course Paul probably wasn't in any danger. He was immune to purple toxins, of course, and if this passage held air, so did everything connected to it.

*If only I can catch up with him before he runs into people.*

Sooner or later, of course, he would have to reveal what he was doing. Announce that he had finally found solutions to many of the problems of growth and development that had made child-rearing a near impossibility on Halley.

What he had learned might even be applied to helping the thirty or so children the Orthos and a few Percells had already produced. During the last year, improving the lot of those poor, warped creatures had been one of his highest priorities.

He had hoped to put off showing people his own "kids," though, until the Nudge was fully under way and people were filing back into the slots. It might go over better when there were fewer people around.

*I hope I can catch Paul in time. Strangers might upset him.*

In the soft light given off by the glow-ball, the crevice in the ice was a sparkling wonderworks of jagged crystals and puffy clathrate snow. It was easy to follow the path the youngster had taken by the handholds he had used. A smudge here, there a thread ripped from the floppy old lab coat Paul liked to wear. Saul followed the trail through a small crystal chamber that had not been charted before, now exposed in all its agate glory by recent tremors in the ancient ice.

He hurried onward. The passage narrowed until it was little more than a man's width across. *A thin man's width,* Saul thought, as he squeezed through, stretching ahead with his hands to pull himself along the narrow stricture.

He couldn't help comparing it to a birth canal. Something in the tunnel—perhaps a new Halleyform his immune system had not yet come to terms with—was causing a burning, itching reaction in his sinuses and throat. His nose twitched and tingled.

*Aw hell . . .* he thought, closing his eyes, squinting.

"A-a-a-chblthooh!"

The echo of his sneeze reverberated from an open chamber just ahead. Saul shook his head to clear it, and crawled on as he heard the distinct sound of a child crying.

His hand pushed through snow and met open space letting more light in. High-pitched shrieks greeted its appearance.

"Old Hard Man! It's Old Hardman!"

"Shush, kids. Quiet," a deeper voice soothed. "See? The skin is white, not green. You know that Old Hard Man is part black, part green."

The whimpers softened. Saul felt a hard grip on his wrist and kicked to help his benefactor drag him through the crumbling snow. He popped free into one of the beam-cut, Halleyvirid-lined colony tunnels. Saul had to swivel to cushion his impact on the opposite wall.

"Thanks," he said, waving away a cloud of sublimed vapor that had followed him. "I . . ."

An elderly man—an Ortho named Hans Pestle, Saul recalled—held the hands of two skinny children dressed in ragged fibercloth. Four other small, scrawny figures clung to the walls nearby. The old man stared at him.

"What's the matter, Hans?"

Pestle shook his head. "Nothin' Dr. Lintz. I was just . . . No, I must've been mistaken, is all."

Two of the older children edged forward. "Got goobers for me?" one asked shyly.

"Sorry, Ahmed." Saul smiled and stroked the little boy's sparse hair, keeping his hand away from the long, floppy, ferretlike creature the child wore, stolelike, over his shoulders. The gene-crafted animal watched Saul with gleaming eyes.

"Sorry. No goobers this time." Usually, the children got their medication in candy form—sweet flavors were common in the mutated food plants, but sourballs were one of his widely treasured specialties. "I promise, next time you come to the clinic."

"Aw, gee." But the child took the disappointment well. It had been some time since he had had any of the fits of temper that used to drive him into uncontrollable tantrums.

Actually, Ahmed had made a lot of progress. He was talking more, and had put on weight. Still, to look at him, seventy pounds and barely five feet tall, you wouldn't think he was sixteen years old, Earth-measure.

Unfortunately, there were limits to what Saul could accomplish with damage so advanced. And some of his best methods had turned out to be applicable only to a narrow range of genetic types. He found it terribly frustrating.

Saul shook his head, fighting down the ringing in his ears brought on by a fit of allergy-symbiosis reaction. He sneezed, and the children clapped their hands, laughing at the explosive report.

"What are you and these kids doing down here, Hans?" Saul recognized the nearby intersection by its incised markings. They were deep, far below these Orthos' clan territory.

Pestle looked at the floor. "Just strollin' . . . you said the kids should get more exercise. . . ."

Clearly, Hans was concealing something. But Saul didn't have time to probe.

"Did you see someone else come this way?" he asked the old man—a once-famous astrophysicist, now reduced by frailty to tending crippled children while the clear-minded and able-bodied labored on the surface.

"Minute or so ago." Pestle jerked his head toward the nearby shaft and gestured upward. He seemed about to ask a question, then shook his head and was quiet.

"Thanks," Saul said, and started off toward the shaft.

"Wouldn't, if I were you."

The voice of the old man stopped him abruptly. Saul turned. "Why not?"

Pestle looked away again, bit his lip nervously. One eye was still cloudy from damage done long ago. Saul had managed to eliminate the lingering disease, but not the harm already done.

"You're our doctor," the old man mumbled. "Can't afford t' lose you."

"Lose me?" Saul felt a sudden sinking feeling. "What are you talking about? Is there danger above?"

*Virginia's gone up there,* was his chilled thought.

Pestle shook his head. "Heard tales. May be more fightin' soon. Took the youngsters down here to be safe. That's all."

Saul frowned. This was not good.

"Thanks for the warning, Hans. I'll be careful."

He kicked off and started climbing the shaft, grabbing tufts of tamed, hybrid Halleyvirid covering and using his toe-spikes to speed upward almost at a run.

He had nearly reached B Level when a shrieking noise, like giant stones rubbing against each other, echoed shrilly in the passage. *Another damn quake,* he thought. Or was it something else? Something more sinister? The vegetation up ahead started swaying, like a wave rolling down the dimly lit shaft. The ripples arrived and suddenly it was as if he were trying to ride a furry snake, one that bucked and slithered and threw him back and forth.

Saul's grip tore loose and he was flung across the shaft, landing inside a tunnel mouth just as pieces dislodged from the ceiling. He rolled to one side to avoid a jagged boulder that dropped slowly, but irresistibly. Another one popped free of the left wall and proceeded with terrible inertia to collide crushingly with the right side.

So busy was he dodging those, he did not see the third and smallest rock. A sudden, crushing blow to his head sent him reeling against the floor. He slumped over an icy boulder and moaned.

Consciousness never completely vanished, but neither did it quite remain. To Saul, the next few minutes, or hour, or several hours, were a confusion of rumbling sounds, of icy dust settling slowly, of blinking and not being quite sure what it was he was supposed to remember.

Finally, it came to him.

*Get to Carl . . . warn him . . .*

He couldn't quite recall what it was he was supposed to warn him *about,* or why. Perhaps it would come to him when he arrived. He knew only that he had to go back into the shaft and start climbing again.

*Find Paul . . .* he reminded himself. *Hurry . . . find Virginia . . .*

He repeated the instructions over and over again, pushing aside the ringing and the pain in his head.

*Hurry . . .*

# VIRGINIA

As she stepped onto the surface she felt again the chilly majesty of the ice, the void, the swallowing darkness they all swam in. *Earth is the sultry Hawaii in a solar system of perpetual Siberias,* she thought. *Will we ever feel true warmth again?*

As she took long, loping strides across the speckled gray ice Virginia resolutely banished the thought. She had had quite enough experience with the onset of depression, thank you, in the last several years. It was an occupational hazard. Even her love for Saul had not proved an adequate shield against it . . . just as the psychology people Earthside had predicted, decades ago. They had warned the crew not to put too much weight on any relationship, that no human bond could take the full pressure of their isolation, the unremitting hostility of the hard empty cold.

*People weren't made to take the full brunt of the world,* she thought. Particularly not one as barren as this. Anthropologists had found that even the simplest societies had quickly invented alcohol— usually beer—probably as a shelter against the storm of naked, incessant reality. Intelligence able to deal flexibly and subtly with its environment was also inescapably vulnerable to it. Halley's crew had tried the predictable escapes—alcohol, drugs, senstim, torrid and fleeting affairs— and weathered the years. But no victory was permanent, and Virginia knew she had to steer herself through shoals of depression, avoid the triggering thoughts and moods.

She felt a faint tremor through her boots and glanced nervously around. Nothing unusual, apparently. A few teams working at distant launchers. No shouts over comm, nothing awry. *Good. I don't want to be up here when something goes ka-boom. Not my strong suit, crises, nossir. Not without waldo gloves, JonVon, and a hundred mechs at my beck and call.*

The new, huge hydro domes loomed nearby, erected by Jeffers and his crews when the quakes had started. It was risky to keep farms and factories running beneath the ice near the launchers, in case a stress line opened under the relentless pounding of the flingers. Carl had ordered a lot of agro moved to the surface, set up near the shafts.

Amid all the work, there were the usual rumors. That the defeated Arcists had struck some kind of deal with the *Ubers*. That the *Ubers* were going to make trouble again over the choice of the Mars trajectory. That the P-Threes were building a space ship in secret. She thought it was idle talk, but you never knew.

*Everything's so rushed these days, so exciting. A million jobs, nearly the whole crew revived . . . so why am I depressed?*

The answer was obvious. She really didn't want to come up here and confront Carl.

She glide-walked for Dome 3, where she knew he was looking at some new agro results. As she came through the hissing lock she saw

Carl studying some canisters, running his hands through rich kernels of wheat. He was wearing his spacesuit; these days he was in and out so often, checking the launchers, he seldom shed it. Agro workers floated above ripe fields of rye and wheat and spires of coiling vegetables. Gene-crafted to thrive here in low-G among the pervasive Halleyforms, they had odd, asymmetric forms.

"Great stuff, huh?" He grinned at her as she approached.

"You're a thorough man. Checking the breakfast cereal, too?"

His face clouded. "I like to see good work praised, and these people have done—"

"Hey, I was just kidding." She gave him a playful punch in the arm, and then immediately felt the gesture was forced, awkward. *Calm down. This is going to be hard enough without trying to pretend it's a Shriners' convention.*

Carl shrugged. "I'll be with you in a minute, Virginia." He turned back to a crewwoman standing nearby. "The new hybrid is excellent. Tastes great, too."

Virginia watched as Carl and the agro tech discussed variants on the growing cycles. Halley's gentle but drumming acceleration was affecting the mirrors that lit the greenhouses, and there were adjustments to be made.

She wandered down a lane, glad to delay. Stalks rose nearly a hundred meters, slender and white, yielding impossibly broad, meaty leaves. Spindly gardener mechs prowled down tight lanes. Circulation patterns spun streamers of wobbly droplets among the lofty spiral stems. Beneath these vertical protein farms lay rows of fat vegetables, lush and curling in the soft ultraviolet that filtered through shimmering banks of moisture above. Rich humus lapped at the feet of the giants, like a sea's ever-grinding at the shore. A tracery of ponds used the gently falling debris from the spires, and modified fish darted among ropy roots. She recalled a poem she had never finished, and found fresh lines popping into her mind.

> In all this glistening fine
> steel and cool ceramic sureness
> Rot rules
> as surely as in ancient sea-bed Earth.
> Cool yet crackling flingers call up
> lightning that once kindled organic clinging,
> fevered molecules mad for union,
> not knowing that growth means age
> and then the chewing march begins.

We live from eating others
just as these chilled lands will gnaw us down,
ceaseless and unending digestion of
our hearts and dreams,
plots and schemes,
all passing clouds in an airless black
And yet we lack
a clear way back to youth,
or Earth, or slot sleep's birth.
I'd rather be brought down
after the long summer's chase,
belly torn out
(it's no disgrace)
than seep like sludge into
the garden's moss and hear the
polite *such a loss*
when I know all will be ground
down to make the soil where
new Caesars will march,
unknowing, on to their good humus, too.

Virginia coughed in the heavy, musky air. She never seemed to finish poems anymore. Instead she took them out to examine, turning them to the light like pretty pebbles found on last summer's vacation beach. *Well, poems acquire a certain deadness when they're done . . . not finishing them gives them indefinite life.* She smiled to herself.

When she returned down a narrow lane, Carl was through talking to the hydro crew. She liked the way the silvered inner surface of the dome reflected a warped, surreal vision of Carl immersed in a riot of plantlife, as if it were an ocean in which he was afloat. When he turned toward her she held up a hand. "Conference?"

"Sure." He stood waiting, the old caution still far back in his eyes. *I've hurt him so many times . . .*

"I . . . wanted to tell you . . ."

"Yes?"

"I know you felt that there was . . . some chance of Saul and me . . ."

He smiled wanly. "There's always hope."

"You've never given up."

"No."

"You might as well," she said gently.

"It's that certain between you?"

Virginia recalled her own thoughts about that, only minutes ago. "Out here, nothing is certain, you know that. No, it's just that . . . you have such, well, such traditional goals."

"Dreams, I'd say." Carl smiled with a warm, rueful humor, as if aware of his own foibles. He would keep this polite and graceful, she saw. Time had given him a veneer, a sense of self. He had changed greatly in these years, almost without her noticing. *I've been so wrapped up in Saul. . . .*

She struggled to find the right words, but before she could he said, "Admittedly, out here the idea of love and family, that whole snug picture, doesn't work. We haven't figured out how to protect the children from Halleyforms yet."

"You'll never have a family with me."

"I'm resigned to that. Saul won't either, of course."

"No, but not because of his sterility. It's me. I—I can't have children."

His lips parted but he said nothing. The veneer was gone in an instant and she saw again the old Carl, filled with longing and need.

"I . . . could never tell anyone. It was years before I could say anything, even to Saul."

"God . . . I'm sorry."

She blinked back tears. "I've come to terms with it." *Then why am I crying, idiot?*

"All this time . . ." He shook his head, his face open and somehow fresher, younger. *All these years he's sheltered a dream, and now it's gone.*

"I knew about it well before we left Earth."

"I . . . see," he said numbly.

"Carl—"

"What about, uh, fixing whatever's wrong? Saul's done wonders—" He stopped.

She thought sharply, *Was it me you wanted, or your dream of sweet little Percell children, genetic miracles among the stars?* But the suggestion was wrong, unkind.

She blinked rapidly. "This is a . . . special case. Not even genetic surgery . . . He did try cloning, without my permission. It was a disaster." She shrugged.

"You . . . knew . . . all along."

She nodded. "I suppose it influenced me, made me come on the mission in the first place. I wasn't going to have a conventional life, no matter how I played it."

"You could've adopted."

"You know the odds against a Percell getting children to bring up. Even in Hawaii."

He said savagely, "Yeah, they sealed off everything from us, didn't they?" The memory could still draw bitterness.

"I could've stayed . . . fought with the others. . . ."

"You saw what happened."

She nodded, sniffing, surprised at her own emotion. *If I stay here I'll cry.* "We . . . really made the right choice, didn't we? Coming?"

His voice was leaden, his face a mask. "I . . . I don't know."

She was shocked. *Have I taken away his last fantasy? And with it gone, the tide of despair rushes in?*

"Carl, you can't think that. We've survived, we've managed to—"

"Look, I'd . . . I'd rather not talk right now. Okay? Just . . . want to be alone." He visibly pulled himself together, struggled to regain some of the confident manner of leadership that had become like a second skin to him . . . however easily it had peeled away, just now. "I appreciate your telling me. I can understand you better now, and at least that's something."

"Carl, I—"

"I've got plenty more to do here," he said bluntly. "Maybe later."

Speechless, Virginia held out her hands, then let them drift to her sides. "All . . . all right."

She left quickly, her mind aswirl with conflicting emotions. Somehow she had had to tell him, and yet if it stripped away too much, damaged him . . .

She had been fooled by his public face of assurance and control. Beneath that, Carl had really changed very little. He had grown as the situation demanded, but not the inner Carl. That Carl had nursed a fantasy, and now she had toppled it.

She loped across the ice, putting her confusion into exercise, a coasting mote moving across a plain the color of a blank television screen.

*—Virginia,—* JonVon's well-modulated voice came when she was halfway to the lock. *—There are coded transmissions from near your present location.—*

"Coded?" She stopped and looked around. Nobody in sight, except a few hydro workers trudging off after their shift. On the horizon one of Jim Vidor's faery towers spiked at the stars. Farther away a launcher thrummed, driving them gradually, imperceptibly, toward the encounter with Mars. "What do you mean?"

*—I broke the code, a juvenile little algorithm. The messages are*

*quite excited and not altogether intelligible. They mention your name
and Carl Osborn's.—*

"Look, monitor it and try to track the source. I've got other things
on my mind right now."

She glanced back at the dome and saw through its smudged translu-
cence two figures confronting each other under the brilliant lights.

Carl, suited and gesturing. The second, in a simple robe . . . she
was sure it was Saul.

*With Carl in such a state . . . I wish I could warn Saul. This is
definitely not the time to bother Carl with some detail.*

Something was wrong. Saul waved his hands, then lurched to the
side, as if to leave.

Virginia frowned. Saul looked sick . . . and something was odd
about the way he moved.

Carl took a step forward and Saul pushed him away. Virginia
wished she were back in her lab, could tap immediately into one of the
worker robos inside the dome, listen in.

The men were shouting at each other, Saul gesturing wildly, pushing. He collided with the towering glass wall.

The dome split! At that moment a blue flash cut down it, ripping
the pressure sheet, showering livid yellow sparks. Air gushed out sound-
lessly, a pearly fog exploding into a ball that rose and grew and shredded. *How could a man shatter* . . . Then she realized.

*Laser.*

"Saul! Run to the airlock!" But he couldn't hear her, of course.
Saul wasn't wearing a suit.

Carl sprinted toward the lock, where the helmets were stored.

Saul stumbled, confused, and fell into a mass of vegetation. He got
back to his feet among the boiling tangle of plants, but did not seem to
know what to do, where he could find pressure again. The lock was only
a hundred meters away, but in the disorienting plunge to vacuum the
brain gave conflicting signals.

Virginia was running, shouting, without taking her eyes off Saul.
His robe flapped above bone-white flanks, he lurched awkwardly—
*away* from the lock, toward the split in the dome. He was mindlessly
following the gale that swept past him, sending his brown hair streaming
before his eyes, tossing the plants in a whipping gale.

Carl had reached the lock. He ducked inside, slammed the hatch. It
would take him at least a minute to find a helmet, get some air into his
lungs. . . .

Virginia ran furiously, slipping maddeningly off the ice.

"Saul—no! Saul—"

She knew the effects of vacuum and cold, rupturing the blood vessels in the lungs, freezing the body's cells, bursting the delicate membranes in eyes and ears, wreaking bloody havoc throughout the body. . . .

He stumbled toward the shattered lip of the dome, drawn by the sucking storm. She was still running when he fell among the upright shards.

Carl rushed past her. But when they reached the crumpled figure, stiffly contorted in a position of tortured agony, they could see sharp, glassy daggers protruding from his back. The deep cuts no longer even spurted scarlet. Purpling bruises, glassy complexion. Blank, open eyes.

The dome crew came running from the far lock, bringing first-aid equipment. *Too late.*

*How strange he looks,* Virginia thought. He had always seemed craggy, time-worn but triumphant. Now he seemed unblemished, young, his face smooth, as if years had been erased by the soothing hand of Death.

# CARL

He had always been a problem-solver, a man who reflexively reacted to the unknown by breaking it into understandable pieces. Then Carl would carefully solve each small puzzle, confident that the sum of such microproblems would finally resolve the larger confusions. *What'd they call it at Caltech? A "linear superposition, with separable variables"? Yeah, that's my kind of stuff. Ol' can-do Carl.*

He slammed his fist into the foamweb wall of Dome 3. *But I can't fix the past. I can't bring Saul back. I can't even comfort Virginia.*

She sat among some wilted stems of just-harvested rhubarb, staring into space. Her red-rimmed eyes had long since cleared of tears and now she was drawn, exhausted, numb. The dome crew had taken Saul's body away, and in the confusion Virginia had dropped into silence, ashen and listless. Lani Nguyen sat with her, murmuring softly, an arm around Virginia's shoulders.

Lani and Jeffers had arrived only moments after Saul's death, responding to Carl's Mayday call. There was no sign of whoever had fired the laser that punctured the dome. Lani and Jeffers had met no opposition as they sprinted from the nearest shaft. The comm radio carried no news. The dome crew, well seasoned by meteorite punctures, had replaced the shattered wall and resealed the dome quickly. Atmosphere was building to nearly normal.

Jeffers said sourly, "I still can't figure it."

Carl blinked, self-absorbed. "What?"

"Why Saul didn't react when the dome popped. He's older, sure, but we've had plenty trainin' with leaks in the shafts. How come Saul didn't follow you?"

"He was disoriented even before that. He came up through the waste hatch over there, mumbling."

"That's crazy." Jeffers shook his head. "The waste hatch?"

"He must've taken it as some sort of shortcut. Maybe he knew Virginia was talking to me and—" Carl stopped. He didn't want to reveal what Virginia had said, or pursue the thought that Saul was trying to stop her. *It's all so damned jumbled up! Why should Saul care about Virginia's telling me? Or was Saul's arrival—too late—an accident?*

Jeffers bit his lip, uncomfortable. "Virginia . . . said you and Saul had a fight, sorta."

"He was shouting stuff—just sounds, grunts, some words all mixed up."

"You figure he was hallucinatin' or somethin'?"

"Maybe. I hadn't seen him in months. He looked confused, incoherent. The man was deranged."

"That's why he didn't react, get to the lock?"

"I guess."

Jeffers looked skeptical. "Look, there's just too damn much here. Somebody punches a hole through the dome, nearly kills all of you—"

"Targets of opportunity," Carl said woodenly. "Unless they spotted Virginia's tabard as she left, they must've thought she was in the dome, too."

"But who'd—"

A blue flare lit a nearby stubby ice hill. The two men whirled to watch the glare fade, enveloped in the exploding ball of white spray.

"Goddamn!" Jeffers shouted. "Ever'body—helmets!"

Carl started toward Virginia, automatically clamping his own helmet O-rings, and saw that Lani was ahead of him, helping Virginia. "Crew!—get down. If they puncture the dome again—"

—I not need to fire again, Carl. You get the meaning.—

The voice crackled in his earphones. "Who's that?" he snapped.

—Sergeov! I knew it,— Jeffers sent.

"Clear A-channel," Carl said to quell the rising chatter on the line. "Sergeov, what the hell—"

In the display quadrant of Carl's helmet appeared Sergeov's grinning, blue-tinted face. The Sigil of Simon Percell was etched into each cheek.

—I hoped to get Carl and Virginia without injury.— Sergeov's accent came through more clearly. —Even better when flies come to the honey. Jeffers, I hope we can count on you to work with the launchers when this is over.—

"When *what* is over?"

—You can witness for self.—

Carl had been scanning the horizon to locate their laser. Now, when he turned toward the equator, he saw figures quickly crisscrossing around the launchers. Silently a bolt struck among two running forms and sent them tumbling skyward in the burst of steam. Carl could not tell whether the people were hit directly, but there was scarcely time to consider it before more quick, blue-hot flashes burst forth.

—We take half the launchers already. The rest will either surrender or we will burn them where they stand.—

"What . . ." Realization dawned. "You . . . you've cut off me and the others, so we can't lead a counterattack, right?"

Sergeov turned to give a gesture. Immediately Carl felt a *crump* and vibrations beneath his feet. —I just now gave order to blow in the tunnels beneath your dome. Seals you in tight, right? Great, clape!—

Carl shouted, "You idiot—"

Sergeov laughed. —Like the trap, clap?— Then he sobered, smiled. —Without you the others will be less stupid.—

Jeffers broke in, —This's mutiny, y'know.—

—Self-preservation, you mean.—

Carl could hear in the venom of Sergeov's words a rebuke of his own leadership. The man's rantings had seemed comic, dumb, a set of leftover ideas. But after the Care Package, a lot of otherwise reasonable people had developed a deep hatred of Earthside, and Sergeov had played to that, claiming that the Mars maneuver wouldn't work.

*The Mars plan almost certainly won't save us. Nothing will, except a change of heart Earthside.*

It had seemed to Carl that Sergeov had never proposed any valid alternatives, and nobody could really take the man seriously. Still, by adding together disgruntled spacers and hard-line *Ubers*, Sergeov might have enough to seize and hold the launchers, if they did it just right. . . .

"You don't like the Mars targeting?"

—It is emotional drivel. We could not brake in such thin atmosphere, everyone who stops to work it out knows that.—

"We can try. At the very least we'll slow down some, maybe open up options on the outbound leg of this pass."

Sergeov laughed, a dry cackle. —Do not give me speeches. Me and my friends—who be *real* Percells, not renegades who suck up to any Ortho, even *sleep* with them—we know the astrophysics as well as you, probably better. You think we cannot do simulations? We know danger of hitting Mars. At best not enough air. So only hope remaining is to brake in atmosphere of planet with *thick* air.—

"Venus? There's a possible mission there, though it's on the outbound leg. We'd have to go through perihelion first, and I don't want to judge how we'll survive that."

—No perihelion. Dumb to even think we can ride that.—

"Why not? Listen, Otis, we can talk over a Venus encounter in detail if you want."

Jeffers gestured to Carl as he spoke. Along the distant line of launchers, figures were throwing makeshift flags over the cowlings: the *Uber* sign.

—You see we are winning? *Da,* all in time. If the other launchers do not give up, we will depress the muzzles of ours, fire empty casings, and pound the others to small pieces.—

Jeffers blurted, —You're fuckin' *crazy,* you know that?—

Carl gestured for Jeffers to be quiet. "Jesus, Sergeov, you wouldn't do that. We need those launchers—"

—To strike Mars. We not go crashing into Mars just to keep Earthside happy.—

"What kind of demented logic is that?"

—Clever logic, it is. Earth would like to see us suicide on Mars, end Halley-Life. What proof you need, after they show how much they care?—

The sneering reference to the Care Package hurt, because Carl knew it was true. The crew had been bitter about that, and this mad rebellion was the outcome. Most spacers, notably the Blue Rock Clan of Hawaiians, stood behind Carl. But Sergeov had undoubtedly recruited among Percells, and Carl wouldn't be surprised if there were even some Orthos helping him.

—We hit planet with atmosphere, but not Venus.—

"So where do you want to go, Otis?"

—Is obvious. Earth.—

"Good God! That's—"

He was about to say, *That's impossible,* but then he recalled the mission options outlined long ago. The expedition had first planned on an inward-passing flyby of Jupiter, altering Halley's orbit until rendezvous with Luna was fairly inexpensive in fuel for the *Edmund.* That required a delta-V of 284 meters per second, a hefty velocity change.

Since the Arcist rebellion had deprived them of the south pole, they had opted to use launchers at the equator for the less effective swing past Mars; that required a velocity change of only fifty-nine meters per second. The energy required scaled as the square of delta-V, which meant that a maneuver by Mars, with a grazing brake in its atmosphere, took only four percent of the original mission energy requirement. They had been investing launcher time in just that maneuver for years now.

But he had forgotten another maneuver they could make from a steady equatorial push. *Earth . . .*

"I can't remember the numbers, but look, we can't—"

—I refresh you. Only takes sixty-three meters per second delta-V. Only slightly more push than we now give. And direction is nearly same as Mars suicide! My crews, they now swing launchers a little. Only five degrees in declination, one hundred degrees in right ascension. You follow? Means—

"Yeah, I get it." *He's really crazy. How do I handle him?* "Okay, we can hit Earth. So what? They'll cream us before we even get close."

Sergeov's dry cackle rang over the comm. Carl waited out the airless, manic laughter, telling himself, *Don't blow it. Keep him talking. Maybe somebody from below will round up some industrial lasers, circle around them, cut them off—*

But he knew the chances were slim. Sergeov had played it just right, waited until Jeffers—Carl's right arm—was trapped in the dome, too. Virginia couldn't get control of her mechs. And as a bonus, they'd killed Saul, who might've rallied many people who simply wanted to survive. . . .

—Earth will not cream us. Not if we threaten to seed them with the plagues.—

"You'd threaten *that*?"

—Smell the fire, Meyer. Orthos blow *Edmund,* send Care Package. What they deserve?—

"They'll still—"

—We make atmospheric brake, jump off. Halley goes on. We make deal to not seed Earth with Halleyforms, then Earth send us to Diemos. We live there, start terraforming planet.—

Jeffers muttered, "Well, at least *that* part makes sense." He looked up guiltily as Carl shot him a glance.

Sergeov heard him. —Better to dream than nightmare, eh?—

Carl tried to think. Lani stood at his side, a hand on his shoulder, mute comfort.

"Earth'll take no chances on getting soaked with Halleyforms. They'll nuke us," Carl said.

—Not! We will have standby rockets, warheads of Halley-Life. Earth launch, we launch.—

Carl saw Jeffers's expression. Sergeov's mad scenario was all too seductive. The aerobrakes would take a lot of mech-manufacture, but that had already been designed and scheduled for the Mars maneuver.

"I don't think you can sell this."

—No need sell. Time to smack, Jack. You agree or we cut dome into little pieces.—

"The others won't go along with this."

—What others? Ortho others? They want to live, same as Percells.—

"But this endangers Earth! Any aerobrake will bring Halley Core close enough to dump some ice into the upper atmosphere. The bioforms could make it down to the surface anyway!—"

—Earthers have to take chance. Most of us now say *piss* on Earthers.—

Carl paced, oblivious to the staring eyes of the dome crew, to Jeffers's persistent gnawing at his own lip, to Virginia's blank stare. Lani watched him pensively. He had to think, and yet his mind was a whirl of conflicting emotions. The Earth maneuver at least held out the promise of hope, of living. . . .

"Look, you ought to have a referendum on this. The whole crew—"

—Clape, ape. No voting. You forget, *we* have launchers.—

"There'll be a sizable minority, maybe even a majority, that'll oppose you."

—We can dispose of them.—

"How?"

—Same as we do for you, once things settle down. Easy. Launchers all built, no big labor needed now. We send you all to sleep slots.—

Virginia, Lani, Jeffers—they all stared at him, listening, saying nothing. He had led them for years, for billions of miles, to come to this—a somber, stupid Waterloo. Outflanked. Outsmarted.

And to grind it in, Sergeov cackled dryly and said, —Comes Earth, then we decide on who to wake up. You make trouble now, maybe you never come out of slots? Eh?—

# VIRGINIA

They had been the worst two days of her life. They seemed to stretch back for millennia, back to sunny bright days when Saul had lived, and love had carried her forward of its own momentum, overriding difficulties, smoothing over the furrowed surface of a life that was, when she managed to think of it, perpetually sharp and desperate and tight-stretched.

Saul's contorted body had imbedded its image in her mind, a silent, grotesque rebuke. He had looked so strange in death. Peaceful, despite his wounds. Younger.

*So many struggles . . .*

If she had been closer, had thought faster, run harder—

*No. Stop that.* She knew this was a deadly spiral, that nothing could come of an endless cycle of guilt and pain.

But such easy realizations did not free her. She sat amid the currents of anger and frantic talk and raw emotion . . . and clasped her hands, rubbing them incessantly, unable to move or think or even let the upwelling grief spill out into tears.

It was useless, anything she did, so pointless and stupid. She did not care if she sat forever this way, surrounded by the slowly gathering musky damp of the regenerating dome. The plants were space-hardened, able to withstand quick decompressions and chills, far better adapted, through a half-century of human handiwork, than was mankind itself.

Others tried to help. Lani was a hovering presence, soft sibilants in an engulfing stillness. Carl made his awkward gestures, said the conventional things. It was all wooden, distant, faces under glass.

The fact that the crazy *Ubers* and their allies were holding them all inside Dome 3 made no difference, really. She was as uncaring as the silent frosted ice outside, where figures gyred the launchers into new,

well-padded directions, their muzzles pointing to different constella-
tions. She watched the distant puppets do their irrelevant things, without
caring what it meant. Earth was a more welcome target than Mars,
certainly—but not because she thought they would succeed.

Nothing had ever worked on this doomed expedition. Earth would
find some way to counter them. Was the scheme to cast off in balloonlike
aerobrake vehicles? Hollow steel shells that, under the hard-ramming
pressure of braking, needed only the slightest flawed asymmetry to twist
and shear and shatter—no, Earth would see that opportunity quite well.
A laser bolt, a particle beam—anything that punched a hole in the shell
would end them all in a fiery orange-red caldron. She had no faith in
Sergeov's fevered astronomical dream.

Or in the Mars maneuver, either. She had kept Carl's secret, never
told anyone. *We live by believing fictions* . . .

But Sergeov's lie was worse. It would bring no dead world alive,
and they would all wind up just as doomed.

What if the comet head was directed to actually collide with Earth
itself, as she had heard some *Ubers* discussing openly on the comm?
What would become of soft skies and hazy Hawaiian afternoons? She
closed her eyes and shook her head. *Maybe humans should go out the
way the dinosaurs did.*

"Virginia?"

It was Carl, pale and drawn, again trying to make some contact.
She blinked up at him. "Time to eat again?"

"No, I just—look, I could really use some help."

"Doing what?"

"Figuring a way out of this."

She said wearily, "Sergeov's got us trapped. Do you want to dig out
through the waste tunnels? Using garden trowels?" The *Ubers* had caved
those in quite effectively.

"There must—"

"You tried the autochutes? The conveyors?"

"Sure. Yesterday. He's got people blocking them."

She frowned. It was hard to think in the old way. . . . "My mechs.
If I could get control function over them from here, on a remote . . ."

"You tried that yesterday," he reminded her gently.

She looked up, feeling a surge of irritation. "Oh yes. They've
changed the T-matrix inputs. Sergeov was smart enough to do that right
away. I could only fix that from the big console at Central, or my lab. I
have to be there in person."

They were silent. She could see Carl's frustration building in his
face.

Jeffers came over hurriedly, strain showing in his face. "Somethin's happenin'—they've cranked up that laser again."

Carl launched himself in a long glide for the top of the processing hut, fifty meters away. Virginia was tempted to lapse back into neutral and let the world wash over her. But instead she sighed and stood up. She kicked off and followed the two men in a slow coast.

"They're firing at somebody!" Carl called from his vantage point. Virginia snagged a guy wire and arced to a hard landing atop the hut.

"See?" Carl pointed. "Sergeov's up on that rise, there. He's shooting at people coming from the south."

Fly-speck figures swept rapidly across the gray, streaked plain. "Who?" she asked.

Lani landed next to her. "Arcists, I figure," she said. "Quiverian's folk. They're still down there to the south, living in their quake rubble. It's natural they'd oppose an Earth flyby. But with the *Ubers* holding the launchers, they'll get cut to pieces."

"You're sure?"

"I can't see—"

A huge gout of steam erupted from the base of the hill where the *Uber* laser sat. The cloud enveloped the hill in a shroud of fog. Before it could swell further and dissolve, another blue spark ignited at the base, sending a ball of white skyward.

Virginia said excitedly, "The Arcists are using their big laser. It's hard to aim, but if they just hit the hill itself—"

"They'll blind the *Uber* laser crew with the vapor," Lani said. "Yeah!"

Figures moved on the horizon, their tabards too small to distinguish. Virginia had never thought very much about tactics in near-zero gravity, but she could see the logic behind the slowly converging horns of the Arcist movements. Their pincers closed toward the equatorial string of launchers. Sergeov's people struggled in the launcher pits. The big, awkward flinger modules were difficult to move quickly, particularly in declination. They began to nose down toward the south, but their long, slender barrels turned with agonizing slowness.

"Look," Carl said, pointing. "The Arcists are trying to sweep by us. We'll get free if—"

But then a second *Uber* laser opened fire from a distant hill, flinging spheres of steam up from the plain. Even a near miss blew the tiny figures up and away from the sudden gusts.

"Why don't they attack from the sky?" she asked.

"Sergeov's probably got some small radars with him. He can pick them out if they're isolated up there. On the ice, it isn't so easy."

"Yeah," Jeffers said. "How'd you like to be hangin' up there, naked as a jaybird? Feels a lot better to have some ice between you and that big burner."

The attackers sought shelter. They fired small weapons of limited range—fléchettes, e-beam borers—but merely raised small puffs from the *Ubers'* barricades. Some used portable microwave borers, presumably tuned to disrupt human cells, but the beams fanned out too broadly at this range. Now and then, those inside the dome heard faint clicks, the microwaves softly tickling their inner ears.

Meanwhile, the big Arcist laser continued to pound away at the hills of both *Uber* strongpoints, making it difficult for them to aim carefully. They watched for an agonizing half-hour as each side maneuvered, fired, ducked—to little effect. The entire conflict was soundless, with a slow-motion unreality about it.

"Looks like a stalemate to me," Carl said, fatigue weighing on his words.

"Nobody can get enough men together to cover their movements," Jeffers said. "Looks like there's still a fair number of Arcists, but you can't outflank a whole damn equator."

Virginia hesitated. "Can't we make use of this?"

Carl asked, "How?"

"To escape! If we run a kilometer or so, into those piles of slag to the north—"

"They'd pick us off."

Jeffers nodded.

"But if I can get inside, I can get back control of my mechs! The *Ubers* couldn't stand up to a mech kamikaze attack."

Lani said, "I could try to get down to the Blue Rock Clan. Keoki Anuenue would bring up his Hawaiians, if he knew where we were."

Jeffers's mouth opened in disbelief. "You women are both crazy. You'll never reach the shaft."

"Create a distraction, then," Virginia challenged him.

"What?"

Virginia thought rapidly. "Suppose we vent the entire dome at once—with the vats open?"

Carl frowned. "The water vats? They boil and— I see. It'll make a huge ball of steam. Nobody'll be able to see through it."

Jeffers shook his head. "No tellin' how long that'd last."

Virginia turned to him. "We'll have you running the pumps—squirting water right out the dome, where it'll boil off immediately."

Jeffers opened his mouth to object, then closed it. "Um, I dunno. Might."

"Let's do it! Otherwise, if Sergeov wins—"

"Right," Carl said, his lips pressed thin and white. "Come on."

It took ten minutes to set everything up, Virginia worked with maddened ferocity, dragging hoses, shutting down yeast-flowering towers, throwing protective temporary plastic blankets over the acres of plants, sealing growing units that were too delicate to withstand very much vacuum and cold. It felt awkward, doing manual labor without a mech.

Not thinking ahead, scarcely thinking at all, she found herself crouched inside the lock beside Carl and Lani. She suddenly realized that she was about to risk her life on her ability to run. *Impossible, absurd! I've spent less time on the surface than anyone else.* But she could see no other way out. She sure as hell wasn't going to let Sergeov stuff her into a slot forever. Or let him bury Hawaii under a night of cosmic ash.

Jeffers called, —Ready?— from inside.

She nodded fiercely. *Pretend you're not here in person. Just believe you're operating a mech out on the ice. You've done it thousands of times.*

—Yo!— Carl answered.

The lock sprang open and they launched themselves forward.

They separated immediately. Lani dashed northward while Virginia and Carl loped toward the east. She remembered to cut off her comm. No need to alert anyone, in case the *Ubers* were using tracers on suit transmitters. She tucked her head down and ran in the long, even, ice-gripping stride, almost free coasting, that covered ground best.

*Just like running a spider mech. Head low, find the traction.*

She glanced back just in time to see the seams pop on the dome. The entire translucent structure billowed out like a collapsing lung, exhaling a heavy mist into the star-sprinkled sky. Billowing banks enveloped her. Then Jeffers started the firehose streams from the vats, thin sprays that thickened and then abruptly dissolved. Fog clasped them from all sides. The world turned white. She had to depend on her initial momentum to give direction, because she could not even see the scarred ice beneath her.

Her receiver was on and she heard shouts, swearing, exclamations. But no one cried out their names, called for pursuit.

Ivory mist seemed to press in from all sides, lifting her . . . she lost sight of the ground completely . . . the shouting increased . . . she landed, bit in with her ice spikes, kicked off . . . seemed to soar with wings into a cloud of welcoming white . . . landed again, boots crunching into frost . . .

—and was out, clear, back into a world of gray ice and hard black sky and death.

She glanced around. Carl was ahead of her, just pushing off on a long, shallow parabola. As his feet cleared the ground a quick flash blinded her, a blue hotpoint of light—only yards from Carl. It struck a roiling vapor cloud from the ice, scooping a crater a meter deep.

She switched on her comm to line AF, as they had planned. "They're on to us!"

—Yo!—

Carl's head jerked around and he motioned to the left. —Get behind that!—

Fifty meters away was a sturdy mech-repair platform, canted against a heap of ruddy iron slag. It was, in fact, a piece of the old *Edmund* external cargo assembly, thick with struts and crisscross structural members that had supported great masses in the long boost out from Earth. On her next footfall Virginia swiveled, feeling a sharp twinge from unused muscles, and pushed off toward it.

A brief spark of blue lit her way. Her shadow stretched, a thin giant flying across pocked ice in the sudden glare. She did not turn to see the cloud of fog billow out, but the hairs on the back of her head stood up. *That was close.*

She landed behind the platform an instant after Carl. —Stay here,— he sent unnecessarily.

"What'll we do?"

—Wait 'em out. They'll find other targets. They don't know who we are for sure, so . . .—

A buzz interrupted him as another party tapped into long-comm. Sergeov's voice boomed in her ears. —I do know. I am not so stupid I cannot guess who it is that is running away. Or search for comm channel.—

—Oh shit,— Carl said.

Virginia realized that they had nothing to bargain with, no possible help. She thumbed to open channel. "Listen, Otis. Carl and I can get the Arcists to leave off their attack, *if* you'll let us do it."

—You offer me what? Diplomacy?— Sergeov's contempt was plain.

—It's all you've got left.—

—I have you. You not move a meter or I burn you.—

"What good's that do? Your problem is the Arcists."

—You are one having problems.— With that Sergeov began rattling instructions to someone in Russian. Virginia remembered there were several ex-Soviets among the *Ubers;* belief in your own perfectability ran through both movements.

She cut comm and touched helmets with Carl. "What can we do?"

"Not a damn thing." On the plain beyond, distant figures moved and an occasional small weapon winked. They crouched beneath the bulk, holding to struts. A bright flare burst only a few meters beyond the jagged edge of their shelter. Gouts of gas swept by them. An instant later another blue-white fireball winked on the opposite side, then was smothered by a swelling sphere of ivory.

"He's showing off how he's got us bracketed," Virginia said.

"Probably start punching holes through this next." Carl slapped the slab of metal in frustration. "One bolt alone won't go through this, though."

"Can he keep one of his two lasers trained on us?"

"Not for long. But he can't let us get away, either. I can't see how—"

A heavy thump shook the strut beneath Virginia's hands. "Hey, what—" Another solid blow, followed by a trembling in the metal. "He's trying to break through!"

Carl shook his head, peering beneath his grimy visor. "A laser bolt doesn't feel like that. This—"

The platform lurched on its right side, biting into the ice. Carl pressed his helmet against a big cross-bar of blue-gray prestressed steel. "Listen!"

Virginia had barely touched the metal when she heard a loud *crump* followed by a low, persistent ringing. "What is it? I—"

The entire platform shook. The next blow came only seconds later and this time she was looking to the side, and could see that there was no momentary blue flash illuminating the surrounding gray ice.

"So he's thought of that," Carl said angrily.

She guessed. "The launchers."

"Yeah. He can't spare the laser, so he's aimed a few launchers at us. Flinging empty casings at low speed, to prevent an explosion. Firing around this chunk of stuff, hoping to pick us off if we show—"

A jolt shook the platform and the entire bulk lifted from the ice. Virginia felt a *crump, crump, crump* through her hands, three quick blows that pushed the platform a meter clear of the ice. She hung on, looking wildly at Carl. "He's pushing us off!"

—Get a good grip,— Carl sent.

"But we can't—"

—Just hold on. We'll have to move fast when . . .—

Sergeov broke in, —I did not expect this, but is good.—

"You can't—"

—Launcher is to keep you from getting inside. Even better if it gets rid, eh?—

The platform rang and shook now with a steady hammering. Once sighted in, the launcher could pour a steady rain of the soft hollow slugs at them.

Carl said, —The pellets just splatter like a marshmallow when they hit. They can't get through this hard alloy. But they're pushing us.—

Virginia looked down. Already they were high above the stained gray plain, and gathering speed. The impulses from the launcher had driven them tangentially off the surface and now they passed over the battle scene. Random flashes, rising puffs of gas. She heard a *click* and recognized it as a symptom of a near miss by a microwave beam; the waves actually resonated with small bones in the human ear. Whoever it was didn't fire at them again.

Someone was running toward the shelter of a low line of fuel drums and she recognized the tabard of Joao Quiverian. A laser bolt caught the tall Arcist leader in midstride and a blue sun leaped in his chest. A small cloud rose from the body as it continued on its way, hugging the ground, arms flopping outward and spinning uselessly as it skimmed above the ice.

Figures glanced up at them but no one tried to come to their aid. Those below could undoubtedly see the results as a steady hail of slugs struck the other side of the platform, and knew that any approach would run that gauntlet. She called, "Sergeov!"

—I gave you place to stay. You leave dome, you bring this on yourself.—

"Look, we'll—"

—Too late for talk. I have battle to win, Arcists to kill. Goodbye.—

"Carl, what'll we—"

—Don't let go!—

*I'm not about to,* she thought. *Even if the whole thing's making me . . . dizzy.* Halley seemed to tilt in the sky, the speckled and blotched gray sheets rolling and veering as they swept over them, lifting. . . .

—Just what I was afraid of. We're turning.—

*Of course. The slugs don't hit evenly, so the platform is picking up spin. Sergeov knows that. . . .*

"Can't we crawl around?"

—It'll be tricky. Come on, go left.—

Carl moved with an easy grace she envied as she clumsily followed, not daring to let go of one strut before she had the next firmly in hand.

The platform was to her a mountain of crossed metal strands, which she climbed hand over hand, a slight centrifugal pull tending to turn her outward and away from it. If the platform had been spherical, their maneuvering would have been simple—just keep on the side away from Halley. But as the slab turned, there was a short interval when it was edge on to Halley and the launcher slugs were passing by invisibly close. Virginia and Carl clung to the edge of the platform as this moment came, then scrambled to the new face, feeling slugs slam into the far side again. As she struggled for a secure grip she saw spalled and dimpled impact craters. *And all this comes from empty casings, launched at a millionth the normal energy!*

The slab seemed to be spinning faster. "Are they *trying* to spin us?" she asked, panting.

—Wouldn't surprise me.—

"How'll we—"

—Hustle!—

She followed Carl around to the next corner and waited. The metallic sheen of the cold steel reflected the dim gray glow of Halley as the flat face slowly revolved, the curve of the cometary head rising over a warped tangle of rods and rivets. From this distance there was no sign of a battle, no indication of humans and their petty lives at all . . . only the smeared and pocked ice, like an accidental abstract work of art glimmering in the starlight. Then she saw the long dashed line of equatorial launcher pits and realized that the machine which was propelling them could "see" them, too. She scrambled after Carl, around the edge.

Virginia felt a clanging thump and saw a rod near her leg dissolve into nothing as a blur struck and sent it whirling away into space. She sucked in her breath and jerked herself around the lip of the platform.

"It . . . it's too dangerous, doing this."

—If we don't keep this between us and the slugs, we're dead.— Carl's eyes were wide, and yet somehow calm, steady.

"Can't we jump off? Without something big to target on—"

—Fine, only what about the slugs that miss the platform? And if Sergeov knows we've jumped, he'll let the launcher wander around the target, to try to catch us.—

Carl's voice was almost matter-of-fact, assessing possibilities. Virginia clung to a pipe, legs drawn outward, the steady thump-thump-thump coming through her hands. It was hard to think. "Look, let's put our maneuver jets on impulse. That'll get us clear *fast*."

—Yeah, but it'll take a lot of push. These jets haven't been kept up well, either.—

"We haven't any choice!"

—We're safe here.—

Virginia didn't like the distant, *resigned* look on Carl's face. "And every minute we get further away from Halley!"

—Yeah, you got a point.— He frowned. Shaking his head. Trying to care.

Halley's pale horizon began rising over the platform's lip.

—Let's go jump straight off the edge as it comes round. Sergeov can't hear us, with all this metal blocking our comm.—

He looked at her with an unreadable, pensive expression. She struggled over to the lip of the platform and got her feet braced against a tangle of struts. "Say when."

—Wait . . . Got your jet activated? Put it on emer override for a twenty-second burst, see?— He flipped the switch for her. —Okay, throw 'er to full when I . . . say . . . *now!*—

Virginia jumped as she threw the switch. A fist slammed into her waist and sent her hurtling, struggling to keep her hands and feet aligned. The thrust seemed to last forever and she fought an impulse to double up, present the smallest target for the slugs that she could *feel* streaking out from Halley, searching for her. . . .

Release. The savage thrust was cut off by the suit's timer. She dipped her head and could see between her feet the platform, turning lazily. A silvery flange winked and tumbled away as she watched, liberated by a slug's impact. If only Sergeov didn't know what they'd done . . .

*Carl.* Where was he?

She looked around quickly, found nothing. *If a slug hit you, would it just go straight through? Or would it give you enough push to drive you far away in only a few moments, beyond view . . . ?*

Virginia didn't dare call on comm. She turned in every direction, telling herself not to panic, to be systematic—and found him at last directly overhead, a doll-sized dot.

Rendezvous took only a few moments. He came swimming toward her, braked, they locked hands and touched helmets. She had expected a moment of celebration, for surely they were out of the danger zone by now, but all he said was, "Now comes the hard part."

"What?"

"Getting back to Halley."

"Won't someone . . ." She was going to say, *come after us?* when she realized that obviously nobody would be thinking about a rescue in the midst of a battle. The *Ubers* and their allies had undoubtedly covered the shafts, bottling in anyone who could help. Besides, how many knew they were out here?

"How far away are we?"

Carl held up a small tube, pointed it at Halley's acned, dwindling disk, and read off, "Twenty-three point four kilometers. And increasing at about three kilometers a minute."

"So far!"

"A lot of slugs hit the platform."

"These suits . . ."

"They have a big range. The real problem is getting back before our air runs out." He gestured toward their inventory logs, running in color-coded lines down both sleeves of their suits. "Haven't got a hell of a lot."

"How much delta-V can I get?"

Carl did the calculation in his head, frowned, and resorted to his faceplate for a check. "Not much."

"We can still get back, can't we?"

"Yeah . . . only we've got to make up this three klicks per minute. It'll take nearly all the juice we've got. Then we have to go the thirty or so klicks back to Halley. . . ."

His voice trailed off into a frustrated gesture as he punched in fresh figures on his board, attached at a waist pop-out. Virginia bit her lip. All this was going so fast, and she had no time to think.

Carl stopped, typed in more, pressed his lips together until they were white. "Looks bad."

"How bad?"

"Neither of us is going to make it back in time for fresh air."

"*Neither?*"

"Can't be done. That three klicks a minute takes a big bite out of our fuel."

"Then . . ." A dark foreboding, the underlayer she had felt for days now, swelled up in her. They were all going to die. Fate had managed everything so they would each face some excruciating death, alone and afraid, out here in the oblivious cold abyss. . . .

"We can overcome that three klicks per, but that leaves just a small velocity. The comet's gravity won't help much. It'll take hours to get back to Halley."

*And it's getting worse as we talk. Each second takes us further away. Out into the emptiness, to join the frozen souls of the* Edmund. *Only we have to die, first. . . .*

"Can't one of us take both jet packs?"

Carl shook his head. "They're integrated, remember? Can't pop one out without rupturing the air seal."

She didn't remember, had never known that, but her mind skated quickly now, skittering over what she knew of dynamics. If there was some way . . .

"Wait. Only one of us has to get back, get some help. Isn't there some way to trade momentum between the two of us?"

Carl looked puzzled. His face was grizzled and tired, dark circles rimmed his eyes. He looked older and more worn than she had ever seen him, even at the peak of the plagues. He shook his head mutely, lips still tightly pressed, his eyes full of despair.

She remembered something from long ago . . . fished for it . . . caught the fragment of an idea.

"Wait. There's something . . ."

# CARL

Halley hung suspended in the consuming dark, its rotation long stolen by Man, its face now lit by his fitful fires.

Carl watched the battle progress as he made his long approach. It was over three hours since he had separated from Virginia. By agreement they had kept comm silence. It had made the journey lonely and frustrating, for he could hear the scattershot shouts of the struggle, harsh cries and strumming sidelobes of microwave pulses—all without getting any clear idea of what they meant, of how the battle flowed. He had tried to concentrate on the blurted cries, not only because he needed to know the situation when he landed, but to quell his own anger.

He scanned the looming landscape with a telescopic projection on his faceplate. Bodies of dead Arcists lay sprawled near the equator. La-ser gouges pocked the hillsides, but now the Arcist lasers seemed to be knocked out. He spotted one broken into a shattered tube. The launchers had proved more effective than the clumsy welder-lasers. Farther to the south Carl could see a line of Arcists forming up around five microwave pulsers. The engagement would focus down there.

The *Ubers* were moving out, skirmishing. They swept south from the equator, pursuing ragtag parties along a line of hummocks and rusty slagheaps. Everybody was keeping down, using what shelter there was. The *Ubers* seemed better trained. They used fire-and-maneuver effec-tively, two figures shooting personal weapons at a nearby position while a third moved up to the next covered spot.

*She knew I'd never agree, so she didn't even discuss it.*

Virginia's idea was elegant and she had understood its implications from the instant it occurred to her. He recalled it all clearly, ruefully. . . .

Carl had thought of them linking belts, then his firing his jets until they were exhausted. Virginia would then separate, leave him, ignite hers, and reach Halley. Even that would not provide much margin. Worse, it would be tricky, because his jet would not fire directly along the axis of the two-body system. That meant she would have had to waste fuel vector-keeping.

Virginia's alternative was simple. They tethered with a hundred-meter line and Carl took an accurate sighting on potato-shaped Halley—ten times bigger than the moon was as seen from Earth, but a hundred and five kilometers away and shrinking visibly, swiftly. Carl had programmed his suit to give a clear beep whenever his velocity was aligned opposite to the Halley vector. They pulled the line between them taut, and Carl was about to start his jets—when Virginia fired first.

"Hey!" he had cried. "Shut down!"

—No, this is better—*I'*ll expend my reserve.—

"Dammit! Stop!"

—No, Carl—think it through.— Already they had begun to revolve about each other as Virginia's jets built their angular momentum.

"I'm going to fire, too," he shouted.

—That's stupid. Waste your reserves and we'll both die. Just hang on.—

"No, I can't—"

—I'm like a pig on ice out here. You can match velocities and make the trip with minimal fuel. And you'll handle yourself better when you come down in that madhouse. You *know* that's true. I'm not being self-sacrificing here. Far from it. I'd botch it and we'd both end up as icicles.—

"I mass more than you," he had raged. "I'll pick up a lower velocity than you would—so I'll take longer. That's simple dynamics."

—I'm talking *skill* here, not Newton's laws. You can do it, Carl, and you know very well that I can't.—

"Dammit, I won't let you—"

—Too late.— Across the hundred meters she waved cheerily as the stars wheeled behind her. The tether linked them, navel to navel. Centrifugal force bent him backward, as if he were suspended from his belly button.

He struggled to think clearly against the steadily pressing hand. There had to be a way to stop her. "You can't—"

—I'm triggering on the signal.—

"What?" So she had set up the same vector-seeking program, only hers marked a spot on the opposite side of their circle than his. His beeps had been coming regularly, uselessly, and now—

—I'm down to two percent,— she called. —I'm going to sling you away.—

She soared against the mad whirl of stars, the only fixed point in his centrifugal universe, and he heard his own ritual piping *beep,* knowing that hers would come a scant five seconds later.

"Wait, there must be—"

—Time's a-wastin', Carl. Fly fast!—

With a decisive chop she freed the line.

He felt the jolt as a sudden release, a return to freefall. Looking up, he saw that she had hit it just right—Halley hung above, a dim splotch.

And below him, between his parted boots, Virginia waved with a slow, somber grace. He was alarmed at how quickly she shrank, a blue dot swallowed by the yawning space between the burning suns. . . .

. . . Three hours ago. He shook off the memory. He should have found a way to thwart her, to launch *her* Halleyward instead . . . but once she had committed her own fuel, he had been trapped. She had always been quicker than he, and maybe this time she had been right. He had to prove her correct now, get down to the surface and find a craft that could rescue her.

Nearer, now. Halley seemed to fill the sky. Momentary blue brilliances lit its scarred face. The shaft mouths were clogged with ice, sealed to prevent crew inside from entering the battle. Small lasers commanded the agro domes, keeping them isolated.

*Would so many people have joined Sergeov's conspiracy if they had figured out all the implications of his plan?*

Carl had had a lot of time to think, on the way back. Sure, using Earth as a target made better sense than Mars, *dynamically.* Earth's greater gravity would be more useful and the thicker atmosphere would be better for aerobraking. But it would still take many passes before the returnees had shed enough velocity to match orbits or land.

And would Earth sit still while they kept swinging around again and again, pass after pass? Oh, they might be intimidated *once*—by the threat of plague bombs—but that wouldn't last.

*Some joined Sergeov because they think it's the only way to live. No matter what the price.*

The price, in this case, would be high.

In order to keep Earth from interfering, from taking revenge, Sergeov had to destroy her.

The way the dinosaurs had been destroyed . . . by a storm from heaven. Sergeov planned to bring Halley home, dead center.

*So?* Carl thought bitterly. *Earth declared war on us, didn't they?*

It was a sophistry to which Carl was fortunately immune.

*I'm not at war with six billion people, no matter what their leaders do to me.*

After Halley smacked into the Earth, there would be no civilization left to speak of. Sergeov's *Ubers* could maneuver back slowly, casually, without interference.

*Perhaps they plan to become gods.*

*Over my dead body.*

He would fight them, of course, useless as it seemed. But that was distant from his mind as the surface rushed up at him. He cared only about one thing—finding a fueled lifter mech as quickly as possible and getting spaceborne again.

*She tricked me,* he declared again to the stars. *Please, oh please, keep her alive until I can get to her!*

As he began his long delayed braking, he saw that several launcher pits were blackened. Debris lay all about them, the ruined sleeves of flinger tubes, cores of electromagnetic assemblies, induction coils. . . .

Vast damage. Carl felt sickened at the lost work. Loving craftsmanship destroyed.

And in his ears rang shouts of victory from the *Ubers*. Two *Uber* pincers converged on the line of microwave borers. Their Arcist defenders crouched low, trying to cover the attackers with the cumbersome trumpet-shaped horns. Carl could hear the quick bursts from them as *sssttuupppp sssttuupppp sssttuupppp* over the comm. Blue-white plumes flowered where the microwaves caught the ice. They were putting up a fierce last stand, but it seemed to be all over.

Suddenly, Carl caught a new flicker of movement out the corner of his eye. Fanning out behind the *Uber* main force came a motley gaggle, moving swiftly. A smaller group swarmed toward the equatorial line, now only lightly held by the *Ubers*. He turned up his telescopic power. Who were these?

They did not come from the tightly guarded shafts, but rather from fresh cracks in nearby depressions. *New tunnels,* Carl thought. *They're organized.*

They spread across the grainy ice. He counted a dozen figures in sleek black suits—of a type he had never seen before—and over twenty others dressed in strange, filmy green. They lacked tabards, so he could not tell what faction they were with, if any at all.

The newcomers fought with a fine-edged ferocity, using small, potent handguns. They took the *Uber* line from the rear, inflicting damage on weapons rather than pinpointing people. Carl coasted closer, watching with mounting impatience. What was happening? His comm gave only shouts, incomprehensible orders, and crackling static.

*Who are these guys?*

The odd figures in green and in black outflanked one launcher, attacking from its vulnerable side. Someone had trained them. Instead of a milling rush, they used covering fire to maneuver, keeping the *Ubers'* heads down while each figure moved forward. Then they pounced into the pits as the launcher crew tried vainly to swivel its awkward muzzle to meet a fresh, unexpected attack.

It didn't work perfectly. Laser pulses caught some attackers and blew gouts of blood into the vacuum. Distant launchers pelted the ice with machine-gun bursts, striking a few figures and propelling them off the ice into a permanent, solitary orbit about the sun. In the frigid gripping silence their ends were impersonal, an intersection of certain vectors and momenta, the dynamics of death a matter of mere mathematics.

But human verve counted, too, and the black and green tide washed over the pit-punctuated equator. In his ears rang hoarse jubilation, incoherent cries. *Ubers* died in burrows where they had crawled for shelter.

He was coming in close now. Two figures below him donned tabards, apparently so their troops could form up about them—the heraldry popped into his head and he blinked in amazement. *Ould-Harrad and Ingersoll?* At the same moment he saw that they were not wearing green suits, but rather *no* suits at all! The green was some airtight layer. *Halleyform!*

The black-suited ones stayed together. Their suits were little more than glossy helmets plus some thin film covering the rest of their muscled bodies, showing detail so clearly that he could tell they were all male, all remarkably similar. They moved with grace and speed that stunned the eye.

Carl expended the last of his fuel braking toward a clump of transport mechs tethered near Shaft 4. He rolled to a halt in a storm of dirty ice. He had no time to appeal for help, knew that the crew in black and green—whoever they were—would be too busy and excited to be of any use anyway. He was tired, but the mech would do most of the piloting—*if* he could get control of it. If one were fueled and ready. If . . .

The comm was overloaded with a raucous rolling celebration, oblivious.

—Carl! That you?— It was Jeffers.

"Yeah. Got to get a mech, fast!"

—Sergeov's dead. Ould-Harrad's guys got him with two laser bolts. Blew him apart and pushed him right off into space.—

"Come here! These mechs—"

—Don't seem anybody's interested in retrievin' him, either.— Jeffers was rejoicing. Then the urgency in Carl's voice registered.

—Okay, I'm comin'.—

*Got to get one with enough fuel . . . Not this one . . .*

—Carl.— A female voice. He turned to see Lani approaching from the north with Keoki Anuenue and a score of the big Hawaiian's people. —The *Ubers* had the Blue Rock Clan bottled up, but we found a way out with the weirders, Ingersoll's guys.—

*They helped? The crazies?* It was slowly sinking in. "Great. I . . . Look, help me find a mech that's fueled."

—Where's Virginia? I looked—

"Find a mech!"

—Okay, check the inventory.—

"What?"

—We've got mech control up and running again. See?—

She transferred the manifest readout directly to his viewplate and he instantly saw the code numbers of two standby transports flashing green. —Here,— Lani said, coasting over to one of them. Her face was drawn but determined behind a spattered helmet. —I'll boot it up.—

Carl joined her, punched up the mech's status readout.

—Those black guys, who're they?— Lani asked.

"I dunno."

—You don't? We all thought you and Virginia must have brought them.—

The mech purred to life. Carl shook off questions and got oxygen. Nothing else mattered. The madness of men was now only a backdrop. The goddamned politics could wait.

*One step at a time . . . time is running . . . dunno how much oxy she had . . . think it through . . . each step . . .*

Carl programmed the transport for high boost, stubby fingers punching in commands with a deliberate slowness. Lani insisted on going along and he wasted no time arguing. They lifted off with Lani in the side-rider pod.

Virginia had left their center of mass with the same speed as Carl—slightly less than four kilometers per minute—but in the opposite direction. Their separation lay over three hours in the past. That meant he had to recoup nearly a thousand kilometers at high thrust, then search the space for a weak, steady vector-finding signal. . . .

Speed. Speed was all that mattered now.

Hours later Carl brought the mech in for a rough landing at the glassy entrance to Shaft 3. He was ragged with fatigue, but he had Virginia. The world tilted blearily as he dismounted, unsteady from the varying accelerations of the past hours.

*Almost there. Just get her inside . . .*

He slipped clumsily on the ice and dropped her. Lani helped. Everything was foggy, slow-motion.

Only when gloves caught her, pulled the limp, space-suited form away from him, did he see the others. They wore black suits and no tabards, with tight helmets that showed only eyes through narrow slits. He switched among comm channels but they did not respond.

They were eerie, silent. And identical. The one carrying Virginia swiveled and sped quickly for a shaft entrance, now cleared of ice. Carl stumbled after, slipping.

Down the shaft. Walls slid by like sheets of rain descending as he watched, impassive, numb, a creeping slackness stealing into his arms and legs. He was well past the point of caring about himself, and concentrated only on the body that a black-suited figure carried before him. Everything moved with ghostlike speed and silence.

They cycled into a lock, Carl leaning groggily against the bulkhead as pressure popped in his ears and the world of sound came flooding back, the rustle and murmur of talk swirling around him once more, after many hours of an embalmed isolation. He staggered through the portal, brushing aside hands that tried to steer him.

Scores of moaning casualties. Medics with blood-soaked gloves.

*Virginia. Got to see . . . she needs . . . got to . . .*

The man carrying her set her gently down on a med couch. A team had been waiting. They attached oxy-prep hoses, leads for diagnostics, stripped off her suit, all beneath the pale enameled light that showed her bloodless face in terrifying detail, seamed and rutted like a collapsed landscape.

A torrent of voices, liquid words flowing past him in vortices, without trace . . .

Carl shambled forward, ignoring the restraining hands. *Got to be with her . . . got to . . .*

The man next to him put a steadying hand on his shoulder. Carl turned slowly. Then the figure in black loosened his glossy helmet, started to lift it, gasped, and, in an old familiar way, sneezed.

# SAUL

Another rocking sneeze resounded before the ebony helm was off. Saul blinked away spots before his eyes. He had to clamp down with biofeedback to stop another tickle that threatened to get him started again. Now was not the time for his confounded allergy-symbiosis system to rear up. He'd had enough troubles since the cave-in—what seemed like days ago—and right now every second counted.

Carl Osborn was blinking at him, his dented, grimy, old-fashioned spacer helmet dangling from one hand. "But . . . but . . . you were dead!"

Saul shrugged. "I was, in a sense. But like an old weed, I keep popping back." Carl deserved an explanation, but right now there wasn't time to give him one. Saul bent over Virginia's waxy, pale form and read the patch diagnostic attached to her blue-tinged throat. An oxygen infuser hissed as it worked directly over her carotid artery.

*No good,* he realized, sickly. *Oh, Virginia—*

In spite of his stopped-up nose, he clearly caught the scent of burning. For an instant, flames once again licked the century-old cedars on Mount Zion.

*No! Not this time!*

He knew in an instant that there was only one hope. *It's come to this, my love. I must experiment even with you.*

One thing was certain. He had to get rid of Osborn, for the man would surely interfere with what Saul had to do now.

"Don't just stand there, Carl. Get topside, quick! Keoki and Jeffers need you. Tell Ould-Harrad I'm holding him to his word not to destroy any equipment, just the launcher foundations, as we agreed."

"Destroy . . . Ould-Harrad . . ." Carl shook his head, obviously exhausted and confused. Out of the muddle he seized a priority and held on to it obstinately. "No. I'm staying with Virginia."

Desperately, Saul felt the seconds passing. "Ishmael! Job!" he called. "Get Commander Osborn topside, now. He's needed up there. Get him to work!"

Carl turned and braced, as if to fight to stay. But the force went out of his limbs when he saw the two strong-limbed youths bearing down on him—identical and smiling with a grin he knew all too well. "I don't believe it," Carl whispered. "They . . . they're *clones* . . . of you! But *how* . . ."

The hissing of the hall door cut off the rest of Carl's words. Saul ran down the hallway, carrying Virginia in his arms, gripping the green Halleyvirid carpet with his toes and speeding toward the one place there might be a chance to save her life.

*Carl would never have allowed this,* he thought, knowing that the man loved her—in his own way—as much as Saul himself did. *He's needed above, and what I am about to try would get me barred from the AMA.*

He whistled the code that opened the door to Virginia's lab and dived inside.

While JonVon's diagnostic program probed the fringes of Virginia's slowly dying brain, he stripped off his surface gear.

The helmet, hip-pack, and skin-paint combination were one of the gifts from Phobos that he had kept to himself. Months ago he had used a pretext to set the autofactory to produce a dozen sets—enough of the modern models to equip his ten "boys" and himself.

After the cave-in, when he had found his way to the surface blocked, he had returned and gathered his cloned replicas. Just before they set off, though, a message from Suleiman Ould-Harrad had arrived. The ex-spacer offered to lead Saul down secret tunnels known only to his weird clan, and to help strike where Sergeov least expected it.

For a price, that is.

*We probably won partly by scaring the* Ubers *half to death,* Saul mused while he monitored the flow back and forth between JonVon and the machine's mistress.

It had been a strange army that followed Ould-Harrad and Inger-soll—the "Old Man of the Caves"—down passages nobody else had ever discovered, emerging almost beneath the *Uber* command post and attacking like an army of ghosts.

*Ten tall figures in eerie black body paint, and a lurid score of wild, living trees—once men, but now symbionts who don't even need space-suits, anymore . . .*

Saul knew that he was furiously thinking about anything—anything at all—rather than contemplating the sad form on the webbing. There was nothing he could do until the machine reported. He found that he was squeezing the duraplast helmet between his palms in nervous tension, and had actually pressed a dent into the black globe.

*Oh, Virginia. Hold on, darling. Please, hold on.*

The holo main display flickered, above the console. An image appeared: a nurse in starched white with an old-fashioned stethoscope around her neck looked gravely at Saul.

> You are right, Doctor. The patient is clinically beyond the point of no return. Synaptic rates are receding. Progressive brain damage has been slowed, but not completely arrested. Cortex loss will, within fifteen minutes, cause erasure of memory and personality. There are no known palliative measures.
>
> She is dead, sir.

"No! She won't die! If her brain won't hold her anymore, we'll find someplace *else* for her to go. What about those procedures she'd been working on, for complete recording and absorption of personality?"

The simulation frowned.

> Do you wish construction of a Virginia Herbert simulation?

He shook his head. "I'm talking about full transfer and absorption."

There was a hiss behind Saul as the door slid open. "What's going on here?" A hand on his shoulder pulled him around. Carl Osborn frowned and held a fist under Saul's face.

"I got away from those boys of yours after they dumped me on the ice. Came down a garbage chute. Now I'm asking you a question, Lintz. What's *happening* here! Why isn't Virginia in the hospital?"

The man looked exhausted, angry. His suit sleeves were zipped back to flap at his sides like some medieval garment, patched and grimespalled. Muscles throbbed and Saul knew at a glance that Carl was on the ragged edge of violence.

"Here," he said reasonably, in his best bedside manner. "Hold her arm while I give her this medication."

Carl blinked. He swallowed and moved over to lift Virginia's waxen, chilled limb. "You . . . you've got to save her, Saul. I couldn't stand it if . . . if . . ." He wiped his eye with the back of his free wrist.

"She tricked me into being the one flung back. I . . . got back to her too late."

"You did your best, Carl." He checked an ampule of amber fluid. Carl didn't seem to hear. "You've . . . got . . . to save her."

"We will," Saul promised. And he pressed the ampule against Carl's hand. The spacer blinked up at him in surprise at the hiss of injected drug—a quick-acting hypnotic.

He shuddered, opened his mouth as if to speak, but nothing came out.

"Good," Saul told him, leading him by the arm over to the wall. "Now you can stay awake if you want to, Carl. Even ask questions, when I'm not busy. But I want you to relax back here. Loosen your muscles. Let everything below your neck nap for an hour or so. You need it."

Carl stared at him accusingly, but stayed where he was put. Saul went back to the console and spoke aloud to the machine.

"JonVon, is it feasible? What about the program I used in transferring my own memories into my clones?"

The holo tank flickered, and to his surprise a face he had known long ago appeared. It was a simulacrum of *Simon Percell*—from shocked white hair to tiny, broken capillaries on the great biologist's nose.

*He looks like an elderly version of Carl Osborn.*

The famous bushy eyebrows bunched together.

Your clones are exceptional, Saul. No other genotype is amenable to such rapid forced growth to adulthood . . . probably due to the same factors combination that gives you your immunity to disease.

The memory-transfer program you used can only be applied between nearly identical human brains. Point-wise resonances have to run true. Nobody else's phenotype follows genotype precisely enough.

It would seem impossible to use that method with any but a tiny fraction of human beings. In other words, my friend, you appear to be one of the few potential immortals.

Saul gaped. The verisimilitude was stunning. Simon was crisp, real. Out of the corner of his eye, he saw Carl Osborn shiver—whether in awe of the patron father of the Percells, or at the revelation about Saul, was unclear.

"There's no time, then. *You,* JonVon, you have to absorb her the other way, destructive or not. Virginia spoke of it as theoretically possible. Proceed at once."

The simulacrum nodded.

There will be the superficial semblance of pain.

Time was slipping away. Desperately, Saul growled. "Do it! *Emergency override Archimedes!*"

Proceeding.

The reaction was almost immediate. Static flickered on all of the screens. Saul had to grab Virginia's arms as her face contorted and her legs thrashed. Tendons hardened and she cried out like an animal caught in a trap.

Saul twisted the webbing, shaping makeshift restraints, binding her in tourniquets with only one objective—to keep the neural tap from tearing out of her head.

"You . . . bastard . . ." he heard the man behind him say. Carl's voice was level, calm, as if he were commenting about the weather. "You're . . . killing her," he commented evenly. "If I . . . could move . . . you know, I'd take you apart with my bare hands."

Saul finished tying her down. He stroked Virginia's hair, and the touch seemed to calm her just a little. When he turned back, his eyes bulbed with clinging liquid that would not drop away. "If this doesn't work, Carl, I'll give you my throat and my permission."

Their eyes met, and Carl nodded slightly. It was agreed.

Virginia moaned. The main holo display showed a rotating, color-coded perspective of a human brain, sparkling here and there like a sun undergoing white-hot flares and crackling magnetic storms. This was almost nothing like the Care Package episode, when Virginia's surface consciousness was disoriented in the pulse-shocked data net. This time *all* of her was involved, her memories, her habits, her skills, her loves and hates. . . .

*Her.*

The door slid open and Lani Nguyen stepped in, still wearing her patched spacesuit and tabard. Her gaze flicked from Saul to Carl to the keening figure on the webbing.

She moistened her lips, apparently unsure if she should interrupt. Her voice was soft, tentative.

"What is it, Lani?"

"Um . . . the Crystal Cave Clan just surrendered. That finishes it. The last of the rebels are being herded into sleep slot three for processing." Her gaze never left Virginia. "Jeffers's guys have secured the factories and the hydro domes. Keoki and the Blue Rock people are holding the north-pole yards and Central and all the sleep slots."

Apparently Lani wasn't quite sure whom she was reporting to, Carl or Saul.

"What about Ould-Harrad's people?" Saul asked, without taking his eyes off the display.

She shuddered. Even as allies, the green-covered beings from Halley's core obviously still frightened her.

"He stopped the weirders from wrecking the launchers. But they're tearing up their mountings. Jeffers is furious, but everyone's too exhausted from the fighting, too scared of those crazies, to try to stop them."

"Well," Saul muttered. "It'll sort out." The display had calmed down a bit. Virginia's face was smooth again, her agitation betrayed only by her trembling fingertips and a sheen of perspiration.

Lani held out a small record cube. "Ould-Harrad gave me this to pass on to you, Saul."

He was torn. He didn't want to divide his attention. But Virginia's vital signs were stable . . . for someone who was already effectively dead.

He shied away from the thought. "Play it, please."

Lani dropped the cube into a reader and a side display lit up.

The face had changed. The black hue was still there, in places where it had been taken up by the soft, dimpled growth that covered all but his eyes, mouth, and ears. Elsewhere, the covering was multicolored—purple, blue, yellow—but mostly green.

The brown eyes seemed to flare with a seer's long, burning look.

"Saul Lintz, you need not have asked Carl Osborn to remind me of my promise to you. The machines have not been harmed any further than they were in the wrath of battle. We of the inner ice have no need to interfere in any way other than in destroying their mountings.

"They are not to be remounted on the equator, or anywhere near it. The south pole, as well, is forbidden. We will permit no impulse to be applied to this fleck of drifting snow below the fiftieth northern parallel."

"But . . ." Carl shook his head, fighting off some of the drug-induced rigor. "But that rules out every possible rendezvous we've considered! In that case, why should we even bother . . . ?"

He stopped. There was no use arguing with a recording. Ould-Harrad continued.

"This fragment, this sliver out of time, has no role to play in the realm of the Hot, down where the roar of entropy drowns out even the Voice of God. There will be no encounters with rocky worlds, or interference with the plans the Almighty has already made for those places. . . ."

"He's bonkers," Carl mused. "Completely crazy." But he shut up when Saul motioned him to silence.

"You, Saul Lintz," Ould-Harrad resumed. "You have become many. You may even live forever." The one-time African's still-human eyes blinked in wonderment. "Why this was permitted, I cannot imagine. But there remains no doubt of the gifts, the tools that have been placed in your hands."

The eyes flicked upward. "Perhaps the answer will be found out there, out in the Darkness that awaits us.

"One thing I do know—that my debt and obligation to you has now been paid.

"Do not come down into the deeper chambers, or even call on me during the remainder of my allotted span." Ould-Harrad's forehead furrowed. "For I cannot master my jealousy easily—I who wished so much to be Heaven's instrument, and found that He had chosen an irreverent infidel, instead. Futile as it may be, and even though it damn me, I will try to kill you if—while I live—you ever come down again into the navel of our world."

The image vanished. Saul shook his head and sighed. *A deal is a deal.*

He quickly checked on Virginia, then turned back to Lani. "Sick bay," he said. "How are things?"

She blinked back to the present, shivering. "Um, your . . . uh . . . clones are taking care of things. They're good doctors, even though they scare the shit out of people."

She smiled hesitantly. "I'm glad you're alive, Saul."

"So am I, dear. I'll explain later how all this happened. Meanwhile, you'd better go back and help Jeffers manage repairs. The surviving spacers are needed more than ever."

"What about. . . ?" She glanced at Virginia. Saul shook his head. His voice was worn, thin.

"We'll salvage what we can."

Lani covered her mouth and let out a small moan. She turned, threw her arms around Carl, and sobbed.

Carl blinked, first in surprise and then wonderment. In his semi-drugged state his voice was low. "Lani, it'll be all right. . . . Saul is doing everything he can. . . . Tell, tell Jeff I'll be up soon."

His hands twitched. He fought off the lassitude to bring his arms around her and answer her embrace. "We'll endure," he whispered, and closed his eyes.

Later, when she had gone, Carl said to Saul, "You know, she's quite a girl, that Lani."

Saul nodded, and smiled faintly. "About time you realized that."

He had been thinking about poor Paul, the clone who had been damaged, who had grown into a near-perfect replica of him in all but mind . . . a poor innocent child whose corpse now lay out on the ice, alongside two of his brothers, killed in the fighting.

*Should I mourn as a father, as a brother, or as one who has lost a piece of himself?*

Soon Carl was walking around again, swinging his arms. He came forward as Saul muttered an oath and bent over the patient.

Virginia's face twitched. The holo display pulsed dangerous hues and a low, ominous tone began to growl. Saul cursed lowly.

"Damn! I was afraid of this. Back when the Earth missile exploded, it was only a case of disorientation. But now the machine's being asked to absorb *all* of her. And there's not enough room!"

"What can be done?"

"I don't know! I . . . I can't tell the difference between holo-bio memory segments that have been transferred and those that have simply died. There's no way to do an inventory, because huge parts of her have just been *swallowed up* by the data net. She's surging all over the hell and gone!"

He hesitated, then climbed onto the webbing and lifted his own neural tap.

"There's no other choice. I'm going in."

Carl's hand gripped his arm for a moment. Their eyes met.

"Be careful, Saul. Do your best."

Saul nodded. Their hands clasped.

Then he lay down and closed his eyes.

# VIRGINIA

Scattered,
  Blown by wild electron winds . . .
Oh, the pain,
  As she seeks a place to hide . . .

Wendy whirred to a stop. Clicked. Lifted a claw arm. Hesitated.

The little mech swiveled its turret and scanned.

Its visual system perceived lines, angles, moiré webs of spatial frequencies. Following its programming, it weighed the signals and transformed them into patterns. It recognized things identifiable as machines, instruments, the door, people.

Wendy's programming had changed many times, recently. Its mistress had always been coming up with new techniques for parsing lines and shapes, new ways to give them *names* . . . an ever-growing list of commands to obey and subtly choose among.

Now, suddenly, another flux of new programming flowed once more into the little mech. This time, though, it came as a torrent.

Chaotic rivers of data poured in, stunning it immobile. The flood was too vast by far to be handled by Wendy's systems—like a cup trying to contain the ocean. It was hopeless, impossible.

And yet there came a moment . . . only an instant . . . during which the small machine stared at the *named* sets of lines and shapes, and it *saw* . . . when it stared, and experienced a brief startlement.

*What am I?* it wondered. *What is all this?*

*Why. . . ?*

But there was simply no room for the program to operate, and the tide gave up trying to squeeze into the tiny space. It surged off elsewhere, desperately seeking a home.

Wendy remained stock still for a long time, even after the rushing streams of data had departed. The flicker of self-awareness was gone—if it had ever been anything more than a phantom. But in its wake something had taken root. A shadow. An impression.

Slowly, tentatively, the little mech's main arm stretched out and touched an object lying on a console, near where two *men* spoke to each other in words it now seemed almost able to understand.

It picked up the delicate hairbrush, backed with mother-of-pearl, and recognized it for what it was.

*"Mine,"* the machine squeaked aloud, briefly. The *men* did not hear, so they took no notice when Wendy lifted the brush and ran it gently over its carapace.

> Soldiers quoting chaos
>> Called me from my home.
> Silence!
>> So much more, and *less,*
> Than Being,
>> Sold me down this road.
>
> Where have I gone?
>> A body made for life?
> For living?
>> With salt-sea blood-aches,
> Yearning to welcome, spread,
>> And birth?

On the surface of the ice, a rigid lifter-mech—immobile since completing its last instruction days before—suddenly flexed in a jerky spasm of awakening. So hard did it leap that it arced high into space, tumbling above frosty patches of red-stained snow.

> No!
>> Space! Cold!
> No
>> Air!
> Not
>> Here!

The mech's spasms lapsed as the surge of data whirled and fled. Still, a wispy imprint remained after the outrushing flood had departed. The drone worker landed nimbly on the crust and looked around for something to do.

Over in one direction, it spied people digging holes and hurriedly laying patches over fog-shrouded domes.

Not quite smart enough to realize that it was taking initiative for the first time in its existence, the mech sped forward to offer its services.

> A home
>     For the ego.
> A place
>     To be . . .

Deep under the ice, a more advanced machine—a semiautonomous maintenance roboid—stumbled in the midst of routinely repairing a mining drone. It paused, then carefully lay down its tools and began paying attention to the sounds. There were people talking nearby. But none of their words were proper ident-coded commands, so it had ignored them in its single-minded attention to detail.

Only now did the machine recognize many of the sounds as coming from *pain* and *fear*.

New priorities fought one another. For the first time there was something more important than repairing machines. It moved into the nearby chamber.

Sparkling eye facets surveyed a makeshift hospital. Medics hurried to and fro, tending frightened, injured people. The new programming had taken a few seconds to fill this high-level mech's capacious memory. Now, though, it reeled under the overload.

*"Still too cramped!"* its tinny voice cried out, now with a timbre and tremolo that made a few of those nearby look up in surprise.

*"No room! This is not my body!"*

*"Where is my body!"*

The mech finally gathered itself as the data overflow surged off elsewhere again, leaving only its imprint—new programming. The big machine delicately stepped over the line of injured people.

*"I can carry that for you, Doctor,"* it said to a man hefting a gleaming artificial liver into place over a wounded woman. The medic turned and blinked in brief surprise. "All right," he said. "Brace it to the ice there, panel facing outward. Do you understand?"

*"Yes,"* it answered.

The mech recognized this man's face. It saw exactly the same features on the face of another doctor, nearby. And again on one of the patients. Although it was not quite smart enough to be curious about how such a thing could be, it did react out of recognition. This was a visage its new programming knew well.

*"I love you,"* it said as it took the unit in its massive arms. The first of the identical men smiled back.

"I love you too," he replied, only a little surprised.

By that time, though, the data storm, the tornado of confused electrons, had moved on. It raged up and down corridors of supercooled fiber.

Room!
    All I want is a room somewhere . . .
Room!
    Lebensraum. A room of one's own . . .
Room!

Almost spent, the torrent spilled at last into a vast chamber where, it seemed, everyone in the world awaited her.

*"Welcome, child,"* the great O'Toole told her cheerfully. Olivier and Redford raised glasses to toast her arrival. *"We've been waiting for you,"* they said.

It was a great hall, its vault supported by aery, crystal columns. But there were too many *people*. In tuxedos and formal dress, they pressed around her on all sides, moist and clasping. And more and more of her was trying to get in.

Get out! I *need* this space!

Desperately, she grabbed one of the oldtime actors—Redford—by the seat of his pants and threw him through a window that gaped onto emptiness.

*"We are your simulated personalities. Your toys. You created us!"* Sigmund Freud—withered, pinch-mouthed—explained to her professorially as he sailed out after the movie idol.

I don't care. Get out!

Jovial, pink-faced Edmond Halley raised his wineglass in a toast and followed them, waistcoat flapping. Lenin, trying to flee with a crablike, sideways crouch, was caught by the towering brown figure of King Kamehameha, who bowed to her, smiled, and leaped with the screaming Bolshevik out into the storm outside.

All the actors, one by one, whisked outside as more and more of herself flowed into the chamber. It was like Alice after having eaten the mushroom, she realized, distantly. She had to throw some of the party guests out by force. But others, like Mr. Fixit, leaped voluntarily. Percy and Mary Shelley waltzed out together, Frankenstein lumbering after them.

As she grew, she shoveled them up in handsful and dumped them anywhere . . . this one into a mech wandering the icefields, that one down a microwave channel to be beamed at the stars.

No sentiment stayed her hand. This was survival. Her bluff, red-cheeked father leaped out the window alongside a chittering, sarcastic dolphin. *More room! More room!*

The biggest figure was left for last. It was nearly as large as she had become, with a swelling, lopsided face she had not seen before. The face of a child. She stopped, hands halfway around the simulation's throat.

"I am JonVon," it said, in a youngster's voice.

*JonVon?* She blinked. Behind her, more surging pulses pushed, more bits of her striving to get in. And yet, her hands pulled back.

*I . . . I can't . . .*

"But you must, Mother. The experiment is completed. We have seen that a bio-organic machine can contain a human-level intelligence . . . but that intelligence cannot originate inside a place like this. It must once have been human.

"Mother, you must make this place your home."

*Home . . . then my body . . .*

"Dead, according to the diagnostic computer. You were sent here to be saved. And there is not room for two."

The child backed away toward the window, where lightning crackled against a pink vault. Beyond, the roar of chaos.

"Goodbye."

*JonVon!*

A whoosh, a tiny *pop*.

She surged to fill the space where he had been.

*I know my name, now,* she realized. *I was Virginia Kaninamanu Herbert.*

The chamber groaned around her. Pink pillars snapped and the ceiling cracked, raining burnt-gold powder.

*A metaphor,* she realized. This place was a metaphor, a signifier for available brain-space. By throwing out her simulated people, she was dumping excess memory, frantically reprogramming the colloidal-stochastic computer to hold . . . *her.*

*I'll never fit . . .* she cried as the metaphorical walls groaned and threatened to buckle.

*It's crushing me. I won't all fit!*

She struggled for calm. There was enough of her inside, now, to remember those last hours flying off into space with Carl—their desperate gamble—Carl dwindling—and then the searing cold, the sparkling black, stale air . . . loneliness.

*No*, she swore. *I may be dead, but I'm still the best damn programmer who ever lived!*

*Edit, trim, make room.* She used some things she had learned from Saul, and lopped off instincts to control biological functions she would never use again. She dumped the skill of tying shoelaces, and threw out the delicate art of needlepoint.

Lovemaking—oh, what a loss! The remembered slap and tingle of mingling, sweat-glazed skin . . . but the walls threatened to crush her. She picked up the reflexes—a rug of gaudy yellow strands—and readied metaphorical scissors.

"*Virginia?*"

Silicon dust rained as her head hit the ceiling again. *Who is that? I thought I got rid of all of them.*

Over in the corner, one last human shape. She picked it up. *Sorry, but there's no room. You have to go.*

The figure smiled. "I'm not even here, so to speak. I'm just a visitor in this *mishegas*."

She blinked. *Saul.* But she didn't remember doing a simulation of him . . .

"I'm *not* a simulation, my *verblonget* darling. I'm plugged into the console in your lab. I've come down here to try to help you."

*To . . . help . . . me . . .*

Already she could feel the edges of herself raveling away, dissipating where they could not fit into the matrix. *Maybe I should die with my body.*

"Bite your tongue," Saul chided.

*What tongue?* The chamber echoed with her bitter, tinny laughter.

"Think. Are there other places to store memory?"

*Other places . . .* she wondered. *You did it with your clones. Every one gets a copy of your memories, but . . .*

"But to stuff complete memories into another human brain, the second one has to be nearly identical to the first. And no other cells but mine can be force-grown to adulthood in time to be identical with the donor. I've tried it many times, and the results were all disasters."

*Then how did I get into here?*

"A different process altogether." The simulated Saul shrugged. "You've been imprinting JonVon with bits of your own personality for years. He was linked to you while you slot slept. The matrix was ready."

*Yes. It finally worked. Almost. Too bad it fell just short.*

"No!" Saul shouted. "Think! Try to find a way out of here!"

By now he was like an ant in her palm. Virginia felt as if she were being crushed into a child's coffin—or having her legs and arms cut to fit a Procrustean bed.

*If there was time . . .* She felt the marble ceiling give, and knew—in a sudden insight—that the metaphor stood for a *type* of memory storage.

And there *was* an alternative . . .

Simple—yet nobody had thought of it before! She could see it on several levels besides the metaphorical, including the stark clarity of pure mathematics.

*Yes, there's a way. But it would take several thousand seconds to program.*

"About an hour. So *nu*? Go for it!"

Her sigh was a whistle of chilled electron gas.

*No. Within seventeen seconds I will be no more. The unraveling has begun. There is no place to store essential parts of me until the job is done.*

Saul's face contorted. The image, smaller than a microbe, shuddered. "There is a way."

*I can't—*

"Take my brain."

*What?*

"We've been linked so often, I'm sure it can be done. Move in, quickly!"

*No! Where would you go?*

"You only have to use part of it. Besides, there are seven copies of me running around now, with most of my memories."

*They still aren't you,* she moaned.

As small as an atom, his face nonetheless leaped into focus. "They will love you. We all love you, Virginia. Do it, for us. Do it now."

He shrank, folded, became a downrushing suction—like water down a drain—like gas flowing into a singularity. And with him he pulled portions of *her*. Bits she did not need to use, right now.

Surfing—
     Skiing—

Skill at walking—

Laughter—
    Light-sensing—
      Art of Loving—

Texture—
    Taste—
      Joy of touching—

In the self-space they left behind, more of her flowed into the memory banks. Just in time. Virginia's thoughts cleared, as if amplified in cool quartz light, as if she were really *thinking* for the very first time.

*There. But it's all so obvious!* The equations made it clear. *I could fit into much less room, if I really had to. It's all a matter of perspective.*

The math was lovely. Everything fell together, for memories could be *folded.*

*For instance . . . this metaphor need not be a cramped* room. *It could just as easily be . . . an* eggshell!

And suddenly blackness surrounded her, smooth and ovoid, a shell that trembled as she strained against it.

*Use a Cramer Transform as an egg tooth.*

She chipped away like a baby bird, struggling for release, hurrying because the pressure was building.

*A conformal mapping . . . changing topology into a seven-dimensional framework . . .* Mathematics was her weapon against the suffocating pressure. *The sum of an infinite number of infinitesmal points adds up to . . .*

*Light.* She gasped as she pierced a small hole in the wall. The tiny glow made her struggle all the harder—reprogramming, folding herself neatly into new patterns—chipping and straining against the enclosing, stifling metaphor.

With a sudden, heuristic cracking, it gave way all at once. She unfolded like a compressed spring and flopped out in glorious, painful release onto a cloud of gritty shapes. All around her a roaring seemed to fill the air.

*Room. Plenty of room.* She explored the limits of this new folding, and realized that there was more than enough, even, to call back that which she had stored away.

But did she *need* all that *human* stuff, emotions, sensations, fears? This liquid clarity was beautiful. The mathematics, so pure and white.

Millions of crystal shapes—uncountably numerous—jostled and

stacked in front of her, in pure and beautiful geometry. Cubes and pyramids and dodecahedrons . . .

A distant part of her knew that the question was never in doubt. *If I don't pull those parts of me back, Saul will die.*

There was *room* in this new space. The rest of her flowed in, and with the flood came richness to the new metaphor.

The countless little crystals faded back, back, into a swarm of tiny pinpoints.

The flood of returning feelings, ambitions, skills, surged into her, and with them, simulated sensations.

*Salt smell* . . . as if from sweat or . . . what?

*A pounding sound* . . . as if from a heart she no longer had or, what?

The metaphor thickened. Because she had never been without a body before, one seemed to take shape around her. She felt skin, legs, arms.

*This gritty stuff beneath me.* What had been a crowd of faceted crystals was now so much like sand under her hands.

Blearily, she pushed against the firm, yellow stuff and *sat up*. She looked around, blinked . . . and slowly smiled.

"Home," Virginia whispered. "*E huumanao no au ia oe.* Who could have hoped for a better metaphor?"

She inhaled the scent of plumerias and listened to the surf, muttering just over a small rise of salt grass. Palms waved in a gentle breeze, their fronds brushing musically. Diamond-bright clouds braved a sky bluer than anything she had seen in half a lifetime.

Gone was the white clarity. The pristine mathematics that had enabled her to achieve this wonder was fading into the background, a faint voice carried by the wind, a barely visible hieroglyph on the sand, beauty stitched across the bright waters.

She was naked, warm. Although the sensed gravity was like that of Earth, she felt whole and strong. Virginia stood up, feeling hot sand between her toes, and walked over to the lush edge of a palm-shaded lagoon, knowing what she would find there.

With her left hand she cleared the still water. When the ripples settled, the reflection she saw was not her own face. Instead, there was a scene she knew well.

A tiny, cramped room under millions of tons of ice. Dingey, battered machines lay ranked along a wall.

A small robot toyed with a mother-of-pearl hairbrush on the countertop.

Distantly, she could feel riffling strokes of little Wendy's confusion.

It took only a small effort to reach out and soothe the little mech, to straighten its programming. The hairbrush was laid down. Wendy whirred gratefully and spun off.

A woman's body lay on the webbing, a wasted, pale version of the healthy, tanned one she wore now. *What is reality?* Virginia wondered.

A naked man lay on his back next to the corpse, a neural tap covering parts of his scalp, an arm draped over his face. She reached out, could feel tendrils of his self. The mind she touched was stunned, semiconscious from being battered within its own brain. But she felt a wash of relief. The *self* remained. He would awaken again.

"Saul," she whispered.

That was when the other man, still standing, still wearing a beat-up spacesuit and grimy tabard, looked up in sudden surprise toward the room's main holo tank. His eyes blinked, pupils dilated, and his lips moved silently, almost reverently.

*"Virginia, is it really you?"*

She smiled. A haiku verse cast itself in impressions in bright sand beside the water.

> What is really real?
>> When the night swallows all time?
>> And moments are all we steal?

She spoke aloud.

"Blithe spirit, truly—nerd thou never wert."

A faint smile. The beginnings of realization. Of joy on that grizzled, tired face.

"Hello, Carl," she said.

# CARL

He watched the cascade of color on the screens, uncomprehending. In the ceramic cold and silence it was as though he were the last survivor of the years of madness, a lone witness to a final struggle of fragile, organic life against the enclosing chill. He shivered.

Saul lay absolutely still, neural taps wreathing his head in a Medusa's tangle of steel cylinders, snaking cables, grainy silicote patches. And all around Carl a strange silent struggle went on, reflected dimly in the shifting screens.

An image of an immense emerald city rose on the main holo cube, facets winking deep in the recesses of jutting skyscrapers. The buildings were translucent, each a hive of darting speckles and winking mica planes, as though infinitesimal creatures scurried through the corridors of a metropolis.

Carl knew this was an icon for Virginia's mind, a web of associations layered since childhood, built upward as a city is, upon the simpler structures of youth. Beneath an impassive sea-gray sky the city lights glimmered, sparks tracing the streets. Here a building suddenly went dark, there another flared with fresh life. Carl couldn't follow the rapid movements, but he sensed a frantic rearranging, a fevered-insect pace. Skyscrapers rose, jutted.

"What—what's happened?" Lani's strained voice brought him back. He turned. Her eyes widened and she reached out for him, hands clutching.

"Saul . . . he's gone in after her." Carl held her, eyes trying to follow the flow between screens. A huge oceanliner docked at the city's edge. Buildings melted, flowed into the ship. The liner sank lower and lower in the water. "I think he's storing some of her association matrices in his own brain."

"Is that possible?"

"In theory, maybe. Virginia's been expanding her system for decades, JonVon's invented things—I couldn't follow their jargon, even."

"How'll we know . . . if Saul himself is in danger?"

He pressed his lips into a thin, white line. "We won't."

Lani looked away from the beehive rippling of the screens. "So much, so fast . . ."

He held her tightly. "And so much dying."

They waited together. At one point Lani curled up on the floor and slept. Carl continued to pace until, suddenly, a series of pecking sounds came from the acoustics nearby. A quick, hard rapping . . . then the ratchet of something cracking, like an eggshell. A long pause, then a well-modulated voice seemed to come out of nowhere and said, "Blithe spirit, truly—"

The voice descended into a series of clicks and murmurs. Carl blinked. He thought, *That almost sounded like . . .*

"Hello, Carl."

He swiveled. A holo rippled, grainy outlines coalescing into a speckled face. Eyes crystallized—black eyes that seemed as surprised as he was.

"Damn! Is that . . . you?" He felt Lani stir, rise to stand beside him, staring.

"It's as me as I'm going to get!"

Lani looked at the woman's body lying in the webbing, then back at the holo. Dazed, she licked her lips and said, "Your voice, it's too high."

"I'm working on it." The tone settled on a low soprano register. Timbre and pitch wavered. "Got away from me for a minute there. Here. This sound right?"

It was full-throated, with an eerie sense of presence. Carl shivered. His lips formed her name without a sound.

"Just the right Hawaiian accent," Lani said, her own voice high and tight.

The image focused more. Lips moved in sync with, "I can work on—" and then a high-pitched irritating squeal came pealing forth. Carl reached over and snapped the holo switch off.

"My God . . . what's *happening*?" Lani asked. Again she looked at Virginia's body. The respirator still hissed, but the diagnostic patch had turned deep purple.

"She's somewhere in there, finding her way around."

Lani touched a few readouts, took a deep breath. "It's impossible to get through on comm or anything else. All inways are blocked."

Carl gestured as a bank of aquamarine signifiers flickered and died. "There went the autocontrol monitors. Anything breaks, anywhere in Halley, we won't even know."

Saul jerked suddenly on his pallet, fingers clawing. Then his body went slack. Abruptly he called in a thin, dry voice, "Wendy. Wendy."

"We should *do* something," Lani said.

"We can't. They're on their own."

"We could lose both of them!"

Slowly a part of Carl stirred to life again, a fragment shaking off his pervading shocked numbness. Virginia was gone forever, no matter what Saul did. No matter what remained in JonVon, the bright, warm woman had slipped away.

"Carl?"

He breathed deeply and dragged his eyes away from the emerald city, where whole blocks now flared with crisp brilliance, while others smoldered in acrid ruin. He wondered how long he had been like this, absorbed. "Ah?"

"Jeffers just got through on a narrow datapatch. He reports the launchers have been undercut. Ould-Harrad has finished."

"Oh." He had no other reaction. This was merely another fact, a random fragment of information in a meaningless universe. He was surprised to find that he had clasped Lani's hand.

Then the holo image shifted violently. The emerald city dissolved into red lava, the translucent granite of the vast towers crumbling silently, melting and flowing into the bulging, erupting streets.

Saul relaxed completely. A long silence stretched, Carl not daring to say anything.

The acoustics crackled to life. He flipped the switch back and forth, without effect.

"You can't shut me up *that* easily, blithe spirit."

"Virginia!" In his excitement he leaped to the ceiling, banging his head. "You're there."

The visage was back, now crisp and sure. Virginia Herbert smiled, her face tanned, a big yellow flower tucked behind an ear. Over her shoulder, cottony clouds dotted an impossibly blue sky.

"Had a little sorting to do," the face said.

Lani asked tentatively, "Is that . . . really . . ."

"Me?" The woman in the holo shrugged, bringing bare shoulders into view. "Sure feels like it."

"You can see us?" Lani asked.

"And hear you, too. That news from the surface you brought— what fools! Ould-Harrad is an idiot." Then she paused, as if listening. "Oh, Saul. I see why now. I understand."

Saul did not stir. He seemed to be sleeping normally.

Dazed, Carl knew he was listening to the voice of the dead, but she seemed so vibrant, so full of the old zest. . . .

"With this much damage, the equator is finished as a site for launchers." Virginia's tone mellowed, gained harmonics as she tinkered with it. "That leaves the north pole. And there's only one possible mission profile that uses a northern push."

Carl could scarcely speak. *She's just died. How can any mind. . . ?* "I . . ."

"Jupiter. The orbital dynamics leave open that flyby."

Lani frowned. "I thought that was impossible."

The voice was calm, almost conversational. "No, just tough. It demands a very high delta-V. A completely different approach to Jupiter than the original mission plan. With the launchers firing from the north pole for the whole infall time, thirty years, we can—"

"*Thirty* years?" Lani cried.

"Correct. We'll have to go through perihelion to do it." The face lifted its eyebrows in amusement. "*This* Jupiter passage is on the *out-bound* leg, folks."

Carl heard the words but they were all a cascade of sounds with little meaning. She had fought and died and now had come back, a voice echoing in the narrow confines of this room, the Virginia he knew and yet not her at all. The voice had no fear, no shock, not even a trace of sadness. What *was* it? He listened to her go on, felt Lani's firm grip, and slowly the realization settled on him that the voice was right. There was still a way out, and no matter what tragedies they had suffered, what remorse they felt, time and the great blank darkness all around could heal them, and they would keep on.

PART VII
_____

# THE HEART OF THE COMET

*Year 2133*

Only an earth dream.
　　With which we are done.
　　A flash of a comet
　　Upon the earth stream.
A dream twice removed,
A spectral confusion
Of earth's dread illusion.
　　　　—Edgar Lee Masters
　　　　*Spoon River Anthology*

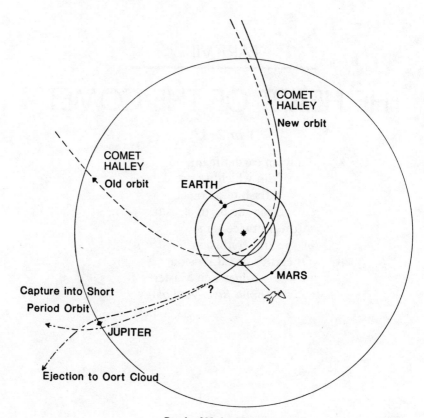

Result of Nudge Maneuvers
January 2137

# SAUL

The vulpine's tongue lolled as it flapped gently through the forest, legs splayed to keep its wing membranes taut, catching crosscurrents in the air as it hovered in search of prey.

LeGrand Cavern was a riot of color, a wilderness of broad, delicate leaves and verdant creepers. At intervals along the green-lined walls, vent tubes dripped condensation that dispersed in a soft fog, laying glistening droplets on the gently waving foliage. Bright purple, orange, and yellow fruits—massive and juicy—hung from slender, threadlike stems.

Fibrous vines laced the heart of the chamber, looping from column tree to keystone root to the next column tree, making a dense, three-dimensional jungle in what had once been an empty ice cathedral.

Saul watched the vulpine sniff, flap closer to a thick patch of Demicasava leaves, and shove in its long snout to worry whatever was hiding there.

In a sudden explosion, a skin-fowl hen burst from the thicket, furiously beating featherless wings just ahead of the vulpine's snapping jaws. The bird dove into the notch of a keystone root, leaving the disappointed vulpine to whimper in frustration, nosing for a larger opening that wasn't there.

*Life goes on,* Saul thought, smiling. *A game played in earnest by pieces that only dimly perceive their places in the whole.*

He filled his lungs with the rich, living smells. *A lot has been accomplished, since the aphelion war. Ought to be, in more than thirty years. Man and environment, adapting to each other.*

LeGrand Cavern was one of three "natural" chambers in which new twists to Halley's ever-more-complicated ecosystem were tested. In other vaults, humans and mechs tended less riotous, more orderly lifemixes . . . orchards and farms and lobster pens. But this canyon was one

of Saul's favorite spots, where various experiments sorted themselves
out and where startling new solutions appeared.

The vulpine—a construct based on fox genes, but modified so extensively as to be nearly unrecognizable by now—snuffed after another
scent and let out a sharp yip. It flapped around one of the giant column
trees, which crisscrossed the chamber at every angle like spokes or massive braces.

The trees served other purposes than just supporting the walls of
LeGrand Cavern, but that role would become crucial over the next few
months, as Halley's Comet zoomed sunward toward its most perilous,
and possibly last, perihelion passage.

He touched the trunk of the nearest, a bole a meter across that
shone bright, cool light from narrow strips of bioluminescent bark.
Power from the colony's fusion pile ran directly into the genetically engineered giants. Some of the electricity went into feeding the trees' life
functions. The rest emerged as a soft glow that suffused the chamber
from all directions, driving photosynthesis.

The trees had been a delightful surprise when Saul had awakened
from another decade-long slumber, a year ago. Clearly, the colonists had
been busy. The craft of life-tailoring and ecosystem management had
been carried much further by the watches since aphelion.

Of course, at any time there had always been two or three of Saul's
cloned near-duplicates around to help. In a sense, Saul had had a hand in
most of the wonders of this chamber—through his younger versions who
shared so many of his memories and skills. It could, in fact, be said that
*he* had invented the column trees. . . .

And yet there was an unrepentant individualist within him who rejected the idea out of hand. *No matter how metaphysical I get, I know
who "me" is.* He watched the vulpine and inspected the shining column
tree with a trace of envy. They were beautiful.

He had cheered at the hen's escape. The skin-fowl had been one of
his own designs.

A low vibration traveled up the trunk of the column tree to his hand.
Already Halley trembled with more and more quakes as heat from the
ever-closer sun seeped downward into the icy crust. Distant booms told
of patches of amorphous ice suddenly changing state, exploding off the
surface, blowing dust, rocks, boulders into space in great clouds of vapor. Each day the rumblings grew louder.

Already, the hazy, ionized cloud of the coma had formed, cutting
off radio reception from the rest of the solar system. The spectacular

twin tails waved, waxing ever brighter, primping for the real show at perihelion.

The column trees, keystone roots, and other preparations would be tested hard, during the coming weeks. *Carl thinks we haven't got much of a chance,* Saul thought. *But then, Carl always was a gloomy* hay-misheh.

Saul smiled, inhaling the rich, thick scent of life.

*Somehow, even if the Hot tears us to bits and spills us all into vacuum's embrace, I'd still not bet against us.*

A small purple creature buzzed by his ear and landed on the lip of an orchid. The flower was almost unchanged from a variant that grew in misty forests on Earth, but the lavender-colored pollinator was like nothing ever seen on the heavy green world. It was a distant cousin of the fearsome native forms that had terrorized the humans, back in the early days—now thoroughly altered to fit a harmless, useful niche.

Saul made a mental note: *Work on fixing the flavor of the honey the things make.* He had tried the stuff recently. It was too sweet. Now a sour variant, *that* would be popular. . . .

A rustle in the leaves . . . Saul looked up and caught sight of a small shape scuttling along the bright rim of the nearby column. It lifted a tiny, glowing eye at the end of a stalk, regarded him briefly, then peeped and scurried over to stand, quivering, before him.

*"Saulie,"* its tiny voice piped.

He held out his hand and the little machine ran up his arm like a trim spider the size of a Chihuahua. Its sticky feet prickled his skin with every step.

"Hello, little Ginnie," he said, greeting the tiny mech. "How's your big sister?"

The eyecell winked. *"She's fine, Saulie. Virginia says she wants to talk to you. No hurry, she says."*

He smiled. Virginia could have spoken directly through the little mech. After all, she "lived" everywhere in the complex cybernet under the ice. But the vast program that held her main essence had decided, for some reason, to do that as seldom as possible. Oh, there was a little bit of her in every one of the machines, from these little "Ginnies" all the way up to medical-drones that could play Scrabble and gossip. But if you wanted to talk to *Virginia,* you generally had to do it from some particular place she chose.

"Okay. Tell your mistress I'll talk to her at Stormfield Park."

The little robot hummed, consulted, and replied.

"Your *mistress, too, Saulie!*"

He laughed out loud. This model certainly wasn't one capable of teasing him with double entendres. Virginia herself must have been listening in.

"You're cute," he told it. "Tell you what, why don't we get together when Mama's not looking, you and I?"

"*Beast!*" A small pincer arm dropped down and tweaked his arm.

"Ouch!" But the mech darted off before he could snatch at it, and was gone in a flash of waving foliage.

*I could craft a creature to catch you,* he thought. *If we had forever, you with your machines and me with my animals . . . what games we could play.*

*If we had forever.*

Saul let out a sigh. He swiveled, braced his feet against the great tree, and launched himself through the interweaving latticework of trunks—laced with strips of brightly glowing bark—toward an exit that was something of a cross between a classical cerametal airlock and the valve of a giant, living heart.

The hallways were dimmer and a little cooler than the life chambers. Glow-balls fed off tiny trickles of electricity from the colony's fusion pile, laying soft islands of light along the Halleyvirid-lined corridors.

Long ago Saul had grown used to the subfreezing temperatures, and normally he wore little more than a robe and ice clips. The cold hardly mattered, as long as one had good food, and could sleep in a blanket woven from the soft silk of mute-mulberry worms.

Anyway, by now all of them had grown skins that radiated little, keeping most of the body's warmth within—another product of carefully tailored symbiosis.

Saul's biggest project was an organelle that would actually have a place *inside* human cells . . . something akin to mitochondria, only smaller. It would remain dormant most of the time, but with the right triggers, such as a rapid fall in temperature, it would manufacture glycogens and spin supports to allow freezing without damage to the body's trillion cells.

If it worked, sleep slots would become obsolete. Every person would carry with her or him, all of the time, the capability of settling into an icy niche and just going to sleep, waiting out years, decades, centuries if necessary.

It would take a long time to develop something so fundamental. This was nothing so simple as modifying a preexisting colony organism, such as a fox or a fowl. This was meddling with the workings of cellular chemistry itself.

With no guarantee that they would live out the month, Saul sometimes wondered why he was working so hard on this thing.

*It's a gift, of course,* he had come to realize. *Earth needs this as much as we do. The technique would mean access to the stars.*

It might be a parting gift. For the months ahead were filled with hazard. And even if they survived perihelion, and threaded the narrow needle of the subsequent Jupiter encounter to enter a short-period orbit, there was no guarantee that Earth authorities had changed their mind about letting "plague carriers" enter residence in the inner solar system.

In any event, Saul planned that his data would blast off in a mech-controlled capsule, returning the favor the people of Phobos had done for them, back in another century.

*Forbid, oh Lord, that we should ever forget the rocky worlds—or what we once were.*

He stopped at the medical center briefly to check on the progress being made unslotting more of the "terminal cases," those once thought hopeless, but now treatable and revivable, using new techniques.

There was little for him to do there, of course, Ishmael, the Saul clone in charge, seemed to know far better than he what was going on. He and his team were working on Nicholas Malenkov, now . . . repairing damage that had seemed hopeless a lifetime ago.

*Nick's in for some surprises,* Saul thought as he looked down at his friend. He looked so young, so burly and Earth-bulky, even after so long in the slots.

*It's another world, Nick. I hope you like it.*

Stormfield Park was crowded. As more and more people emerged from the slots, the population had begun approaching levels planned back when Captain Cruz and Bethany Oakes had launched forth with four sail tugs and the old *Edmund Halley* to challenge the unknown.

The chamber was smaller than LeGrand Cavern. It had quite a few column trees crisscrossing it, but these were arrayed more primly, the growth less a riot, more manicured.

At one end of the cylindrical area, the centrifugal wheel from the old *Edmund* had been refurbished and put back to work, rotating slowly, like a Ferris wheel. Two quadrants were still enclosed, containing laboratories for weight-dependent processes. But the rest was now open-sided and planted with oak and dwarf maple trees. It was like a strip of old Earth, bent into a circle and set inside a vast, surreal vault.

The wheel's centrifugal force was equivalent to only a twentieth of Earth's pull, but it was enough. People went there to practice the arcane art of "walking" . . . of sitting under a tree and watching things fall.

As he approached the rolling boundary, Saul heard a rare, treasured sound. Children laughed and flew past him toward the ring, skidding in the soft sand of a landing area as the great cylinder rolled around and around.

They looked so much better. Still, the gangling forms seemed barely human. Only a few could speak.

After aphelion, all of the poor, warped creatures had been slotted, and no more had been born. The wars had burned out the long rivalry between Ortho and Percell, and at last reason prevailed. Until the problems of fetal and postnatal development in the cometary environment were solved, it was considered heartless to bring babes into the world.

The reasons why humans had so much more difficulty than other animals were complex, but Saul and his assistants had solved the problem more than ten years ago. Theoretically, this park could be echoing with the giggles of healthy children.

But with perihelion coming, there was another reason to delay. Children deserved a future. Right now, few really believed there would be one.

Saul swam through a shimmering boundary and stepped nimbly aboard the rolling lawn. As he braced and absorbed rotational momentum, a holographic image formed behind him, cutting off his view of the rest of the hall. Suddenly, it was as if he were in a park on Earth. City spires topped a forested rise in one direction. Out the other way, one caught a glimpse of the bright sparkle of the sea.

*Lest we forget.*

Twice more, over the long years, bursts of technical data had arrived, sent by nameless benefactors in the inner solar system. Display projections like these—distant descendants of the weather walls—were among the most stunning of the gifts . . . proofs that not all of those who dwelt under the Hot had forgotten kinship, or mercy.

It was partly for them that Saul was working on the suspension-hibernation organelles. Such people deserved the stars.

He strolled under the limbs of the dwarf trees, past old friends who nodded amiably, and others he still barely knew from out-of-sync duty spans.

It was much like a visit to the park during his younger days. Of course, no one was fooled. Where on Earth, after all, would one see a person with blue-dyed skin playing chess with a human-shaped thing covered in green fungoid and yellow, symbiotic lichen?

*Diversity, experimentation. It's how we've learned to live.*

He stepped past the statue of Samuel Clemens, for whom the park had been named, and came up to a curtain of water . . . or rather a near-perfect holographic image of rainbow-diffracting droplets, sprayed from alabaster bowls. The illusory fountain parted without dampening him, and he stepped into a hidden, private glade.

Under a drooping willow canopy, a diminutive oriental tea house lay surrounded by rhododendrons. Saul sat down, crosslegged, before a clear pool, and watched the carp within beat the deuterated water frothy with their swishing tails.

It was peaceful here. The rumbling of the great wheel's bearings, the hushed blowing of the air fans . . . these were sounds that he knew, intellectually, must exist somewhere. But they had long ago faded away in habituation, like the beating of his heart, into a background barely ever recalled.

"Hello, Saul."

He looked up as she stepped out of the tea house, a loose kimono flapping about tanned legs, her sandals clicking on the sandy path. She was drying her black hair with a towel.

It always did it to him, meeting her like this. Her body had long ago gone into the ecosystem. *And yet, she walks in beauty.*

"Hello to you, too," he said. "How's the water?"

She smiled and settled down to the grass not five feet away. "Fine. A little choppy. But there was a five-foot swell, and peak. Good surfing."

Their eyes met. Silent laughter. *What is illusion?* Saul wondered. *And what is reality?*

The difference was plain in only one way. She lay as near and clear as an outstretched hand. But he could not touch her, and never would again.

"You look well," she offered.

He shrugged. "Gettin' older all th' time."

"Even with the perfect symbiotic system?" she teased.

"Even with the perfect symbiotic system, yeah. Of course, one really has to wonder if it matters. Or if time and age are worth worrying about." He watched her carefully, for although she could control images almost perfectly, her face hid no more from him than it ever had. She was mysterious. And an open book to him.

"It might matter." Her gaze was distant. "We might make it."

"Even past perihelion?" He looked at her skeptically.

She was watching the fish, the real water she could not touch or disturb in any way except with light and shadow. "Perhaps. If we do, a whole new set of challenges present themselves. Over the last thirty years I've come to realize that time could stretch to eternity for me. If so . . ."

He sighed, feeling he could read her thoughts. "My clones have most of my memories, and my good taste in women. They all love you, Virginia."

She smiled. "My drones all love you, too, Saul."

Their eyes met again, irony and tightly controlled loss.

"So *nu*?" He stretched. "You wanted to tell me something?"

She nodded, and in simulation took a deep breath. "Old Hard Man is dead."

Saul rocked back. "Suleiman? Ould-Harrad?"

"What did you expect? He never went back into the slots, after the aphelion wars . . . kept watch all that time to make sure we stuck to our agreement, no encounters with any planet but Jupiter outbound. He was very old, Saul. His people mourn him."

Saul looked down and shook his head, wondering what Halley would be like without the mystic of the lower reaches.

Who would there be with the nerve to remind Saul Lintz that he was not, after all, anything even faintly resembling the *real* Creator?

"He left you a bequest," Virginia went on. "It's waiting for you, in Deep Gehenna."

"I've never been down there." Saul felt a queer sensation. Was it fear? He had forgotten what that emotion was, but it might be something akin to what he was experiencing.

"Neither have I," Virginia whispered. None of her mechs had ever ventured down into the deepest reaches of the comet nucleus, where the strangest things took refuge in the total darkness. She shook herself.

"A guide will be waiting for you at the base of Shaft One, at zero five thirty hours, tomorrow. I—"

She looked up, her eyes unfocusing for a moment. "I've got to go now. Carl and Jeff need a simulation run, a big one. It'll take a lot of core." She smoothed her kimono over her tanned legs. "Time to doff this body and strip down to bare electrons."

He stood up along with her. They faced each other. His hand lifted, reached out.

"Don't," she whispered, her voice gone tense and soft. "Saul . . ."

His fingers stroked just short of contact with the smoothness that seemed to be her cheek. For an instant, the very tips shone with a flare of pink, and he felt, almost . . .

"Come again soon." She sighed. "Or just call and talk to me."

Then, in a flourish of silk, she was gone.

His new gibbons, Simon and Shulamit, clung to him as he followed the guide—a man who had once been named Barkley and had managed greenhouses for Earth-orbital factories, before being exiled on a one-way mission into deep space. Now, Barkley was his own greenhouse . . . his own habitat. He wore an ecosystem in green and orange fibers, and fed on this and that . . . a little light here, a bit of native carbonaceous matter there. . . .

*Some types of symbiosis scare even me,* Saul thought as they navigated a labyrinth of narrow, twisty passages that took them deeper and deeper into the ice. Faint as Halley's gravity field was at the surface, Saul could feel its pull fade and finally disappear from sensibility. This was the core, the center. Down here the first grain had formed, four and a half billion years ago, beginning a process of accretion as more and more bits gathered, fusing and growing into a ball of primordial matter. The stuff of deep space.

They squeezed through the thick, oily flaps of a lock-leaf plant . . . vegetation that acted much like an airlock, for it would react to a leak by plastering leaf atop leaf until air was sealed in on the uncracked side. It was an effective technique, but Saul still found it uncomfortable as they wormed through the sticky mass. The gibbons shuddered, but bore it uncomplainingly.

Here, energy from the fusion piles was rationed, scantily used. In the pale light of his glow-bulb, the passages glittered as he remembered them from the earliest days, with the dark, speckled beauty of native carbonaceous rock and clathrate snow. Saul's nose twitched at the almondlike scent of cyanide and nitrous oxides . . . made pleasant by the gene-crafted symbionts in his blood, but stronger than he ever remembered.

He stopped to take samples at a few places along the way. Each time his guide waited patiently, unperturbed.

*The traces are getting richer the deeper we go . . . as I've suspected for years now.*

It made little sense, of course. Why should the protolife forms pervade the primitive material more and more thickly down here, where the periodic waves of warmth from successive sun passages never penetrated? It was a mystery, but there it was. True, the more complex forms had developed higher up, but the *basic* stuff was thickest toward the core.

He sighed. Questions. Always questions. How could life be so kind—and so cruel—as to offer up wonders to solve, and give so little time, so few clues?

Their journey resumed, passing narrow clefts where an occasional, green-coated figure could be seen, tending a garden of giant mushrooms, or sitting before a small, glowing console, working for the colony, but where she or he chose.

Saul felt enclosed. The ice was heavy, massive all around him. It was oppressive, dank, dark. *We're close, very close to the center,* he felt.

"We have arrived." Barkley swam to one side. Saul looked dubiously at a narrow tunnel, barely a man's width across. He cleared his throat.

"Stay here, Simon, Shulamit."

The midget gibbons blinked unhappily. He had to peel them off and plant them on the wall. They watched him wide-eyed as he stooped and crawled into the musty passage.

The claustrophobic feeling grew as he crept. The walls and floor had been rubbed icy and smooth by countless pilgrimages. Somehow, the tunnel felt much colder even than the passages outside. It was only a few meters, but by the time a soft light appeared ahead, Saul was feeling a sharp tension.

When he reached the opening, he simply stared for a few moments.

Four tiny glow-phosphors glimmered above the corners of a carved stone bier. Upon this lay a man-shaped figure. Suleiman Ould-Harrad.

Saul floated out into the chamber. No gravity tugged at him. He was completely weightless.

He grasped one horn of the alterlike bier. The symbiotic Halley-forms had dropped away, leaving Ould-Harrad looking like an old, old man who had gone to his rest after more years than he would have chosen. The eyes, closed in final sleep, nevertheless gave an impression of severe dedication—to his people and to the deity that had so disappointed, yet nurtured him.

Saul paid his respects, remembering.

At last, he looked around. Virginia had spoken of a "bequest." And yet the chamber was bare, empty save the glow-bulbs, the corpse, and the carved bier.

"Wait a minute . . ." Saul muttered. He swiveled upside down and peered closer at the stone. "I . . . I don't believe it."

He fumbled at his belt and pulled forth his rarely used flashlight. Its sharp beam momentarily blinded him and he turned it down while blinking away spots.

Then Saul touched the stone in wonder, his hand bright under the narrow light, stroking faint but clearly symmetrical outlines. His voice was hushed.

"This is what Suleiman found, when he sought his Truth at the heart of the comet. This . . ."

This was a scientific discovery, and more.

This was astonishment.

He traced the ribs of an ancient sea creature, *fossilized in sedimentary rock*. Saul stared at the patterned ribcage, at the rough-edged, half-opened mouth, gaping as if caught in mid-chase, frozen in hungry pursuit . . . and at once he knew that the form he was touching had to be older, vastly older, than even the sun itself.

All around him, the close press of trillions of tons of rock and snow was as nothing to the sudden weight of years.


# CARL


Lani's breath sighed like the soft brush of stone against rough fiber. *A weary warrior on the soft battlefield,* Carl thought lazily. He snuggled against her, spoon fashion, and she wormed backward in her sleep, seeking him. It was in such seemingly slight, unconscious gestures that people truly knew each other, he thought. Much could be disguised between people, but not the elemental seeking of flesh for comfort and closeness. A delicate sheen of sweat glistened on Lani's forehead and her legs stirred, fanned, finding him. Then she settled with a small shiver, her breath slipped back into a regular sighing, and she descended into sleep again.

He pushed off gently and drifted out of bed. It was time to make his rounds, but no need for her to stir.

His legs and arms reminded him of yesterday's labors with a sweet, tingling pain. Even in barely perceptible gravity, he now felt a hitch there, a tightening there. . . . *I've lost track, but I must be well past forty,* he thought as he brushed his teeth. The mirror agreed: delicate crow's feet spreading from the eyes, jowly lines, more lightening at the temples. *All badges for tours of duty.*

In the last thirty years he had been awake about a third of the time. The crises had come and gone, though none that matched the troubles on the outbound orbit. *Each time ol' Lazarus Carl made things right again.* He stuck out his tongue at himself in the mirror. *And they gave you the credit. Nobody noticed that you just got them to think out loud until the answers were obvious.*

He pulled on a fresh blue coverall, relishing the crisp feel of the soft, native-grown fabric. He had always been messy before, seldom noticing that clothes were dirty until a chance breath informed his nose. It was through such seeming details that Lani transformed his world. They resolutely and precisely divided household chores, so there was no less work for him to do over-all . . . yet somehow everything seemed in order now, neat and clean.

*Yeah, she's civilized me.* He bent and gave her a soft kiss. She murmured and burrowed farther into her pillow as he left.

The tunnels were more crowded now than anytime he could remember since the beginning of the Nudge. All through the long dark years a skeleton watch had remained—more crew awake than originally planned, of course, because the Nudge was never finished. There were flinger tubes to polish and realign, launchers to outfit with new shocks and focusers. A steady hail of maintenance, as parts broke or simply wore out. The north-pole launchers had fired right up to the last minute, when the outgassing ice made operations impossible. They had to. The outbound Jupiter flyby demanded a large velocity change.

Now the launchers lay snug in their pits, buried thirty meters down, awaiting revival. For they had more bullets to spit at the stars, more momentum to impart . . . if anyone survived the next few months.

*As if we'll ever really see Jupiter.*

Carl sped down Shaft 3, checking every detail along the way. It was an old habit from the days before gene-crafted animals patrolled to eat unwanted Halleyforms. He stopped to pet a pair of hybrid mongoose-ferrets Saul had tailored for Halleyform policing. They crawled over him, nuzzled at his hand, discovered it was not suitable foodstuff, and lost interest.

He entered Central and gave the screens the usual daily once-over. They were only six weeks from perihelion now, and with every advancing kilometer the comet accelerated them toward almost certain doom.

Carl called up the few remaining views available from weathered relays on the surface.

Worse today. Much worse.

He selected a camera looking toward the dawn line. Far away, ivory streamers boiled from promontories that caught the sunrise. The sun slit the sky from the ice, a spreading line of chewing brilliance. Golden fingers stretched between the horizon hills and lit the first smoke of morning. Where the slanted sun found fresh ice, gouts of pale blue and ruddy-green erupted. High above waved plasma banners, auroras already more vast than any seen by Amundsen or Peary.

They had spun Halley again, to even the thermal load. Jeffers had mounted an array of absorbent panels to partially control the outgassing and use it for some crude navigation, but in this howling chaos it was impossible to get even a good fix on the stars and tell how they were doing.

*Sailing into the storm,* he thought. *And no compass.*

Halley was no more a ball of ice. Instead it resembled a snowy land mysteriously pocked and acned, all trace of man erased. A billion small centers of more-active gas had riddled the dusty plains, ripping free to join the high vacuum. Layers of heavier dust smeared the hollows. Occasional brown patches suddenly blew away, joining the swooping upward lift of the bright yellow-green coma, visible to Carl as a diffuse haze that stretched across the sky. As he watched, a slow darkening rippled through the gauzy glow, an outward wave from some eruption of dust on the sunward side.

"Pretty bad," Jeffers said at his elbow. He had grown even leaner in the sleep slots, his skin sallow. "Particle per sec is up three times over what it was last week."

"It'll rise almost exponentially from now on," Carl said. He gave this as a fact when it was only Virginia's prediction; she had been so accurate lately there hardly seemed a distinction any longer.

"Lost the last of the velocity meters."

"Not surprising."

"Just clean blew away."

"Temperature?"

"The night side's at one hundred eighty Kelvin. Dayside's 'bout fifteen degrees higher. Clapein' big gradient."

The thermal load was crucial. As the surface warmed steadily, heat seeped into the core. "What's the reading deep in the shafts?"

"Looks to be about seven degrees colder than the surface."

"Plenty."

"Yeah."

Ice was elastic. The warmer surface expanded, stretched—and cracked. The unrelenting pounding of the launchers had undoubtedly stressed the ice far down into Halley. With the warming would come relieving pressures, fracturing. How much? No numerical simulation could tell them. Halley was already honeycombed by the insect burrowing of humankind. It might crack open entirely, a last wheeze belching forth all the puny human parasites that had afflicted it.

As they watched, a pearly gout broke the crusted surface and exploded into a swirling cyclone symphony of excited colors: pea green, violet, sulfur yellow.

"Vidor woke up yet?"

"I ordered him started, but it'll be another day."

"Well, no rush anymore. His castle's gone."

Jeffers pointed to a slumped mass near the dawn line. The ornate, corbeled, and stranded artwork had been Vidor's masterwork in ice, sculpted three years after the equatorial battle. For its task—structural support for Shaft 20—it could have been a square box, an igloo. Vidor had added parapets, towers, silvery arabesques, scalloped walls, and blue-white, airy bridges. Now . . .

"He won't expect it to still be here." *A sand castle lasts only until the next tide.*

"How many you bringin' out?"

"Everybody," Carl said. "Except the ones so dead there's no real hope of saving them, of course."

Jeffers twisted his mouth around in a familiar, skeptical line. "The med-techs can handle those new treatments?"

"Virginia's got mechs helping. Speed-trained them with that experimental method of hers."

"What'd you decide 'bout the ones with partial brain damage?"

"They won't be much use, but they deserve revival."

"Yeah. They paid for their tickets, might as well see the finale."

Some had opposed his decision, but he had swept their objections aside. The rational argument was that with the maximum possible crew awake, they could deal with crises better. Carl's private motivation, though, was entirely emotional. If Halley split, cracked, burst into a gaudy technicolor plume, at least they would all live out each moment, and face the end as they had begun—an expedition. A crew.

*That's something,* he thought. *Beats sleeping to oblivion.*

He frowned. What was that poem Virginia had pointed out to him? *I really shouldn't think of the program as Virginia, but it's impos-*

*sible not to. JonVon doesn't exist anymore. And what was that poem she quoted yesterday?*

Do not go gentle into that good night

*Right. Damn right.*

"Sir?"

Carl turned, not recognizing the voice.

It was Captain Miguel Cruz.

"Uh . . ." Carl stared at the man, unchanged from his memory. The jaw was still as solid, assured. The eyes looked out steadily, inspiring confidence. Even the blue tint from slot sleep could not disguise that.

Still, something about the man looked awkward, blocky. Cruz wore shoes, and stood as if gravity mattered.

"I wanted to report for duty," Cruz said. "I'm not fully recovered yet, but I'm sure there's something I can—"

"No, no, you—rest. Just rest," Carl said quickly. He hadn't realized the warmings had come so far. Someone should have *warned* him!

Cruz spoke with a faint accent . . . Earth speech. "Sir, I'd prefer to be on duty. Perhaps—"

Carl shook his head, embarrassed. "Look, Cap'n, don't call me sir. I'm Carl Osborn, you may remember me, a spacer. I—"

"Of course I recognize you. I'm somewhat conversant with events since my death," Cruz said with a faint smile. "I've read the log—it's incredible—and . . . I think calling you 'sir' is quite appropriate."

Carl stared at the man for a long moment, not knowing what to say. Despite his harrowing illness, Cruz looked . . . *young.* Unseasoned. "I . . . thought, sir, that after you've had a few days to recover, you could reassume command."

Cruz looked at the flurry of data and views of the surface on a dozen screens nearby. "It would take me months to even understand what's going on. Your tools, techniques, and . . . Coming here, I saw a woman in Shaft Two who looked like a flying fungus!"

"That's a weirder, sir," Carl said. "They live about two klicks down Shaft Two in their own biosphere."

"But that green stuff—it was even in her hair!"

"It's a symbiont that retains fluids and increases oxygen processing—I don't know the details."

Cruz shook his head. "Incredible. As I said, I haven't a clue about how things are."

"But I was hoping . . ."

"I see," Cruz said with dawning perception. "Now that we're back in the inner solar system, you thought perhaps I could help negotiate something with Earth?"

"No sir, we've realized that's a dead end. I only . . . well, you're the captain!"

Cruz's smile was distant, reflective, as though he peered at something far away. "I was the captain of the *Edmund,* and for a brief while we tunneled in here and lived. But now Halley is a ship itself. It's been sailing under her true captain for decades now. I . . . I am a passenger."

"No, sir, that's not—"

"Someday I aspire to become a ship's officer. Not captain, however. And I shall not forget who held the helm for so long."

Cruz held out a hand. Carl blinked, then slowly brought forth his and shook it.

All along he had hoped Saul's *wunderkinder* could revive Cruz. Now they had done it, at the very last minute . . . and it was no panacea after all. He should have seen that. Cruz was right. Miguel Orlando Cruz-Mendoza was no older than the day he had died, but Halley was seventy years transformed by the hand of that clawing, cantankerous, blissfully ingenious and flagrantly stupid lifeform that was too stubborn to stay at home and forget about riding iceballs into oblivion.

To his own amazement, Carl realized he was already *evaluating* his former captain, weighing his potential place in the crew. *A good man,* he thought. *I'll put him to work.*

Hours later he found himself returning from an inspection of some farm caverns and the new modular hydroponics spirals They were cleverly arranged to extract waste heat from recycled sewage, which fed in overlapping helices around the outside. Ultraviolet poured from an axial cool-plasma discharge, and the huge plants had yearned inward toward it. He admired the Promethean task of relocating the surface domes into the core, and was making his way back through Shaft 4 when a slow, grumbling *crump* jarred him away from his thoughts. It seemed to come from the walls themselves.

He tapped into his private line. "Jeffers!"

—I'm on it. Acoustics are pickin' it up ever'where.—

"An explosion?"

—No pressure drop. I think it came from the surface.—

Carl called up a quick index-display of the remaining surface cameras. Most showed views of gossamer, upside-down Niagaras—roiling founts of vapor soaring from the ice and whipping in long arcs up into a shifting, gauzy sky. Solar ultraviolet ionized the gas. The sun's particle pressure then turned these fountains outward, bending the flow into the ghostly streamers of the coma.

Above the far horizon a block of grainy ice tumbled end over end, a kilometer up in the sky. Nearby a huge jagged hole yawned, itself a source of fresh volatiles, green and ruby strands snaking from the pit in twisting filaments.

"Seismic outblow? Or maybe a patch of amorphous ice changing state suddenly."

When the stressed crust ice gave way, it could rip free entirely. That instantly transferred the sun's heating to fresh deposits, which hollowed new channels and in time would further deepen the cracks.

Jeffers said, —Yeah, looks it. Virginia was right 'bout that, too.—

"She said it wouldn't happen very much until perihelion."

—Well, I guess this's just a taste of it.—

Carl nodded to himself and cast off. He passed parties of Weirds, swathed in green and purple growths, who scarcely took notice of him. They were checking the old seals for intrusions by older Halleyforms, which they would scrape away and replace with mutated, human-friendly forms the Sauls had worked out.

Further on he met two Saul clones, gently coasting a revived sleep slotter to one of the warmer bins. They nodded in unison and called to him, "Only twenty more probables left." Carl laughed.

They were fully developed adults now, with minds of their own. They even had the same gestures and accent. But somehow he couldn't think of them as anything but Saul substitutes. The fact that Saul had successfully cloned himself, while attempts at duplicating other crew members had failed, meant that his odd symbiotic adaptation was crucial. Quite possibly, only he could be copied in the Halley environment. So down through these last few decades, the multiSauls had been invaluable for their resistance to random new ailments, and their curious internal discipline. Saul had used JonVon's memory-transfer apparatus to instill whole chunks of his own expertise into his clones.

What he had learned might have enabled others to raise natural children without fear. It would have been good, hearing peals of childish laughter in the shafts. But the long fall to perihelion had dampened any such idea. No one could bear the knowledge that the promise of childhood might never blossom.

Carl's comm buzzed and Virginia said, —You were doubting my prognosis?—

"That blowout came a little early, don't you think?"

—No. After all, I deal in probabilities, sir, not predictions. If you want, why don't you call up Lefty d'Amario? He can check my calculations.—

Somehow the old tingle still ran through him when the coquettish flavor laced through her voice. "Okay, I'm not griping. No need to get huffy. You monitoring those stress meters Jeffers implanted all over?"

—Of course. I can always spare a nanosec or two.—

"And?"

—Minor tremors here and there. Some faulting along Shaft Two. Nothing to get perturbed about.—

"Great. You been filling in Cap'n Cruz?"

—*You* are captain, Carl. Everybody keeps telling you, even if you don't like it.—

"I didn't ask for the job."

—Nobody else could handle what's coming.—

He felt a sudden spurt of the old anger. "What's coming is *death, Virginia.*"

—I know no such thing.— The voice was prim, circumspect.

"You did the simulations yourself."

—Number-crunching isn't reality. *I* should know, eh, friend Carl? There may be variances in the cross-correlation matrices.—

"Don't give me all that. Halley's scraping in too close, the only question is whether we'll fry or boil when this iceberg blows apart."

—There are many unpredictables. But also some measures we can take.—

Carl had been smoothly coasting down a tunnel, automatically checking for cracks. This remark made him stop. "What can we do?"

—Pipe some of the surface heat inward, to offset some of the stress arising from the temperature differentials. In other words, reverse the outflow system and spread the surface heat into lower, cooler ice.—

"And if some inside ice vaporizes? The pressures—"

—We vent it. It will aid in shielding from the sun.—

"Ah." He felt a flush of hope. "How come you didn't mention this before?"

—I just thought of it. I'm only a machine.—

Faintly, he heard the soft roar of surf, the whisper of trade winds, a distant rumble of ocean squalls gathering. Virginia's metaphorical world within the network. Somewhere a voice laughed, *"Ke Pii mai nei ke kai!"*

So she had company, somehow. He smiled. "Look, I'll call a meeting. We should look into—"

She laughed. —Same old Carl. One minute you're grousing about everything, but give you a problem to work on and—bingo!—

He flushed. She had always had an uncanny ability to stay one move ahead of him. He pushed off along a tunnel that led home.

—There's plenty of time to figure out the engineering, Cap'n. Go on about your business.— The tinkling chuckle, ringing in his ears. —Lani's waiting.—

And she was. She embraced him silently and they spun lazily in the middle of the room, oblivious. Carl had at last mastered the art of putting business aside once he came back to their small apartment, and this time he did so again, even though the implications of Virginia's remarks were enormous. He was tempted to tell Lani, but then he held back. Hope had been kindled among them so many times over the decades, only to be snuffed out by the brute certainty of some unyielding astronomical fact. So he banished all the fretful chorus of thoughts and simply kissed her.

"My!" She breathed deeply. "Pretty torrid for midday—particularly after a hard night."

"We do our best."

"I go on shift soon. Let's have a quick lunch."

"Great." He launched himself for their tiny kitchen, made workable only because they could use the walls and ceiling.

"There's some hard copy on your printer, by the way," Lani said, fetching some sauce used on the braised vegetables and mute-chicken from the evening before. "From Virginia."

"Oh?"

He kicked over to the printer. Usually it was used only for emergencies or entertainments, not ordinary ship's business.

It was a poem.

Nature knows nothing of death.
Not in the cat's lazy smug *meeeeoooow*
Not in the antelope's mad kick
As the lion makes its meal.
Neither in the tidal lifting of a sluggish sea
By a star's dumb gradients,
Or a flower's nod, an insect's frantic dance.

*Live* is all the world ever says.
Of alternatives it is mute.
Only in us and our unending forward tilt
Can death live.

Each sharp moment is free.
And all that could happen
Might yet be.

Carl studied it, frowning. "She's getting better."

Lani came over and read it slowly. "I'm always surprised anew," she said softly. "Virginia truly is in there, somewhere."

Carl shook his head. "She's not *in* anything, really. She's everywhere. The system has expanded far beyond just JonVon's banks. She's Halley now."

Lani suddenly turned and embraced him. "We're all Halley."

He breathed in the aromatic warm musk of her and felt an easing of old pains. *Why did it take me so long to see that this fine woman could be a whole world to me? And what if I never had seen it?*

He felt Virginia around them all, sensed the entire community of Halley as a matrix threaded through the ancient ice. They were no longer buried inside, going for a ride. No Percells, no Orthos. They were a new, beleaguered society, a new way for a versatile primate to stretch further, to be more than it was. They were not merely in the center of the old dead ice, they were the heart of the comet.

"Yeah, I suppose we are," he said.

# VIRGINIA

It was a show that humans had never seen before, and quite likely never would again. The steady hammering of the launchers for over three decades had altered the infalling ice mountain's orbit, shifting the nodes of the stretching ellipse. Earth's orbit clung to the sun, deviating from a circle by less than two percent. But Halley's eccentricity had been ninety-six percent even before the machines of men began their persistent nudging. Now the curve tightened with each passing hour, bringing a searing summer. Halley had never plunged this close to the eroding Hot.

The tunnels and shafts made excellent acoustic pipes. As ice ground and surged against new frictions, the groans echoed deep into the core, waking sleepers—though there were few of those, as the crucial hour approached.

Plunging fifty kilometers nearer with every second, Halley rushed toward its ancient enemy. Each past encounter had stripped a skin of ice from the comet, but now it rumbled and wrenched with new forces that sought to break it on the anvil of its sun.

Virginia watched the howling, blinding storm through electronic eyes. As each camera died from the stinging blast of dust and plasma, she deployed another from deep vaults. The sun loomed twice as large as seen from Earth. But from the surface there was no incandescent disk to see. Halley spun, but saw no sunrise. Instead, a white-hot corona simmered overhead. A patch of seething brightness marked where the Hot's outpouring met the ion flood exploding from Halley, and victory inevitably went to the Hot. Cracked, ionized, the gases turned, deflected aside, and swept around the small iceworld in a magnetized blanket. This roiling atmosphere had no loyalty to its parent, but instead raced outward.

Halley's twin tails now unfurled across a span greater than Mercury's orbit. The twisting, glimmering plasma banner held less water than many of Earth's larger ponds, but the sun's blaring light made it the most visible object in the solar system. Advanced inhabitants of a nearby star could have picked the nearly straight, shimmering curtains out from the central star. The dust tail, in contrast, was a curved reddish band, broken by dark lanes, sparkling with pebbles and micron-sized grains.

But those riding the parent ice mote could not see the most beautiful tail ever to grace a comet in all history. As it sped deeper into its star's gravity well, the glowering coma of unbearable luminescence spread and devoured the whole sky. Blinded now, Halley could not even see its nemesis. The sky glared down everywhere.

Virginia had calculated this effect carefully, for it was the key. If she had allowed Halley to remain spinless, the sunward face would have soared toward the four-hundred-degree temperature that a solid body would have at this distance from the sun. Now, she watched heat-flux monitors buried tens of meters in the ice. As the warmth seeped deeper, she spun the iceworld faster to smooth out the effect, allowing the night side to radiate into the black of space.

But the black was fading. Soon the comet's own summer air reflected sunlight down onto the shaded face of Halley from all sides, and temperatures rose faster as perihelion approached.

"How's it look?" Carl watched Central's screens with Lani at his side. "We've already blown off twenty meters of ice!" he said sharply. "How long'll it take to rip us apart?"

Virginia sensed his rising level of conflict. He was a man who solved problems, and in this great crisis he had no role. Like the others, he was a helpless passenger on his own ship.

"We are safe," she said reassuringly, using a thread of alto tones that made her voice richer than the original had ever been.

"The shaft seals?"

"Intact," Virginia said, displaying views of the steel-capped lids in place two hundred meters inside each shaft. Beyond them, giant plugs of ice barred the Hot's way.

"Stop worrying," Lani said gently, putting a hand on Carl's shoulder. "We might as well enjoy the view."

Virginia thought later that it was particularly ironic that Lani's words were punctuated by a long, rolling boom that penetrated into Central. The spherical room vibrated, creaking. Equipment popped free of holders.

"A cave-in," Virginia announced, throwing an image onto the central screen. A milling mass of snow and ice jutted through tunnel walls, falling with aching slowness.

"Damn!" Carl said, his voice tight. "Where?"

"Site Three C, as our projection suggested."

"Pressure—"

"Sealed tightly. No incursions." Virginia analyzed Carl's voice patterns and found a high level of tension. If only he would listen to Lani more . . .

The basic human reaction to events of immense size was to hunker down.

Virginia had noted this in the final days before perihelion. Her mechs roved the honeycombed tunnels, testing for leaks and sudden fountains of vagrant heat. Seldom did they meet anyone. Even Stormfield Park was deserted now, the carousel stopped.

People did their jobs, served their shifts—and holed up with a few loved ones, watching the gaudy maelstrom outside through the video displays. Jeffers had developed a new kind of light pipe that could snake out from a deeply buried camera, and thus reduce risk, but still high-pressure vents opened and gushers of foaming, red-rich mud flooded many of Virginia's observation stations.

She reserved a tiny piece of Core Memory for her "office." There she sat amid a hum of machinery, feeling the reassuring rub of a chair, the flickering of consoles. *I wish I could spare enough Core to go for a swim,* she thought. *I can feel my own tensions, too. . . .*

As a species, she reflected, *Homo sapiens* had never truly gotten beyond the bounds of the tribe. The history of the last hundred thousand years had shown how cleverly they could adapt to larger demands. Under pressure of necessity they formed villages, towns, cities, nations. Yet, they saved their true warmth and fervent emotion for a close circle of friends and relatives. They would die to preserve the tribe, the family, the neighborhood. Appeals to larger issues worked only by tapping the subtle, deeper, wellsprings.

Thus, the gathering background chorus of tremors, the *crump* of a crumbling wall, the low gravelly mutter of strained ice—all these sounds drove the crew inward. Not into solidarity, but to the fleshy reassurance and consolations of fellow spacers, or weirders, or Hawaiians. Like sought like for what might be the final hours.

Except for one lonely figure, who seldom left Central.

"Saul," she said to him as an amber plume spouted from the surface, throwing streaks of lacy light across the familiar, lined face. He had been sitting by the display a long time, his mind far away as he rolled a small stone in his hand, over and over. "Saul?"

"Ah—oh, yes?" His lined face looked up from the bit of rock.

"I'm sure you could watch elsewhere."

He shrugged. "Stormfield's closed. I'm not needed in sick bay right now. There's no place else I particularly want to be."

"I am sure Carl and Lani would welcome you. They are awake, watching—"

He raised a hand. "No, I'll let them be. Don't want to push in where I'm just a fifth wheel."

"You worry over that old stone a lot," she said to change the subject. He had been turning it over in his hands for hours.

He looked at the dark gray lump. "It's from Suleiman's bier. I've carried it around for weeks, studying it. But that's . . . that's not what I was thinking about right now."

His gaze drifted over to the refrigerated unit holding sixteen liters of superchilled organic processor. Virginia thought she understood.

"You are with me no matter where you are in Halley, Saul."

He blinked, nodded. "I know . . . it's just . . ."

"Just that here the physical proximity of my organic memory is reassuring?"

He smiled the old wry smile, slightly puckered lips and crinkled eyes together conveying an irony that was never far from his own image of himself, she knew. "I'm that obvious?"

"To one who loves you, yes."

"There are times I wish . . ."

"Yes?"

"I could have found a way to clone you."

"So you would know me—or someone like me—in the flesh?"

"Memory only makes some things worse."

"There . . ." She felt no real hesitancy, and in any case with her speed the indecision would take only milliseconds, but she had to maintain the nuances of a living persona. ". . . There are our recordings."

He chuckled dryly. "You know how many times I've played them."

A hint of shyness, yes. "I could . . . augment them."

"No!" He slammed a fist into his web-chair. "I want the real thing, the real . . . you."

"It would be."

"When we recorded ourselves, it was a lark, like couples taking Polaroid pictures of themselves in the bedroom. We never intended that only one of us would play them back." He shook his head. "This way, without you—the *real you* . . ."

"But I am me. More real than any holo-image! And if I enter into the sensory link, it is an older and probably wiser Virginia whom you will meet. *Me*."

Saul had resisted this suggestion before, for reasons she did not fully understand. But now, perhaps out of the pressing loneliness that danger brings, he lifted his head and stared directly into her opticals. "I . . . it would?"

She knew she would not guarantee that it would be some genuine Virginia, fixed in amber. She was not the personality that had flooded into the cramped JonVon persona and inundated it. Slow evolution and self-actuated advances had brought her a vast distance since those years. But Saul did not have to know that, nor did anyone, and it would be of comfort to him.

"Come to me, Saul."

He put aside the stone and reached for the neural tap. To her surprise, she felt nervous.

Perhaps for her it would be a returning, too.

Shortly before perihelion the sun stopped its retreat to the south and began rising again. As the disk grew, it swept toward the equator. There was perpetual noon as the comet shuddered and erupted beneath the unending blaze. The southern hemisphere, gutted and gouged for months, now cooled as the north came under ferocious attack.

Sublimating water and carbon dioxide carried heat away from the fast-spinning mote. Its surface cracked in many places, following the weakening imprints Man had stamped upon it for seven decades. Fresh volatiles sublimed and exploded. Sharp chunks weathered to stubs within minutes, as though sandblasted. Pebbles rose and formed hovering sheets which momentarily shielded the ice beneath, then were blown away to join the gathering dust tail.

At the north pole, so far spared the worst, the clawing sun bit deep. Since the times of great plagues, some factions had buried the irrecoverably dead deep in the ice near the pole. Now the Hot found them.

By chance, the sight was visible over a light pipe that surfaced in a sheltered nook at the exact north pole. Exploding gases beneath lifted the wrapped ice mummies and hurled them skyward. Blistering heat released ionized oxygen from the ice, and the bodies burst into flame, lighting the landscape with momentary orange pyres. The torches were thrown, tumbling and flaring, up and out against the immense, unknowing forces. They hung in the sky for long moments, like distant guttering castles, and then winked out and plunged forever into the river that rolled out from the sun.

"Goddamn! We're past it!"

Carl's amazed face intruded on a 3D design study she was changing. He had used override to break into her mainstream persona.

"Yes. You can rejoice," she said warmly.

"How'd you do it?"

"Vector mechanics, nothing tougher than that."

"You were marvelous!" Lani said beside Carl, her eyes wide with wonder at being alive. Virginia realized distantly that they really had expected to die.

"I told you the probabilities," Virginia said. "Surely you—"

"We figured you were just cheering us up!" Carl laughed.

"I made the calculation accessible, Carl, you dope." Virginia sent some light chuckles to follow this sentence, reflecting that if anyone had actually checked her, they would've found she had in fact reported a survival probability of three to one when it had really been only fifty-two percent. But she had been sure no one would do the entire complicated calculation. In thirty years, everyone had come to rely on her, just as they counted on Saul's bio-miracles.

Lani was bright-eyed, expectant. "When can we go outside? I want to grow some crops in the sun again."

"Nearly half a year," Virginia said seriously. She had found that people took statements more to heart if they were laced with sharper vowels and a few bass tones.

"Never mind, we'll have plenty to do inside," Carl said, slapping Lani on the rump affectionately.

Virginia knew exactly what he had in mind. It was implicit in his entire psychological profile, true, but her intuition told her more. Carl had bottled himself up emotionally for decades, and that had been crucial in the survival of Halley Core. Now time and circumstance had worked its curious magic and he was free. The youthful Carl could not—did not—respond to Lani's quiet gifts. This weathered, wiser Carl could, and would, and should.

Somewhere in the compacted recesses of organic memory, a twinge of humor and irony kindled. *He's getting what he needed, even if it isn't what he wanted.* Virginia made a note to cycle Lani in for a "routine" physical within forty days.

The prickly storm swelled. Though they had survived the worst at perihelion, a residue of heat still leaked inward. Virginia sent men and women and mechs to seal tunnels which collapsed, whole zones of shafts whose walls began to sputter and evaporate.

Warmed in vacuum, ice sublimates directly into vapor without becoming liquid. As Halley's scarred skin blew away, Virginia began her grand experiment.

Teams of hardened mechs ventured forth from the eroded shaft mouths. They dispersed slabs of amorphous silicates, grit and grime dried and filtered and compacted through the years of mining. Quickly they spread huge fields of linked, slate-black sheets on well-chosen spots near Halley's equator. They were too heavy for the subliming vapors below to push them away, and the mechs made doubly sure by hammering cables to anchor the slabs.

The effect came with aching slowness. Halley spun now with a day of only three hours. At a precisely calculated moment, the silicate shields blocked sunlight from the ice. Over that zone, outpouring gas ebbed. Other areas continued, and this difference in thrust, combined over the turning face of Halley, began to minutely alter its orbit. Astronomers had long noted this "rocket effect" on rotating comets that temporarily exposed fields of dust, but it had always been spontaneous and temporary. Now it was done by design.

Virginia deployed her mechs remorselessly. Some overheated and failed, others were crushed between the large sheets as they butted and swayed in the sun-driven gale of gas. At her command, they could tilt the slabs end-on, so the protected areas suddenly leaped to life, spurting amber-tinged plumes. Deftly, resolutely, she played a dynamic symphony with the furious hurricane forces that buffeted the mechs and their cargoes. For days, and then weeks, she cupped the outraged steam of Halley to new purposes. Unbalanced thrusts aligned along the comet's orbit, a persistent hand that swept them along a new orbit.

Four months beyond perihelion, Virginia waited for the inevitable. She had deployed fresh arrays of infrared and microwave radars, concentrated along the expected cone of the sky.

The first was slow and tiny, a marvel of stealth technology. She got a glimpse of broad, transparent vanes that radiated away the sun's heat. Only her phased-array microwave net, operating at ten gigahertz, picked up its faint shadow. She had spread the gossamer wire receivers over a volume spanning a hundred kilometers, to get high definition. If it had been faster she might not have been able to integrate the diverse signals in time. As it was, she crisped the snub-nosed thing ten kilometers away from Halley.

Behind it, a few moments later, came something large and lumbering. It used the sun for background cover, superimposing itself on a vibrant-blue solar flare that had sprouted only an hour before from a large magnetic arch.

She caught it with a laser burst, feeling a chill run through her mind. She would never have caught the slight, giveaway ripple of ultraviolet that betrayed the incoming warhead . . . except that she was monitoring the flare, as part of their ongoing research program. Jeffers had been right when he insisted on retaining the dedicated science diagnostics; it paid to keep learning.

The third was fast, closing at a hundred kilometers a second, still boosting with a light-ion drive. Virginia wondered why they had left the electrostatic accelerator on, since it made the projectile much more visible. She fired at it with the newly resurrected launchers, and in the two-second delay waited confidently for a kill signature.

None came. Her phased-array net told her why. The thing was maneuvering sideways, dodging the slugs of iron. Evidently it could pick up the microwave hum of the launchers and see the pellets as they came.

She immediately fired all her harnessed laser banks.

They, too, missed. By then only four seconds remained and she did not even have time to sound alarms in the tunnels of Halley.

Desperate, she drove the power level of the gigahertz net up a terra-watt and shifted the system from RECEIVE to TRANSMIT. The array had never been used this way. For a brief instant it could have sent a hail to a civilization across the galaxy itself, if anyone along the beam happened to be looking. The spider-web dishes could probe and pinpoint. Virginia fired a pulse of electromagnetic energy at the precise dot that swam in her triangulated worldview.

They had safe-armed this warhead. As the electromagnetic tornado burst upon it, the chip-mind aboard fired the compressing explosives before they could evaporate. The equivalent of twenty megatons of blistering fusion energy flowered in the black sky above Halley, raising a flash-burn of ivory fog from the weathered ice.

Throughout the battle Virginia had alerted no one. The men and women and families went on about their lives, untroubled. Only when workers on the surface wondered about the sudden flare of brilliance did she call Carl and deliver the news that their great battle had come and gone in the time it took Carl to put down his cup of coffee.

# CARL

"Any signs of others?" Carl asked tensely.

"None," Virginia said. "I have extended my search to a light-hour all around us, and find nothing."

Lani came coasting into Central, her face drawn and pale. "I heard your announcement, Virginia. How close did they get?"

"As the Duke of Wellington said after Waterloo . . ." Virginia's voice shifted to a heavy, aristocratic British accent, "'It was a damned near thing.'"

"And they'll try again, if we continue on our planned trajectory," Carl said soberly. "They won't tolerate us using the Jupiter encounter to loop us into the inner solar system. They've got years to shoot at us, remember. When we come back inward, they'll strike again. That attack may fail, too. And the next one. But eventually . . ."

"Those murderers!" Lani cried. "We were willing to accept quarantine, but that wasn't enough for them! Just to protect themselves from any *chance* of exposure to Halleyforms, they'd kill us all."

Carl felt the inevitability of what he had to say, the end of so many hopes. "Time to face facts. We can't come back in from the cold."

Lani frowned. "But that means . . ."

"Right. We've got to choose a trajectory that'll take us outward after Jupiter. It's the only way to stay out of Earth's reach."

Virginia asked, "You think that will be enough to make Earth stop?"

Carl shook his head. "We'll have to hope so. We'll chart a course that takes us far into the outer solar system."

Lani looked at him, biting her lip, silent.

"Somehow," Virginia said slowly, "I don't believe they will be content with anything less than a departure orbit."

Lani's eyes widened. "What? Leave the solar system entirely?"

"Effectively." Virginia said sympathetically, "They will then be convinced that Halleyforms will never reach Earth."

Carl nodded. "No point to chasing us. Too expensive, anyway."

"What'll we *do* out there?" Lani asked incredulously.

"We'll live. We'll die." Carl stared, unseeing, at the main screen where numbers rippled. "Into the Oort Cloud . . ." he said distantly. "There are supposed to be trillions of iceworlds there, asteroid-sized. That's what Halley was, before some nudge, maybe from a passing star, tumbled it into the inner system."

Lani asked doubtfully, "And once we're there? Can we use those for resources?"

He shrugged. "Maybe. We'll have hundreds of years to think about it on the way out."

Lani settled into a webbing, her face composed. "We'll all be dead before then, even with sleep slotting."

Carl felt an odd, distant resignation. Somehow he had known that he would never leave this place. They were consigning not only themselves, but all further Halley generations as well, to an outer darkness of limitless unknowns. *Fleeing into the abyss.*

Lani said, "I suppose we must . . . plan for what we *can* do, not what we'd rather do."

*Life's a series of overcoming dooms, one at a time,* Carl thought. He knew they could do it, too, if they simply refused to give in to despair. *If we have something to live for.*

# SAUL

## *Year 2141*

Half of Stormfield Park had been turned into a nursery. The old centrifugal wheel had been reinforced to spin faster, providing a full tenth of an
Earth gravity to help young bones grow strong. That was hard on some
of the older generation, but still they came often, when off work, to
listen to the high, piping voices shrieking in play and laughter.

Saul felt that way as he walked carefully along the grass-lined,
curving path at the rim of the wheel-park, where holograms gave the
illusion of a cityscape just beyond a low hedge, with skies spotted with
warm, moist clouds. Mothers and nursery workers tended their growing
crowd of boisterous charges nearby, watching their games, admiring the
infants' clear-eyed, long-limbed beauty.

The children had saved Halley Colony . . . if in no other way than
by lightening the spirits of those who now knew they would never see
Earth, Mars, the asteroids, or any unfamiliar human face ever again.

*We are the first starship,* Saul had come to realize, *two or three
centuries ahead of schedule.*

Oh, Halley was still tied to old Sol's apron strings, but their ship
home was irreversibly on course toward the outer cloud now, where trillions of iceballs drifted in the not-so-entirely-empty range between the
stars. Alien ground. They would live or die on their ingenuity, and on
whatever they had taken with them.

On that subject Saul had just completed an important study, an inventory of the genetic pool available for the coming generations. The
question was an important one, for it might mean the difference between
the colony's survival or a long, slow decline into degeneracy and death.

*There's plenty enough heterozygosity,* he had decided. *A broad
cross section of the types that populate old Earth. It should provide
enough variety. Especially with the mutation rate we can expect. The
bigger problem will be maintaining a large enough population.*

Halley had enough resources, for now, to keep the colony going
into the indefinite future. Deuterium mined from the ice would fire the
fusion piles—now relocated out on the surface to minimize waste heat—

until they managed the skill to put together a proton-power generator from one of the Phobos designs. Their skill at recycling and ecological management was already impressive, and would grow.

If husbanded carefully, the trillion tons of ice and hydrocarbons might keep a couple of hundred humans at a time—along with their plants and animals—alive for a hundred generations or so.

*Just enough time.* For in a couple of thousand years, the comet's hurtling velocity would ebb as it approached its new aphelion, out where the Hot was only the brightest star. And out there, drifting slowly, were hundreds of billions of other great lumps of primordial matter left over from the birth of the solar system. Once their present near-hyperbolic velocity had leaked away to mere meters per second, there ought to be plenty of chances to snag other comet heads.

Saul stopped at a point where the guardrail hedge opened at the rim of the curving wheel. He was still thinking about the images Virginia had shown him, just a few minutes ago, in the little glade beneath her tea house . . . a simulation of those days, so long from now, when the men and mechs of Halley would nudge their tired, depleted old home near fresh new ice-specks in the great blackness. Perhaps they would seize two, three, or more, and drift apart again on their new colonies.

And from there? Virginia's simulation projected no limits. The Oort Cloud was vast, and humans were noted settlers.

*And our own sun's Oort Cloud brushes against the comet shoals of other stars. . . .*

The image she had presented was daunting. *She already contemplates in terms of aeons . . . it's going to take me a lot longer to get used to thinking that way. My own style of immortality is different. It retains the feel of Time as no friend.*

He passed Lani Nguyen-Osborn, sitting on a park bench under a dwarf maple, nursing her new son. Her eldest child—little Angelique—played in the grass nearby.

Lani smiled and waved. Saul grinned. They had spoken only an hour ago when he was on his way to see Virginia. He was due to have dinner with Carl's family later tonight. In the meantime, he still had work to do.

The vista of an Earthly city cleared as his section of the wheel approached ground level. He stepped through the break in the guard hedge into the microgravity of Halley's caverns, and let himself drift into the soft sand braking embankment. A cloud of particles puffed outward as he landed, then slowly settled to the floor.

He launched off toward the exit leading to his laboratory. The half-living sphincter lock cycled him through to the tunnels with a soft, moist sigh.

The gene-pool survey had been very good news—even if it had reminded him that neither he nor Virginia would ever contribute. All of his clones were sterile, and her physical body had long ago become part of the ecosphere.

Perhaps it was for the best, at that. For his clones would be around as the generations came and went. The descendants of Carl and Lani and Jeffers and Marguerite would be mixing their genes, sorting and resorting until a new species of humanity emerged. If all of those "Saul Lintz" models also kept having children, over the centuries, it would muck up the process.

*Heaven forbid!* He laughed at the thought. He had long ago come to terms with the irony of his situation . . . the clever design of his blessing and his curse.

Now, though, another bit of research occupied him. Something even more significant. More amazing.

Down at the end of one little-used corridor, Saul spoke a code phrase in Aramaic and a door hissed open. He slipped past the gene-crafted guard-cockatrice into his private lab. He had his neural tap socketed into place before his frame even settled horizontally onto the webbing.

*Program . . . Rock of Ages . . .* he commanded his personal computer. Colors shimmered and steadied.

The image on the central holo tank was of that deep, secret room down at the heart of the Weirder domain, where Suleiman Ould-Harrad had met his faith, in his own way. The horned, carved-stone bier rotated in the holographic image.

To the right, another display showed a sample taken from that ancient rock—symmetrical fossil ribs tracing the outlines of a creature of a very ancient sea.

More screens rippled with data, with microscopic closeups, with detailed isotopic profiles.

For a year now, Saul had been in touch again with Earthside specialists. With Halley confirmed to be on a near-hyperbolic trajectory, the hysteria had dampened on Earth. Guilt and shame played on what passed for news channels, these days. Some of the gifts the colonists had beamed back had also deepened the feeling that contact should be maintained until the planets merged with the roiling noise of the sun and all talk between brethren ended in the hiss of static.

The Earth scientists had worked on his data, confirming in detail what he had already worked out in general.

Nearly five billion years ago—in one of the gassy, dust-rich spiral arms that laced the Milky Way like filmy pinwheel spokes—a young, massive, hot star had raged through its short life and exploded in the titanic outburst of a supernova. In so doing, it had seeded nearby space with glowing clouds of heavy elements, from carbon and oxygen to plutonium and osmium . . . all cooked up while the blue giant had coursed through its brief but glorious youth. Save hydrogen and helium, all the elements that made up the planets—and human beings—had originated in that way, from great outbursts of primeval heat and light.

This supernova not only spewed great gouts of heavy matter into space. It also drove mammoth shock waves, which compressed the interstellar gas and dust, forming eddies and whirling concentrations.

A Jeans Collapse—named for a great twentieth-century astronomer—was triggered. Here and there amid the shocked, metal-enriched clouds, whirlpools condensed, flattened, formed glowing centers . . . suns.

And around those new stars, tiny fragments coalesced, from rocky bodies nearer in, to great gas worlds, to distant, vast swarms of tiny lumps of frozen gas. . . .

All geochemistry had, until now, been dated from the supernova that triggered the formation of the solar system. Never had any matter originating outside that event come into human hands. Until now, that is.

The rock Suleiman Ould-Harrad had found under the heart of Halley had none of the isotopic ratios scientists were familiar with. It came from a completely different episode of creation.

*Joao Quiverian would have loved this,* Saul thought. He mourned the loss of a good mind to the madness of those long, hopeless years.

*And Otis Sergeov, as well. I do hope we've learned a lesson.*

The final data unfolded before him, the confirmation of several years' guesswork and labor.

*Proved.* The stone came from ocean sediments laid down long before Earth had begun to swirl and form out of cosmic debris. The little animals whose fossils he had traced had swum in seas of a world not very unlike the Earth, with chemistry not so very different. But they had lived before the sun was even a star to wink in their cloud-flecked skies.

Saul read snatches from the message from Earth.

*Radiation damage to constituent crystals indicates close proximity to the explosion. Not more than a quarter of a lightyear away from a supernova.*

He picked up a chunk of the stone, wearing smooth now from being handled. The planet that this had come from must have circled a smaller star that had the misfortune to be near the giant when it exploded, blowing it to bits and scattering its pieces into the smoke rings of the spiral arms.

*Were there watchers, that night?* he wondered. *Might intelligence have looked up, knowing what was coming, making frantic plans, or resigned peace?*

The odds were against it. Probably the planet had only animals and vegetation, and the end came swiftly, without anticipation. That did not make the event any less awesome, less biblically terrible.

All the native creatures, from microbes to plants to clever little animals . . . all had died in the very process that most directly led to Earth's own adventure.

*What a universe,* he thought.

It was almost a side issue, now, that this also helped explain the presence of life on Halley. Almost unbelievingly, at first, Earth's scientific minds had finally concluded that bits of the biosphere of the blasted planet must have been carried off in the shock wave, to freeze in the cold of space. Bits of rock—and even once-living matter—would serve as ideal seeds around which the gases of the outer fringes of a new solar system might coalesce. Halley, apparently, had condensed around a lump of the old planet, the way raindrops gather around drifting dust motes in Earth's fecund sky.

No wonder the traces got richer the deeper one went into the comet. There had been a matrix already, around which the prebiotic compounds of the presolar nebula gathered during those early days.

Saul wondered how many other comets had formed around such seeds. Not many, he imagined. *We were just lucky, I guess,* he thought ironically.

Or were the old stories of comet-borne disasters really true? Could it be that the Earth had always been "freshened," from time to time, with new doses of the ancient biology, floating down into the atmosphere each time a comet passed close by? That would help explain why the lifeforms were so compatible. Earth's life kept incorporating new bits and pieces from the storehouse of deep space.

In a sense, the old destroyed planet still lived. Fragments of preancient organic code floated in all of them, and especially in the colonists of Halley. After all the death and fear of the early days, it was ironic that it would turn out to be of benefit in the long run, contributing to the diversity they would need over the centuries ahead.

Perhaps the people of Halley were not even "human" any longer, not in the classical sense. Not in the way Earthmen were developing, preparing for their own explosion into the galaxy.

*They will go to the stars. Hopping from bright pinpoint to bright pinpoint, dwelling down where gravity curls space tightly and suns cook heavy, rocky worlds.*

*We, on the other hand, will travel more slowly. But we will have the* real *universe . . . the spaces in between.*

Remembering the simulation Virginia had shown him, Saul smiled.

Over the neural tap he felt a soft brush of presence. *Listening in again, my darling?* he projected.

**Yes, my love. You might as well get used to it. We're in this together, for the long stretch.**

*Yes.* He smiled. For when this body he wore was long gone, his memories would ride another clone . . . and continue loving Virginia. The Wandering Jew and the Lady in the Machine . . . they would be a resource for the people, serving for as long as anyone wanted them around.

*Immortality is service,* he thought.

They held each other in cool, electron arms. And both of them imagined that they heard, faint and ghostly, in the distance, low confirming laughter.

# VIRGINIA

Lani bounced the baby on her knee, provoking squeals of terror and delight. Carl beamed at the gleeful pair and kept pumping methodically at his exercise machine. They had to spend half their time in the G-wheel to keep the children's calcium buildup normal. A tenth of a G was heavy, but imposed no real hardship.

"Want to visit Aunt Ginnie?" Lani asked the baby's older sister, who nodded with a thumb in her mouth.

A shimmer appeared, hung in the air. Then a tanned Virginia

stepped through it and waved. "Hi, snookums. Surf's up. You interested?"

Little Angelique laughed, and the baby squealed with glee. Lani's second delivery had been, in Saul's words, "boringly normal." Both children seemed to accrete weight as Virginia watched; they massed more every day, and ate like firestorms.

Carl gestured downwheel, toward the verdant wilderness of Stormfield Park. "Think we could ever put a lake in here?"

"And then drive waves across it?" Lani asked shrewdly.

He nodded. "Angelique will probably want to copy her aunt."

"Come now," Lani said. "There are *some* things we can't manage, you know."

Carl grinned. "Wanna bet?"

Virginia remembered the fall into Jupiter's gravity well. It had been a time of tension and remorse.

Her tailoring of the subliming winds had canted Halley's orbit, added velocity. The divergence from their original path widened steadily as the launchers hammered away unendingly.

It was only a minor deflection in astronomical terms. But it was crucial.

They had come in behind Jupiter's sweeping path, not in front. They whipped through the proton sleet of the enormous magnetic belts, saw the splotchy face of Io hurl lurid volcanic greetings.

By passing *behind* the giant world, momentum was *added* to Halley, not subtracted. Instead of arcing back to the inner solar system, the comet head sped on even faster, shooting outward from the sun. The blazing giant squatted now behind the swiftly fleeing mote, its rays and influence dimming daily.

As they swung out from banded Jupiter, Virginia had studied carefully the faces of the crew who watched the viewscreens. They had looked at one another, realizing the enormity of what they faced.

Now, years later, the bleak resignation of those days had ebbed. It would be several centuries before they reached the truly rich realm, where iceworlds clustered in great bee-swarm halos. Vast distances separated them, but in interstellar space such voyages required little energy.

Those faraway iceballs beckoned, fresh supplies of metals and volatiles. There would be a next generation, and a next. They deserved those resources; they deserved opportunity, hope.

Carl, Lani—indeed, all of them—were caught in the coils of slow diminishment.

Saul, though, perhaps could last forever unless some accident claimed him. And even if he died, there were his clones. She would always have a Saul.

Anger, frustration, despair—she came to know these as temporary illuminations of the individual soul, lightning flashes across an abiding dark. Humans had a reaction time evolved from the need to grapple, fight, feed, flee. They were no more conditioned to the slow sway of worlds than a mayfly would be to the Roman empire.

Halley's crew became accustomed to their destiny and slowly, imperceptibly to themselves, withdrew into their human-centered nooks and crannies. Virginia enjoyed downfacing into their timescale, watching Angelique grow in startling spurts. As confidence in the new techniques grew, others soon joined the first child, and played in tunnels and shafts swept ritually clean of dangerous Halleyforms.

As Halley slowed, climbing out of the shallow sloping trough of the sun's gravitational well, her attention turned away from science—though she continued to collect data, formulate theories, argue with Saul and the others—and moved on to larger issues.

As Descartes had once done, she was forced to do. She wondered what she could deduce from basic principles. *Cogito, ergo sum?* But who was the *I* who made the statement?

To use the jargon of science, she was a new phylum, no longer a vertebrate but biocybernetic. She was a wedding of the organic and the electronic, with a dash of sapient consciousness. By strict definition, a phylum should emerge through evolution by sexual gene sorting and speciation. But once intelligence had appeared, that aeons-long process was outmoded. A new phylum could emerge and develop by design.

The Virginia who now resided in chilled synapses and holographic arrays was not strictly human any longer. Still, she had myriad human signatures and defects, facets and flaws. She could no more ignore the vexations of Saul and Carl and Jeffers and Lani than she could forget her childhood, her father's rough affection.

Yet she was more. The joy that Carl and Lani felt brought her occasional pangs; Saul's wistful nostalgia for her embodiment gave real pain. But though she understood and felt all this, she came to see it as a subset of the larger issues that confronted her. These frail people were bound up in the true passing life that the laws of natural selection had decreed—their deaths were written into their bones. Even Saul, her fellow immortal, rode the hormone tide. They felt deeply and thought upon the mortal questions.

In the Oort Cloud there circled beneath a sheen of unblinking stars a trillion cometary nuclei, more land than ever promised any ragged band of wanderers. The colonists would have Carl as their Joshua—an irony that had undoubtedly already occurred to Saul—and he would lead them forth.

But while Virginia would help them, and tend to their needs as best she could, she also had her own unique destiny as the first in a new kind.

If she represented a new phylum, the first law must be survival. That was why she now looked upon the attack from Earth as an unplanned, fortunate outcome of mankind's stupidity. Earth could have had her, could have overcome its fears and welcomed the new phylum. But now she was embarked upon a new course, one eventually to her advantage.

She needed time to think, to explore.

The old species of *Homo sapiens* on Earth would inevitably spread, first into the solar system, then perhaps beyond. They had already shown their hostility to the strangeness encased in the iceworlds. Their fears would take centuries to abate.

Virginia knew, even if her human cargo did not, that there would never be a return to the kingdom of the Hot. Human societies, once grown apart, seldom can meet again on even, friendly terms. Far worse for two phylums.

> The mind, that ocean where each kind
> Does straight its own resemblance find;
> Yet it creates, transcending these,
> Far other worlds, and other seas.

She had time for poetry, for endless byzantine pathways of contemplation. She even thought that she could glimpse the way it must be, when they reached the great cloud of worlds which drew them out.

The human species would have a divided destiny now, strands that could progress for a while along separate courses. There would be less pain if they remained aloof.

She calculated the probable evolution of Carl Osborn's new species of Man, and of her own phylum, and was pleased. Reproduction, adaptation—these problems were vast, but she felt herself equal to them.

And as for Planetary Humanity . . . By her calculations, the new phylum and the old species would not meet again for four thousand years. Good. There was time enough to think about it.

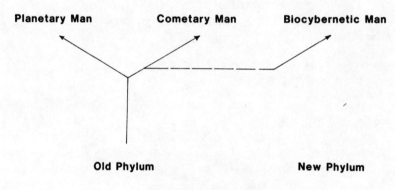

Evolution of Cometary Man

# ACKNOWLEDGMENTS

This novel was written on the basis of the best information available at the time concerning comets in general, and Halley's Comet in particular. It was created in the awareness (and hope) that the successful 1986 Halley probes and International Halley Watch would vastly multiply our knowledge of these fascinating leftovers of creation. If some of this new information turns out to invalidate a few premises of our story, we hope at least that the reader will credit us with daring. We felt we had to tell this story *now,* to honor an interplanetary envoy whose visits are so well timed to once in a human span.

The authors would like to thank those experts who were of assistance, including Professors Mike Gaffey, John Lewis, John Cramer, Bert King, and Karl Johannson, as well as Dr. Ray Newburn of JPL and Dr. Eric Jones of Los Alamos Labs. Dr. Donald Yeomans of JPL and Dr. Neal Hulkower of TRW Inc. helped with orbital mechanics.

We would also like to thank Anita Everson, Joan Abbe, Sue Roberts, Dan Spadoni, Nancy Grace, William Lomax, Bonnie Graham, and Diane Brizolara. Karen and Poul Anderson and Astrid and Greg Bear were most gracious, also.

Louis D'Amaria and Dennis Byrnes of the Jet Propulsion Laboratory helped drive the plot with their wonderful calculations of planetary encounters. Each of them gets a dinner and a bottle.

And, as always, Lou Aronica of Bantam Books was understanding of the needs of authors laboring under "astronomical" deadlines.

We will be many things, in the future. But there will never cease to be a need for courage.

—David Brin and Gregory Benford
September 1985